HEARTSTOPPER

VOLUME 1

Heartstopper: Volume 1 was originally published by the author in 2018, and then in England by Hachette Children's Group in 2019.

Library of Congress Control Number: 2019944235

ISBN 978-1-338-61744-3 (hardcover)
ISBN 978-1-338-61743-6 (paperback)

15 14 13 12 11   22 23 24 25

Printed in China 62
This edition first printing, May 2020

ALICE OSEMAN

HEARTSTOPPER

VOLUME 1

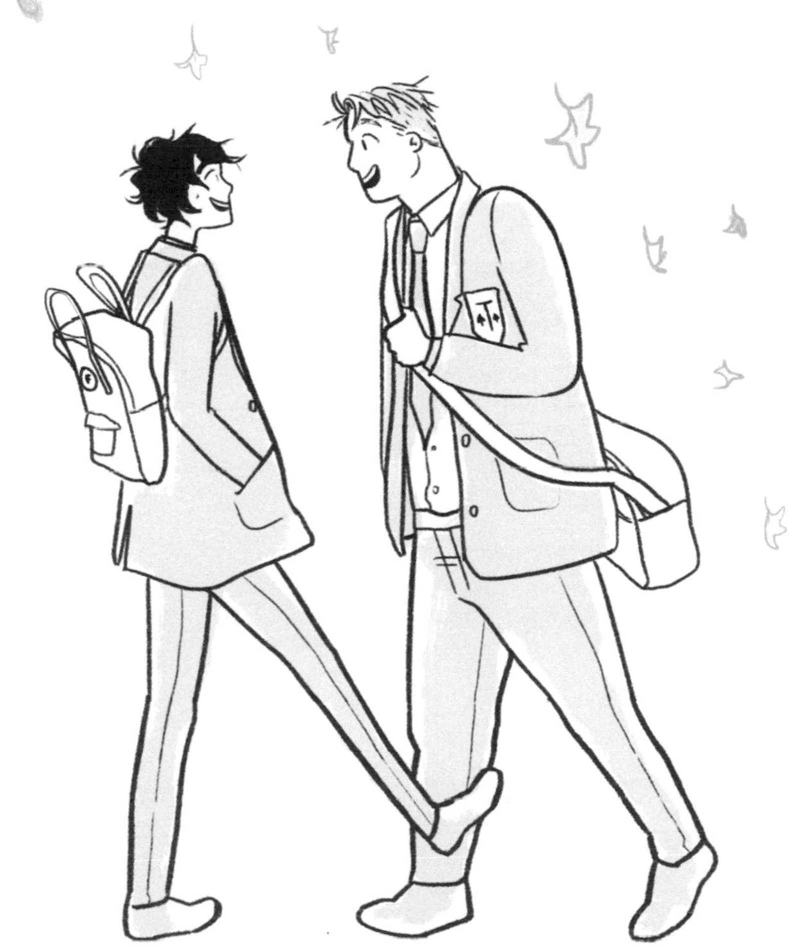

graphix
An Imprint of
SCHOLASTIC

1. MEET

January

8:01
Ben
Library?
Mon
K
Music Room 2?
Wed
Ok
Library?
Thur
Yep

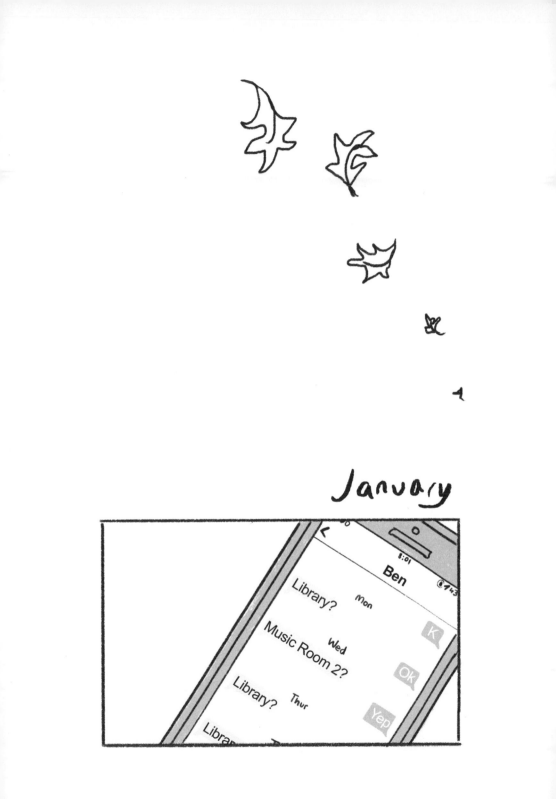

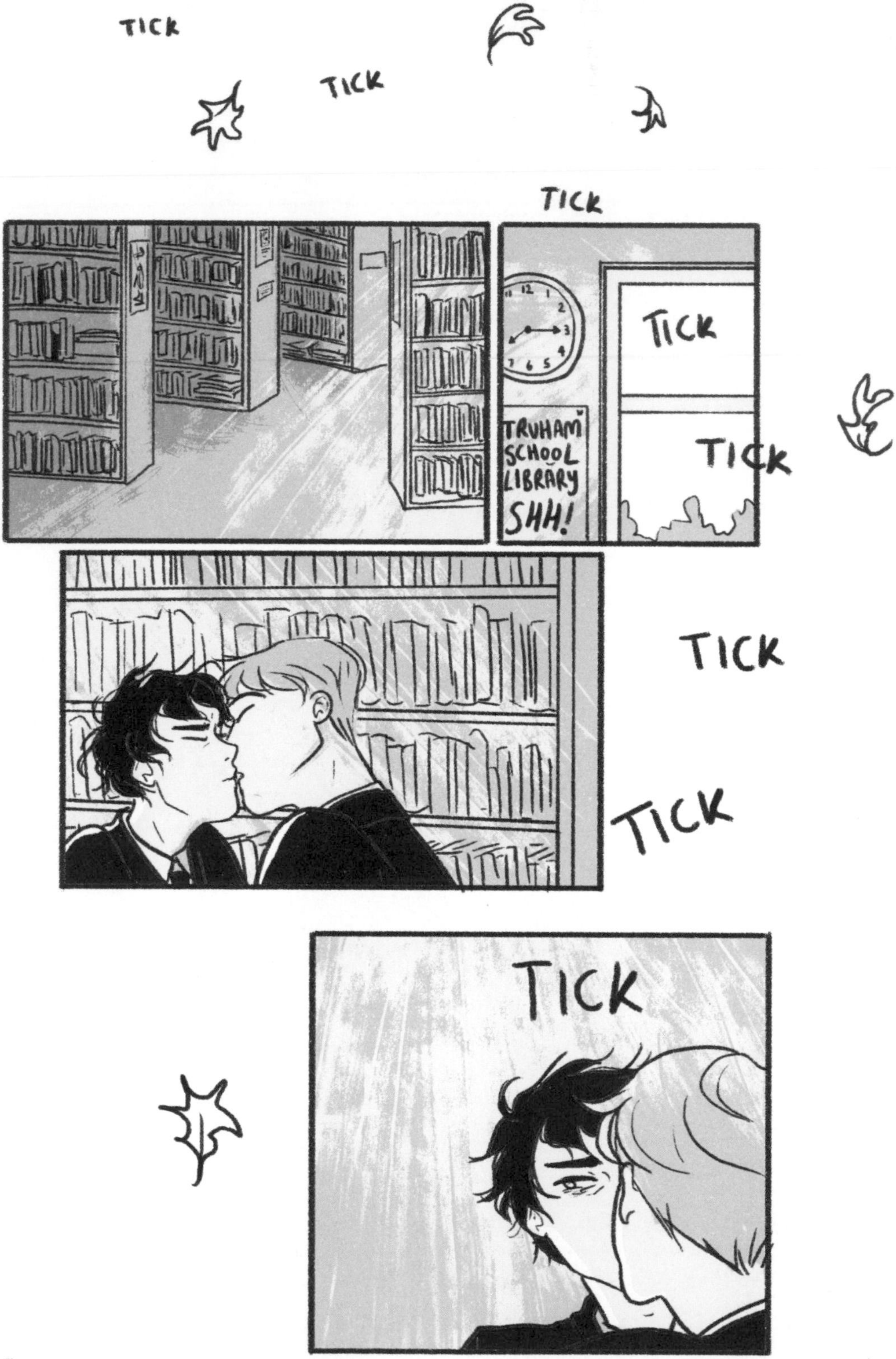
TICK
TICK
TICK
TRUHAM SCHOOL LIBRARY SHH!
TICK
TICK
TICK
TICK
TICK

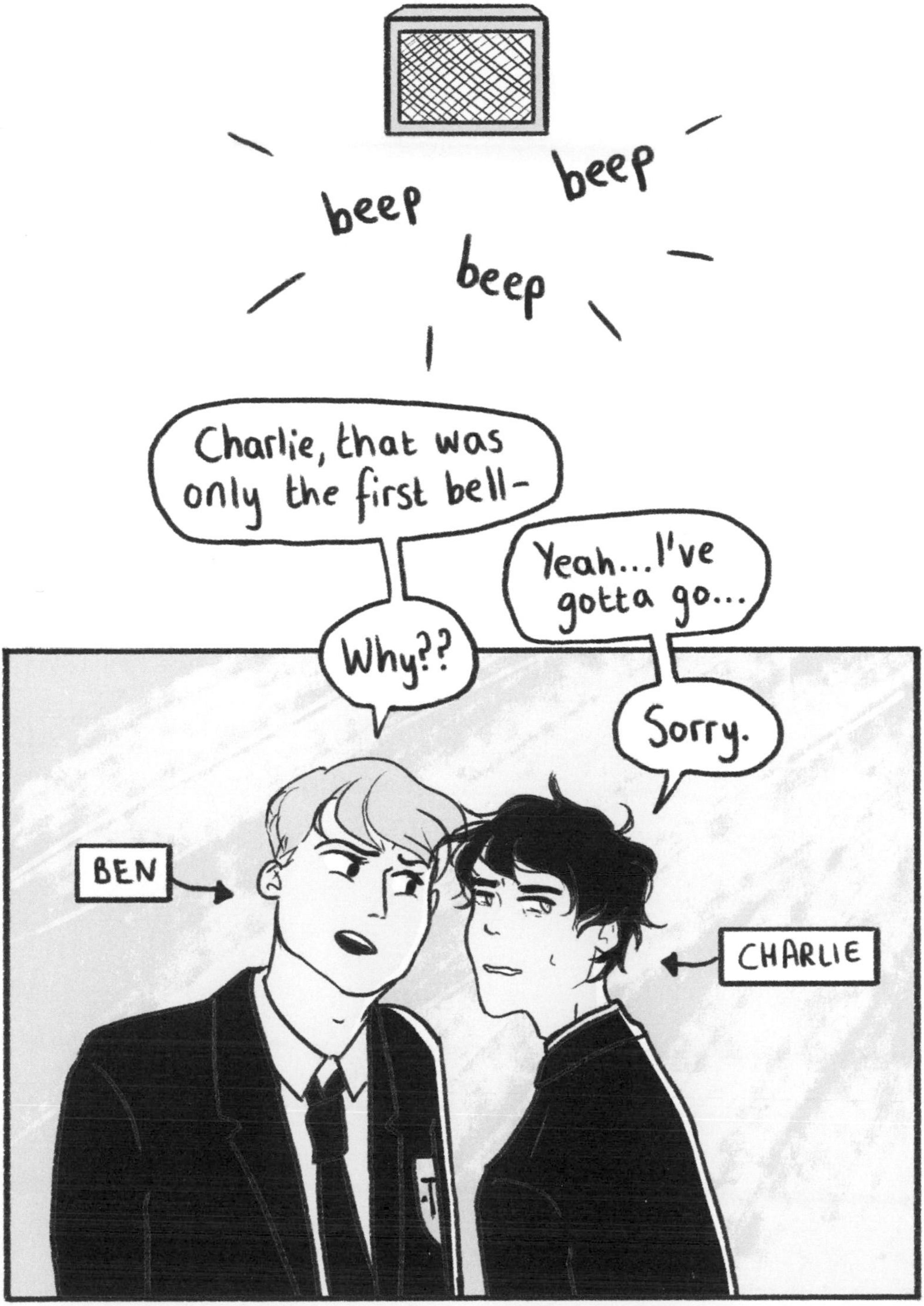
beep
beep
beep
Charlie, that was only the first bell-
Why??
Yeah... I've gotta go...
Sorry.
BEN
CHARLIE

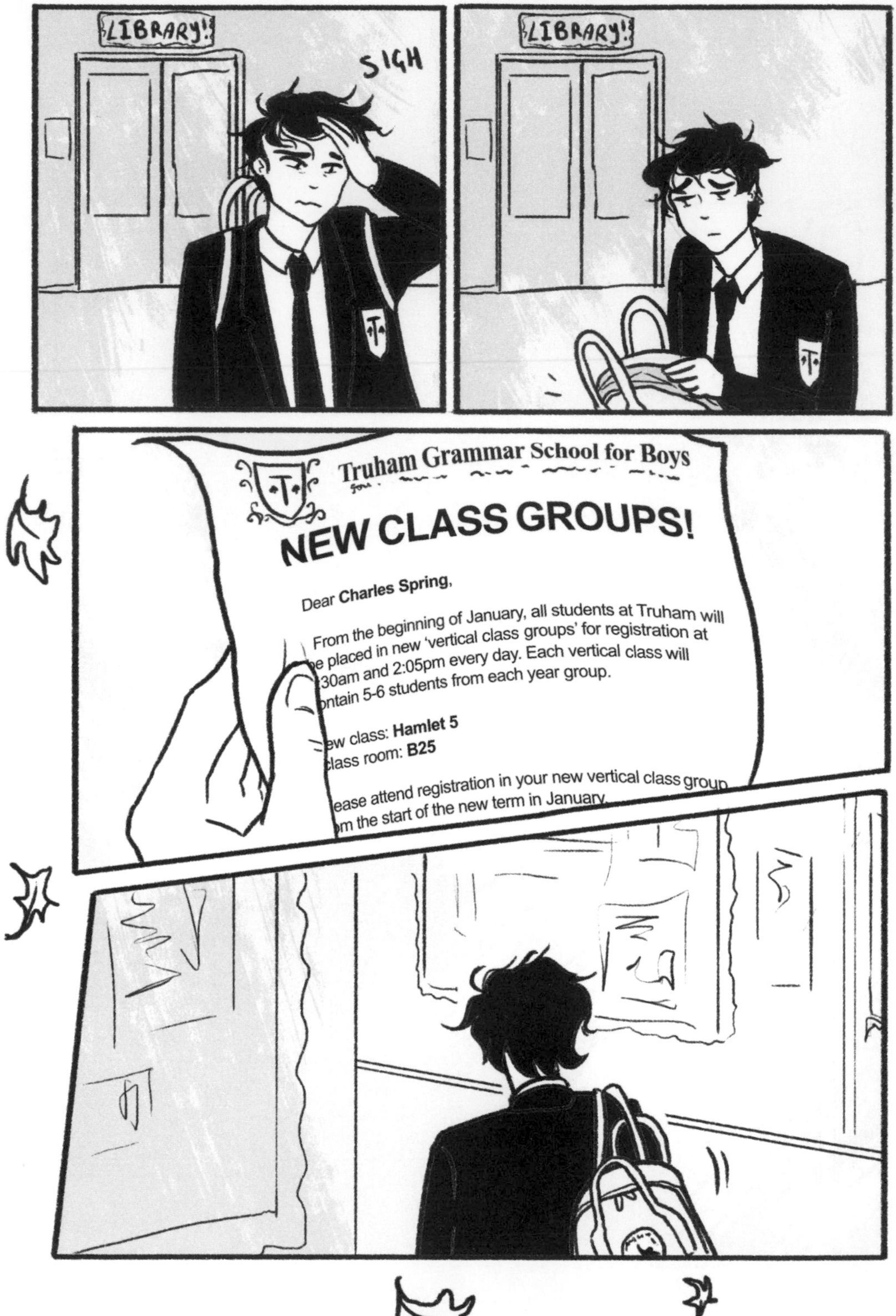
LIBRARY!
SIGH
LIBRARY!
Truham Grammar School for Boys
NEW CLASS GROUPS!
Dear Charles Spring,
From the beginning of January, all students at Truham will
be placed in new 'vertical class groups' for registration at
30am and 2:05pm every day. Each vertical class will
ontain 5-6 students from each year group.
ew class: Hamlet 5
class room: B25
lease attend registration in your new vertical class group
om the start of the new term in January.

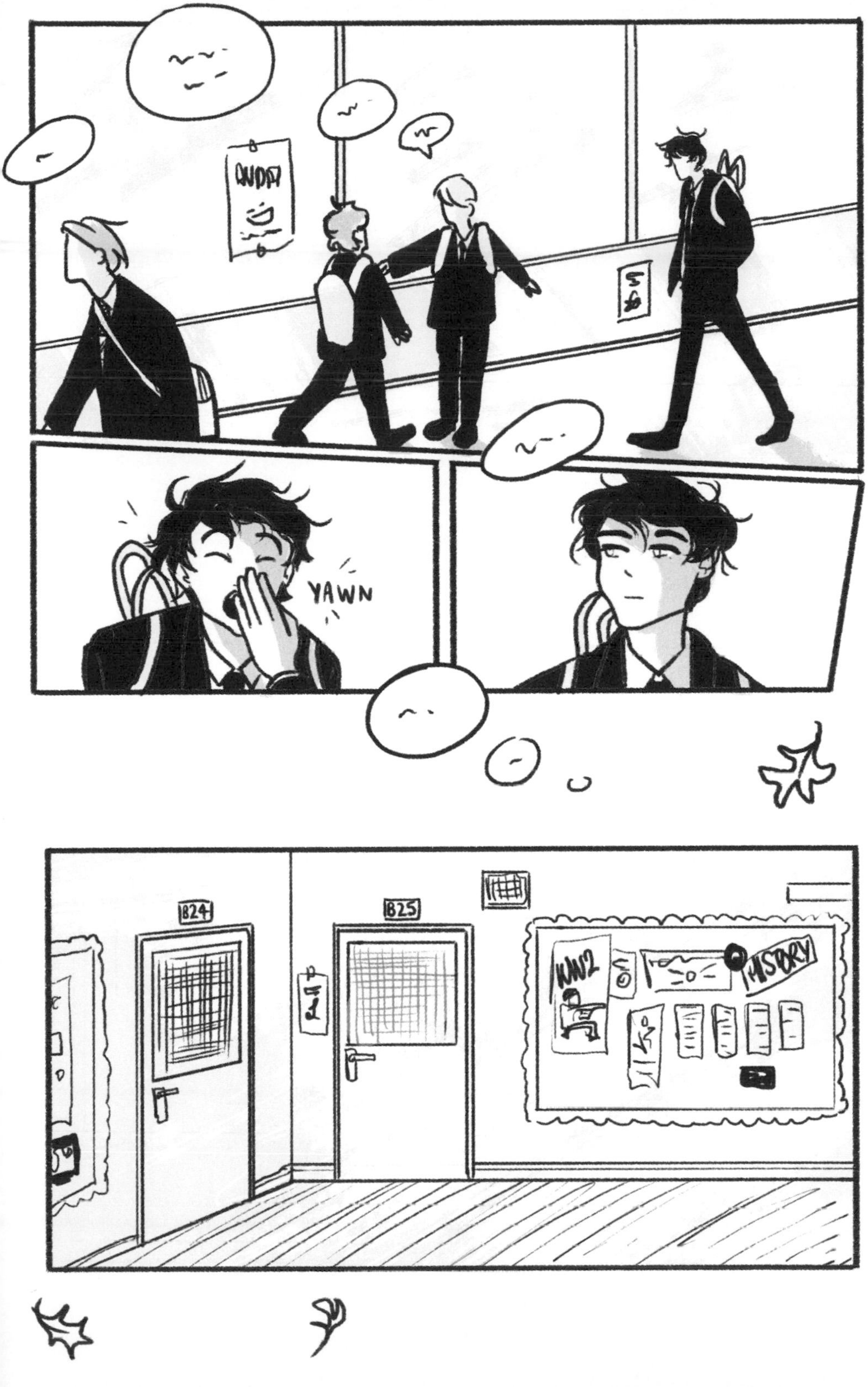
YAWN
B24
B25
WW2
HISTORY

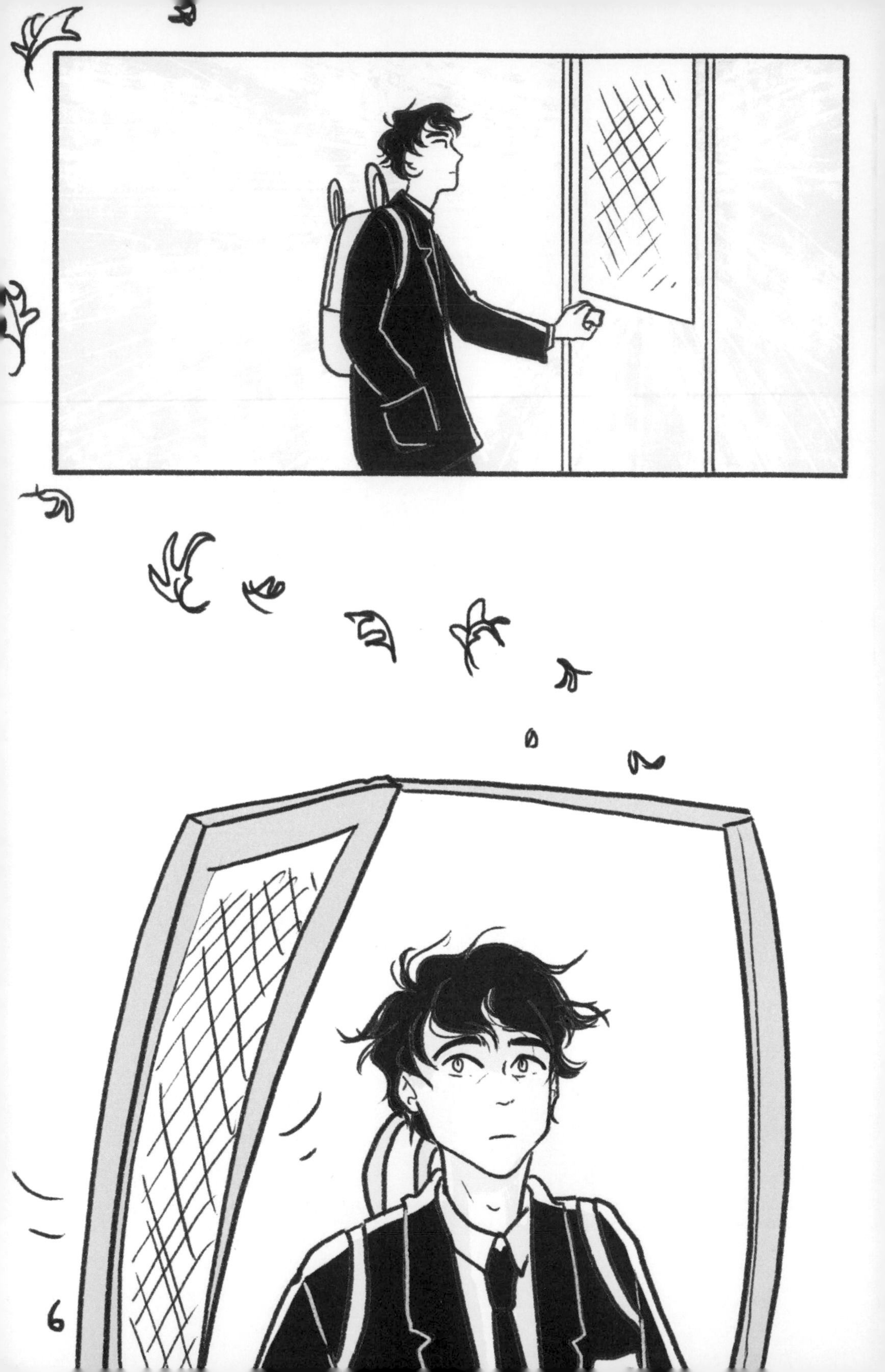

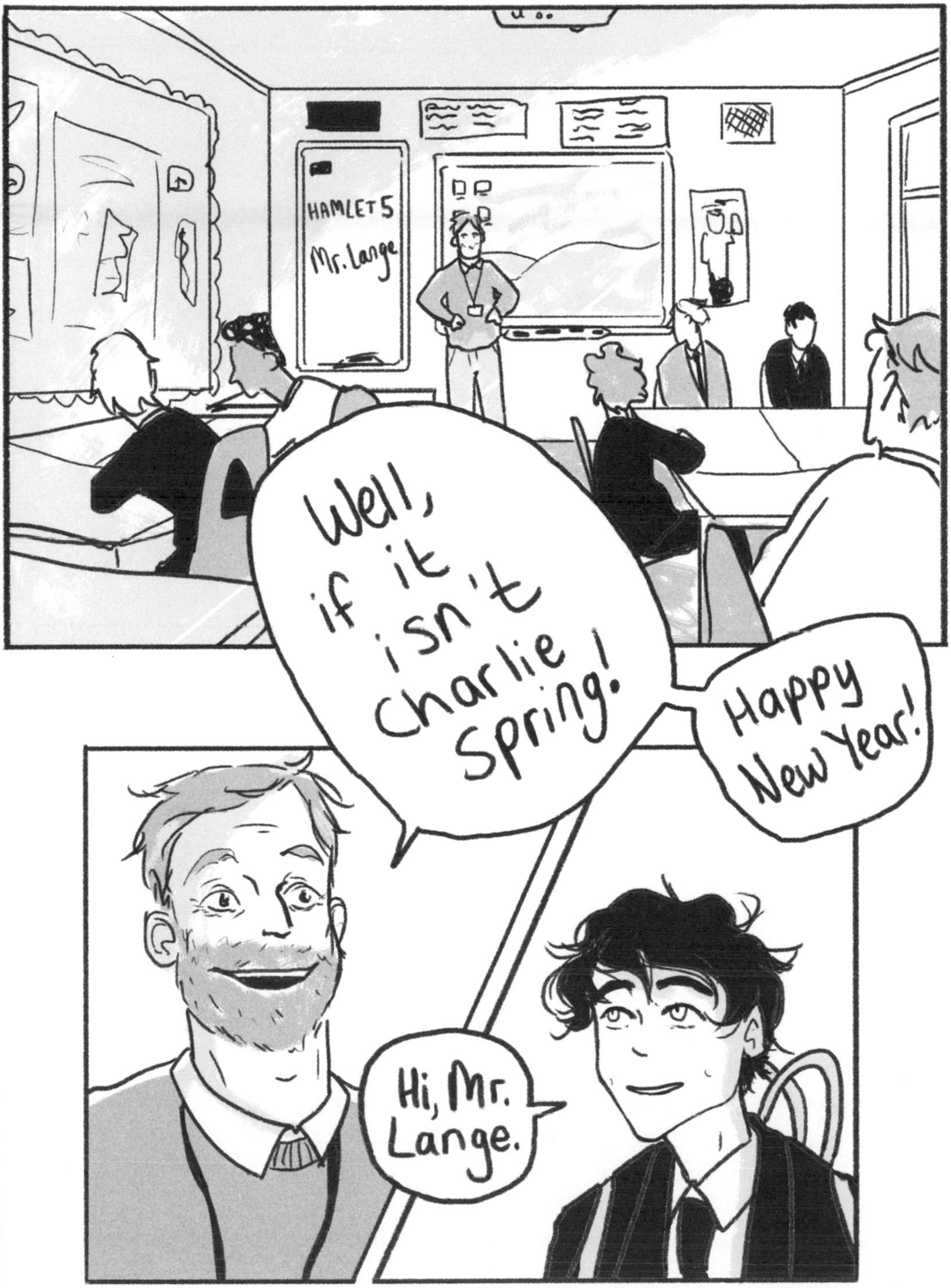
HAMLET 5
Mr. Lange
Well, if it isn't Charlie Spring!
Happy New Year!
Hi, Mr. Lange.

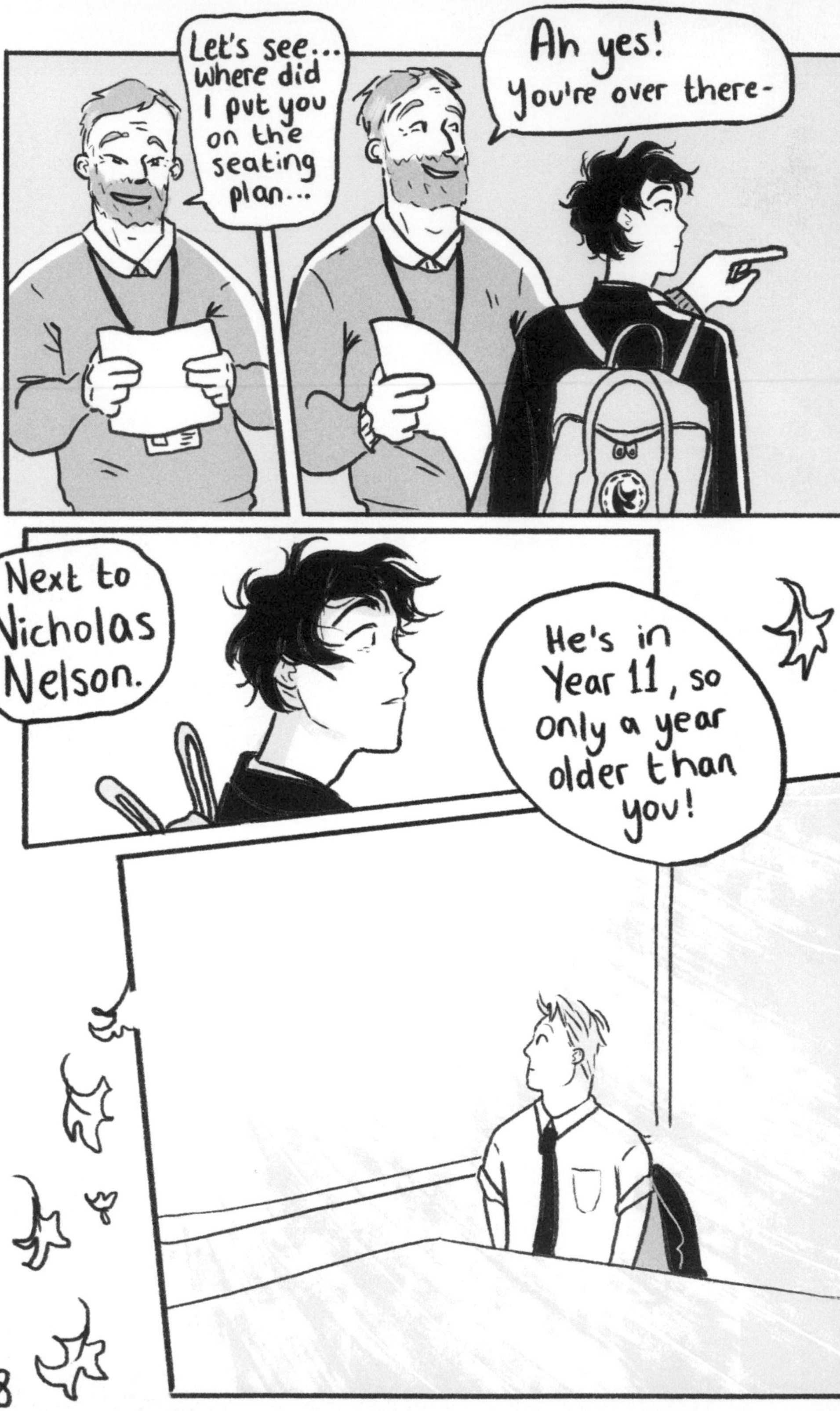
Let's see... where did I put you on the seating plan...
Ah yes! You're over there-
Next to Nicholas Nelson.
He's in Year 11, so only a year older than you!

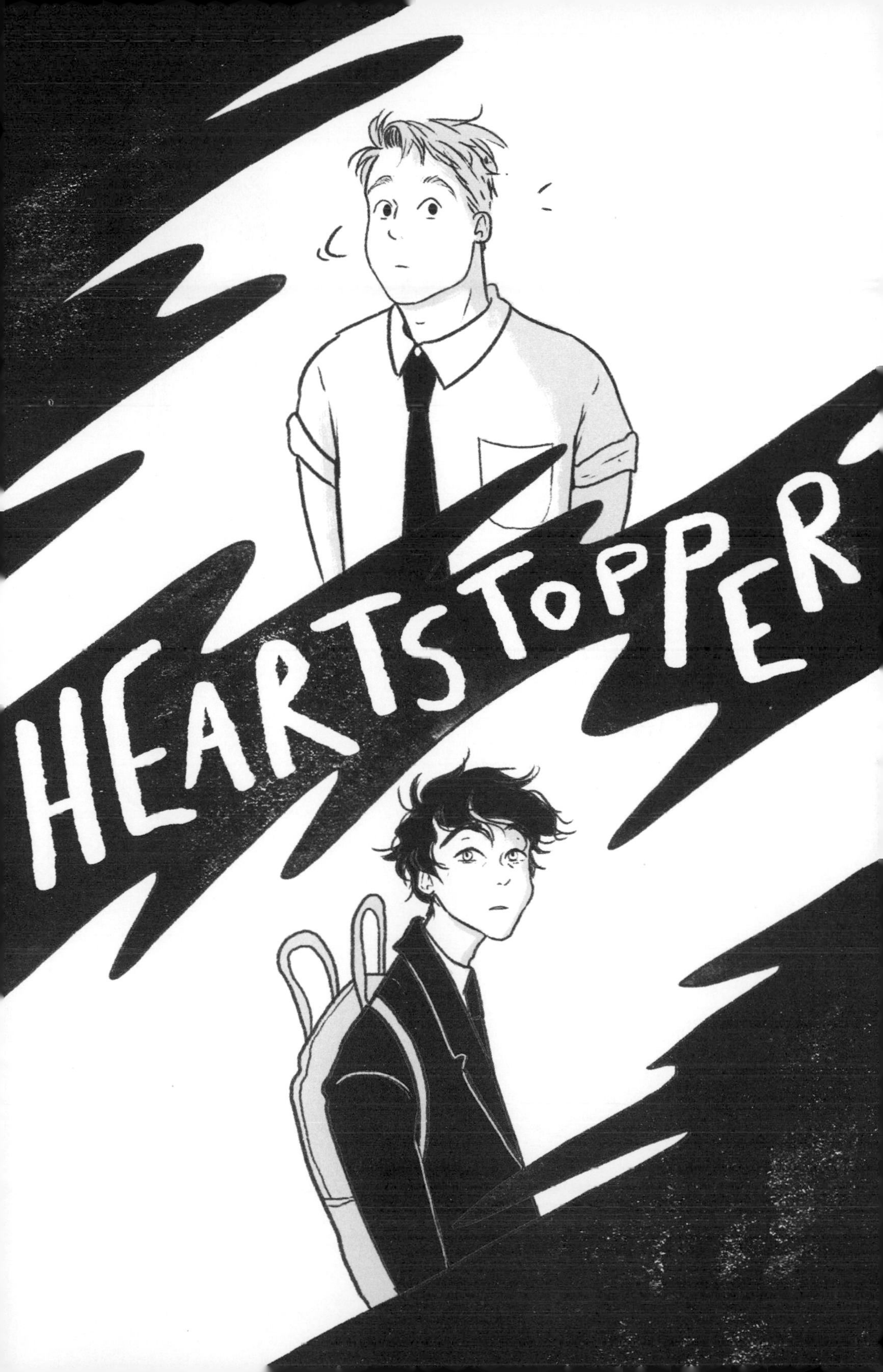
HEARTSTOPPER

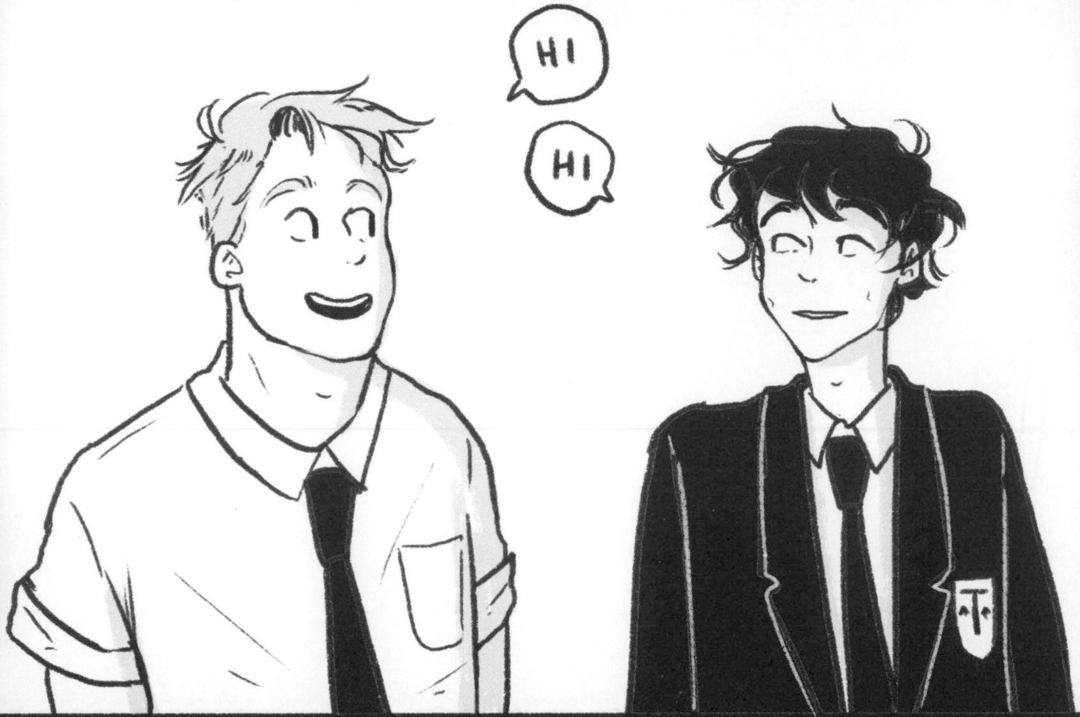
HI
HI

A COMIC BY

ALICE
OSEMAN

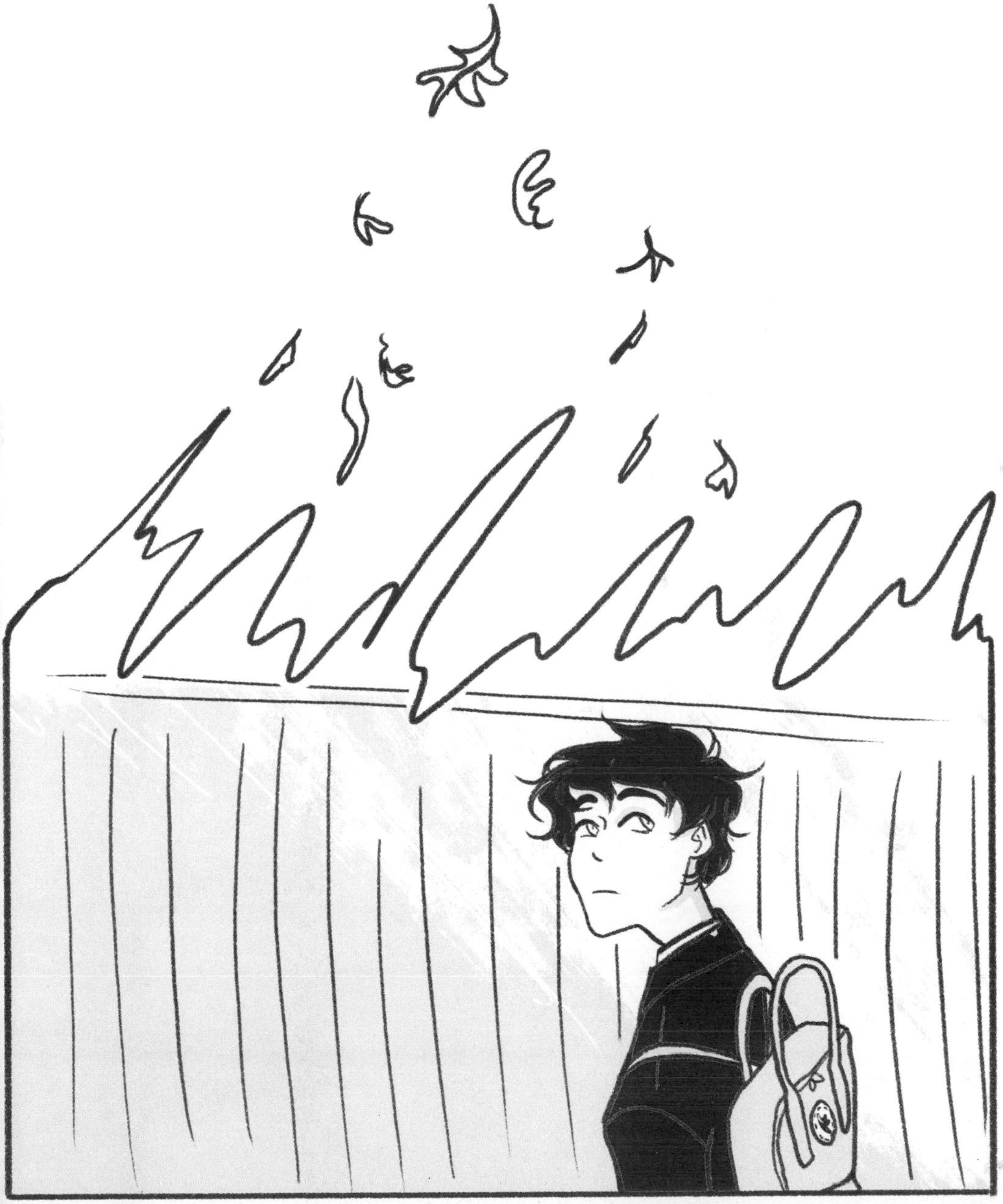

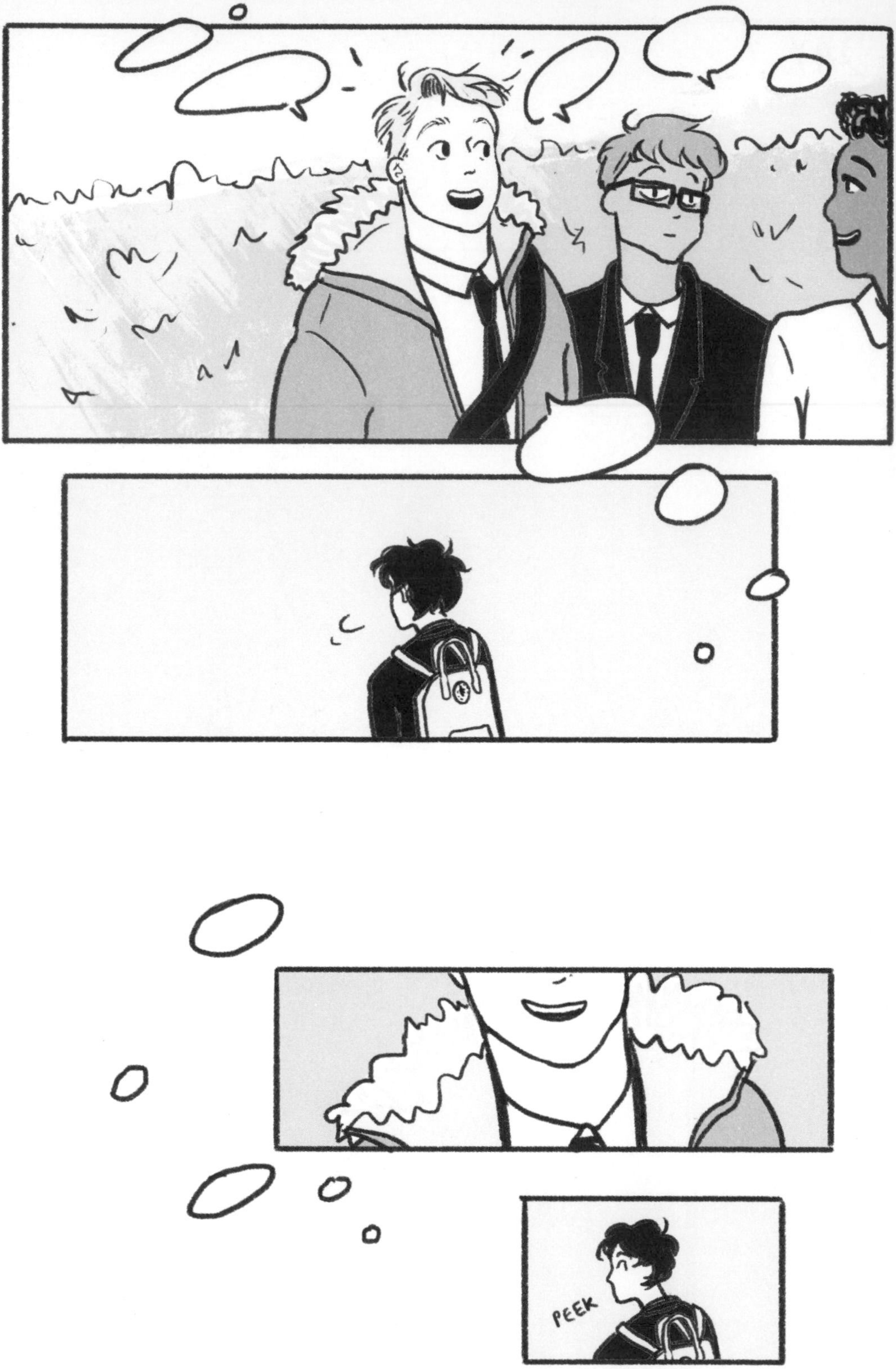
PEEK

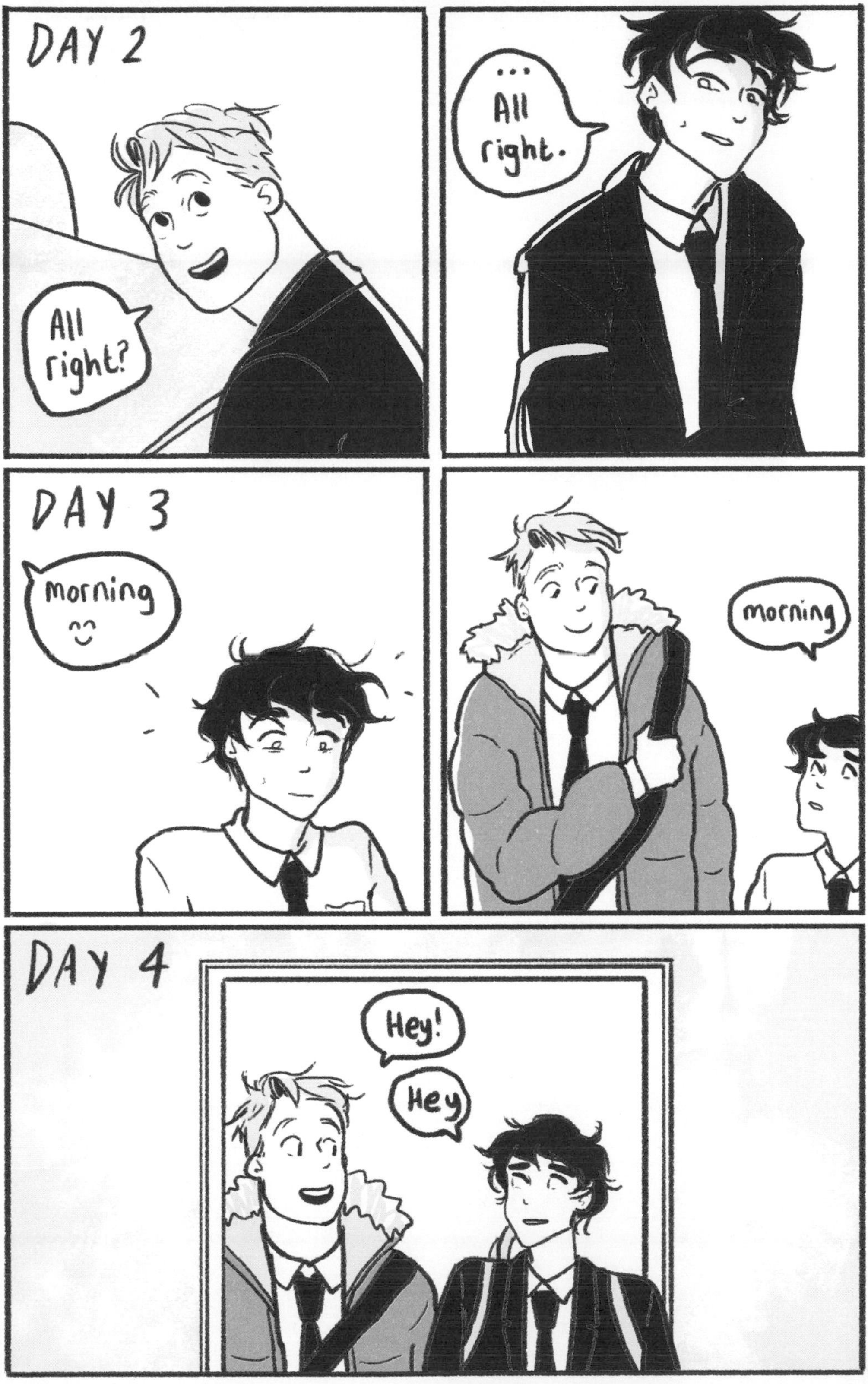
DAY 2
All right?
...
All right.
DAY 3
morning
morning
DAY 4
Hey!
Hey

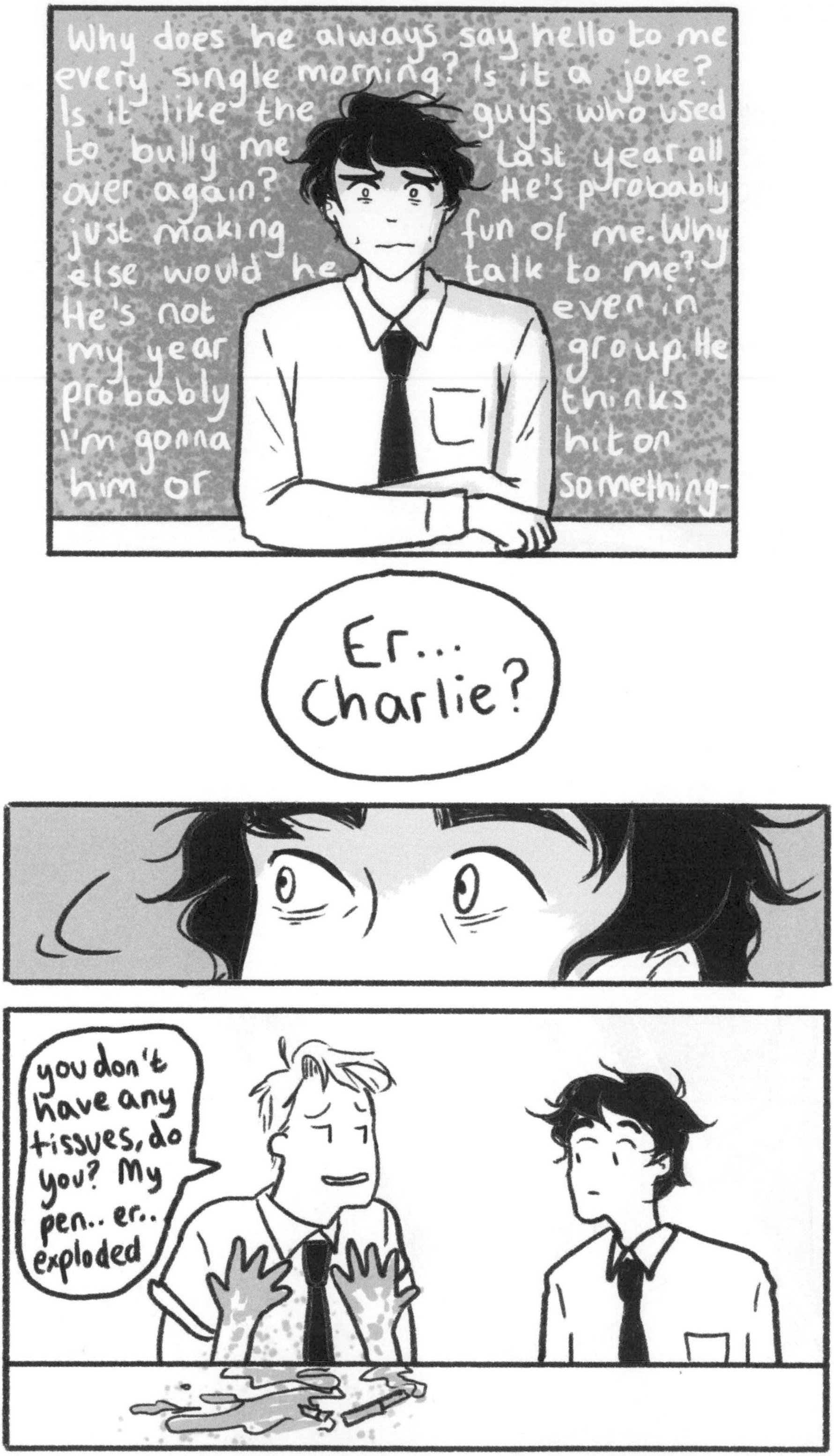
Why does he always say hello to me every single morning? Is it a joke? Is it like the guys who used to bully me last year all over again? He's probably just making fun of me. Why else would he talk to me? He's not even in my year group. He probably thinks I'm gonna hit on him or something-
Er... Charlie?
you don't have any tissues, do you? My pen.. er.. exploded

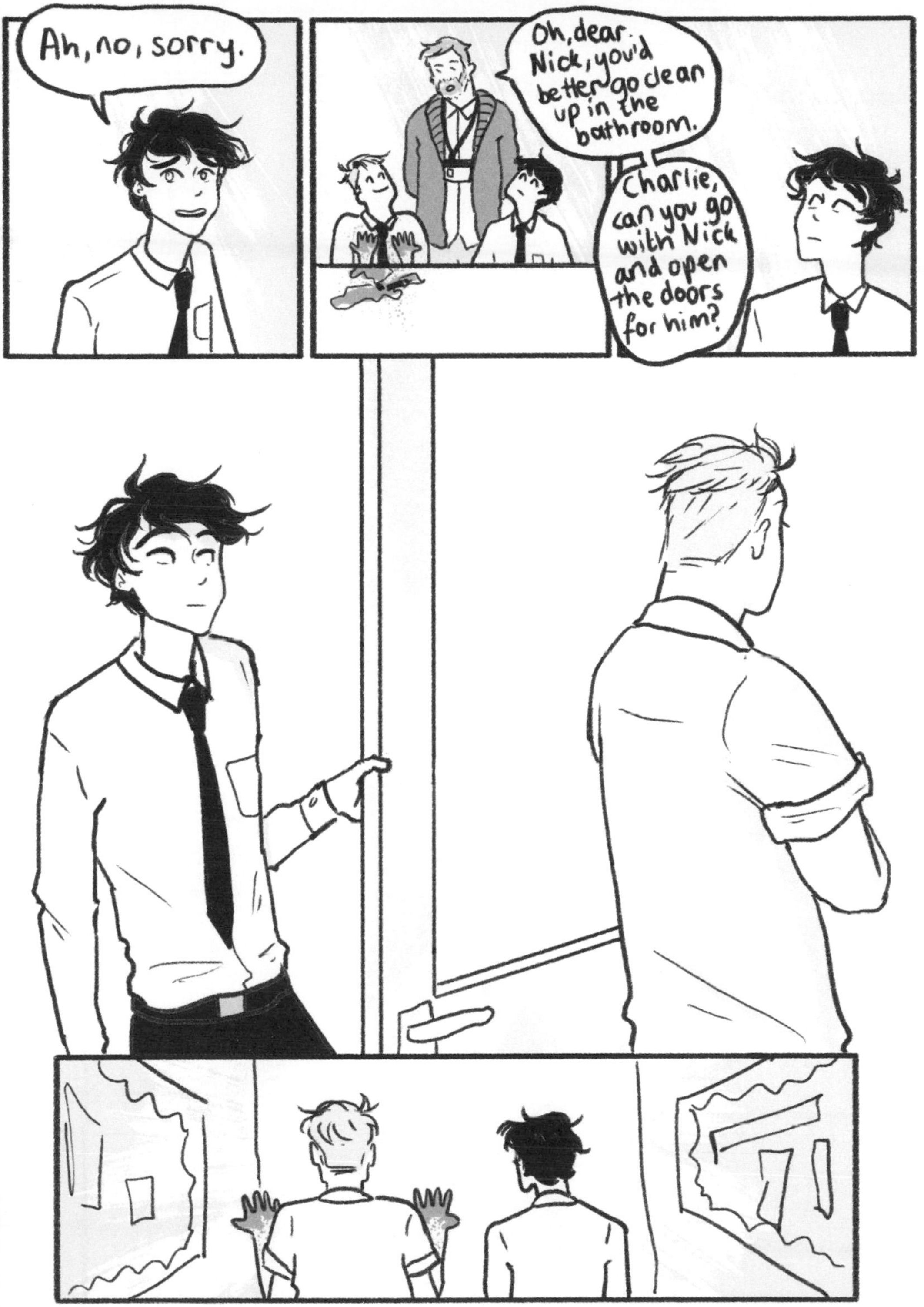

Ah, no, sorry.
Oh, dear. Nick, you'd better go clean up in the bathroom.
Charlie, can you go with Nick and open the doors for him?

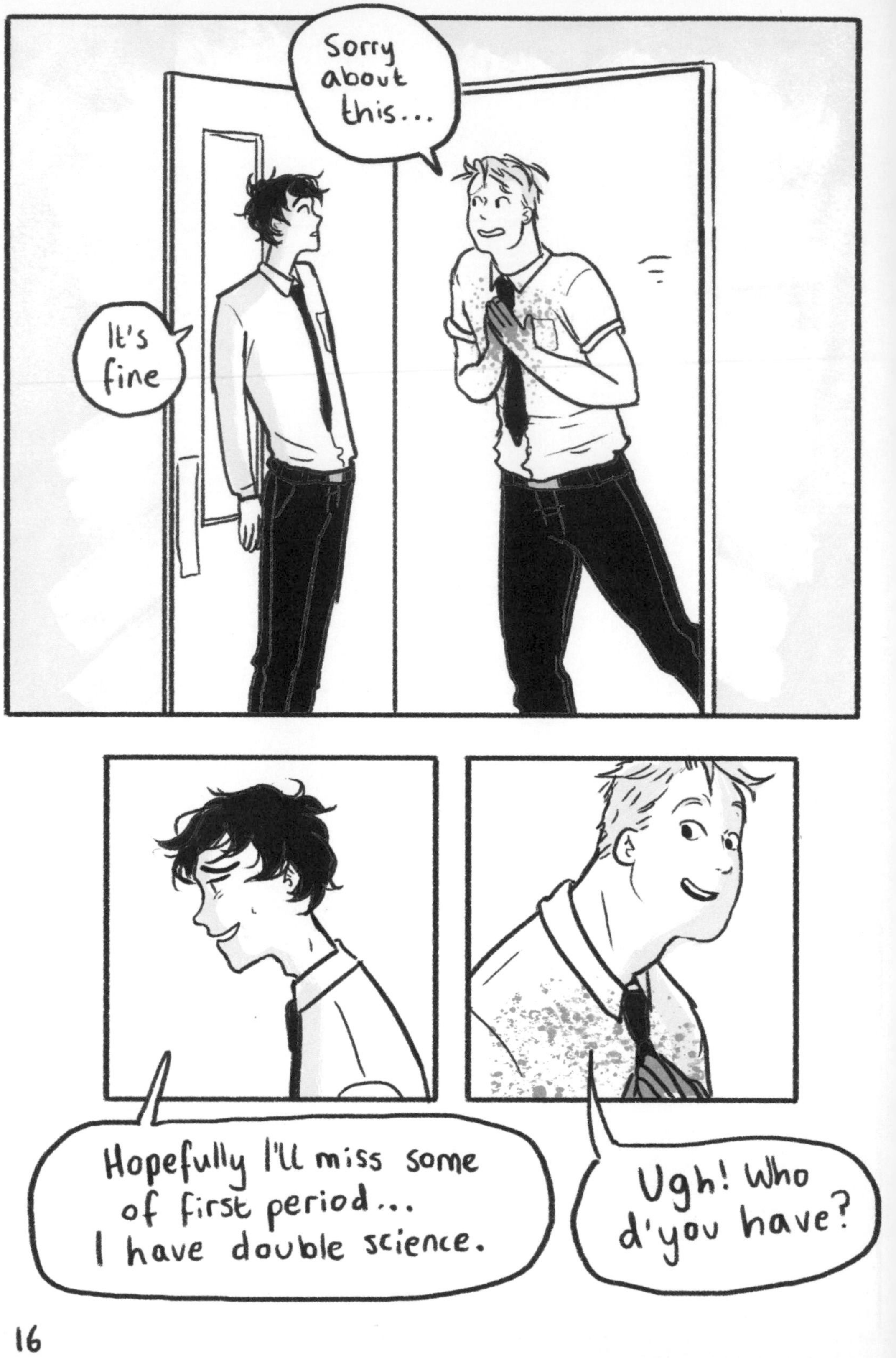
Sorry about this...
It's fine
Hopefully I'll miss some of first period... I have double science.
Ugh! Who d'you have?

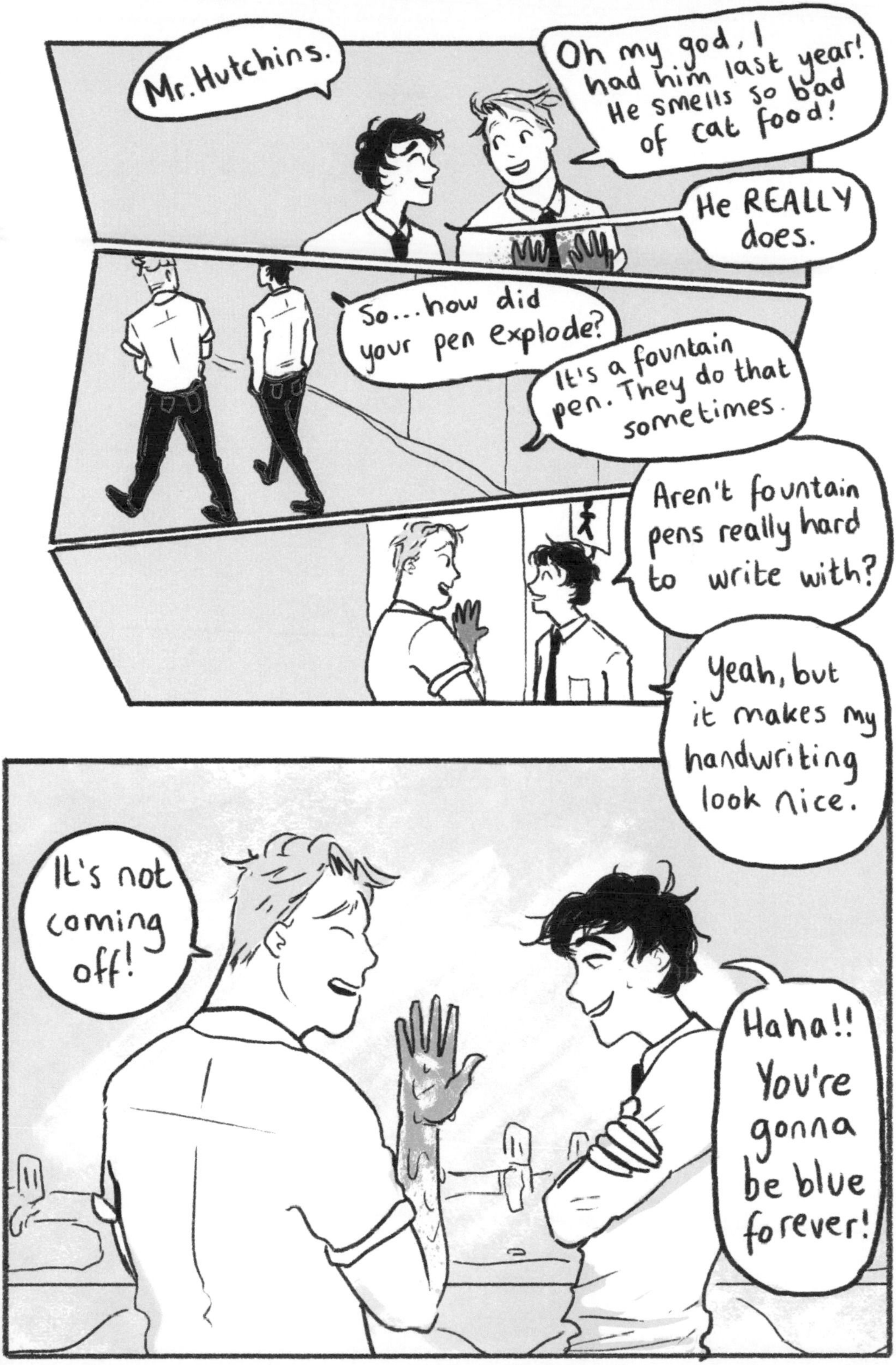
Mr. Hutchins.
Oh my god, I had him last year! He smells so bad of cat food!
He REALLY does.
So... how did your pen explode?
It's a fountain pen. They do that sometimes.
Aren't fountain pens really hard to write with?
Yeah, but it makes my handwriting look nice.
It's not coming off!
Haha!! You're gonna be blue forever!

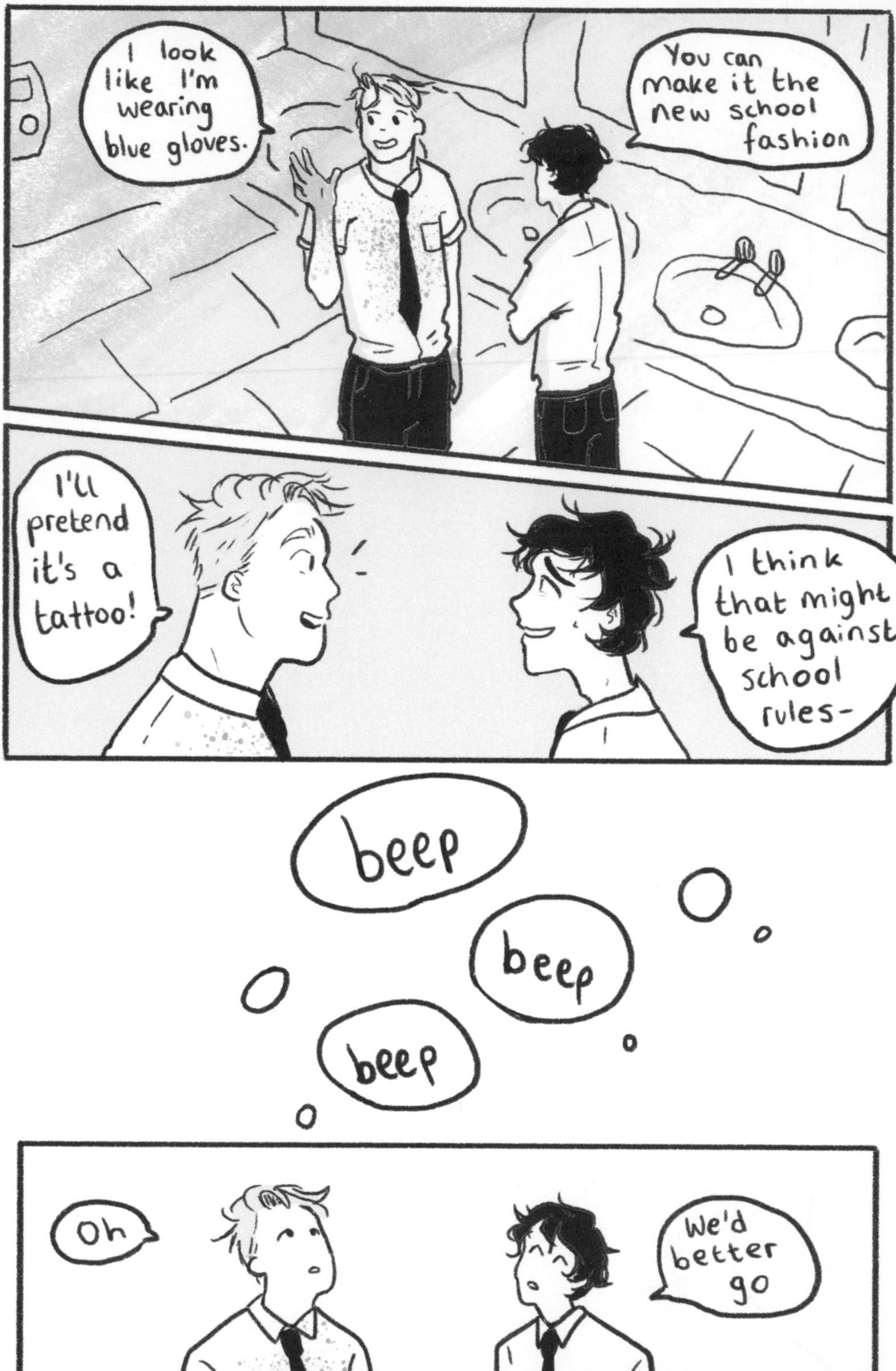
I look like I'm wearing blue gloves.
You can make it the new school fashion
I'll pretend it's a tattoo!
I think that might be against school rules-
beep
beep
beep
Oh
We'd better go

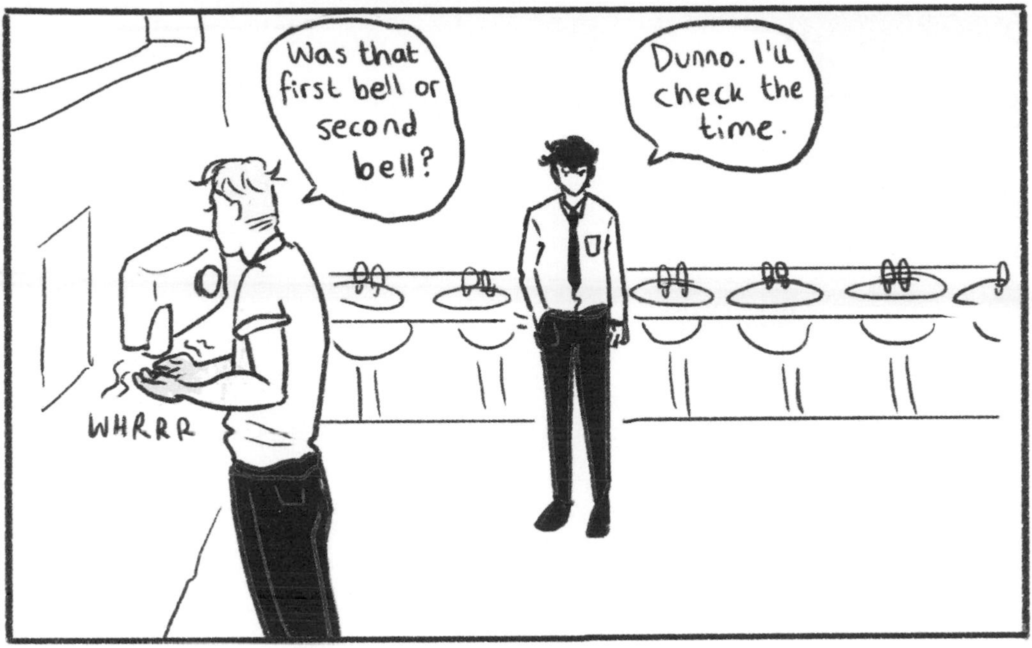
Was that first bell or second bell?
Dunno. I'll check the time.
WHRRR

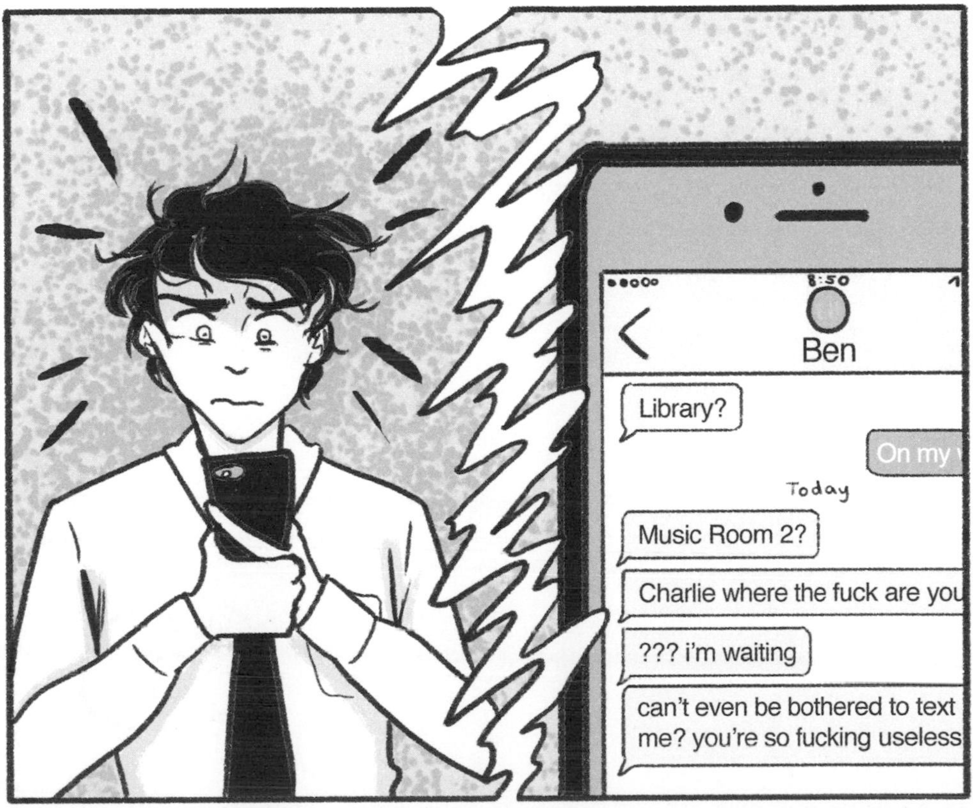
8:50
Ben
Library?
Today
Music Room 2?
Charlie where the fuck are you
??? i'm waiting
can't even be bothered to text me? you're so fucking useless

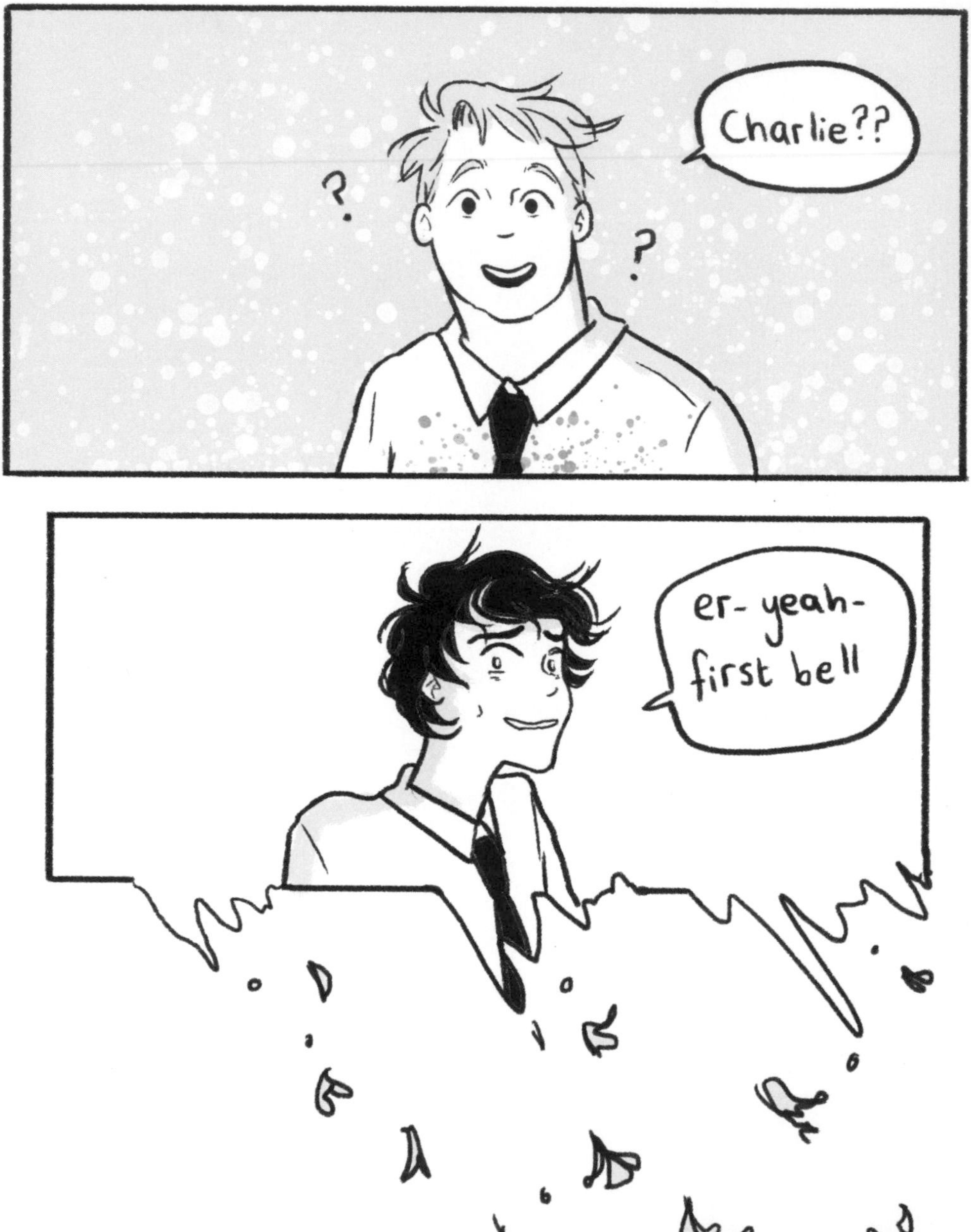
Charlie??
?
?
er- yeah-
first bell

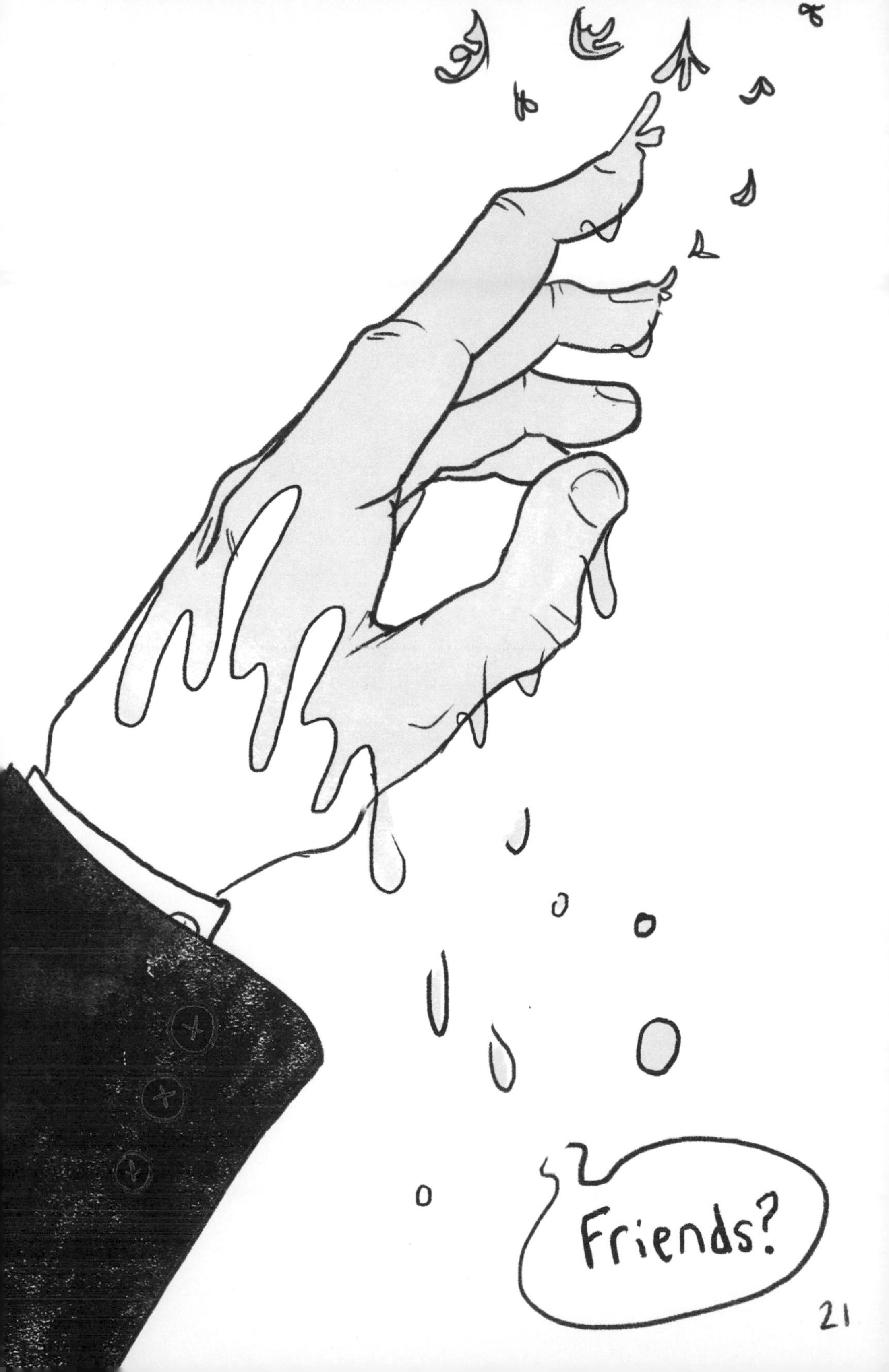
Friends?

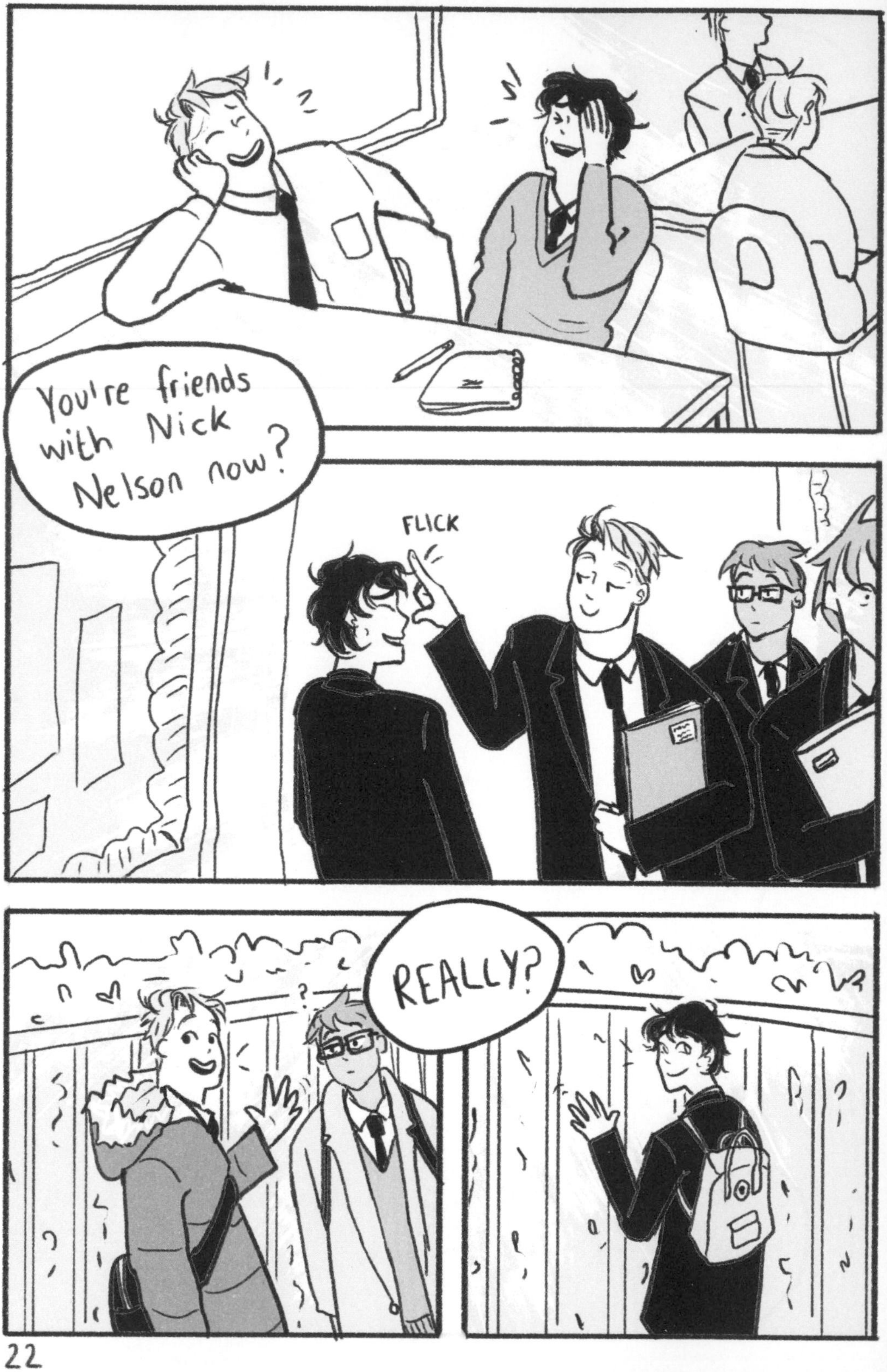
You're friends with Nick Nelson now?
FLICK
REALLY?

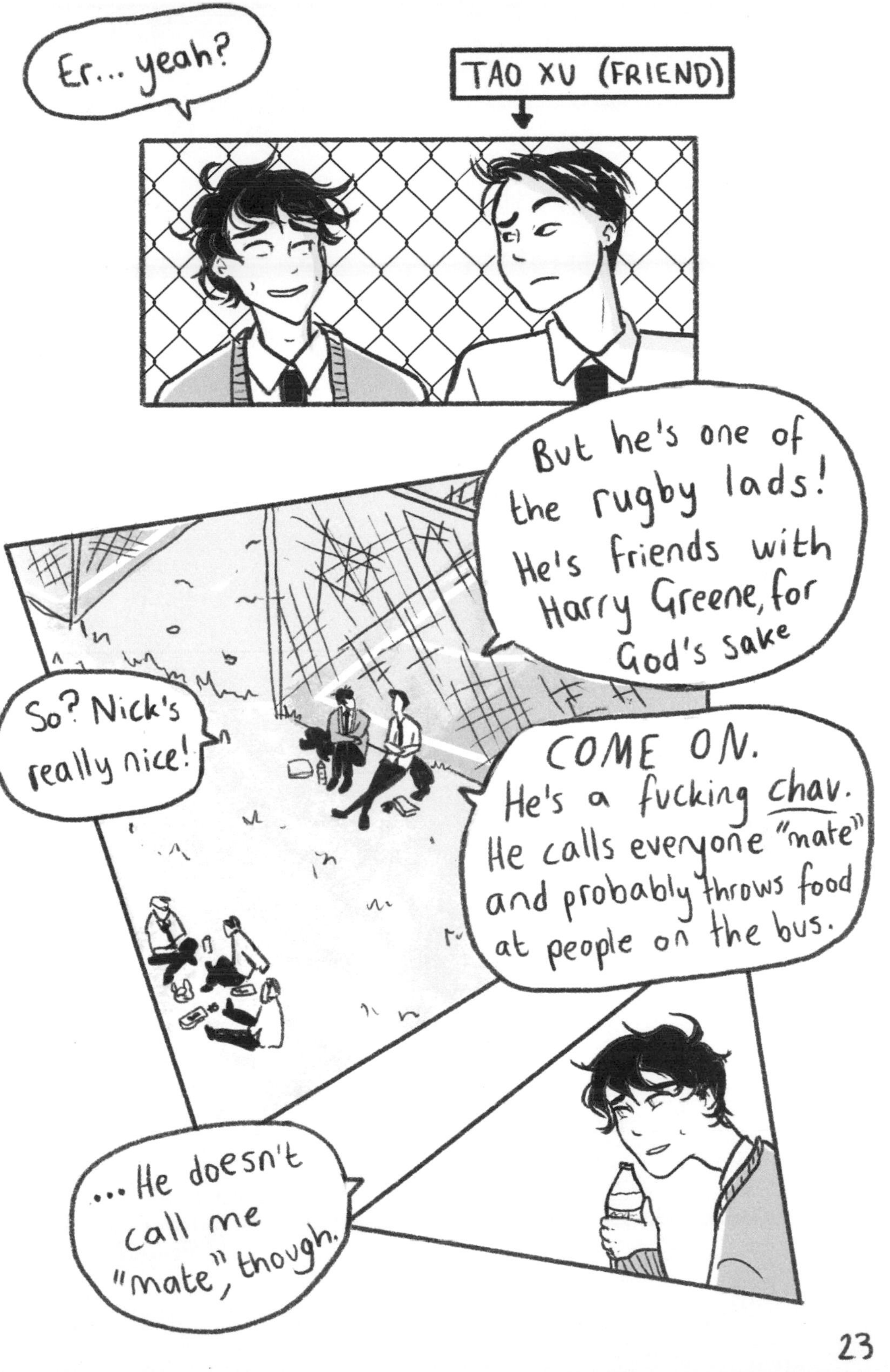
Er... yeah?
TAO XU (FRIEND)
But he's one of the rugby lads! He's friends with Harry Greene, for God's sake
So? Nick's really nice!
COME ON. He's a fucking chav. He calls everyone "mate" and probably throws food at people on the bus.
...He doesn't call me "mate", though.

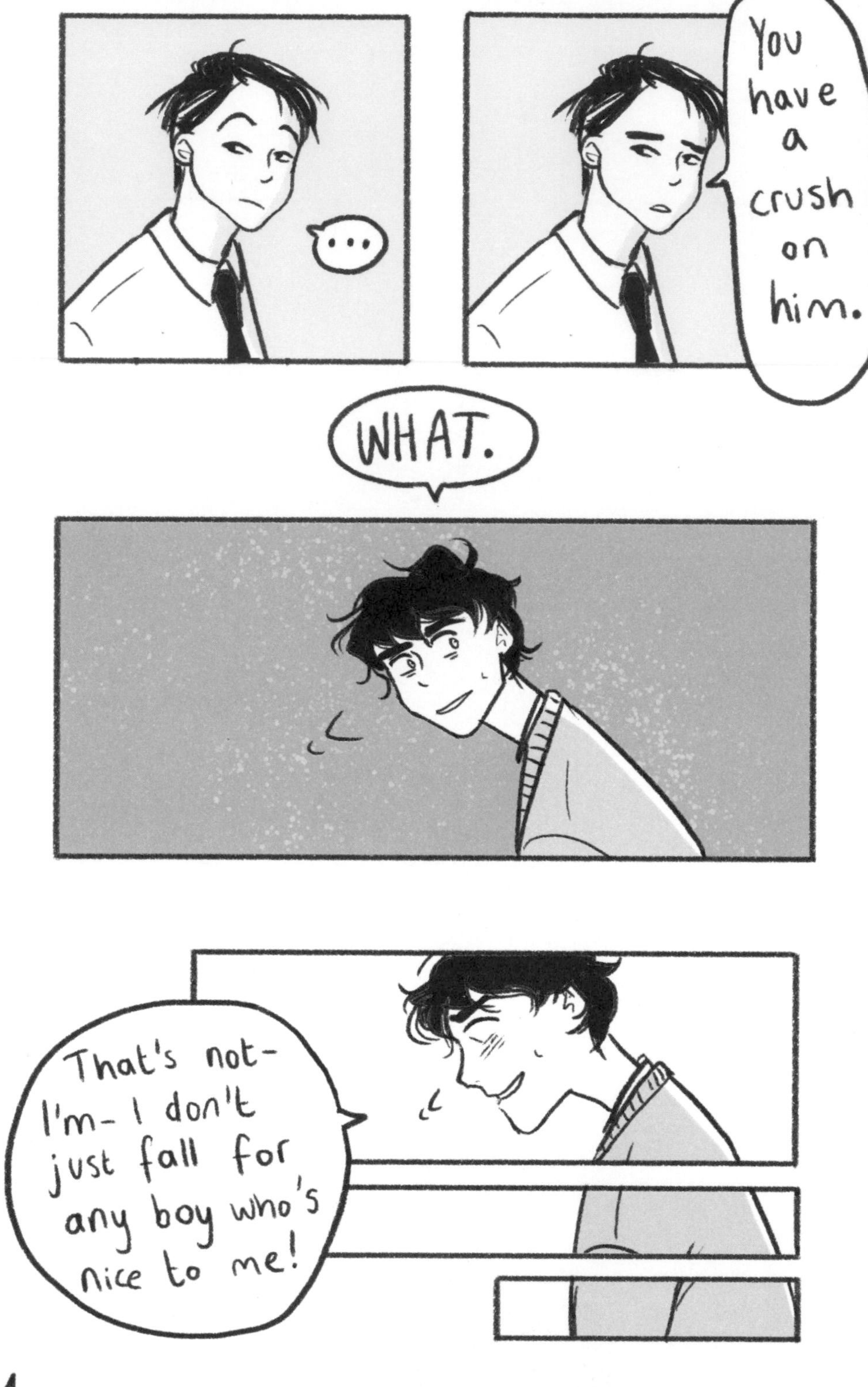
...
You have a crush on him.
WHAT.
That's not- I'm- I don't just fall for any boy who's nice to me!

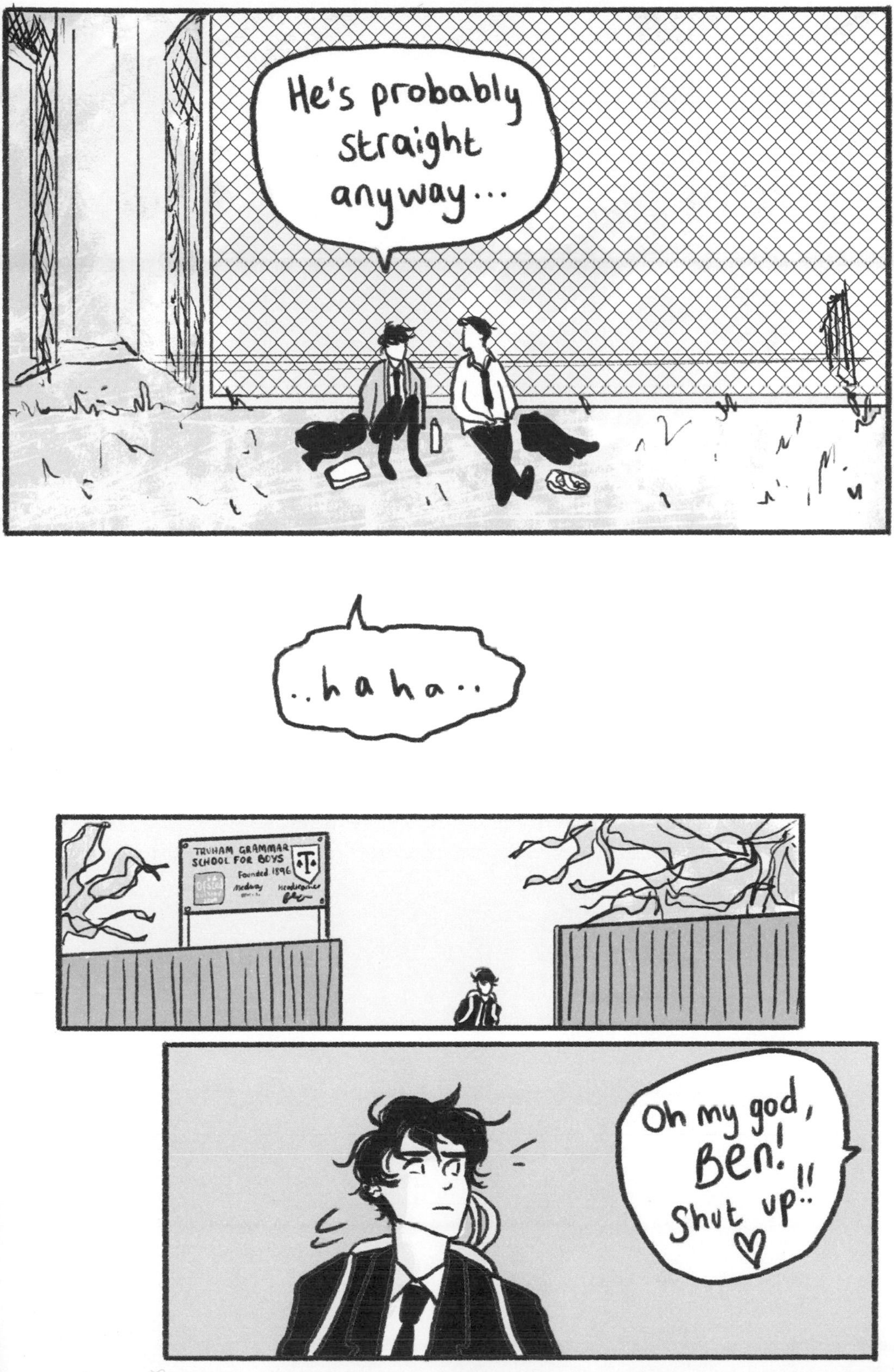
He's probably straight anyway...
..haha..
TRUHAM GRAMMAR SCHOOL FOR BOYS
Founded 1896
Oh my god, Ben! Shut up!! ♥

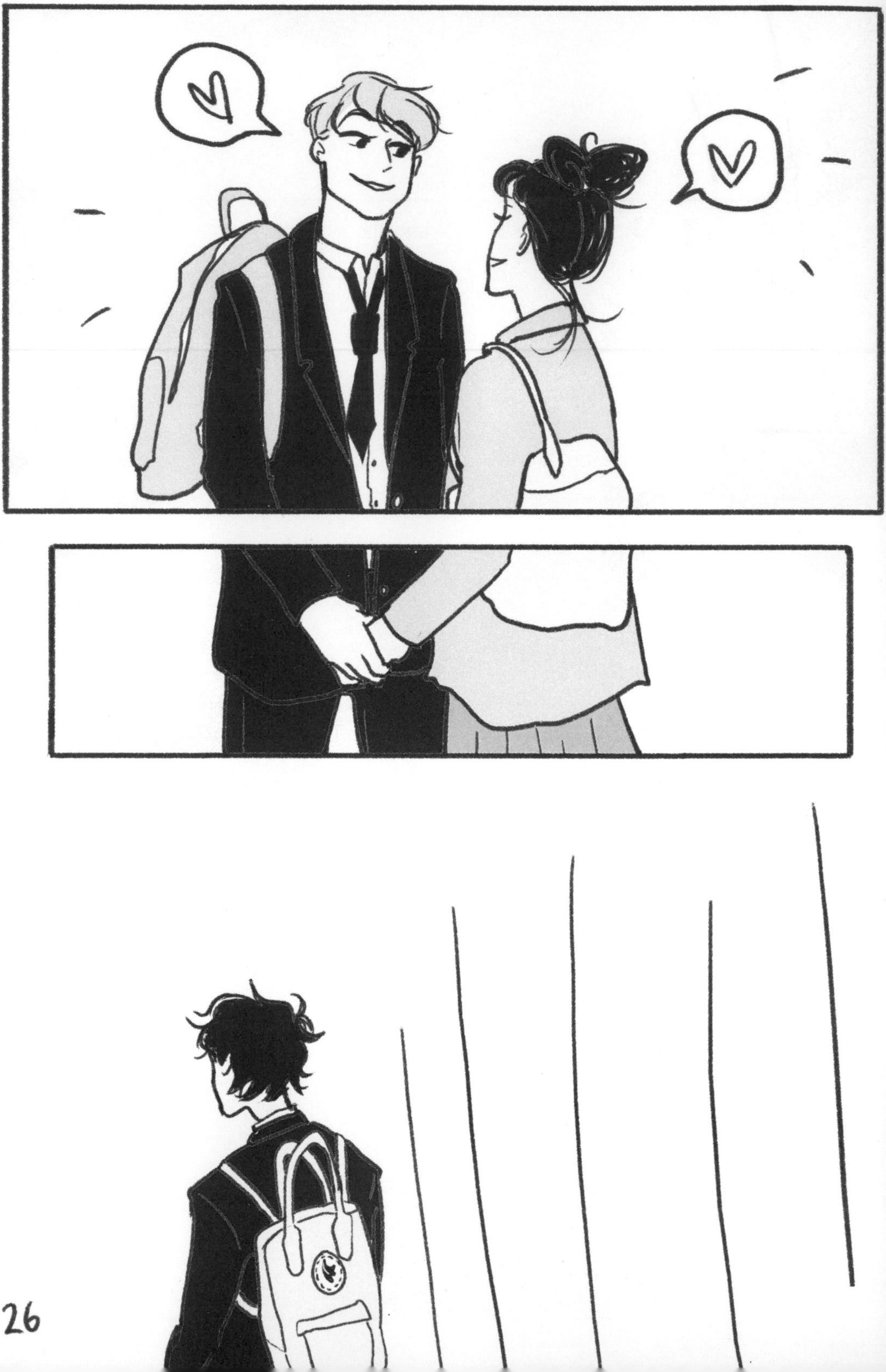

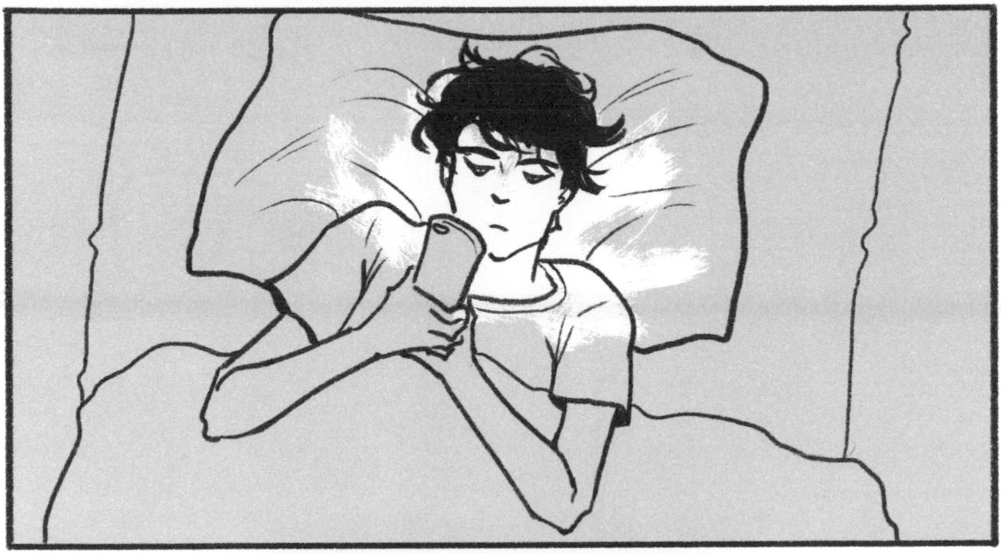

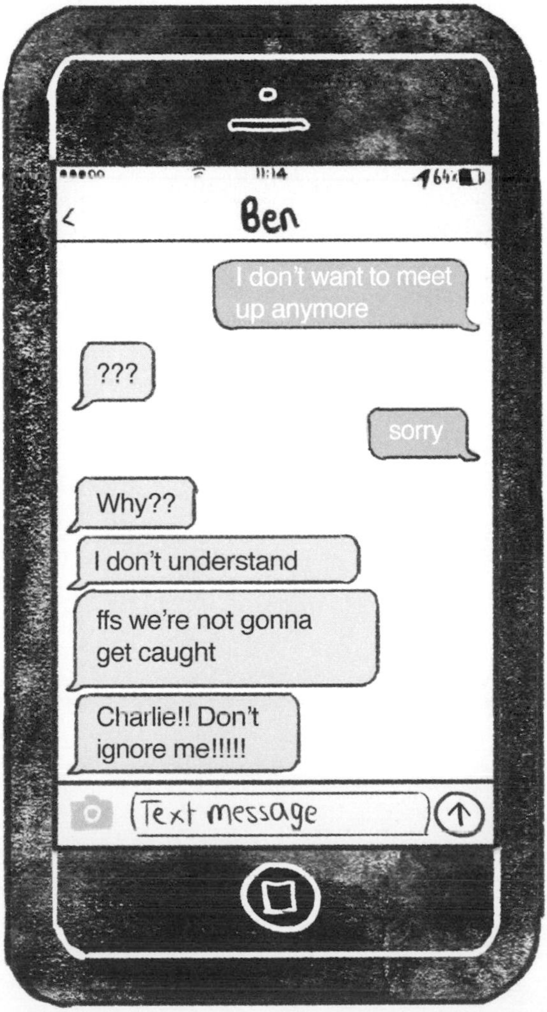
Ben
I don't want to meet up anymore
???
sorry
Why??
I don't understand
ffs we're not gonna get caught
Charlie!! Don't ignore me!!!!!
Text message

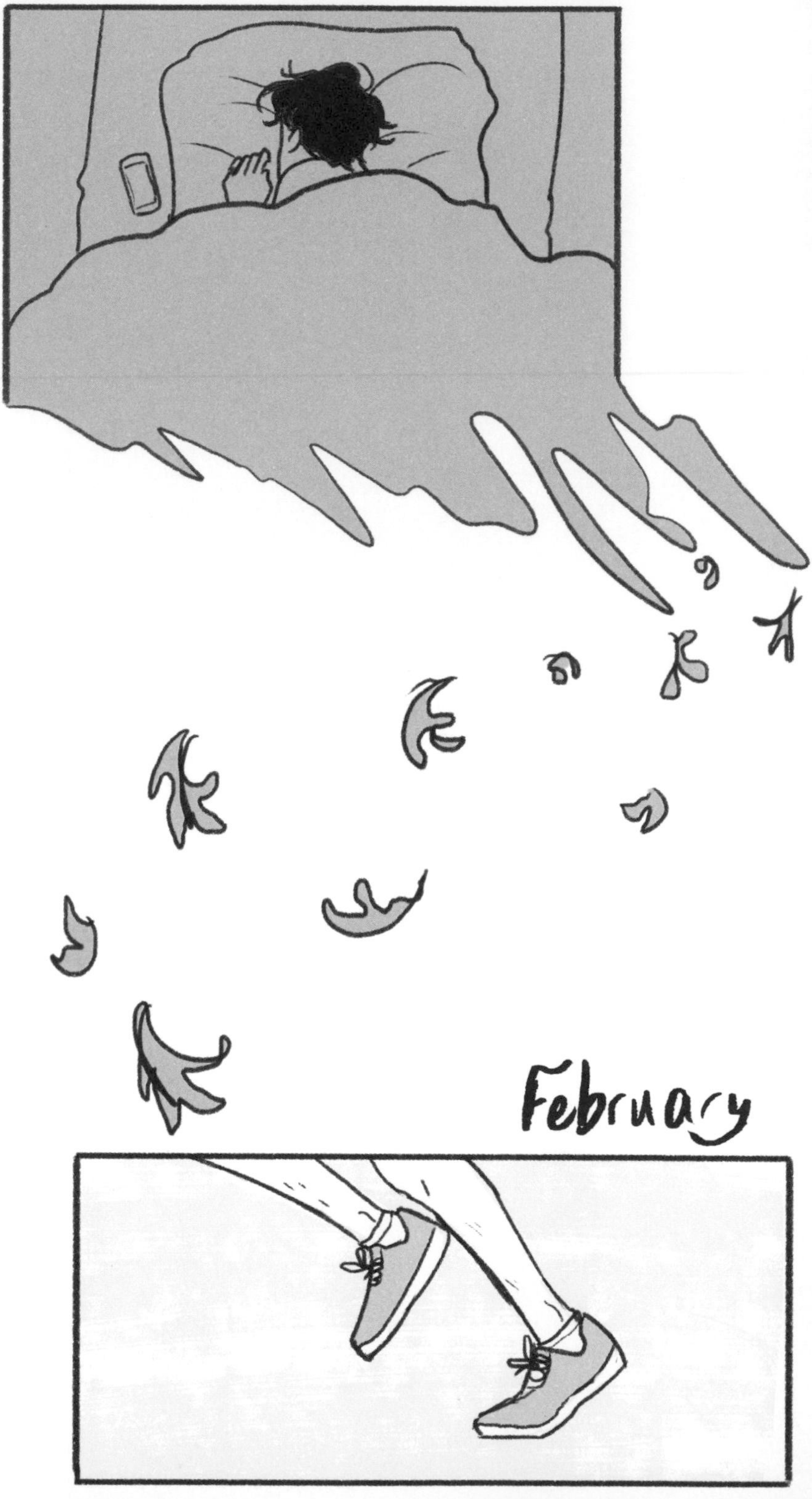
February

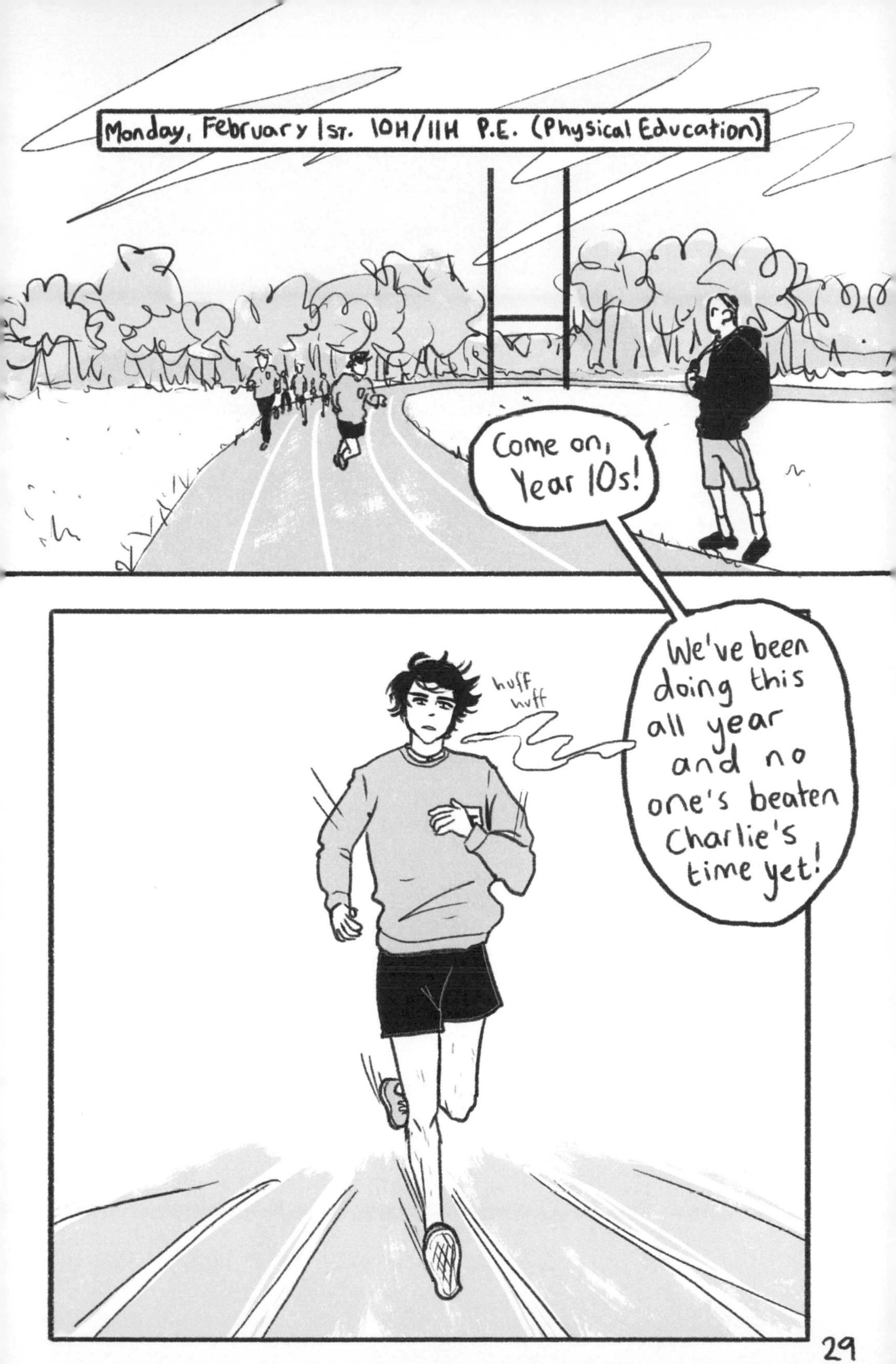
Monday, February 1st. 10H/11H P.E. (Physical Education)
Come on, Year 10s!
We've been doing this all year and no one's beaten Charlie's time yet!
huff huff

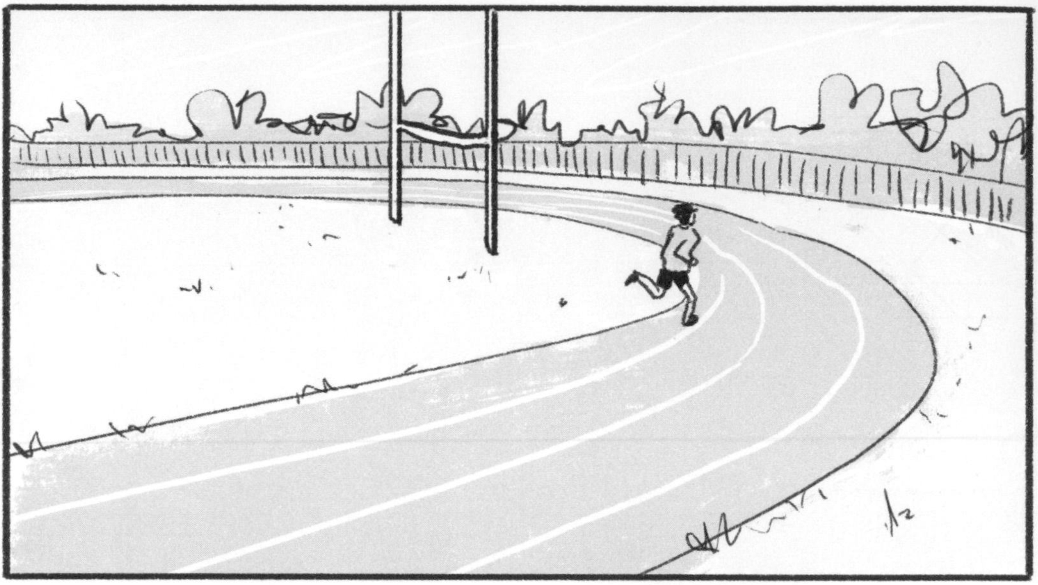

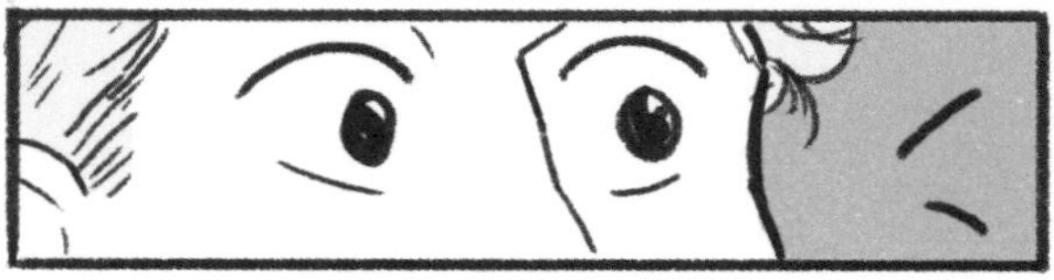

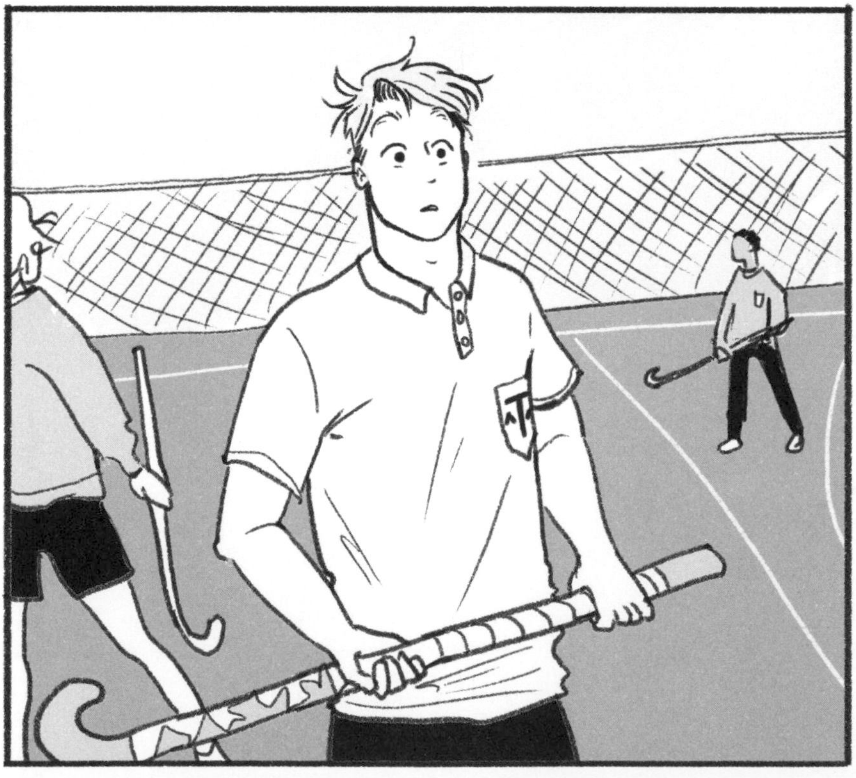

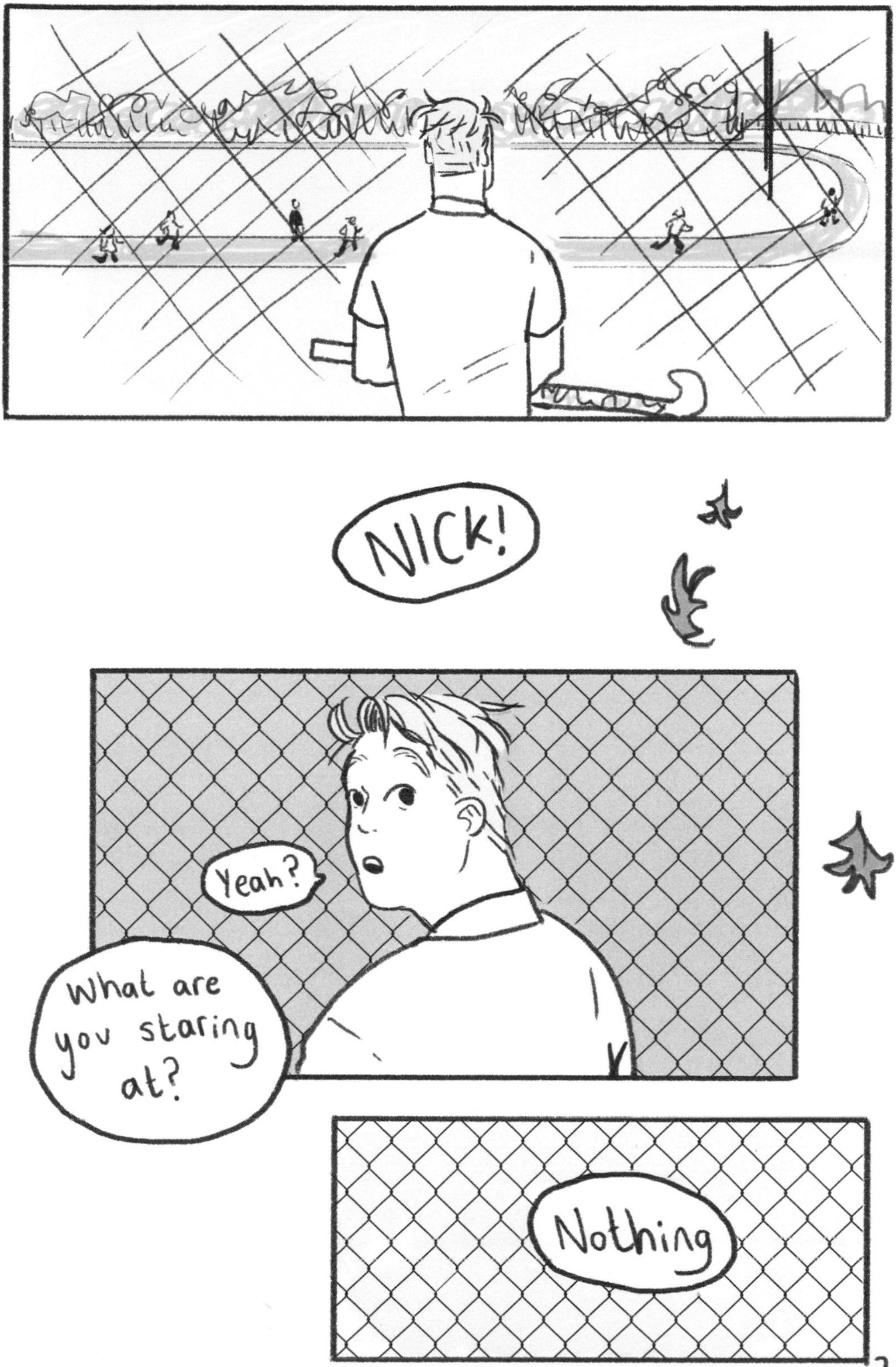
NICK!
Yeah?
What are you staring at?
Nothing

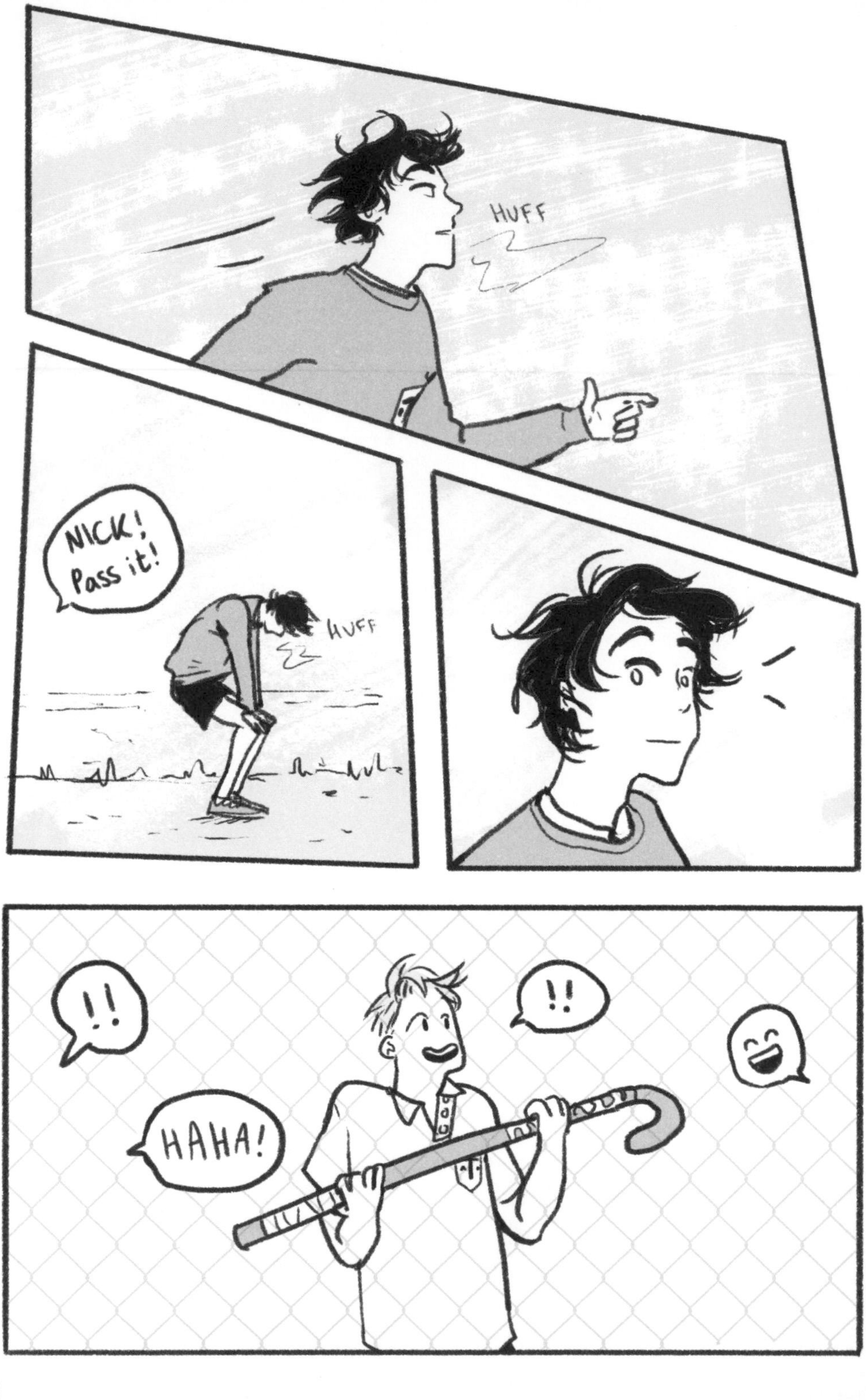
HUFF
NICK! Pass it!
HUFF
!!
!!
HAHA!

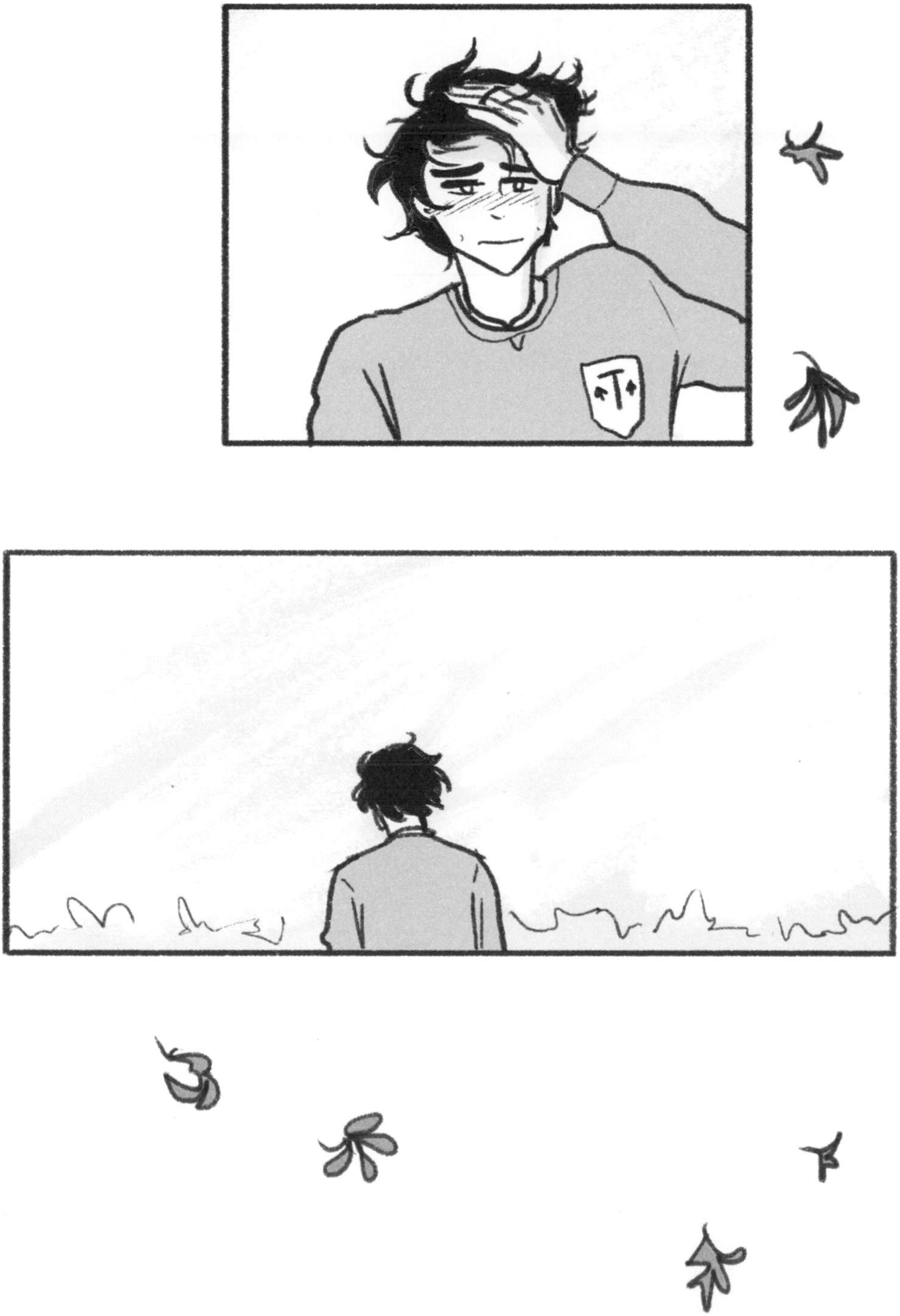

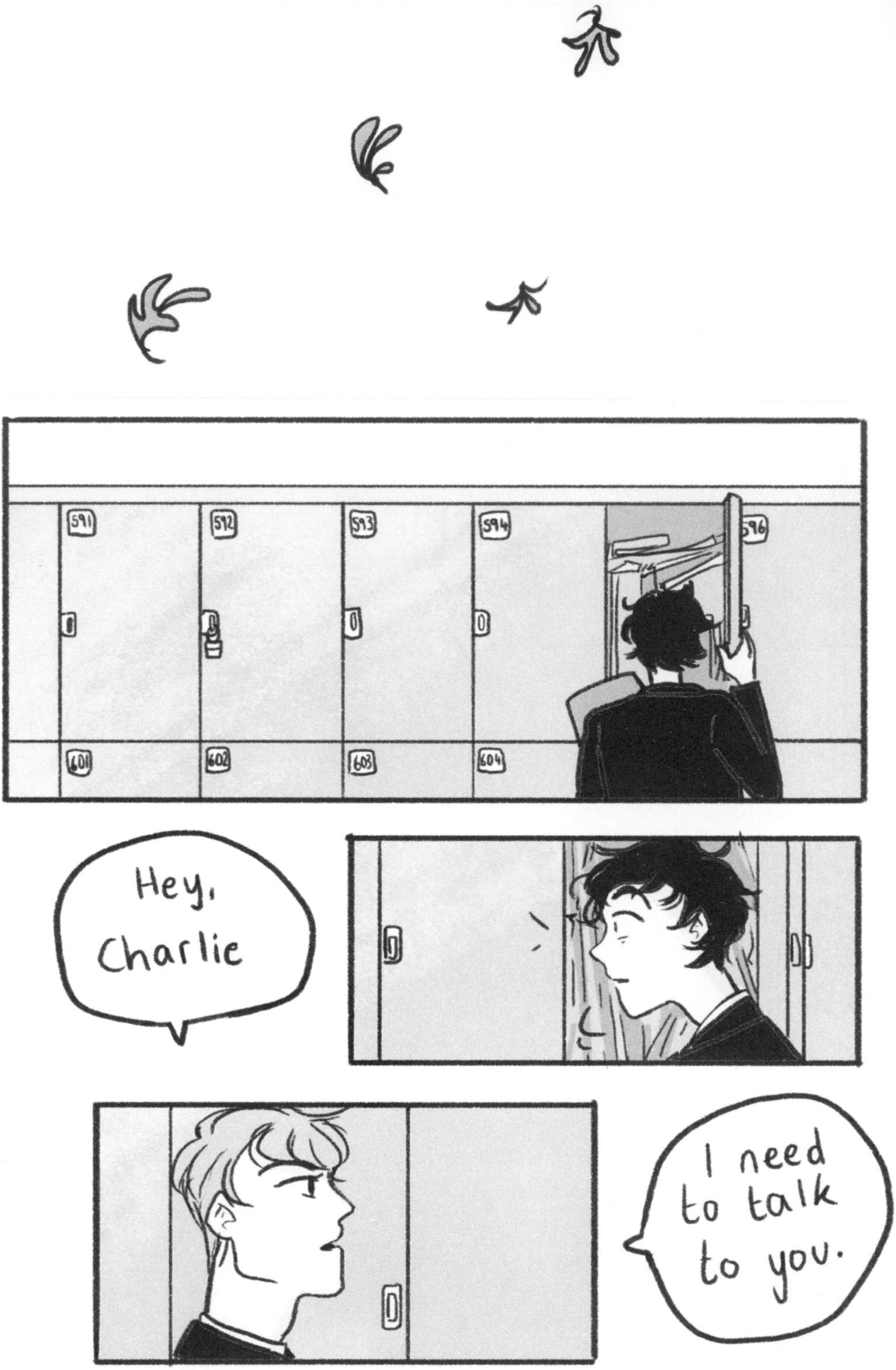
591
592
593
594
596
601
602
603
604
Hey, Charlie
I need to talk to you.

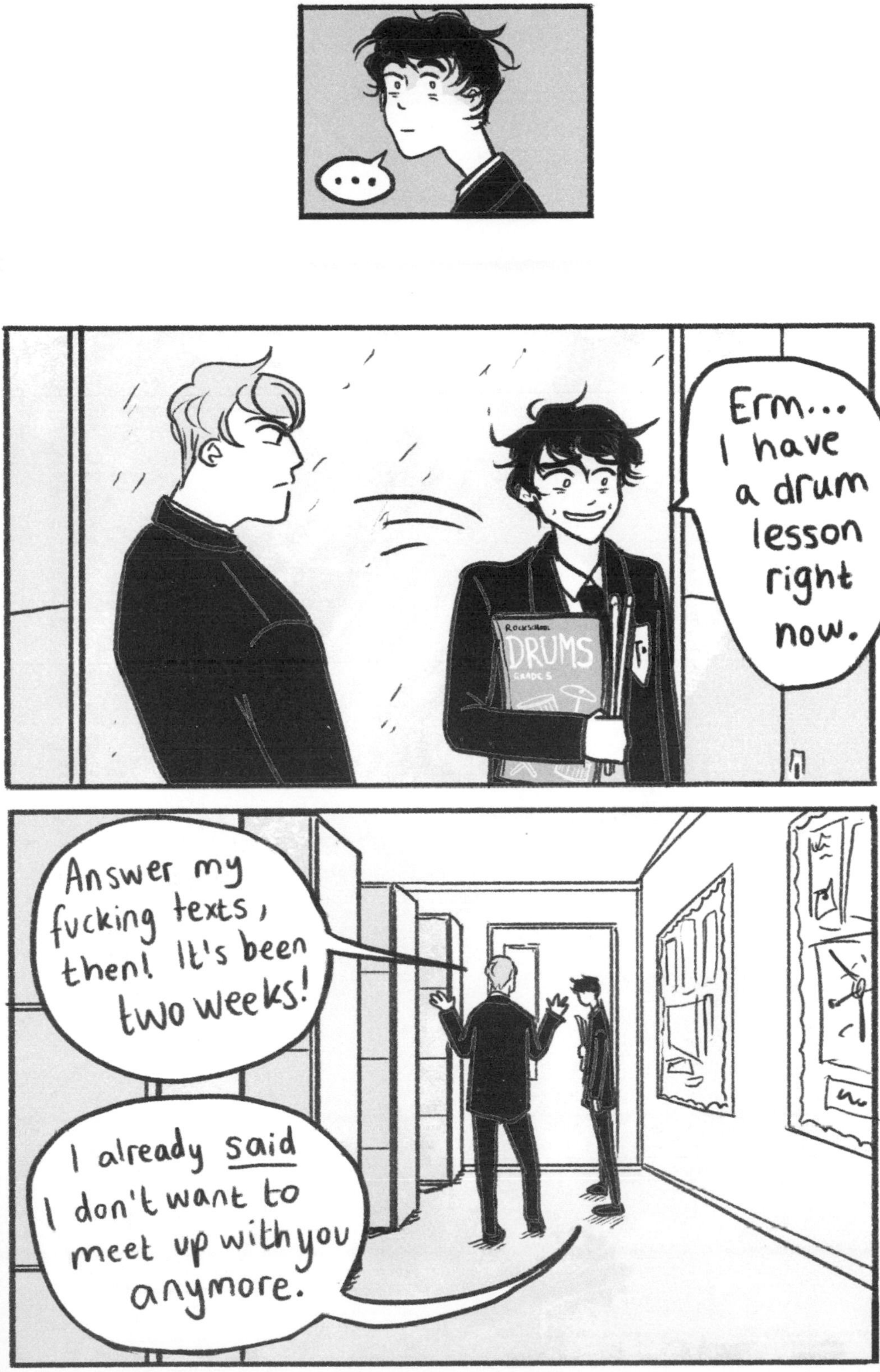
...
Erm... I have a drum lesson right now.
ROCKSCHOOL DRUMS GRADE 5
Answer my fucking texts, then! It's been two weeks!
I already said I don't want to meet up with you anymore.

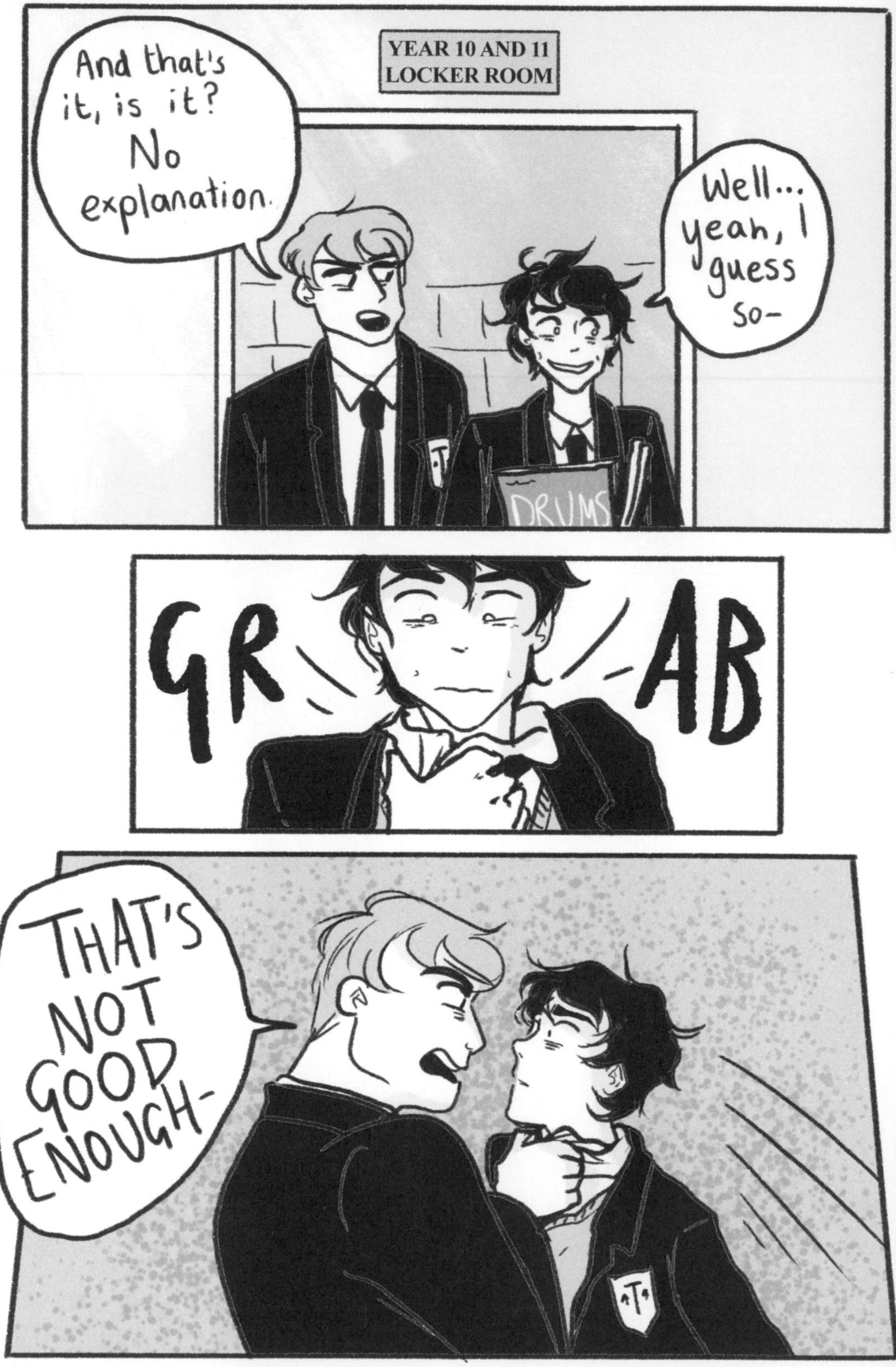

YEAR 10 AND 11 LOCKER ROOM
And that's it, is it? No explanation.
Well... yeah, I guess so-
DRUMS
GRAB
THAT'S NOT GOOD ENOUGH-

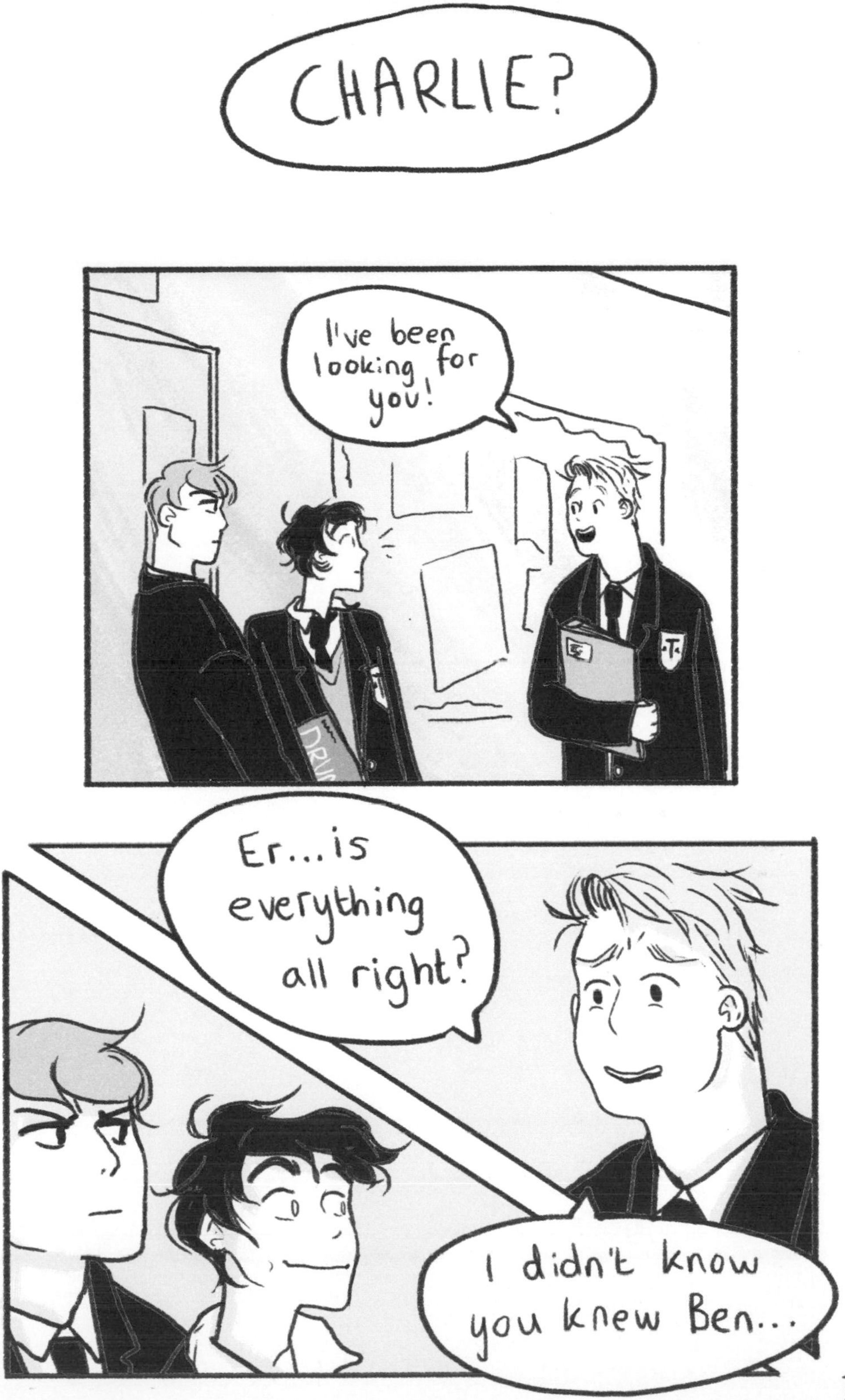
CHARLIE?
I've been looking for you!
Er...is everything all right?
I didn't know you knew Ben...

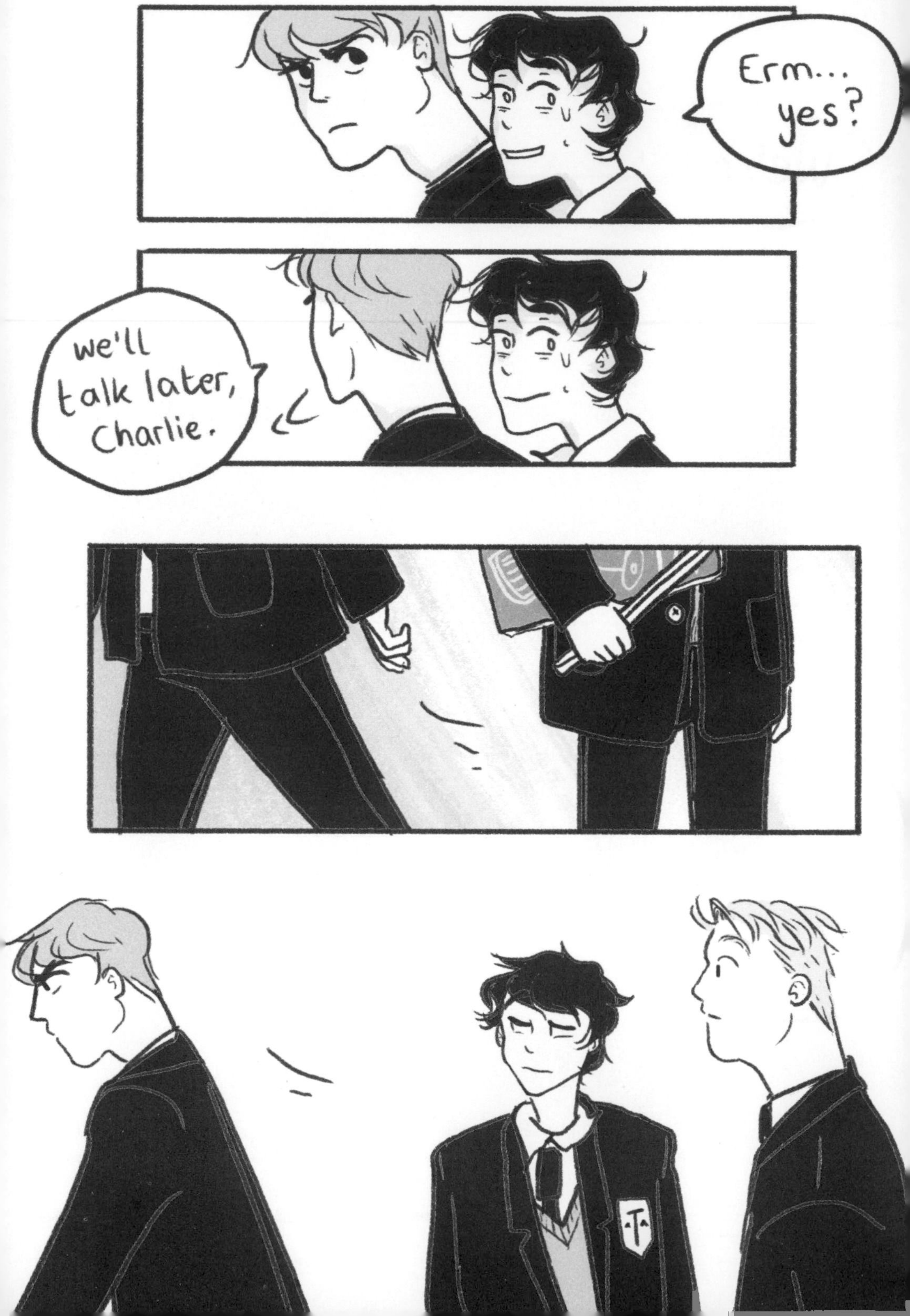
Erm... yes?
we'll talk later, Charlie.

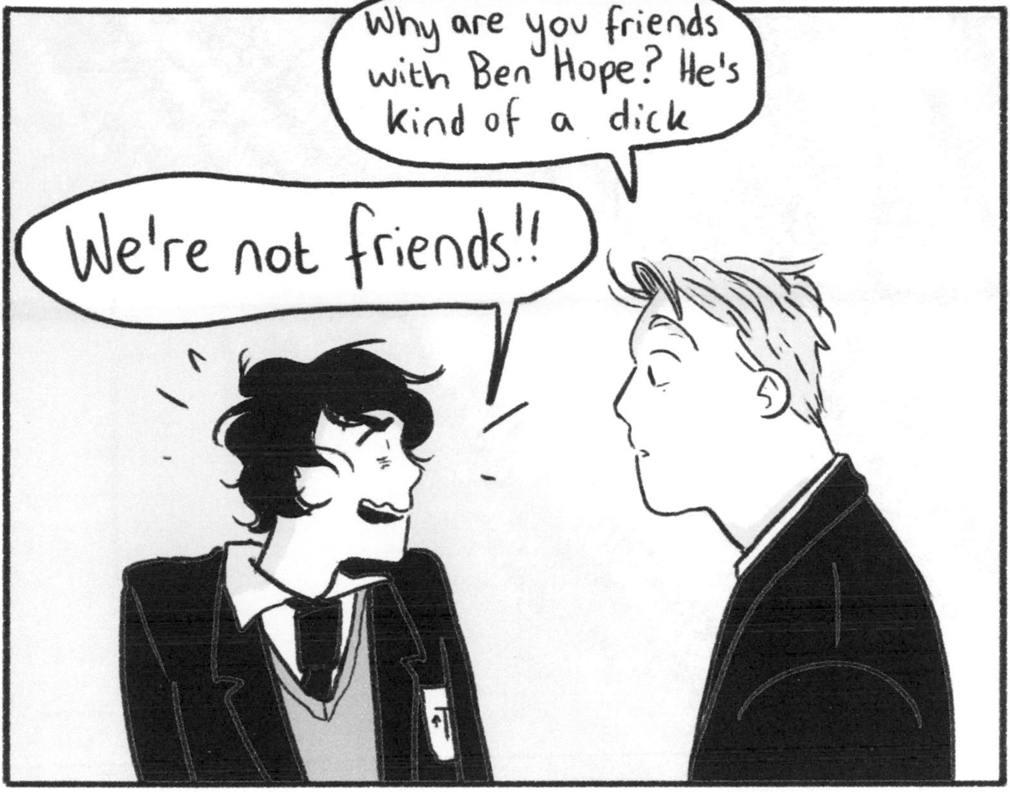
Why are you friends with Ben Hope? He's kind of a dick
We're not friends!!

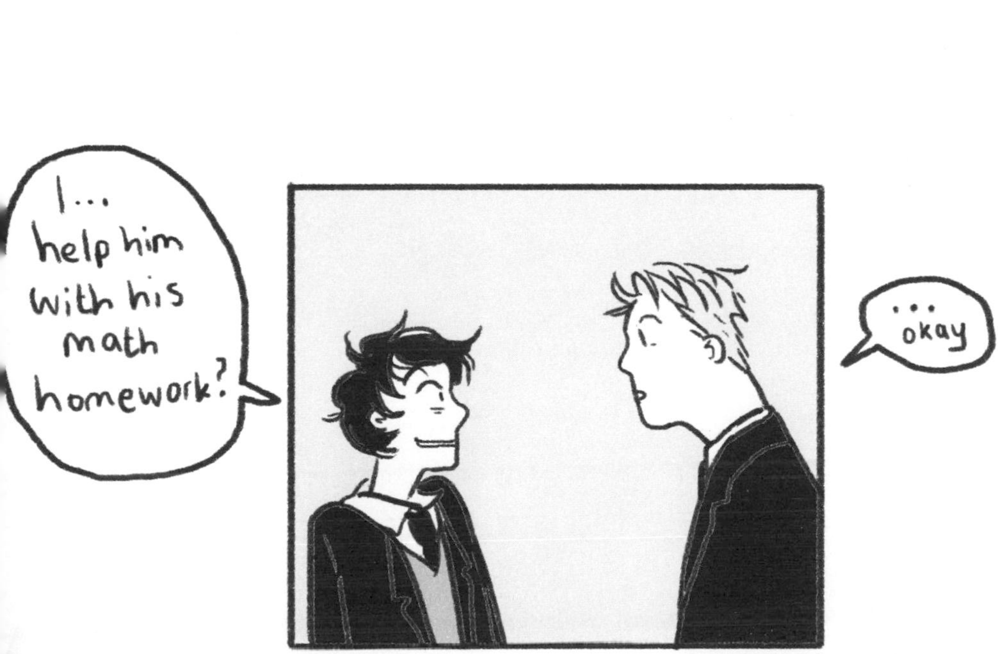
I... help him with his math homework?
...okay

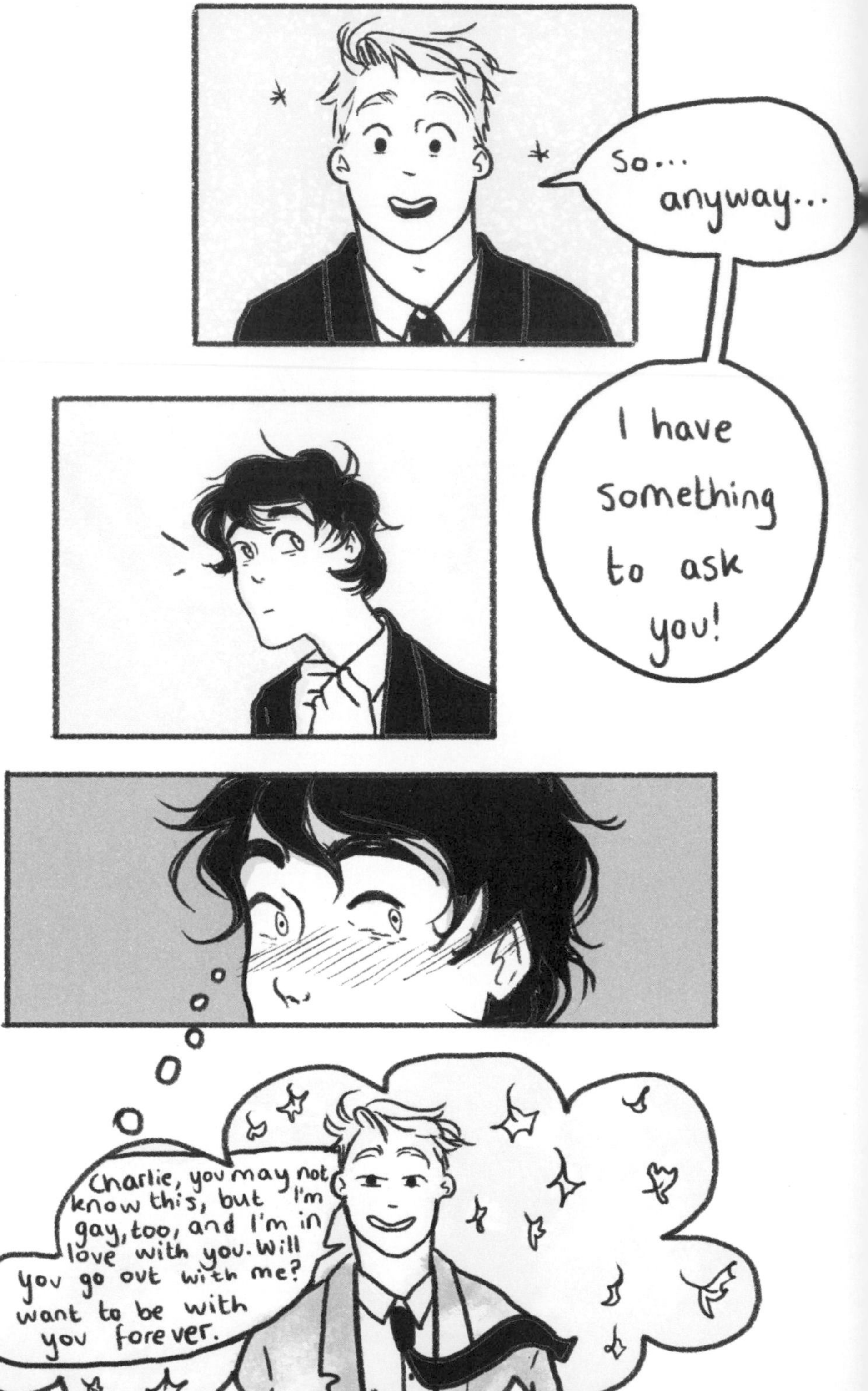
So... anyway...
I have something to ask you!
Charlie, you may not know this, but I'm gay, too, and I'm in love with you. Will you go out with me? I want to be with you forever.

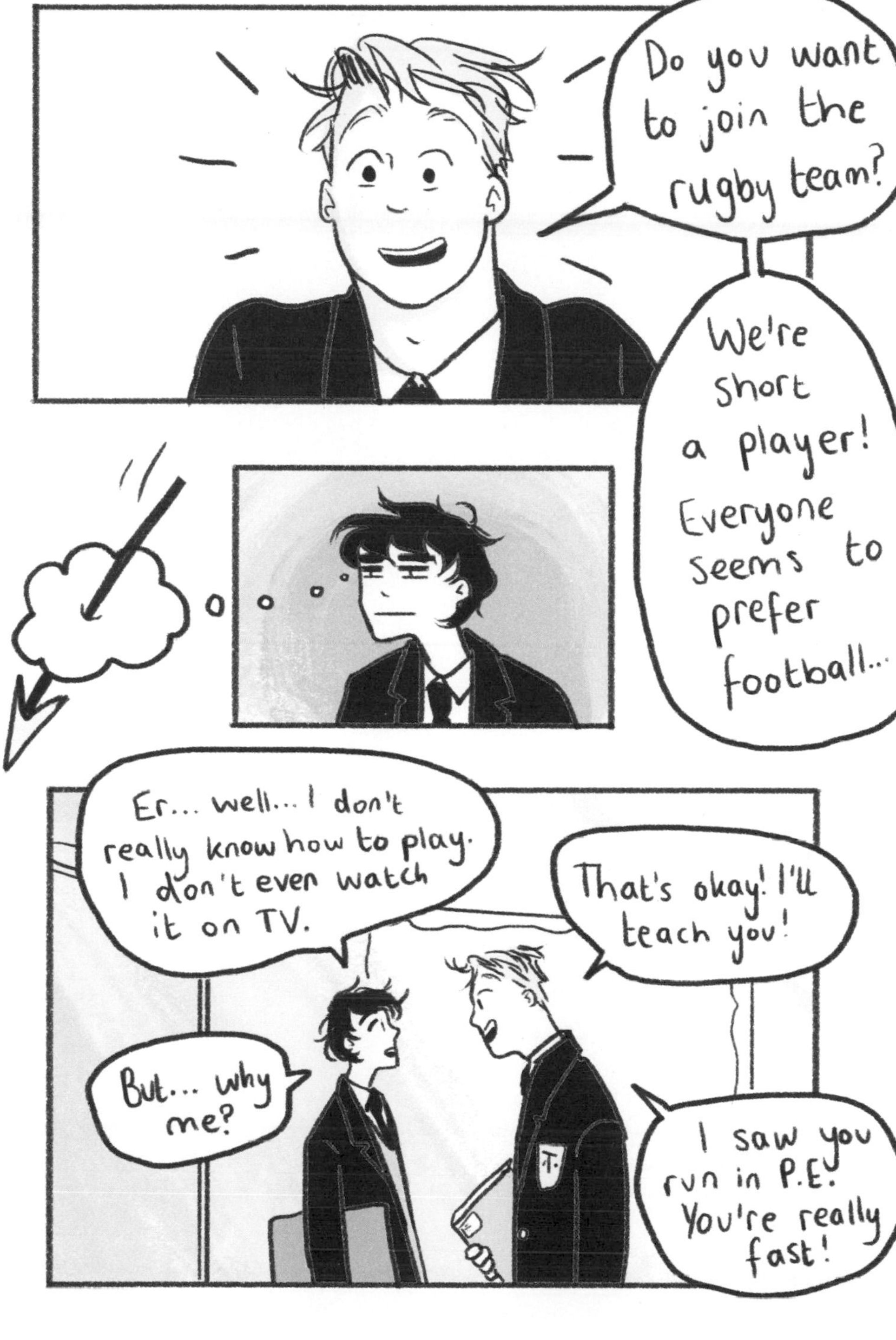
Do you want to join the rugby team?
We're short a player! Everyone seems to prefer football...
Er... well... I don't really know how to play. I don't even watch it on TV.
That's okay! I'll teach you!
But... why me?
I saw you run in P.E.! You're really fast!

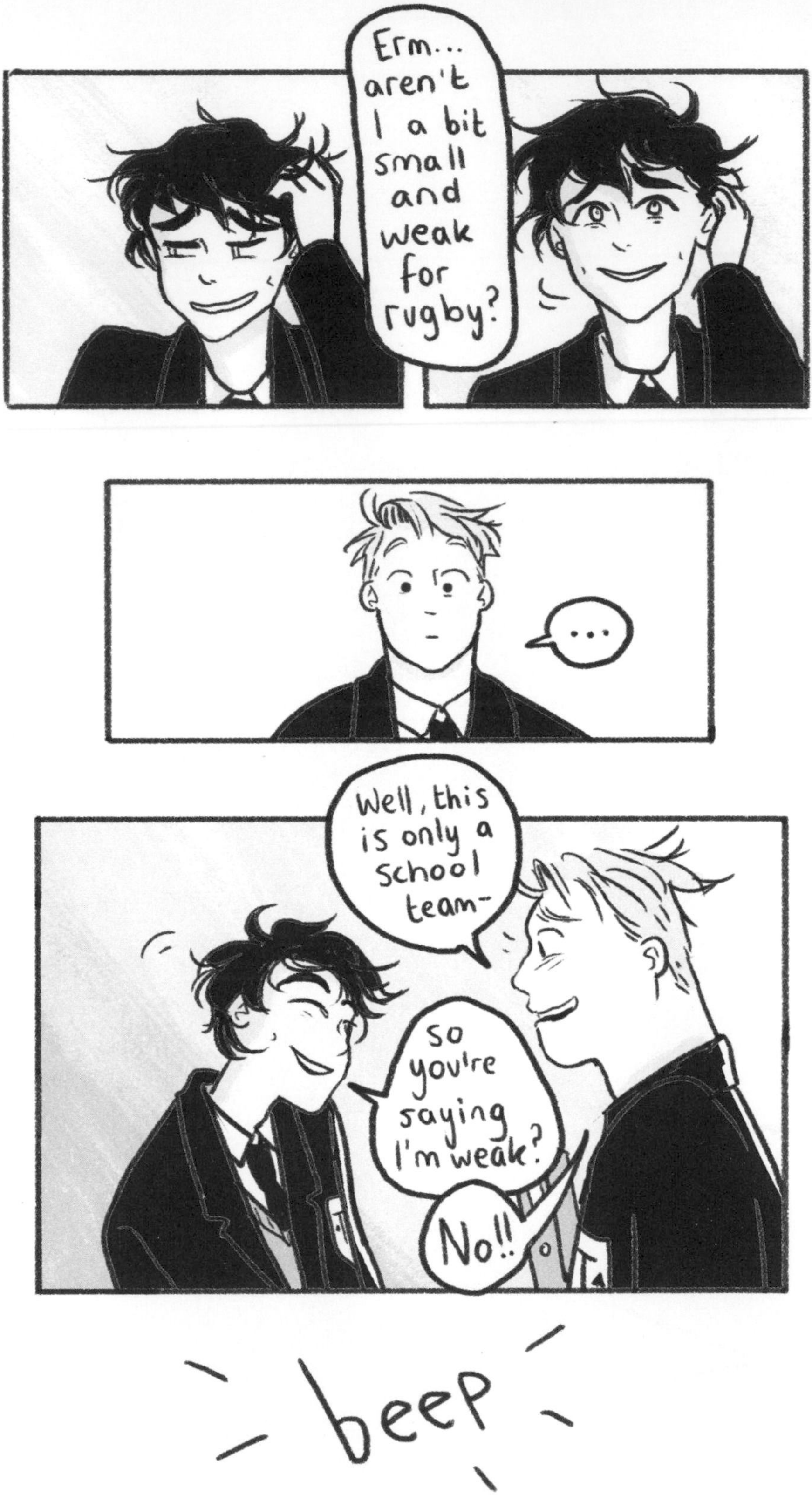
Erm... aren't I a bit small and weak for rugby?
...
Well, this is only a school team-
So you're saying I'm weak?
No!!
beep

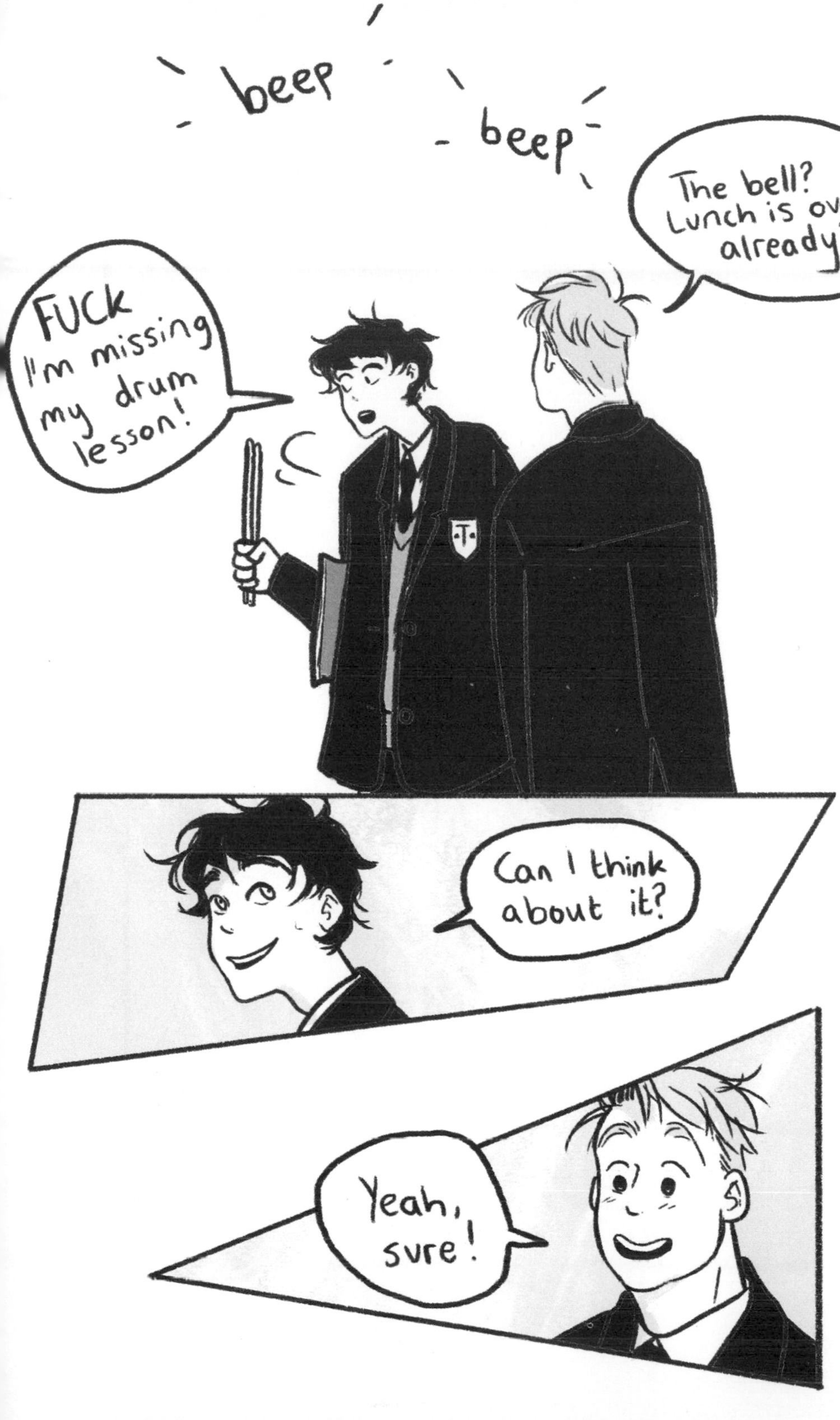
beep
beep
The bell? Lunch is over already?
FUCK I'm missing my drum lesson!
Can I think about it?
Yeah, sure!

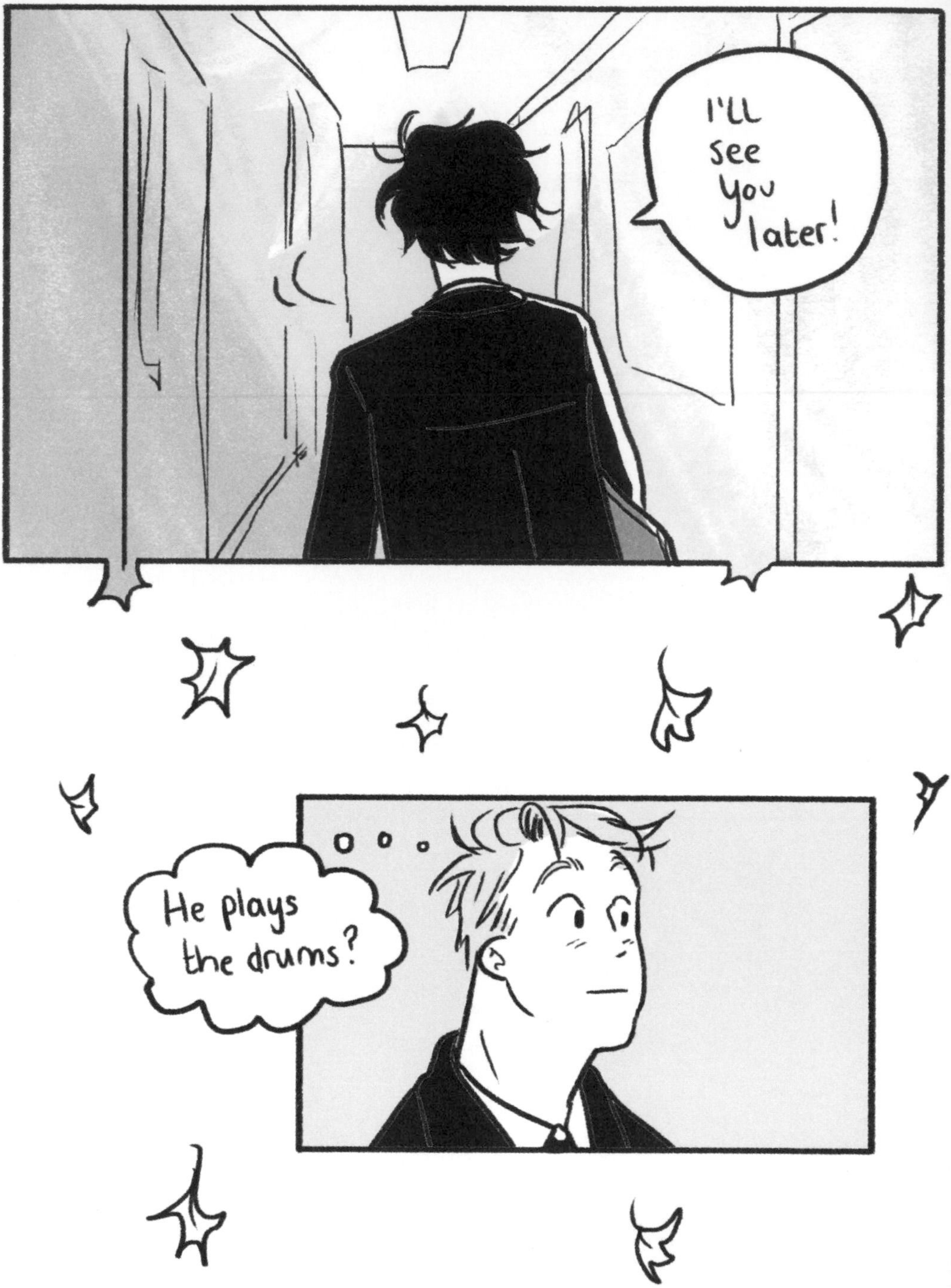
I'll see you later!
...
He plays the drums?

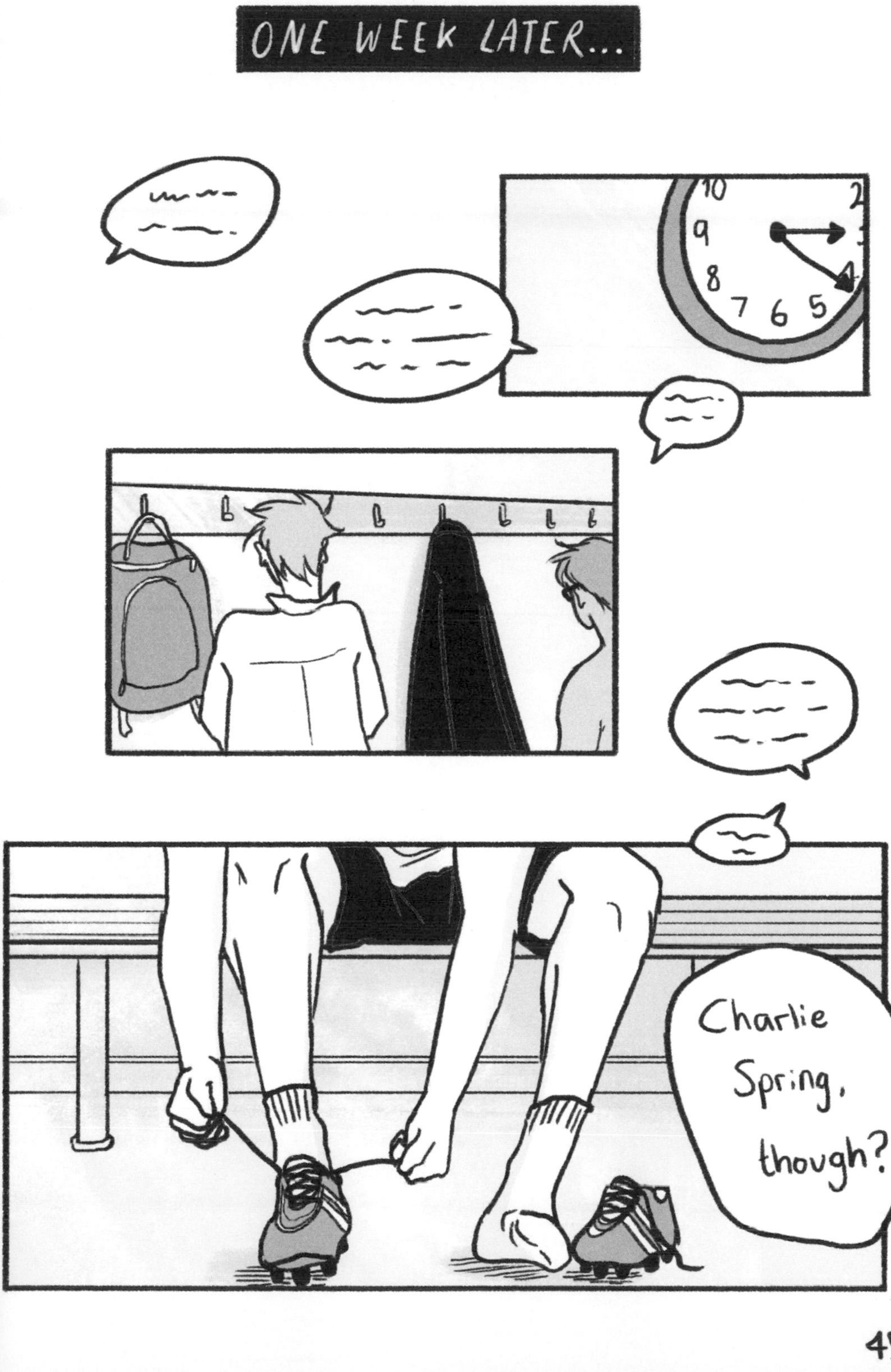
ONE WEEK LATER...
Charlie Spring, though?

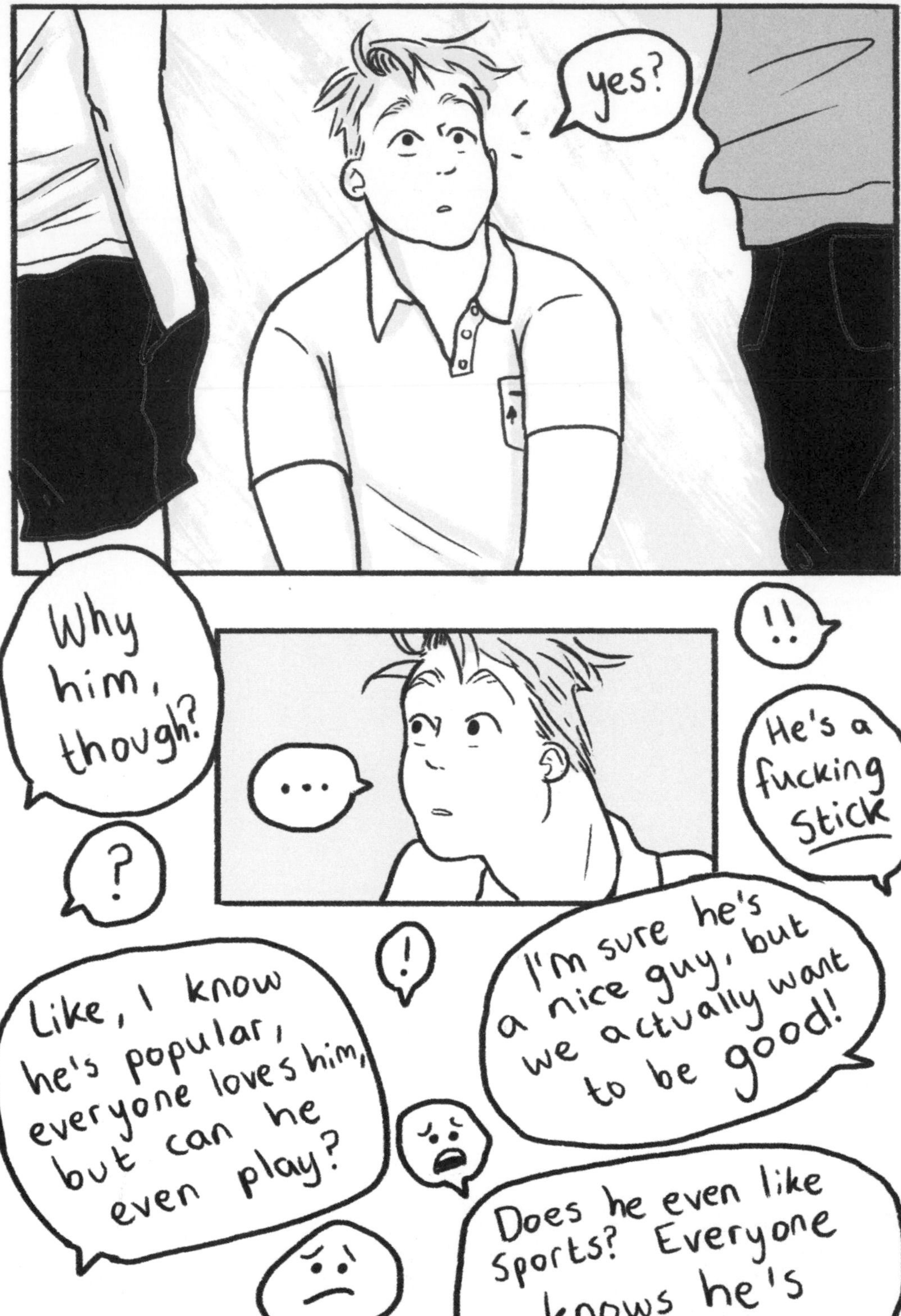
yes?
Why him, though?
!!
...
He's a fucking Stick
?
!
I'm sure he's a nice guy, but we actually want to be good!
Like, I know he's popular, everyone loves him, but can he even play?
Does he even like Sports? Everyone knows he's gay-

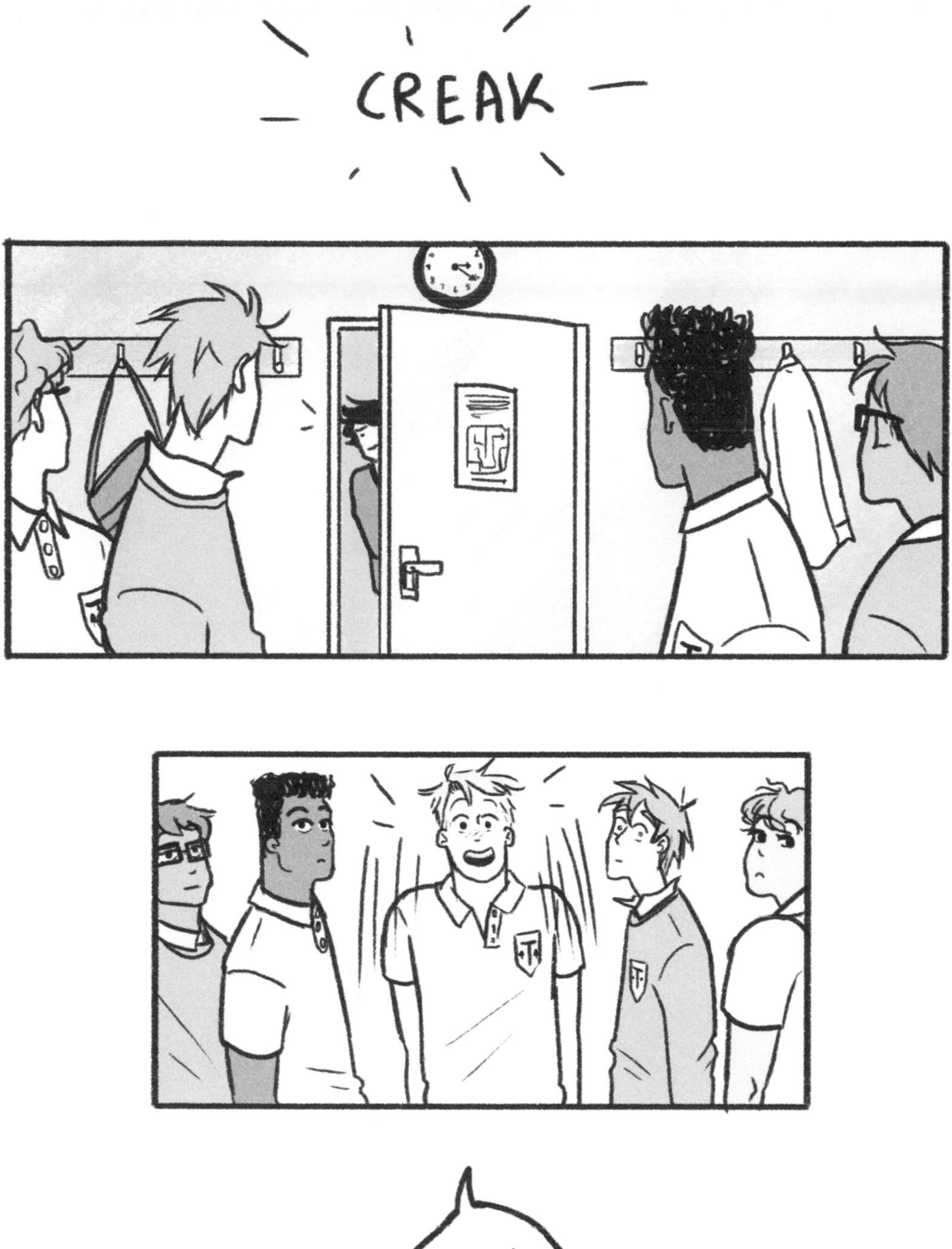
CREAK
Hey!

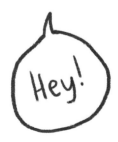

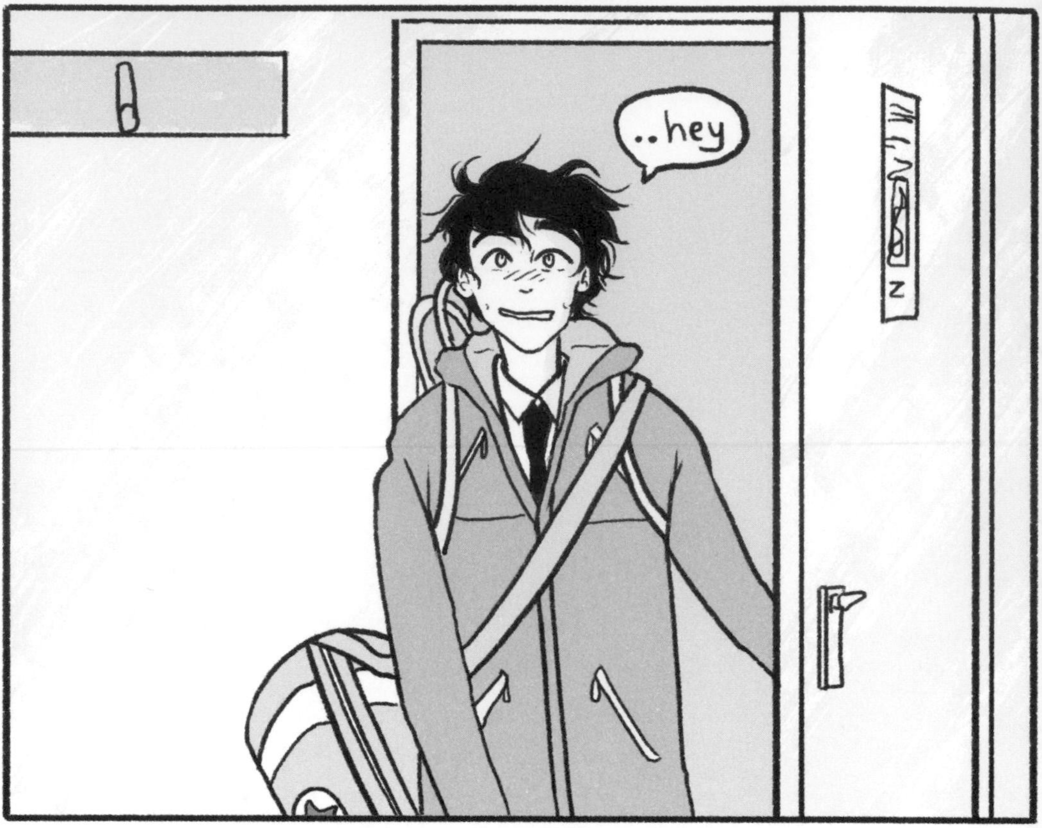
..hey

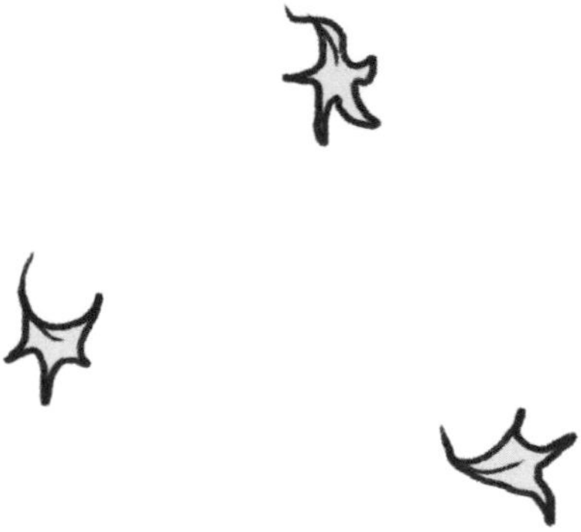

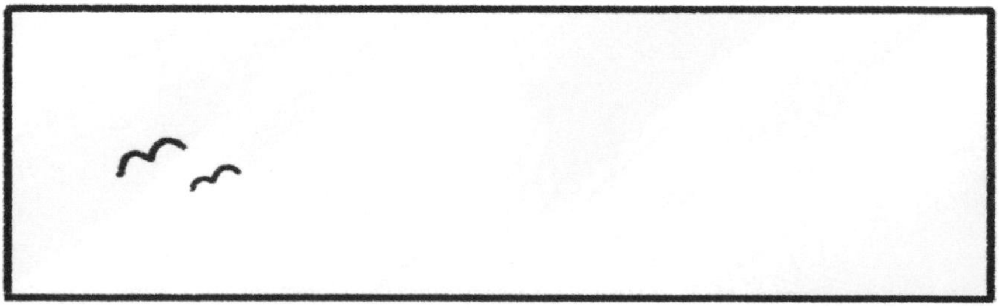

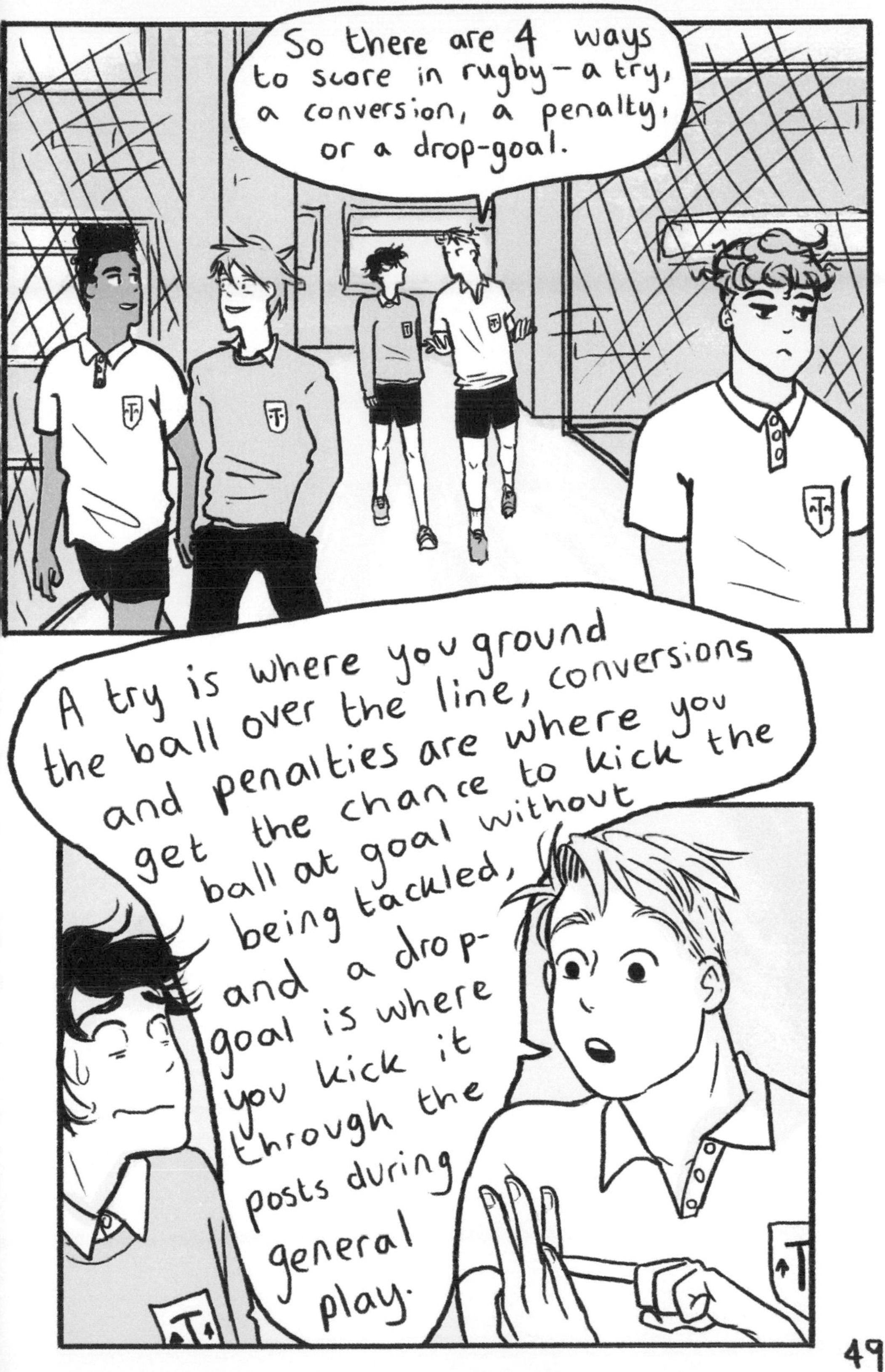
So there are 4 ways to score in rugby—a try, a conversion, a penalty, or a drop-goal.
A try is where you ground the ball over the line, conversions and penalties are where you get the chance to kick the ball at goal without being tackled, and a drop-goal is where you kick it through the posts during general play.

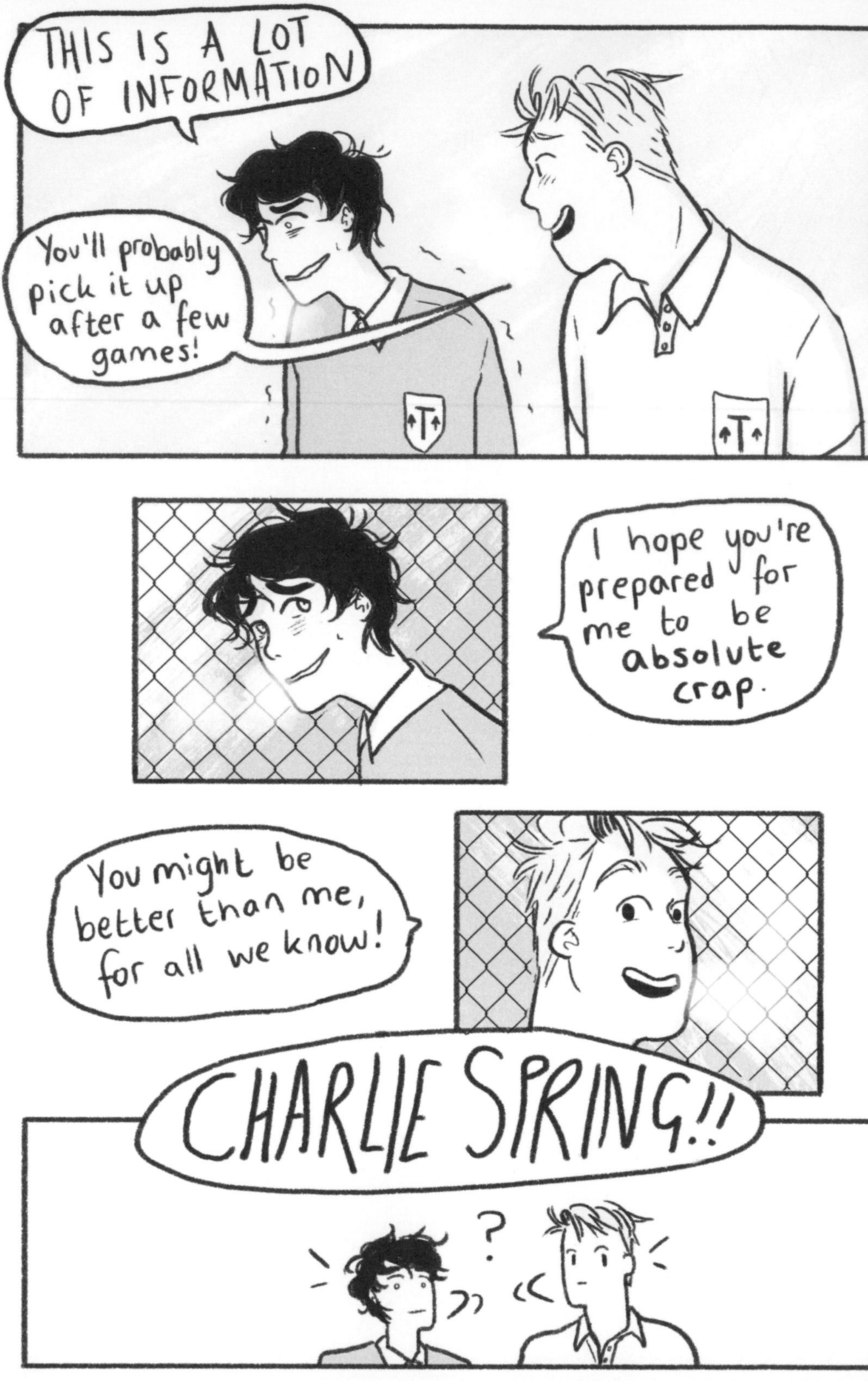
THIS IS A LOT OF INFORMATION
You'll probably pick it up after a few games!
I hope you're prepared for me to be absolute crap.
You might be better than me, for all we know!
CHARLIE SPRING!!
?

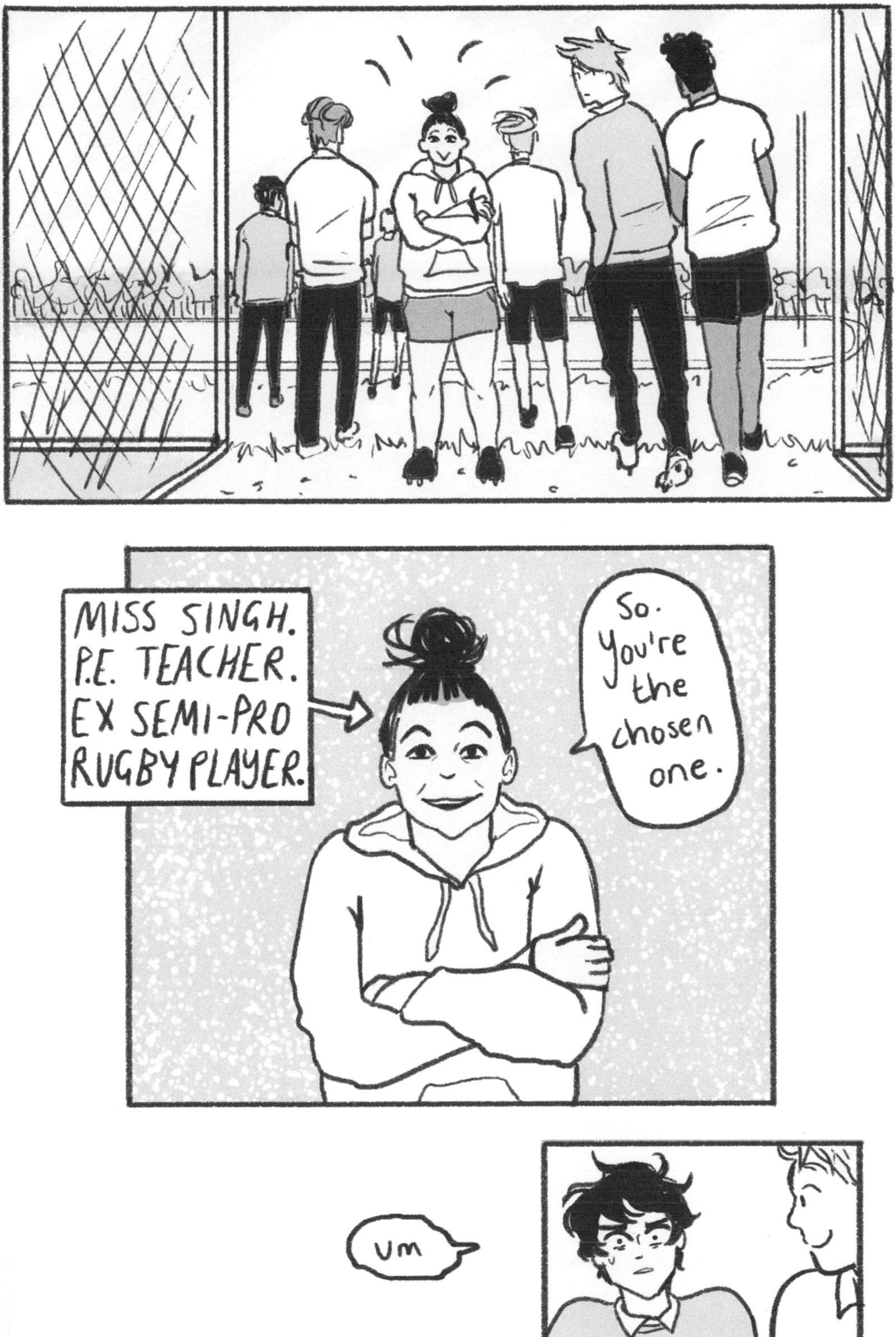
MISS SINGH. P.E. TEACHER. EX SEMI-PRO RUGBY PLAYER.
So. You're the chosen one.
um

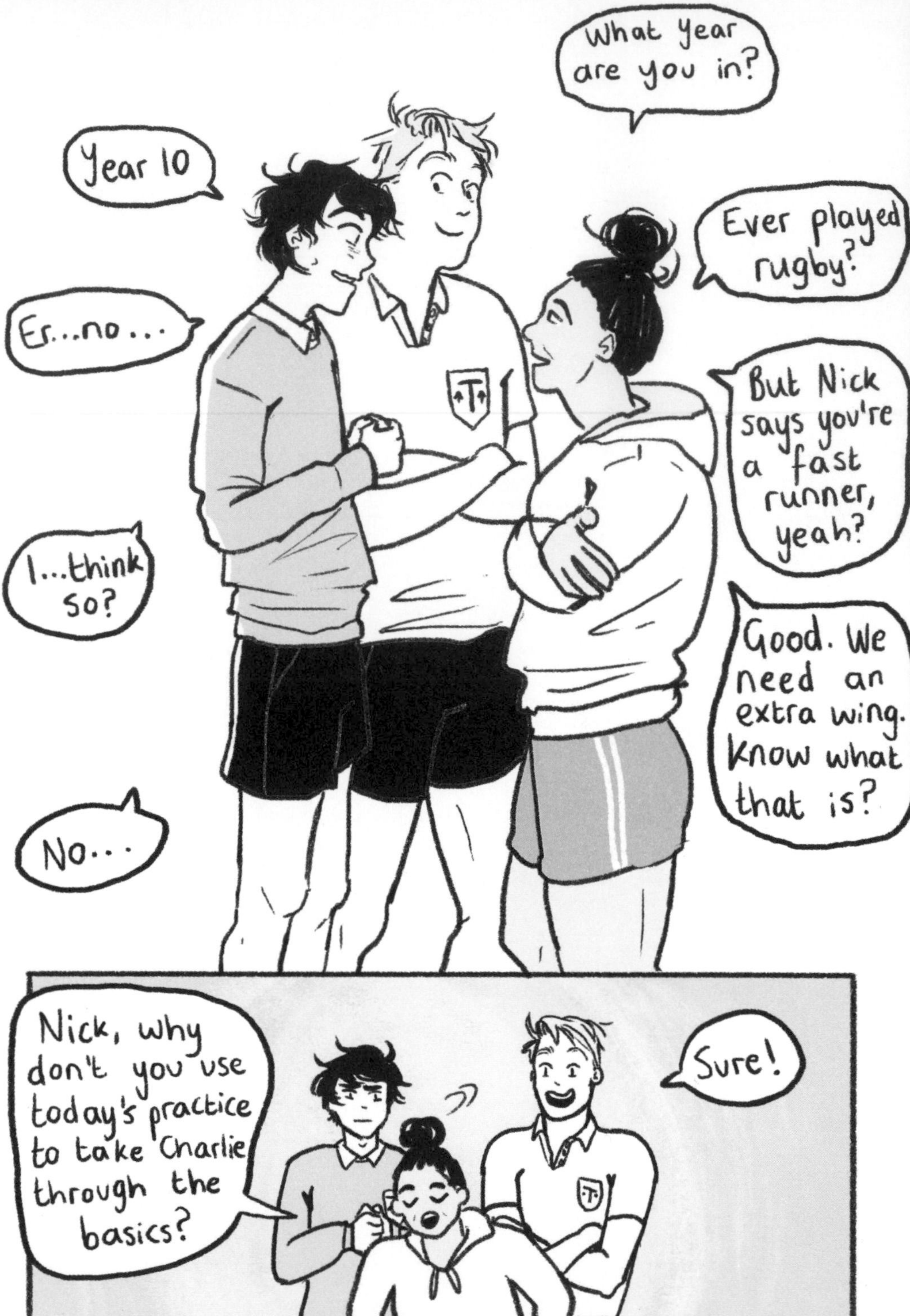
What year are you in?
Year 10
Ever played rugby?
Er...no...
But Nick says you're a fast runner, yeah?
I...think so?
Good. We need an extra wing. Know what that is?
No...
Nick, why don't you use today's practice to take Charlie through the basics?
Sure!

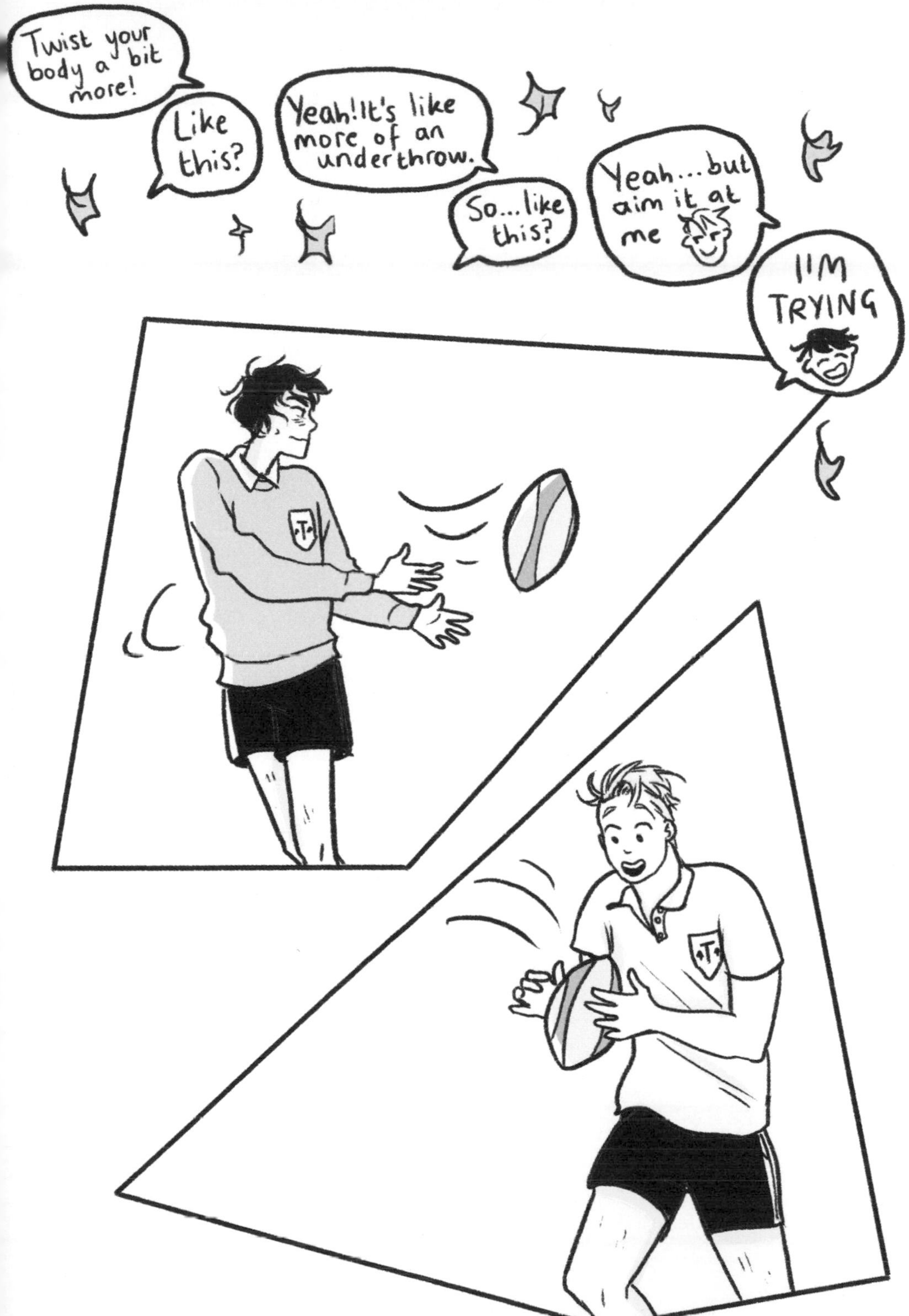

Twist your body a bit more!
Like this?
Yeah! It's like more of an underthrow.
So...like this?
Yeah...but aim it at me
I'M TRYING

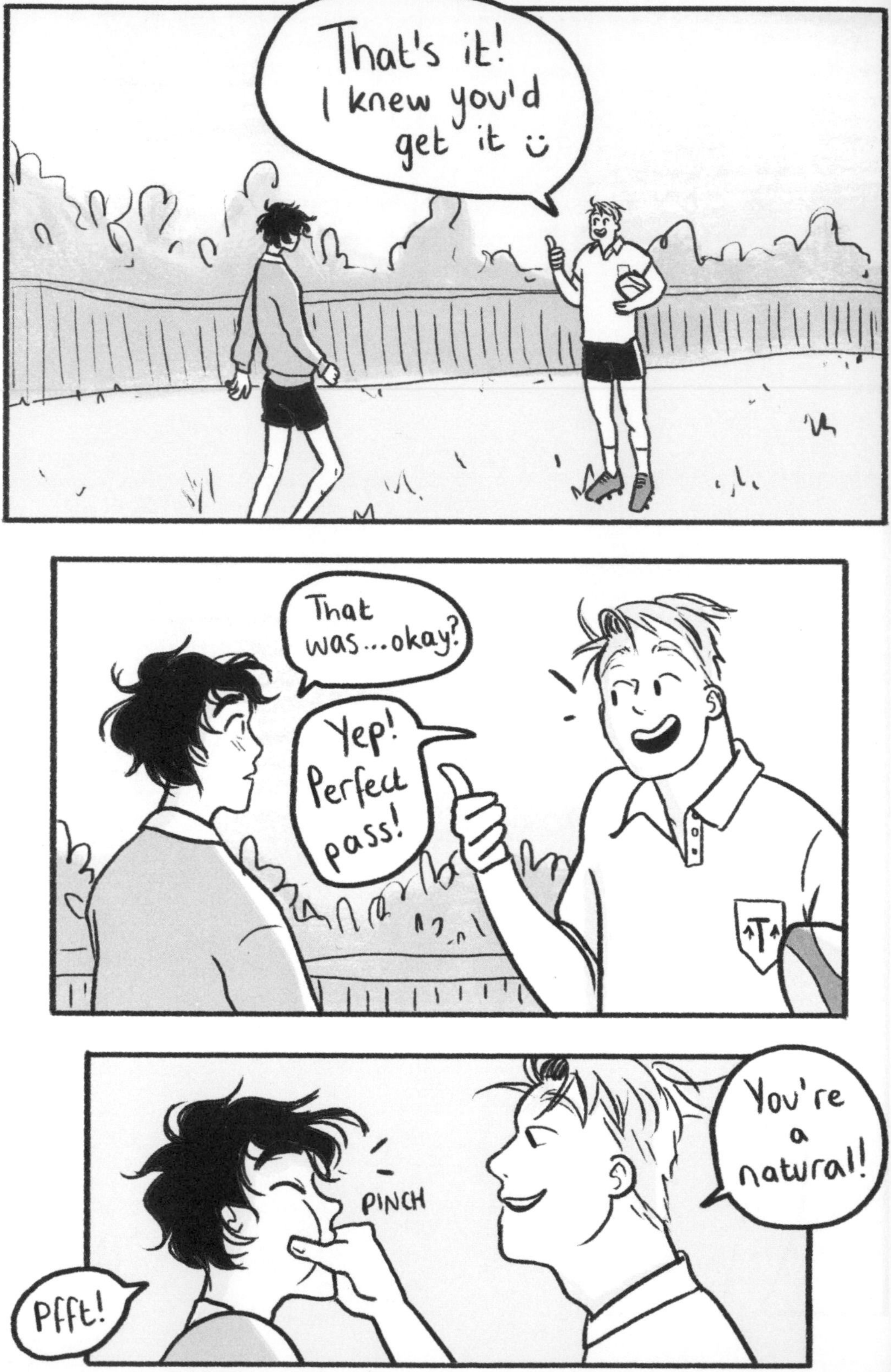
That's it!
I knew you'd get it ☺
That was...okay?
Yep! Perfect pass!
PINCH
You're a natural!
Pfft!

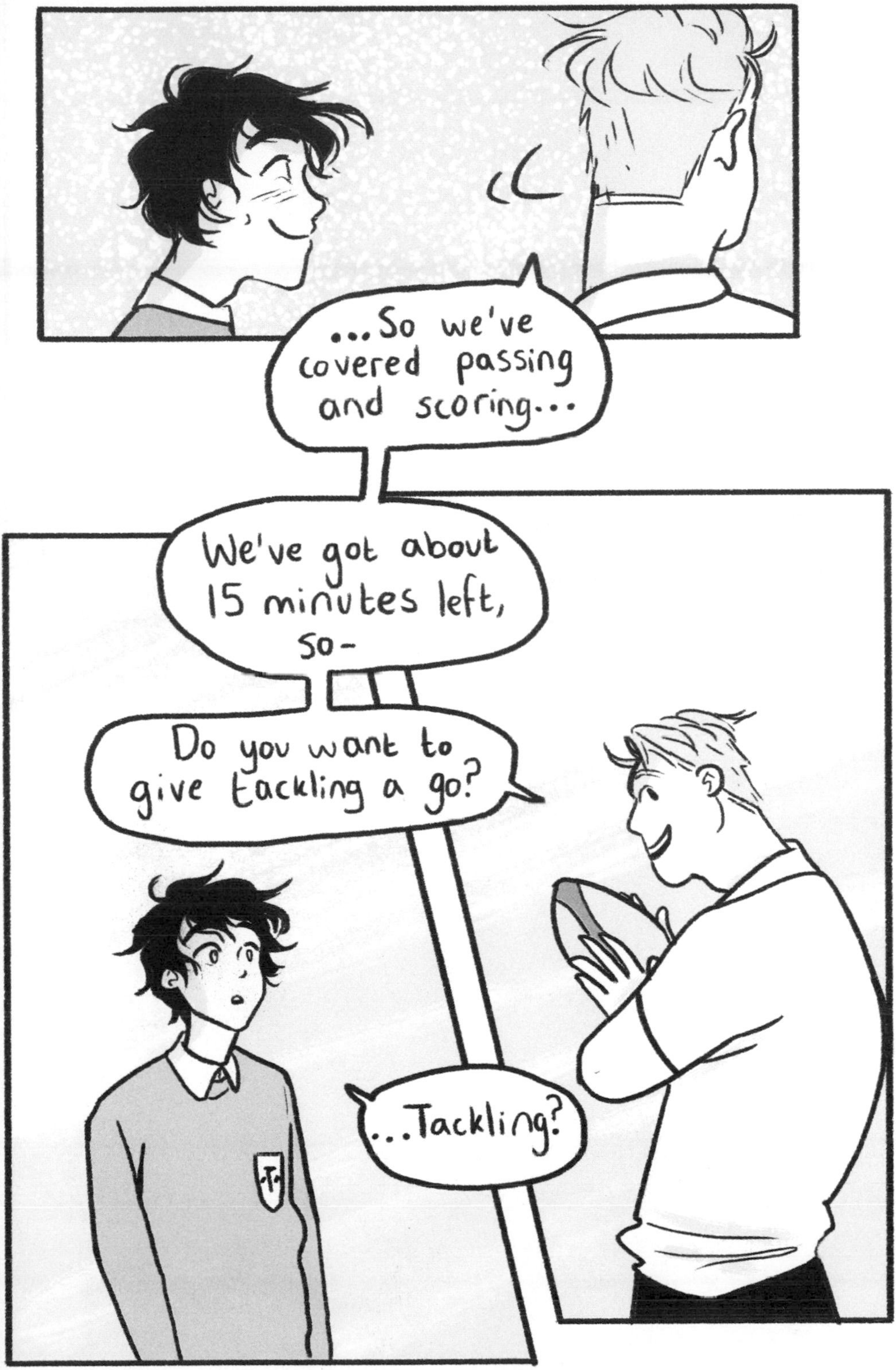
...So we've covered passing and scoring...
We've got about 15 minutes left, so-
Do you want to give tackling a go?
...Tackling?

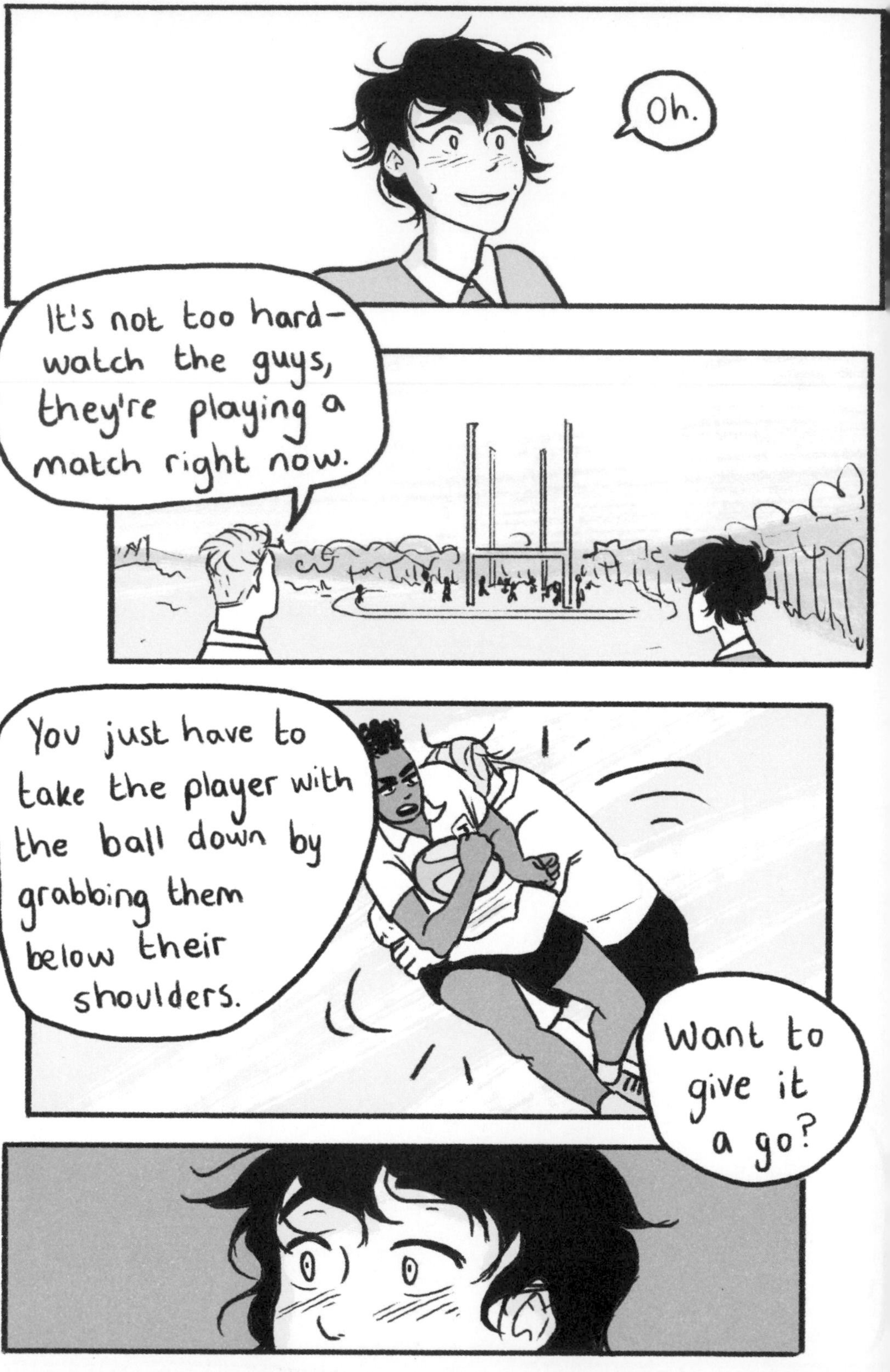
Oh.
It's not too hard- watch the guys, they're playing a match right now.
You just have to take the player with the ball down by grabbing them below their shoulders.
Want to give it a go?

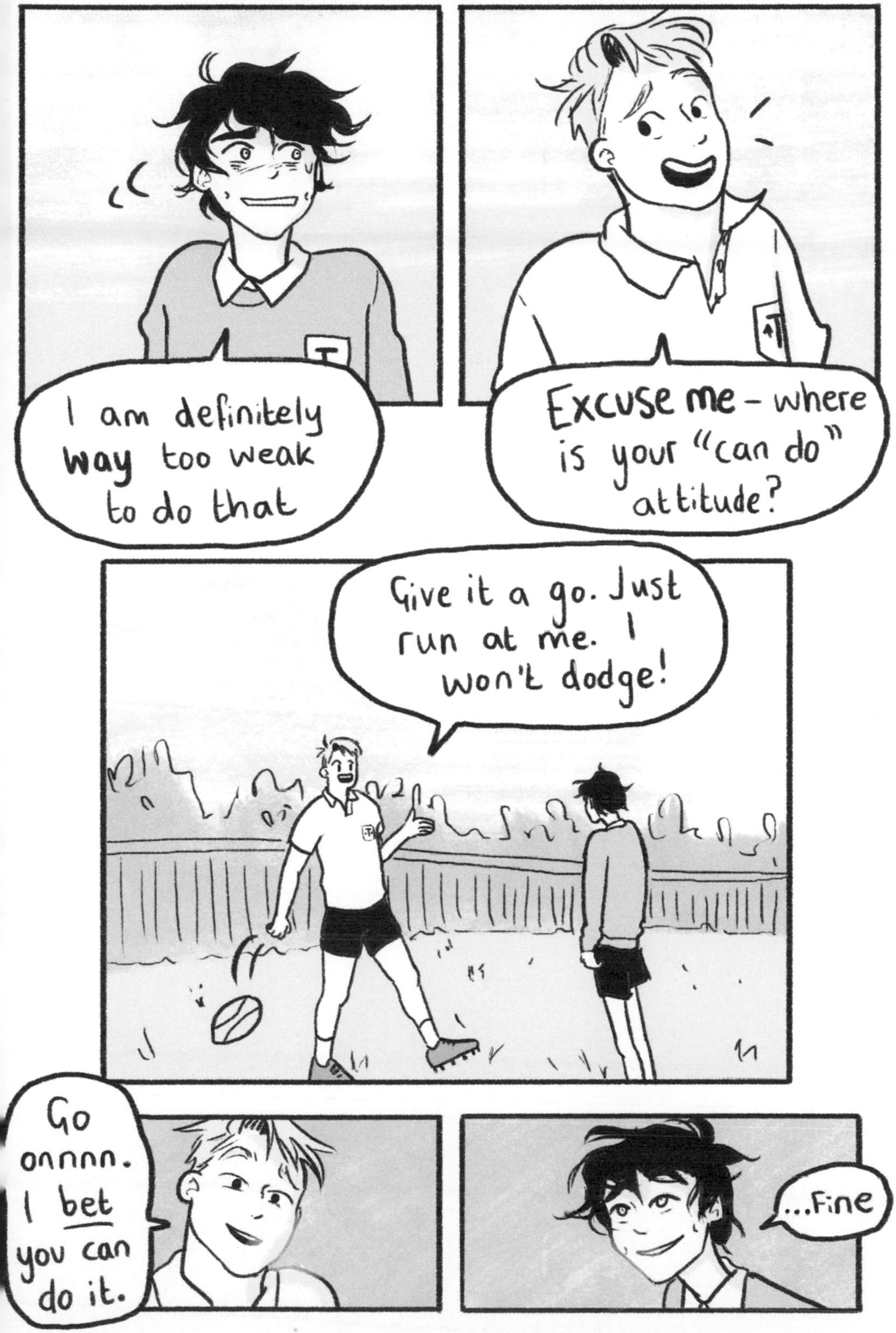
I am definitely way too weak to do that
Excuse me - where is your "can do" attitude?
Give it a go. Just run at me. I won't dodge!
Go onnnn. I bet you can do it.
...Fine

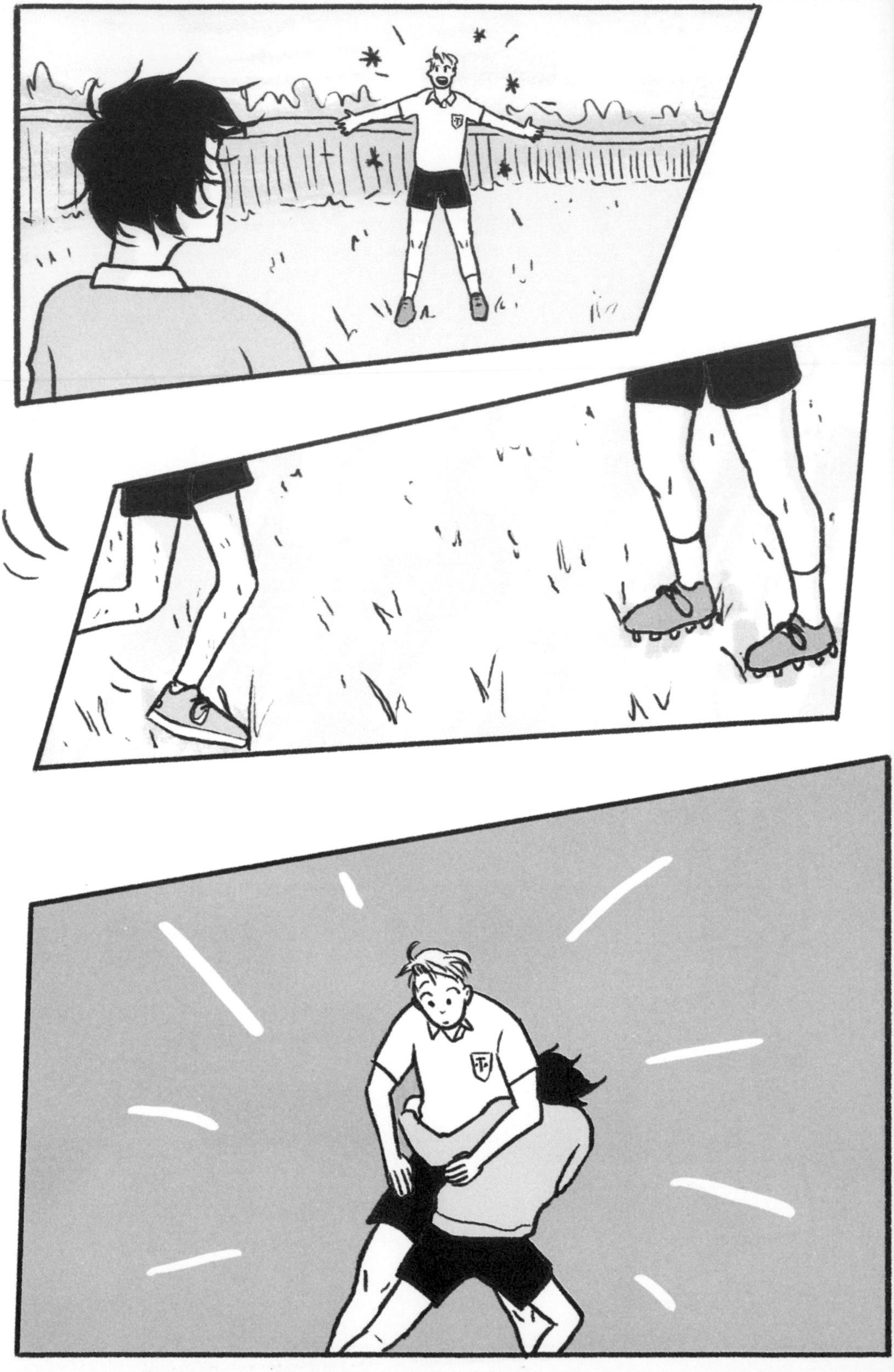

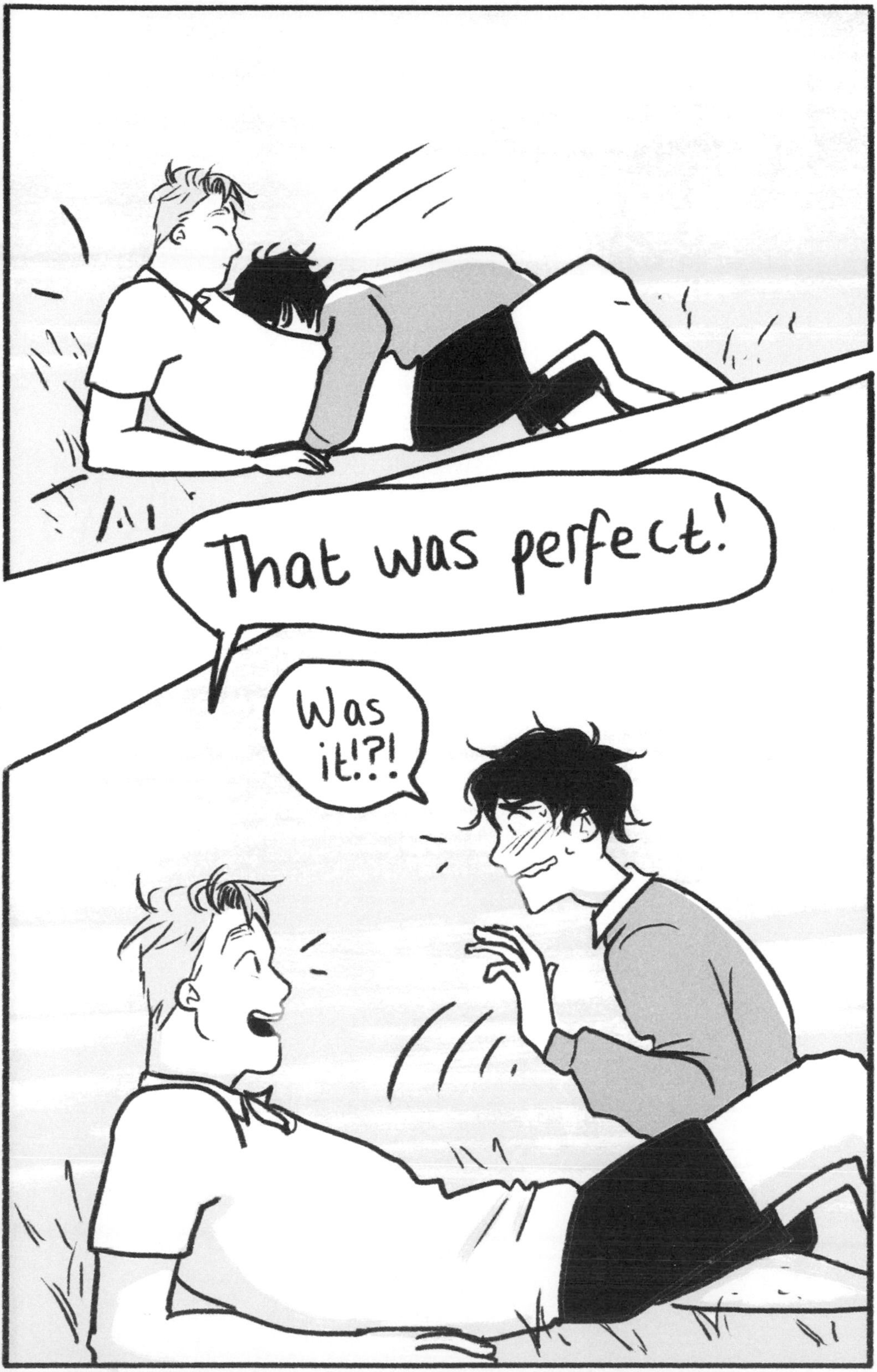
That was perfect!
Was it!?!

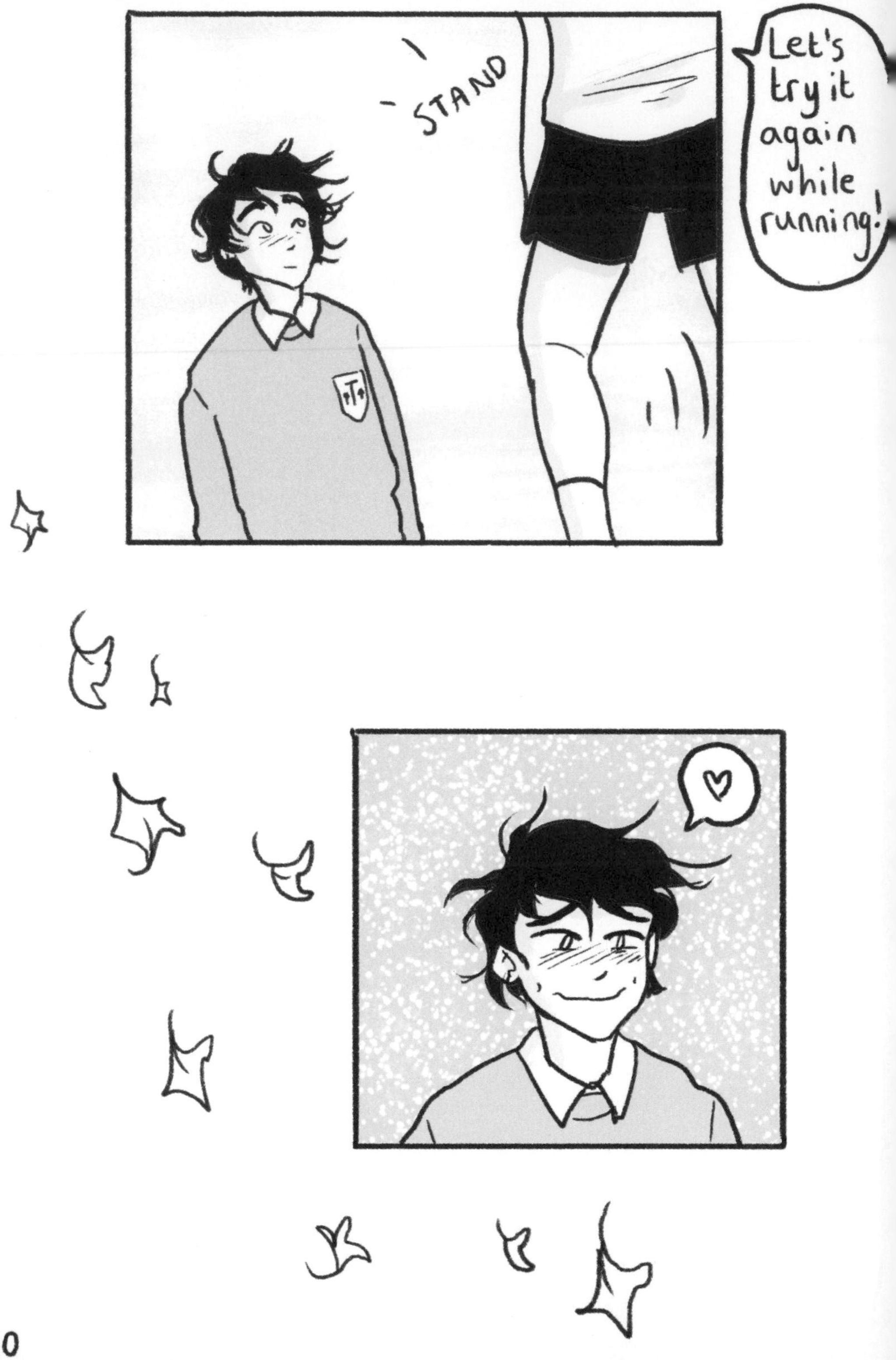
STAND
Let's try it again while running!

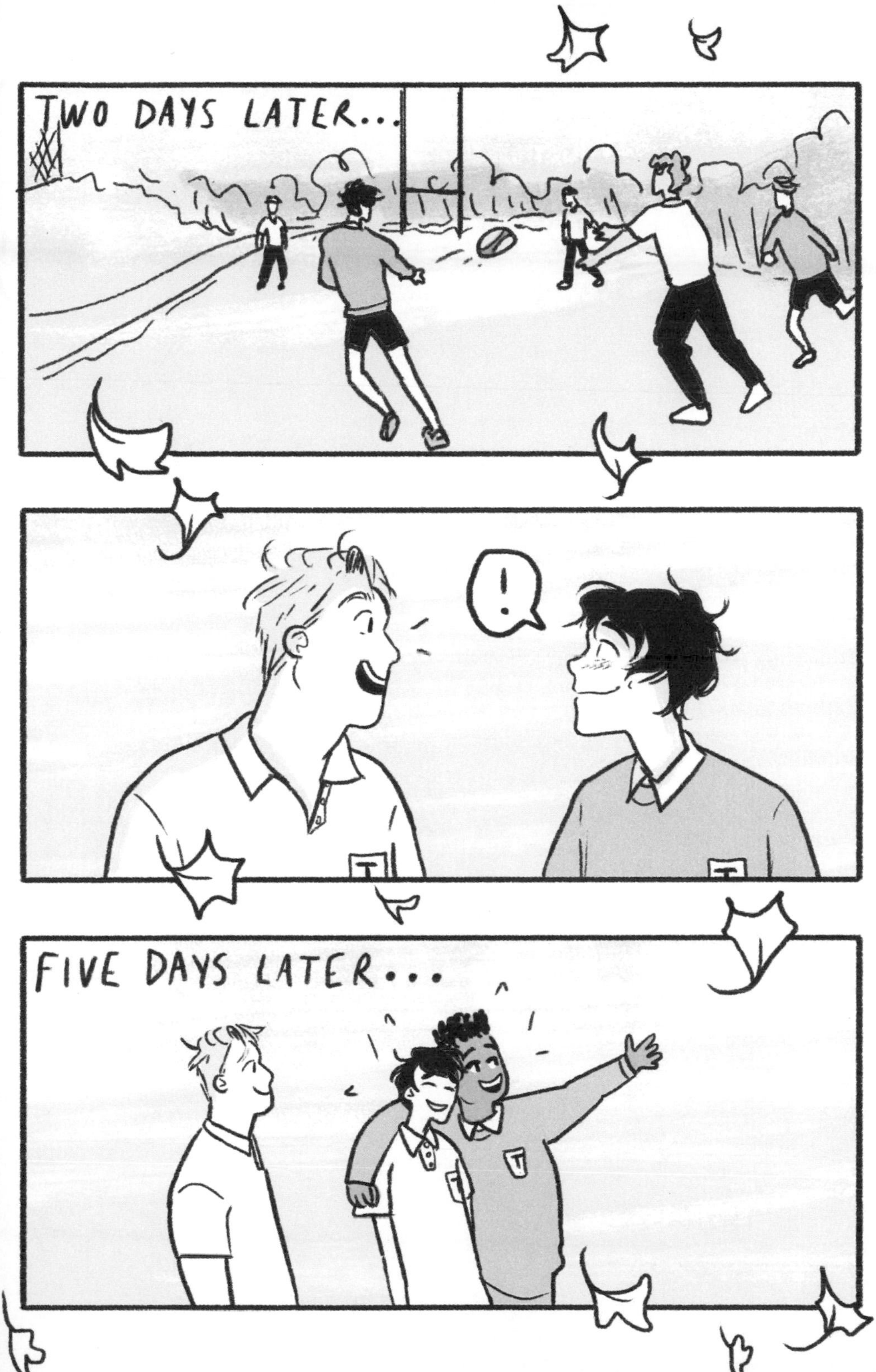

TWO DAYS LATER...
!
FIVE DAYS LATER...

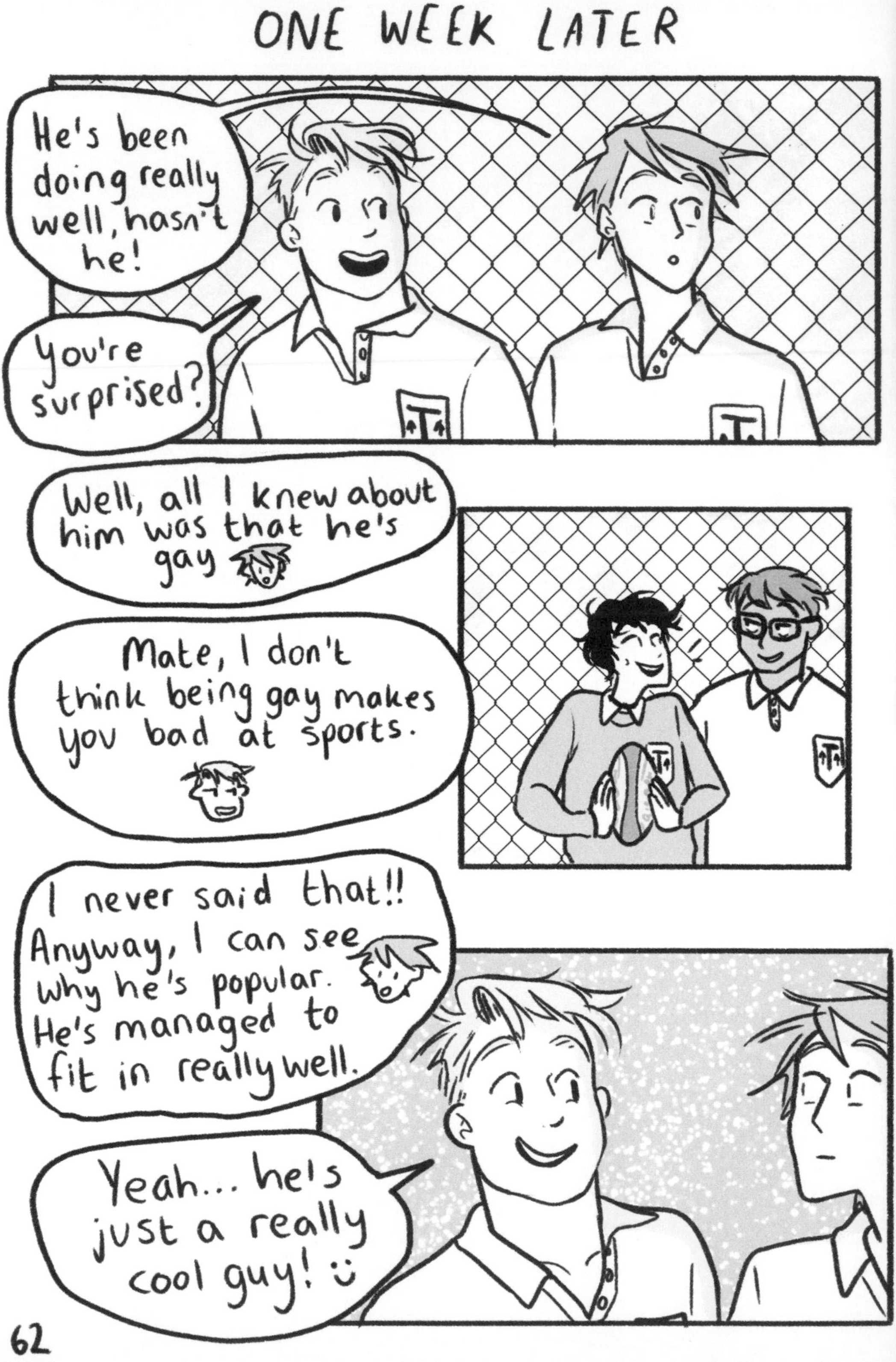
ONE WEEK LATER
He's been doing really well, hasn't he!
You're surprised?
Well, all I knew about him was that he's gay
Mate, I don't think being gay makes you bad at sports.
I never said that!! Anyway, I can see why he's popular. He's managed to fit in really well.
Yeah... he's just a really cool guy! :)

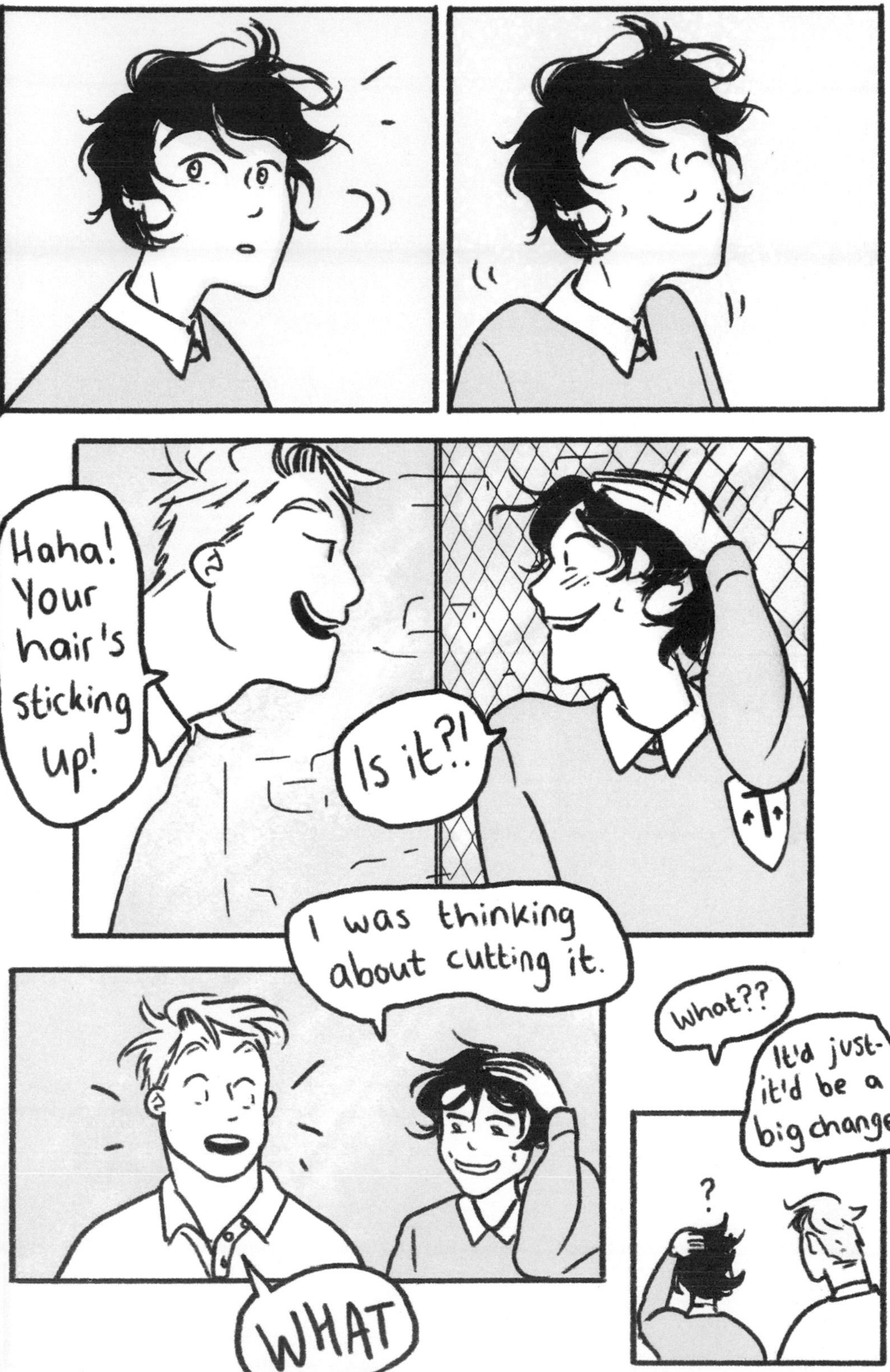
Haha! Your hair's sticking up!
Is it?!
I was thinking about cutting it.
WHAT
What??
It'd just- it'd be a big change!
?

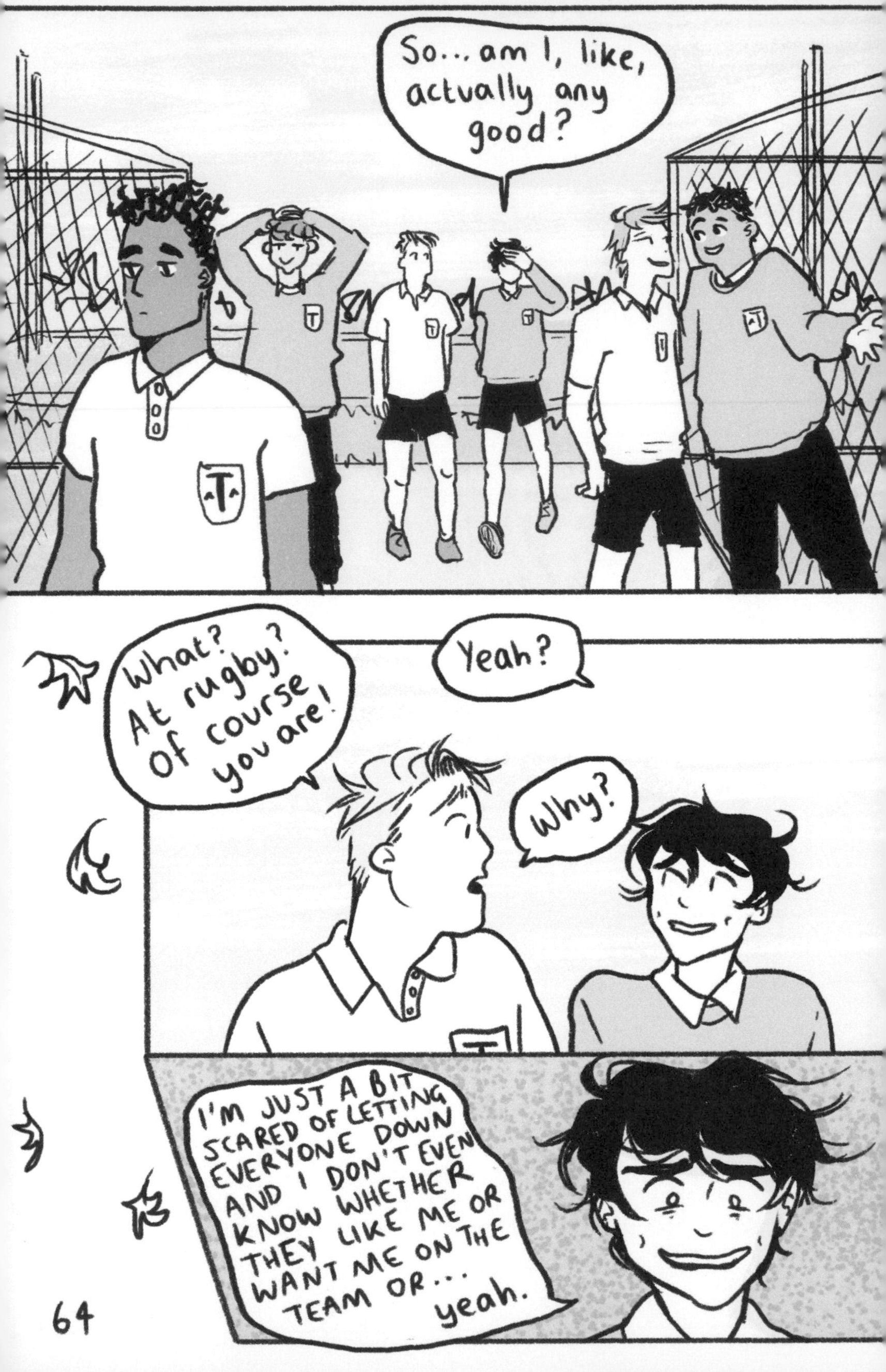
So... am I, like, actually any good?
What? At rugby? Of course you are!
Yeah?
Why?
I'M JUST A BIT SCARED OF LETTING EVERYONE DOWN AND I DON'T EVEN KNOW WHETHER THEY LIKE ME OR WANT ME ON THE TEAM OR... yeah.

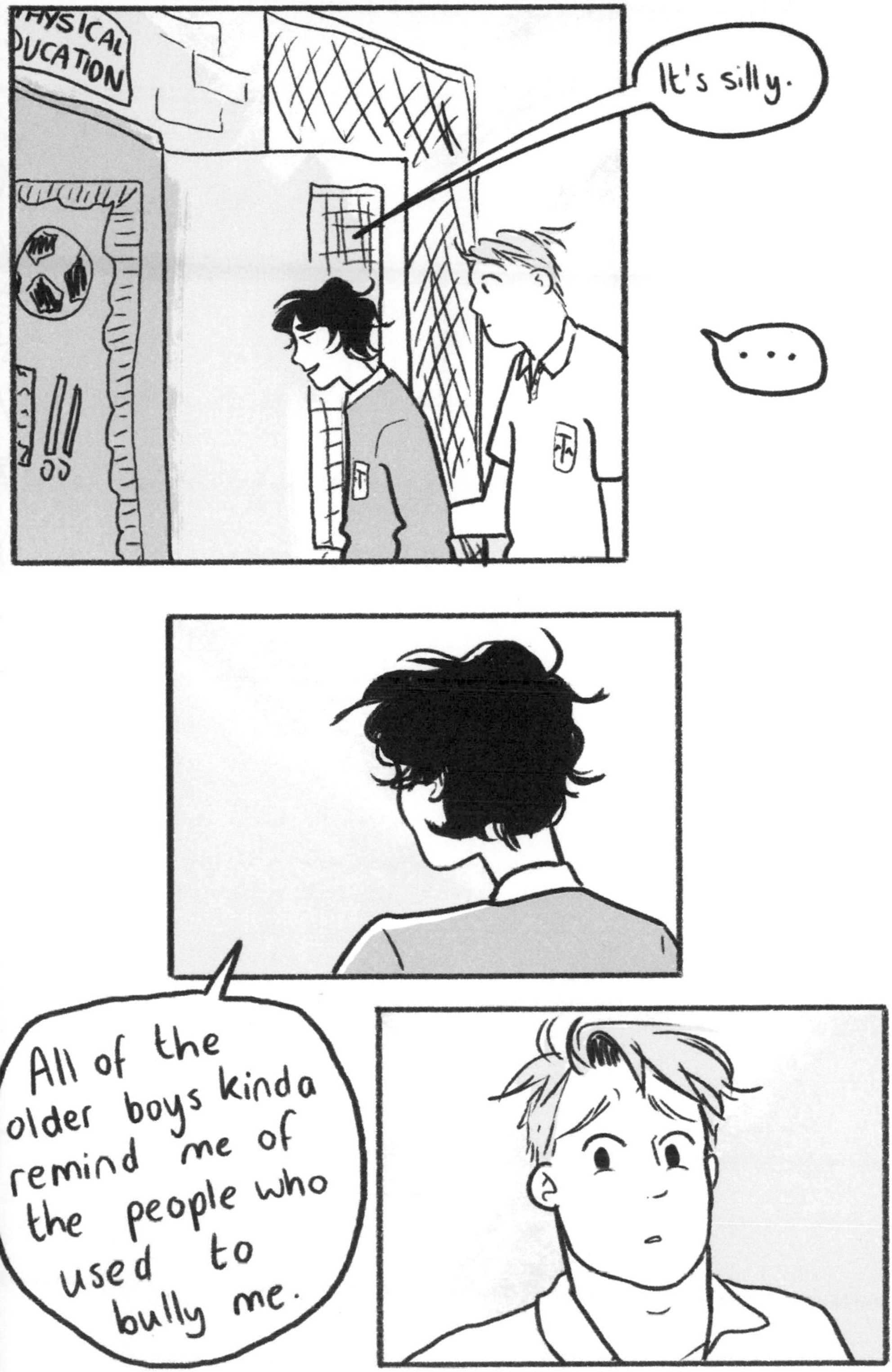
PHYSICAL EDUCATION
It's silly.
...
All of the older boys kinda remind me of the people who used to bully me.

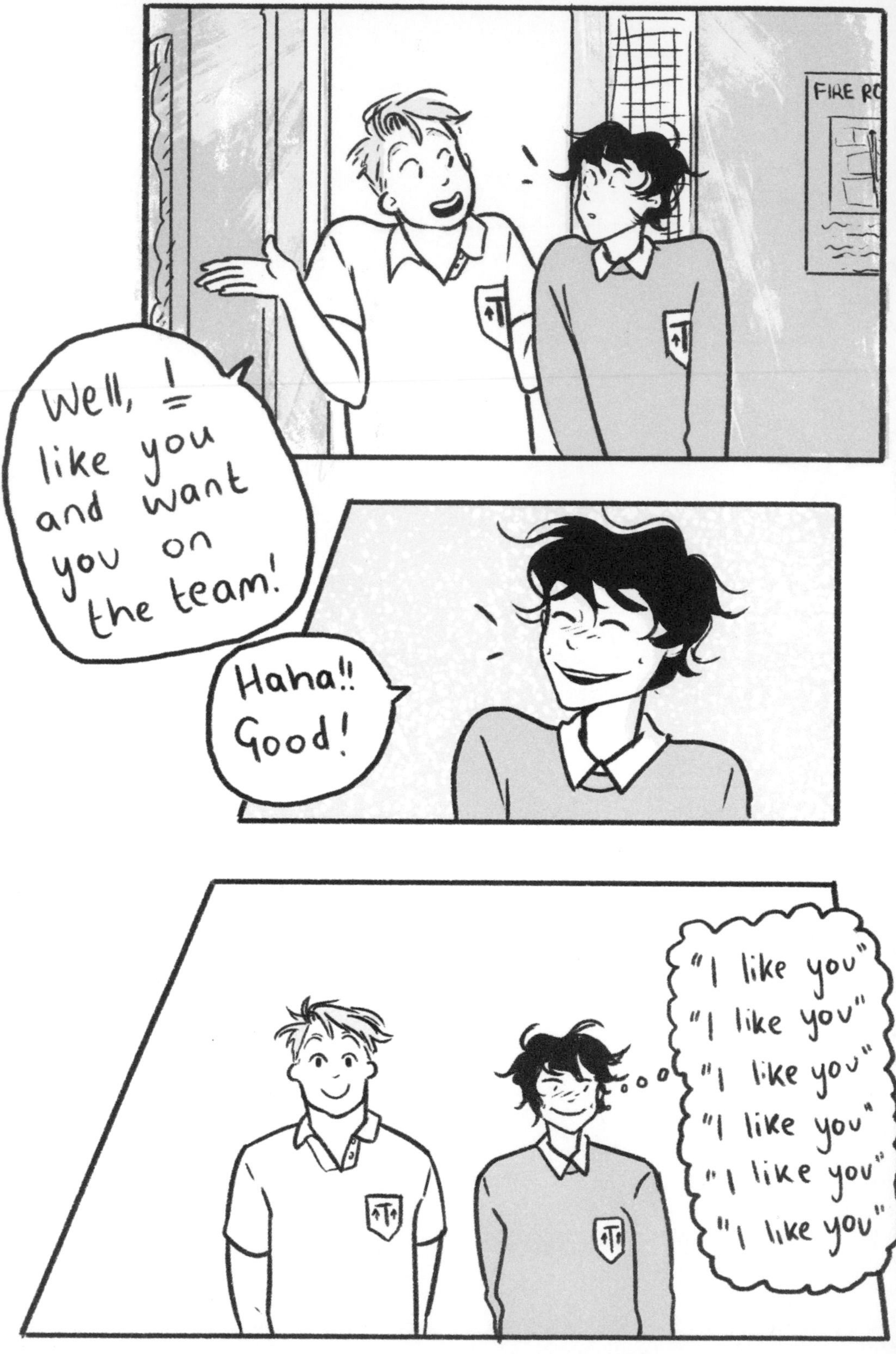
FIRE RO
Well, I like you and want you on the team!
Haha!! Good!
"I like you"
"I like you"
"I like you"
"I like you"
"I like you"
"I like you"

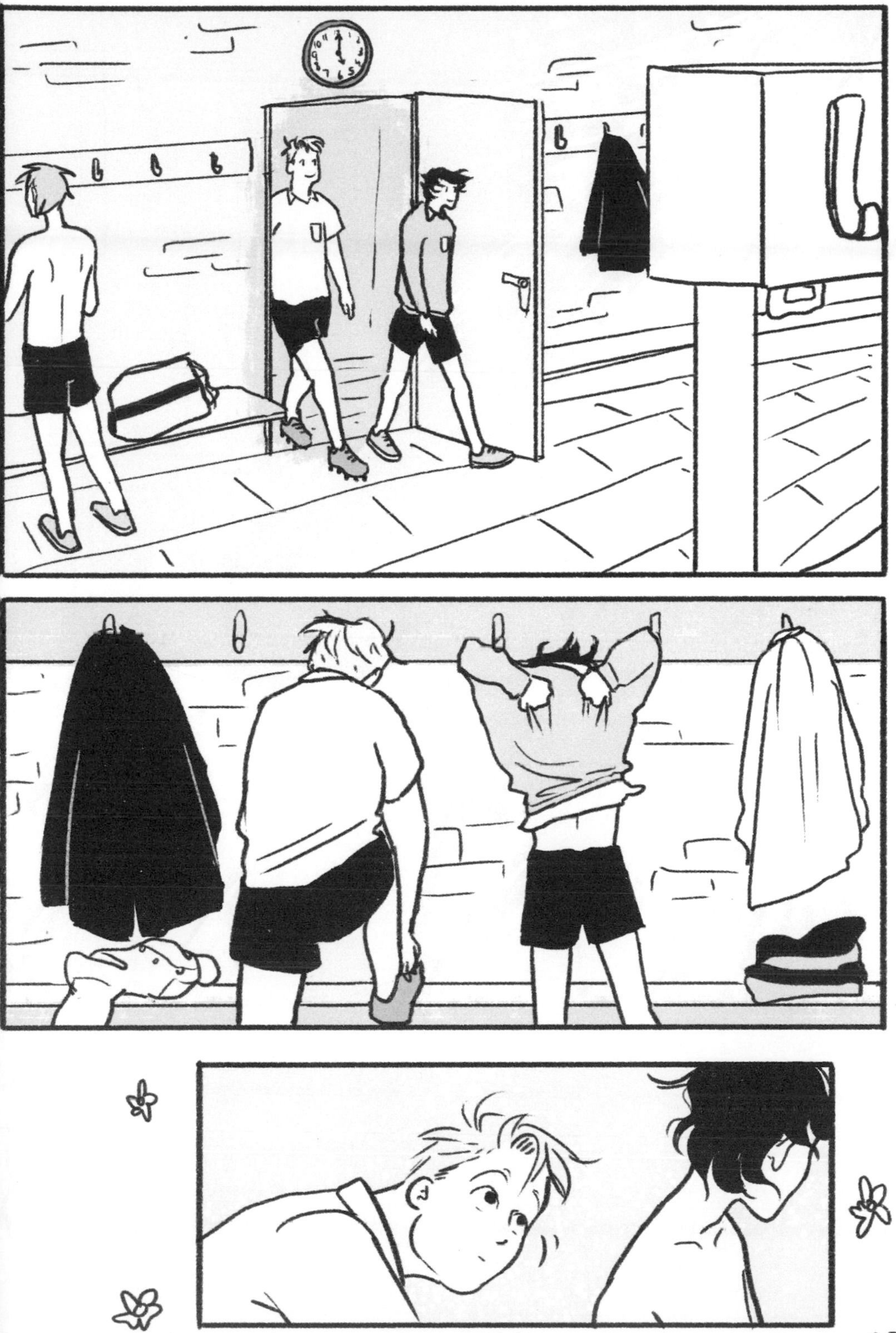

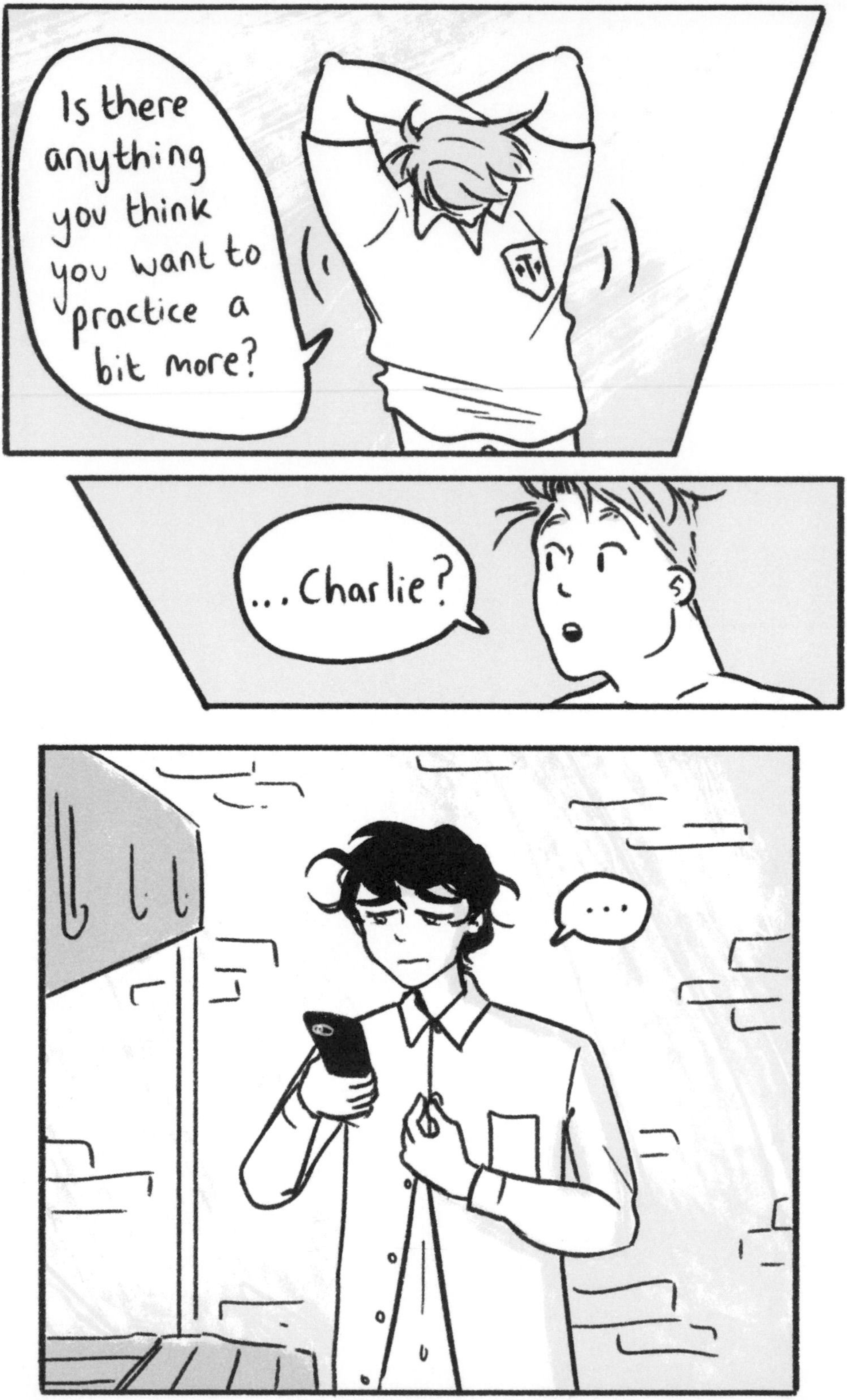
Is there anything you think you want to you want to practice a bit more?
...Charlie?
...

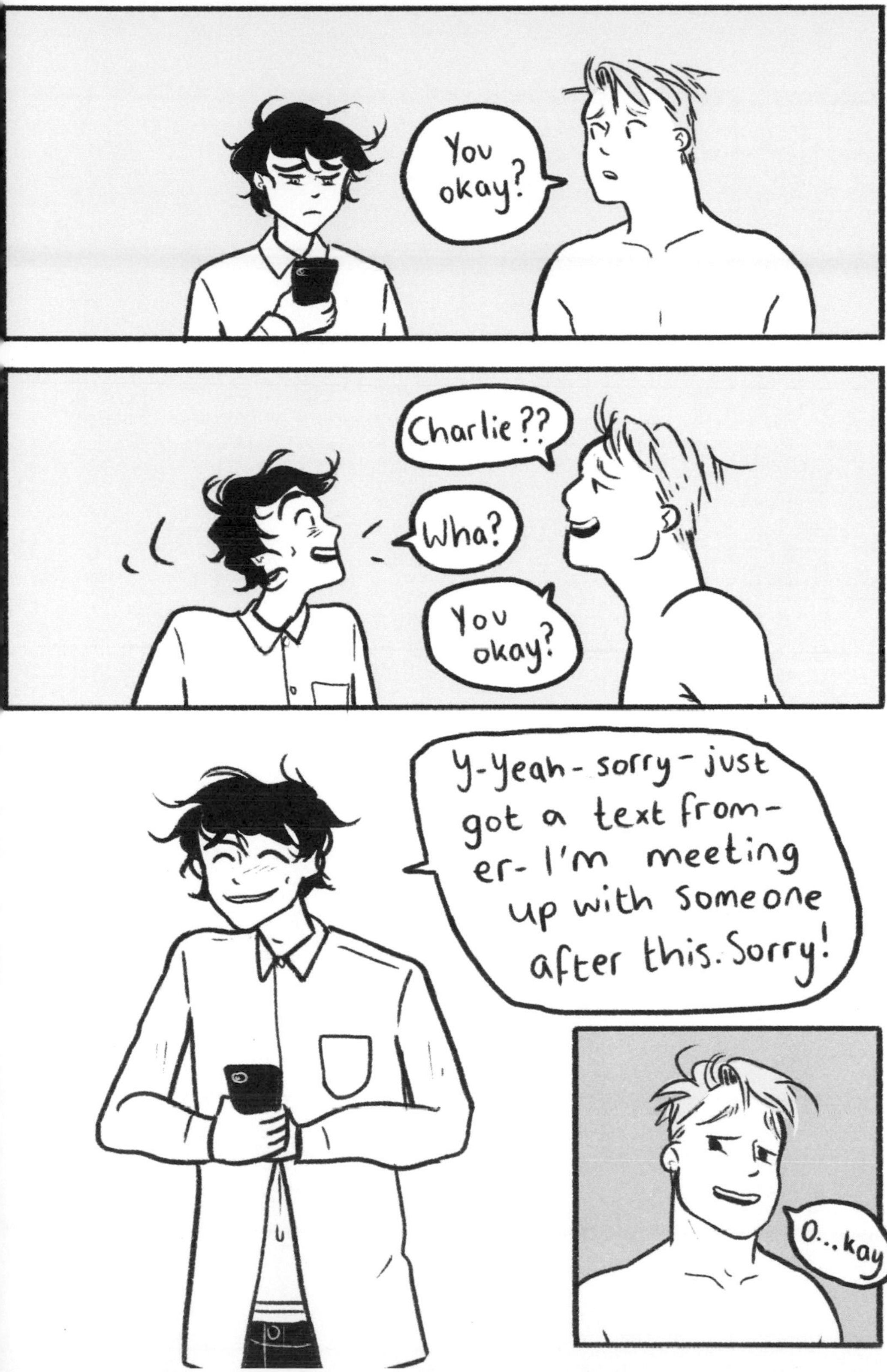

You okay?
Charlie??
Wha?
You okay?
Y-Yeah- sorry- just got a text from- er- I'm meeting up with someone after this. Sorry!
O...kay

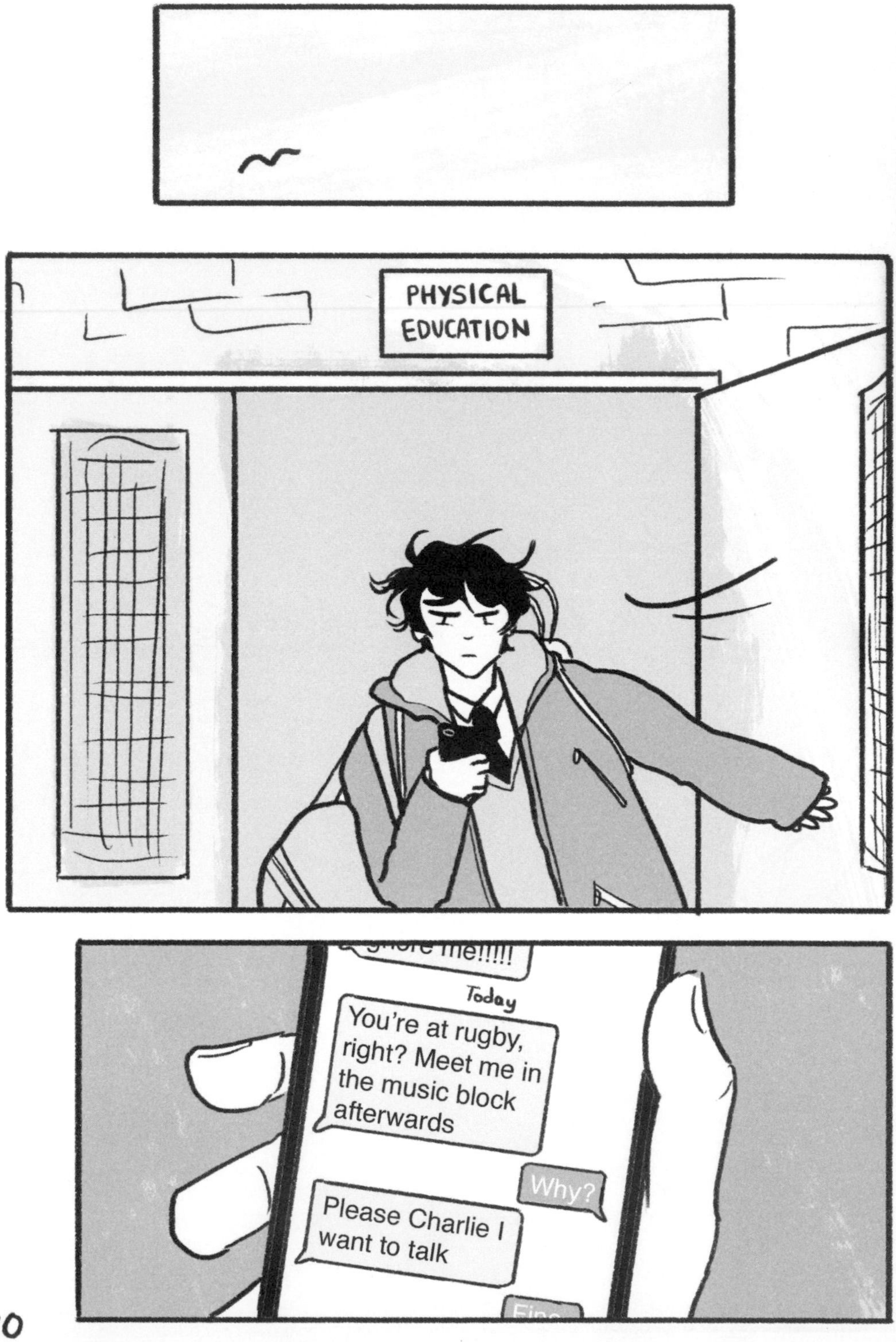
PHYSICAL EDUCATION
Today
You're at rugby, right? Meet me in the music block afterwards
Why?
Please Charlie I want to talk

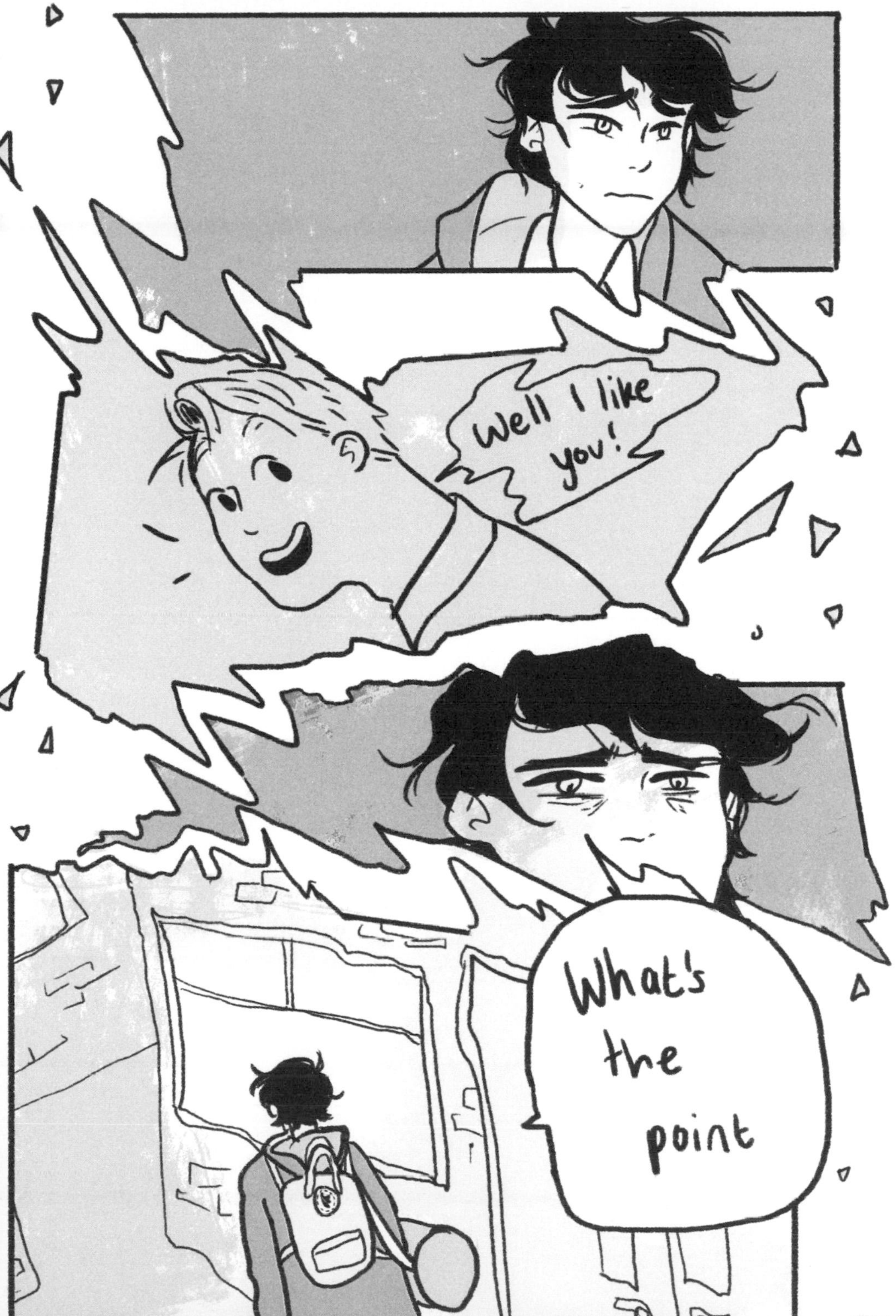
Well I like you!
What's the point

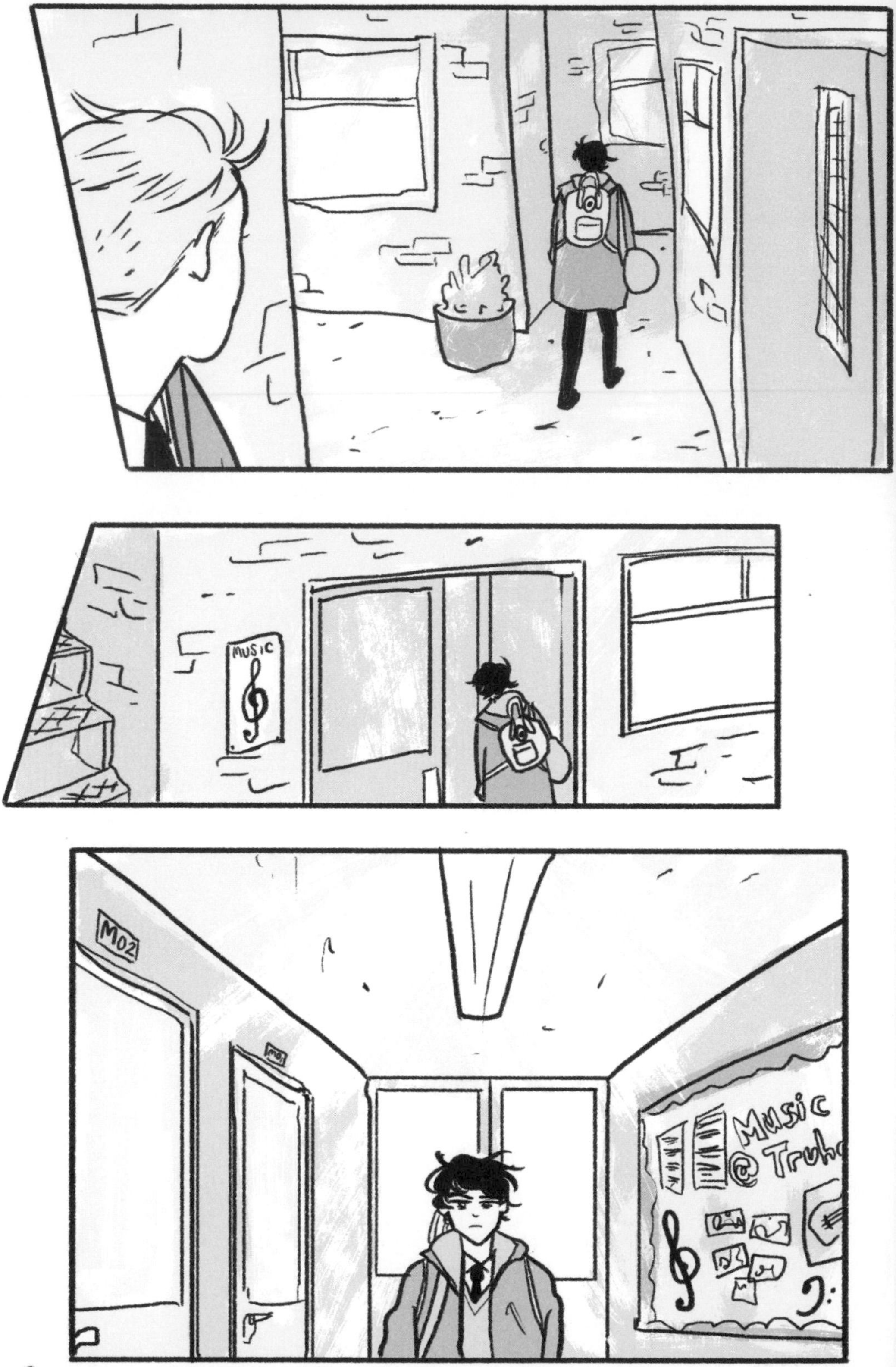
MUSIC
M02
Music

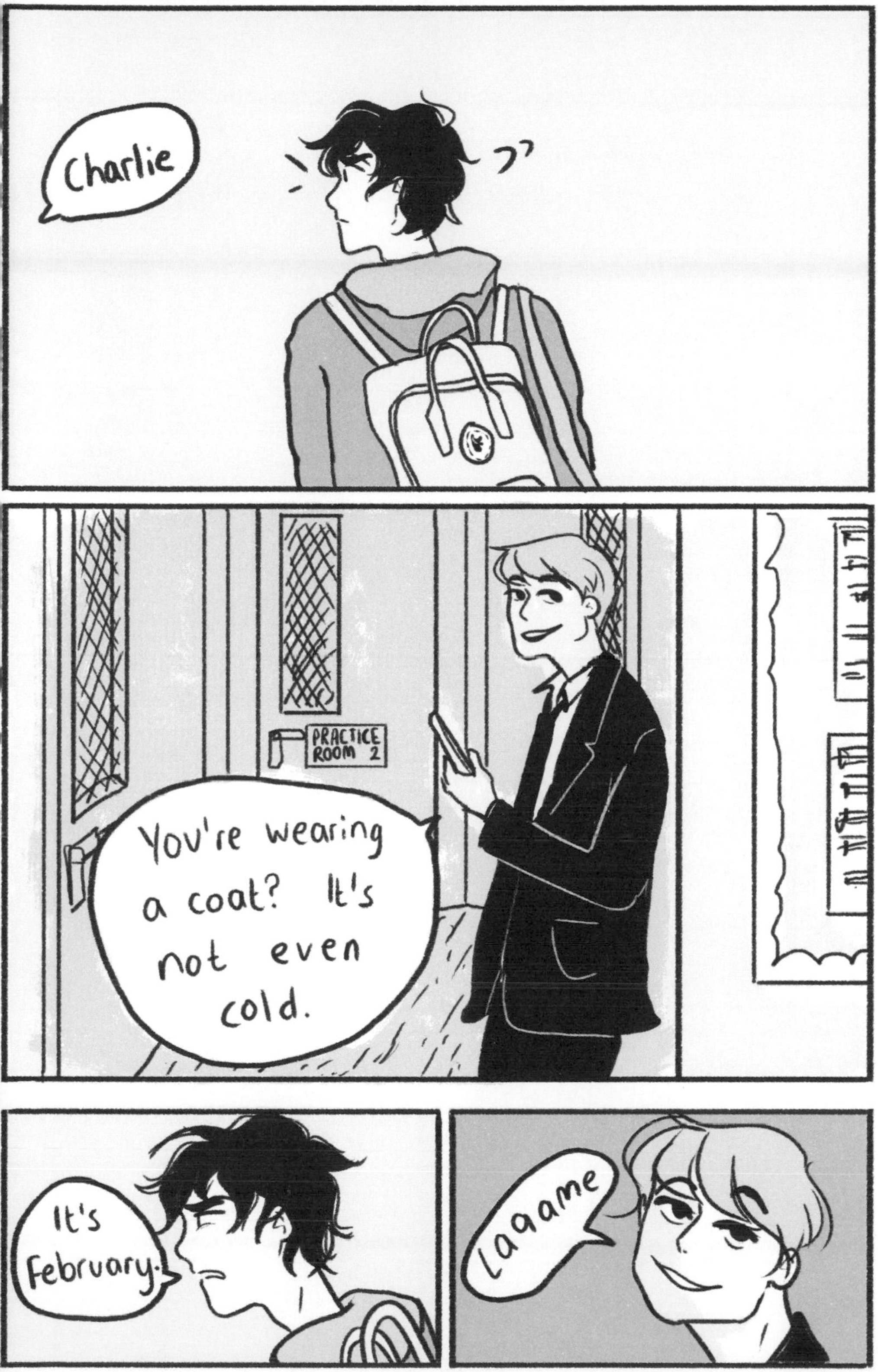
Charlie
PRACTICE ROOM 2
You're wearing a coat? It's not even cold.
It's February.
Lagame

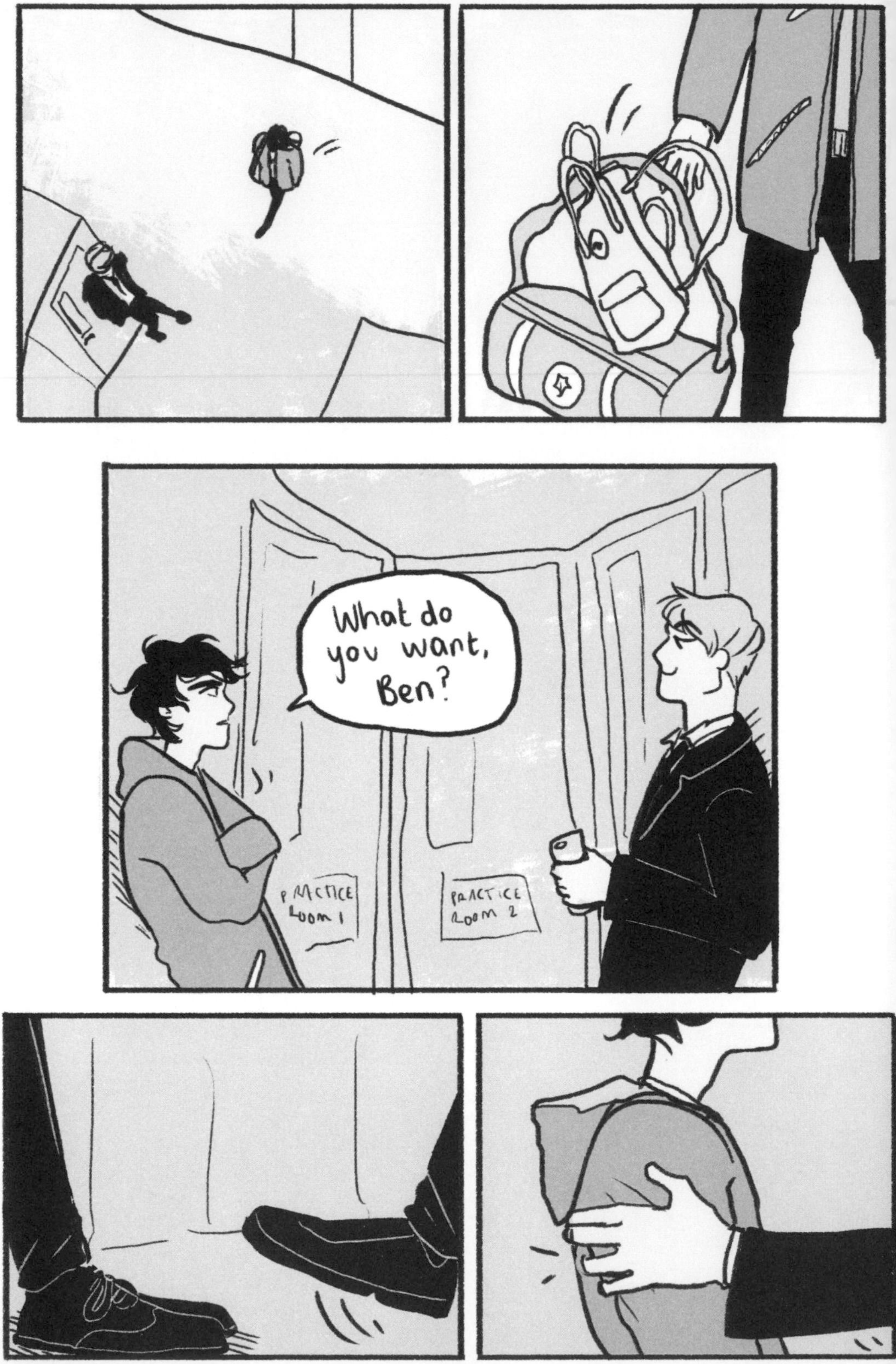
What do you want, Ben?
PRACTICE ROOM 1
PRACTICE ROOM 2

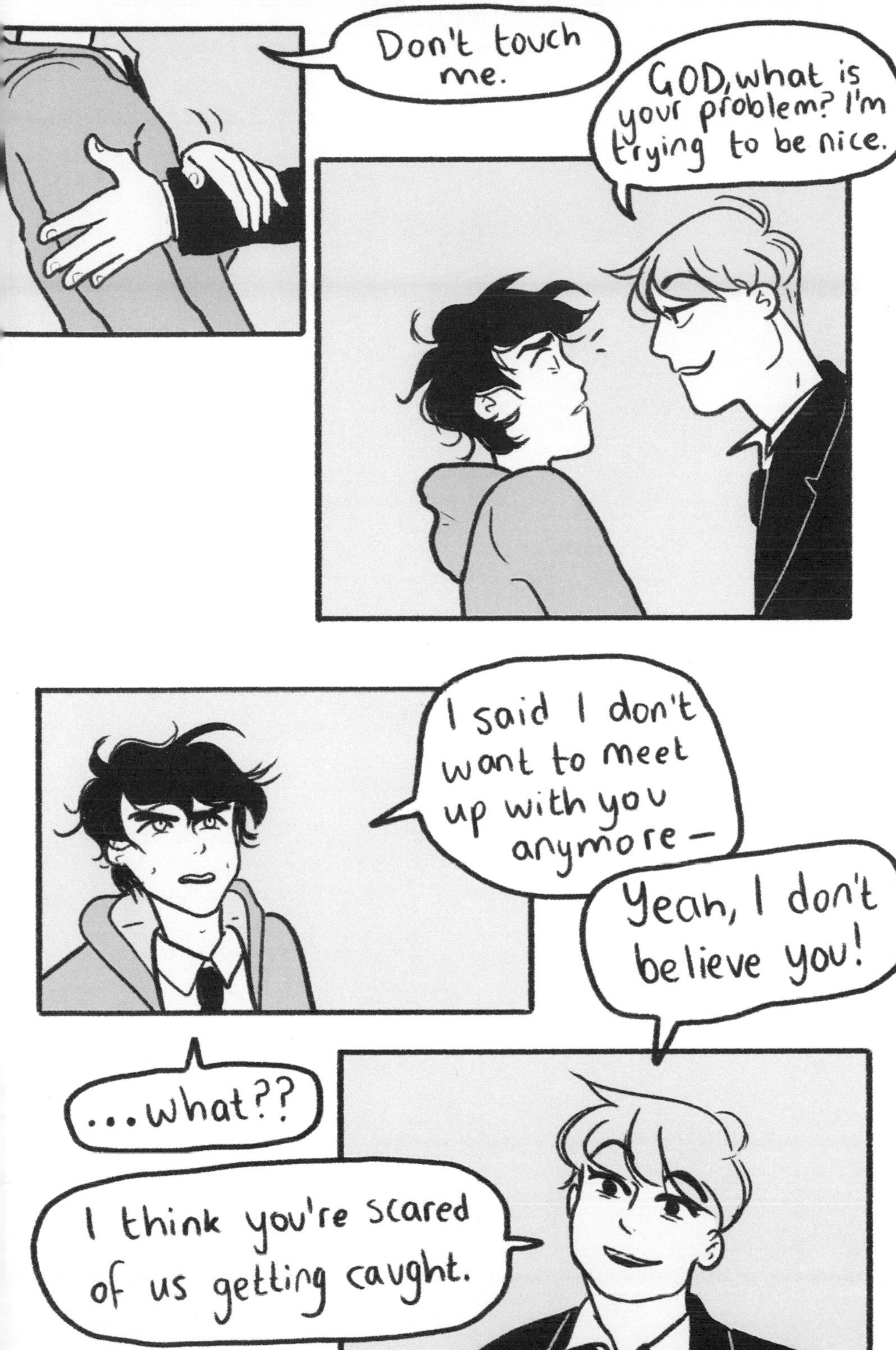
Don't touch me.
GOD, what is your problem? I'm trying to be nice.
I said I don't want to meet up with you anymore—
Yeah, I don't believe you!
...what??
I think you're scared of us getting caught.

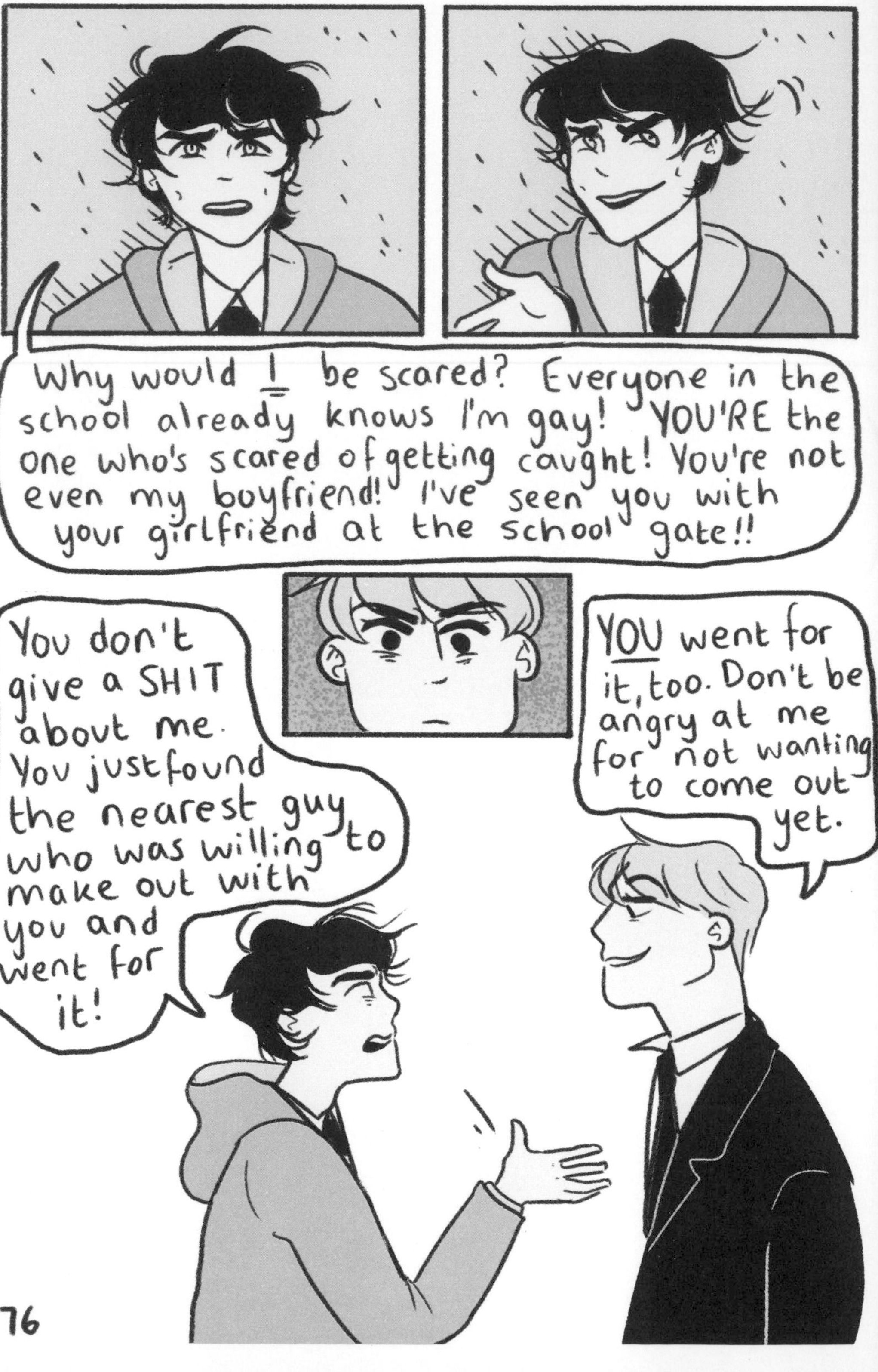
Why would I be scared? Everyone in the school already knows I'm gay! YOU'RE the one who's scared of getting caught! You're not even my boyfriend! I've seen you with your girlfriend at the school gate!!
You don't give a SHIT about me. You just found the nearest guy who was willing to make out with you and went for it!
YOU went for it, too. Don't be angry at me for not wanting to come out yet.

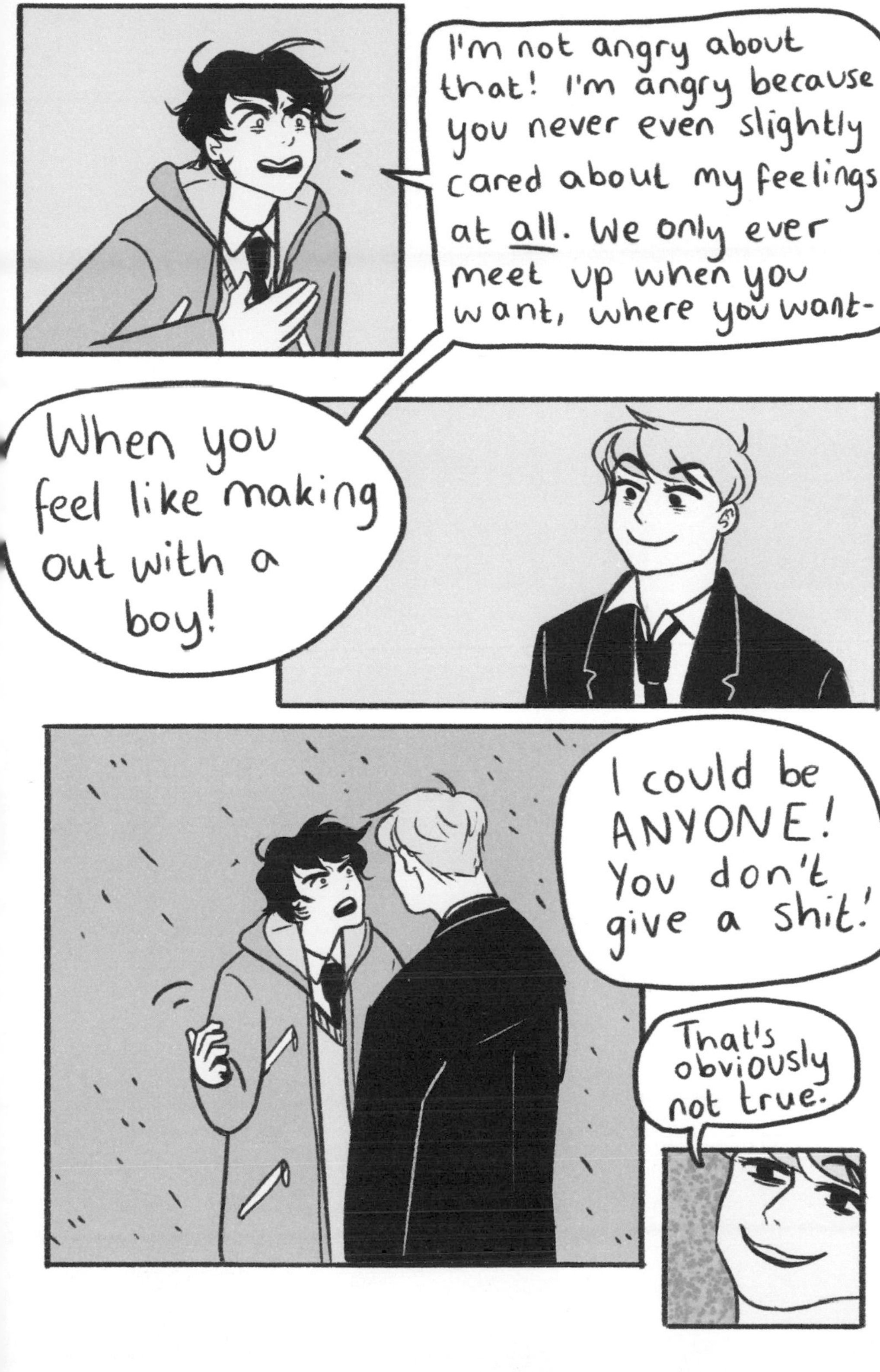
I'm not angry about that! I'm angry because you never even slightly cared about my feelings at all. We only ever meet up when you want, where you want-
When you feel like making out with a boy!
I could be ANYONE! You don't give a shit!
That's obviously not true.

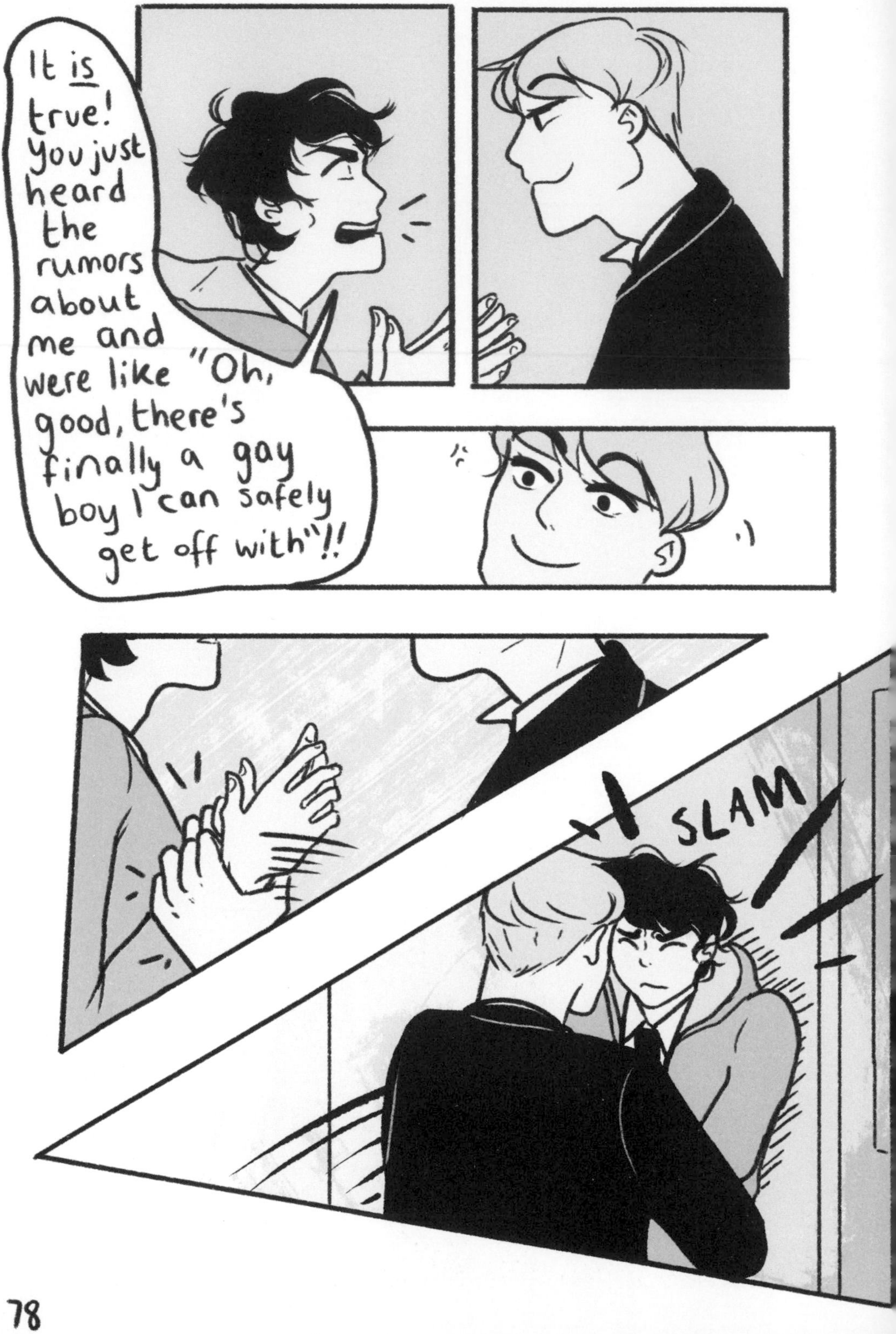
It is true! You just heard the rumors about me and were like "Oh, good, there's finally a gay boy I can safely get off with"!!
SLAM

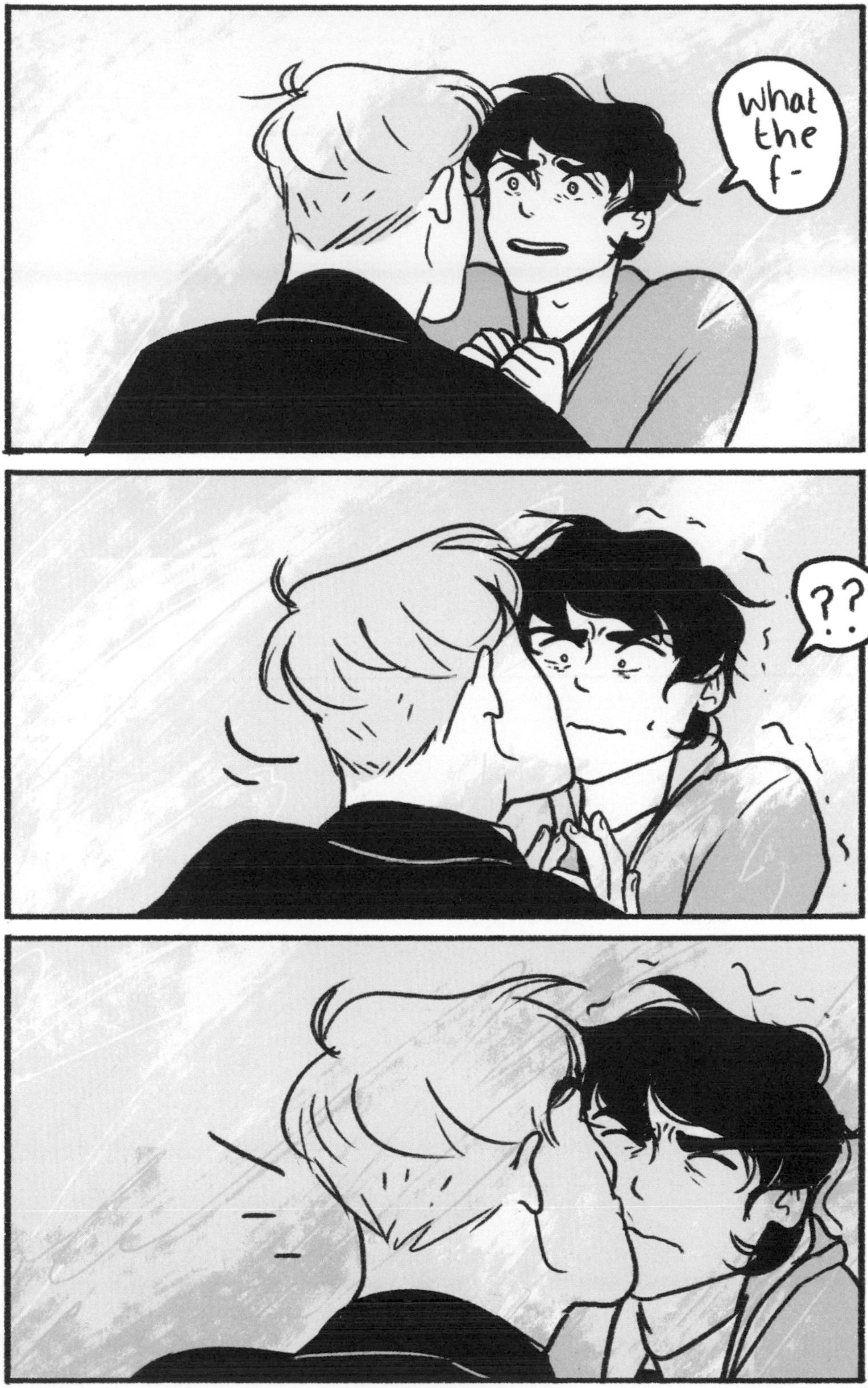
what the f-
??

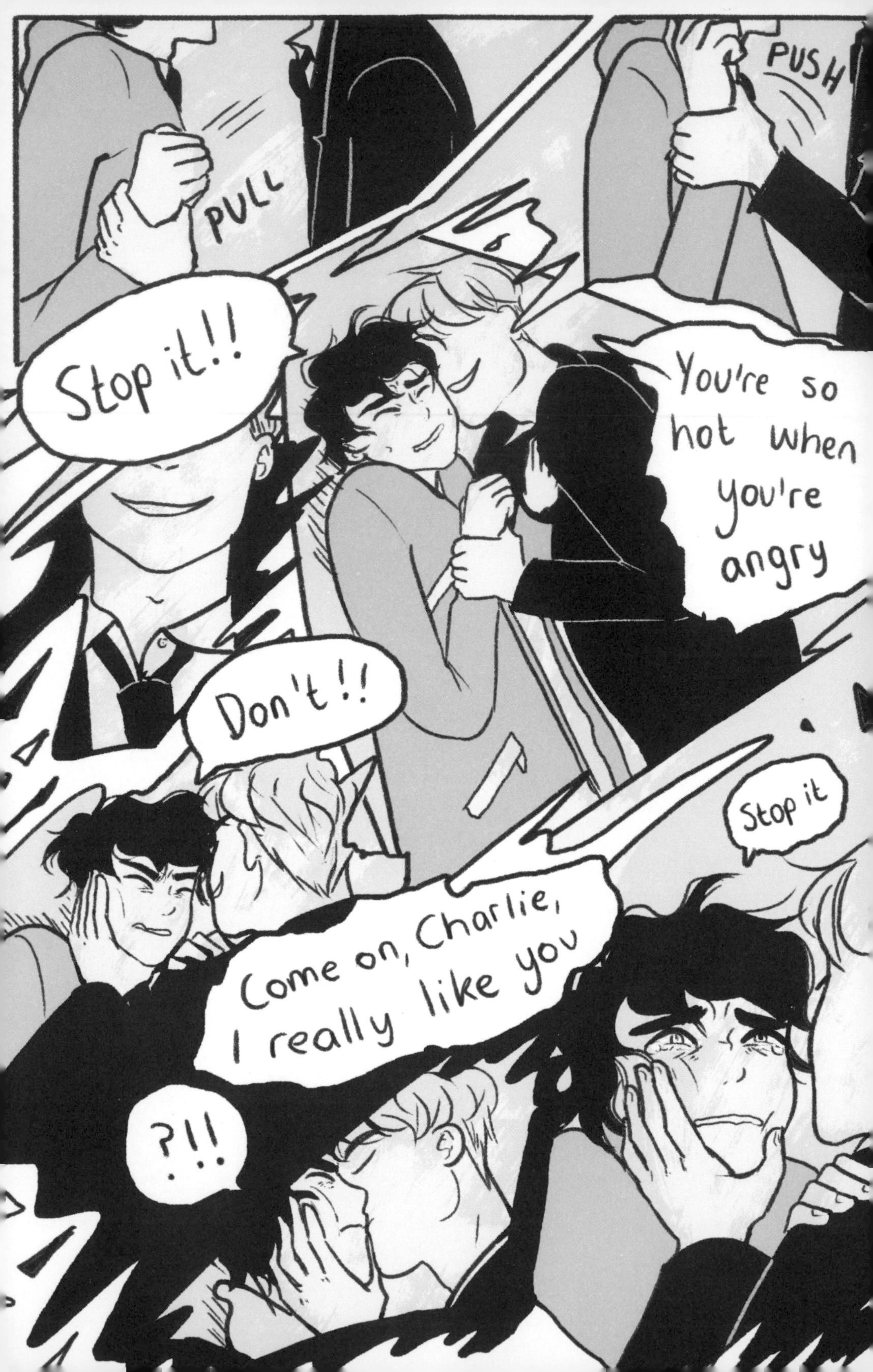
PULL
PUSH
Stop it!!
You're so hot when you're angry
Don't!!
Stop it
Come on, Charlie, I really like you
?!!

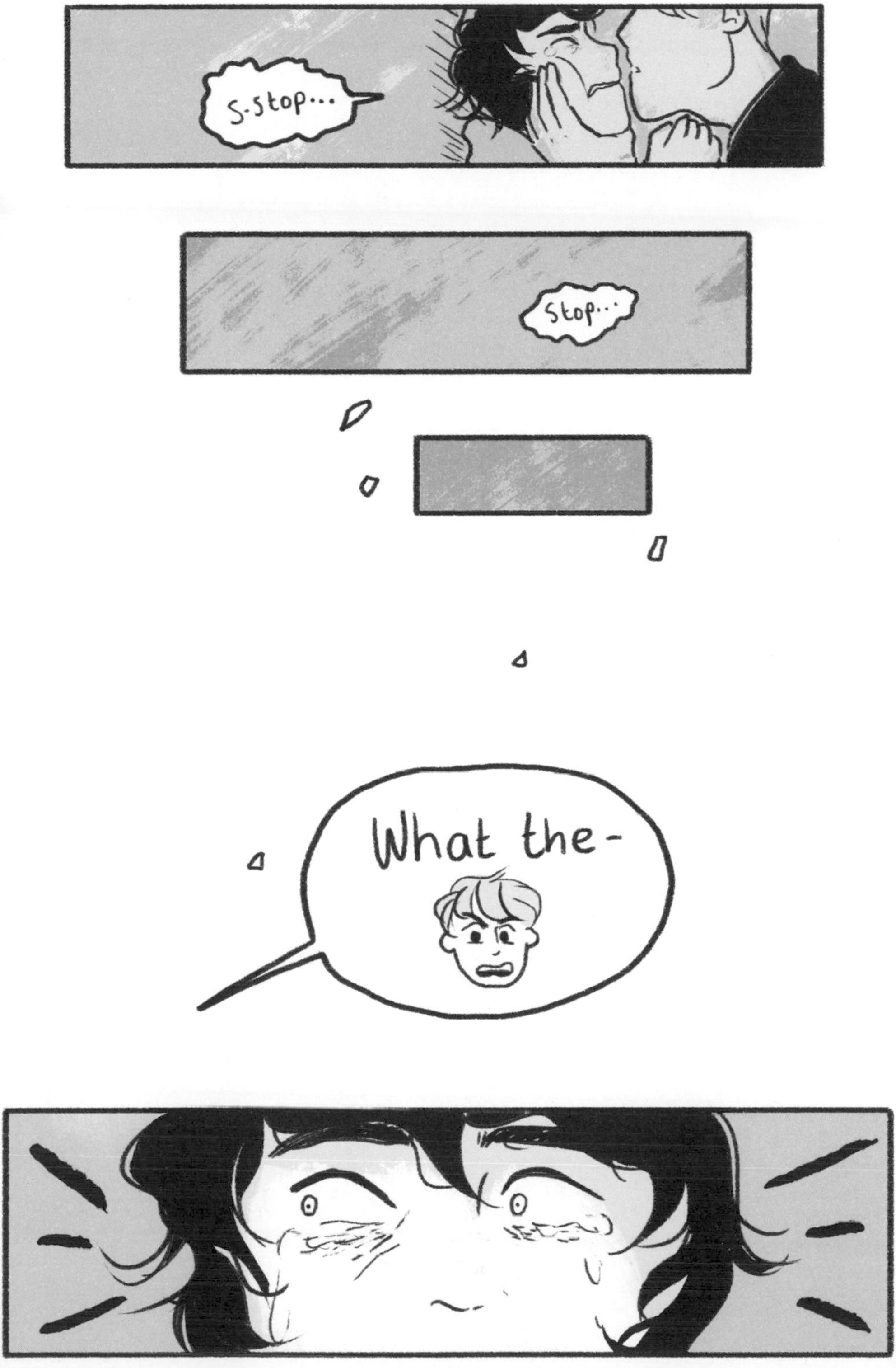
S-Stop...
Stop...
What the-

He told you to stop, you fucking prick!

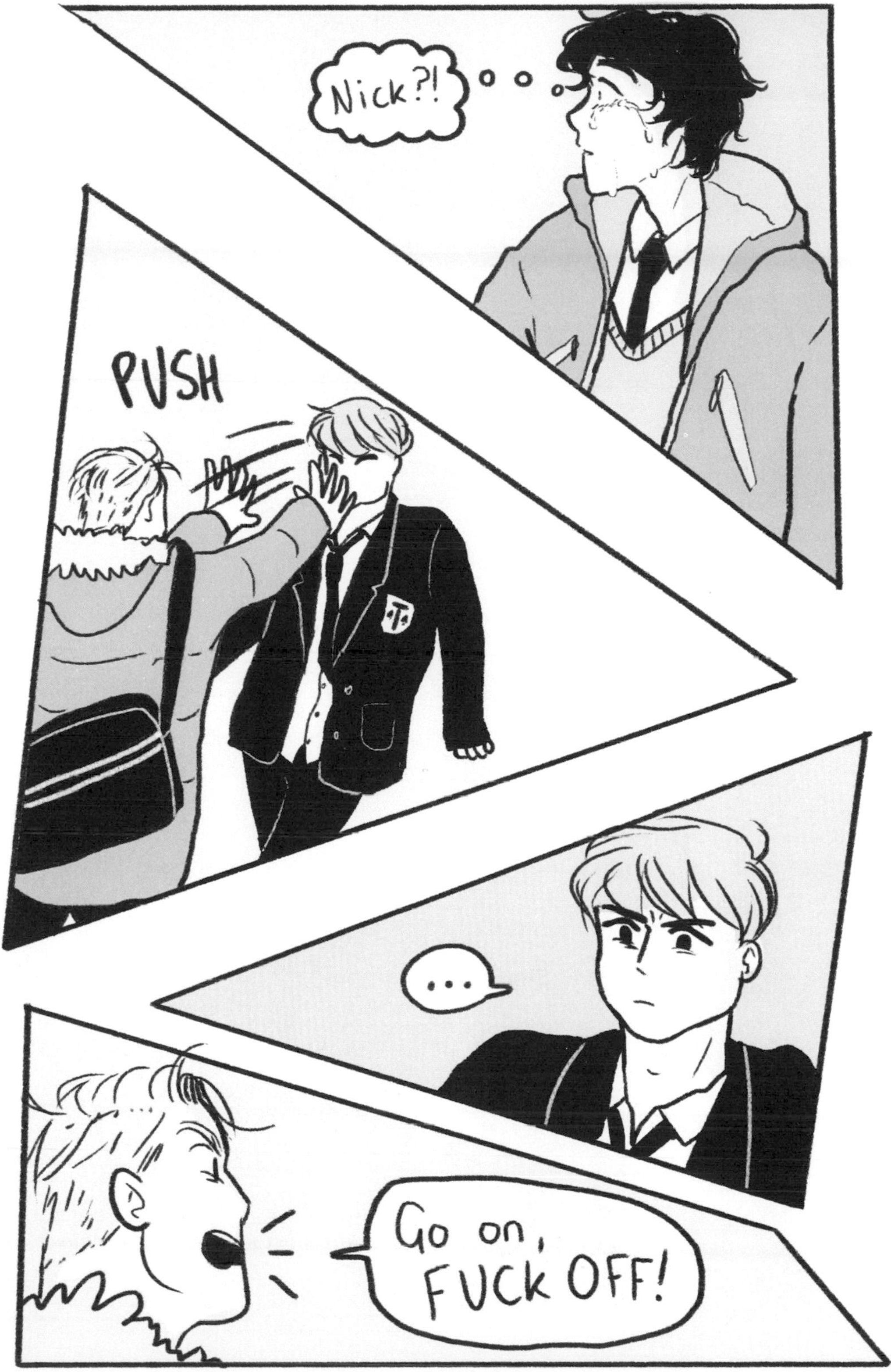
Nick?!
PUSH
...
Go on, FUCK OFF!

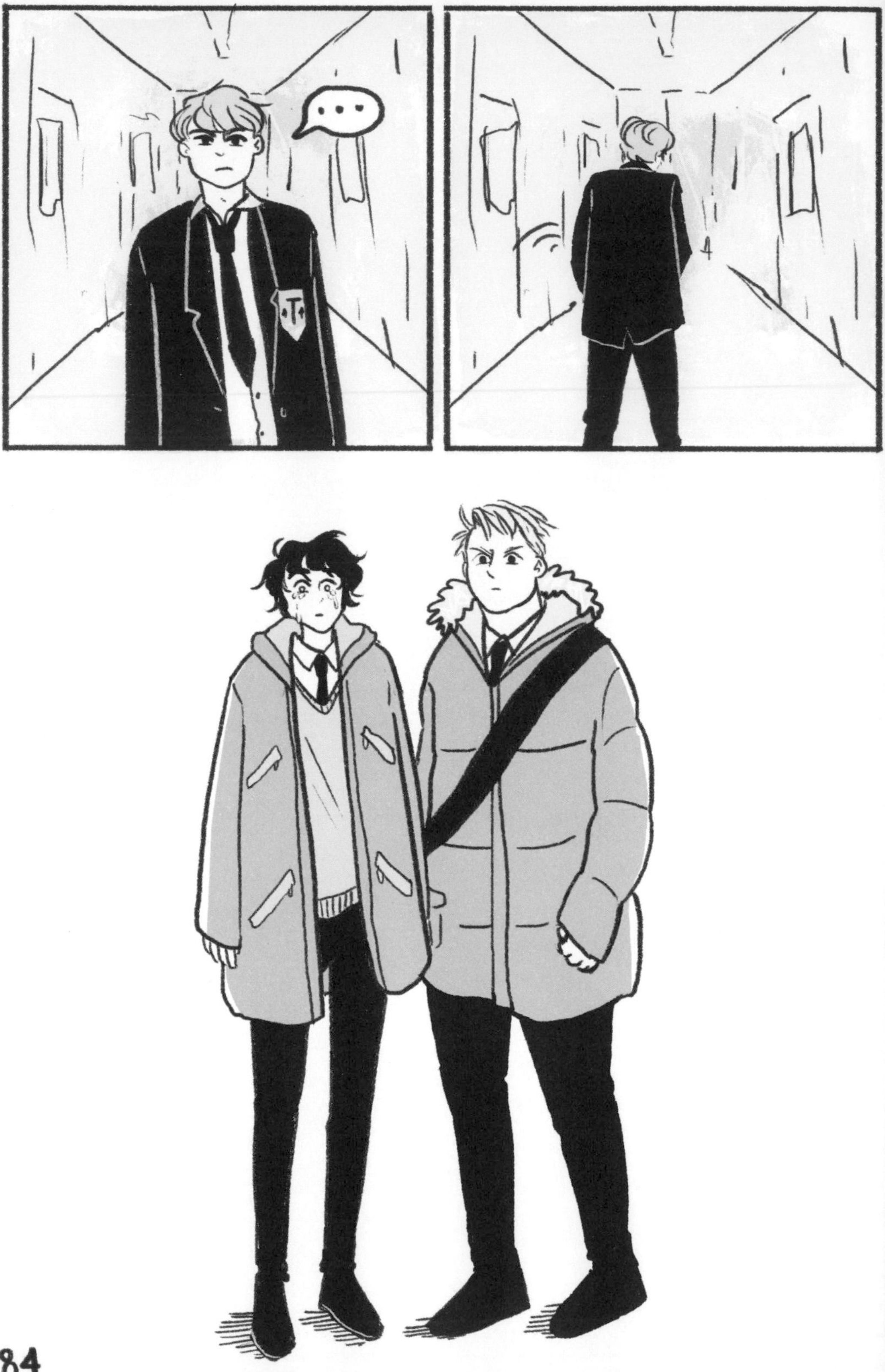
...

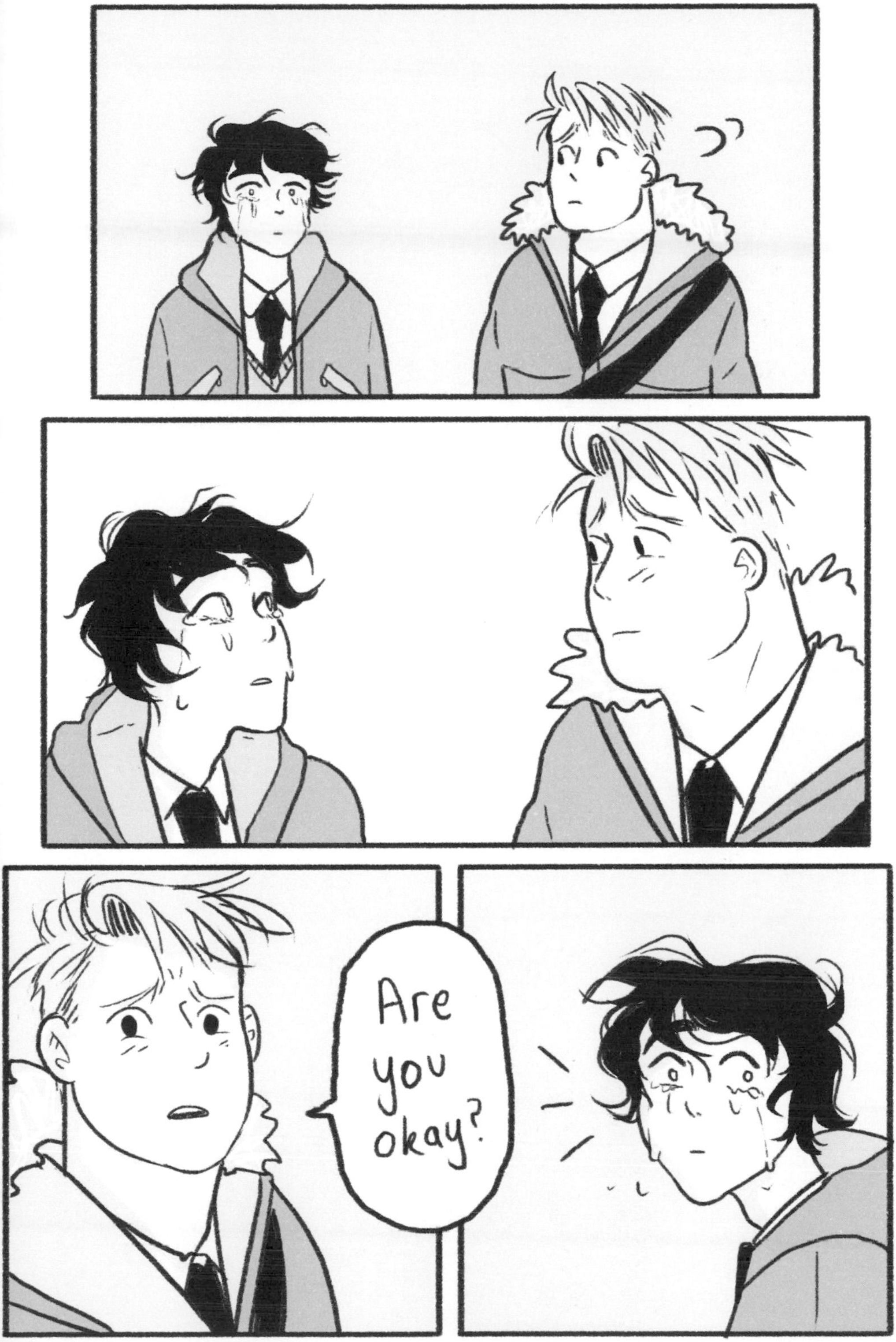
Are you okay?

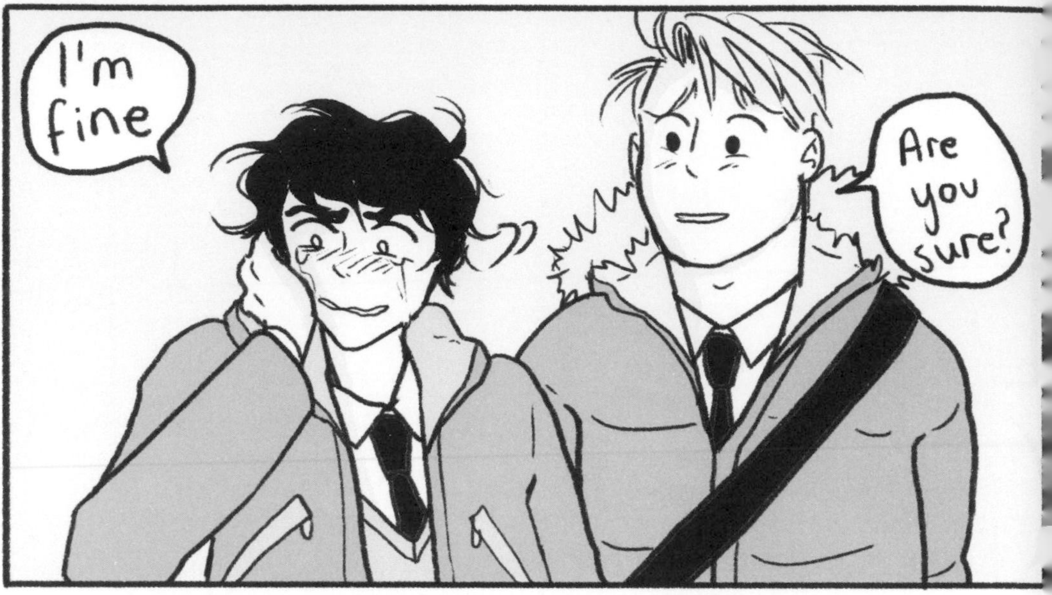
I'm fine
Are you sure?

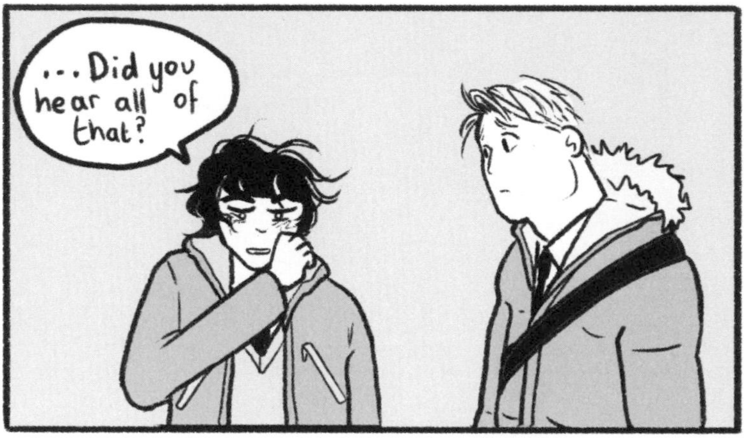
...Did you hear all of that?

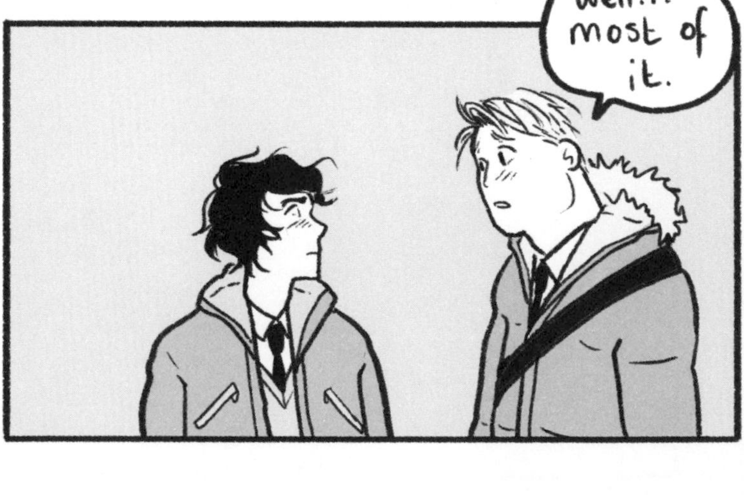
Well... most of it.

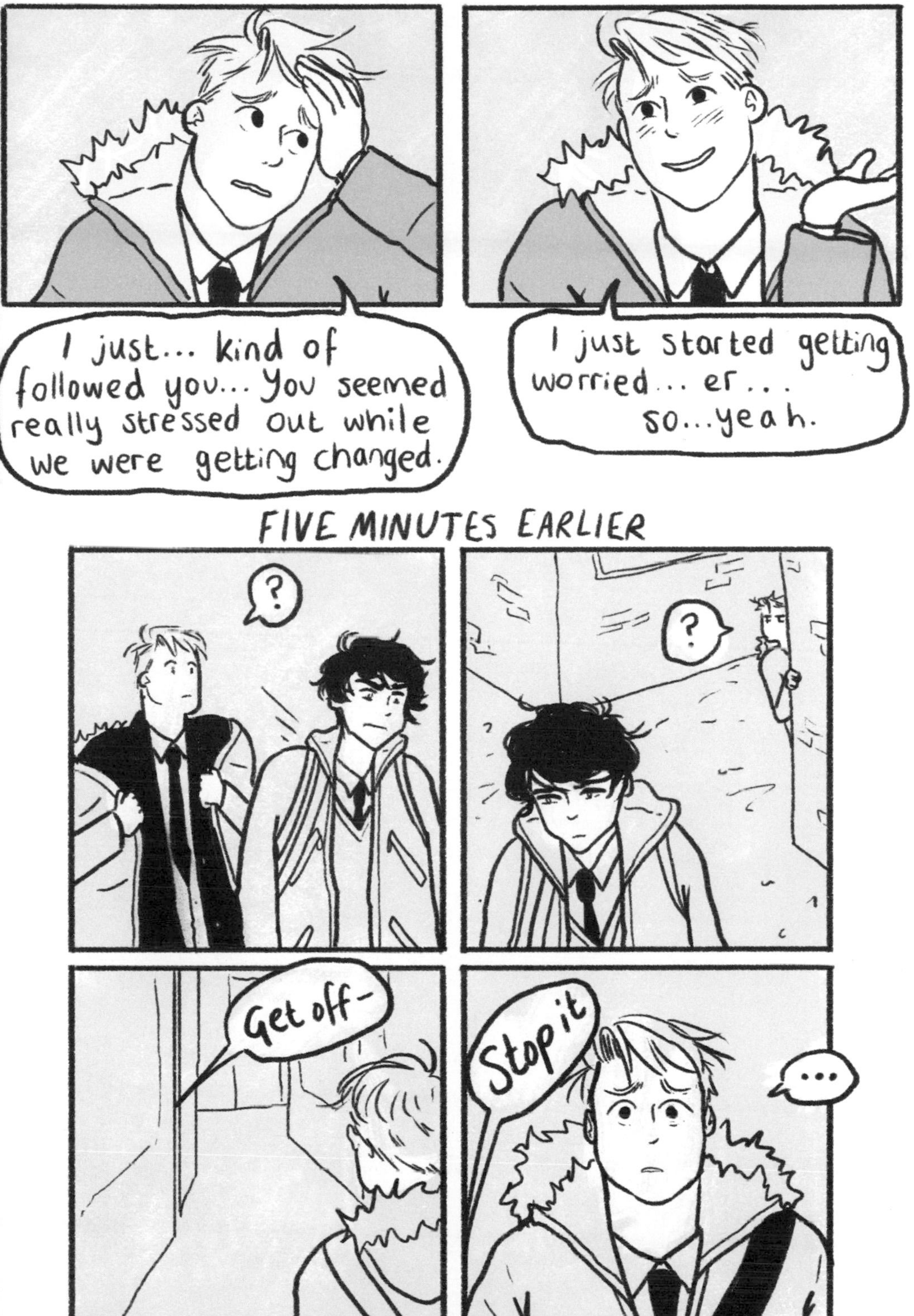

I just... kind of followed you... You seemed really stressed out while we were getting changed.
I just started getting worried... er... so...yeah.
FIVE MINUTES EARLIER
?
?
Get off-
Stop it
...

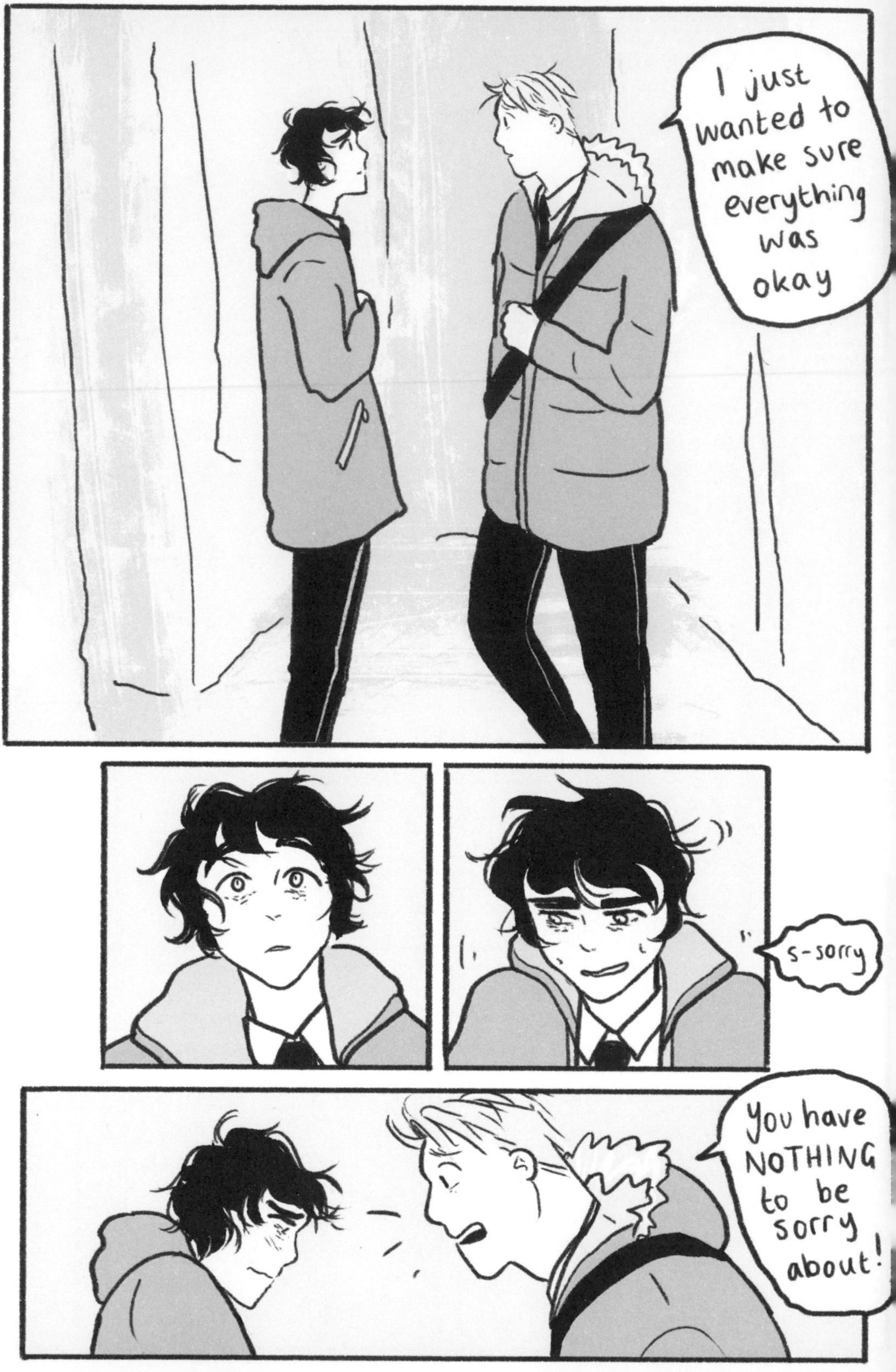
I just wanted to make sure everything was okay
s-sorry
You have NOTHING to be sorry about!

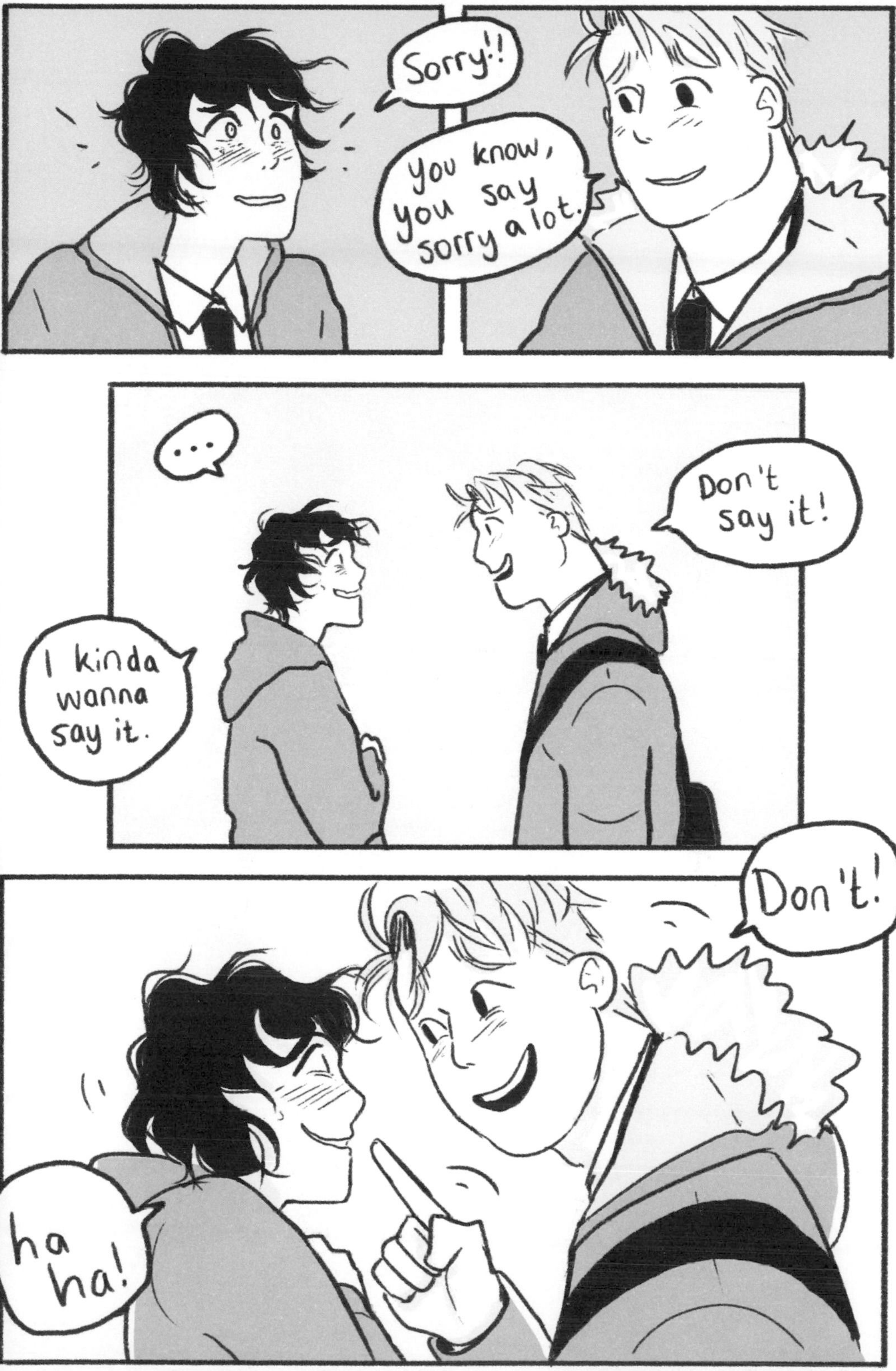
Sorry!!
You know, you say sorry a lot.
...
Don't say it!
I kinda wanna say it.
Don't!
ha ha!

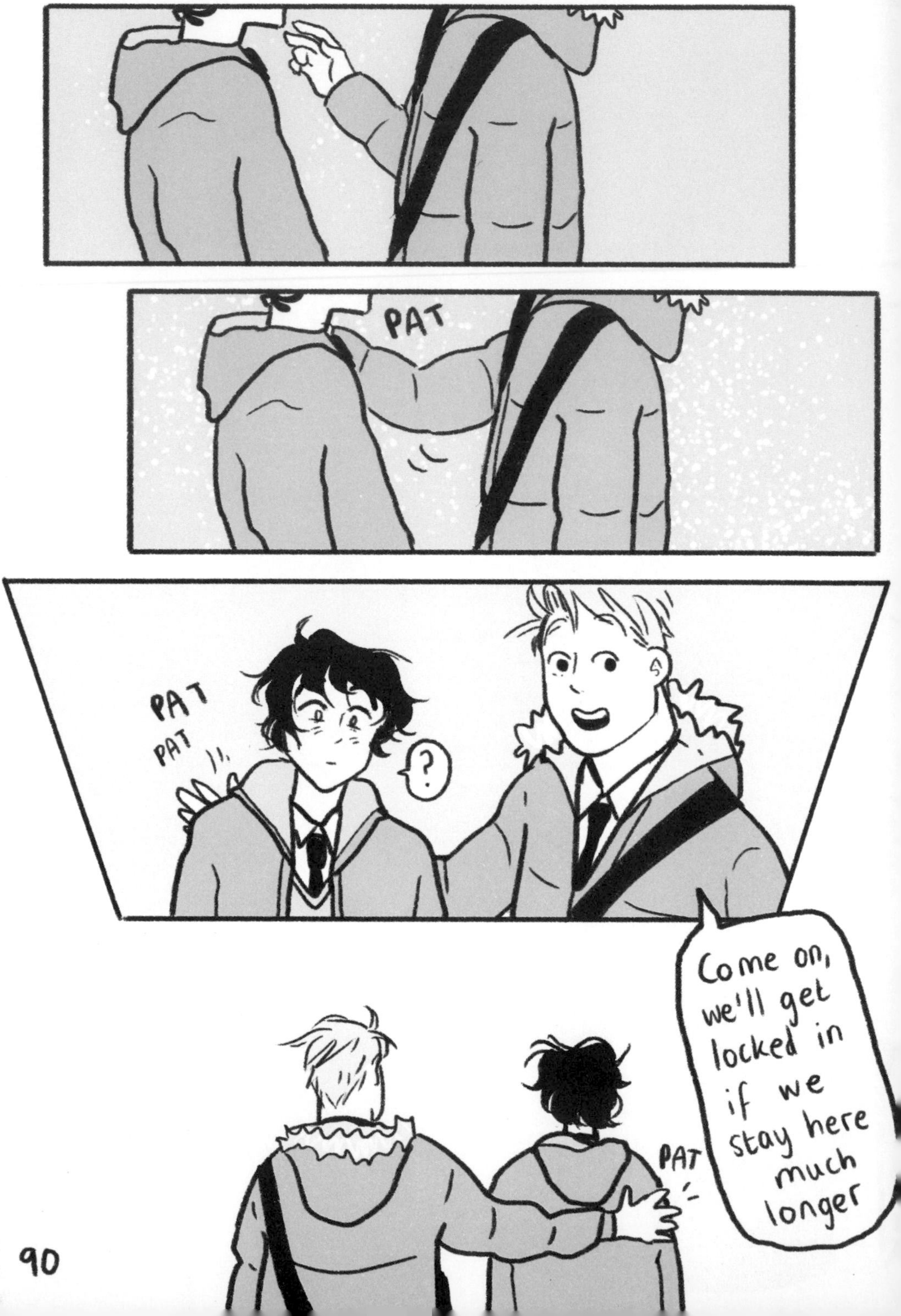
PAT
PAT
PAT
?
Come on, we'll get locked in if we stay here much longer
PAT

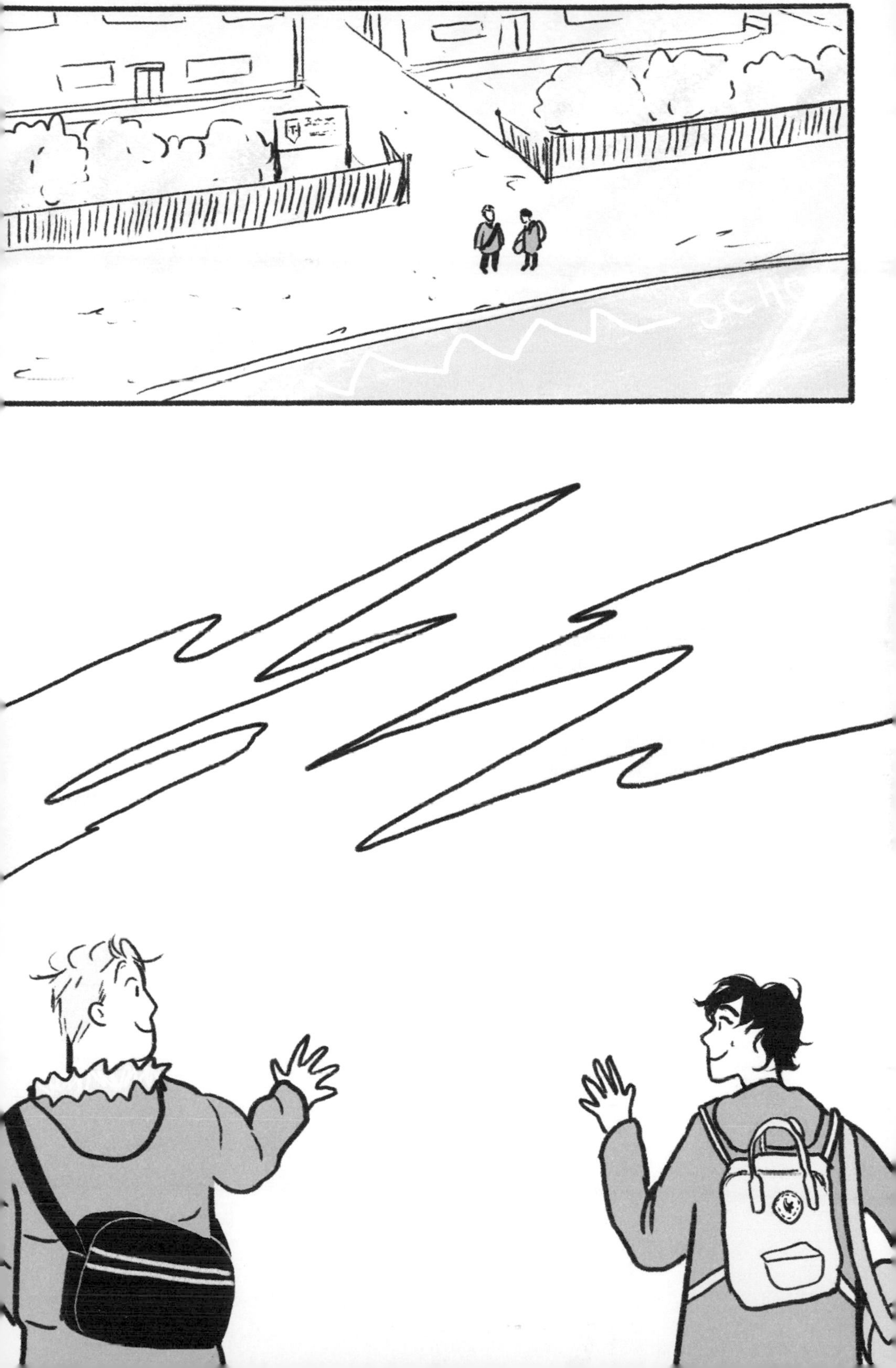

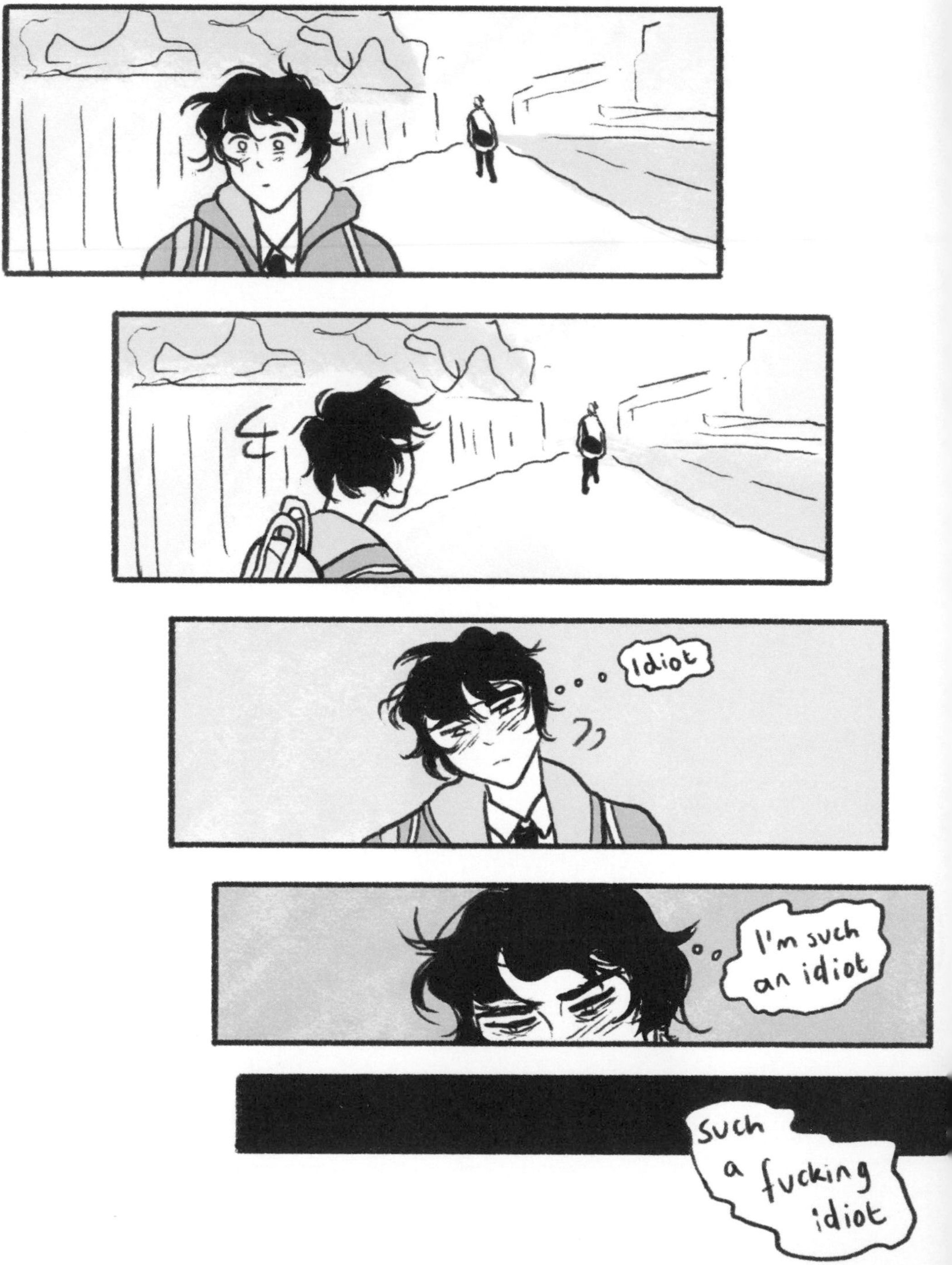
Idiot
I'm such an idiot
such a fucking idiot

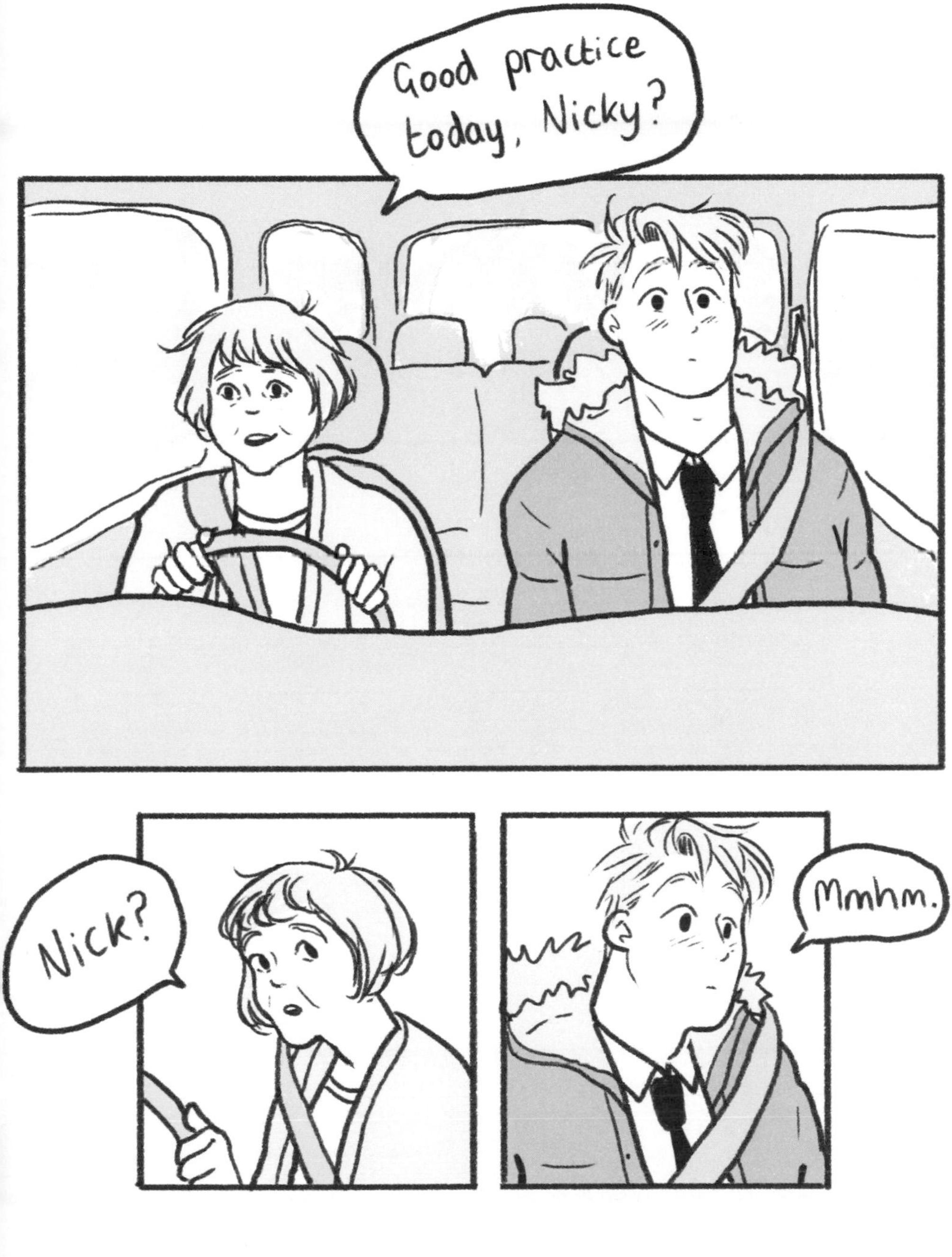
Good practice today, Nicky?
Nick?
Mmhm.

2. CRUSH

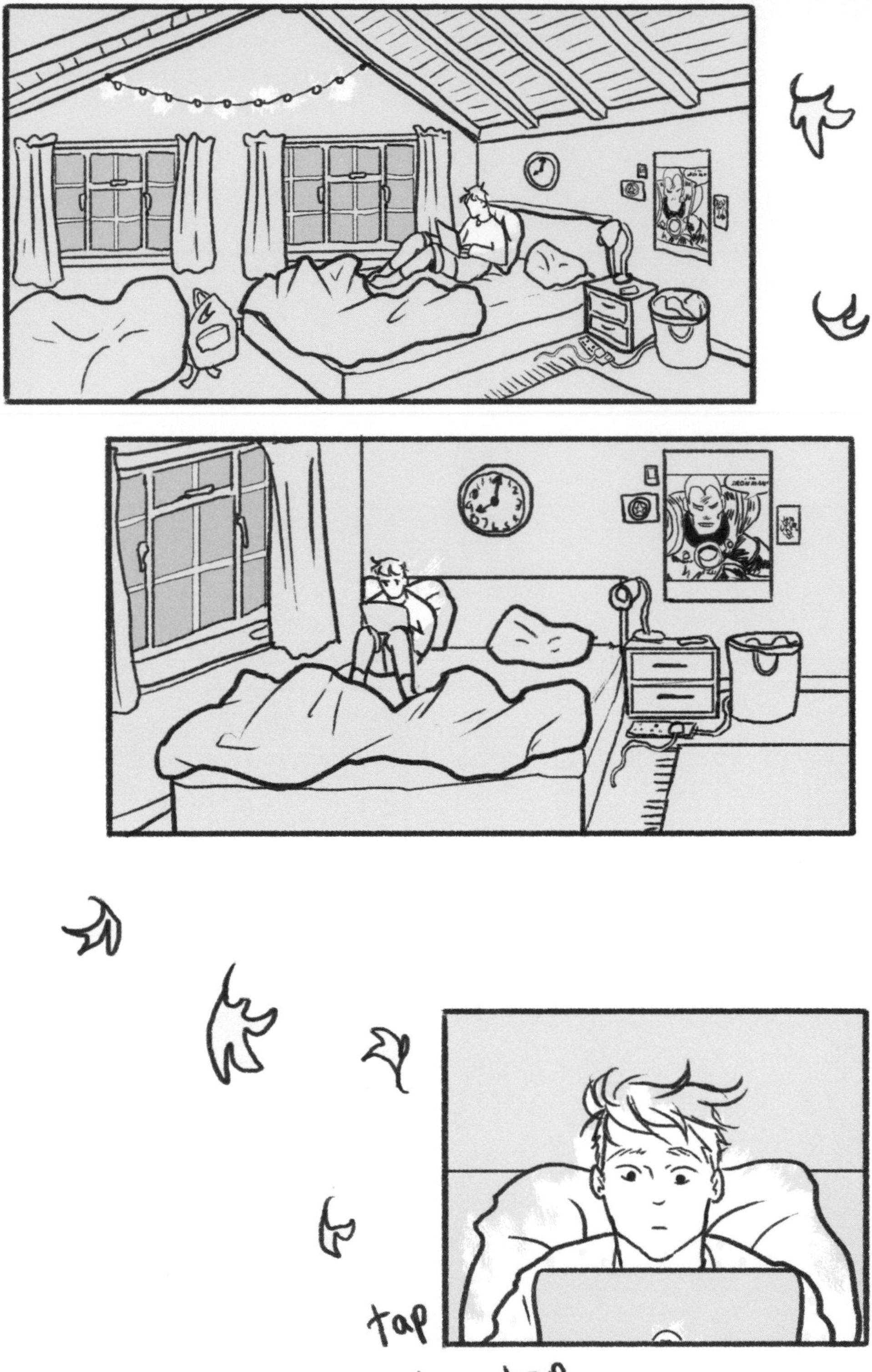
tap
tap tap

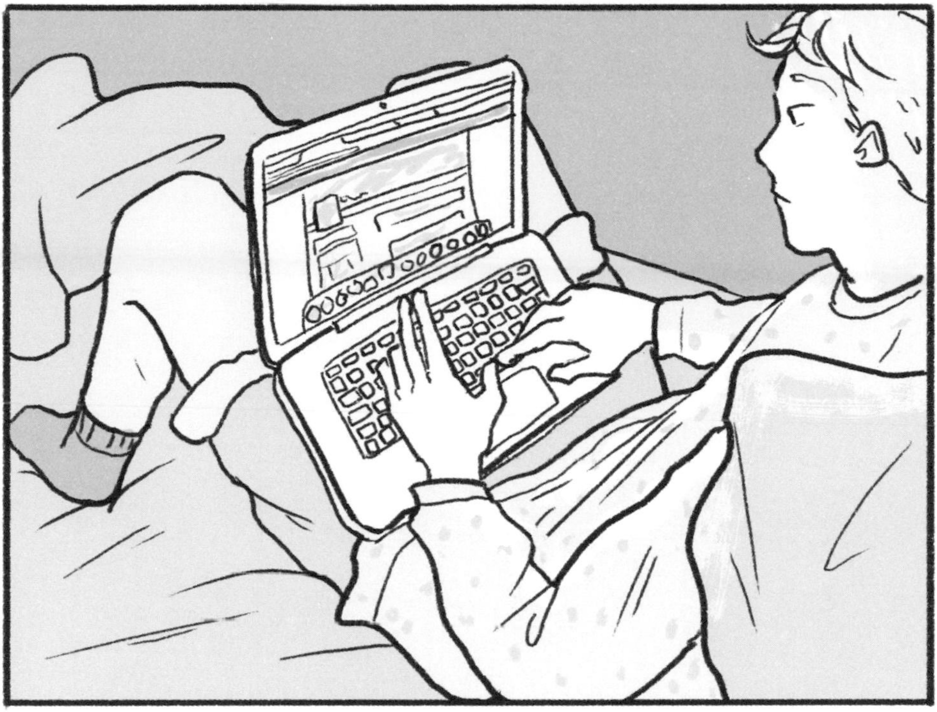

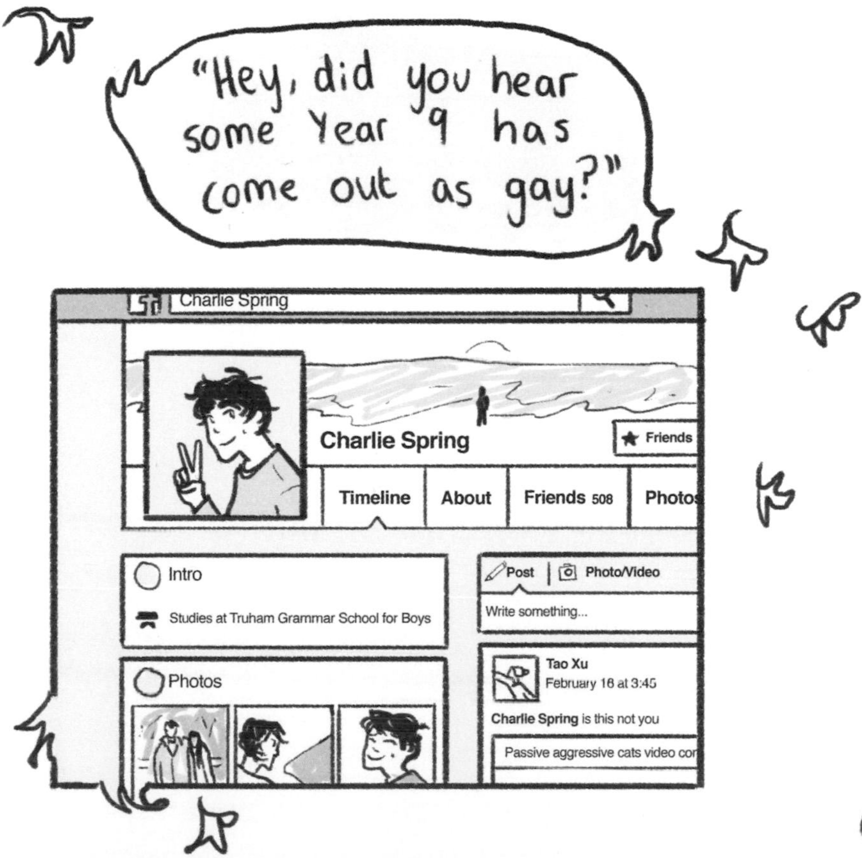
"Hey, did you hear some Year 9 has come out as gay?"
Charlie Spring
Charlie Spring
Friends
Timeline
About
Friends 508
Photos
Intro
Studies at Truham Grammar School for Boys
Photos
Post
Photo/Video
Write something...
Tao Xu
February 16 at 3:45
Charlie Spring is this not you
Passive aggressive cats video co

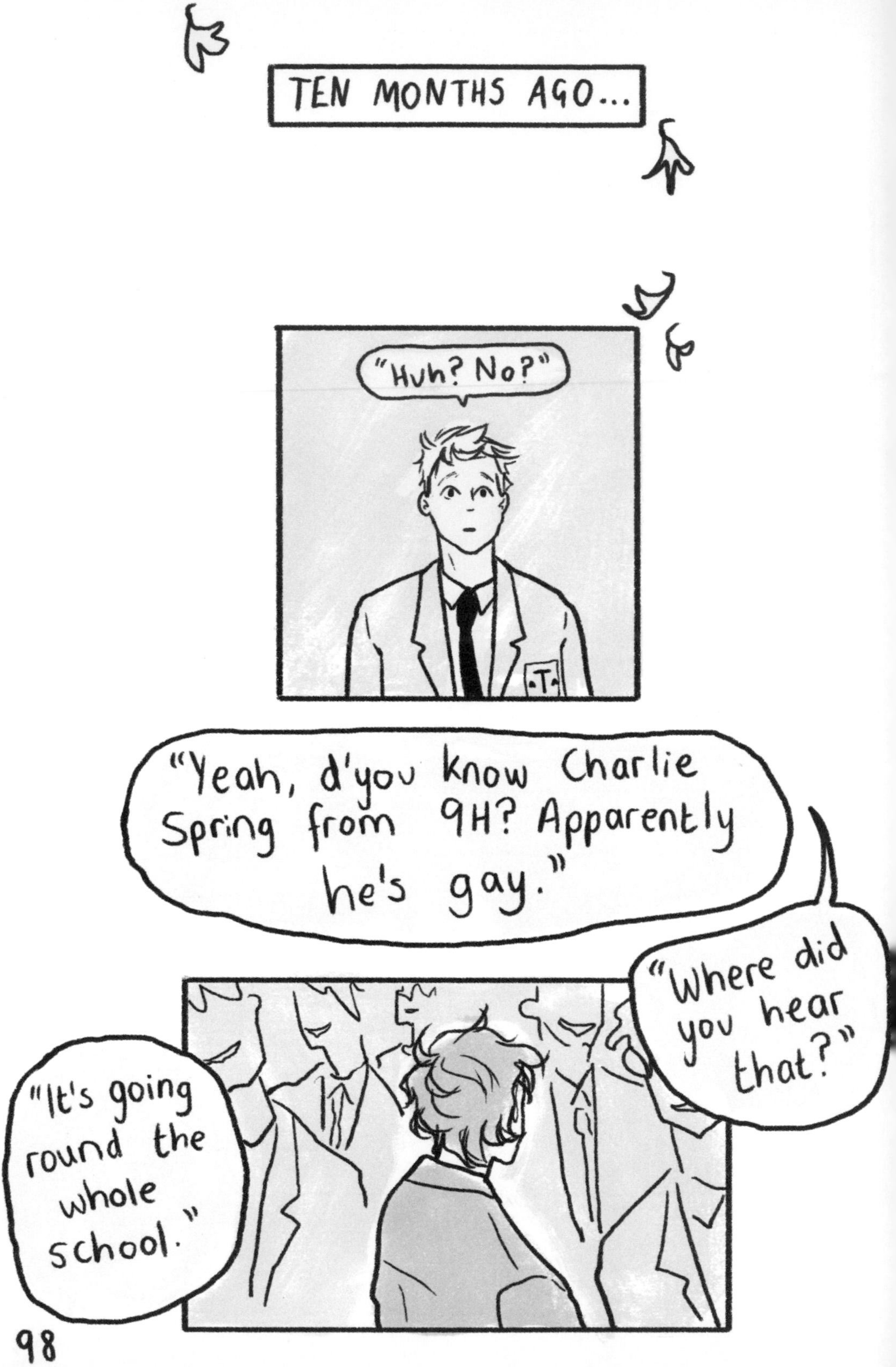
TEN MONTHS AGO...
"Huh? No?"
"Yeah, d'you know Charlie Spring from 9H? Apparently he's gay."
"Where did you hear that?"
"It's going round the whole school."

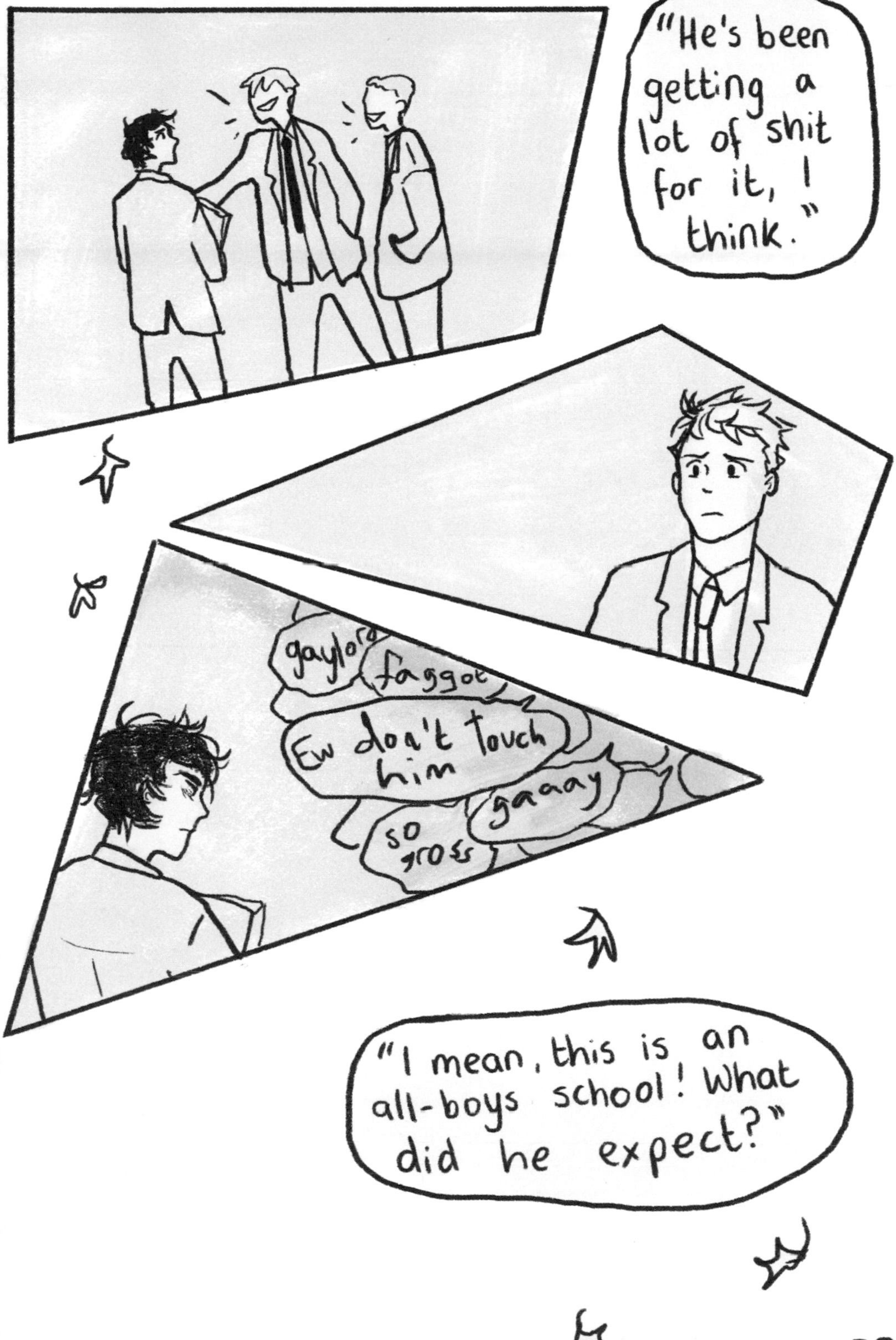
"He's been getting a lot of shit for it, I think."
gaylord
faggot
Ew don't touch him
gaaay
so gross
"I mean, this is an all-boys school! What did he expect?"

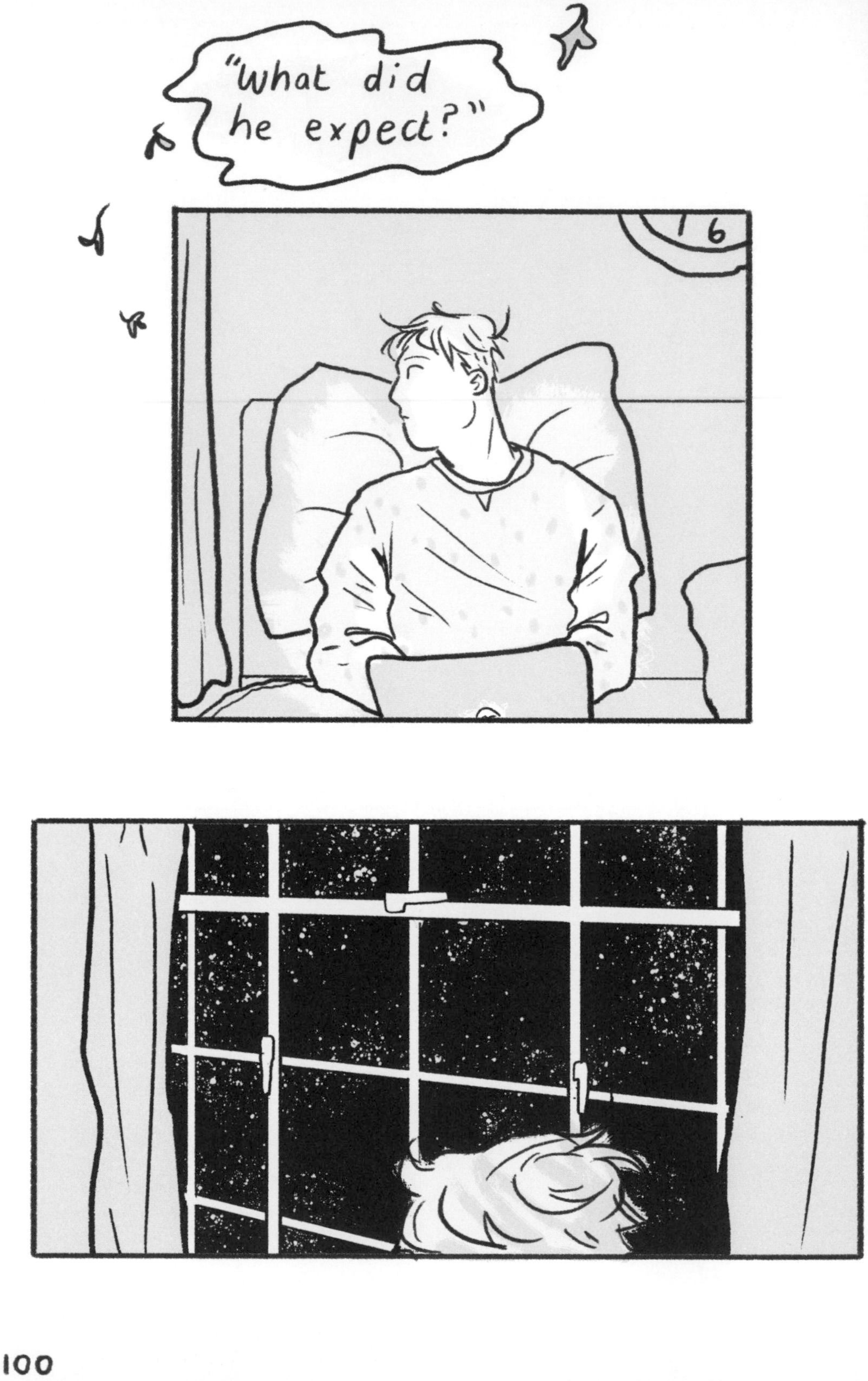
"What did he expect?"

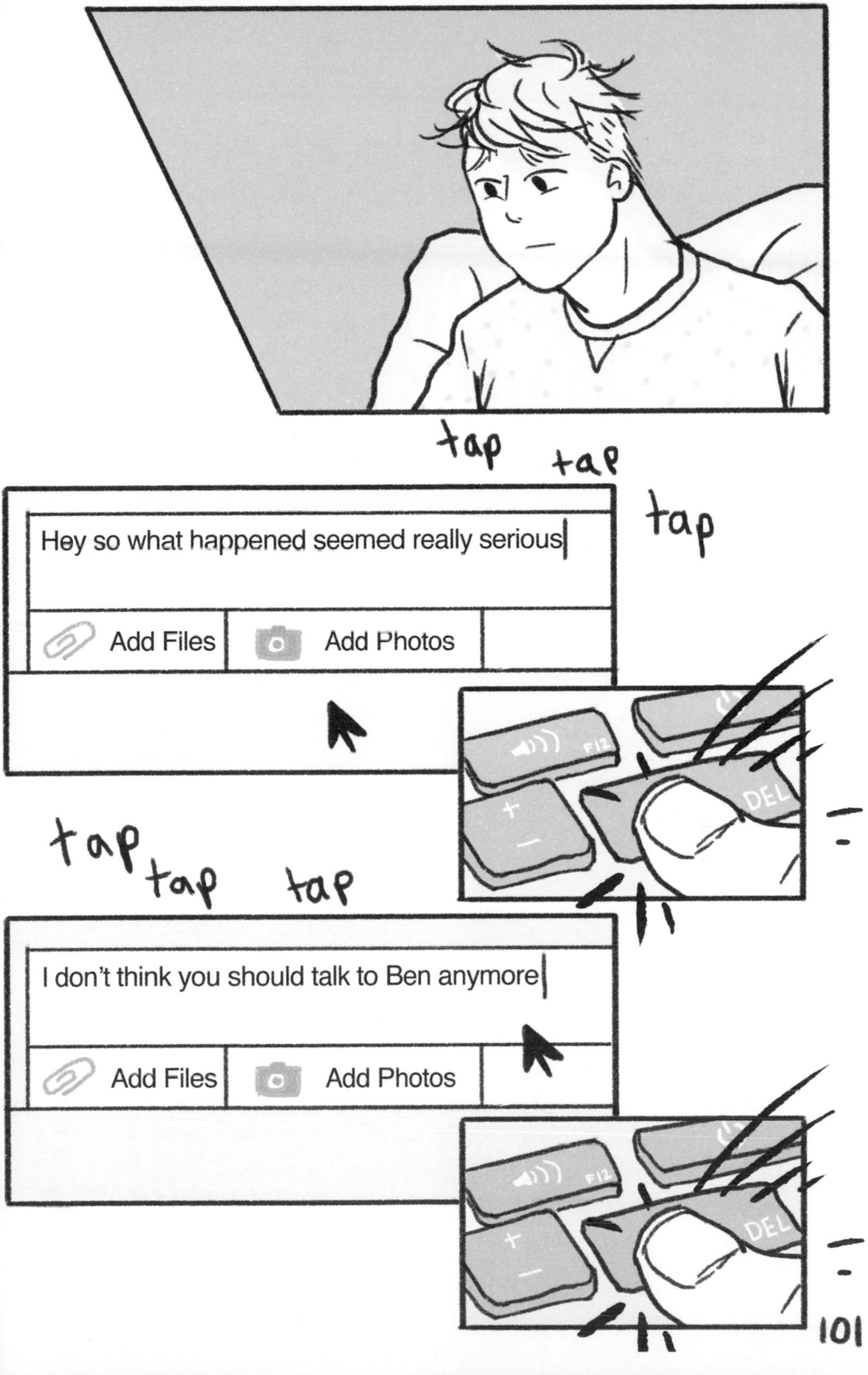
tap tap tap
Hey so what happened seemed really serious
Add Files
Add Photos
F12
DEL
tap tap tap
I don't think you should talk to Ben anymore
Add Files
Add Photos
F12
DEL

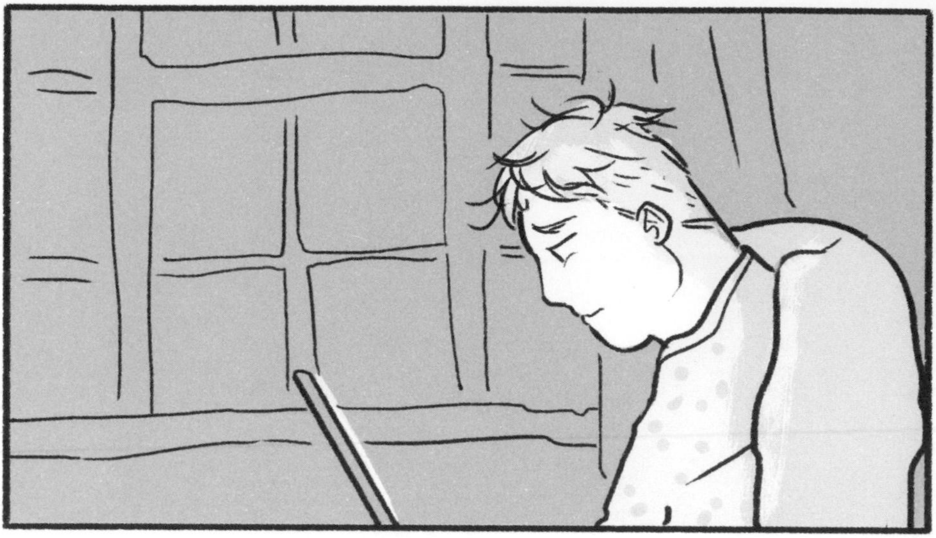

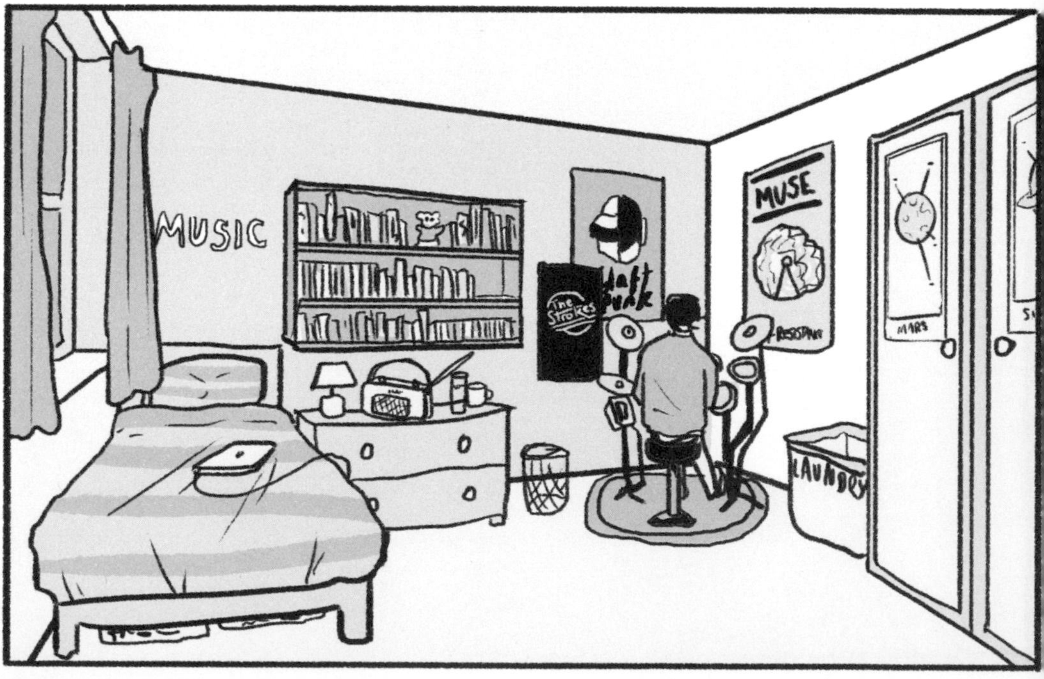
MUSIC
The Strokes
daft punk
MUSE
MARS
LAUNDRY

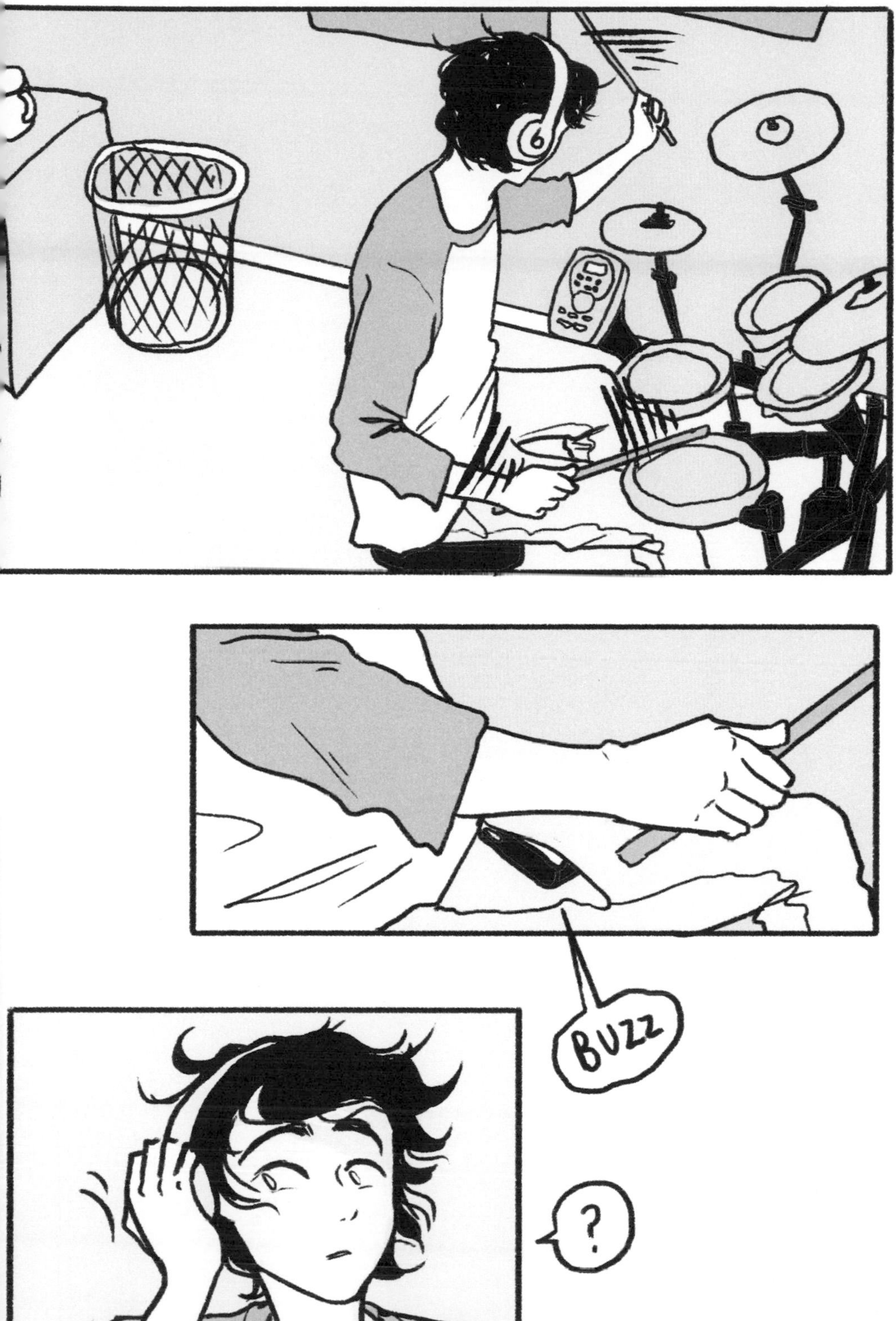
BUZZ
?

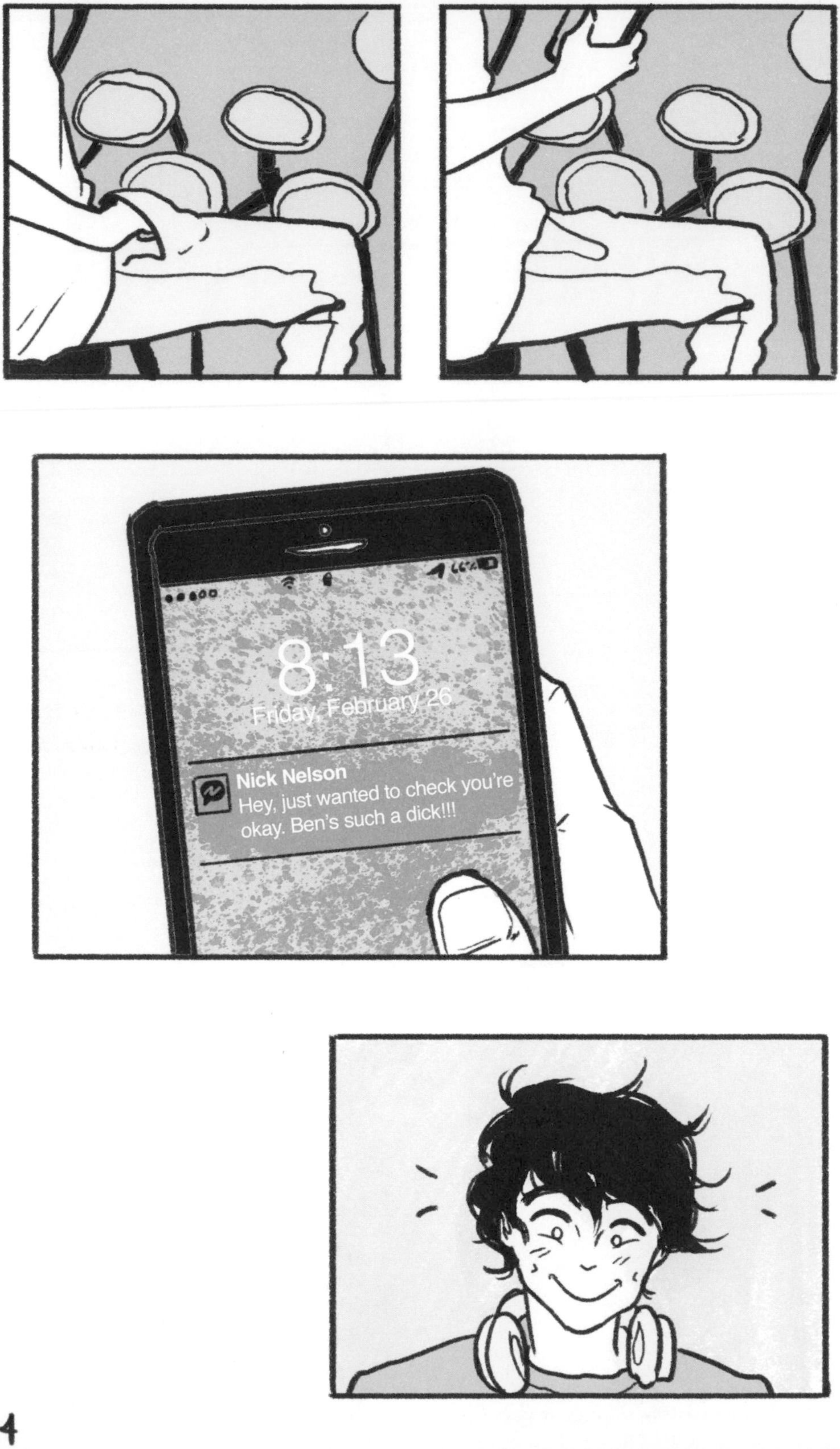
8:13
Friday, February 26
Nick Nelson
Hey, just wanted to check you're okay. Ben's such a dick!!!

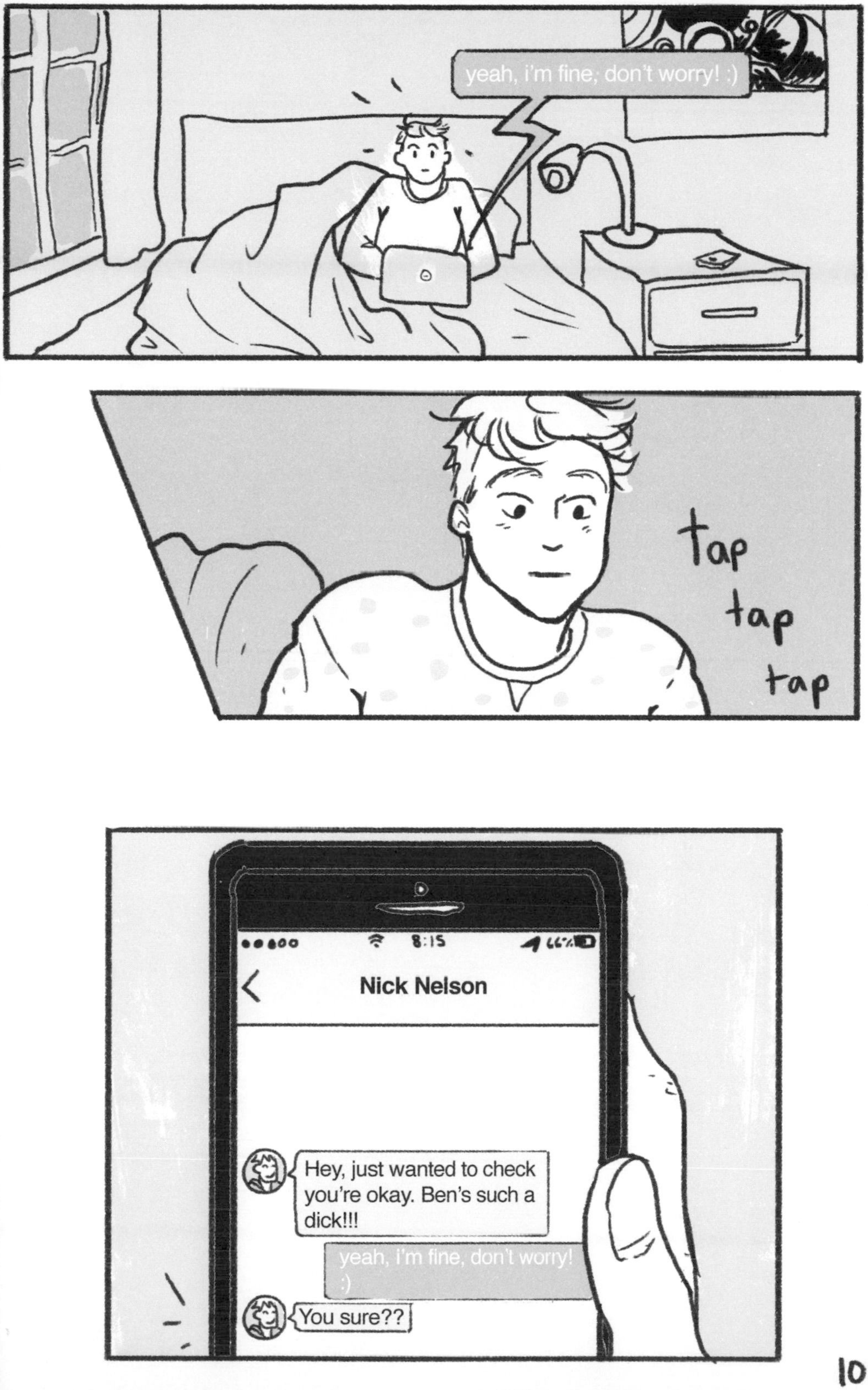
yeah, i'm fine, don't worry! :)
tap
tap
tap
8:15
Nick Nelson
Hey, just wanted to check you're okay. Ben's such a dick!!!
yeah, i'm fine, don't worry! :)
You sure??

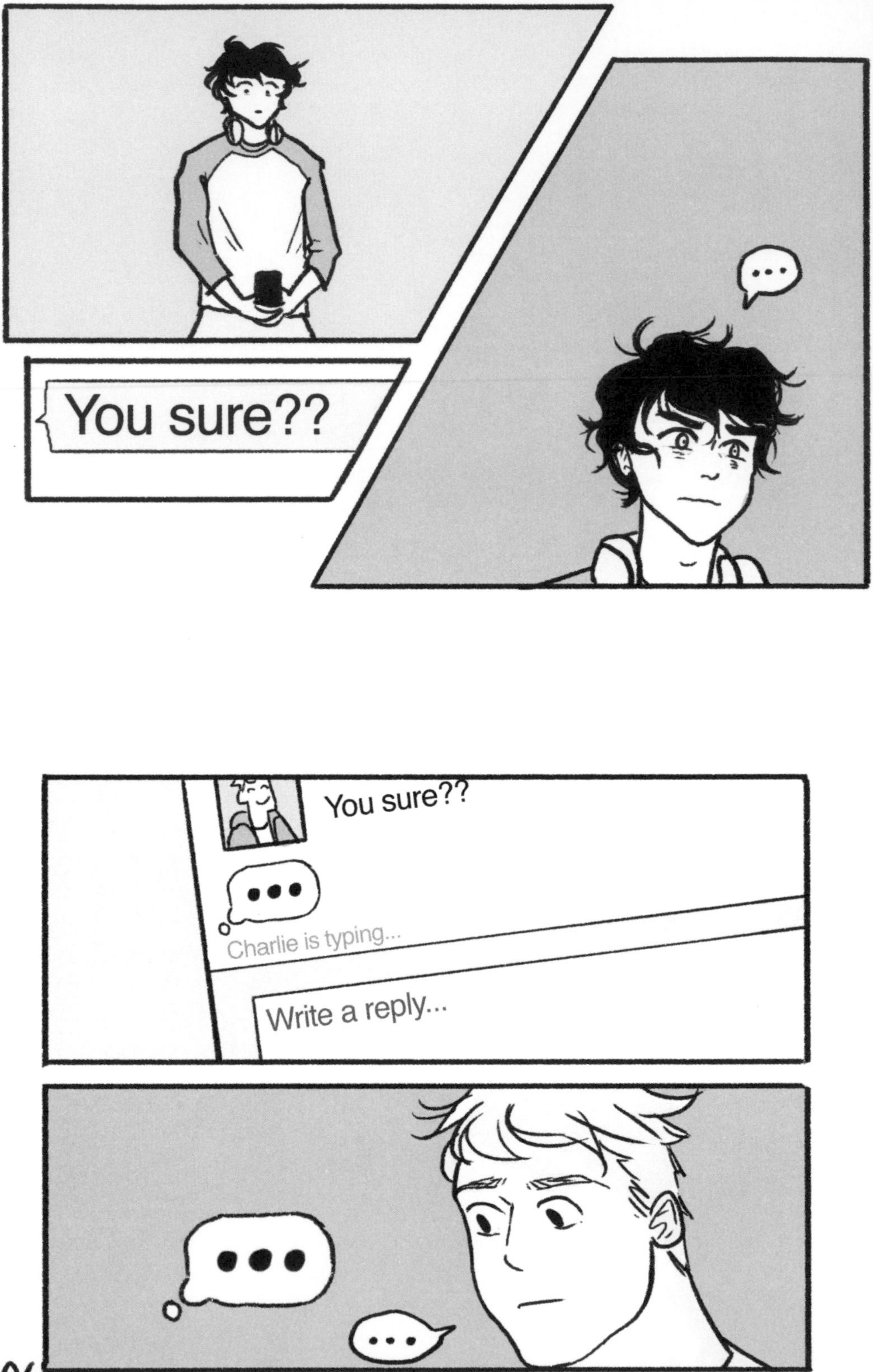
You sure??
...
You sure??
Charlie is typing...
Write a reply...
...

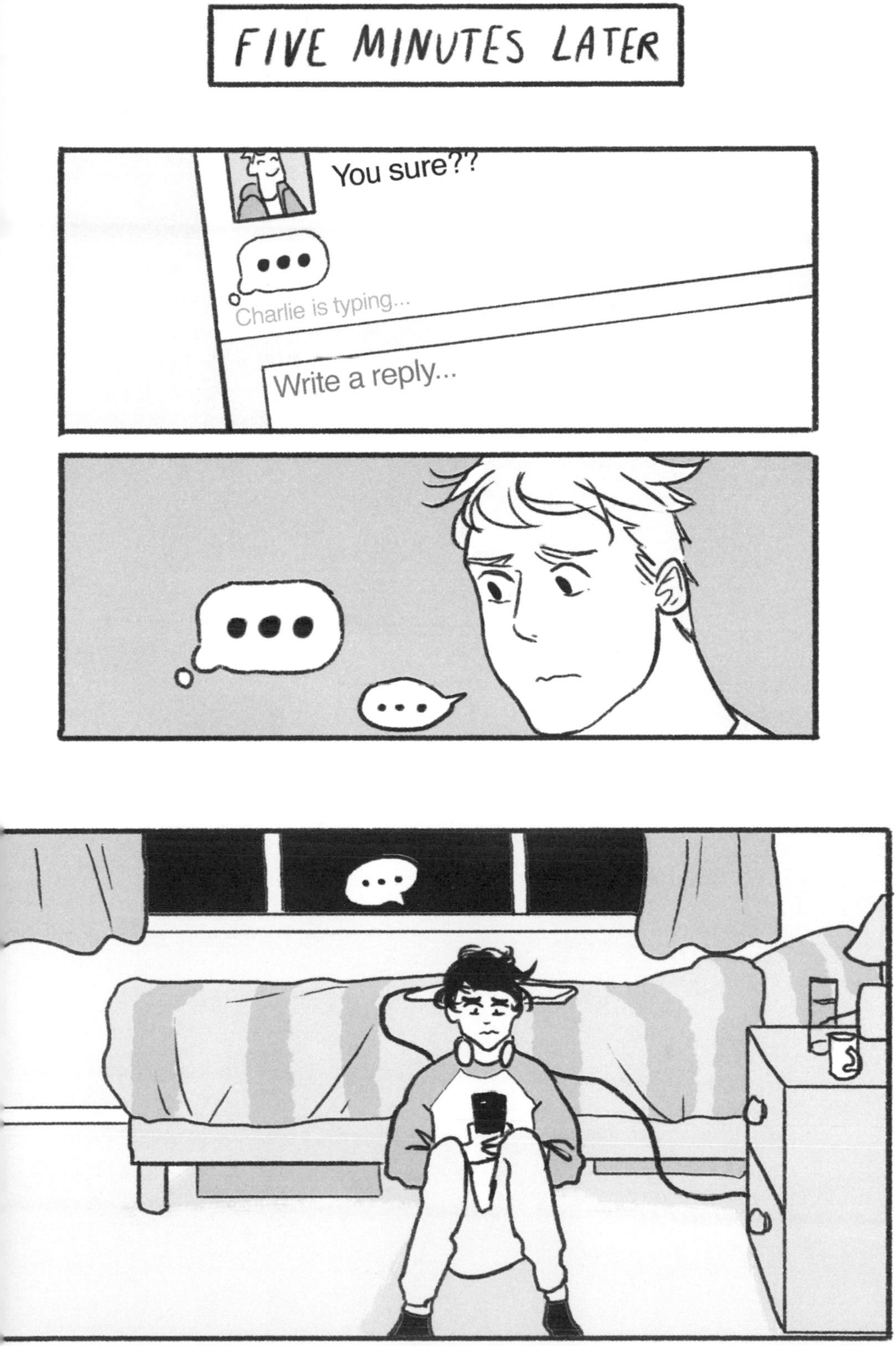
FIVE MINUTES LATER
You sure??
Charlie is typing...
Write a reply...

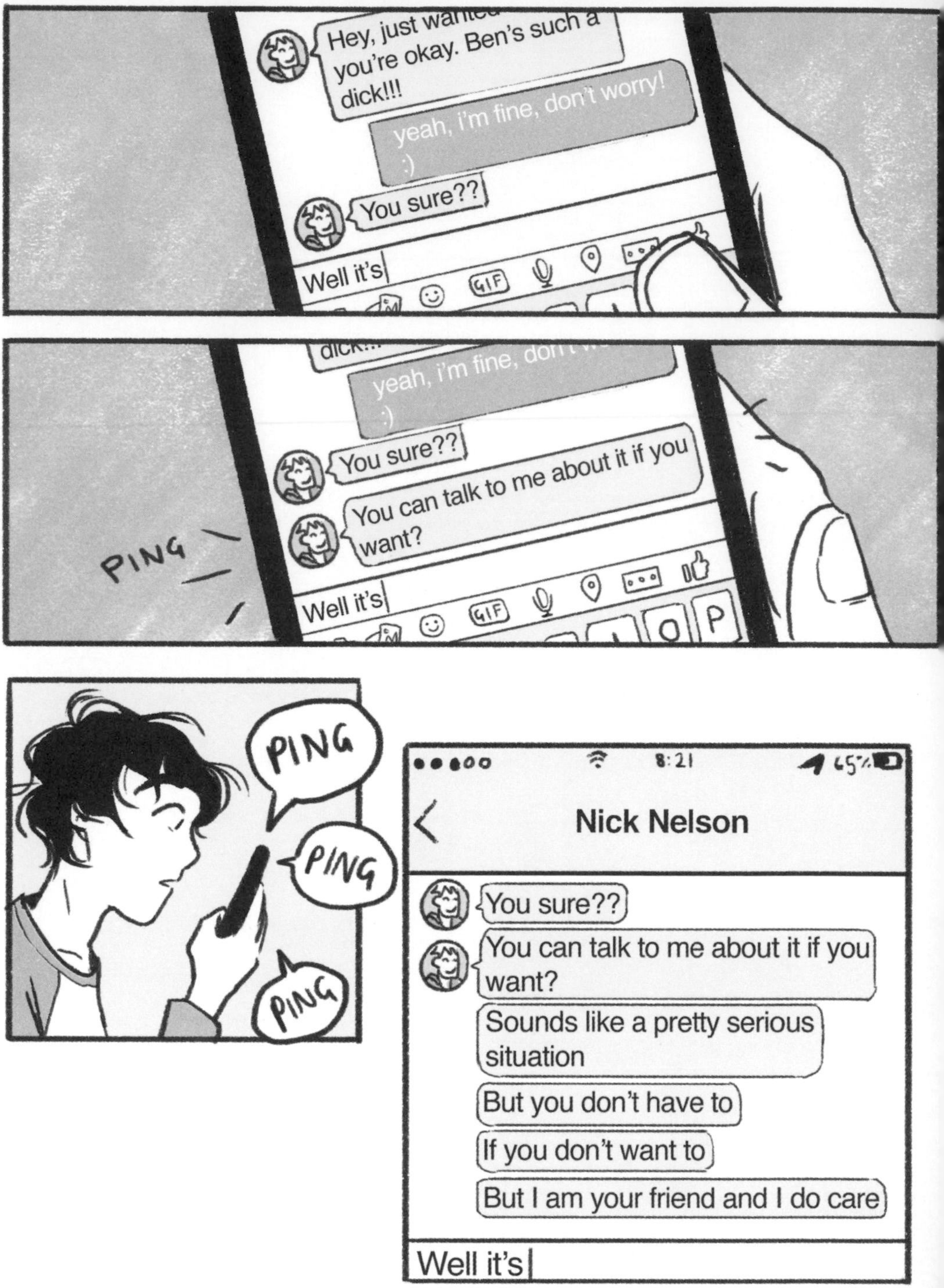
Hey, just
you're okay. Ben's such a dick!!!
yeah, i'm fine, don't worry! :)
You sure??
Well it's
yeah, i'm fine,
:)
You sure??
You can talk to me about it if you want?
PING
Well it's
PING
PING
PING
8:21
Nick Nelson
You sure??
You can talk to me about it if you want?
Sounds like a pretty serious situation
But you don't have to
If you don't want to
But I am your friend and I do care
Well it's

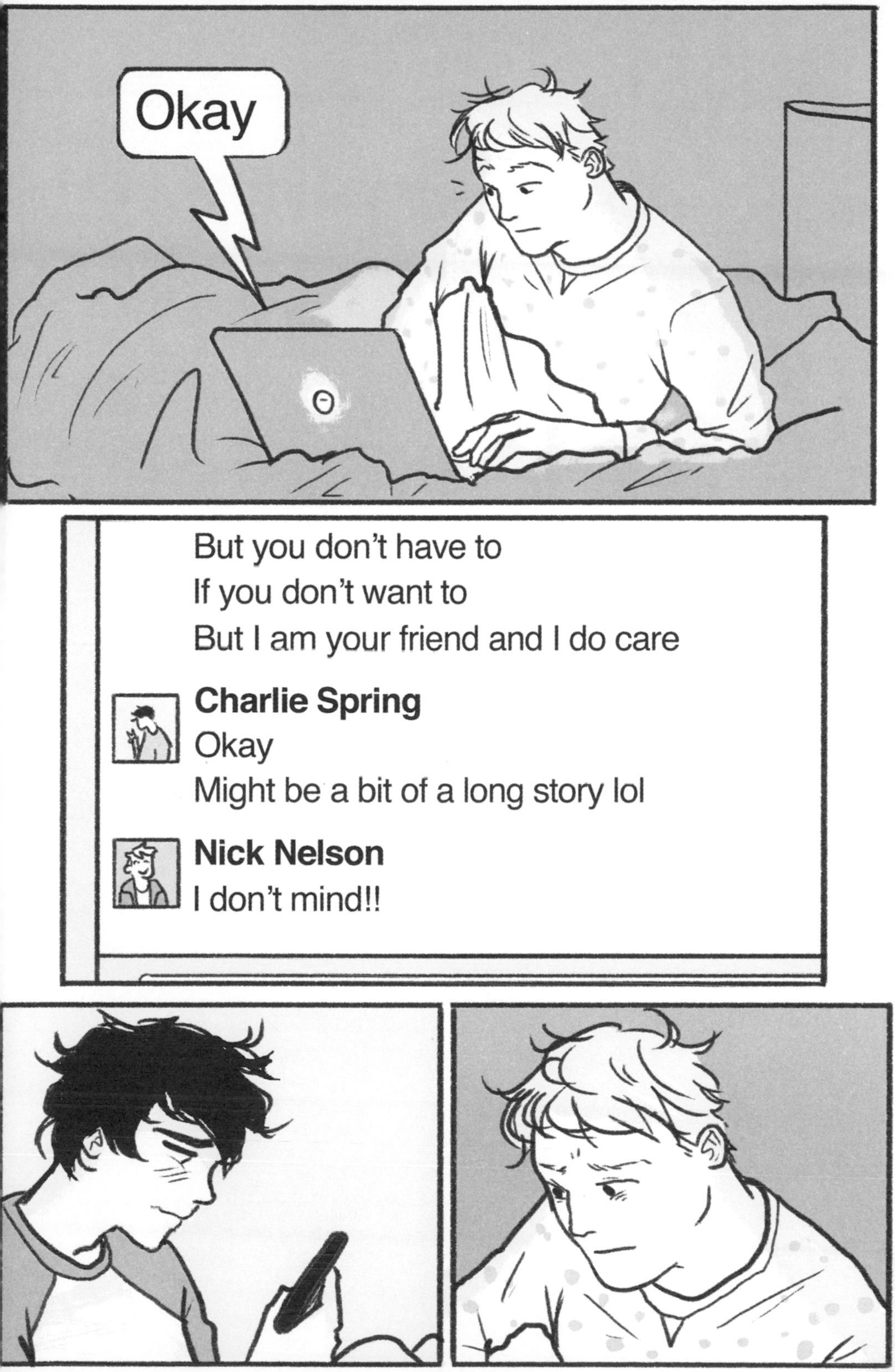
Okay
But you don't have to
If you don't want to
But I am your friend and I do care
Charlie Spring
Okay
Might be a bit of a long story lol
Nick Nelson
I don't mind!!

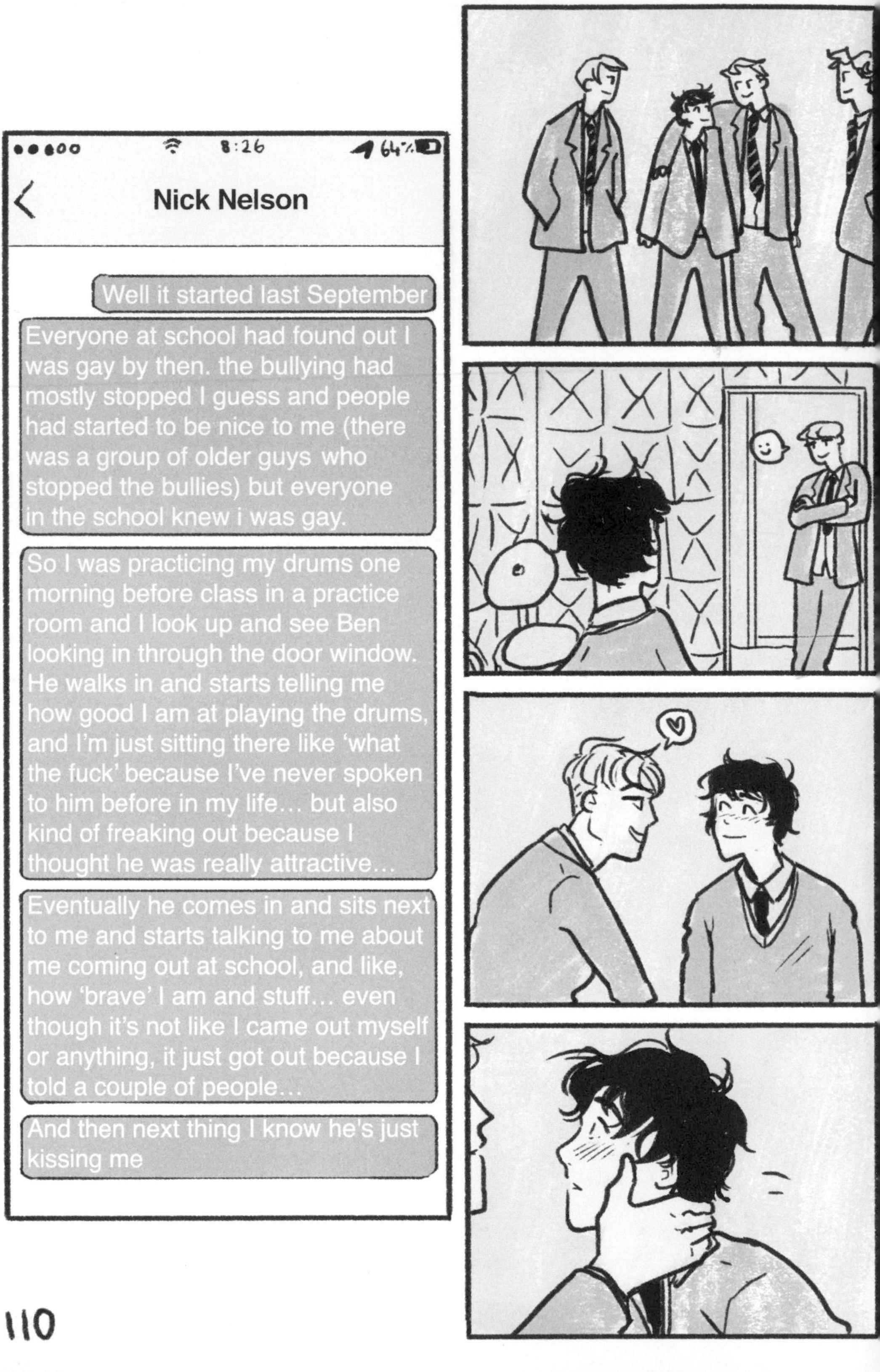
8:26
64%
Nick Nelson
Well it started last September
Everyone at school had found out I was gay by then. the bullying had mostly stopped I guess and people had started to be nice to me (there was a group of older guys who stopped the bullies) but everyone in the school knew i was gay.
So I was practicing my drums one morning before class in a practice room and I look up and see Ben looking in through the door window. He walks in and starts telling me how good I am at playing the drums, and I'm just sitting there like 'what the fuck' because I've never spoken to him before in my life… but also kind of freaking out because I thought he was really attractive…
Eventually he comes in and sits next to me and starts talking to me about me coming out at school, and like, how 'brave' I am and stuff… even though it's not like I came out myself or anything, it just got out because I told a couple of people…
And then next thing I know he's just kissing me

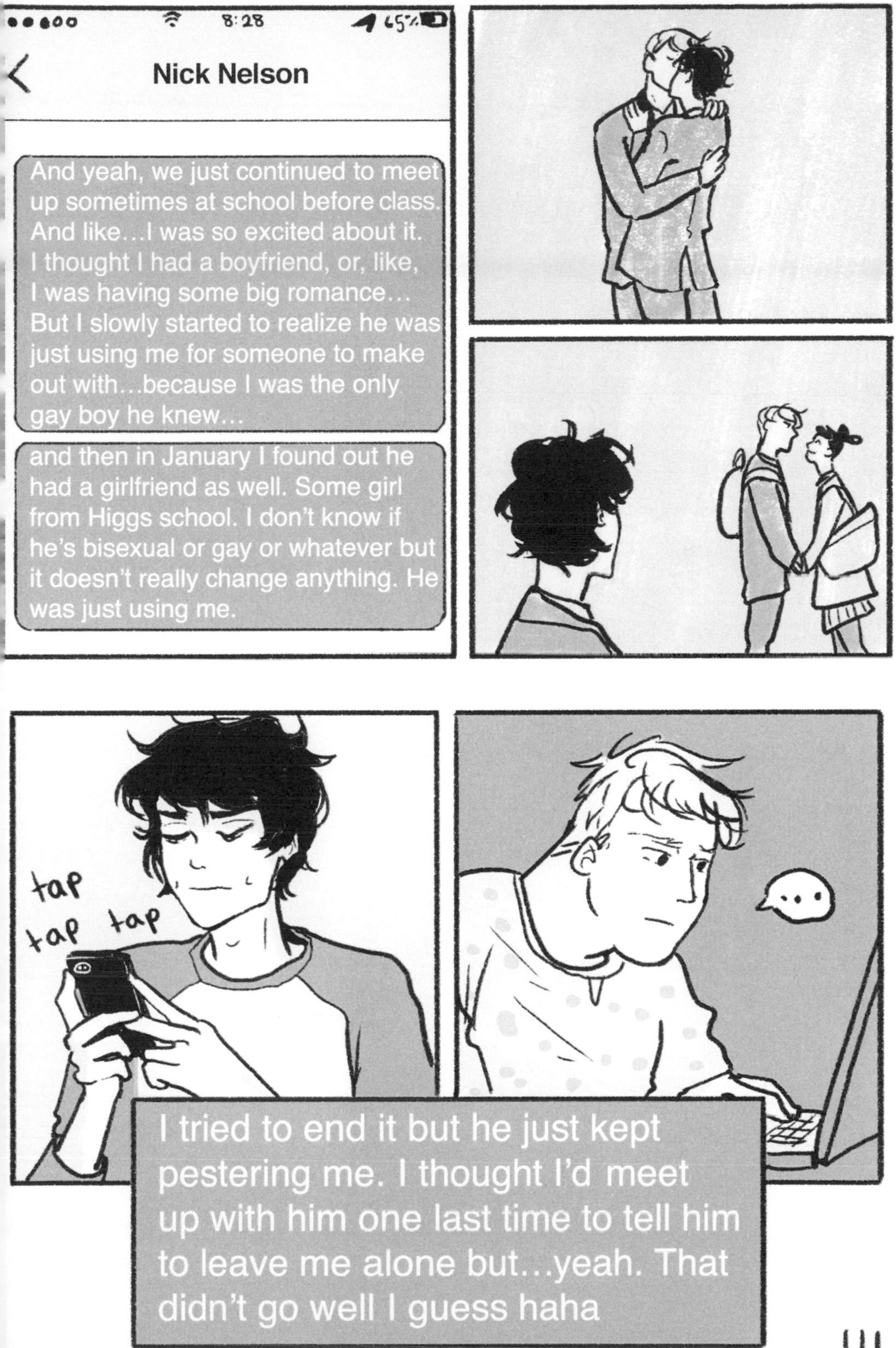
8:28
65%
Nick Nelson
And yeah, we just continued to meet up sometimes at school before class. And like…I was so excited about it. I thought I had a boyfriend, or, like, I was having some big romance… But I slowly started to realize he was just using me for someone to make out with…because I was the only gay boy he knew…
and then in January I found out he had a girlfriend as well. Some girl from Higgs school. I don't know if he's bisexual or gay or whatever but it doesn't really change anything. He was just using me.
tap
tap tap
I tried to end it but he just kept pestering me. I thought I'd meet up with him one last time to tell him to leave me alone but…yeah. That didn't go well I guess haha

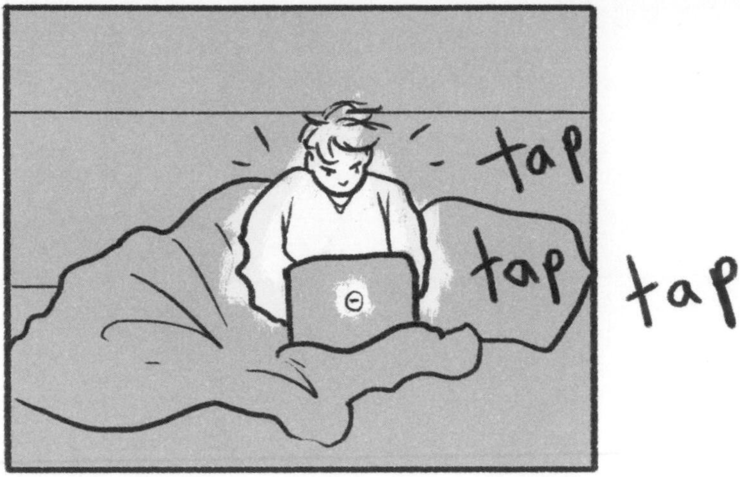
tap
tap
tap

Nick Nelson
FUCK I hate Ben so much. I knew he was a dick, but... jesus.

Please don't ever talk to him again

Charlie Spring
I definitely won't!!!!

Nick Nelson
I will kick his ass if he tries to come near you

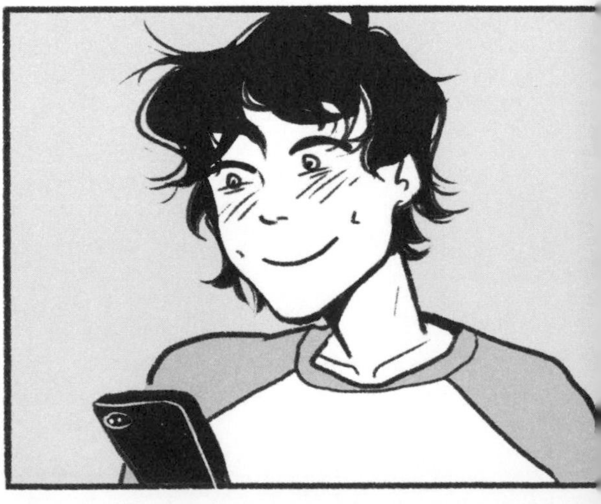

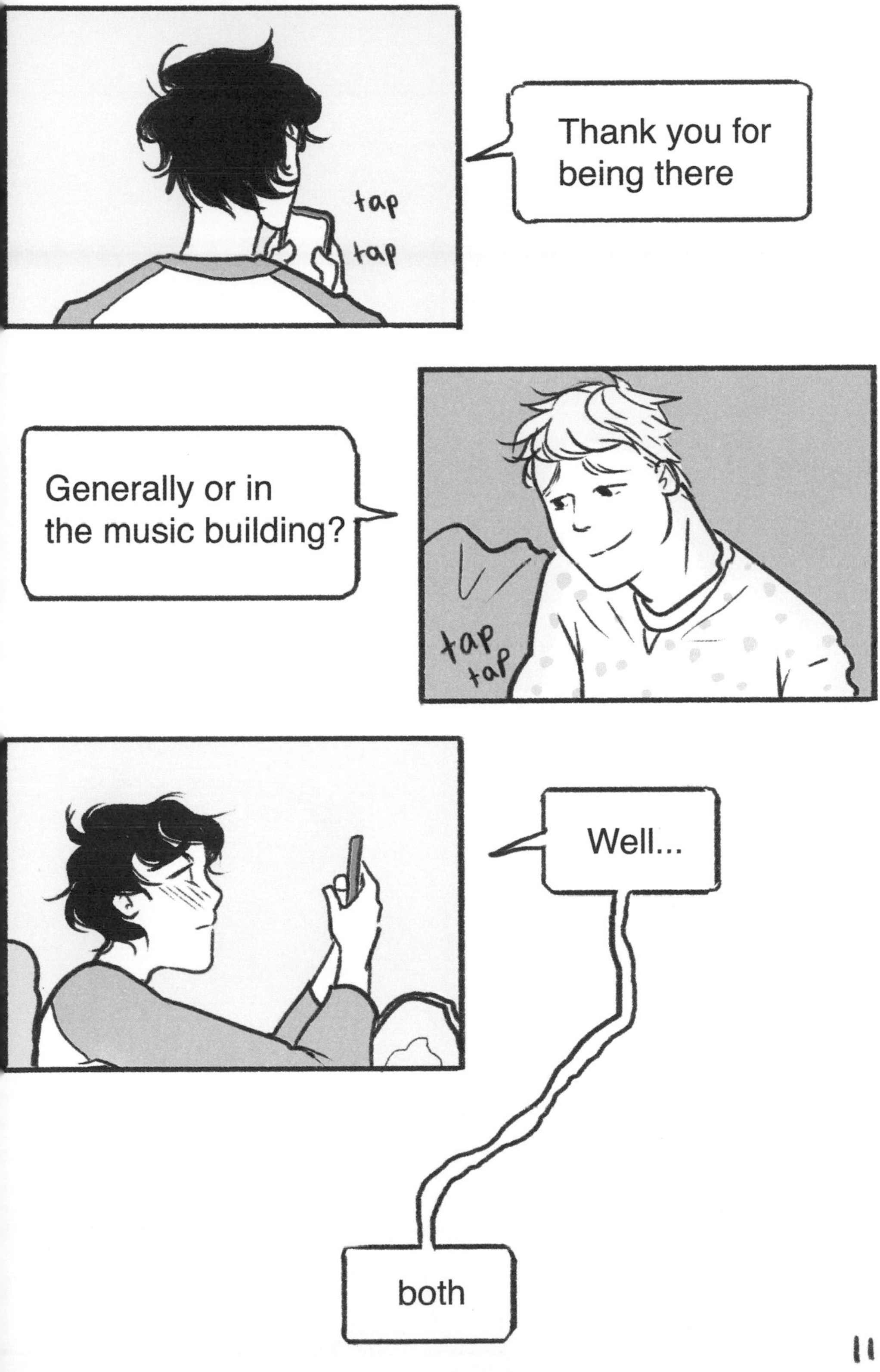
tap
tap
Thank you for being there
Generally or in the music building?
tap
tap
Well...
both

Not a problem
Not a problem
I love talking to you
GIF
QWERTY
ASDFG
Not a problem
I'm so glad we're frien
GIF
QWERYU
ASD
Not a problem

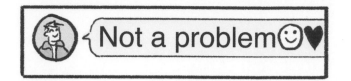

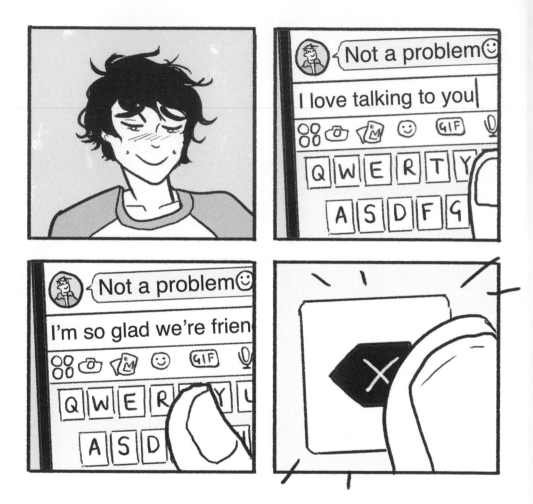

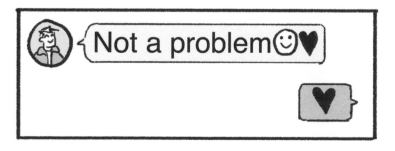

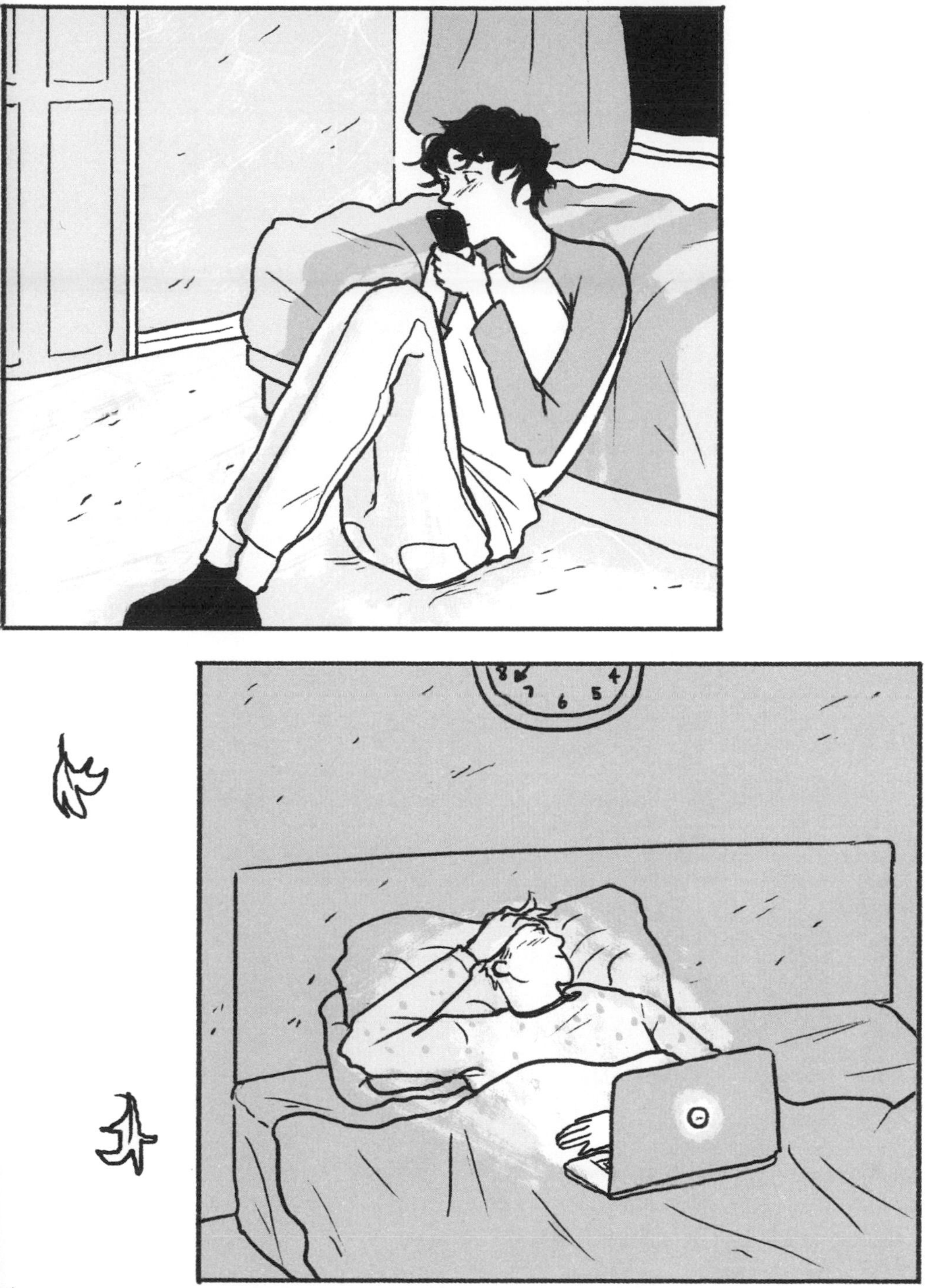

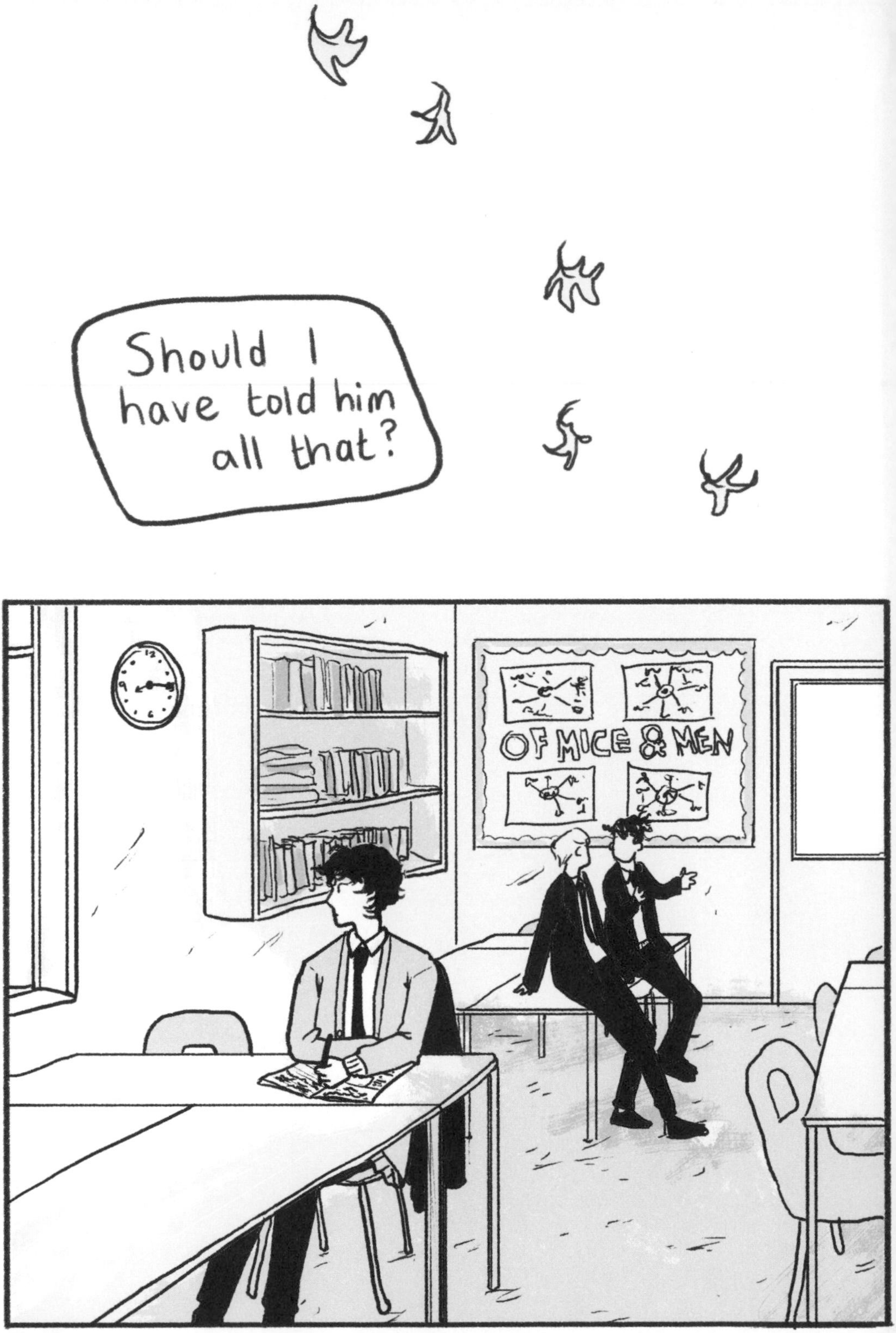
Should I have told him all that?
OF MICE & MEN

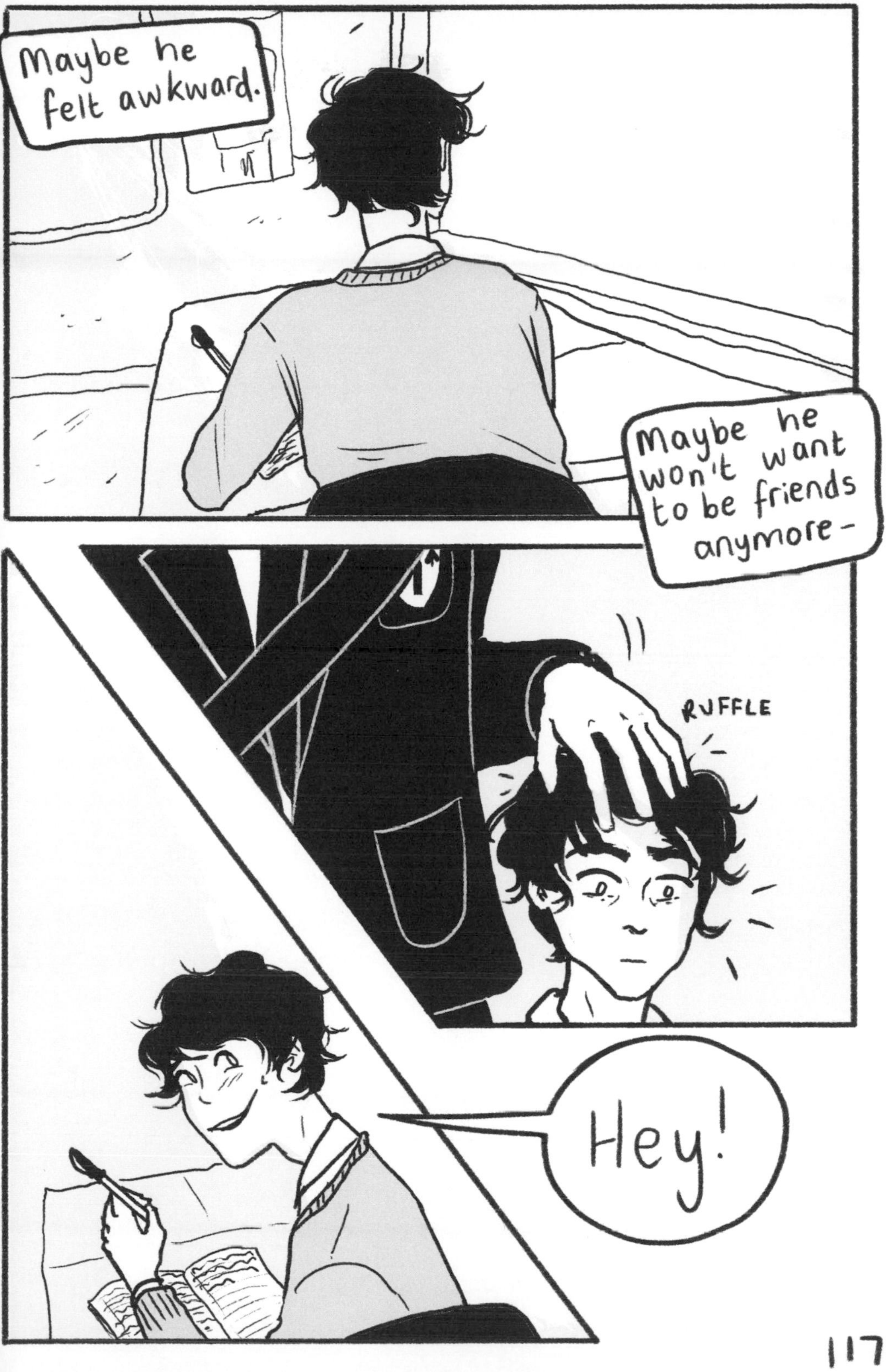
Maybe he felt awkward.
Maybe he won't want to be friends anymore-
RUFFLE
Hey!

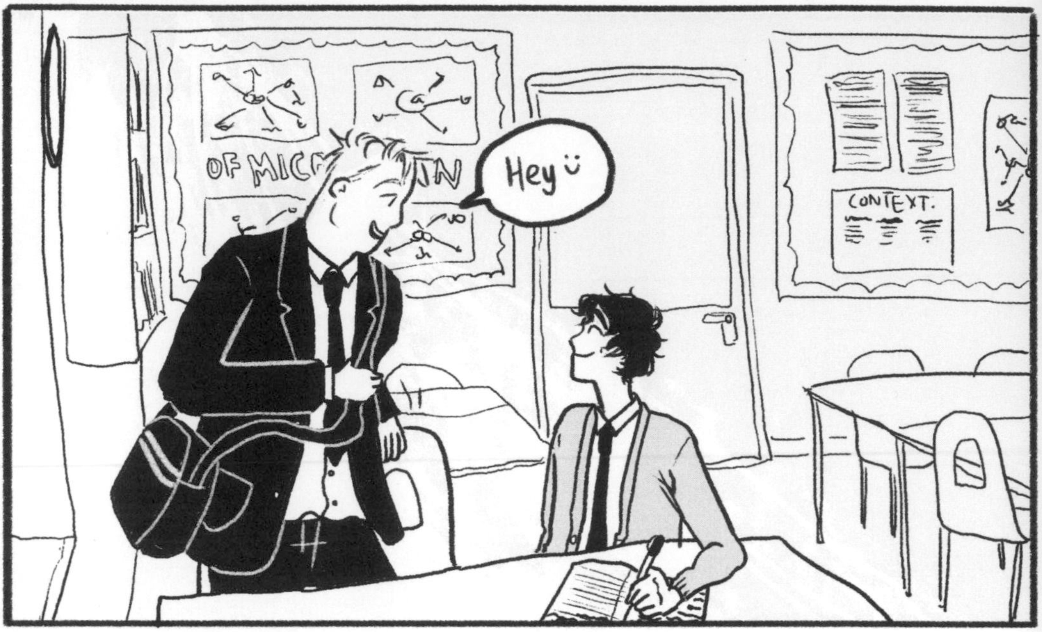
CONTEXT.
Hey

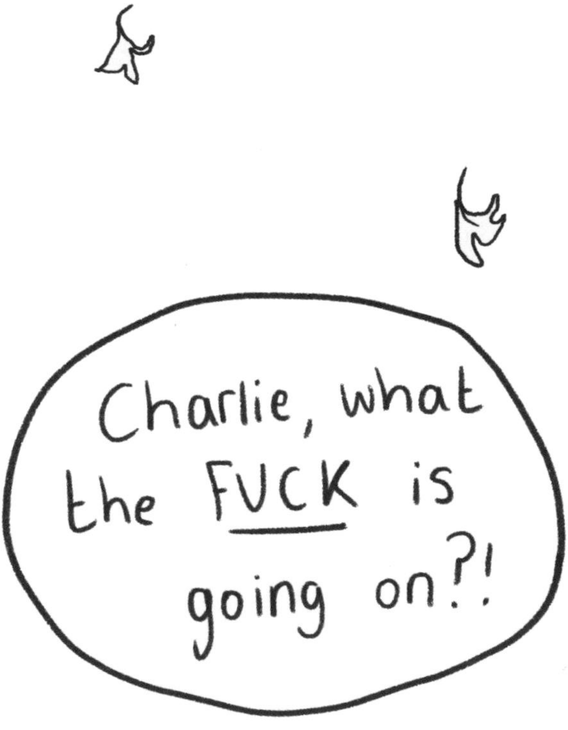
Charlie, what the FUCK is going on?!

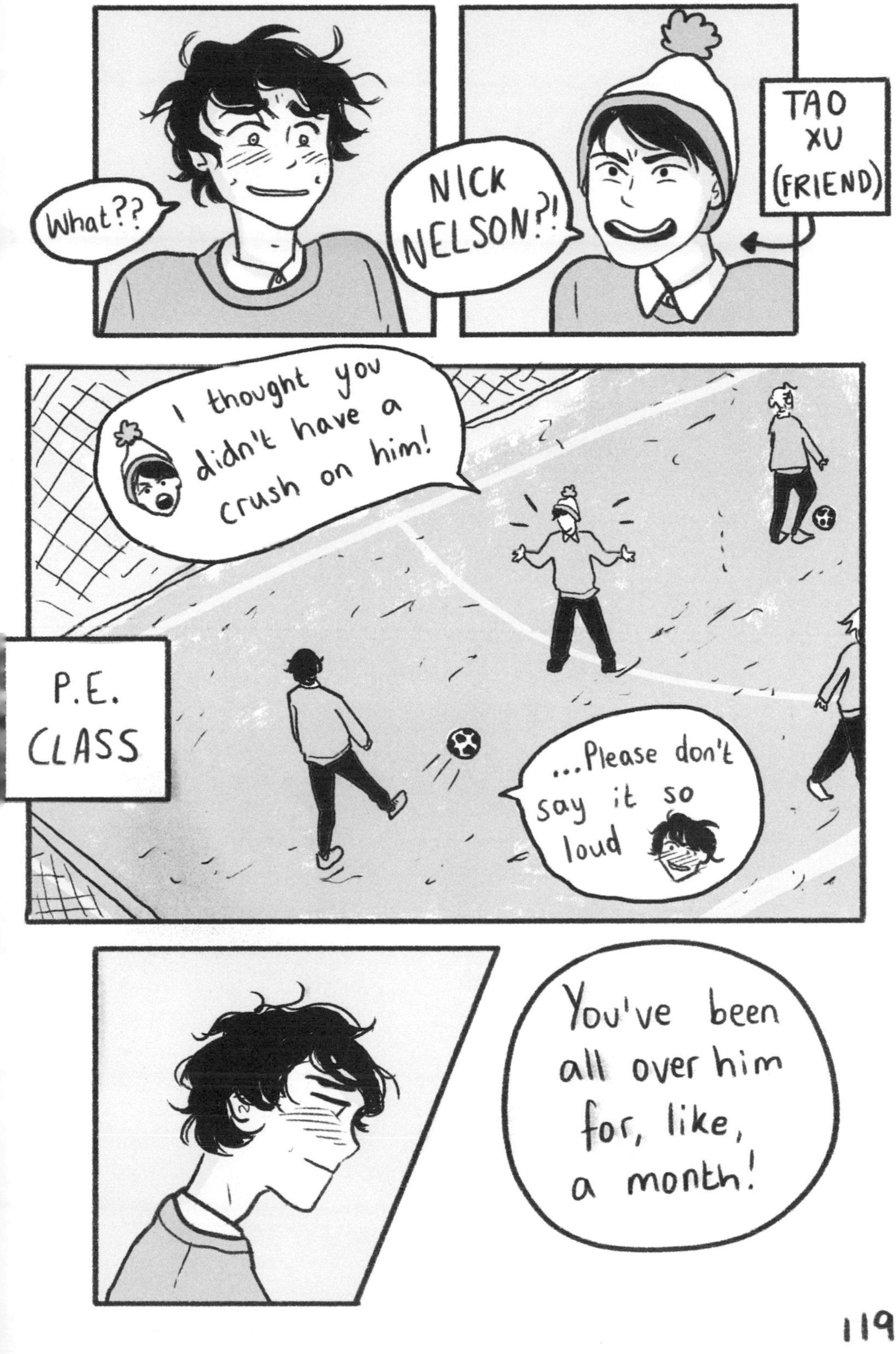
What??
NICK NELSON?!
TAO XU (FRIEND)
I thought you didn't have a crush on him!
P.E. CLASS
...Please don't say it so loud
You've been all over him for, like, a month!

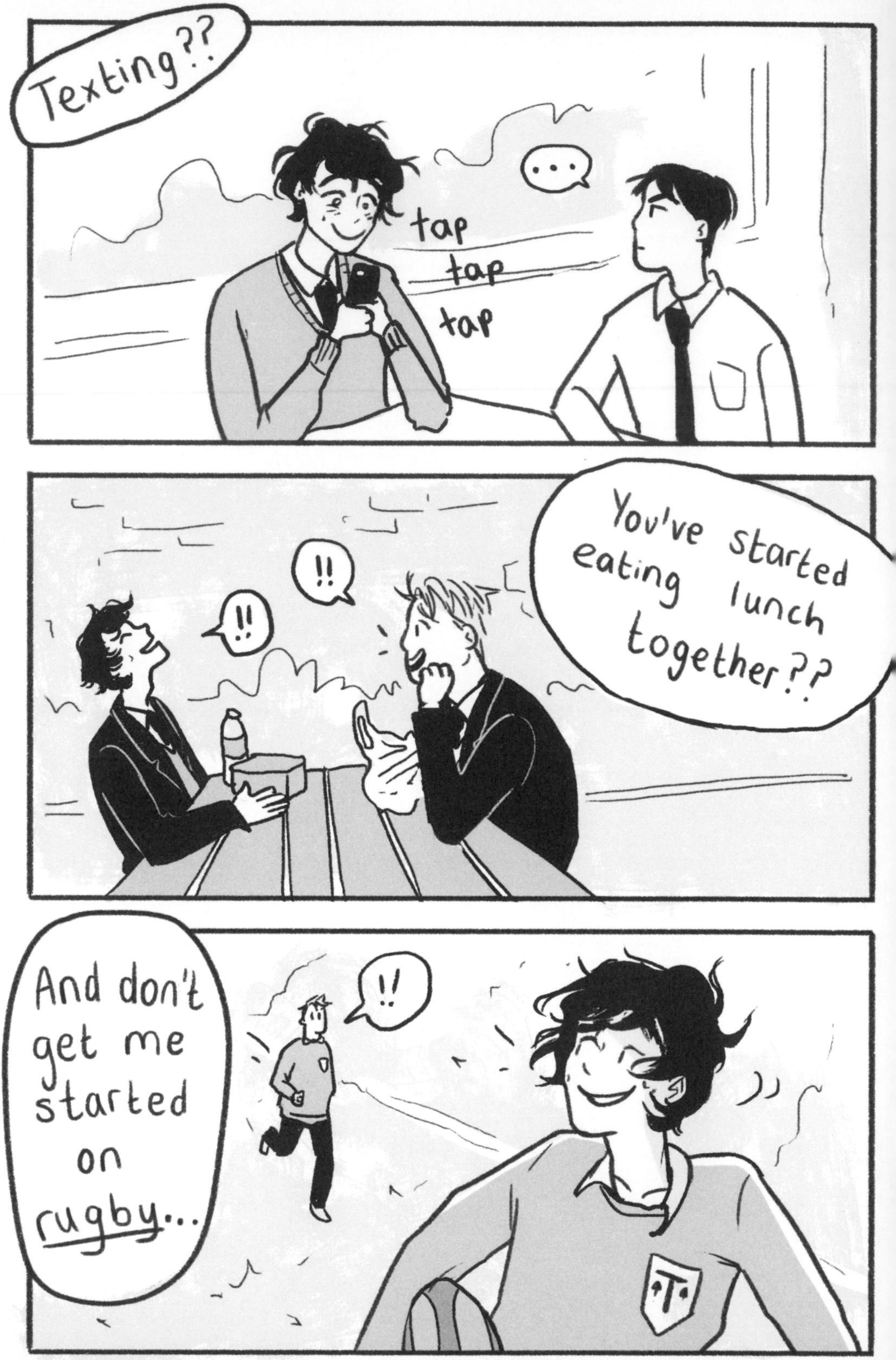
Texting??
...
tap
tap
tap
You've started eating lunch together??
!!
!!
And don't get me started on rugby...
!!

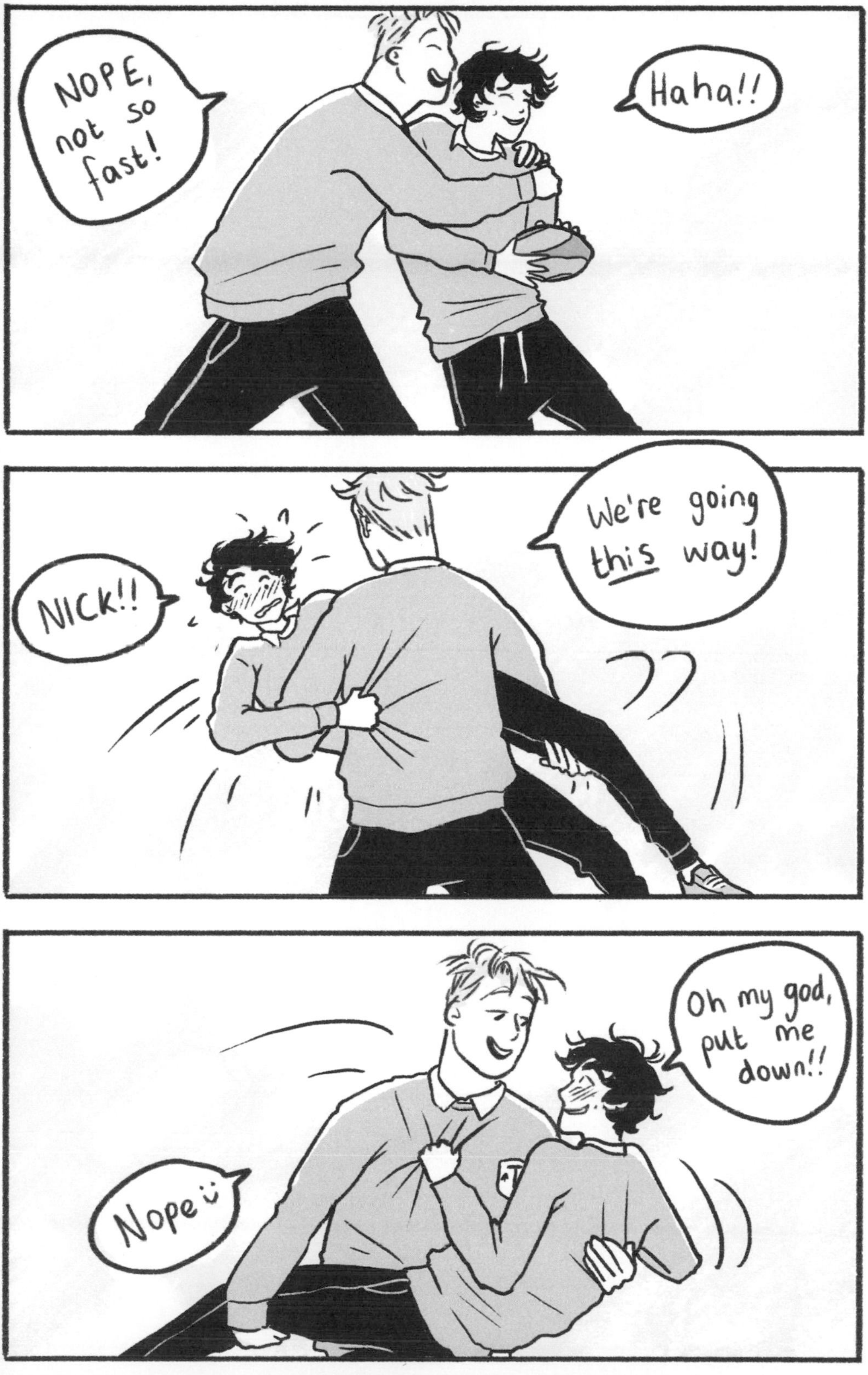
NOPE, not so fast!
Haha!!
We're going this way!
NICK!!
Oh my god, put me down!!
Nope

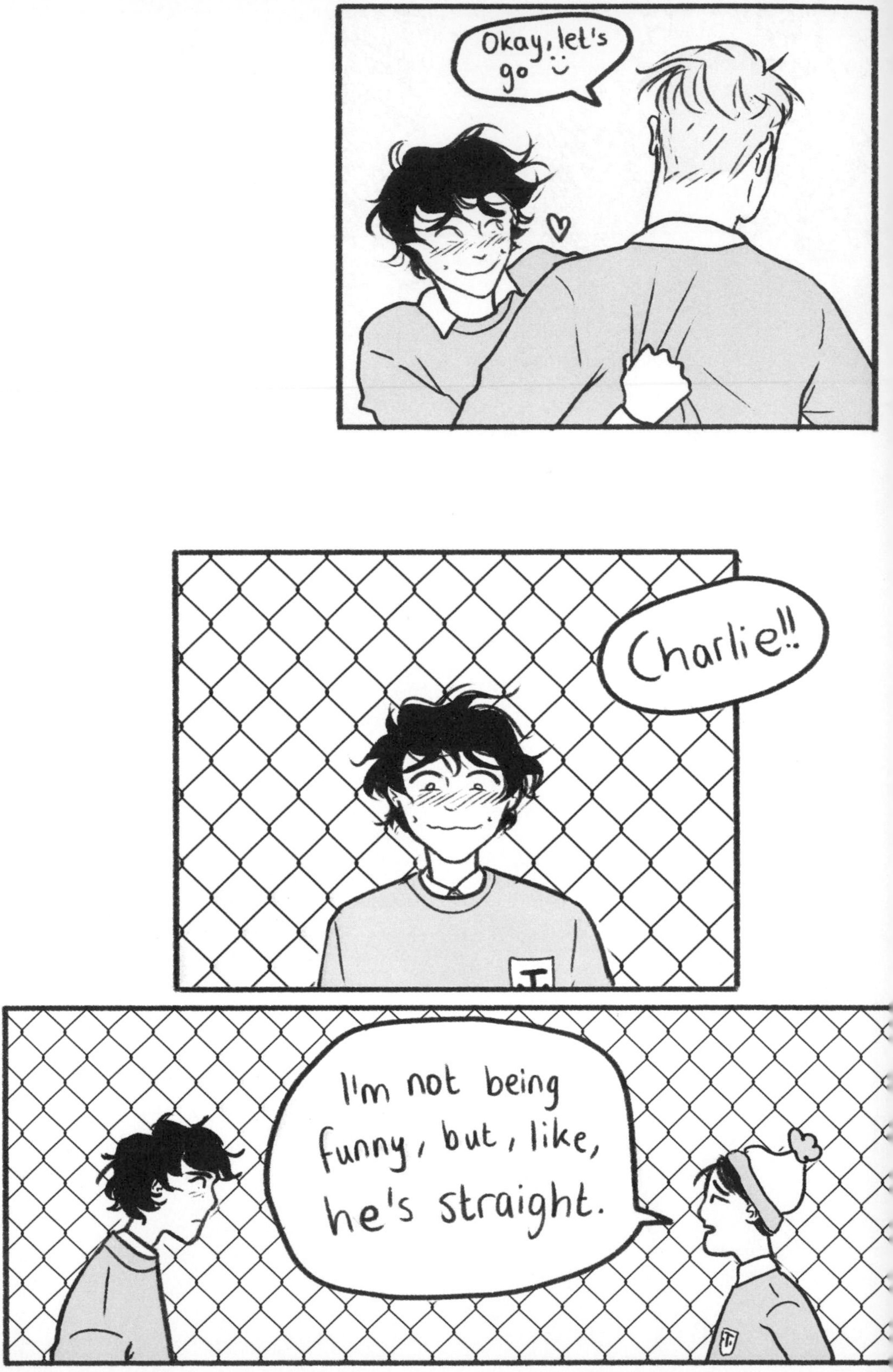
Okay, let's go
Charlie!!
I'm not being funny, but, like, he's straight.

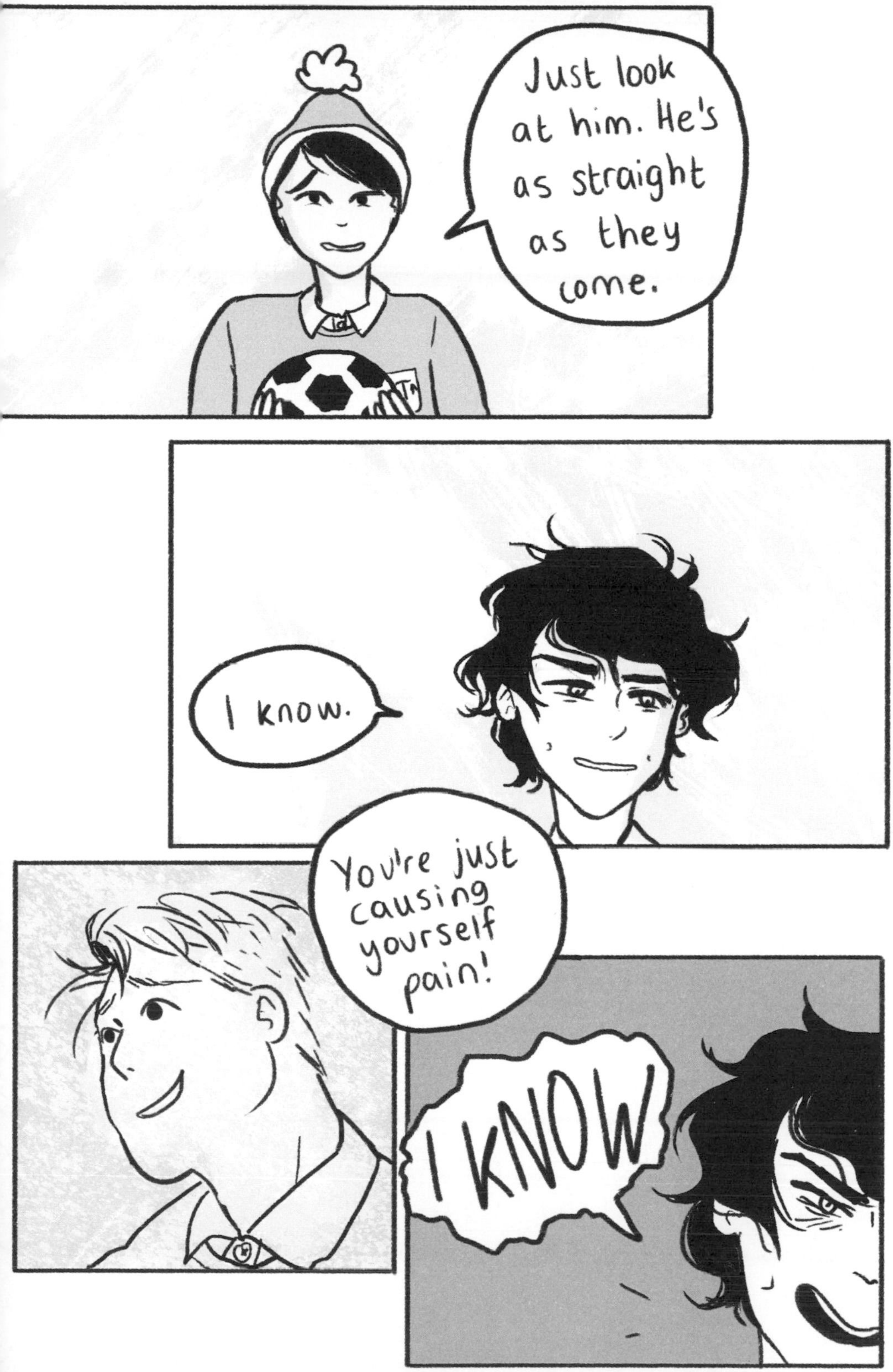
Just look at him. He's as straight as they come.
I know.
You're just causing yourself pain!
I KNOW

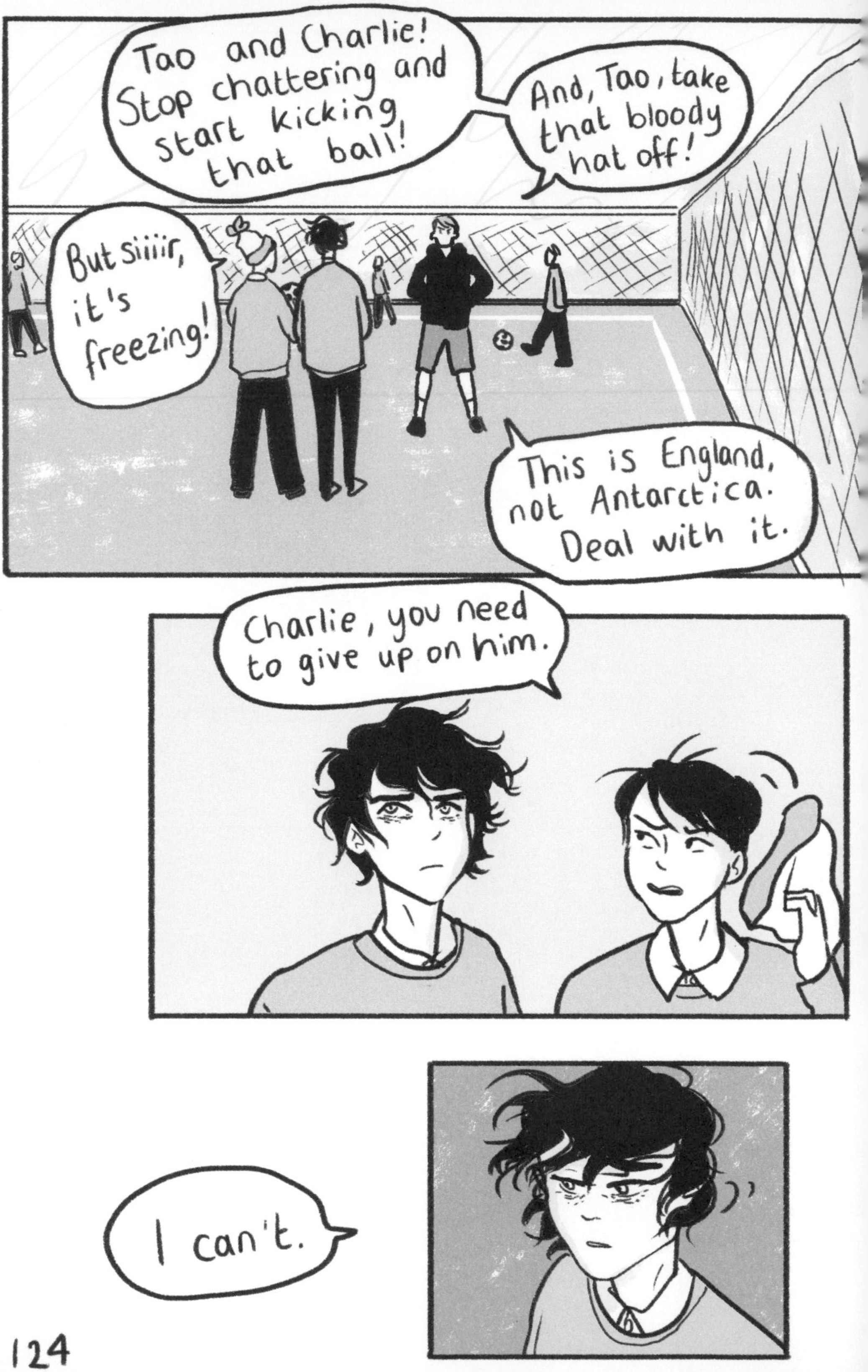
Tao and Charlie! Stop chattering and start kicking that ball!
And, Tao, take that bloody hat off!
But siiiir, it's freezing!
This is England, not Antarctica. Deal with it.
Charlie, you need to give up on him.
I can't.

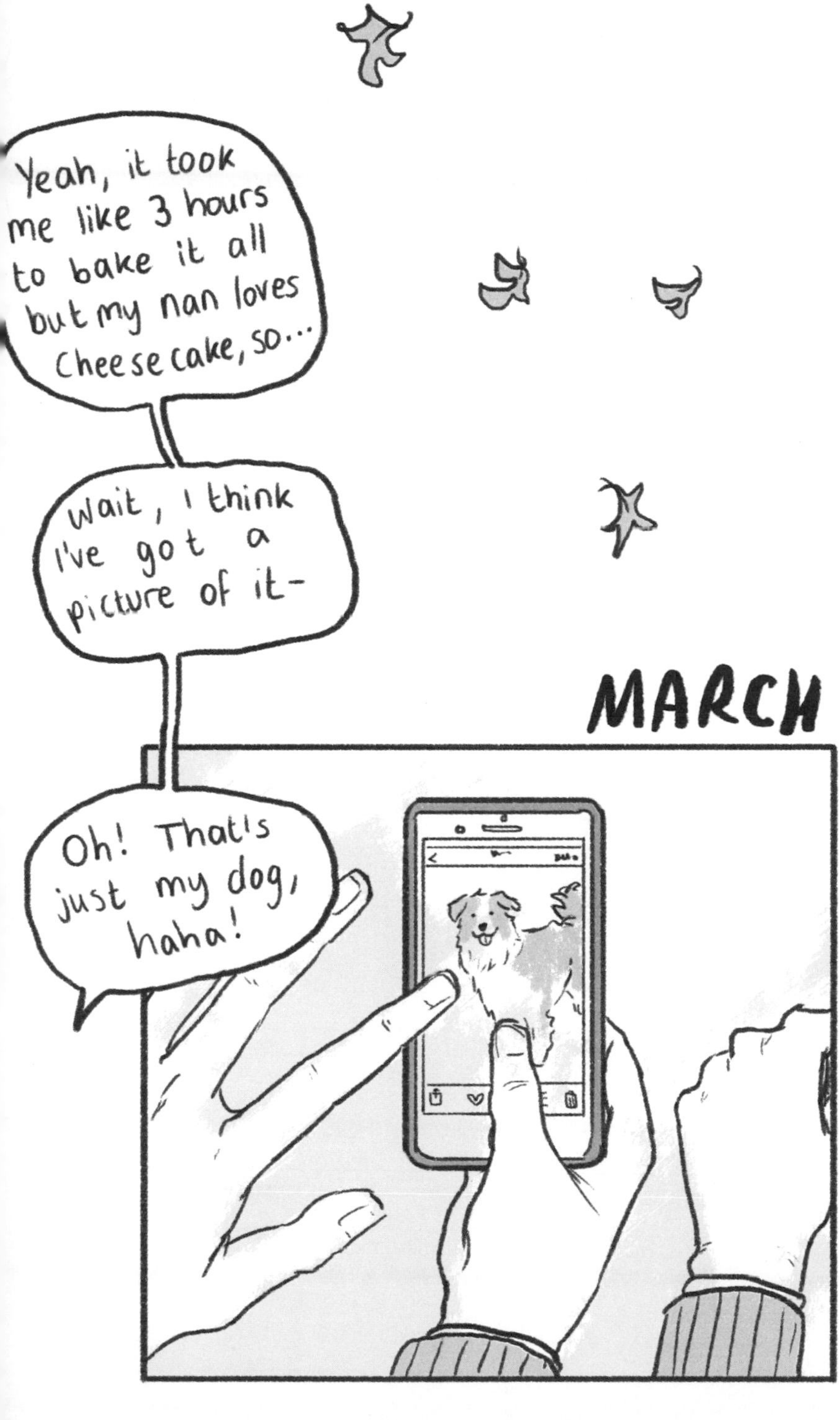
Yeah, it took me like 3 hours to bake it all but my nan loves Cheese cake, so...
Wait, I think I've got a picture of it-
MARCH
Oh! That's just my dog, haha!

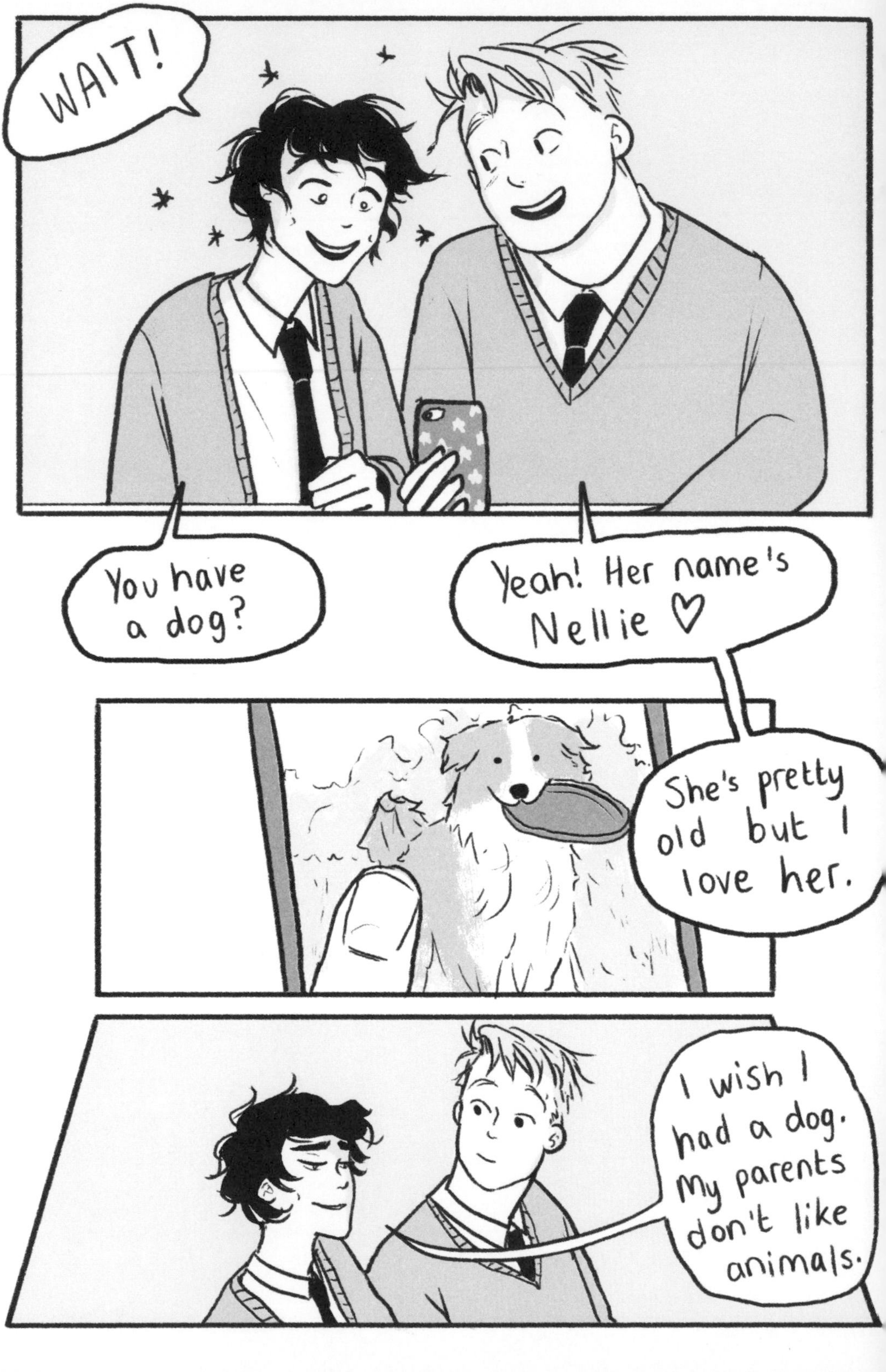
WAIT!
You have a dog?
Yeah! Her name's Nellie ♡
She's pretty old but I love her.
I wish I had a dog. My parents don't like animals.

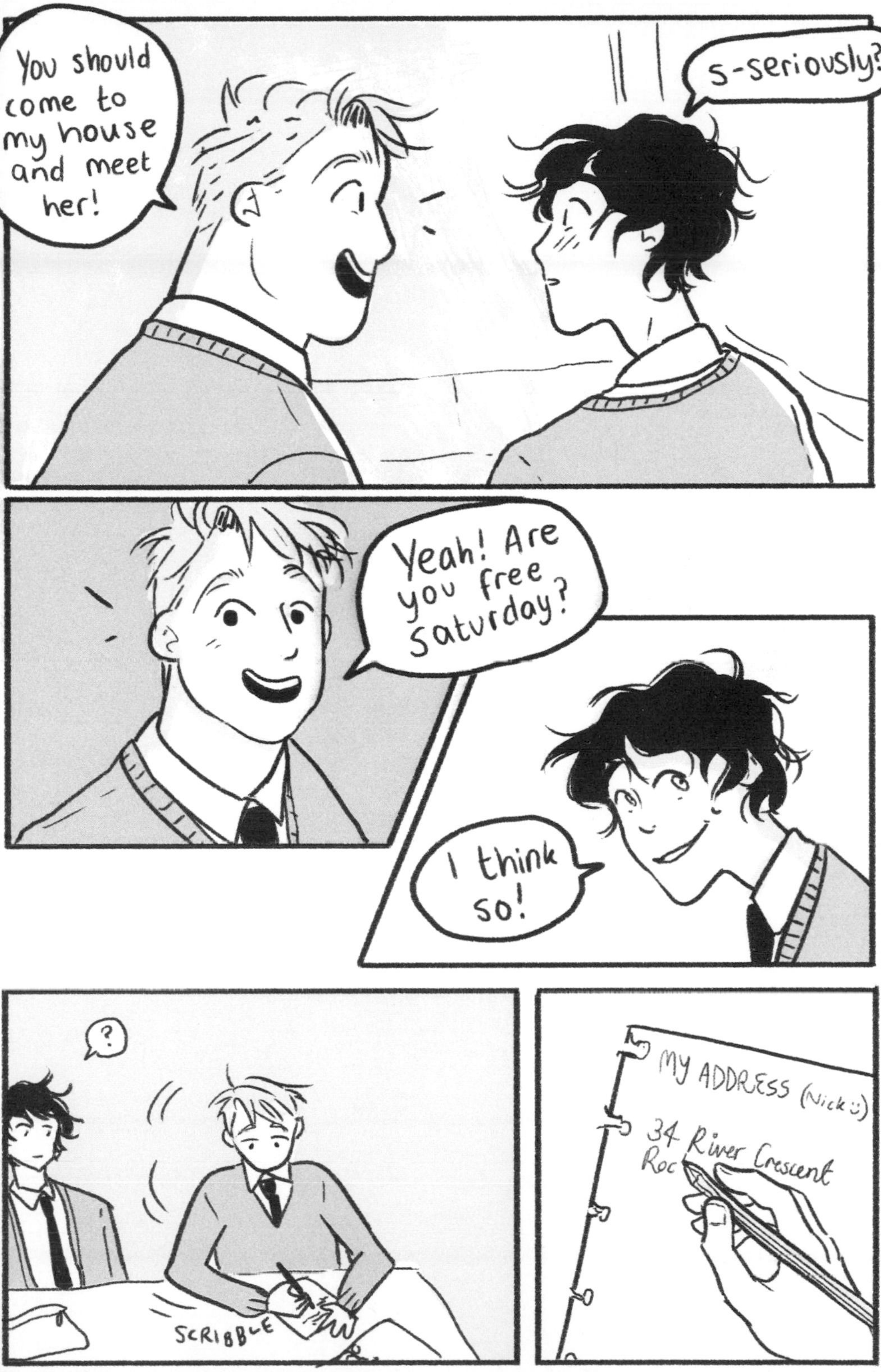
You should come to my house and meet her!
s-seriously?
Yeah! Are you free Saturday?
I think so!
?
SCRIBBLE
MY ADDRESS (Nick :))
34 River Crescent
Roc

Wow, that's only a 10-minute walk from my house!
Is it?!
Yeah, I live on Britannia Road!
Saturday, then?
Okay!
Did you two swap seats?

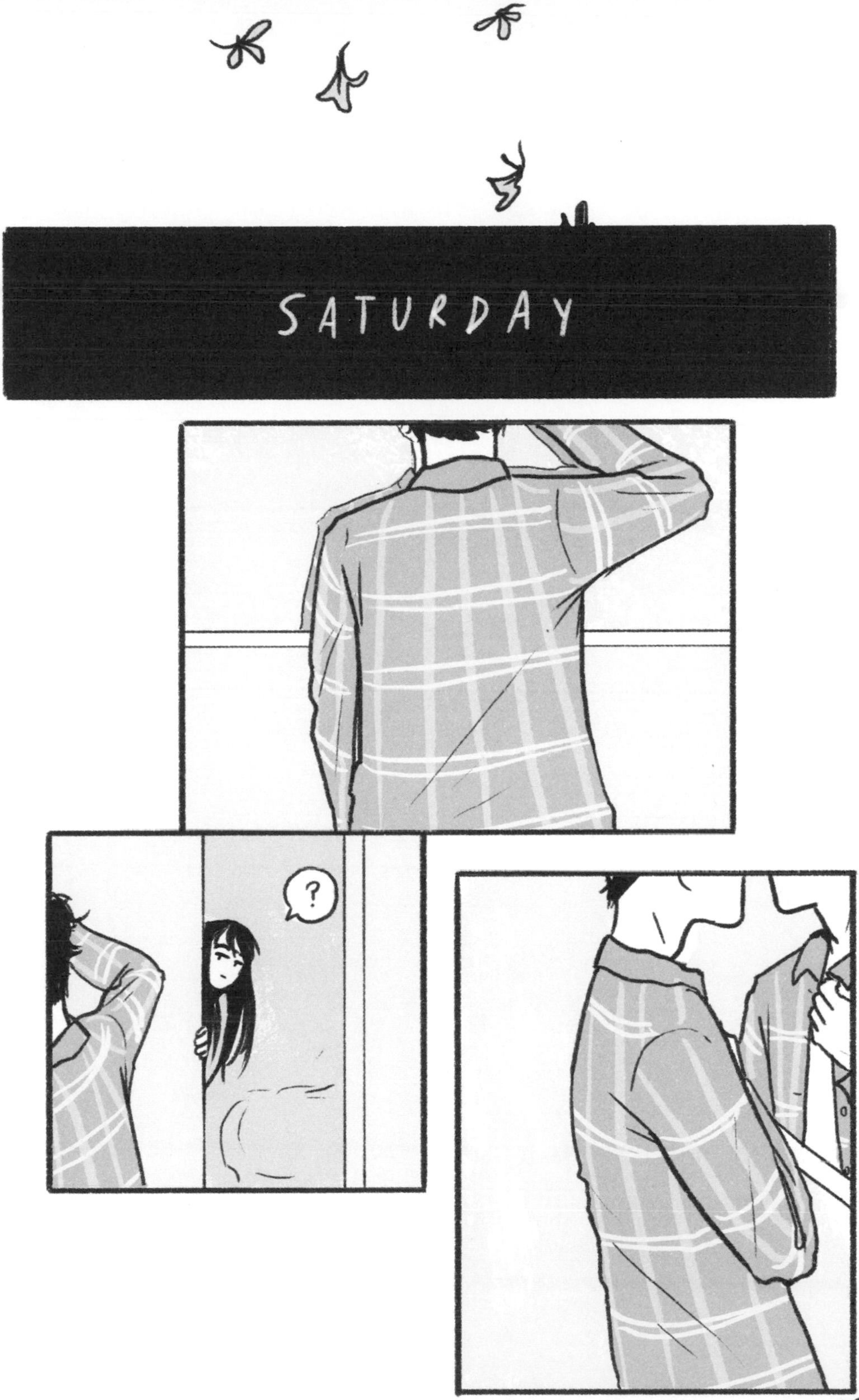
SATURDAY
?

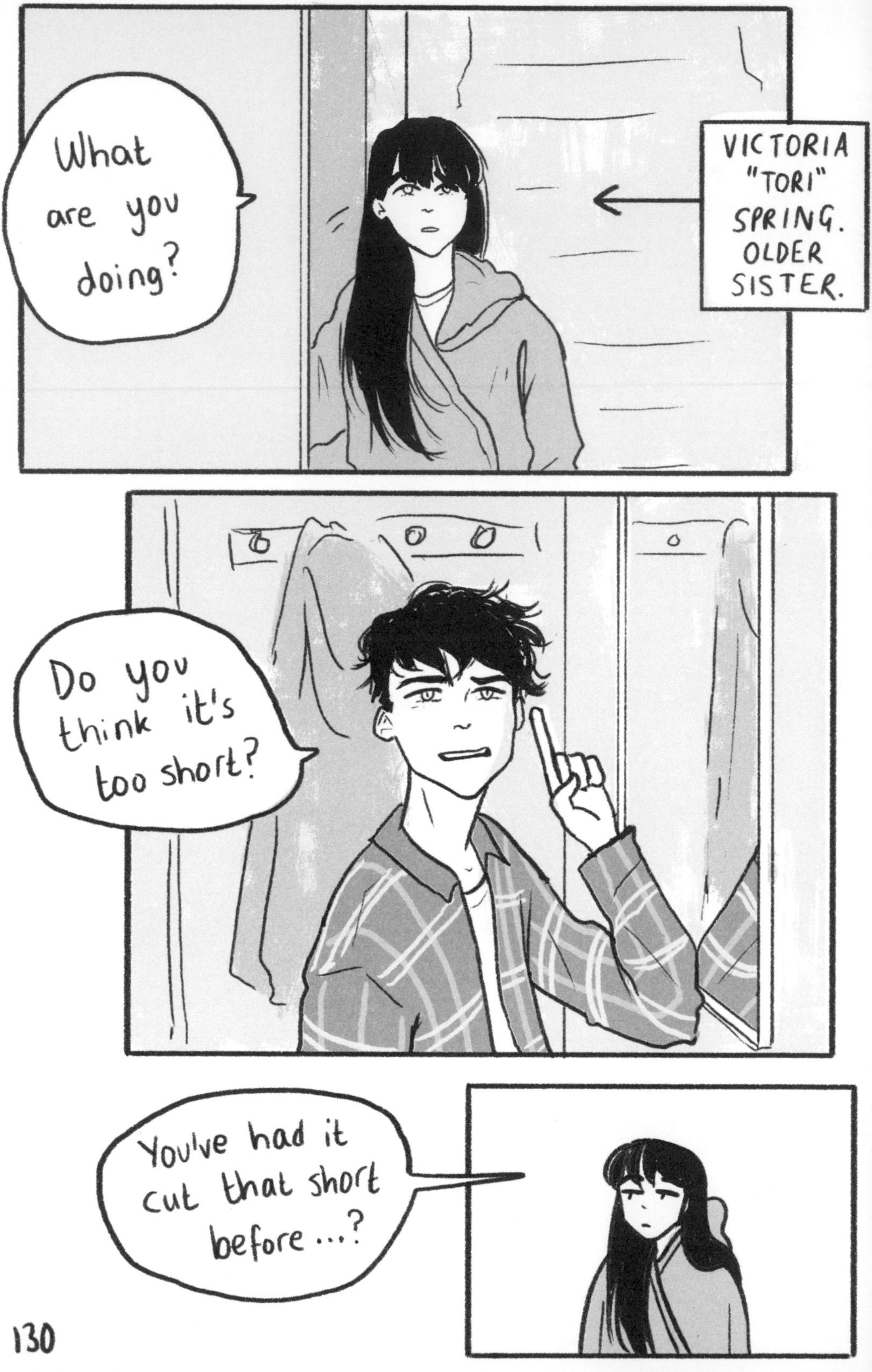
What are you doing?
VICTORIA "TORI" SPRING. OLDER SISTER.
Do you think it's too short?
You've had it cut that short before...?

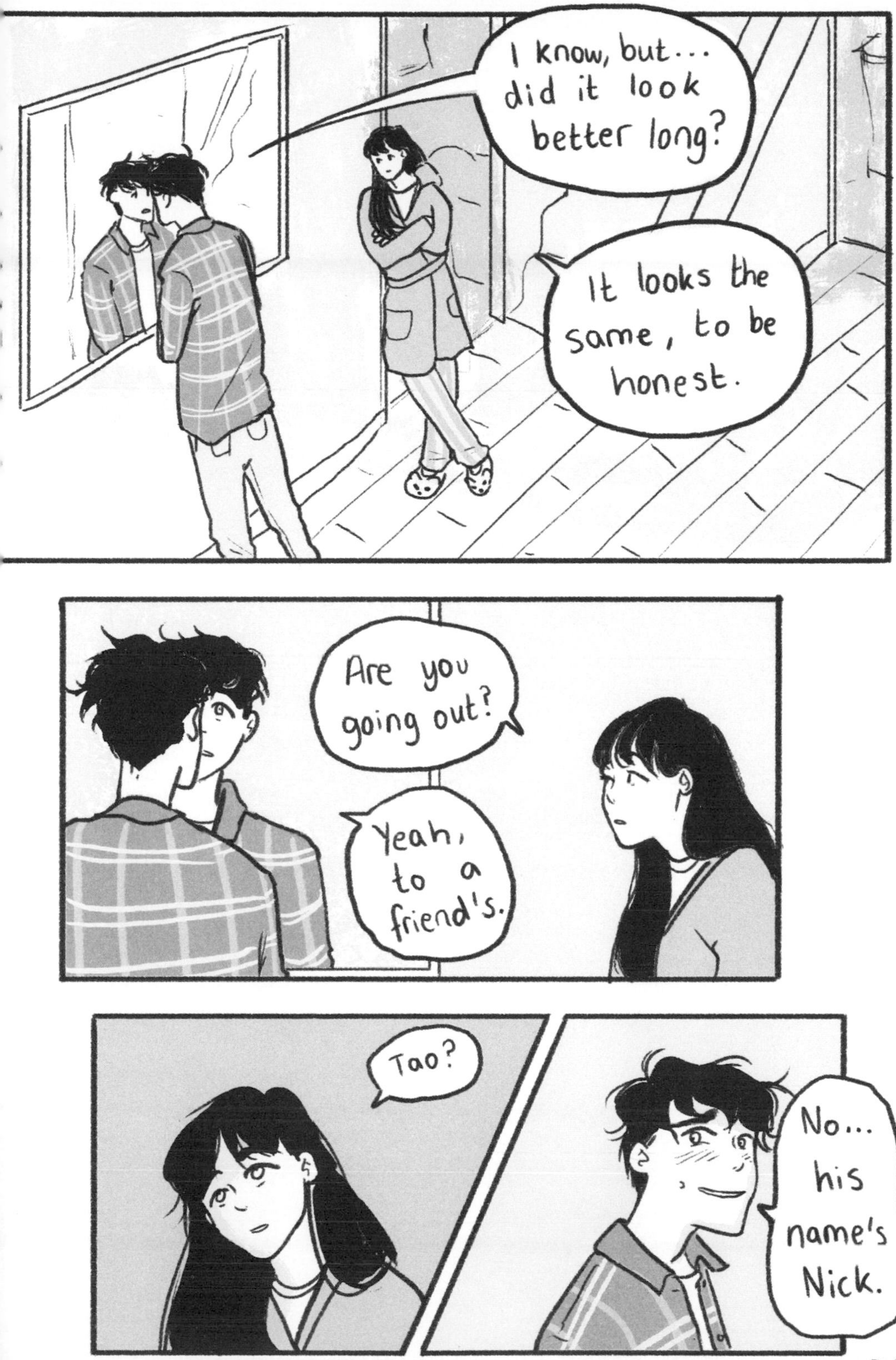
I know, but...
did it look
better long?
It looks the
same, to be
honest.
Are you
going out?
Yeah,
to a
friend's.
Tao?
No...
his
name's
Nick.

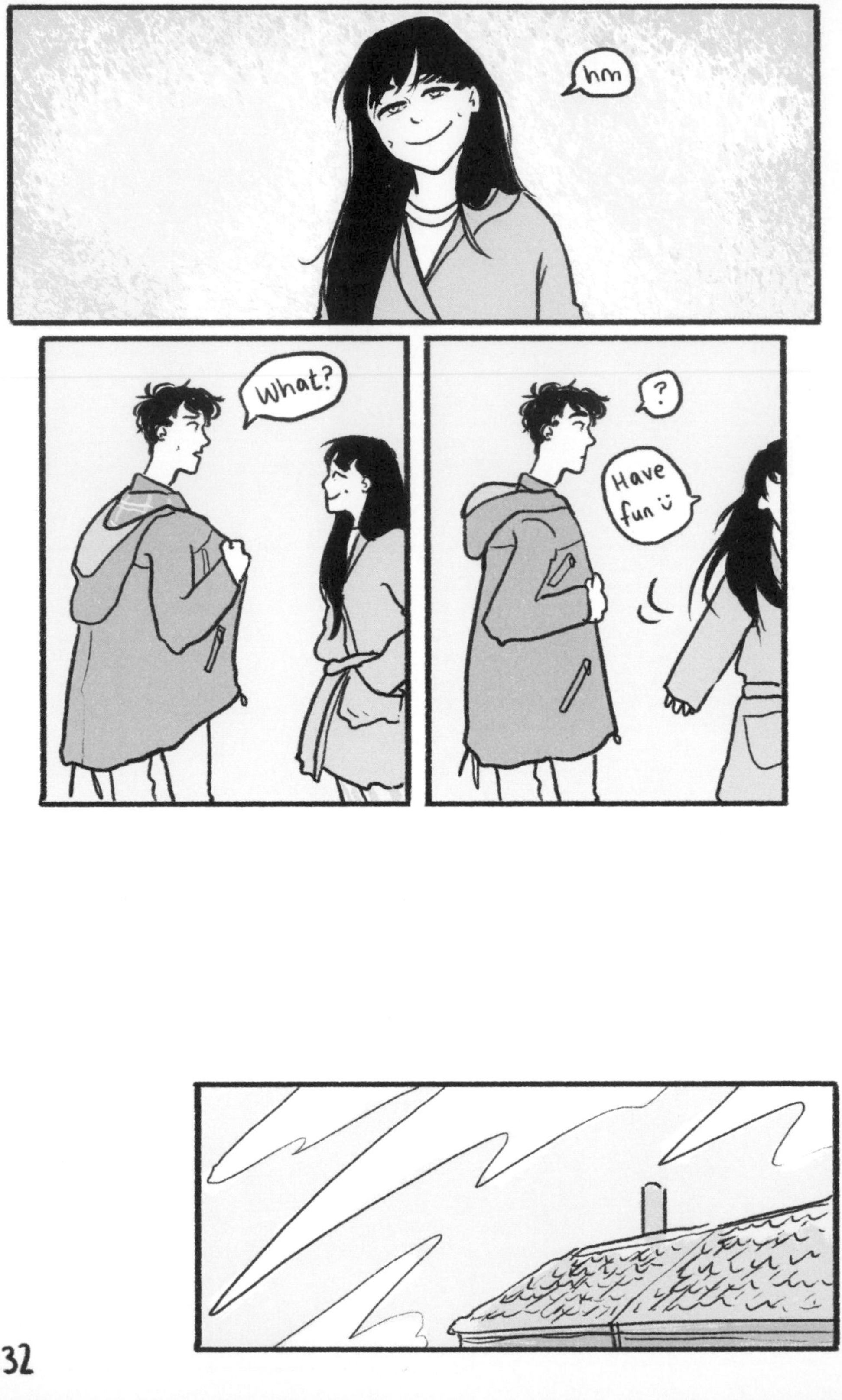
hm
What?
?
Have fun

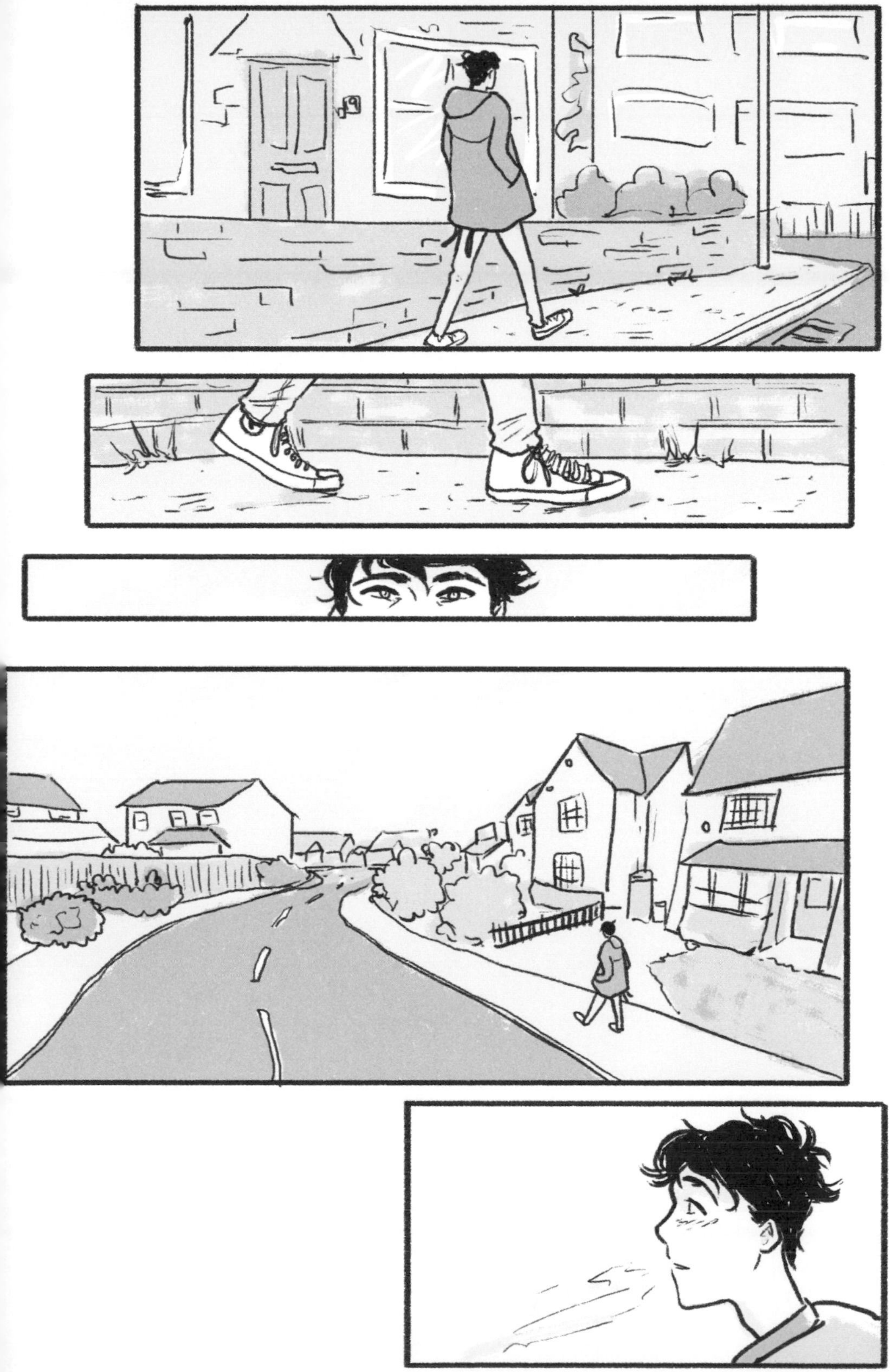

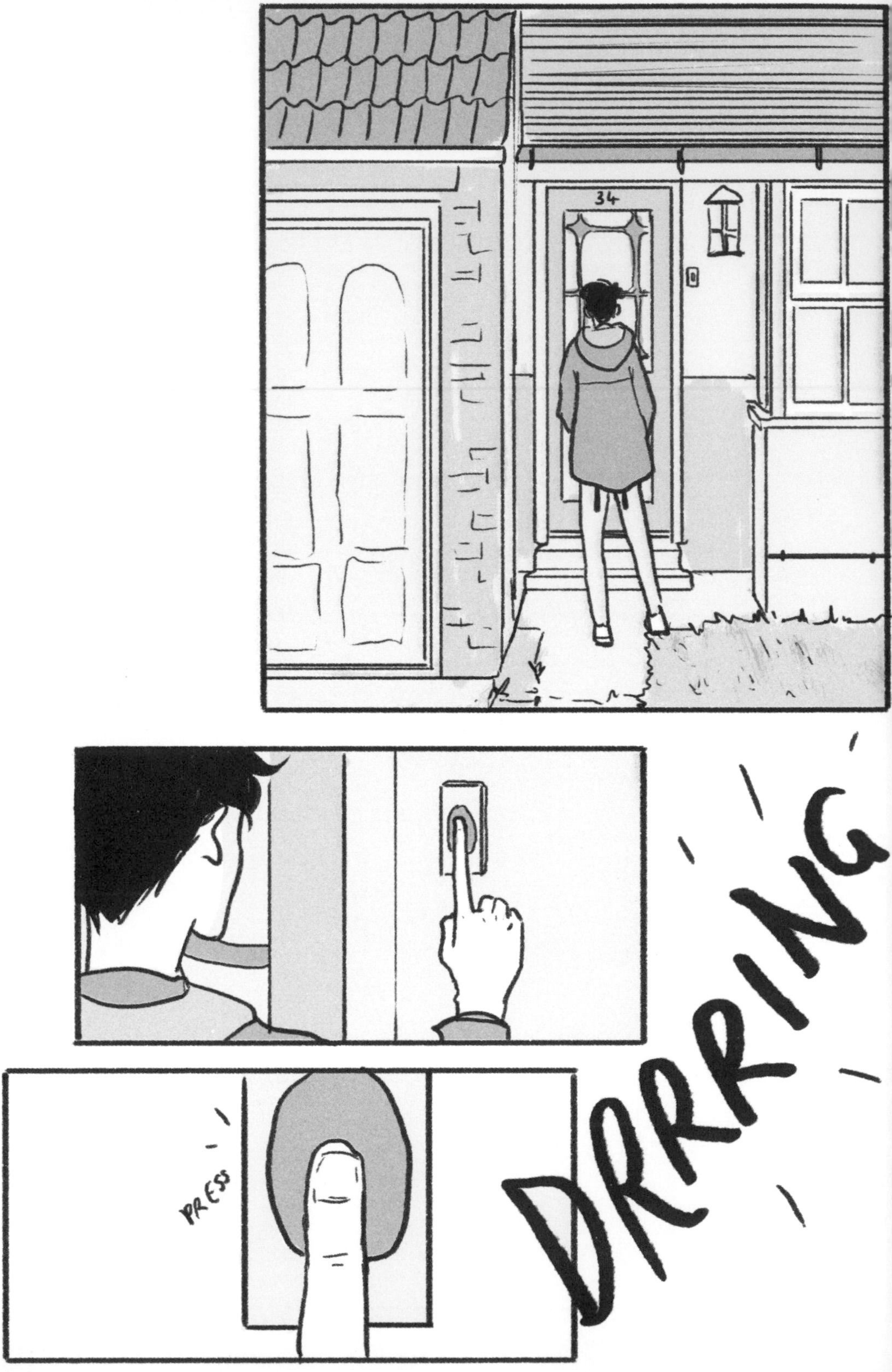
34
PRESS
DRRRING

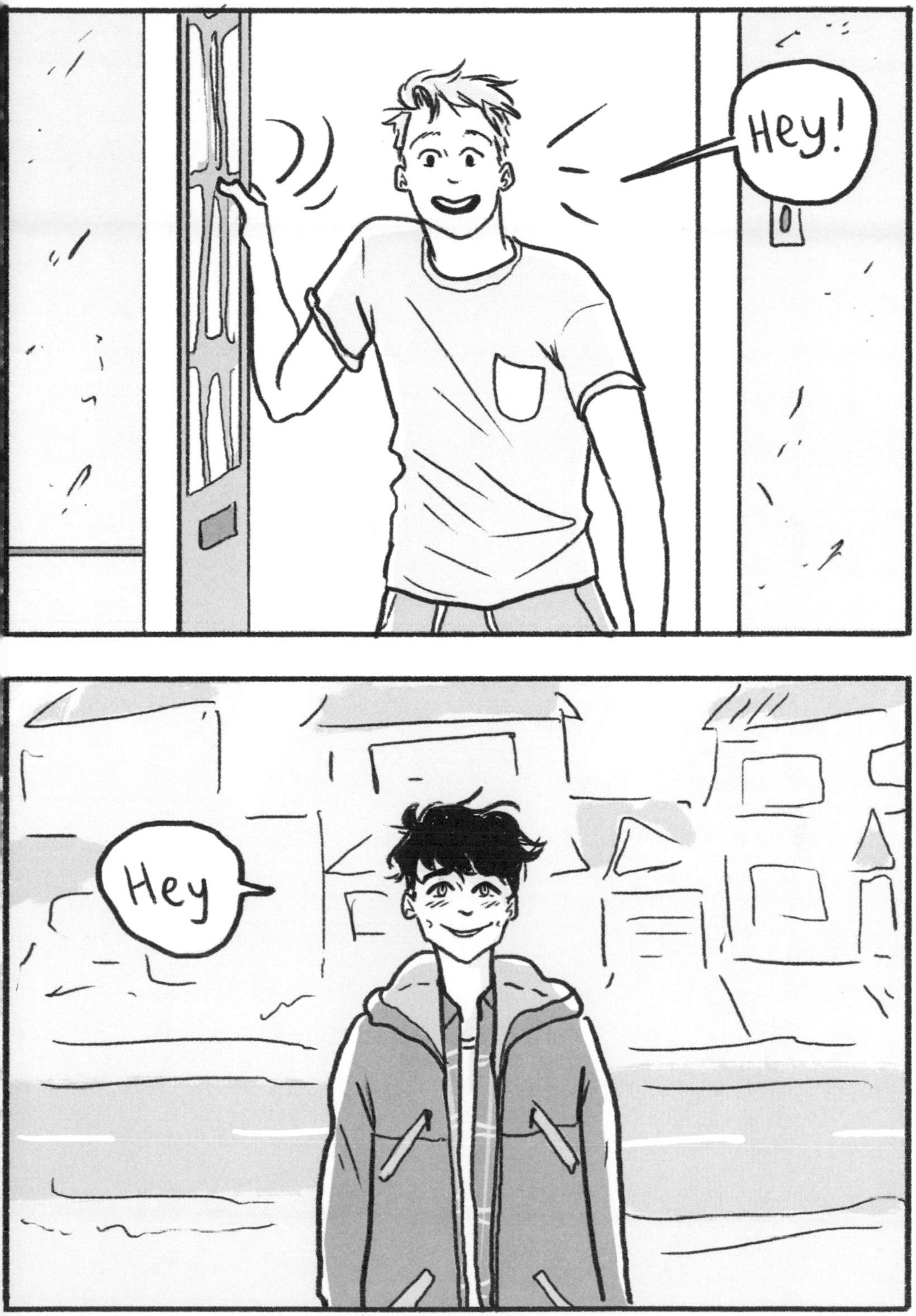
Hey!
Hey

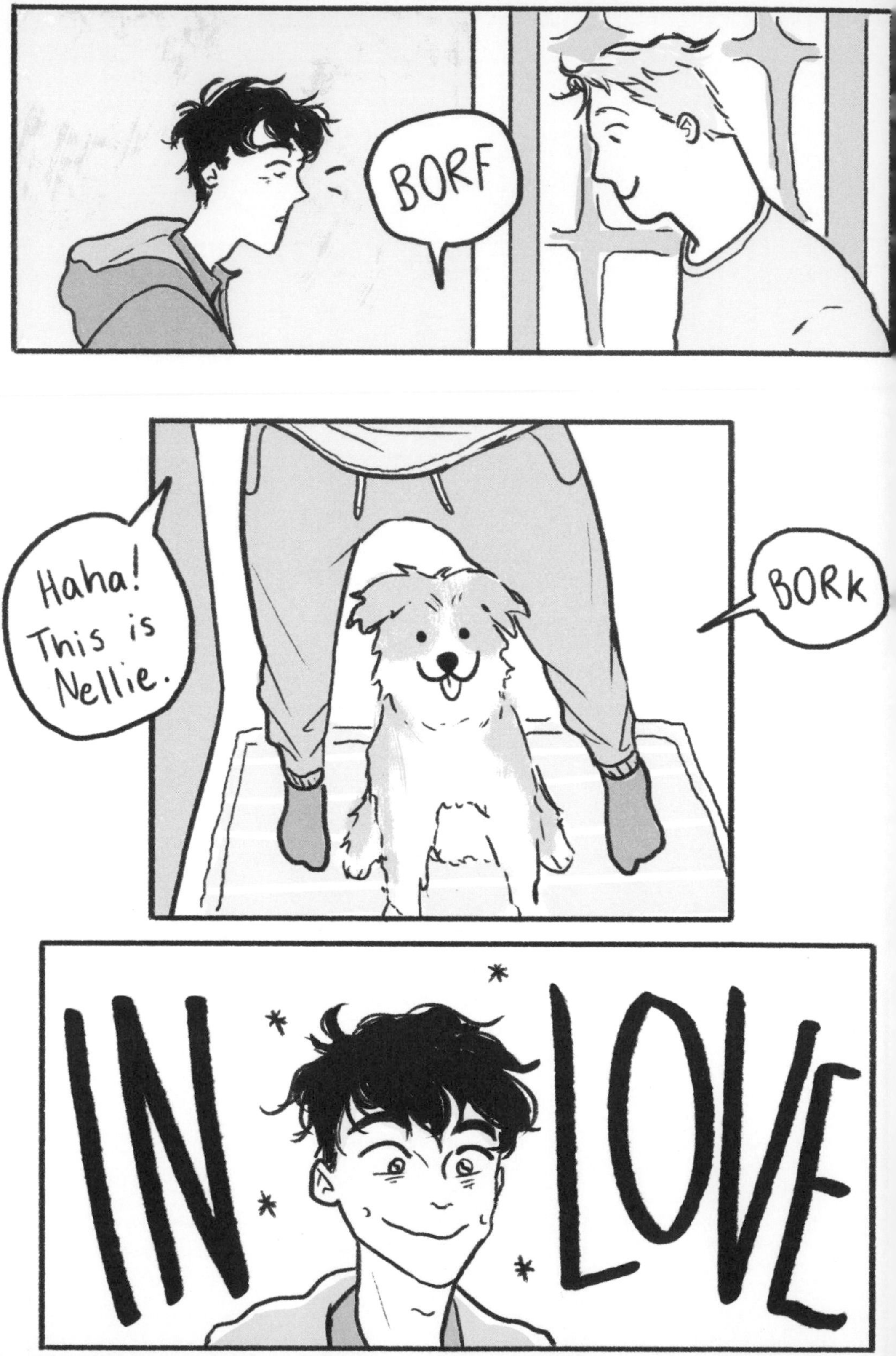
BORF
Haha! This is Nellie.
BORK
IN LOVE

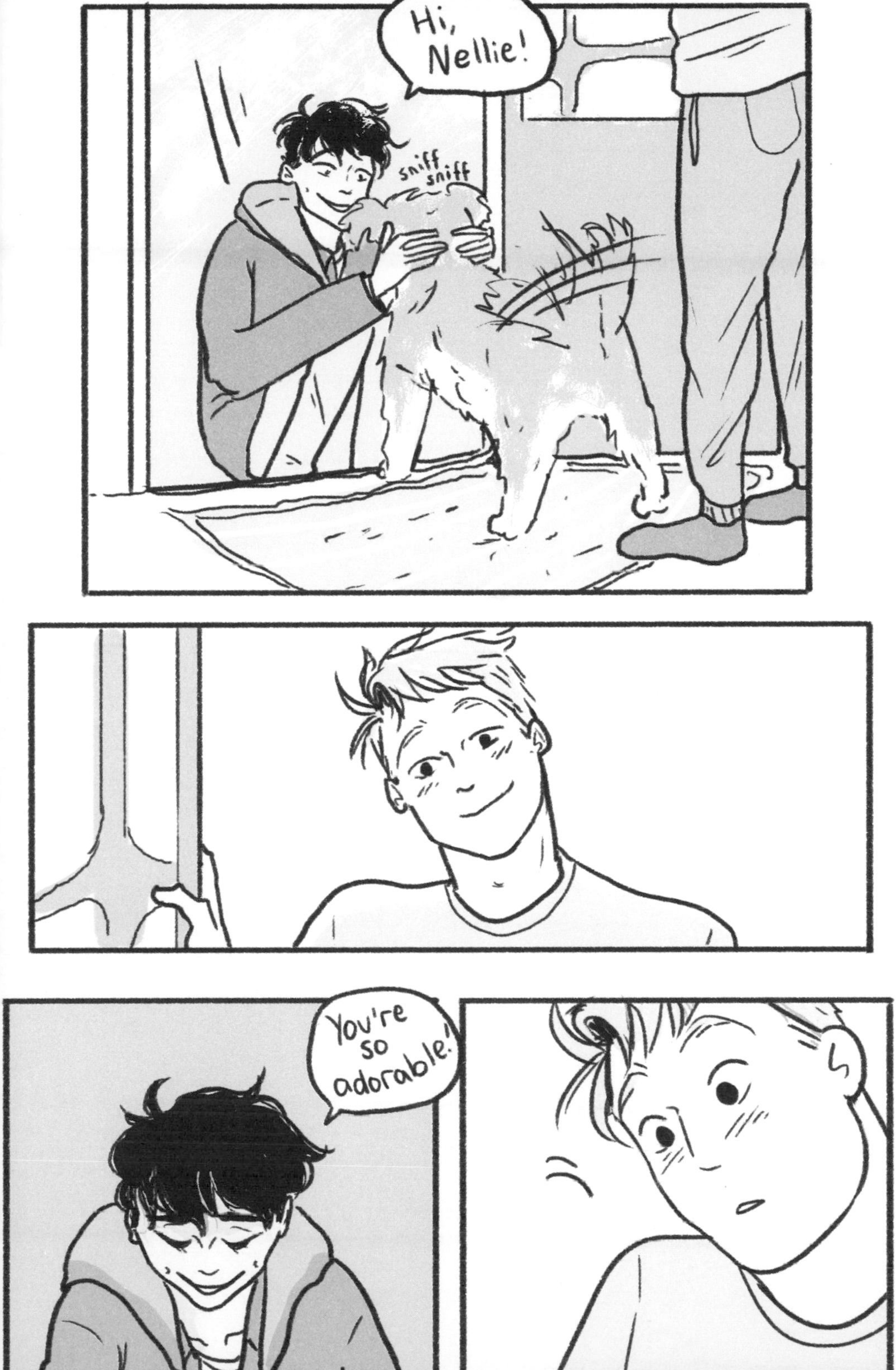
Hi, Nellie!
sniff sniff
You're so adorable!

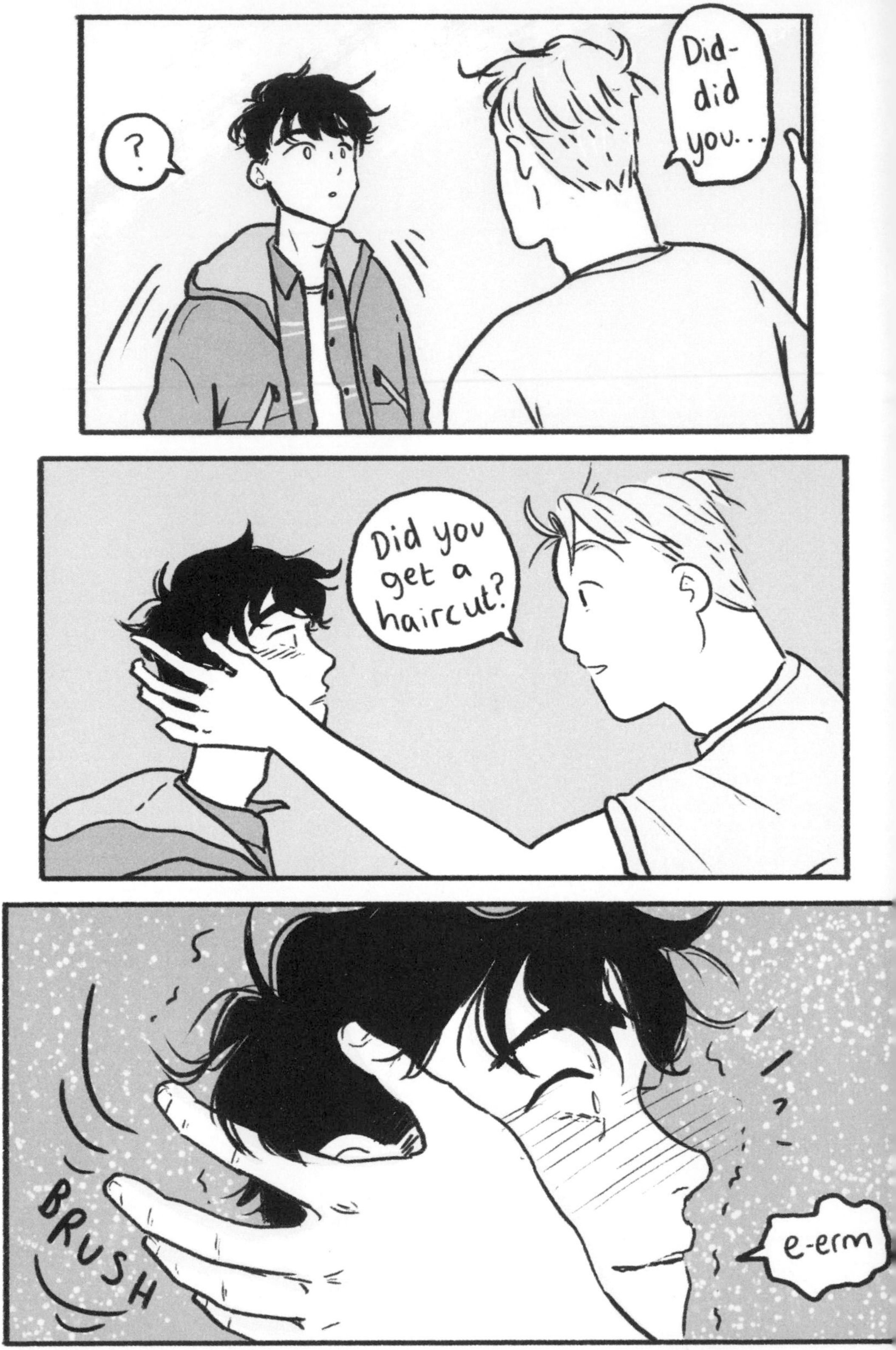
?
Did-did you...
Did you get a haircut?
BRUSH
e-erm

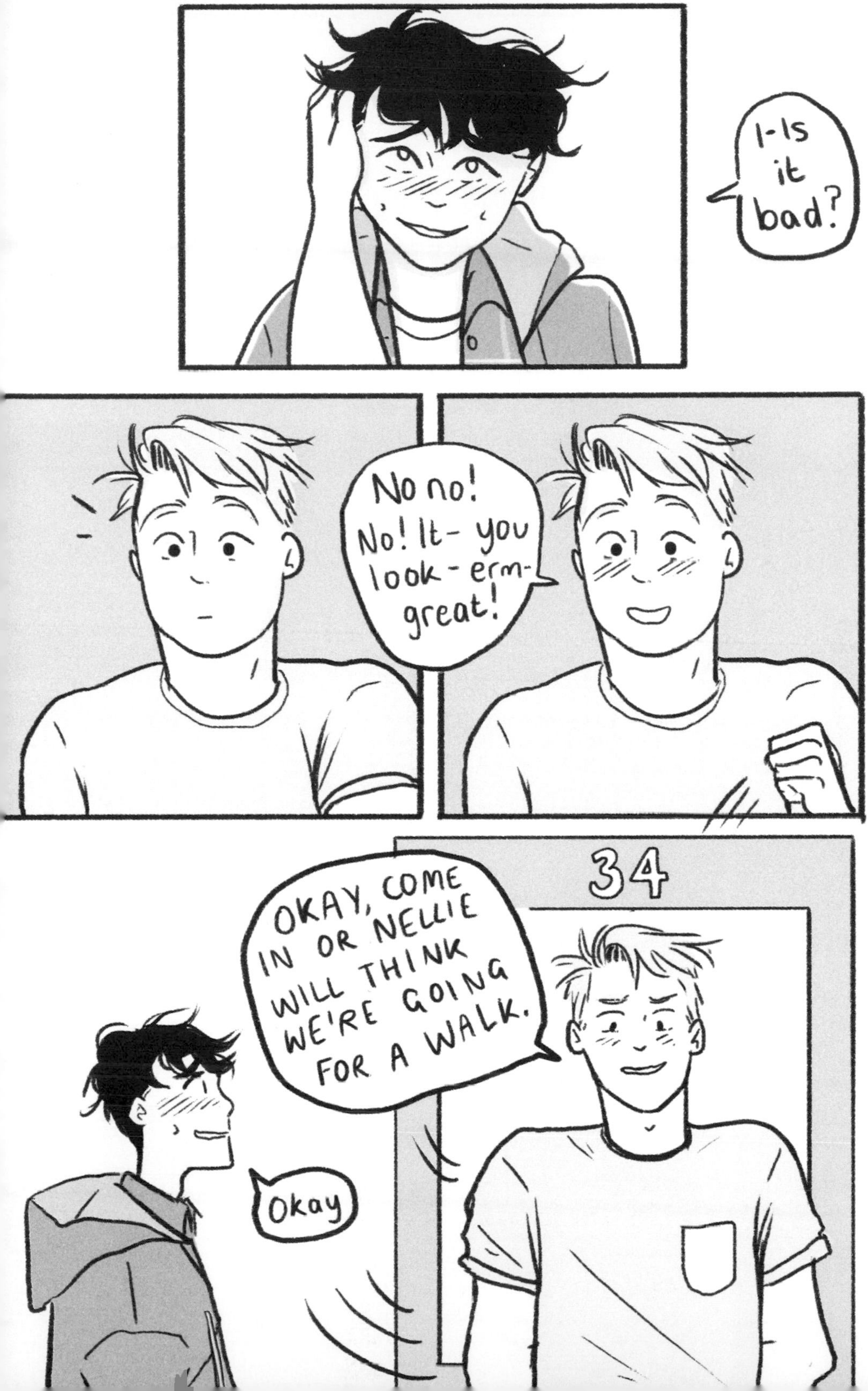
I-Is it bad?
No no! No! It- you look - erm- great!
OKAY, COME IN OR NELLIE WILL THINK WE'RE GOING FOR A WALK.
34
Okay

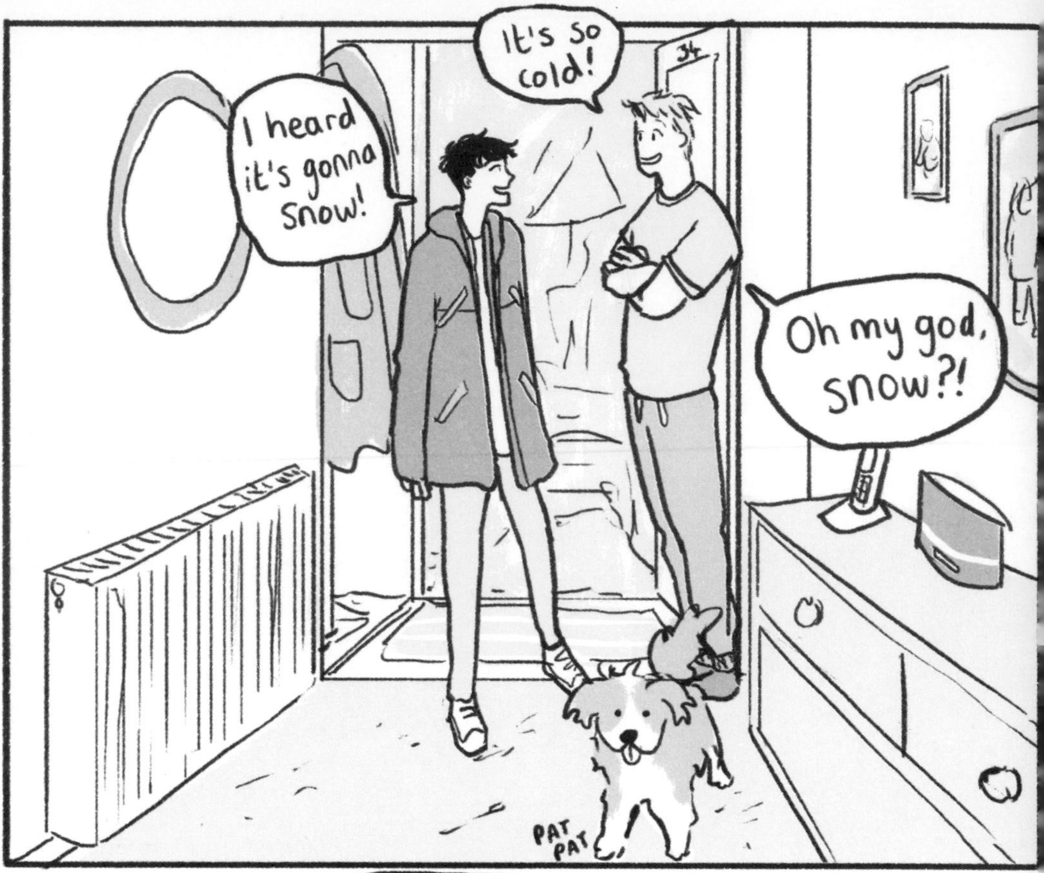
I heard it's gonna snow!
It's so cold!
Oh my god, snow?!
PAT PAT

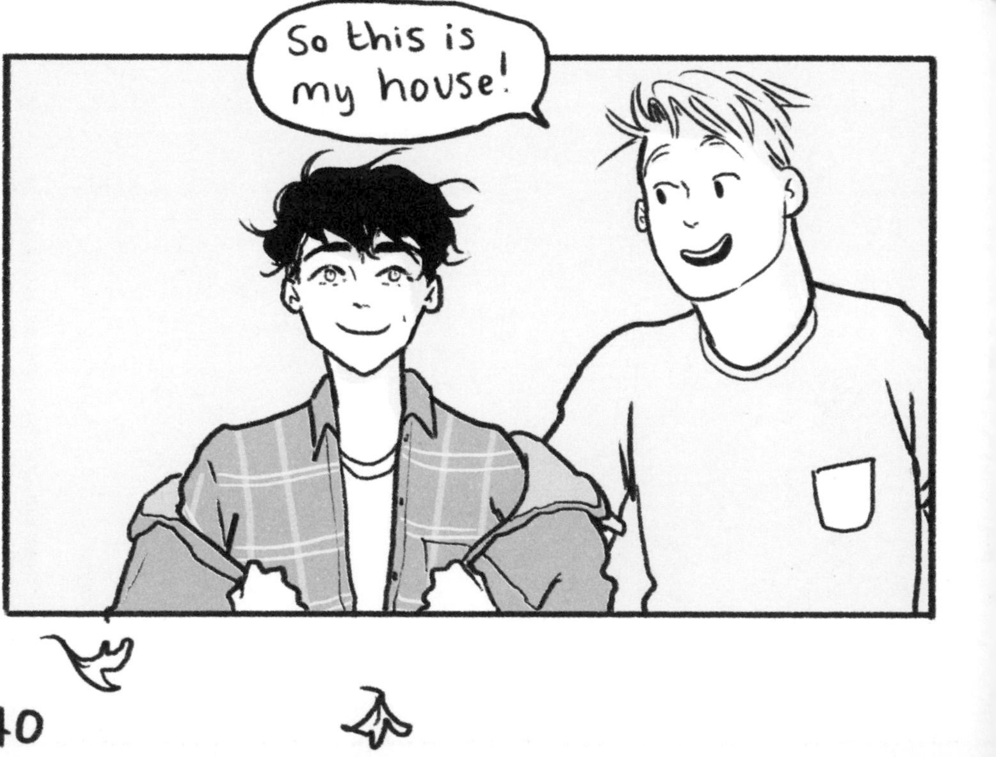
So this is my house!

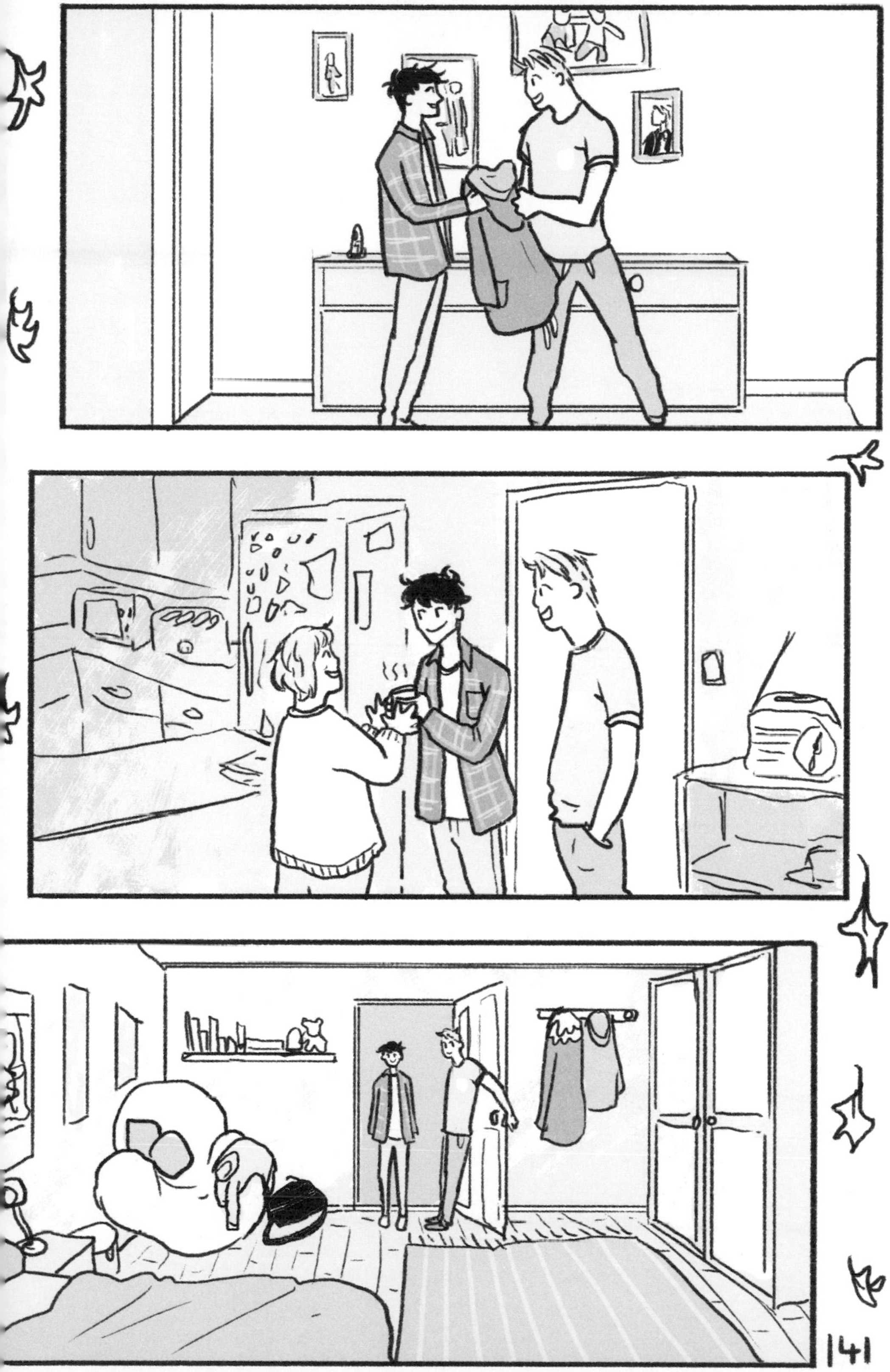

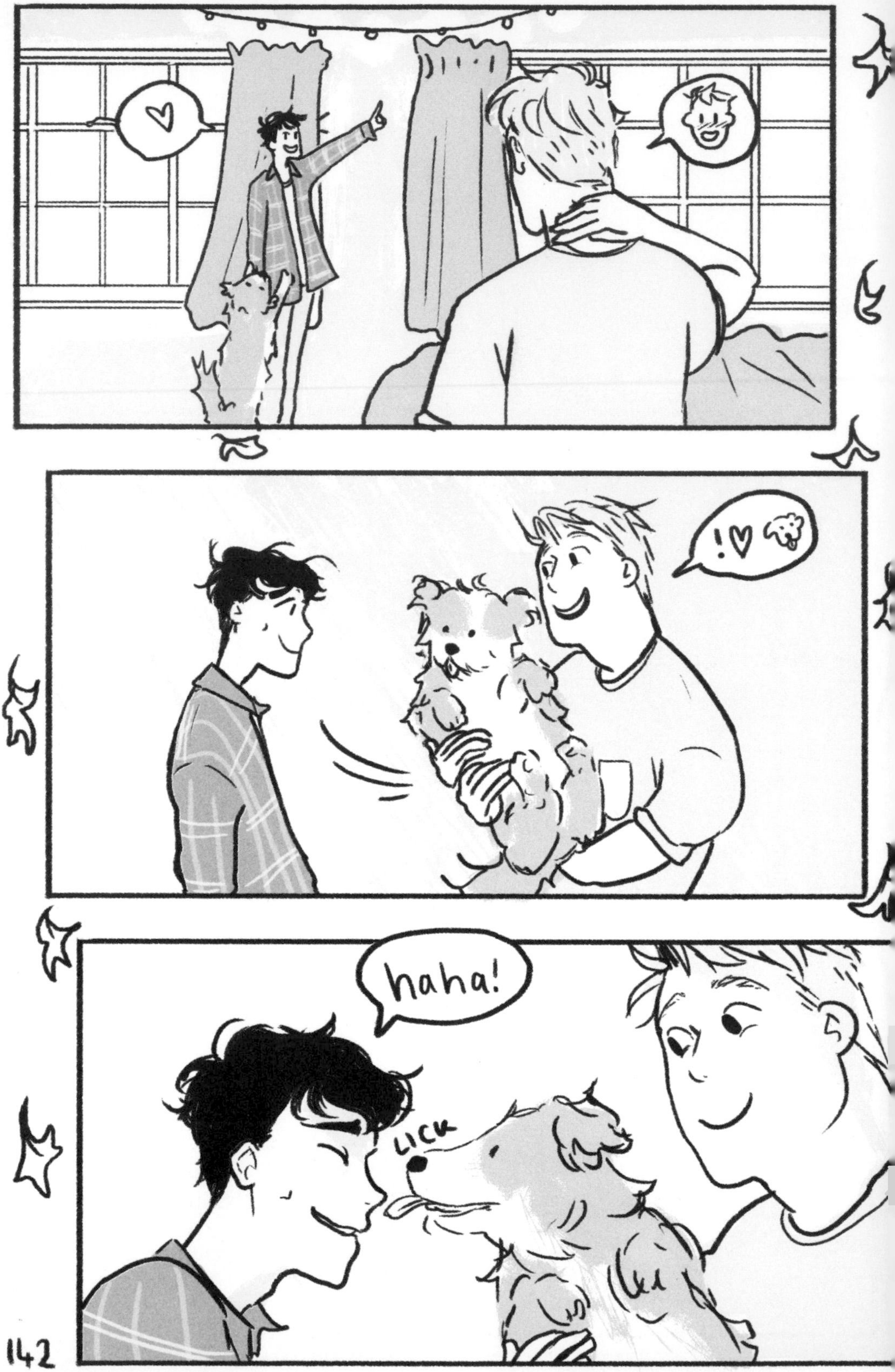
haha!
LICK

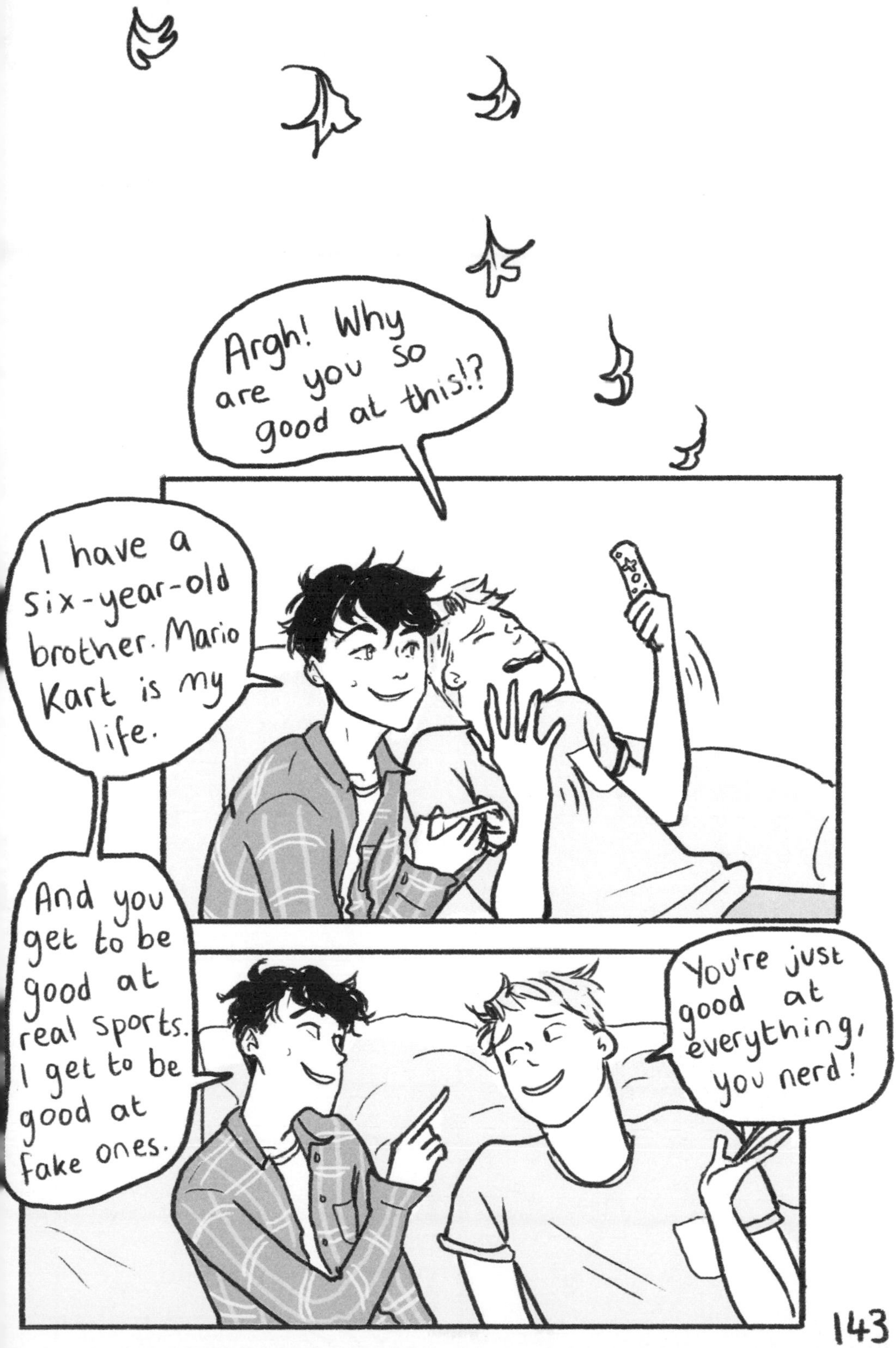
Argh! Why are you so good at this!?
I have a six-year-old brother. Mario Kart is my life.
And you get to be good at real sports. I get to be good at fake ones.
You're just good at everything, you nerd!

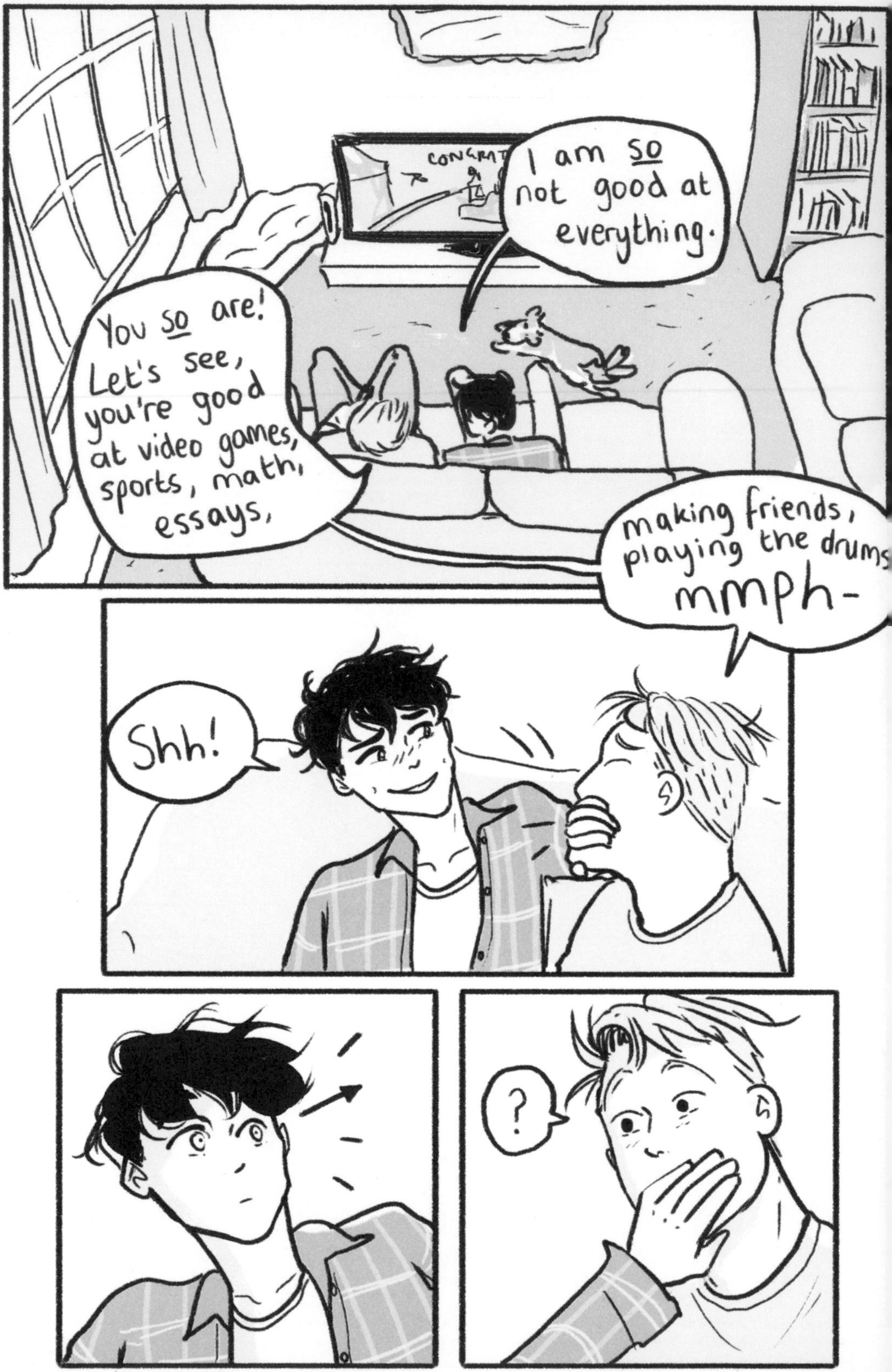
CONGRAT
I am SO not good at everything.
You SO are! Let's see, you're good at video games, sports, math, essays,
making friends, playing the drums
mmph-
Shh!
?

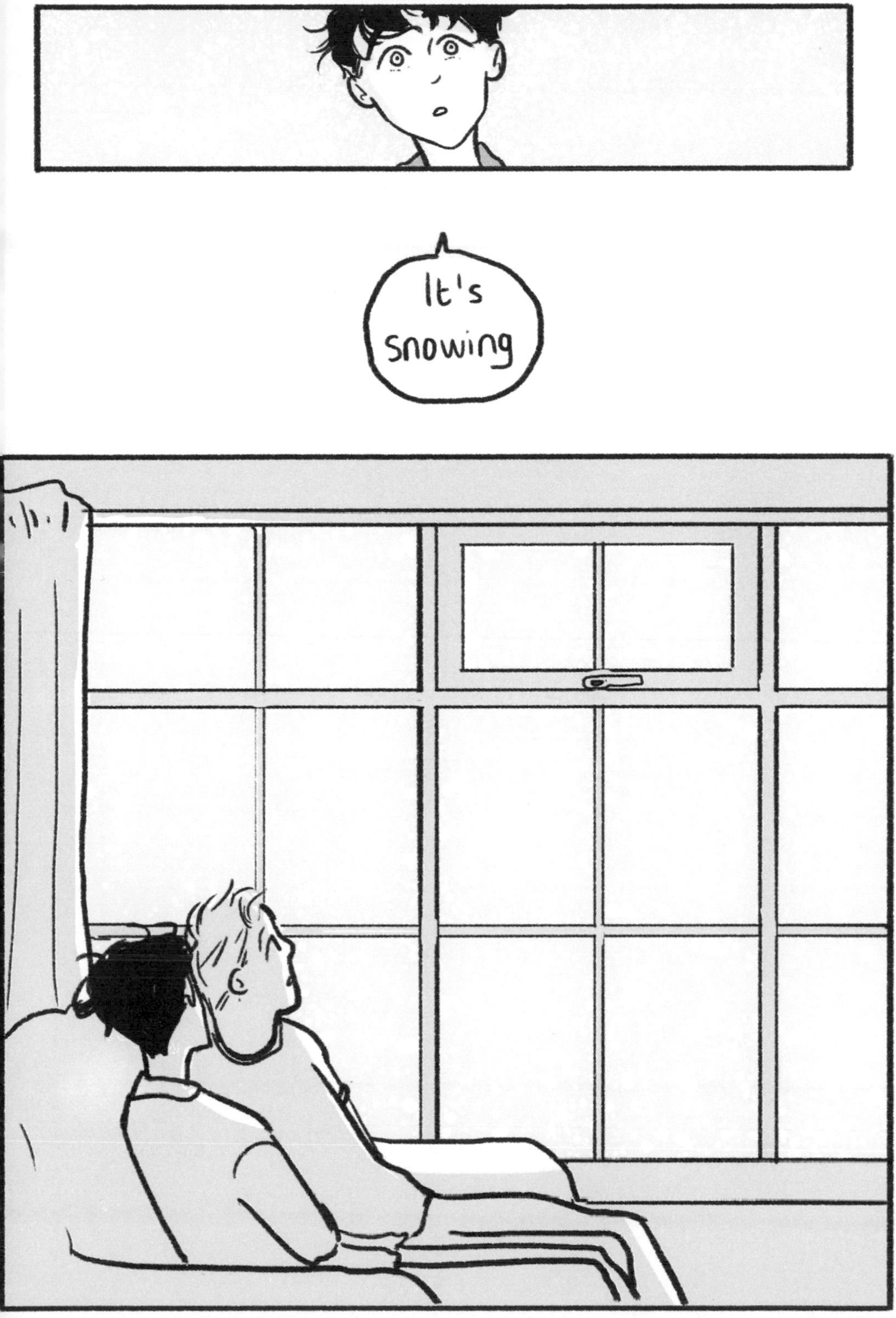
It's snowing

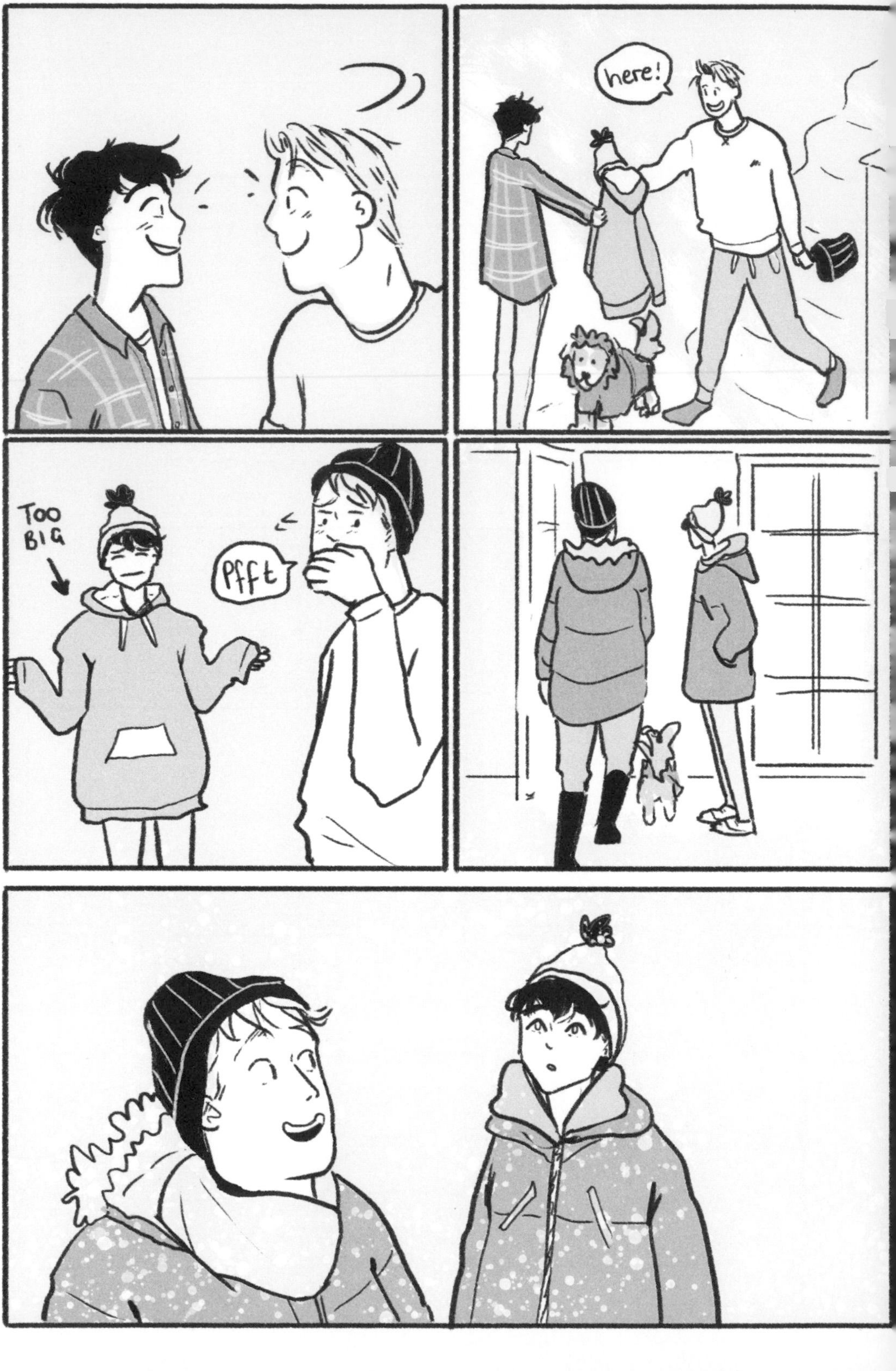
here!
TOO BIG
Pfft

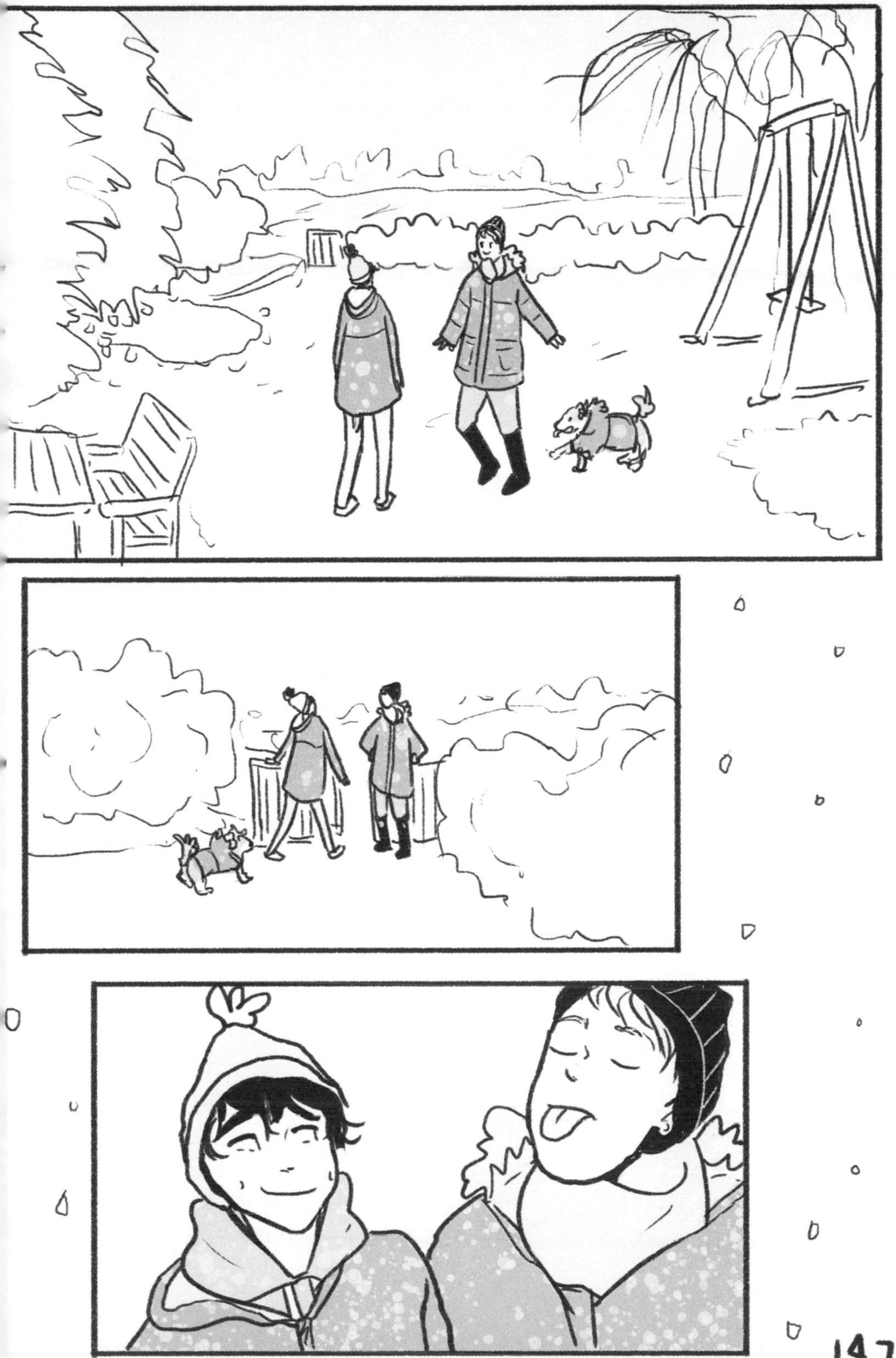

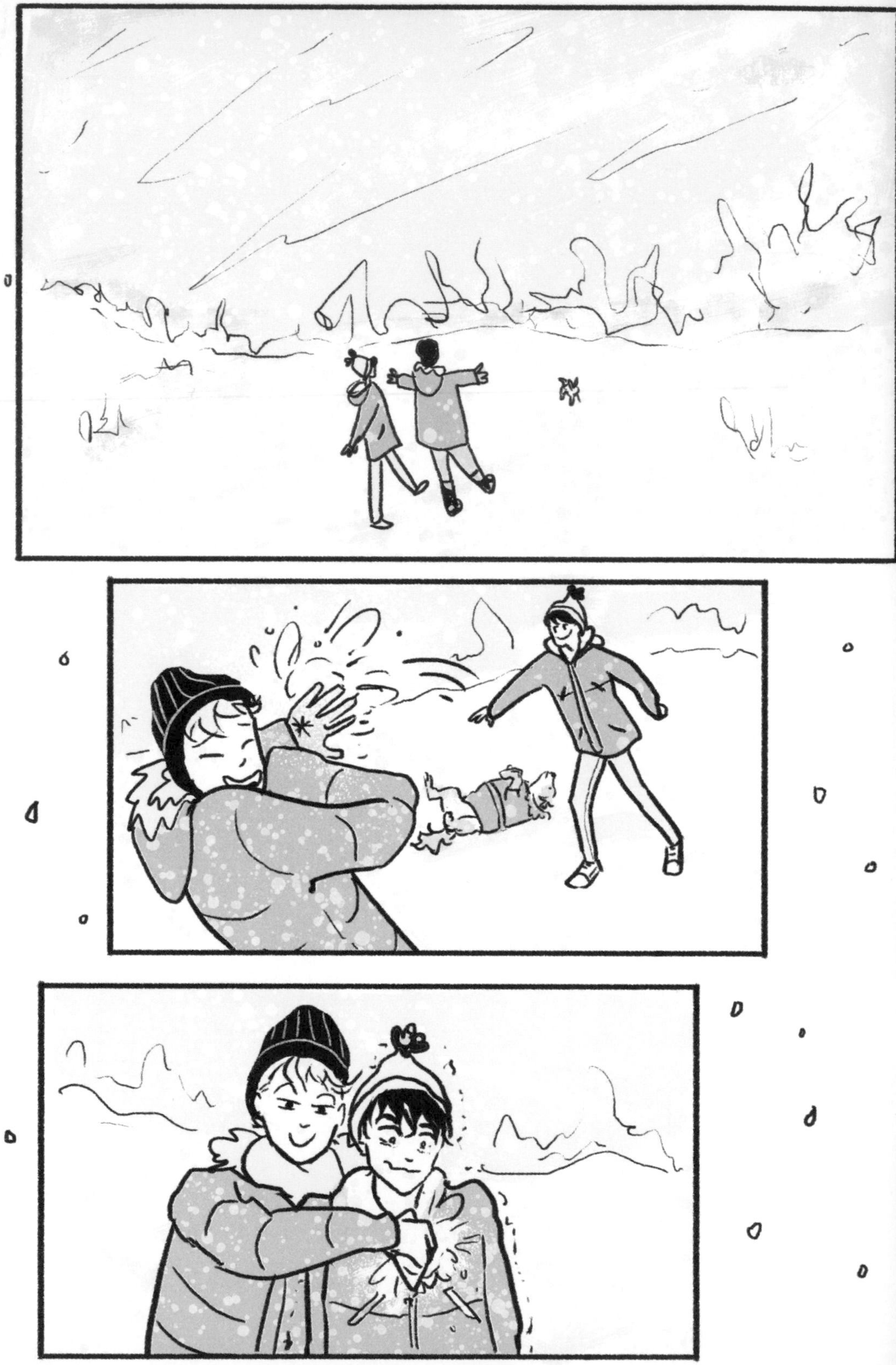

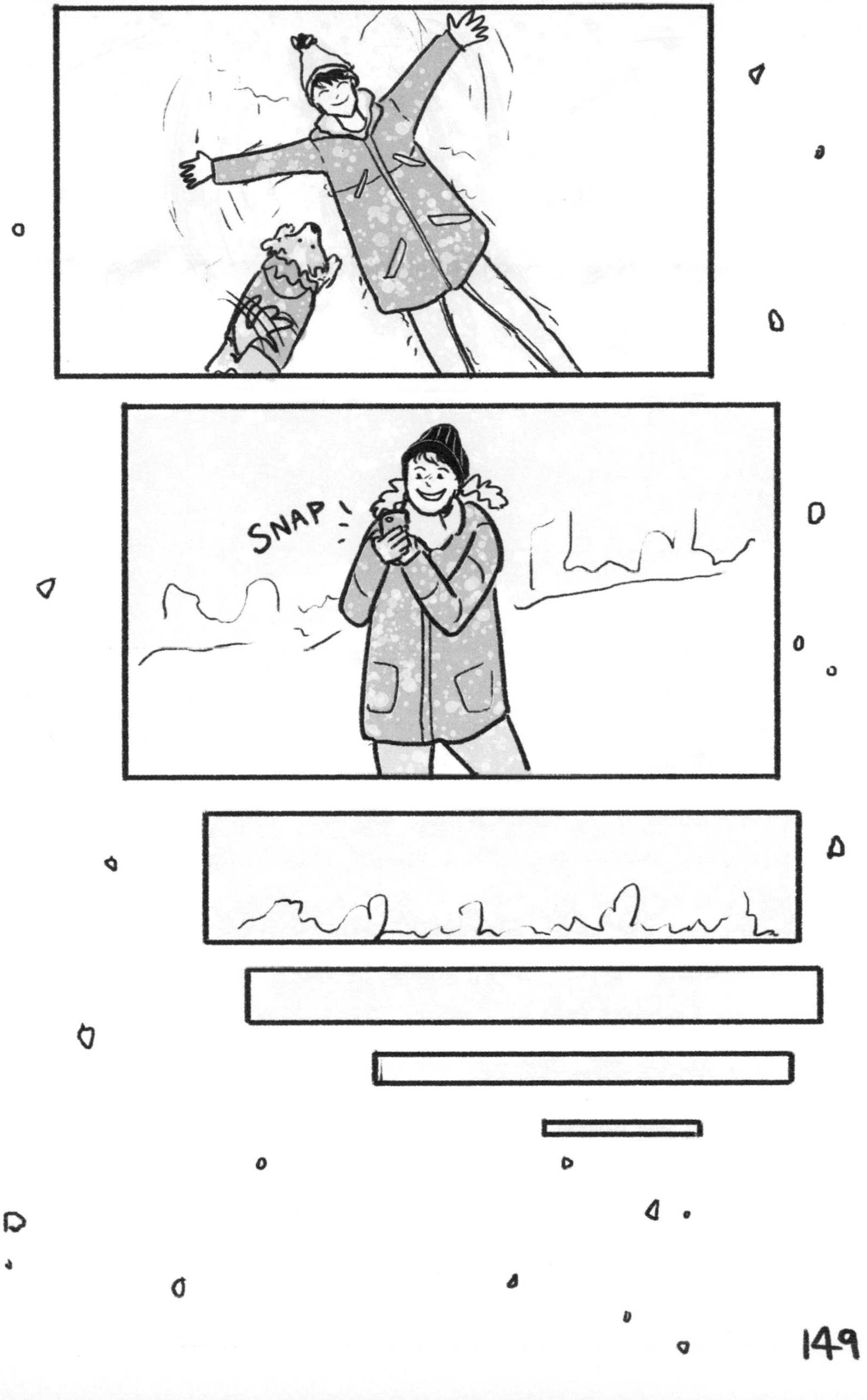
SNAP!

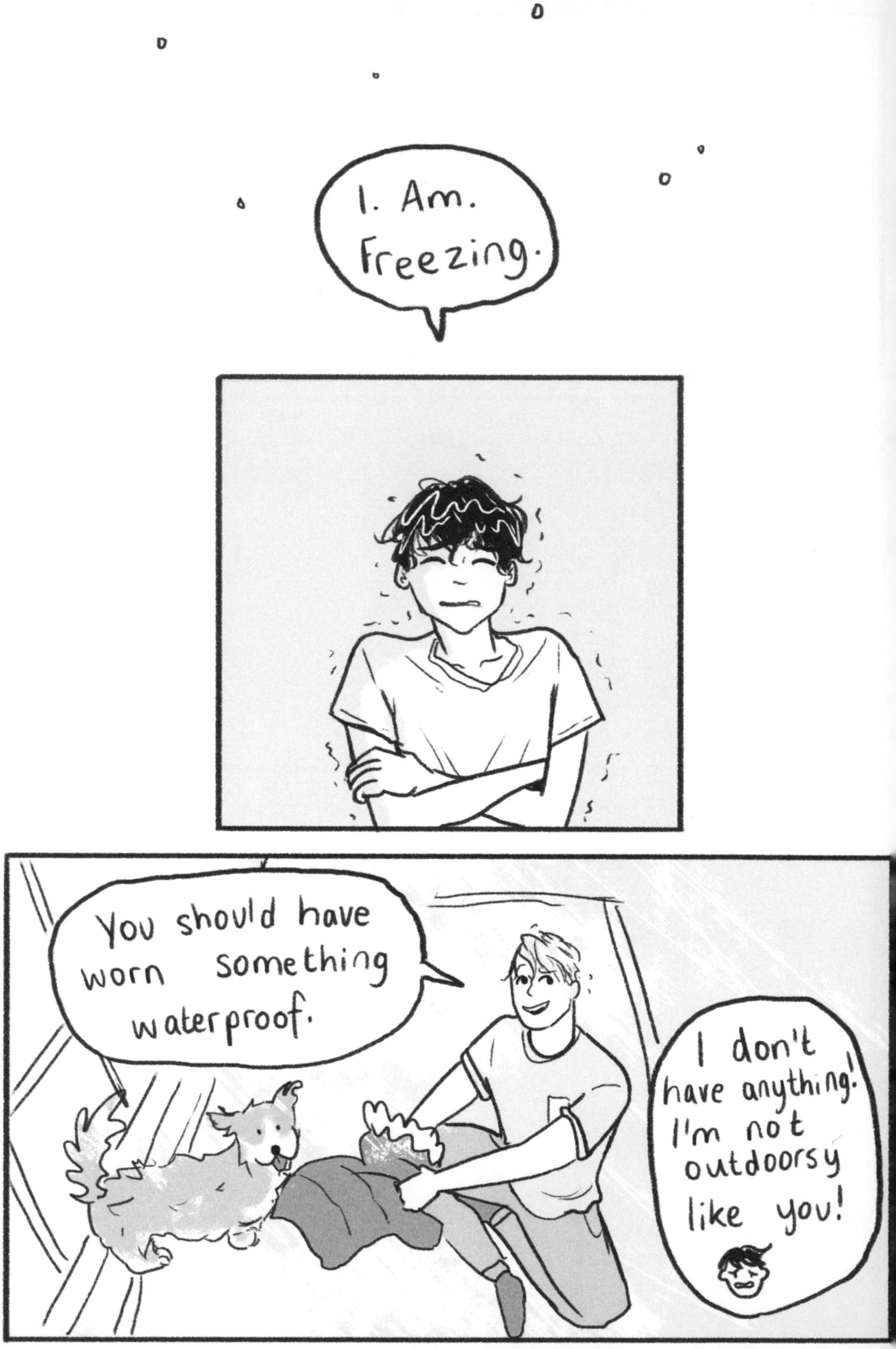
I. Am. Freezing.
You should have worn something waterproof.
I don't have anything! I'm not outdoorsy like you!

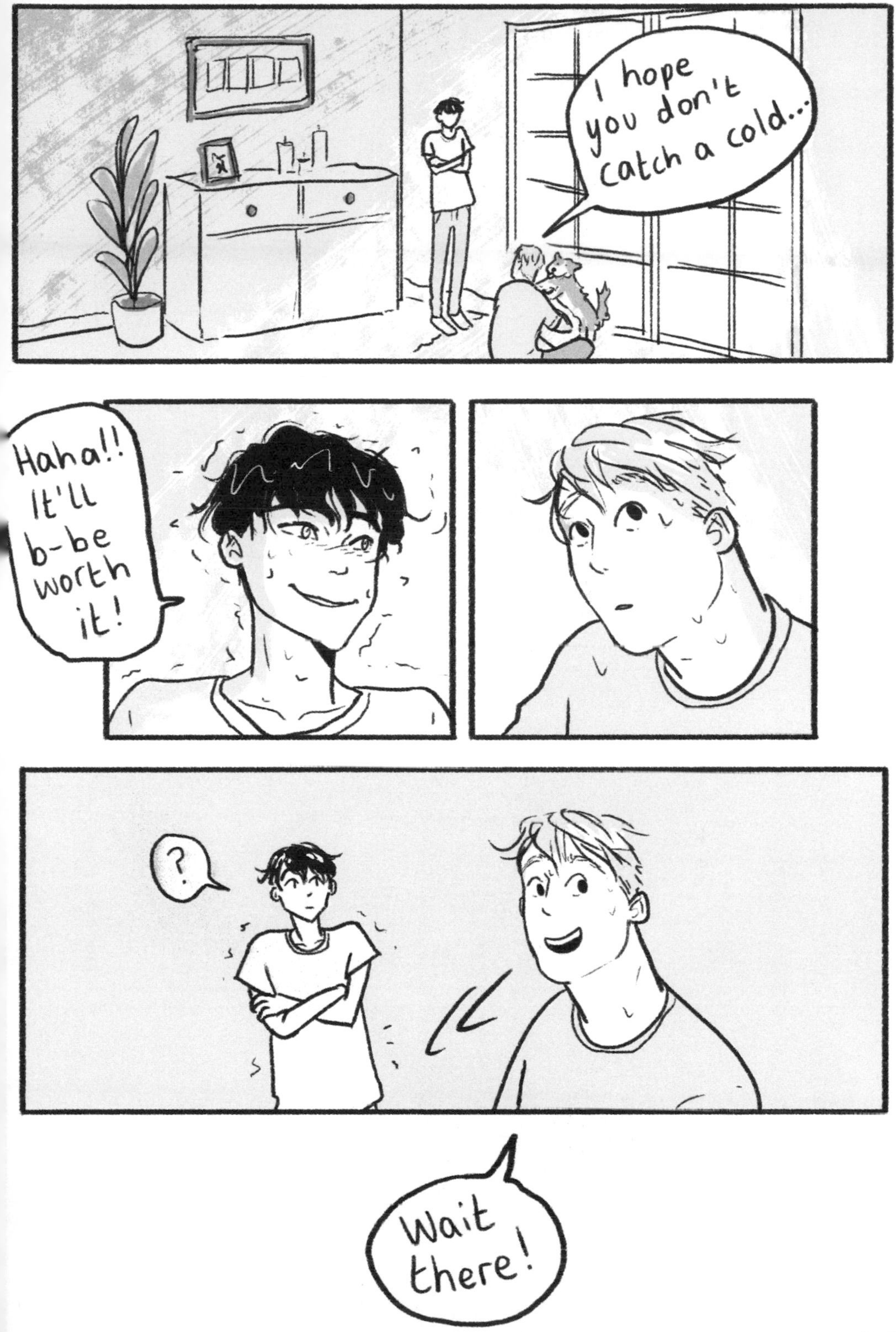
I hope you don't catch a cold...
Haha!! It'll b-be worth it!
?
Wait there!

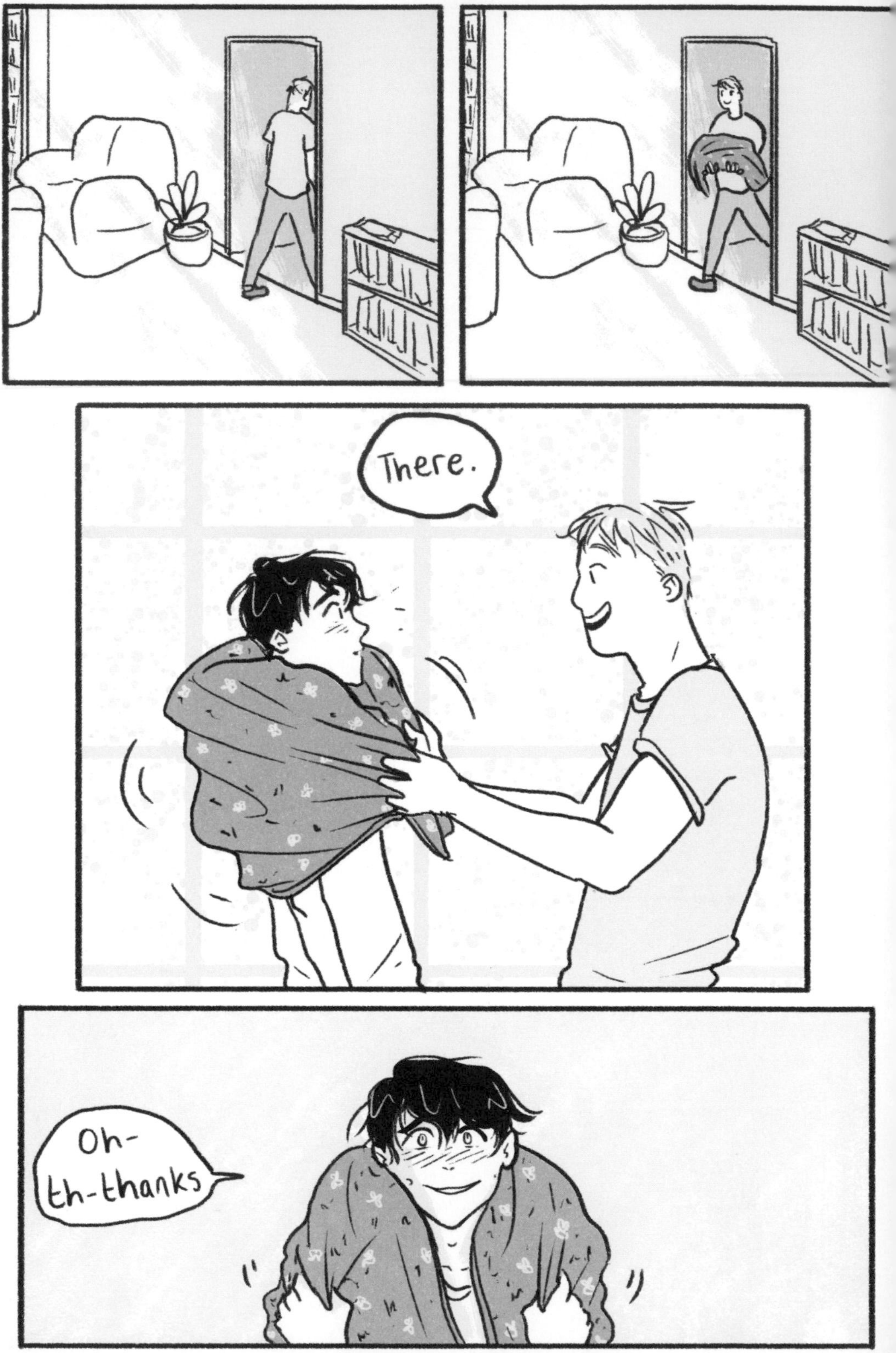
There.
Oh-
th-thanks

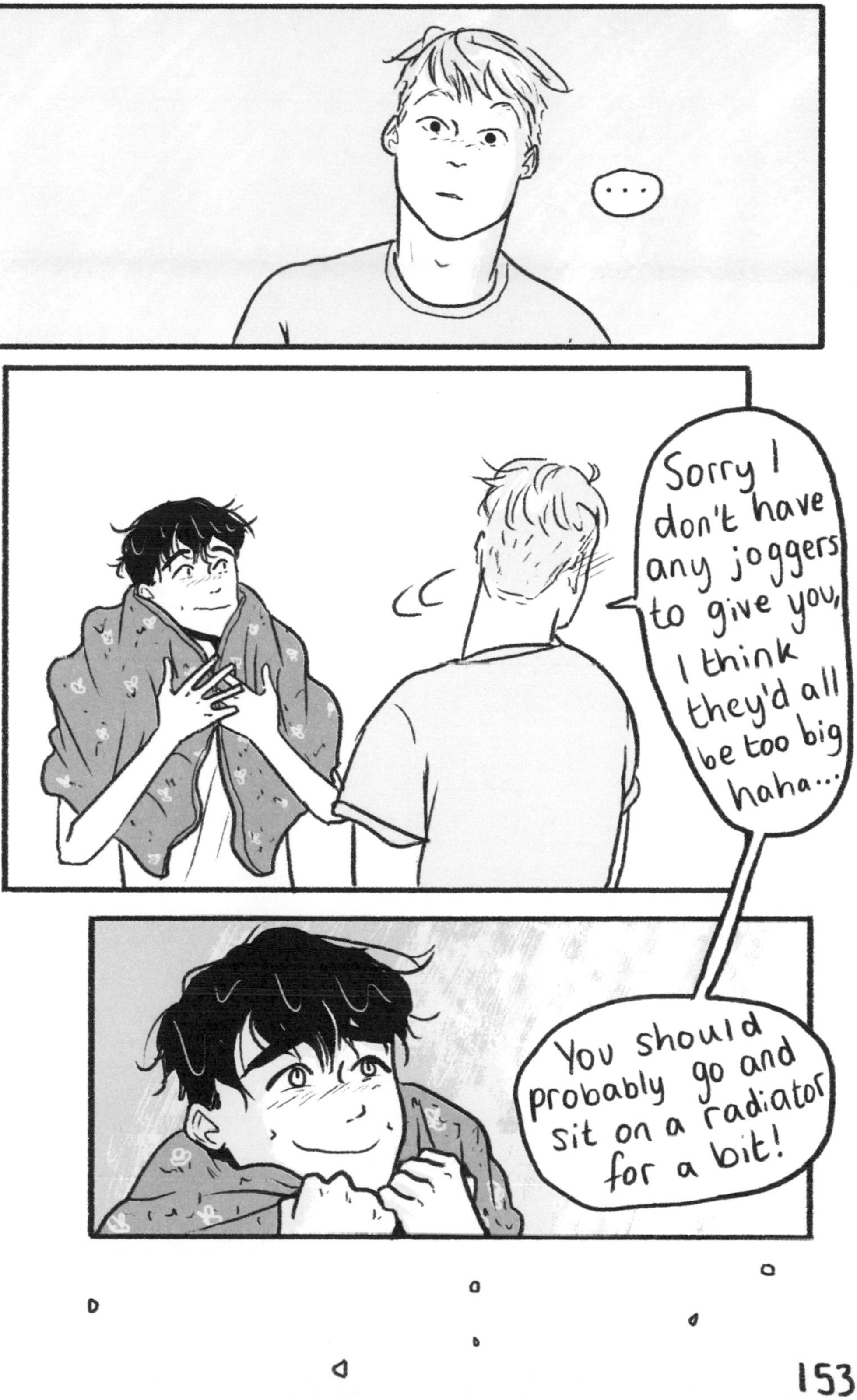
...
Sorry I don't have any joggers to give you, I think they'd all be too big haha...
You should probably go and sit on a radiator for a bit!

You really have to go home?
Yeah... My dad said I had to be home for dinner.
Well... Nellie will miss you!

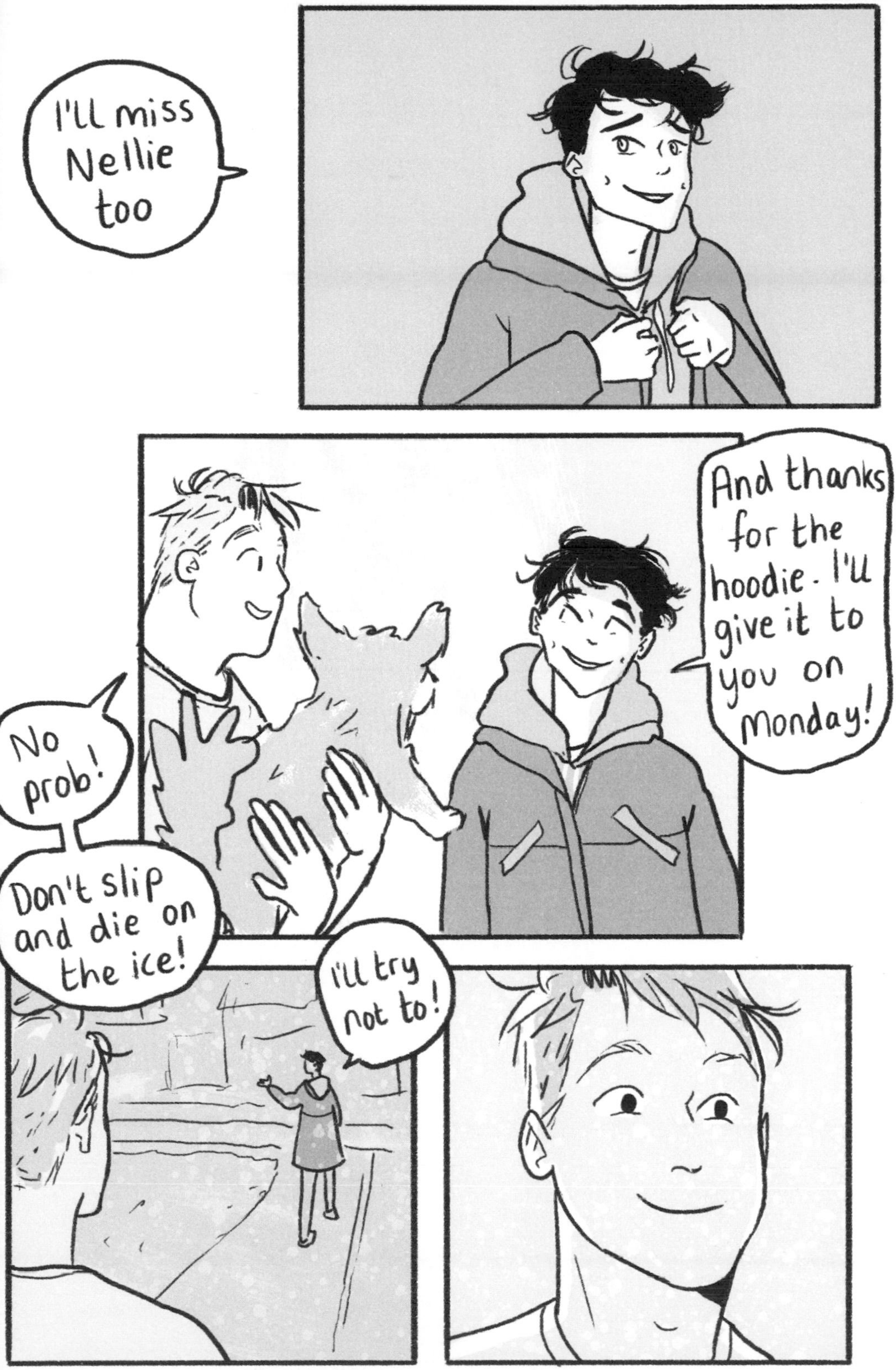
I'll miss Nellie too
And thanks for the hoodie. I'll give it to you on Monday!
No prob!
Don't slip and die on the ice!
I'll try not to!

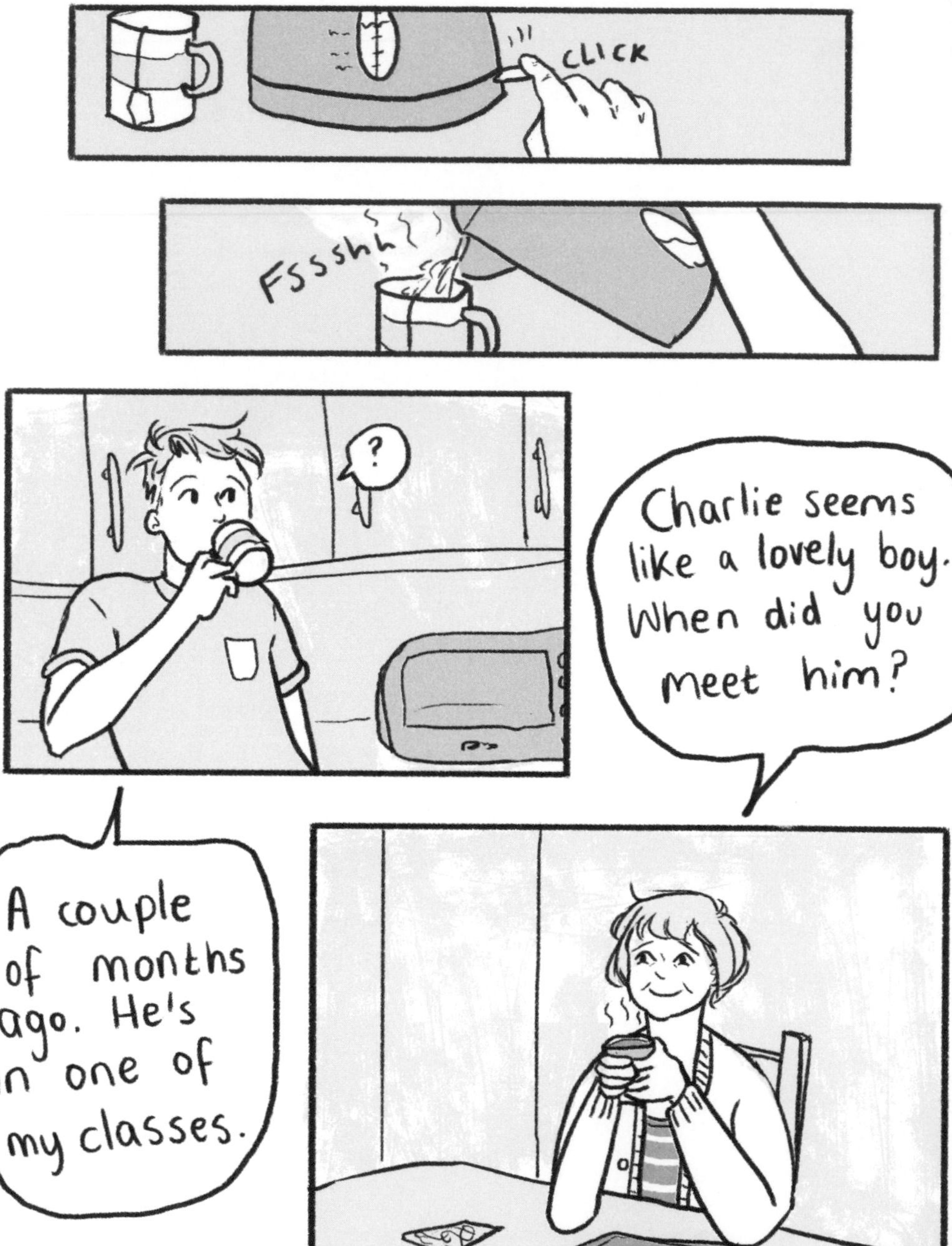
CLICK
FSSSHH
?
Charlie seems like a lovely boy. When did you meet him?
A couple of months ago. He's in one of my classes.

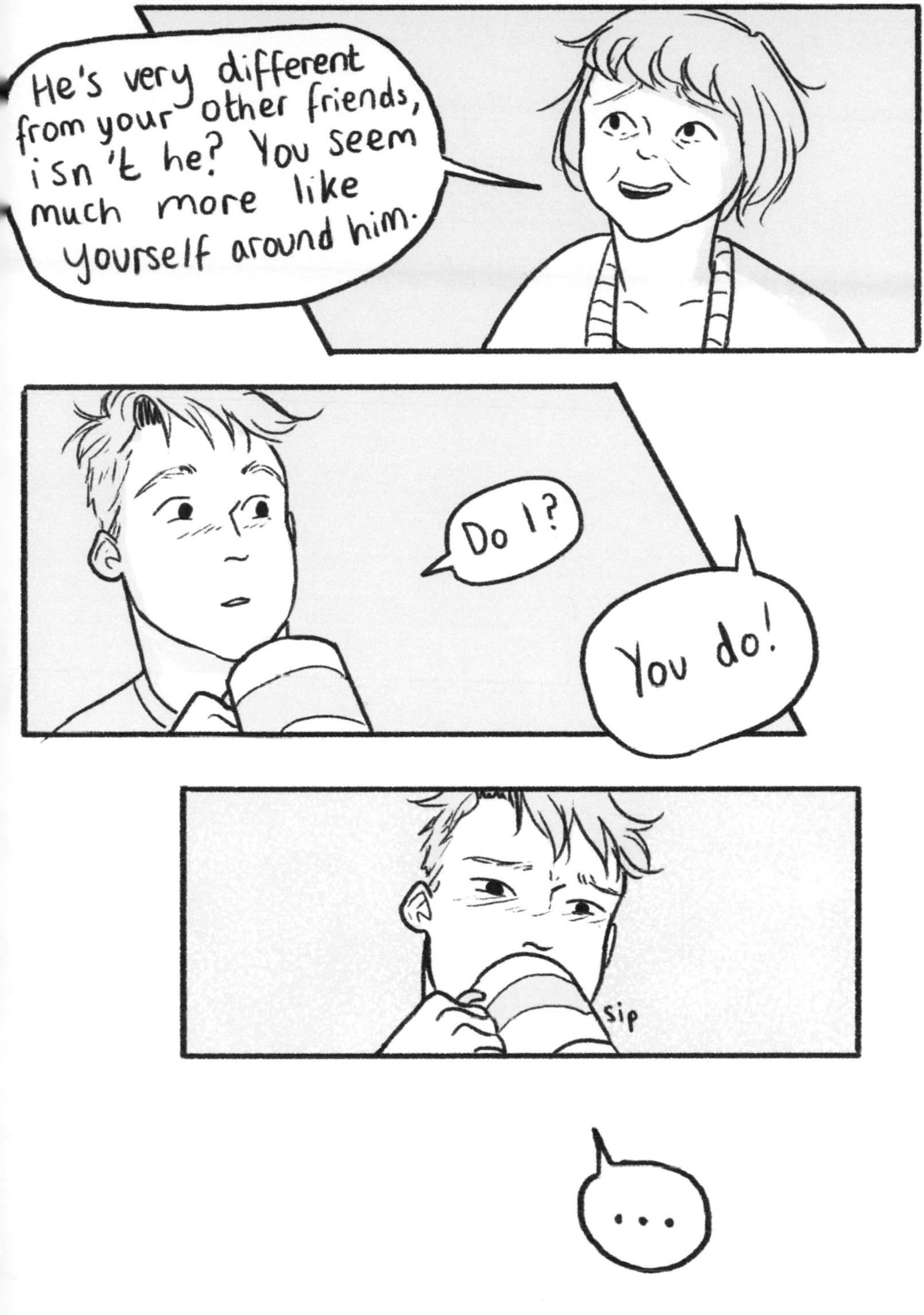
He's very different from your other friends, isn't he? You seem much more like yourself around him.
Do I?
You do!
Sip
...

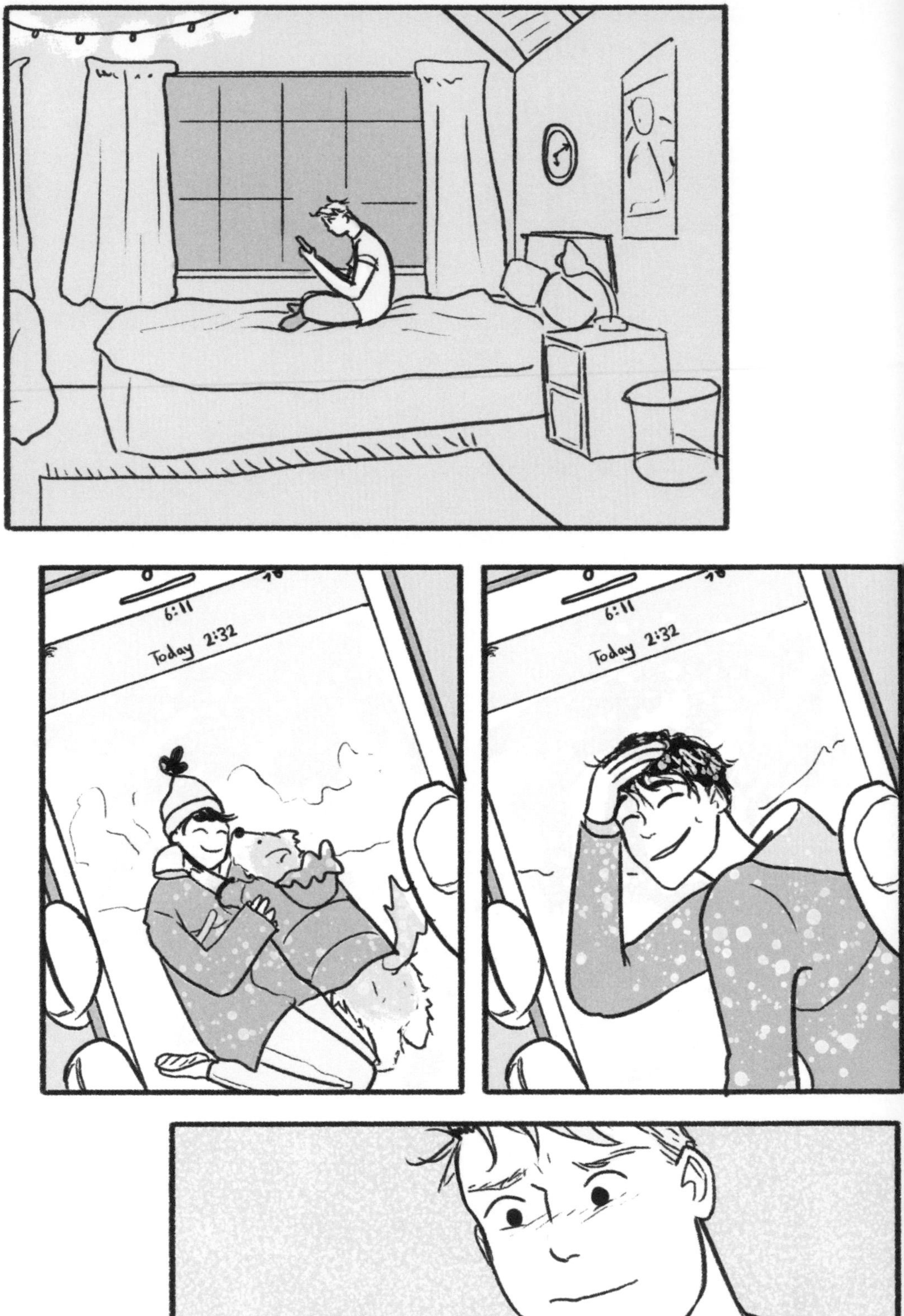
6:11
Today 2:32
6:11
Today 2:32

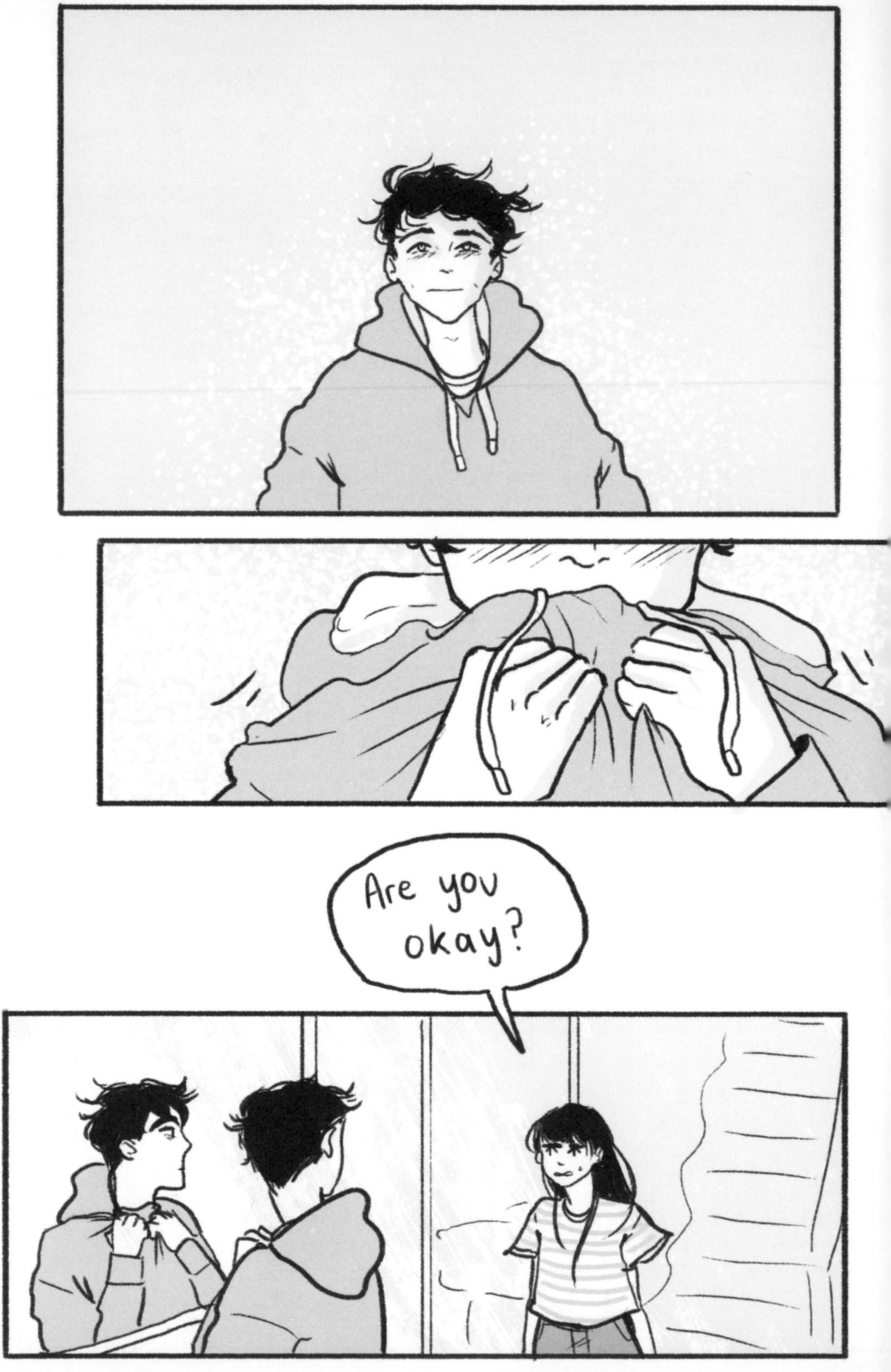
Are you okay?

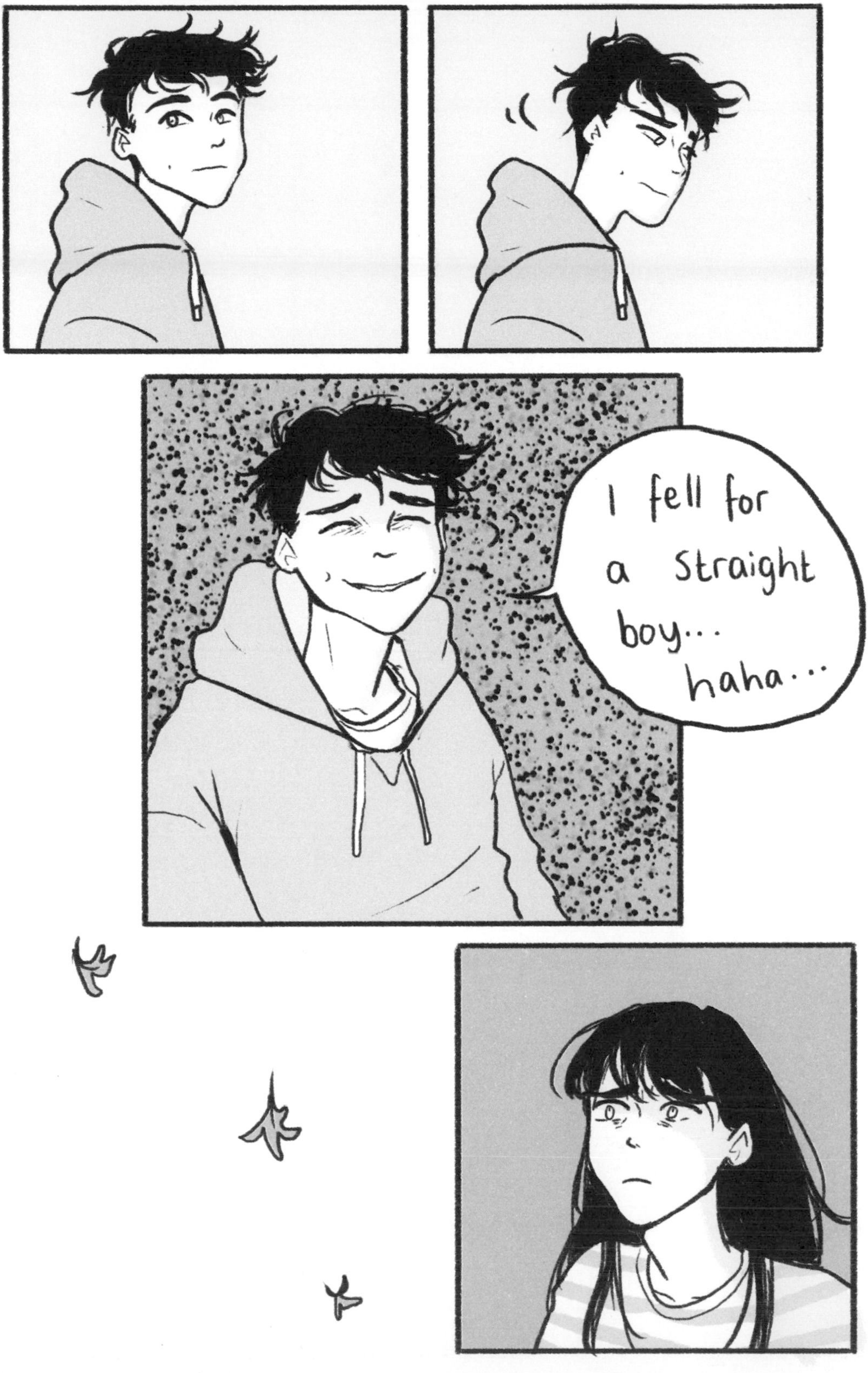
I fell for a straight boy... haha...

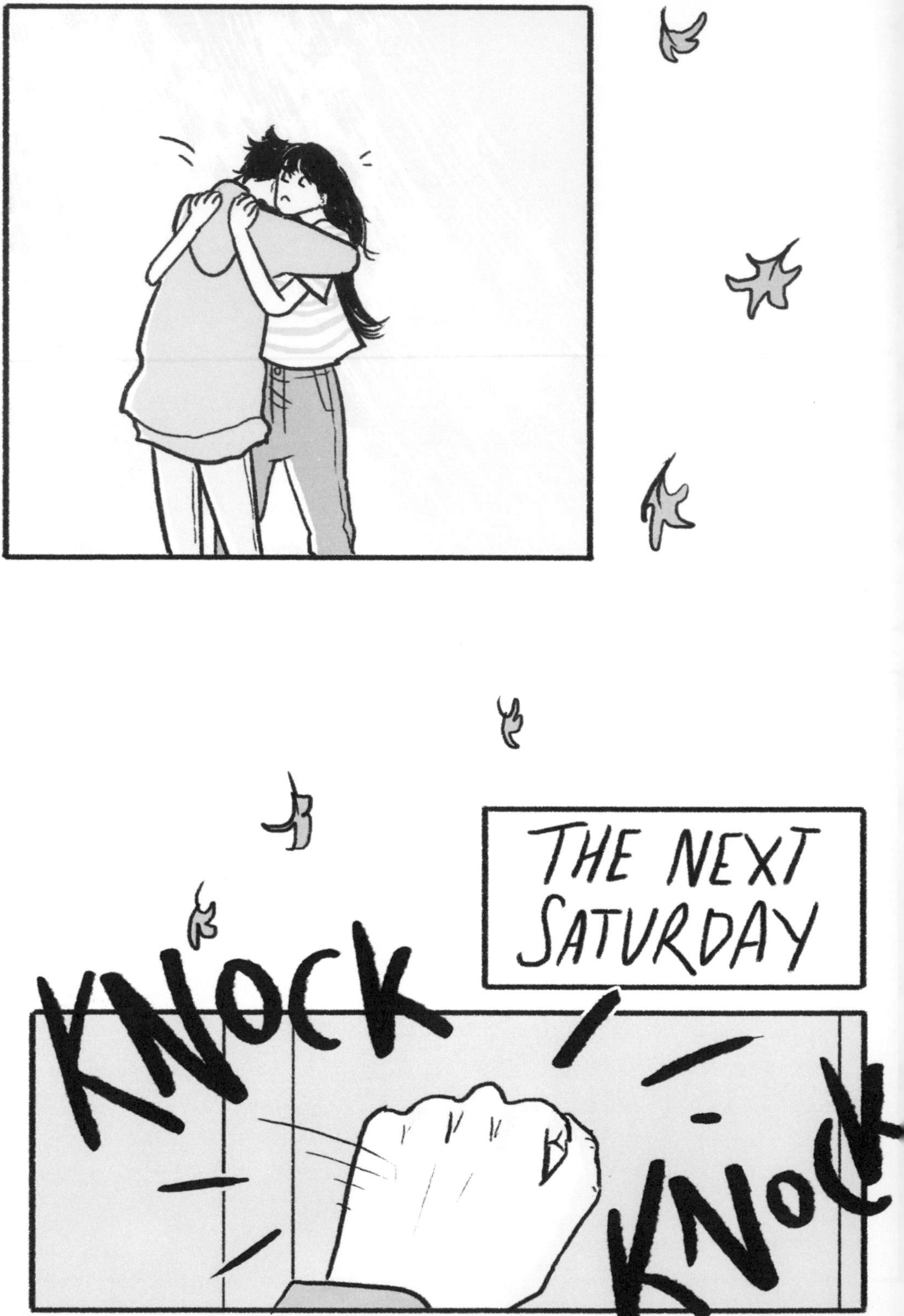
THE NEXT SATURDAY
KNOCK
KNOCK

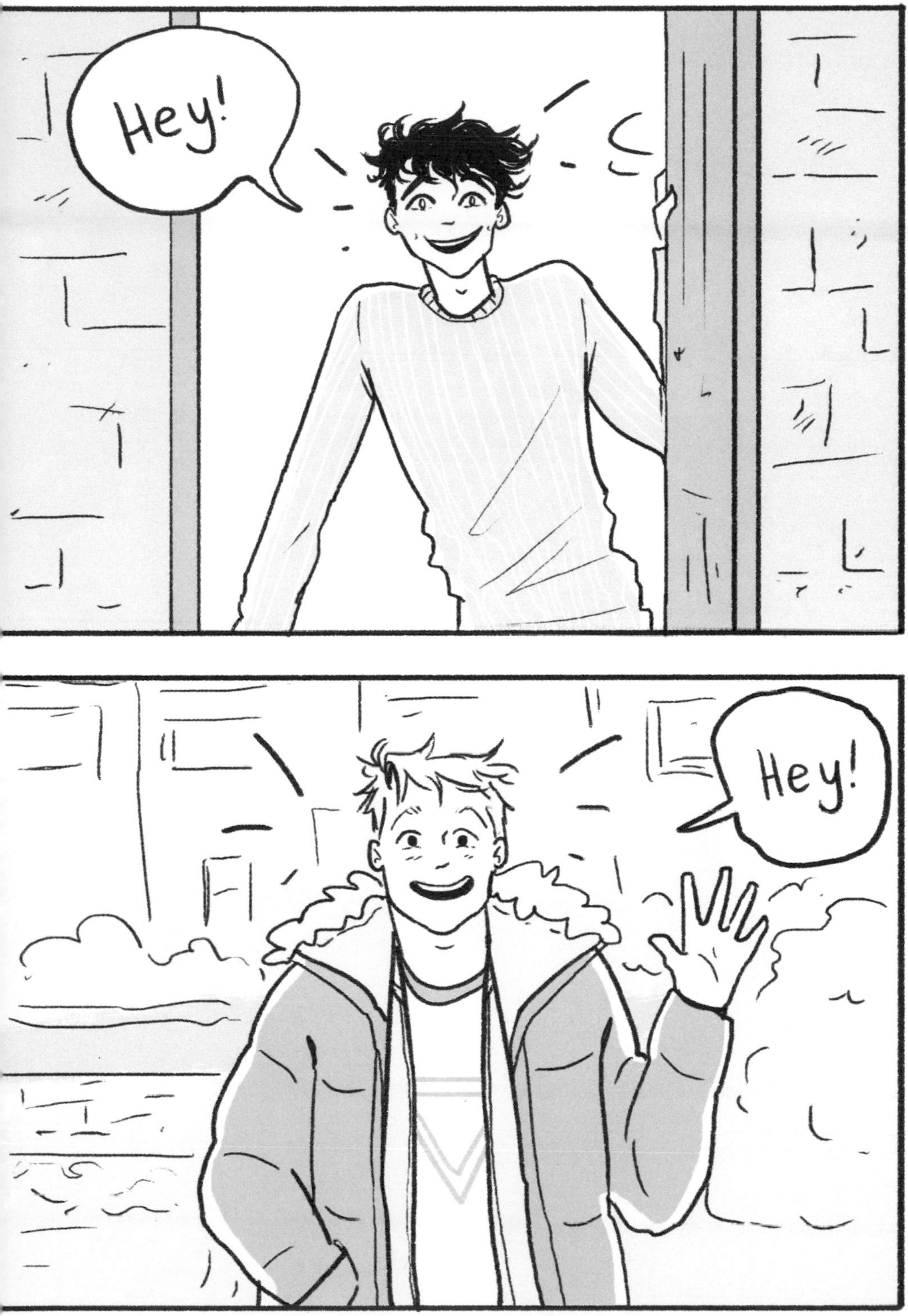
Hey!
Hey!

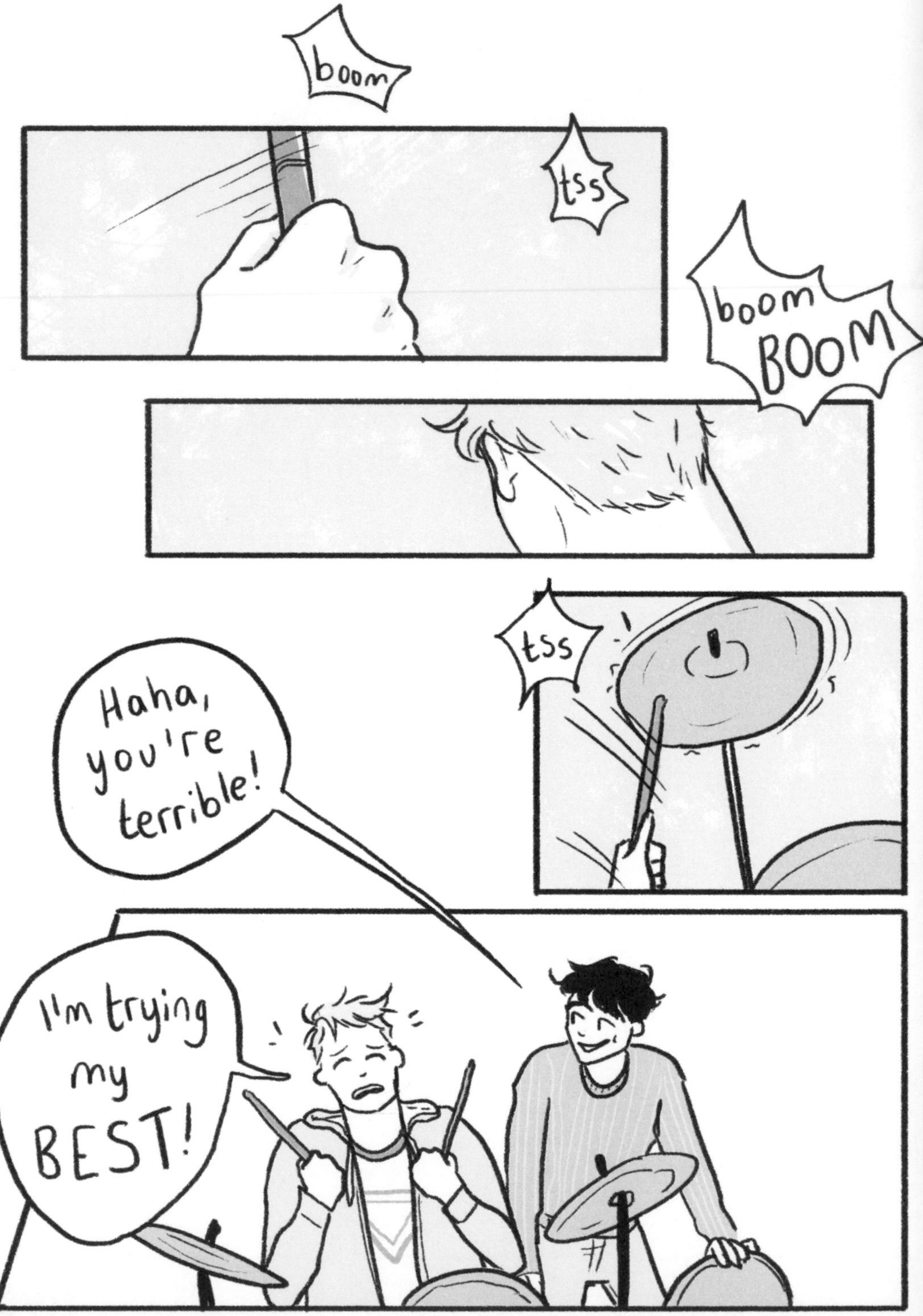
boom
tss
boom BOOM
tss
Haha, you're terrible!
I'm trying my BEST!

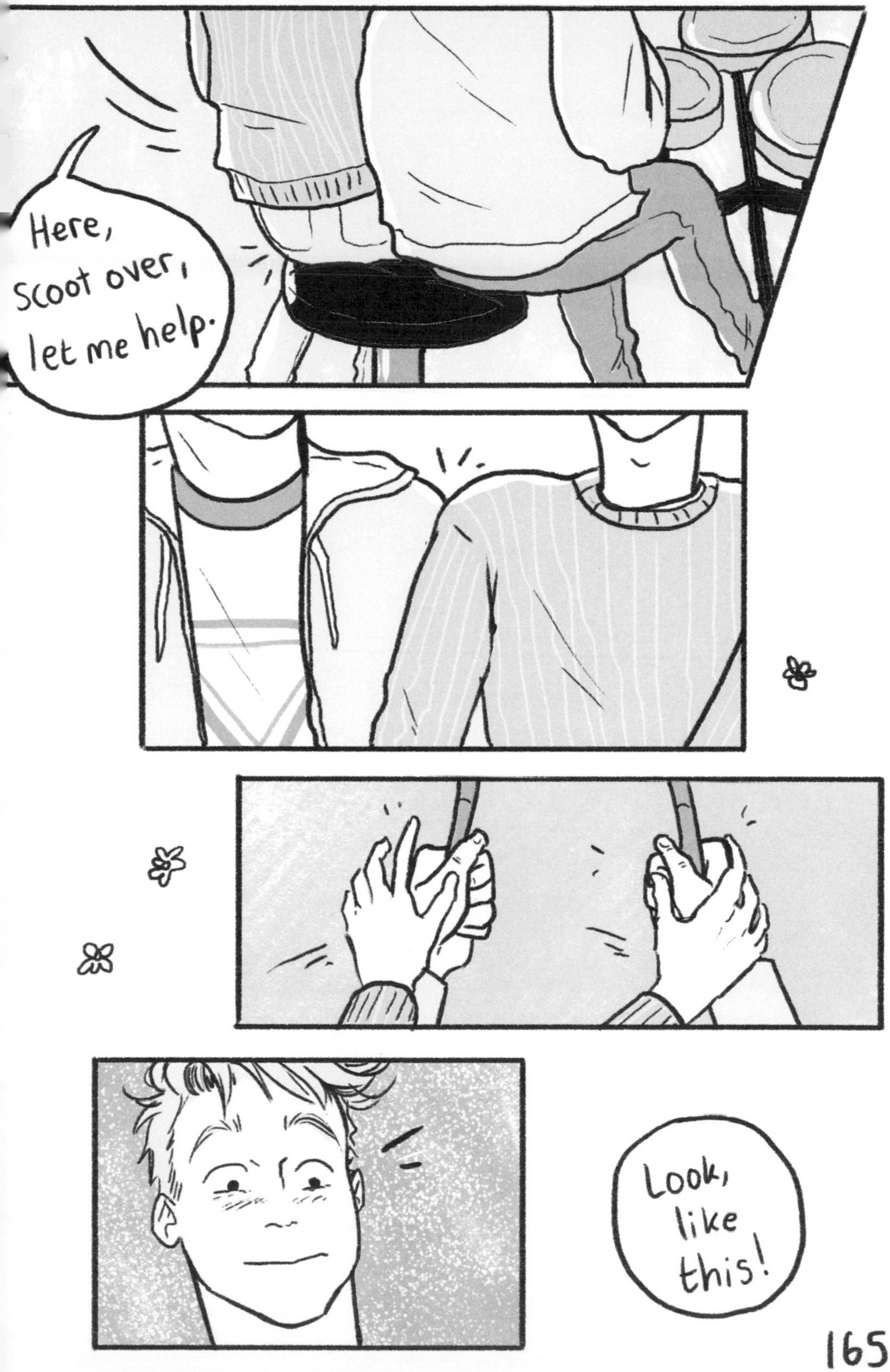
Here, scoot over, let me help.
Look, like this!

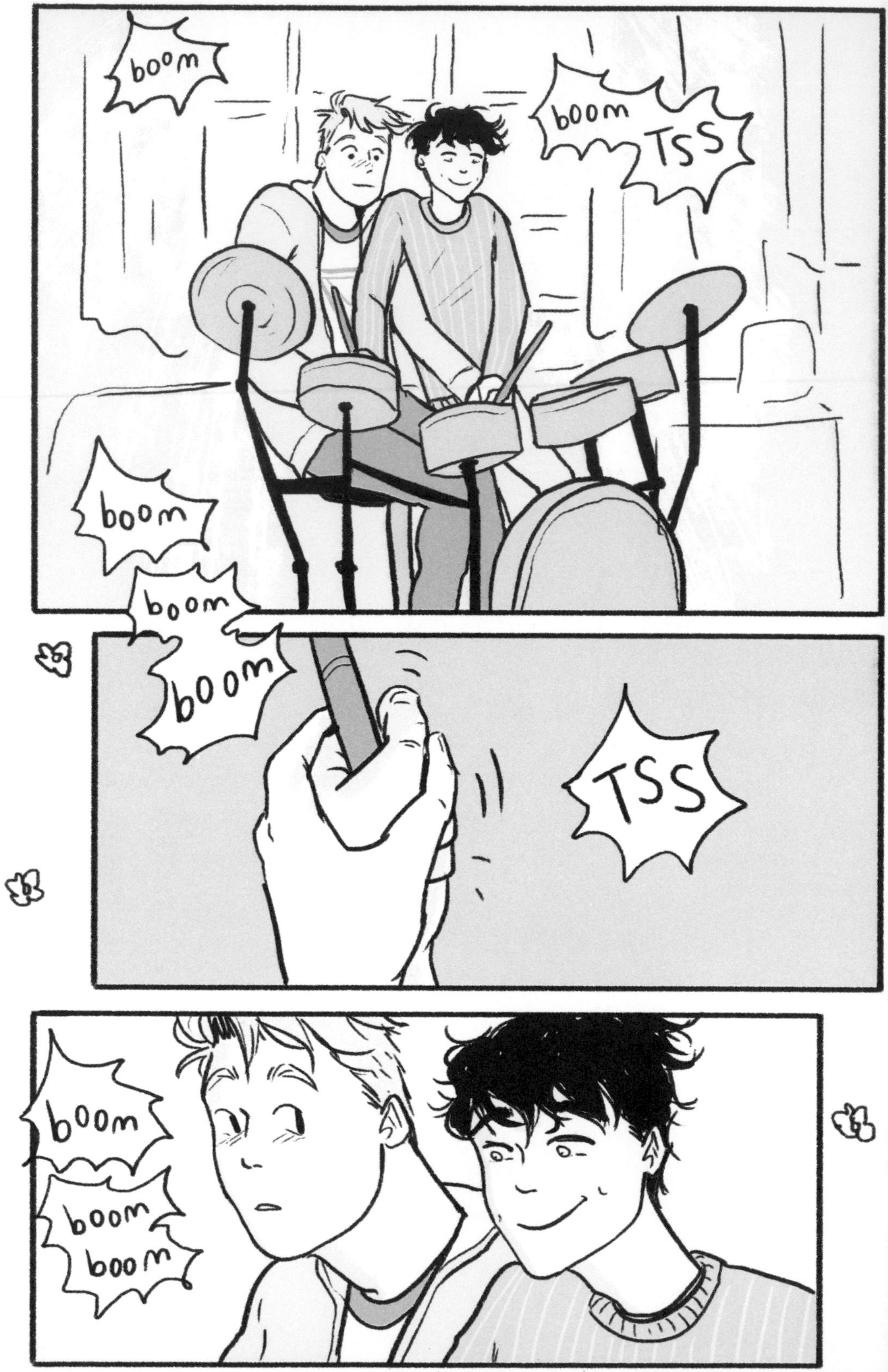
boom
boom
TSS
boom
boom
boom
TSS
boom
boom
boom

There, you're a pro now!

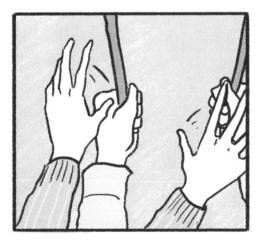

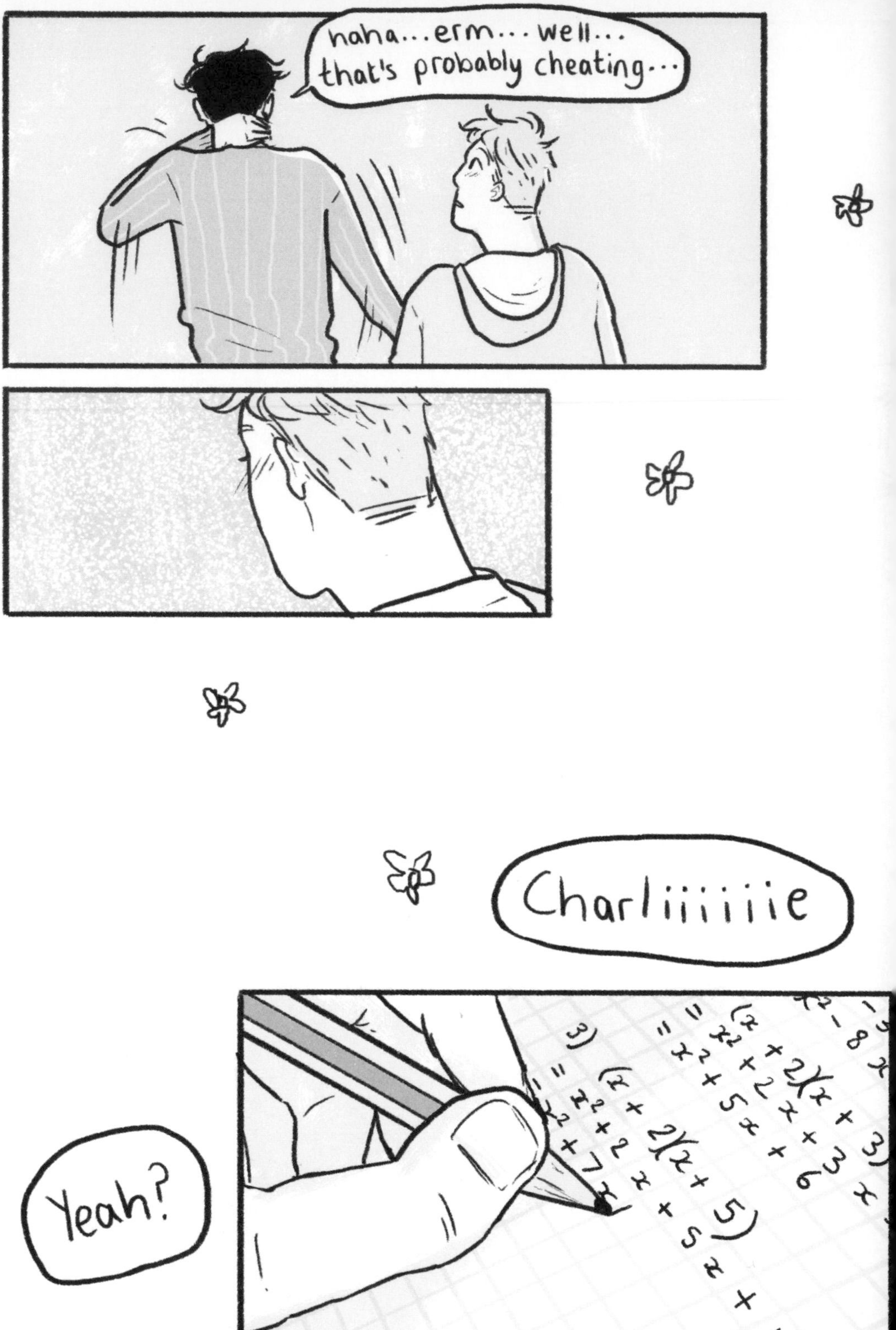
haha... erm... well... that's probably cheating...
Charliiiiiie
Yeah?

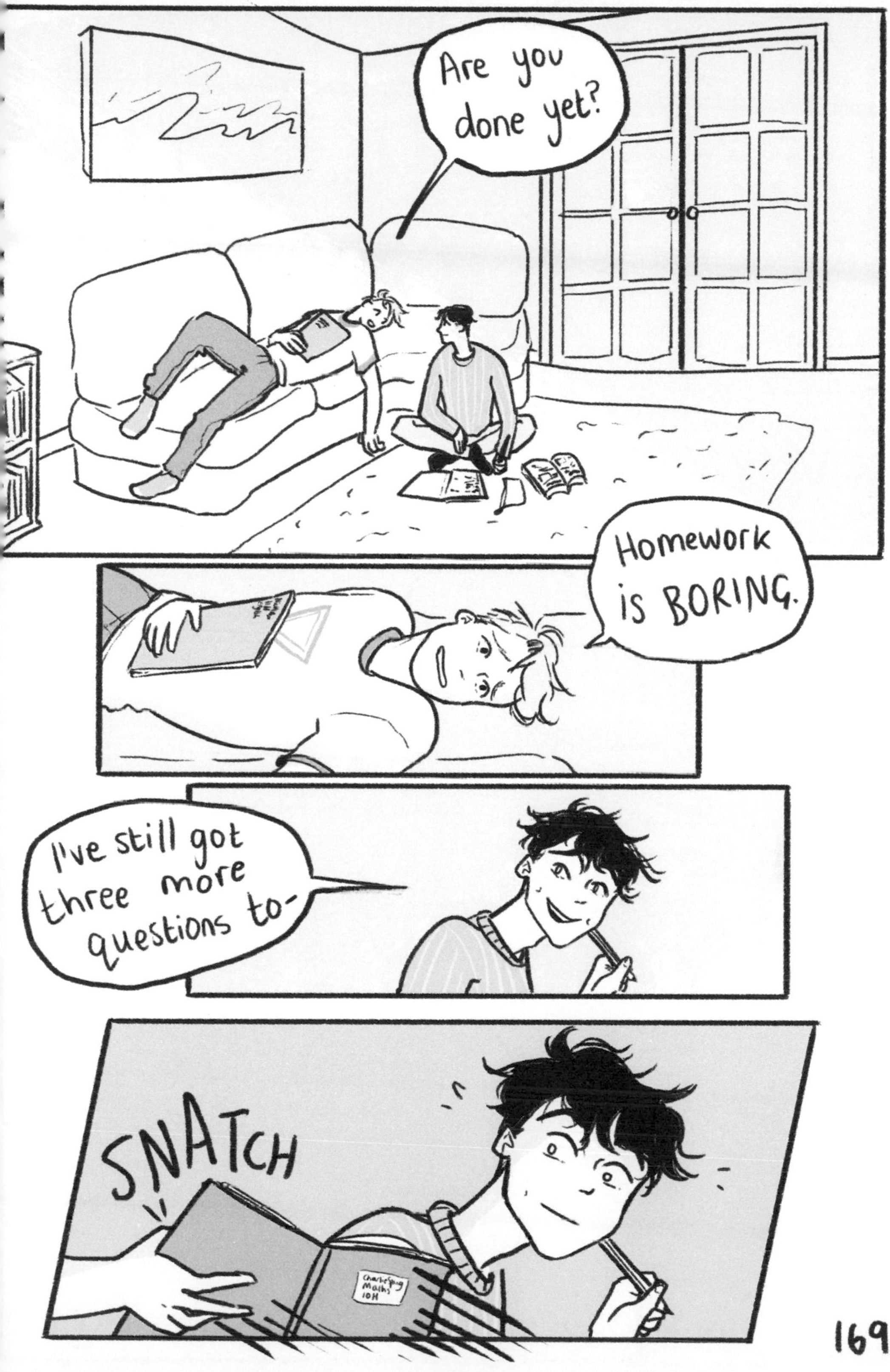
Are you done yet?
Homework is BORING.
I've still got three more questions to-
SNATCH
Charlie Spring Maths 10H

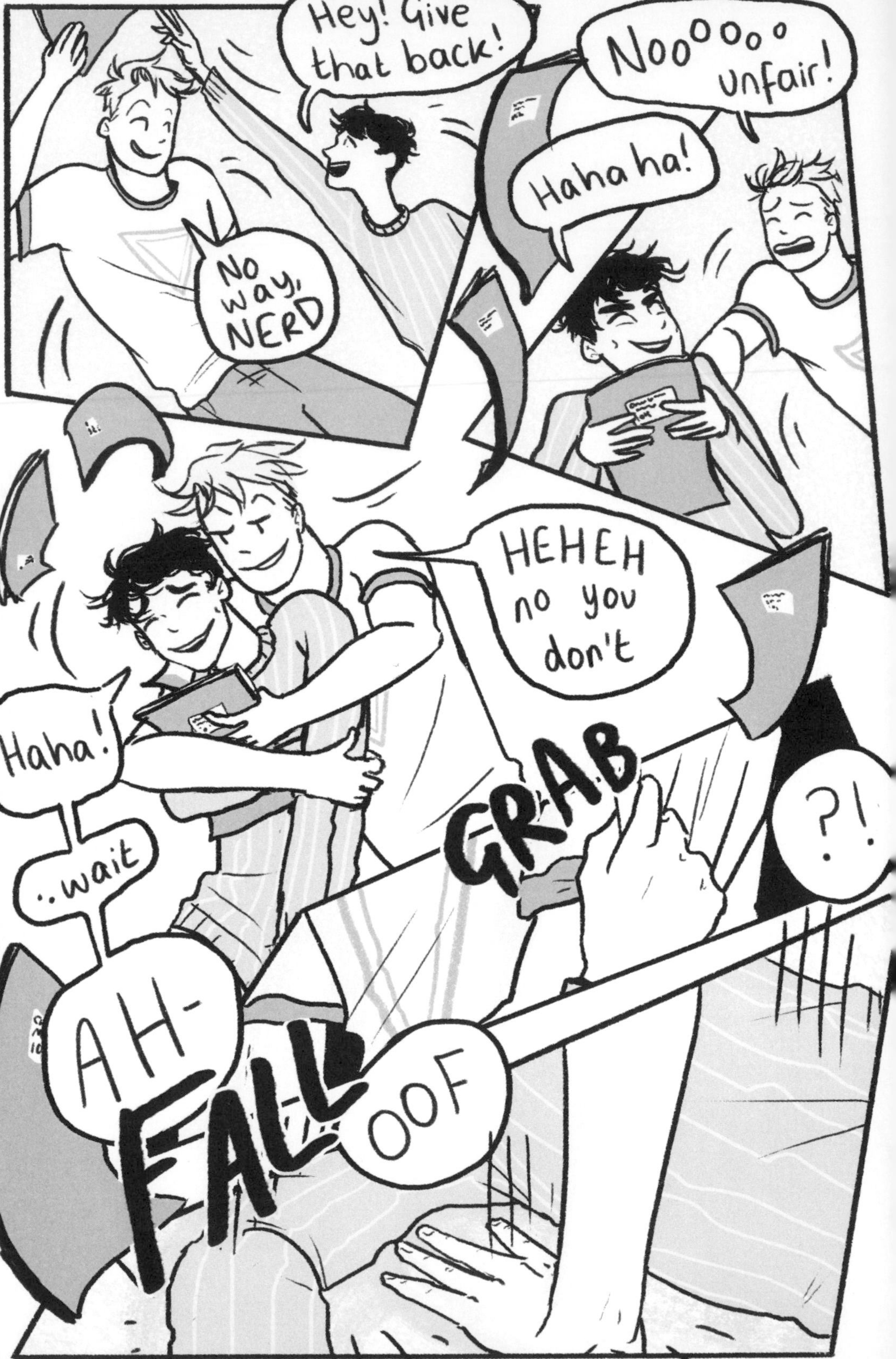
Hey! Give that back!
No way, NERD
Nooooooo unfair!
Hahaha!
HEHEH no you don't
Haha!
..wait
GRAB
?!
AH-
FALL
OOF

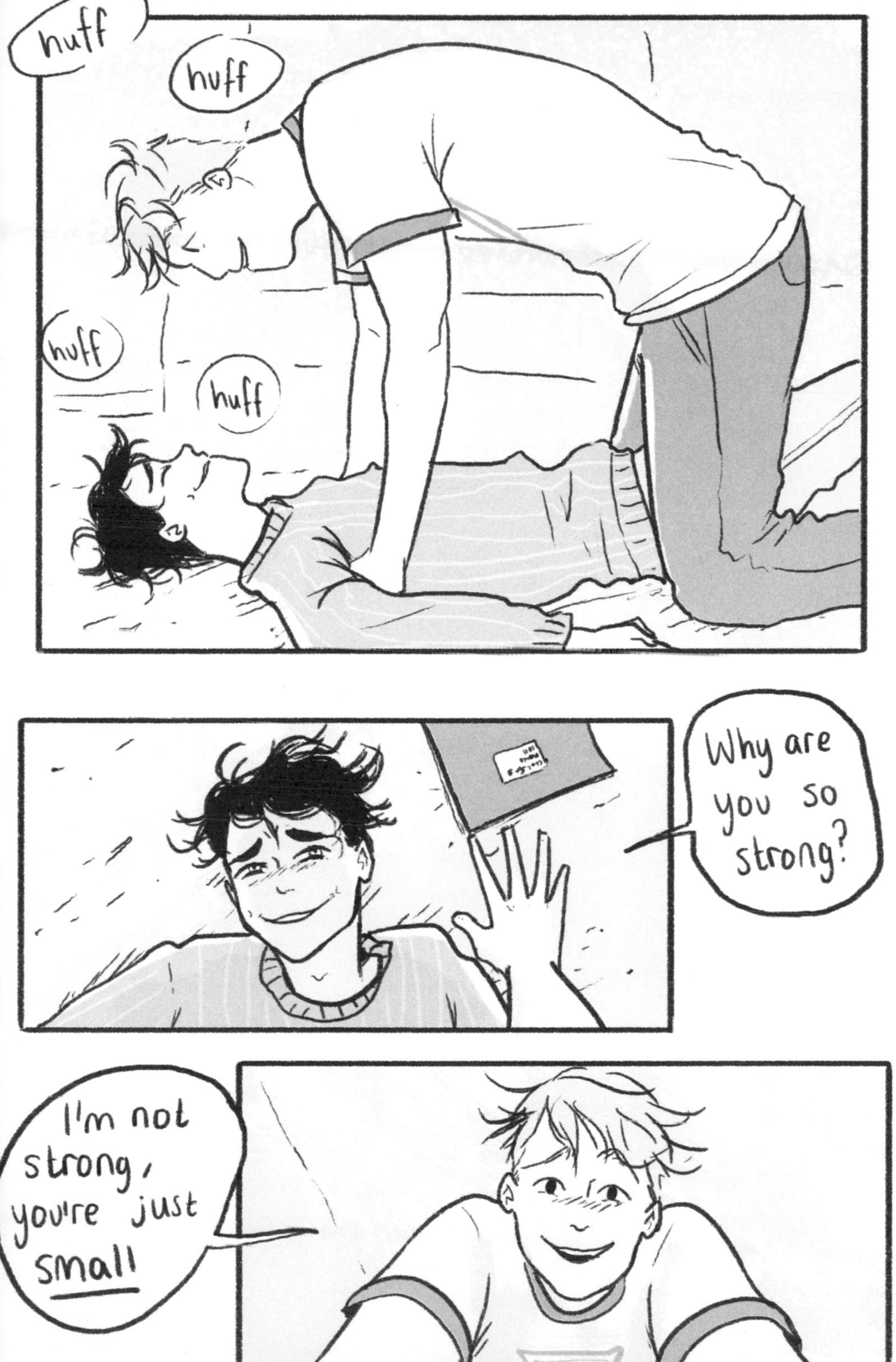
huff
huff
huff
huff
Why are you so strong?
I'm not strong, you're just small

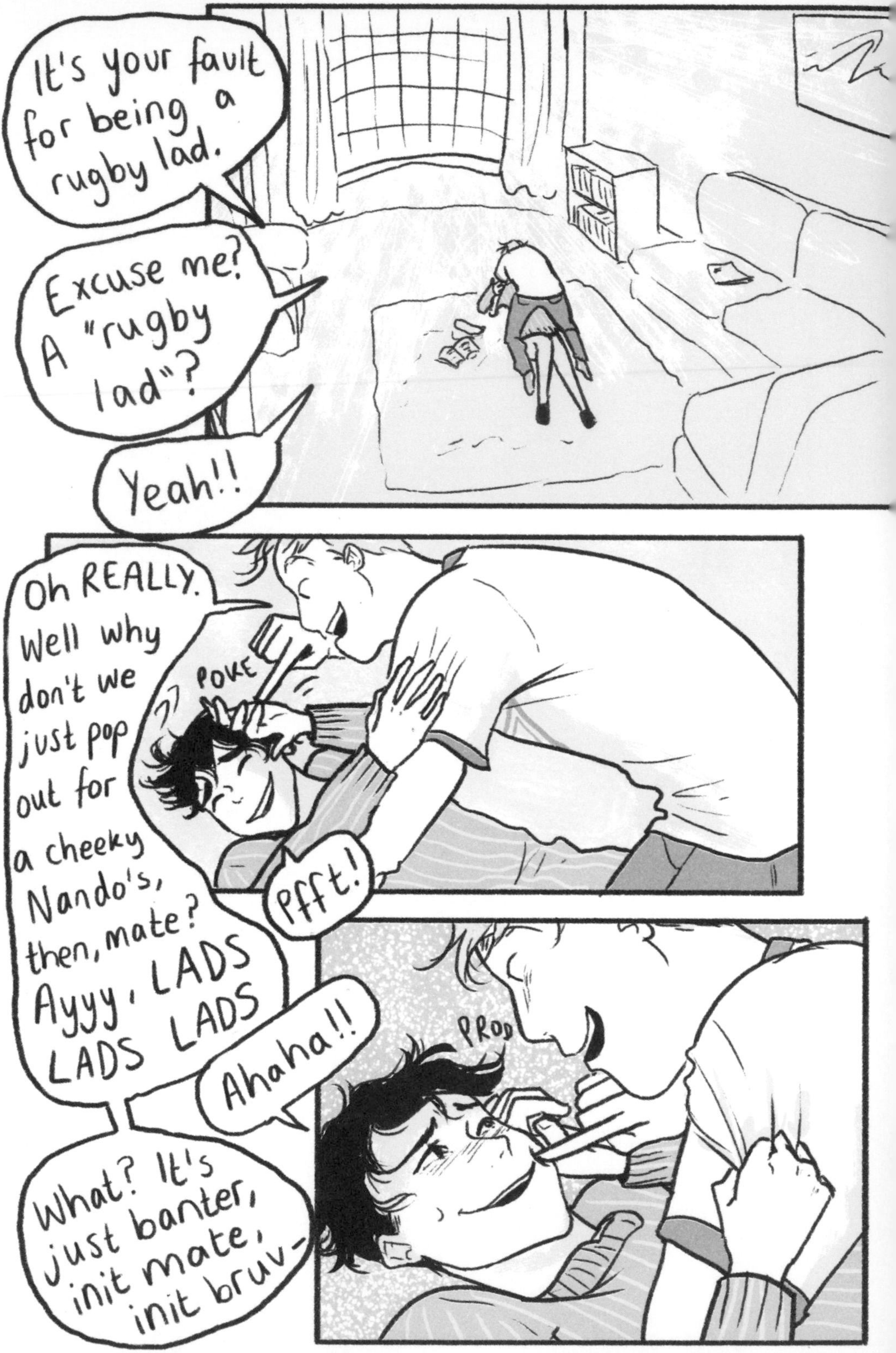
It's your fault for being a rugby lad.
Excuse me? A "rugby lad"?
Yeah!!
Oh REALLY. Well why don't we just pop out for a cheeky Nando's, then, mate? Ayyy, LADS LADS LADS
POKE
Pfft!
PROD
Ahaha!!
What? It's just banter, init mate, init bruv-

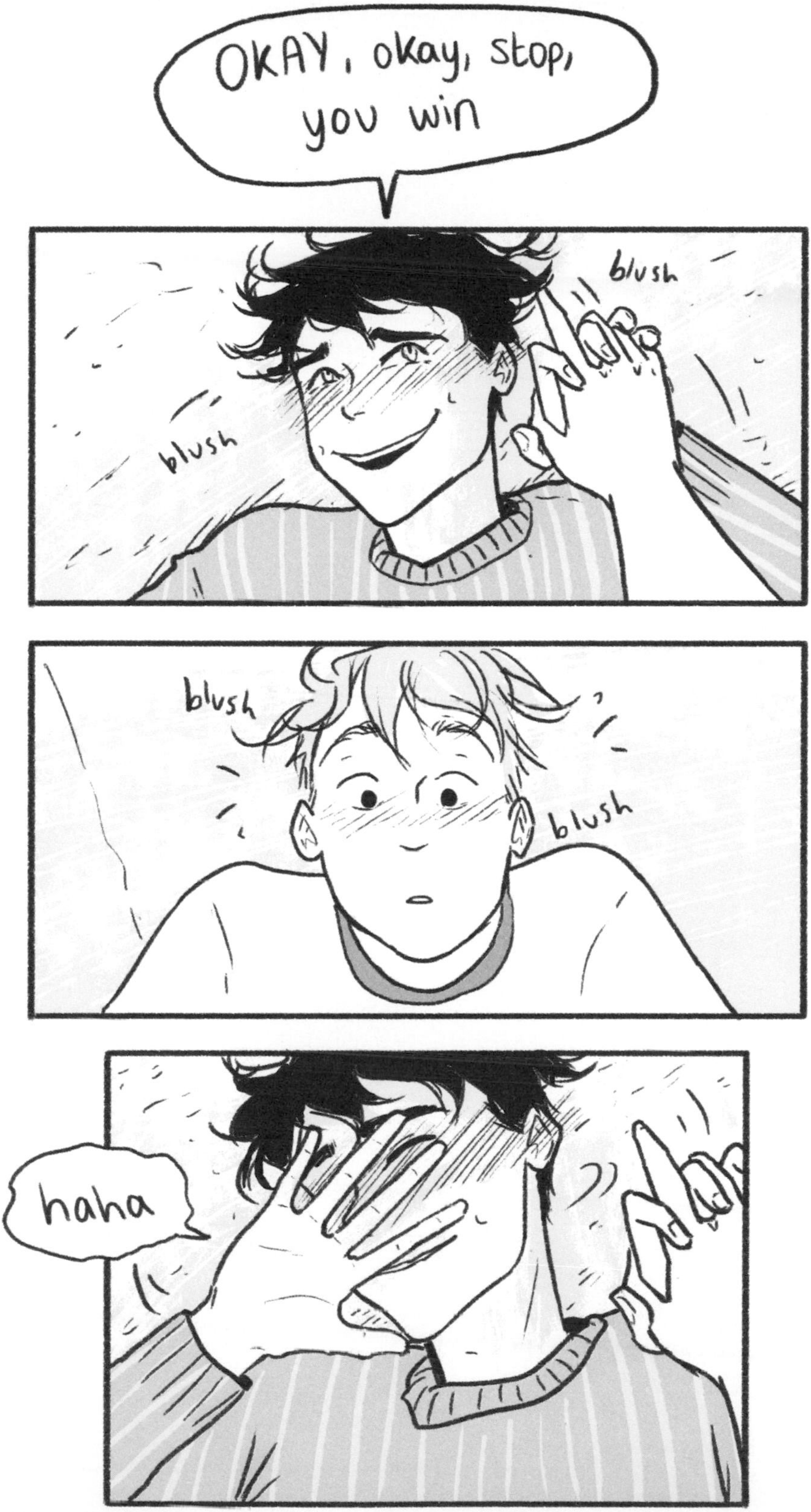
OKAY, okay, stop, you win
blush
blush
blush
blush
haha

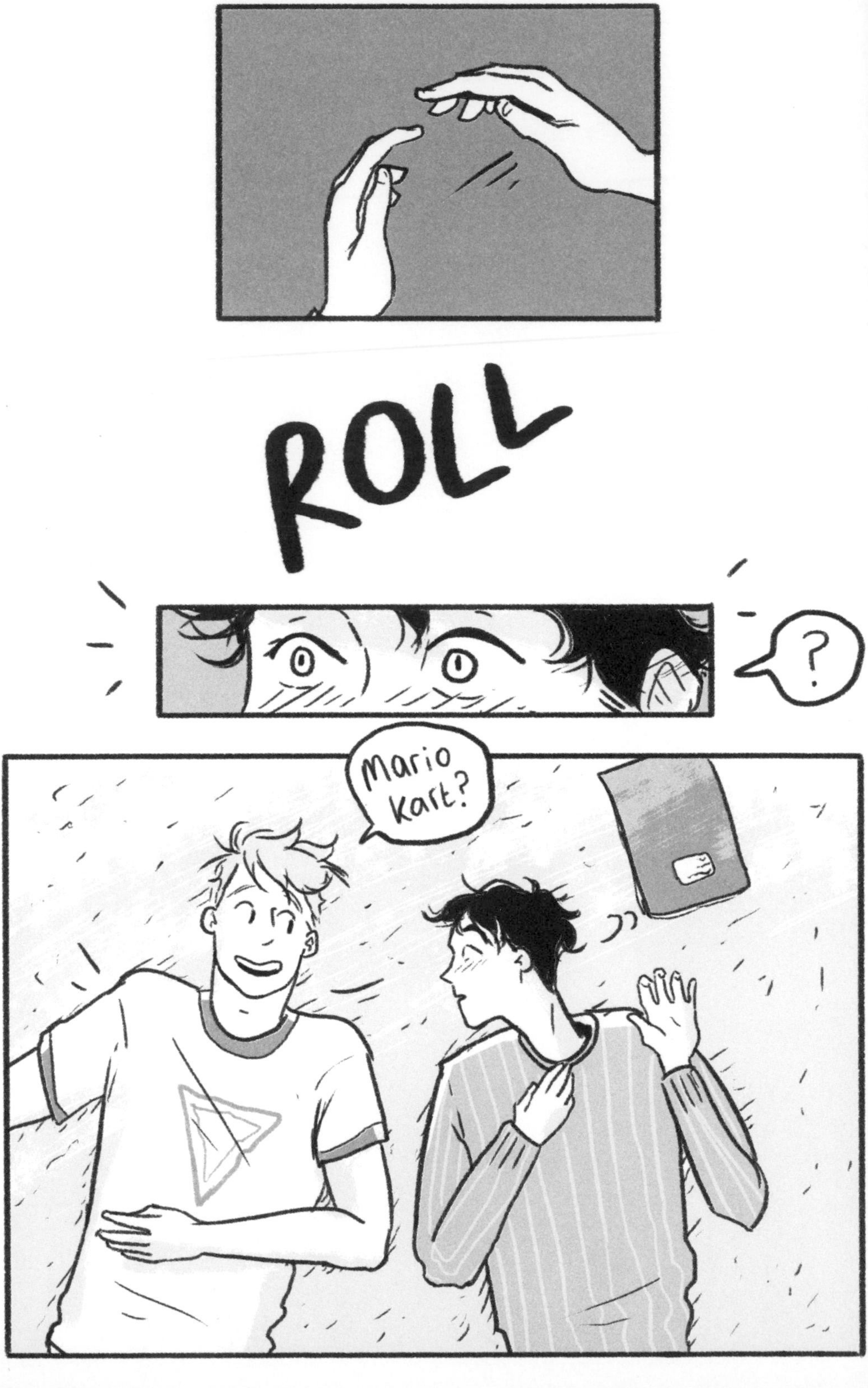
ROLL
?
Mario kart?

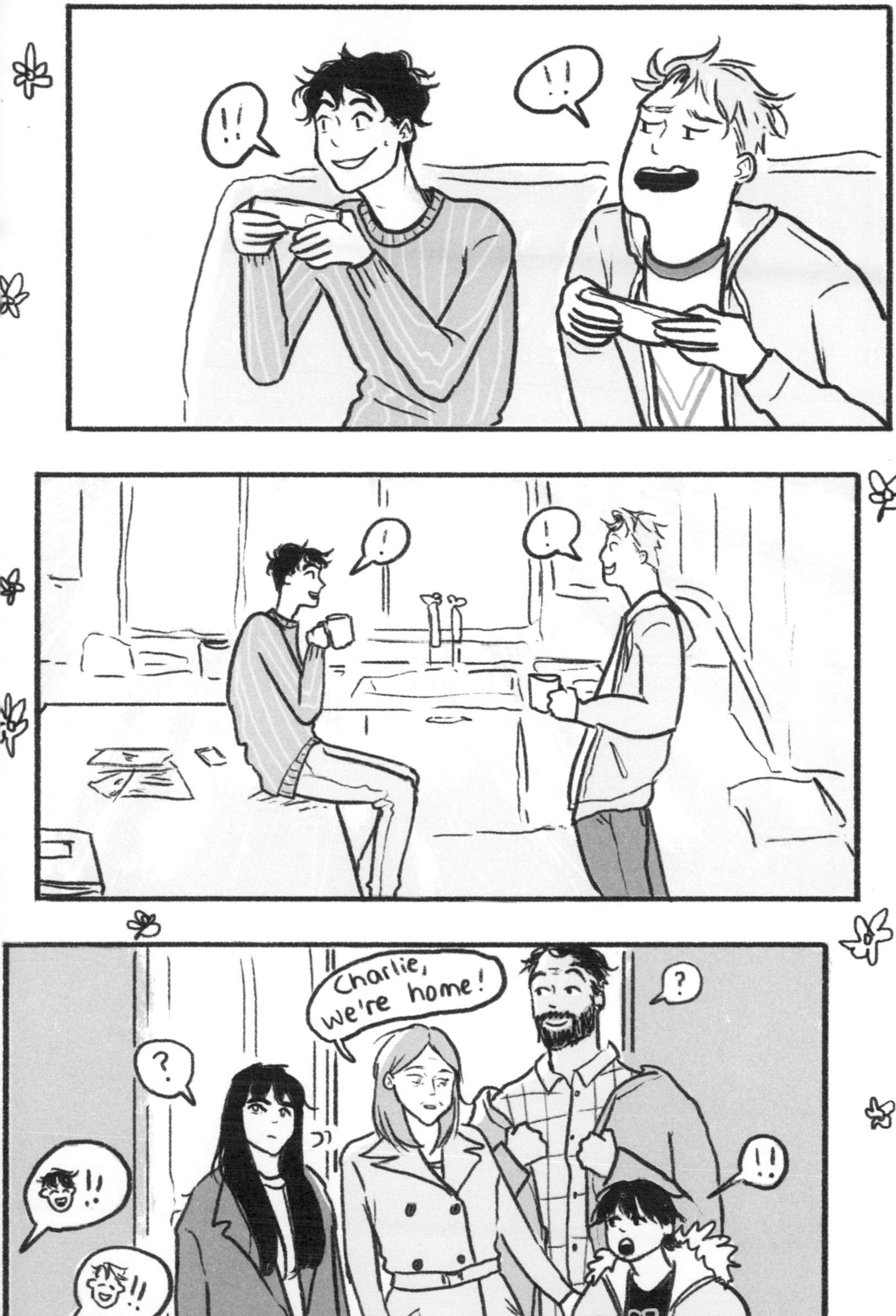
!!
!!
!
!
Charlie, we're home!
?
?
!!
!!
!!

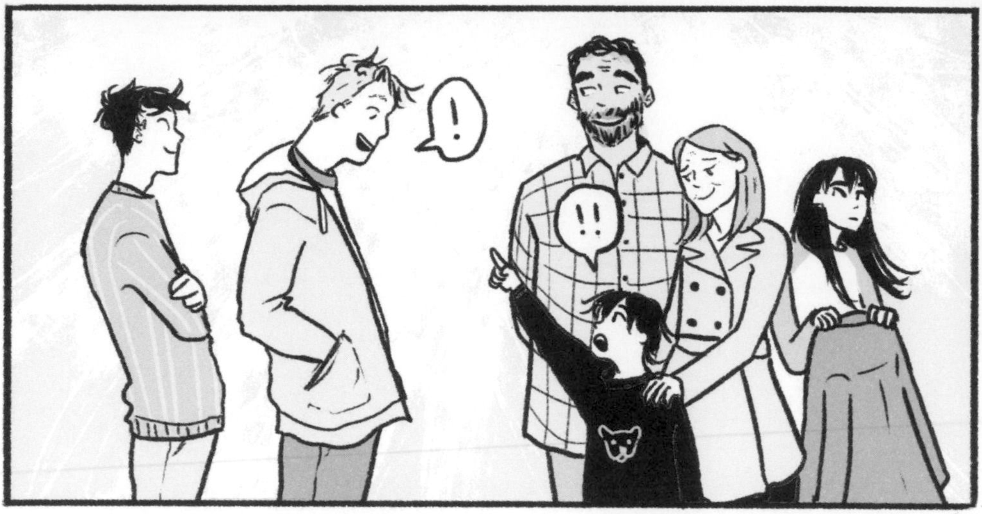
!
!!

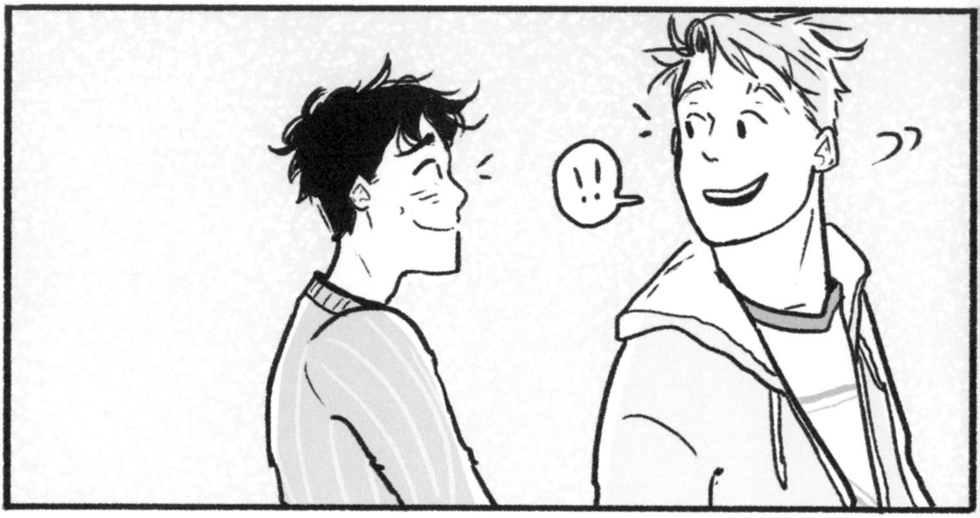
!!

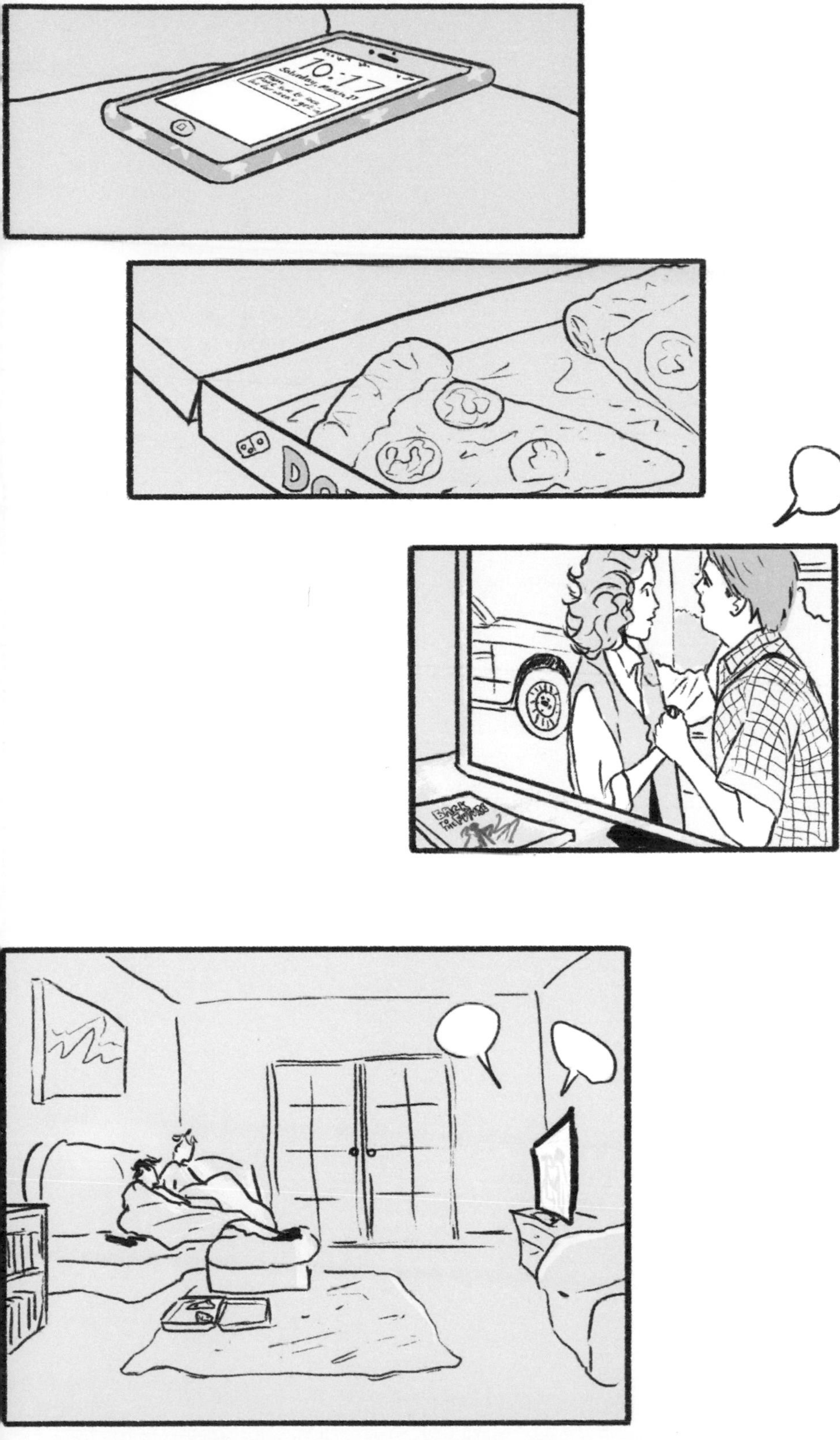
10:17
BACK TO THE FUTURE

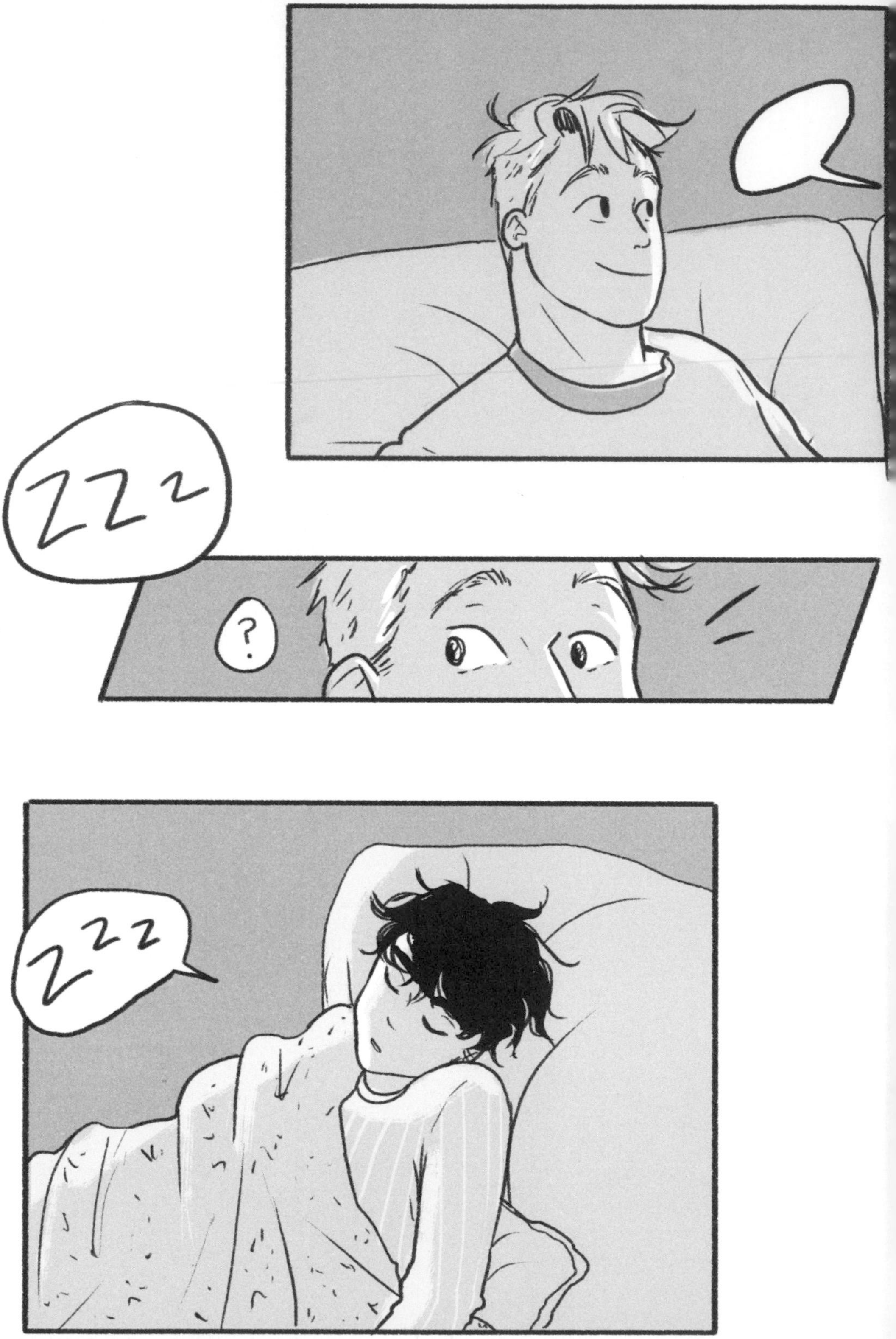
ZZZ
?
ZZZ

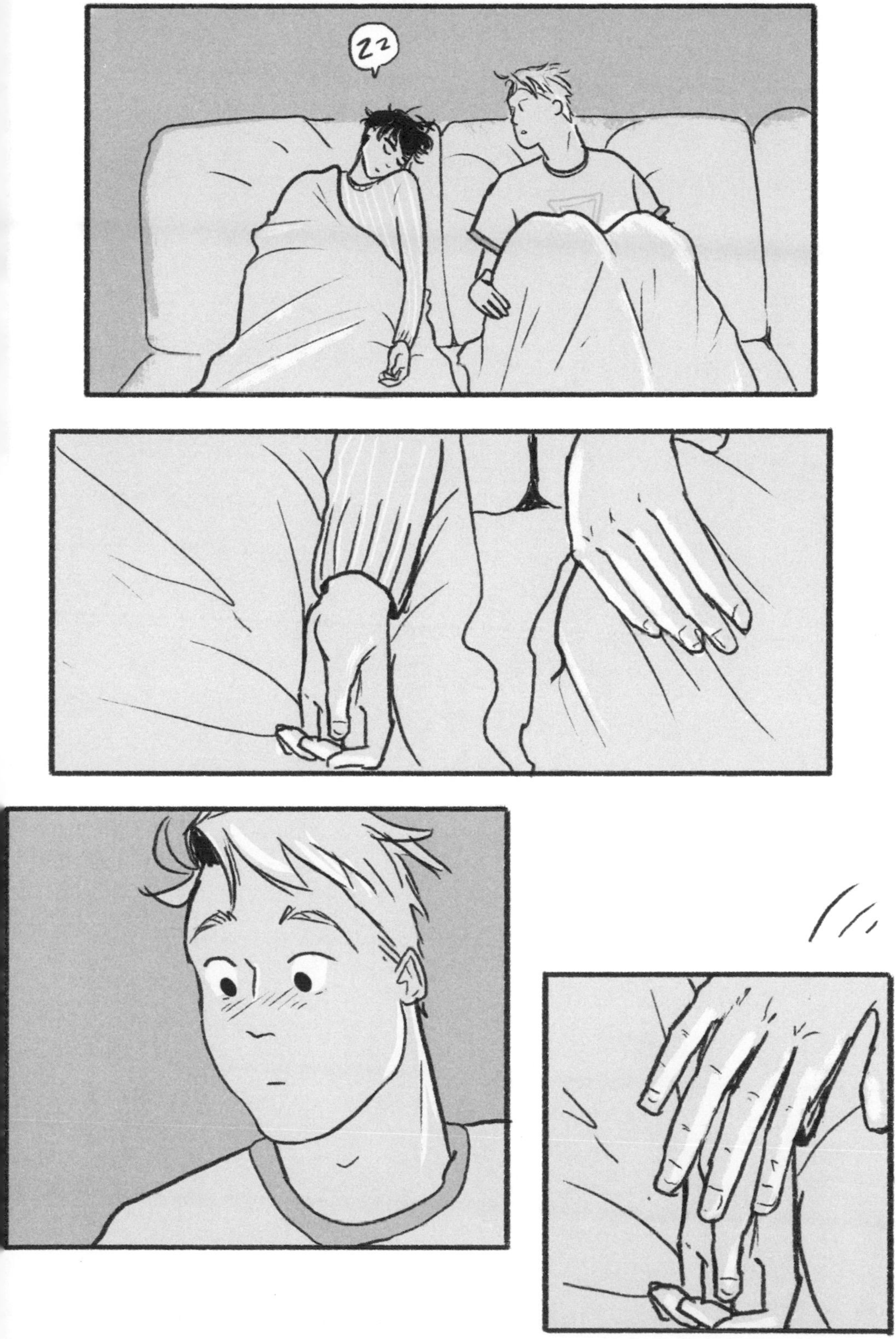
Zz

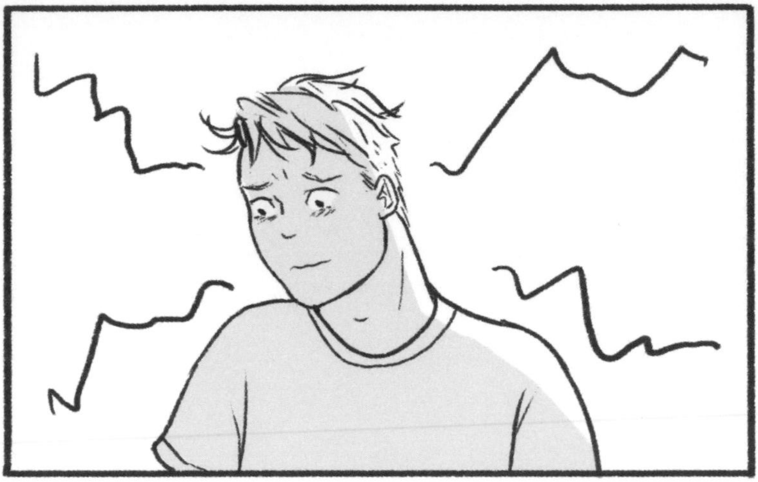

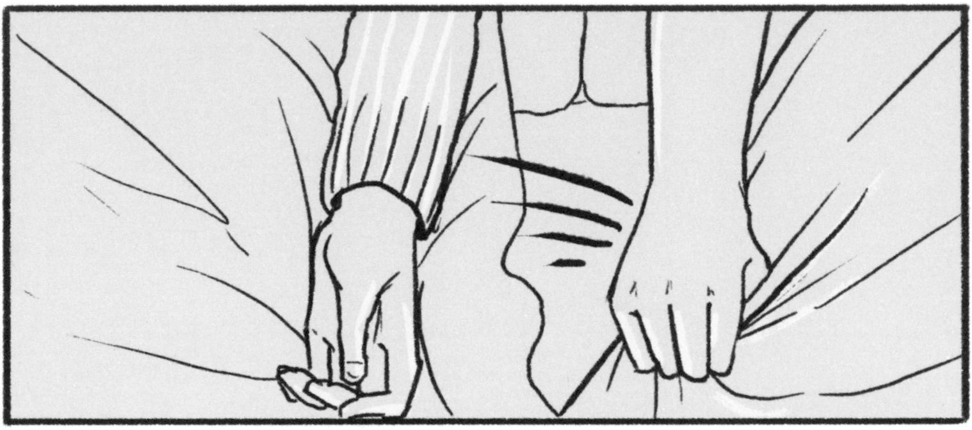

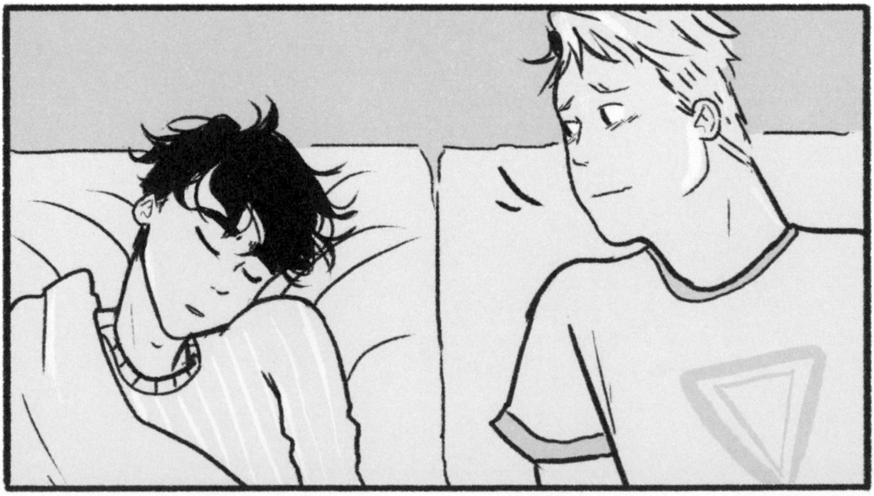

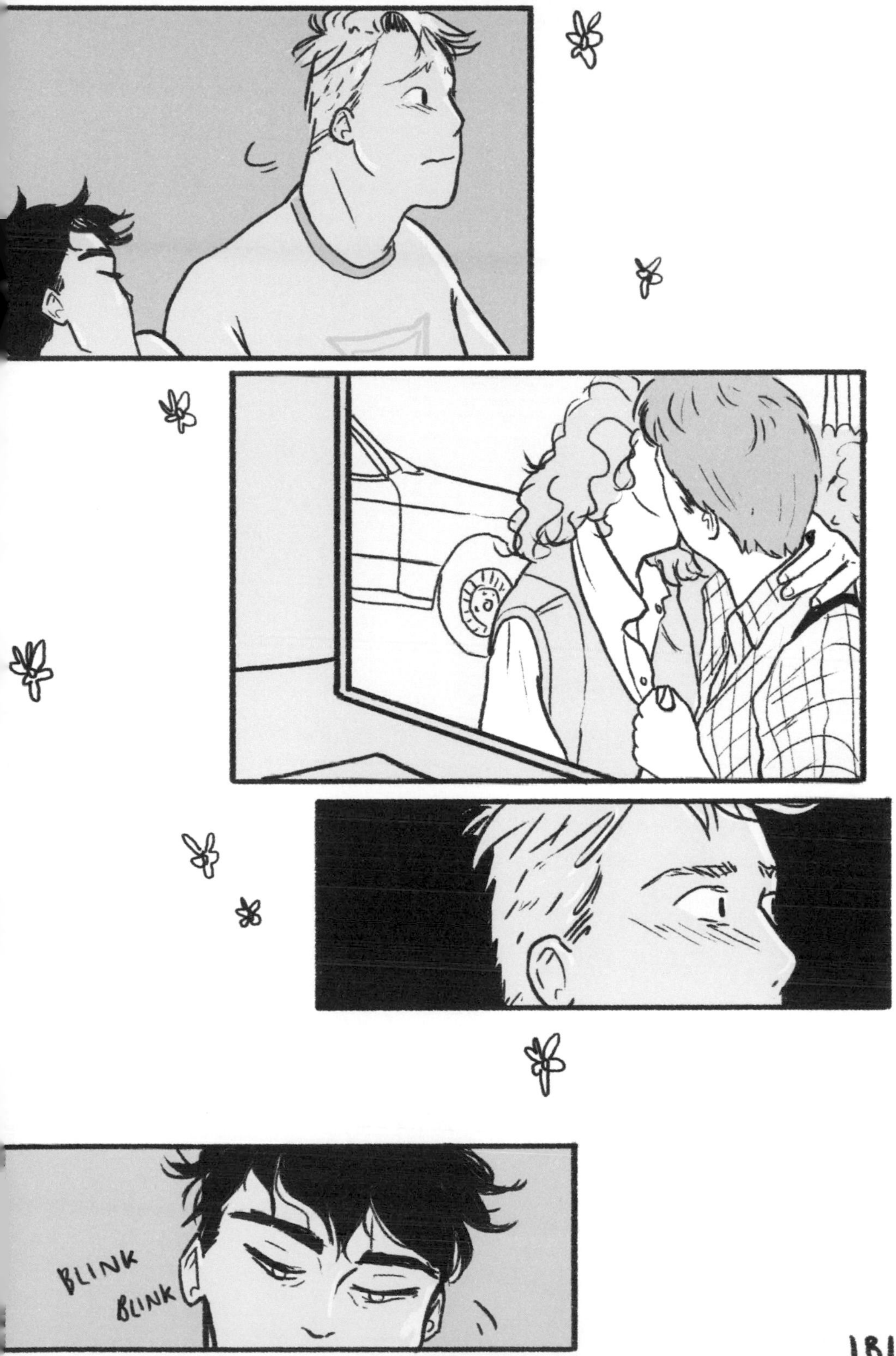
BLINK
BLINK

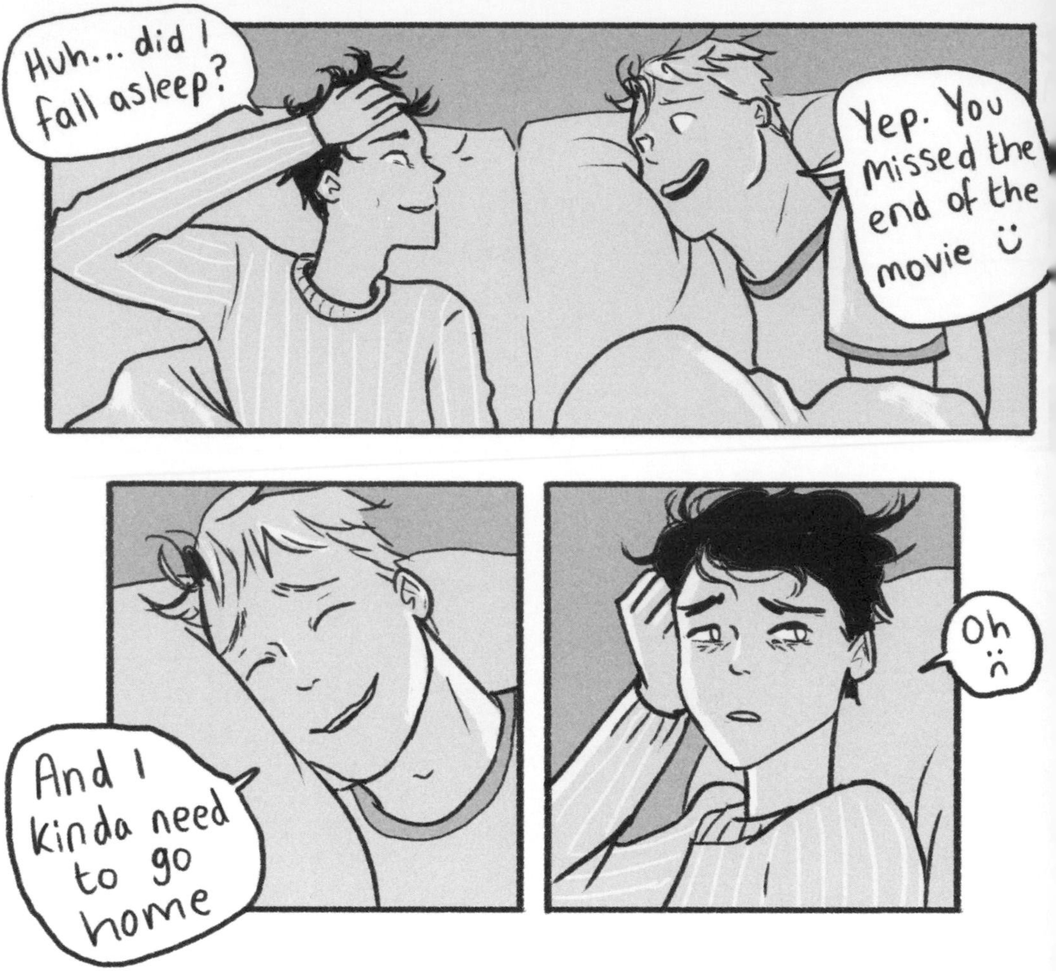
Huh... did I fall asleep?
Yep. You missed the end of the movie :)
And I kinda need to go home
Oh :(

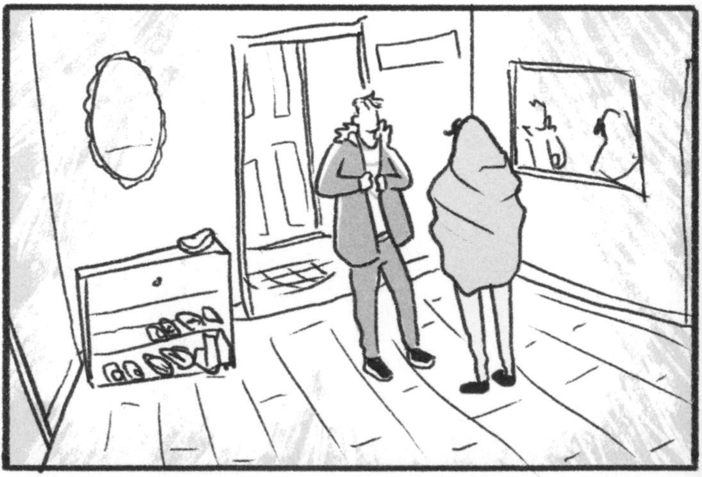

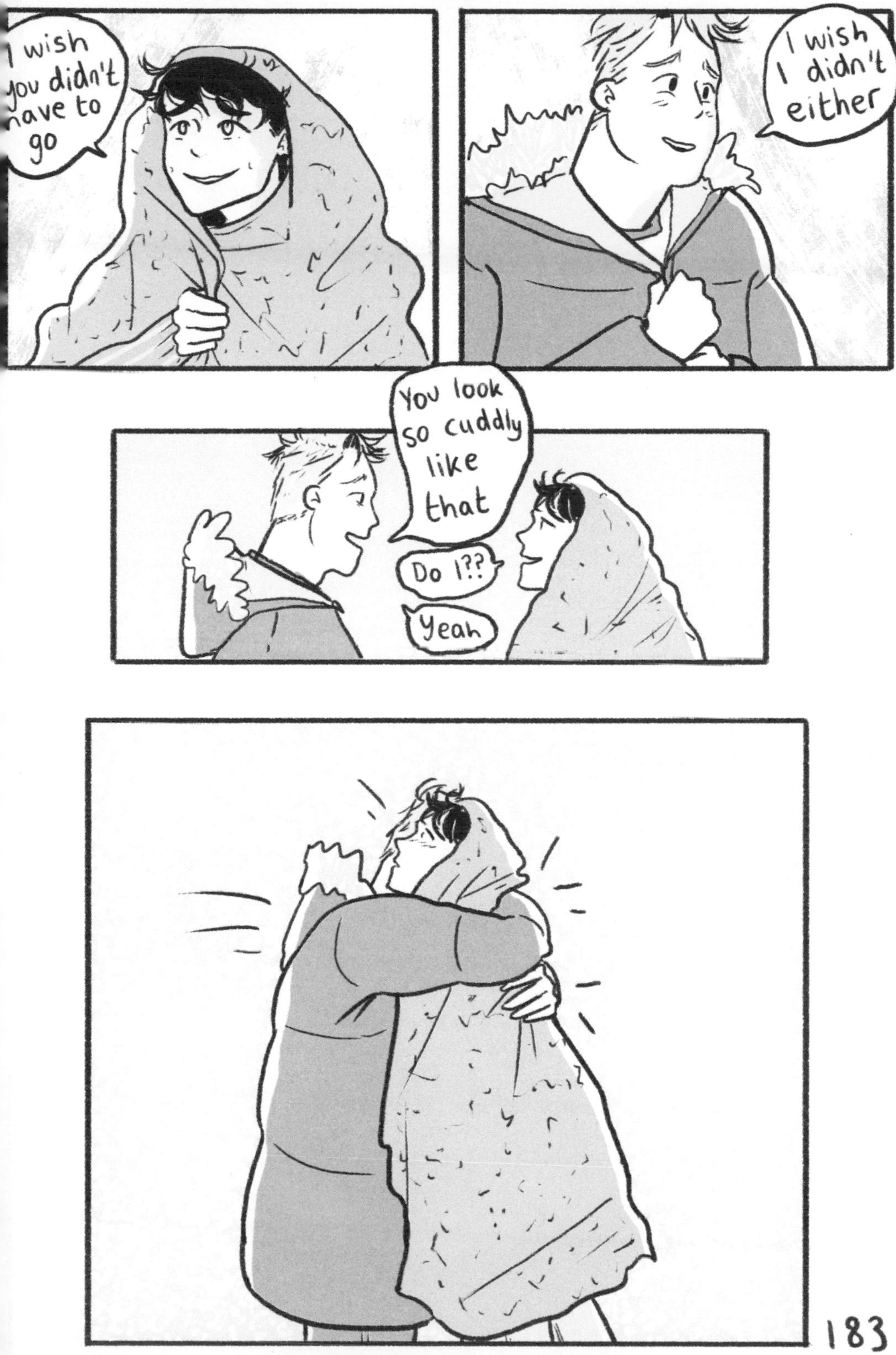
I wish you didn't have to go
I wish I didn't either
You look so cuddly like that
Do I??
Yeah

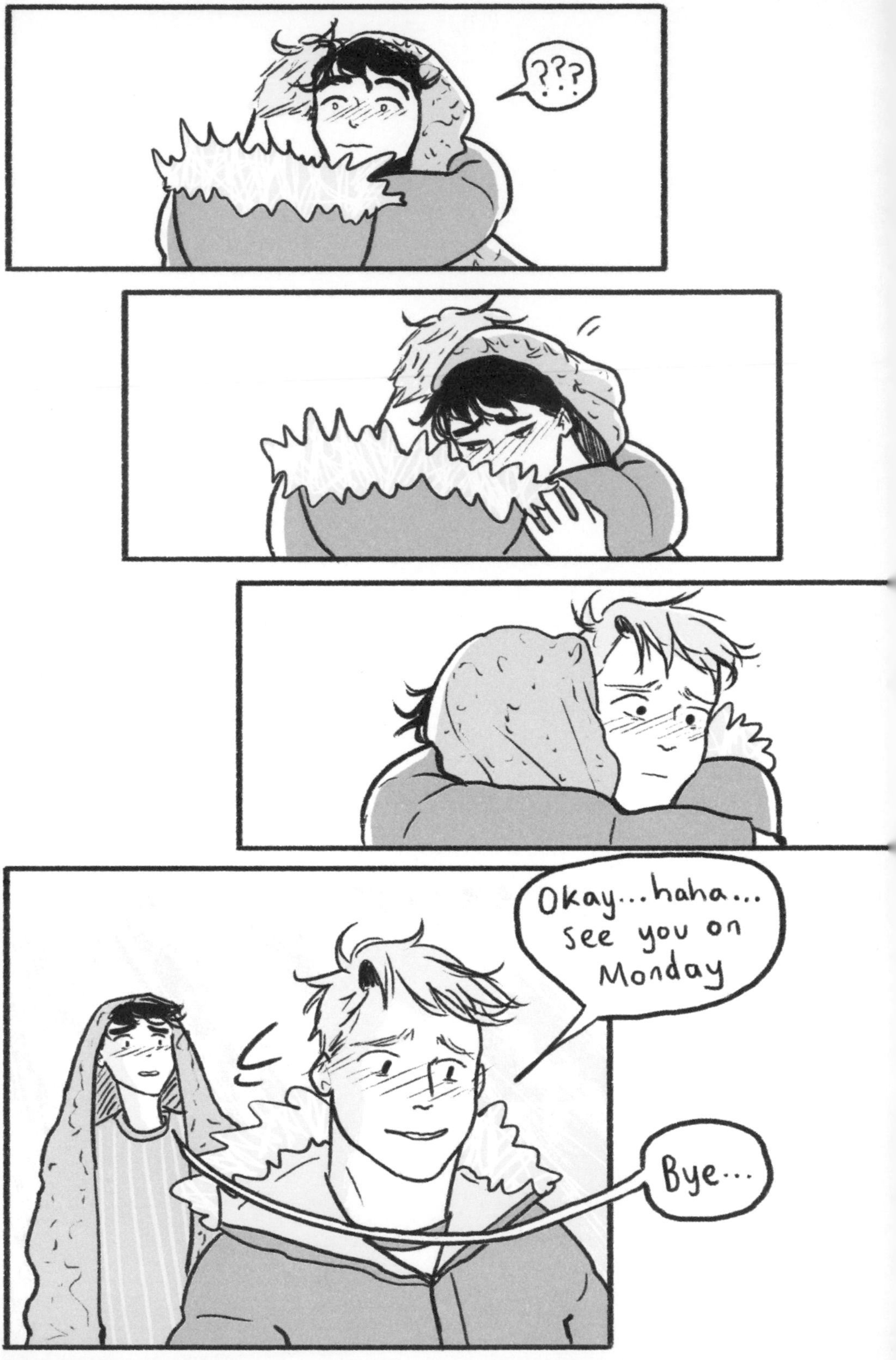
???
Okay...haha... see you on Monday
Bye...

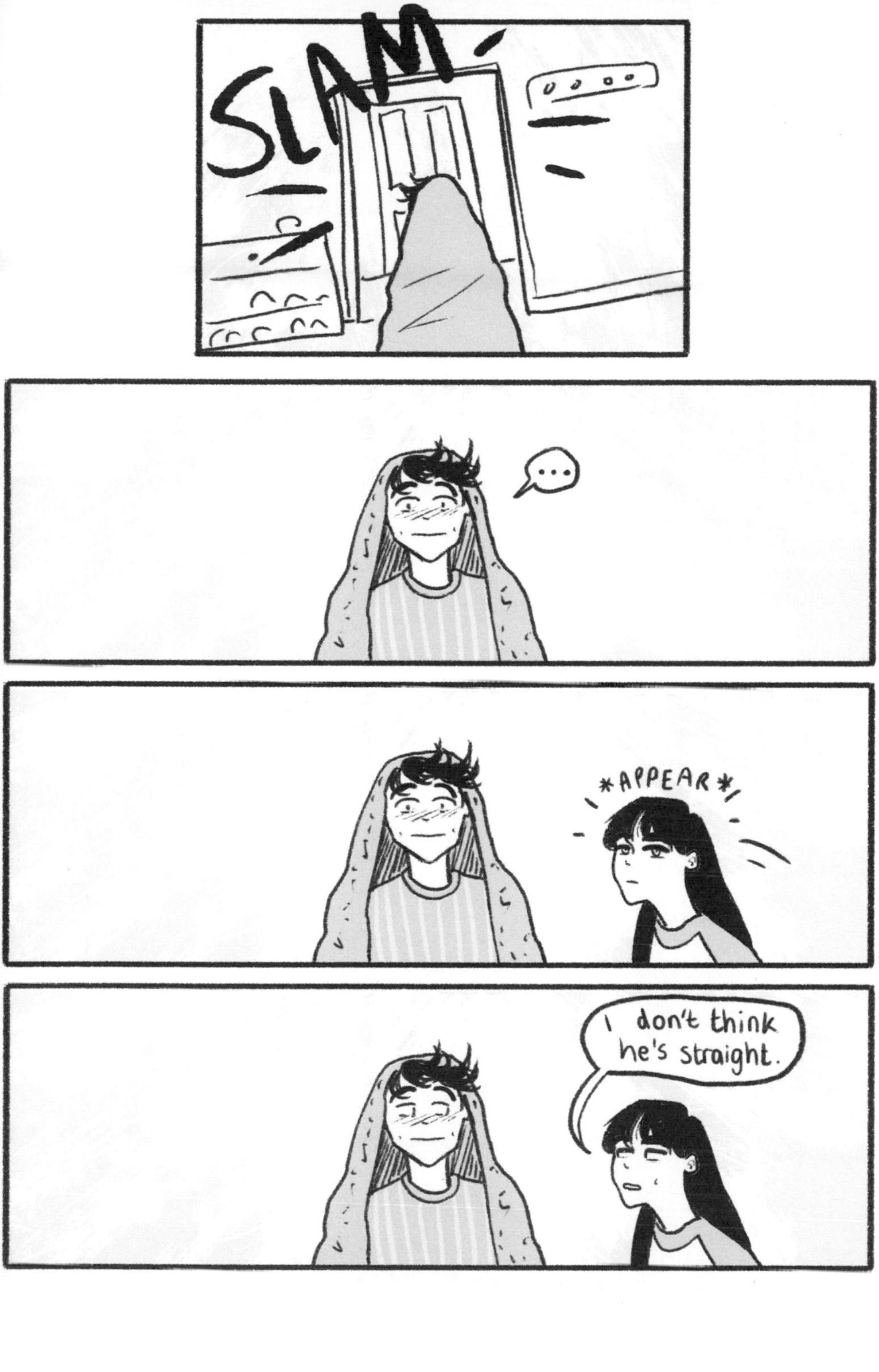
SLAM
...
APPEAR
I don't think he's straight.

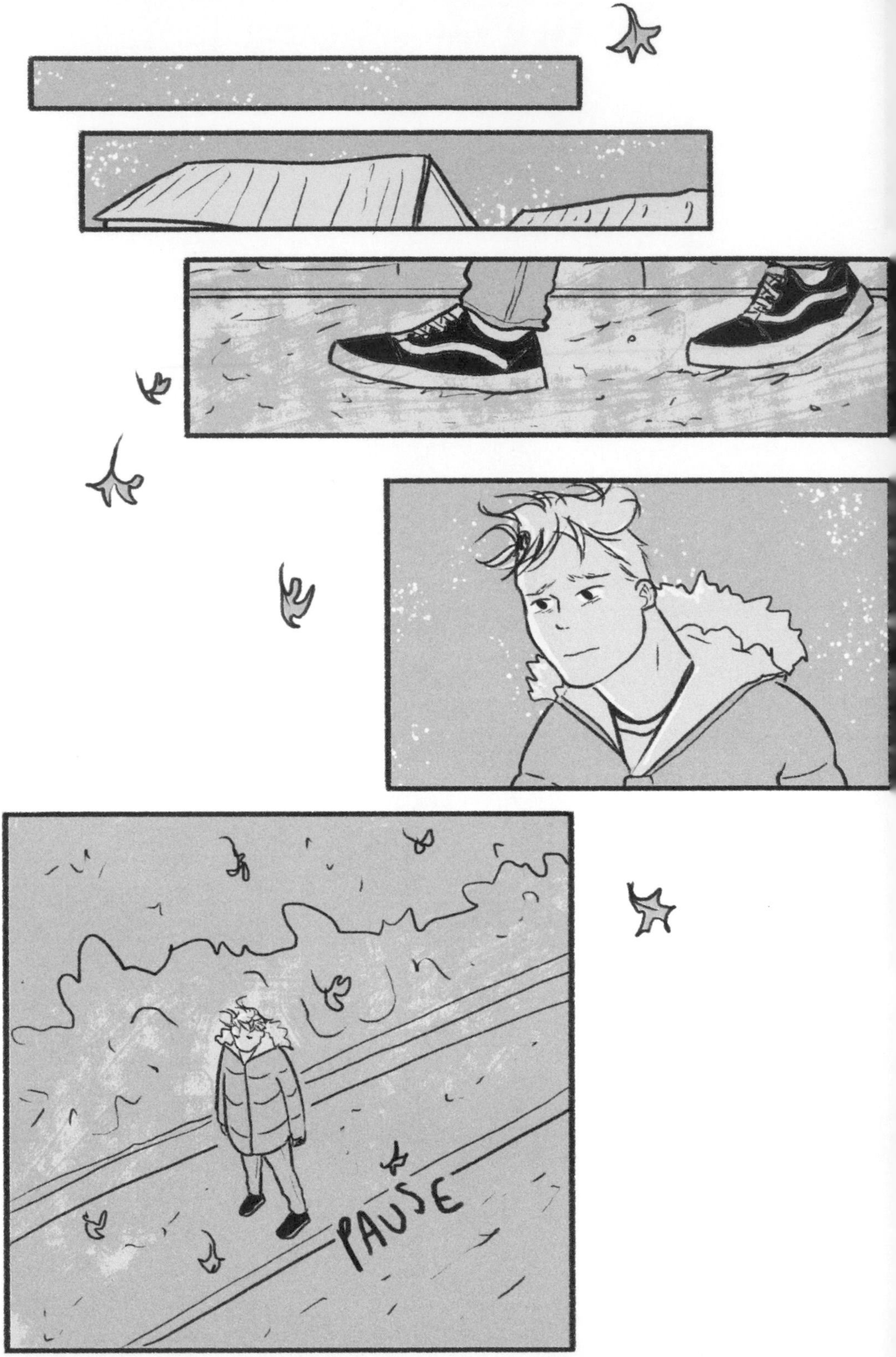
PAUSE

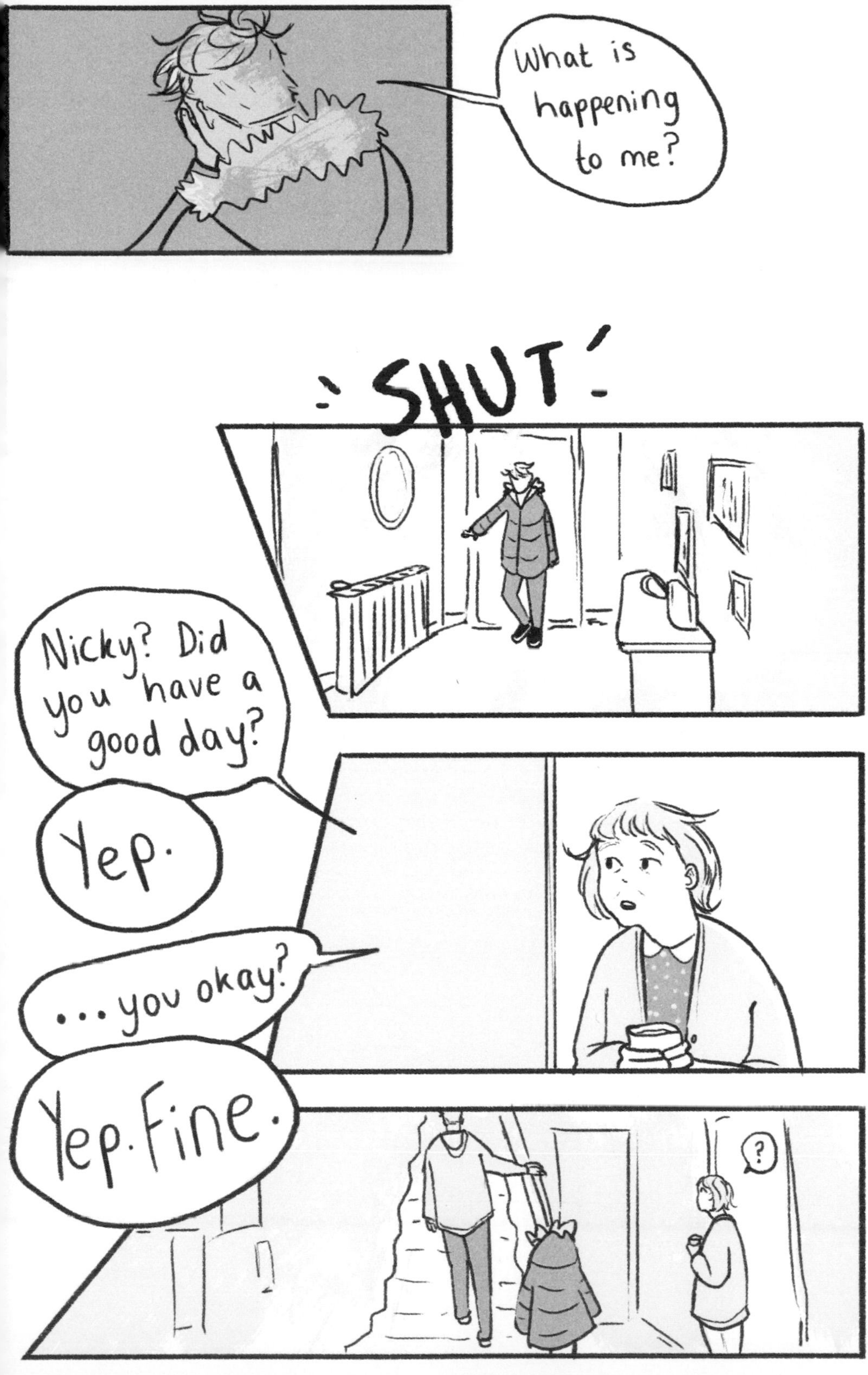
What is happening to me?
SHUT
Nicky? Did you have a good day?
Yep.
...you okay?
Yep. Fine.
?

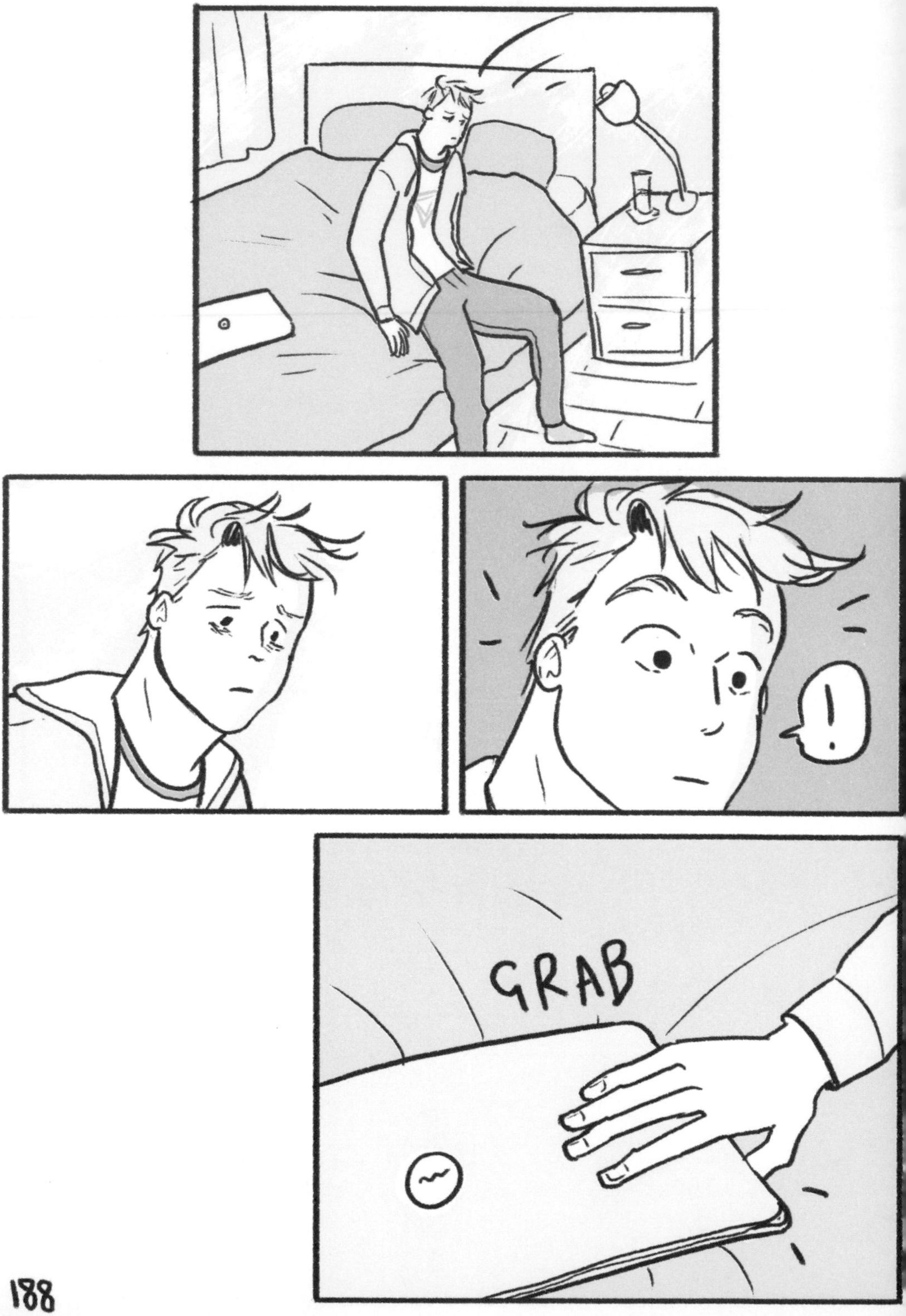
!
GRAB

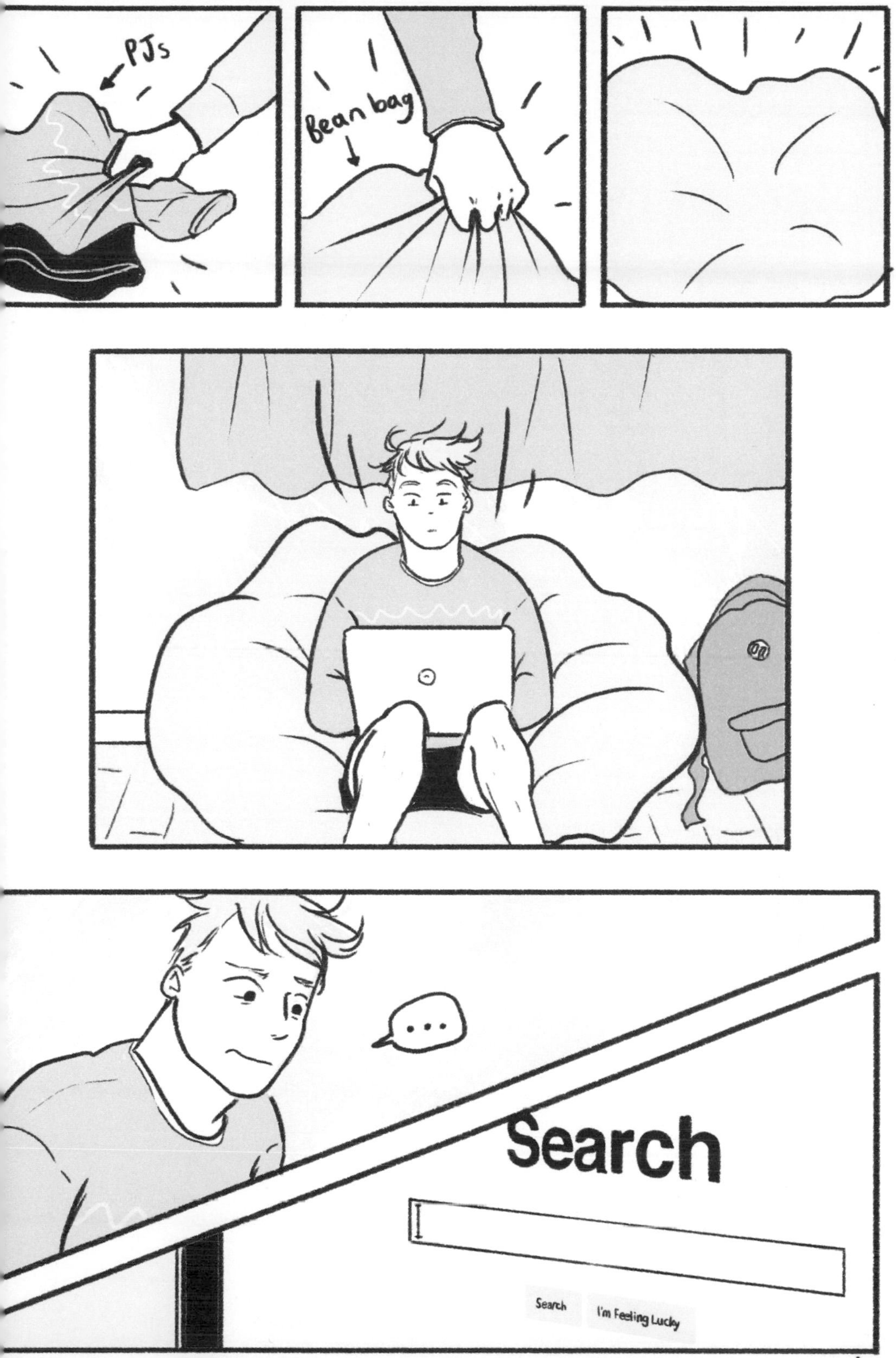
PJs
Bean bag
...
Search
Search
I'm Feeling Lucky

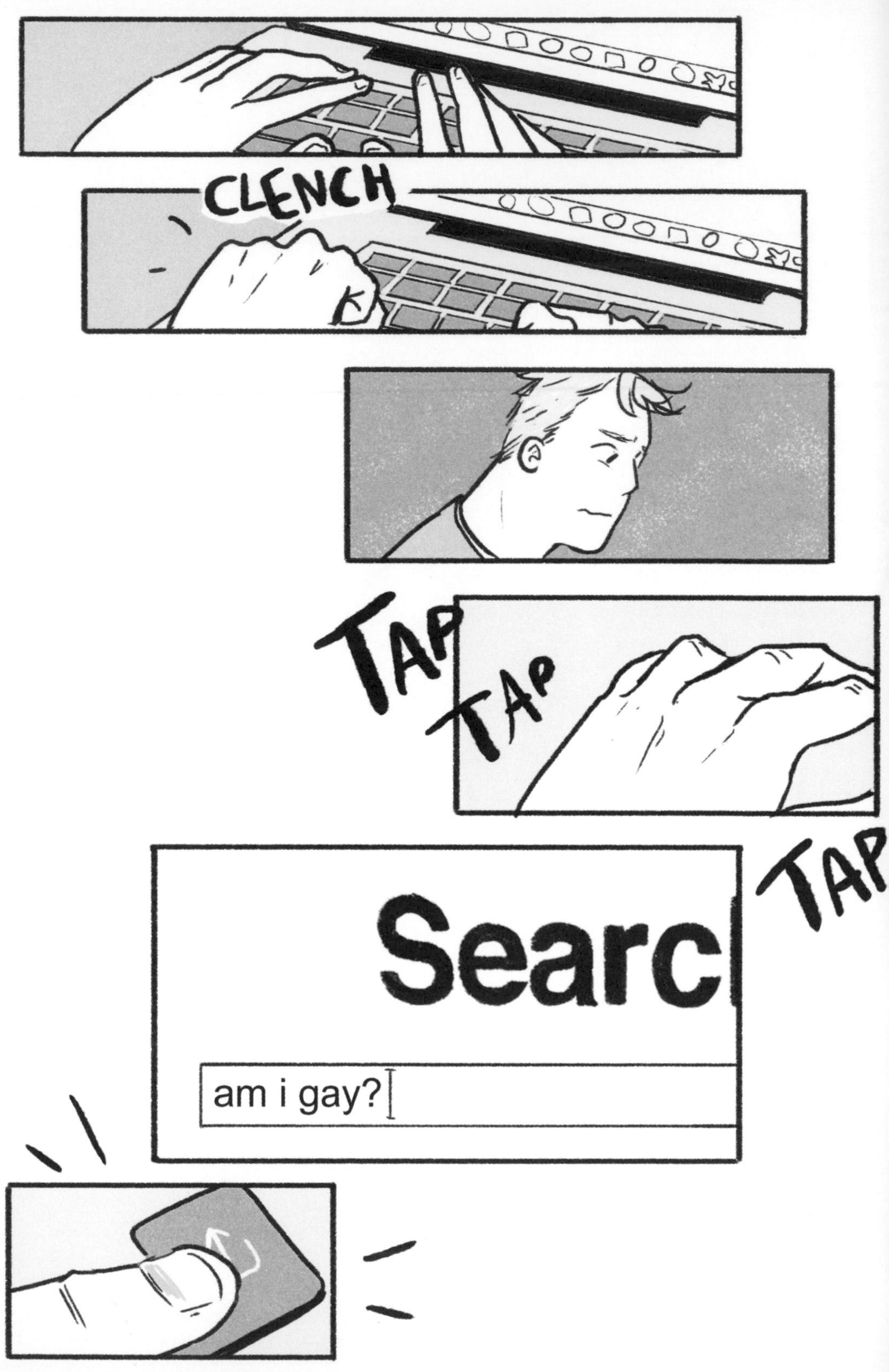
CLENCH
TAP
TAP
TAP
Searc
am i gay?

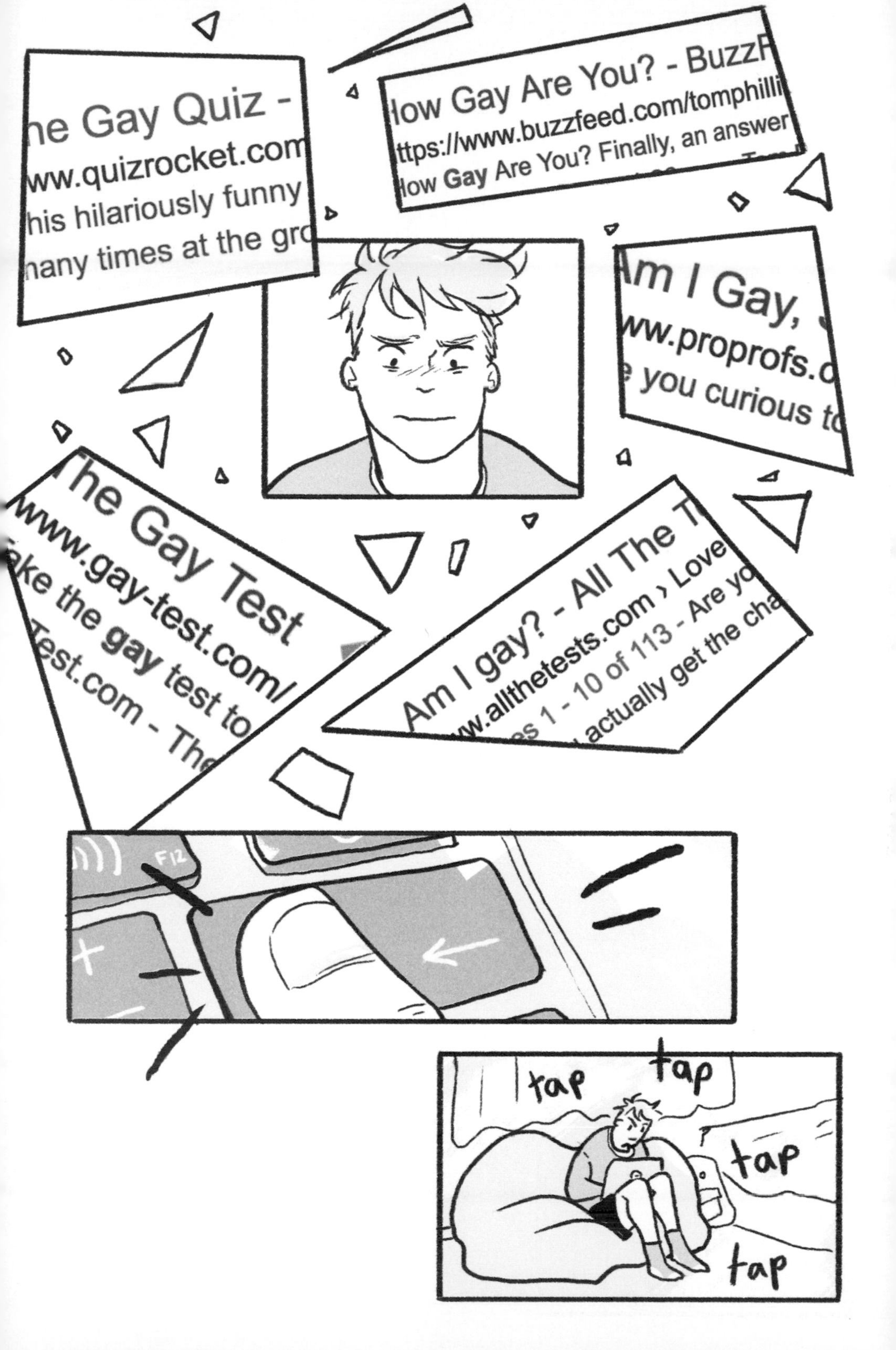

he Gay Quiz -
www.quizrocket.com
his hilariously funny
many times at the gro
How Gay Are You? - BuzzF
https://www.buzzfeed.com/tomphilli
How Gay Are You? Finally, an answer
Am I Gay,
ww.proprofs.c
e you curious to
The Gay Test
www.gay-test.com/
ake the gay test to
Test.com - The
Am I gay? - All The Te
www.allthetests.com › Love
1 - 10 of 113 - Are yo
actually get the cha
tap
tap
tap
tap

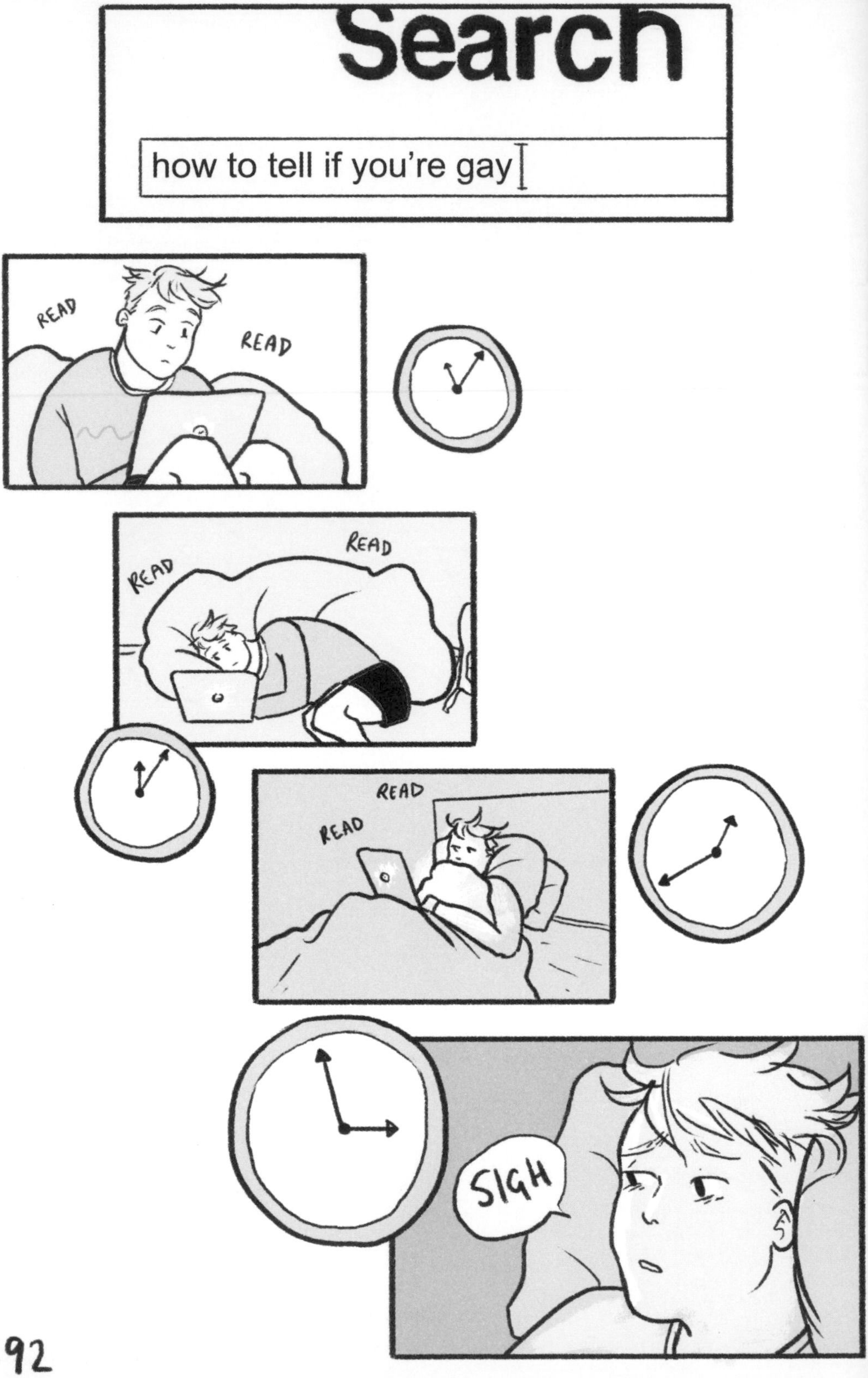
Search
how to tell if you're gay
READ
READ
READ
READ
READ
READ
SIGH

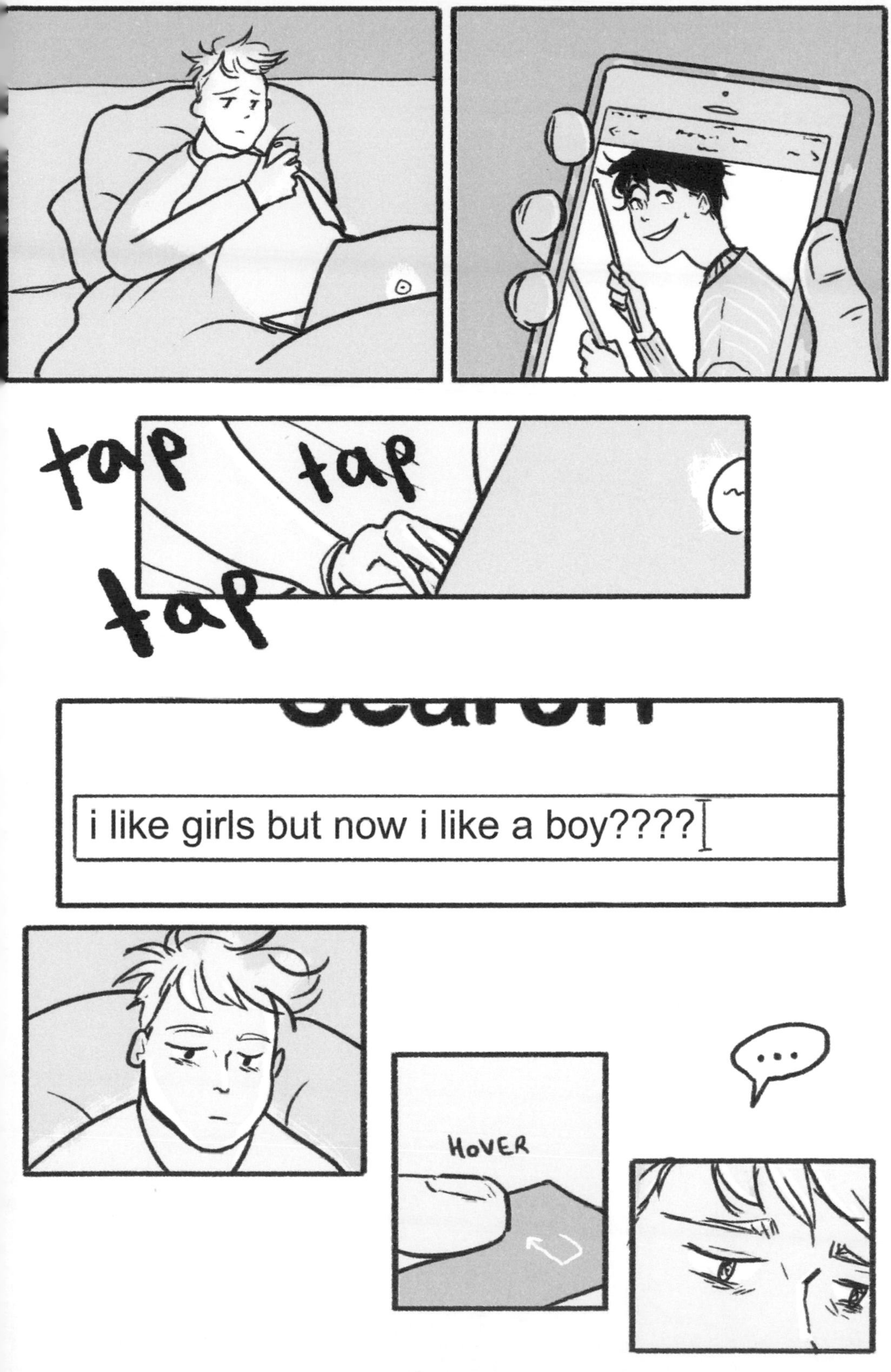
tap
tap
tap
i like girls but now i like a boy????
HOVER
...

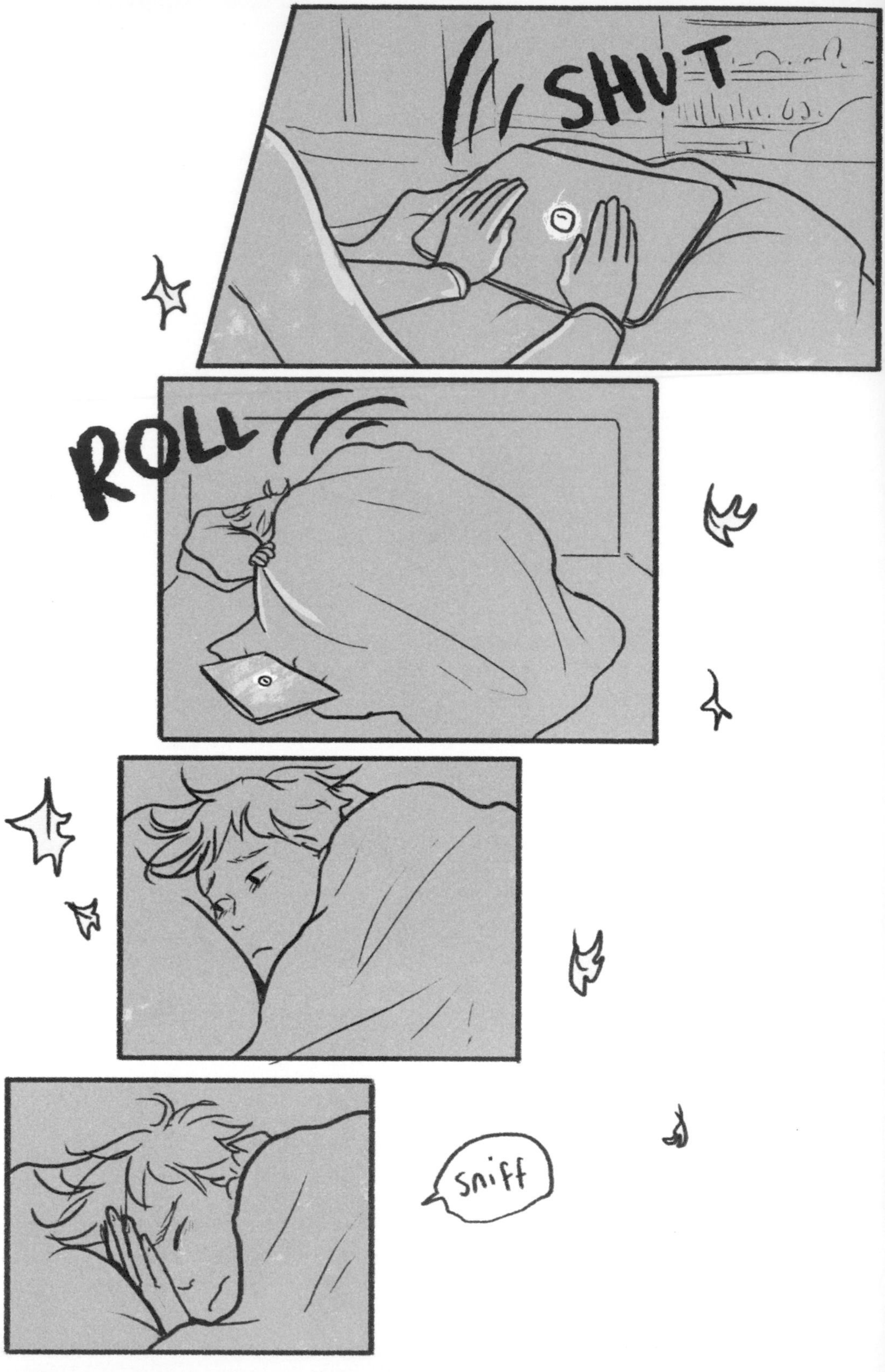
SHUT
ROLL
sniff

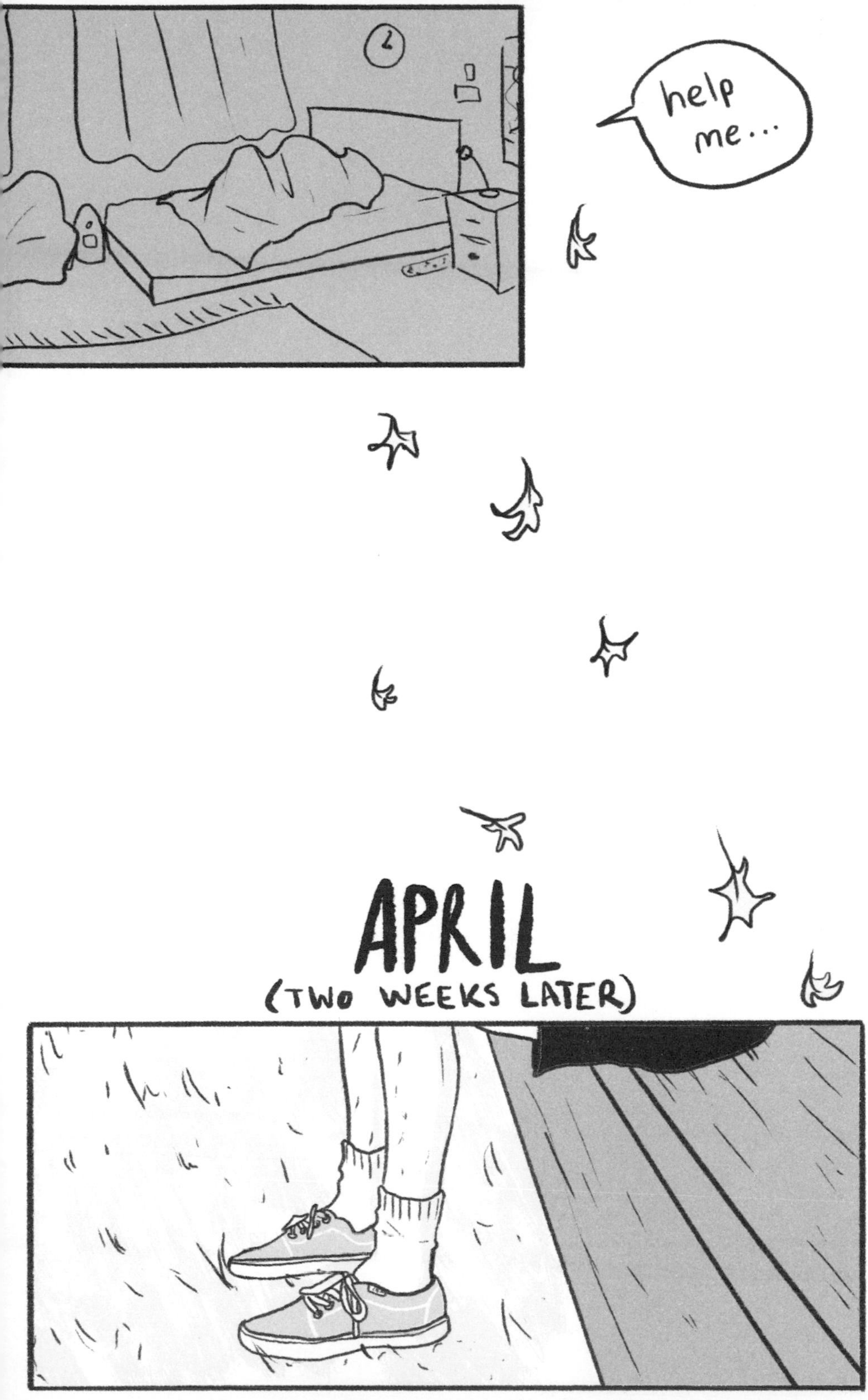
help me...
APRIL
(TWO WEEKS LATER)

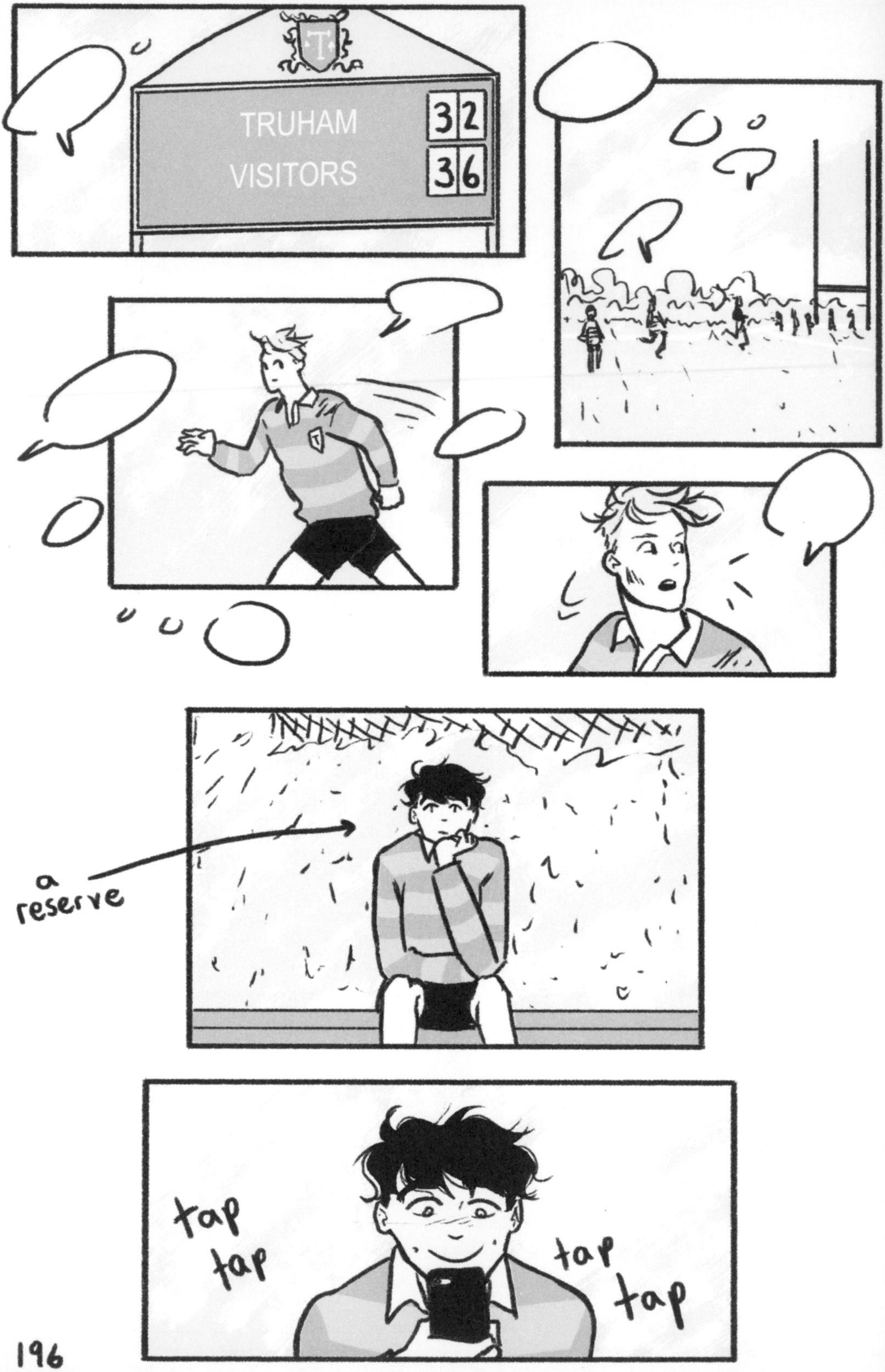
TRUHAM
32
VISITORS
36
a reserve
tap
tap
tap
tap

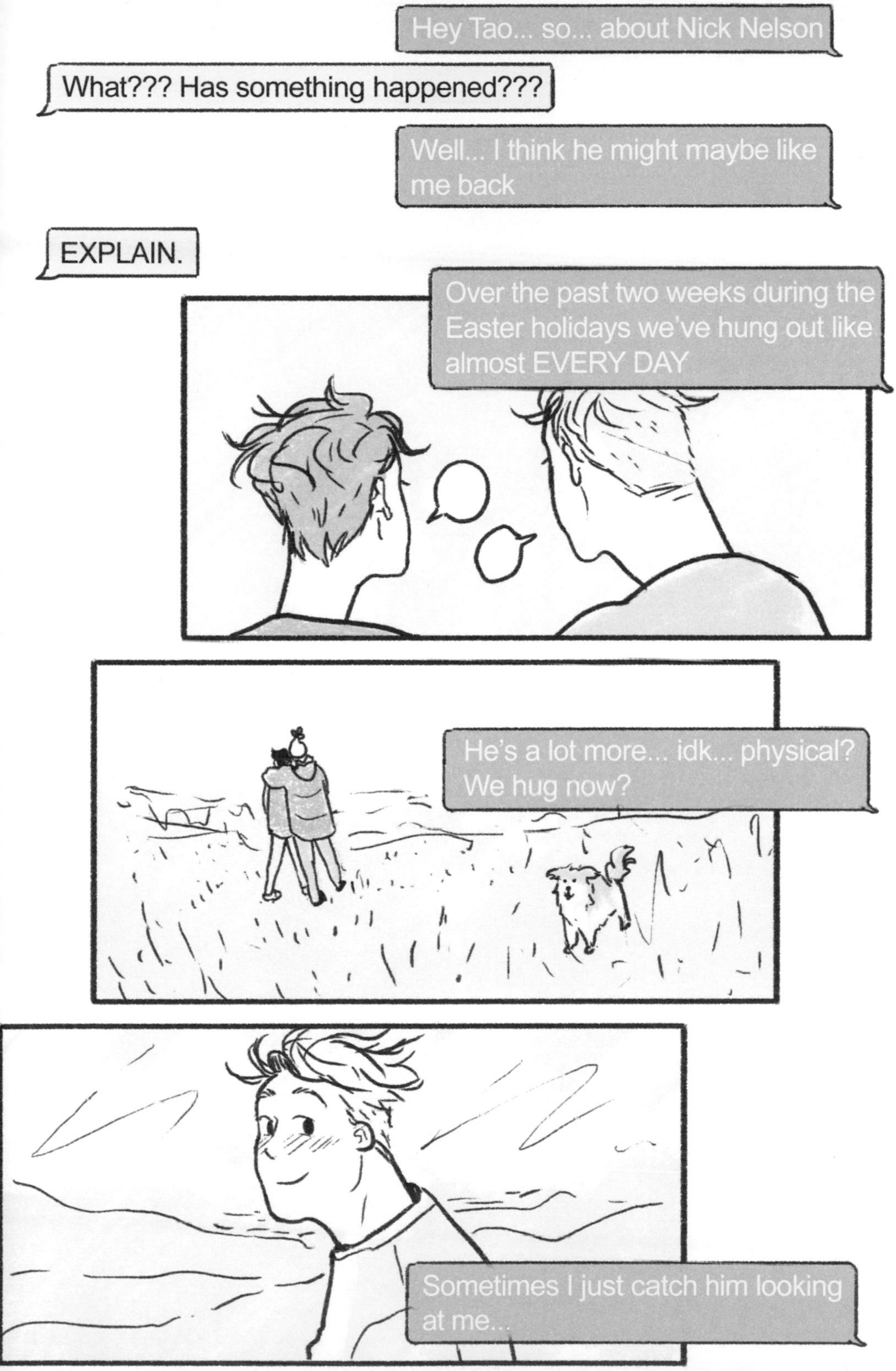
Hey Tao... so... about Nick Nelson
What??? Has something happened???
Well... I think he might maybe like me back
EXPLAIN.
Over the past two weeks during the Easter holidays we've hung out like almost EVERY DAY
He's a lot more... idk... physical? We hug now?
Sometimes I just catch him looking at me...

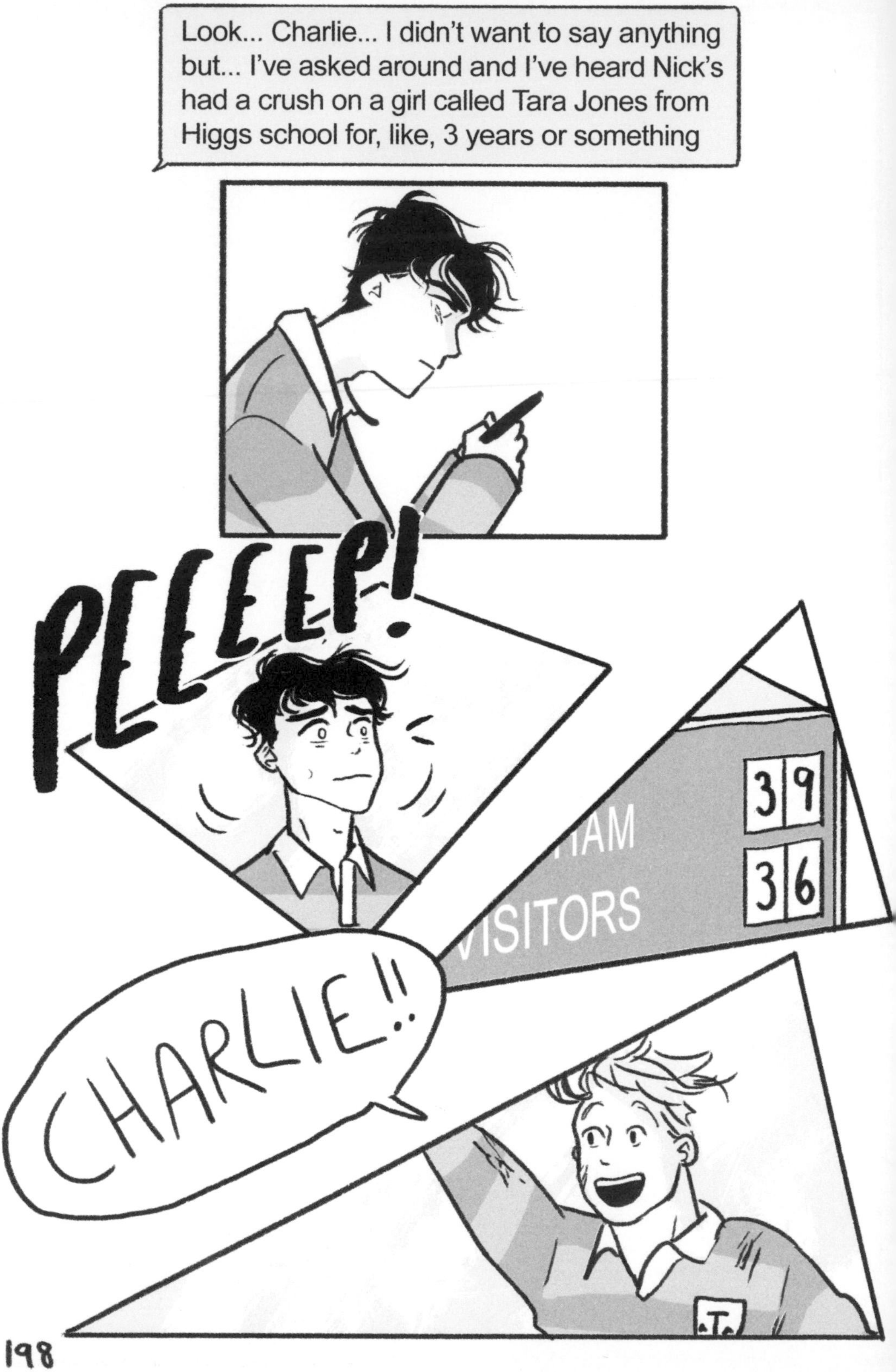
Look... Charlie... I didn't want to say anything but... I've asked around and I've heard Nick's had a crush on a girl called Tara Jones from Higgs school for, like, 3 years or something
PEEEEP!
HAM
VISITORS
39
36
CHARLIE!!

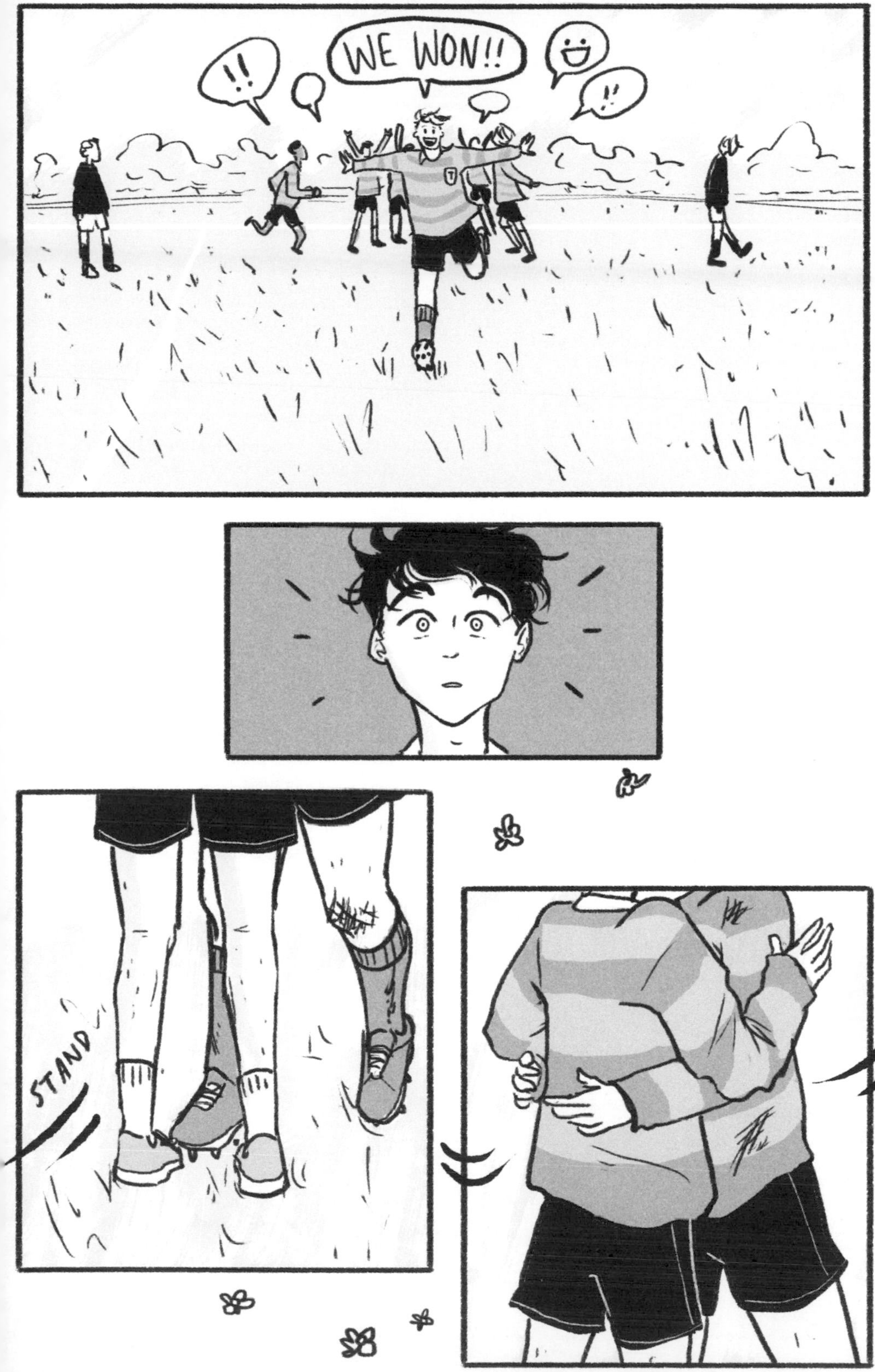

!!
WE WON!!
!!
STAND

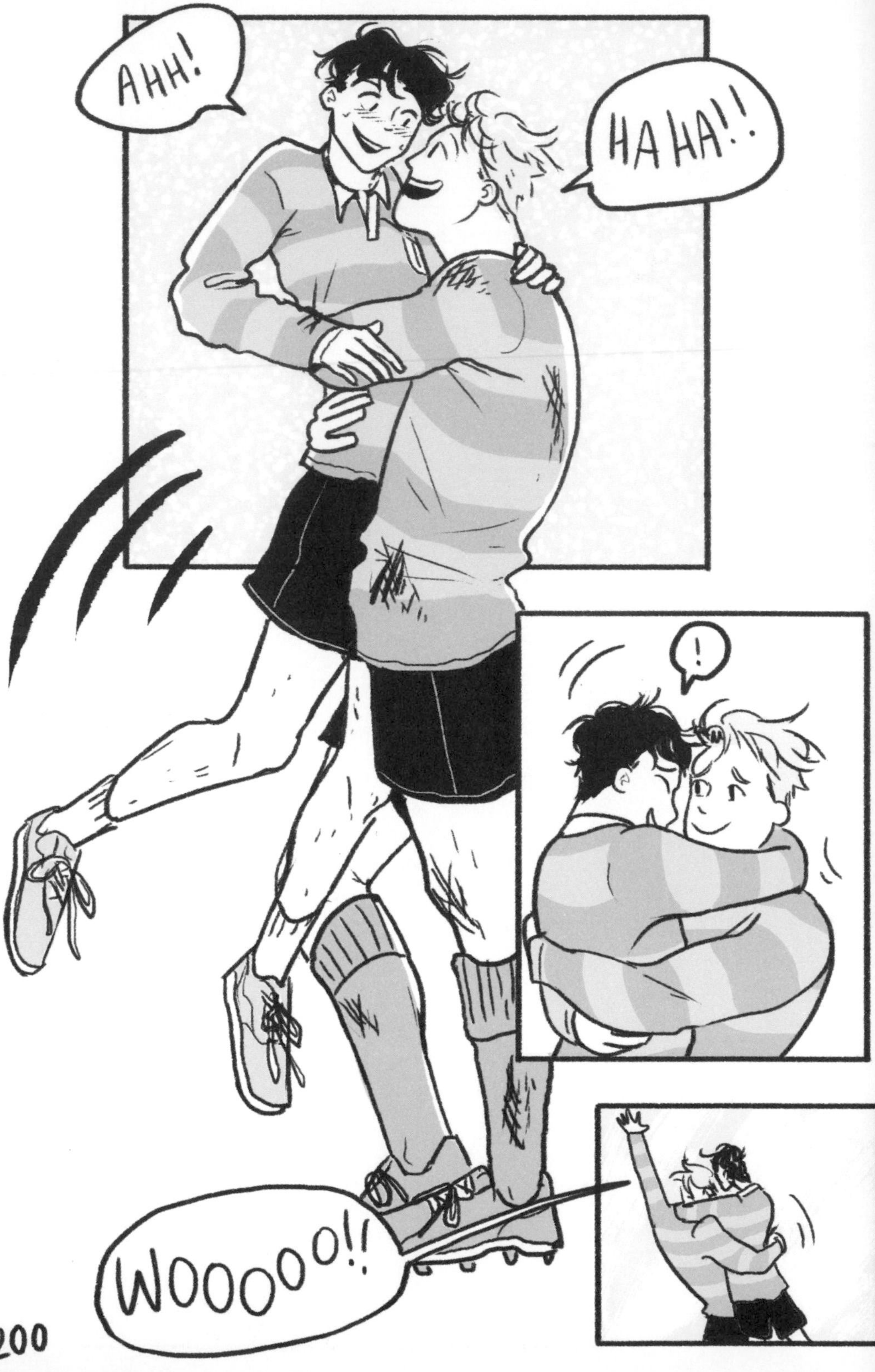
AHH!
HAHA!!
!
WOOOOO!!

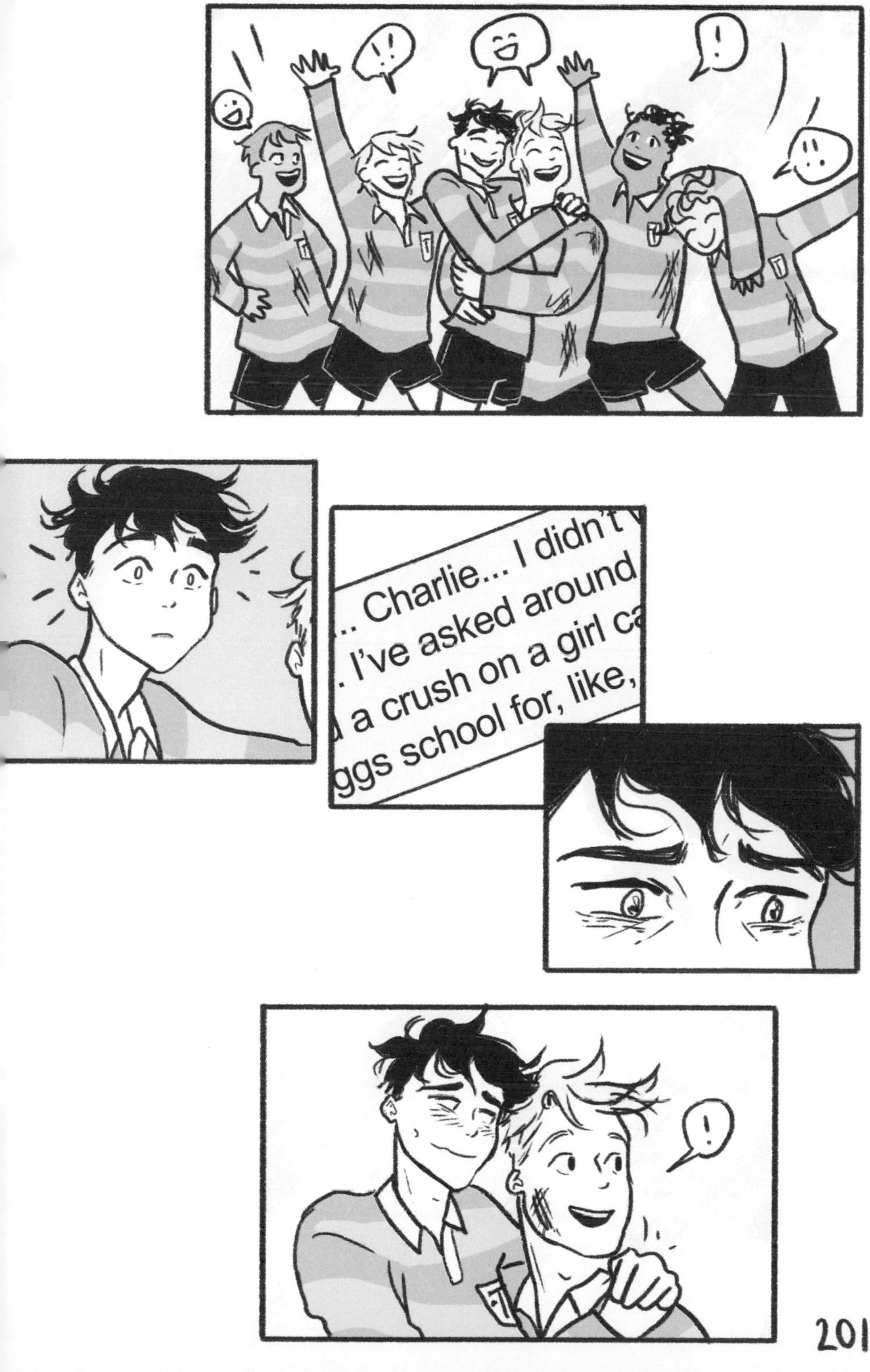
!!
!
... Charlie... I didn't
. I've asked around
a crush on a girl ca
ggs school for, like,
!

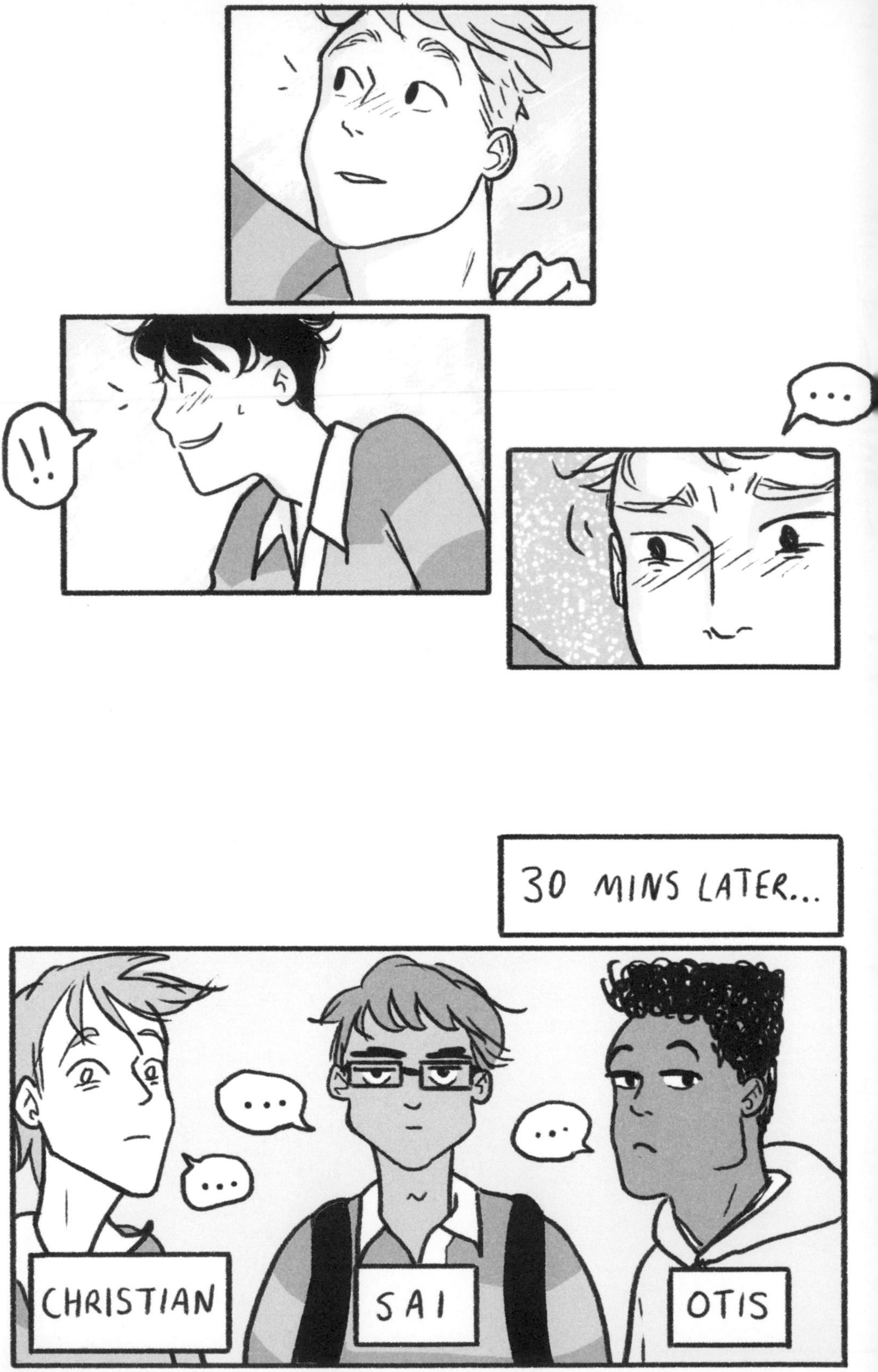
!!
...
30 MINS LATER...
...
...
...
CHRISTIAN
SAI
OTIS

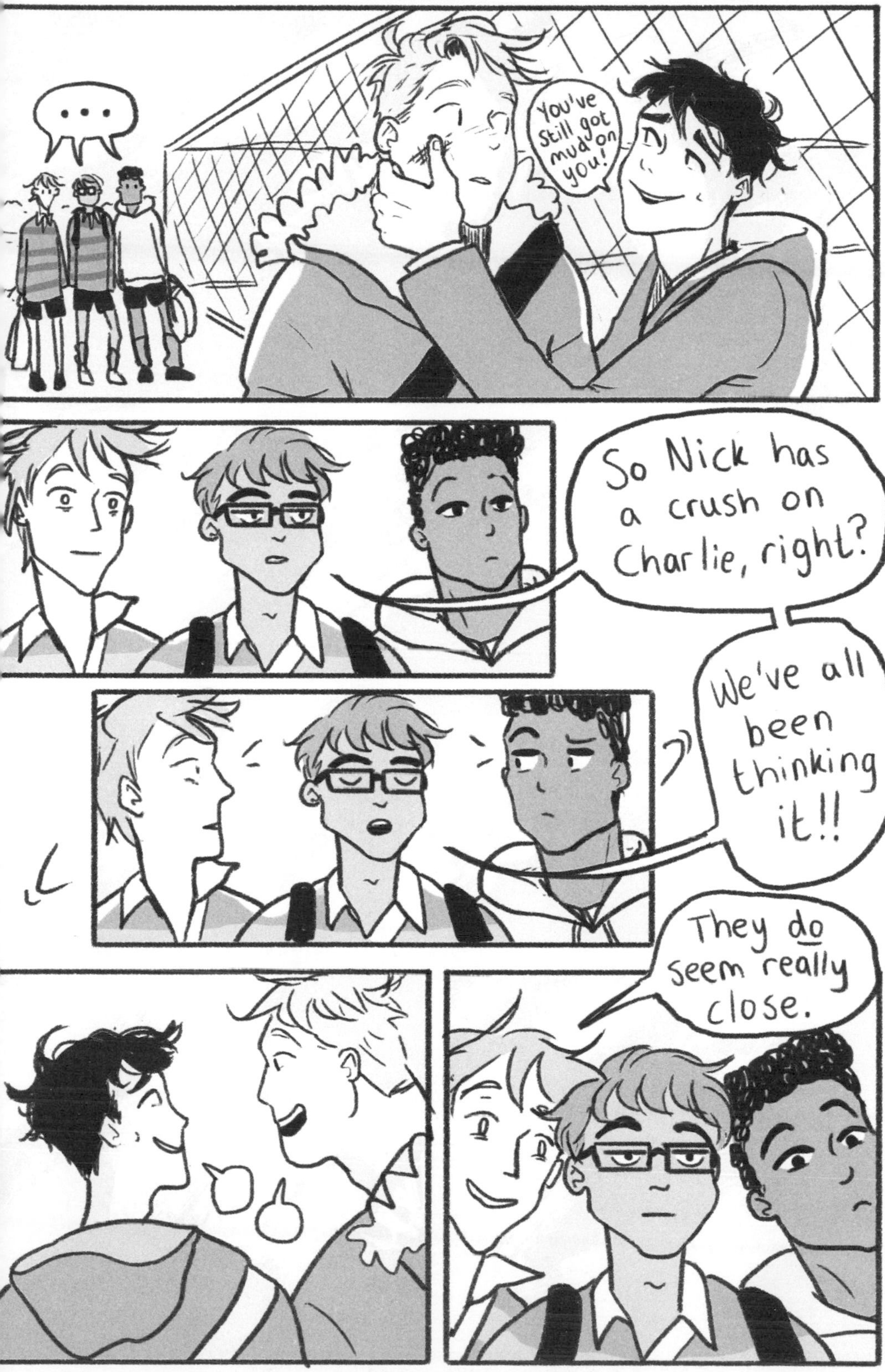
...
You've still got mud on you!
So Nick has a crush on Charlie, right?
We've all been thinking it!!
They do seem really close.

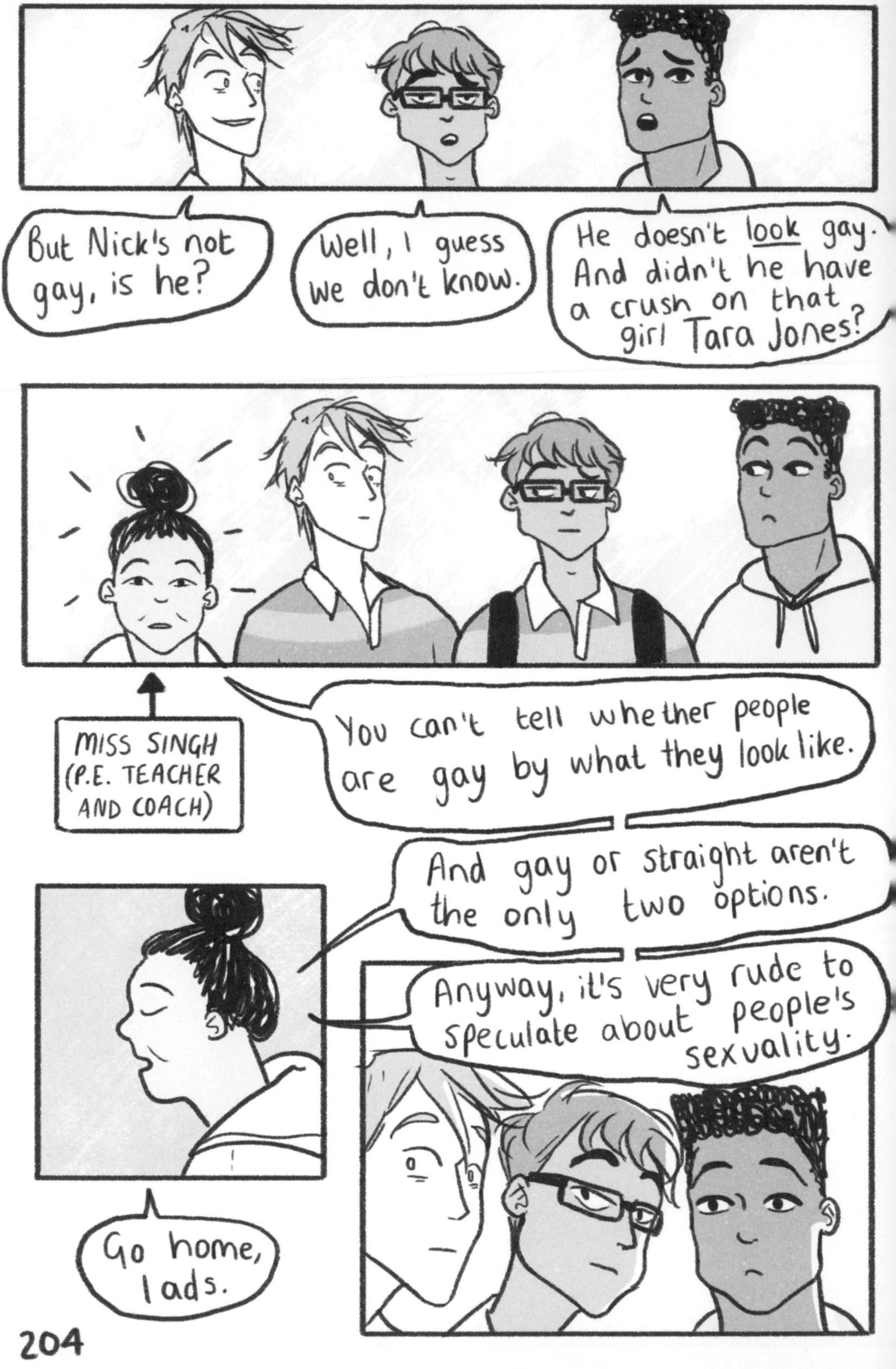

But Nick's not gay, is he?
Well, I guess we don't know.
He doesn't look gay. And didn't he have a crush on that girl Tara Jones?
MISS SINGH (P.E. TEACHER AND COACH)
You can't tell whether people are gay by what they look like.
And gay or straight aren't the only two options.
Anyway, it's very rude to speculate about people's sexuality.
Go home, lads.

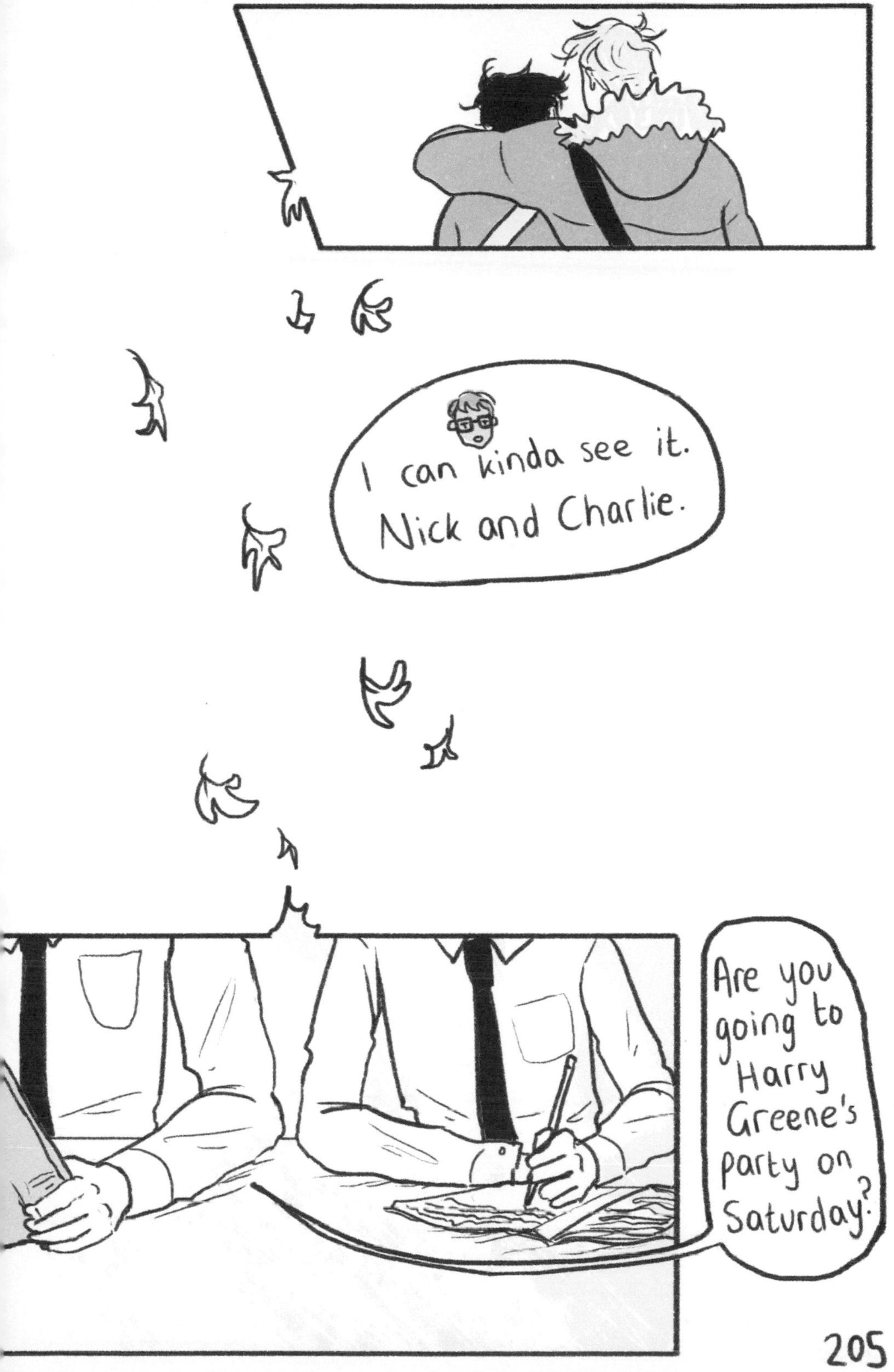
I can kinda see it. Nick and Charlie.
Are you going to Harry Greene's party on Saturday?

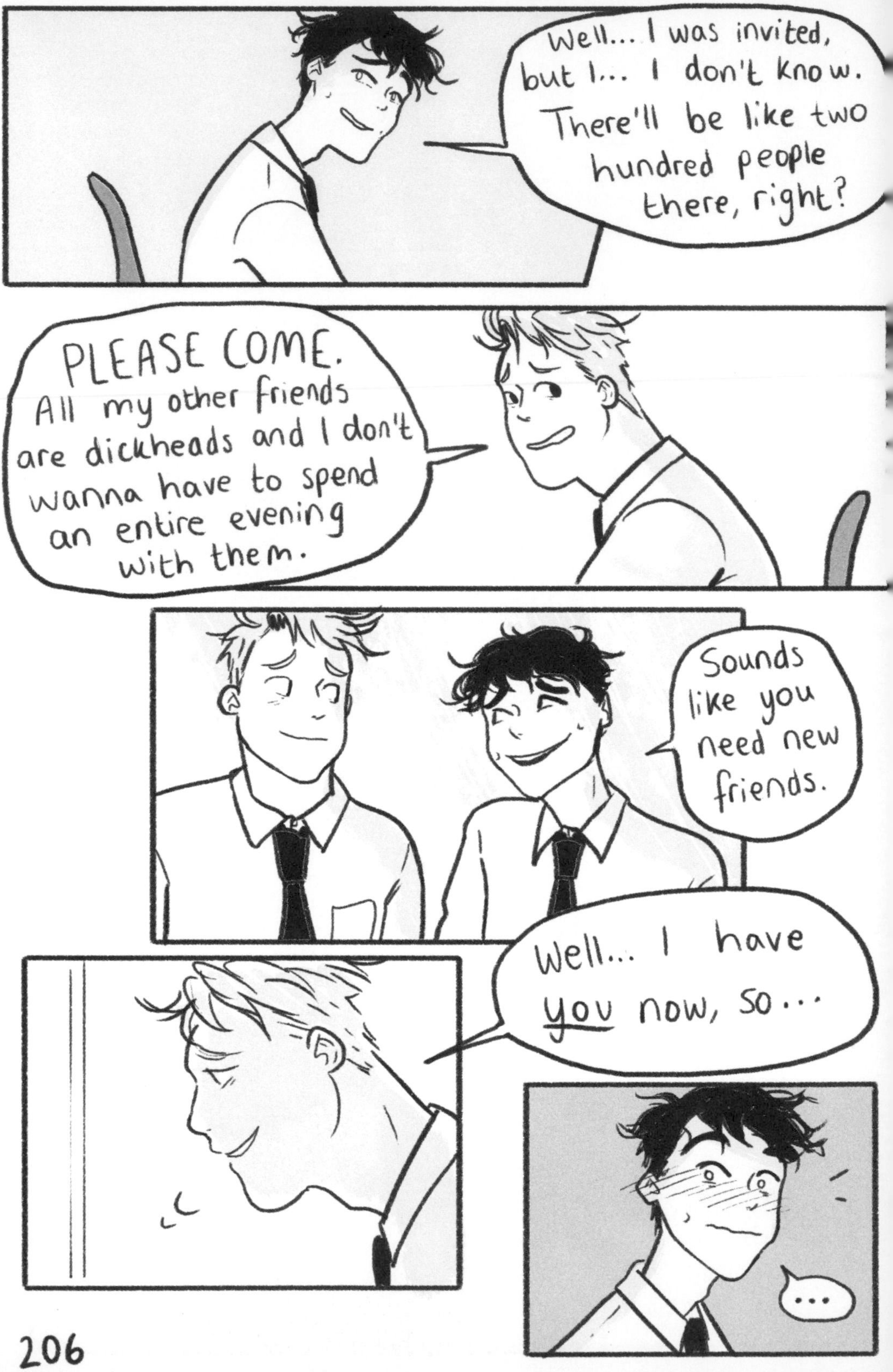
Well... I was invited, but I... I don't know. There'll be like two hundred people there, right?
PLEASE COME. All my other friends are dickheads and I don't wanna have to spend an entire evening with them.
Sounds like you need new friends.
Well... I have you now, so...
...

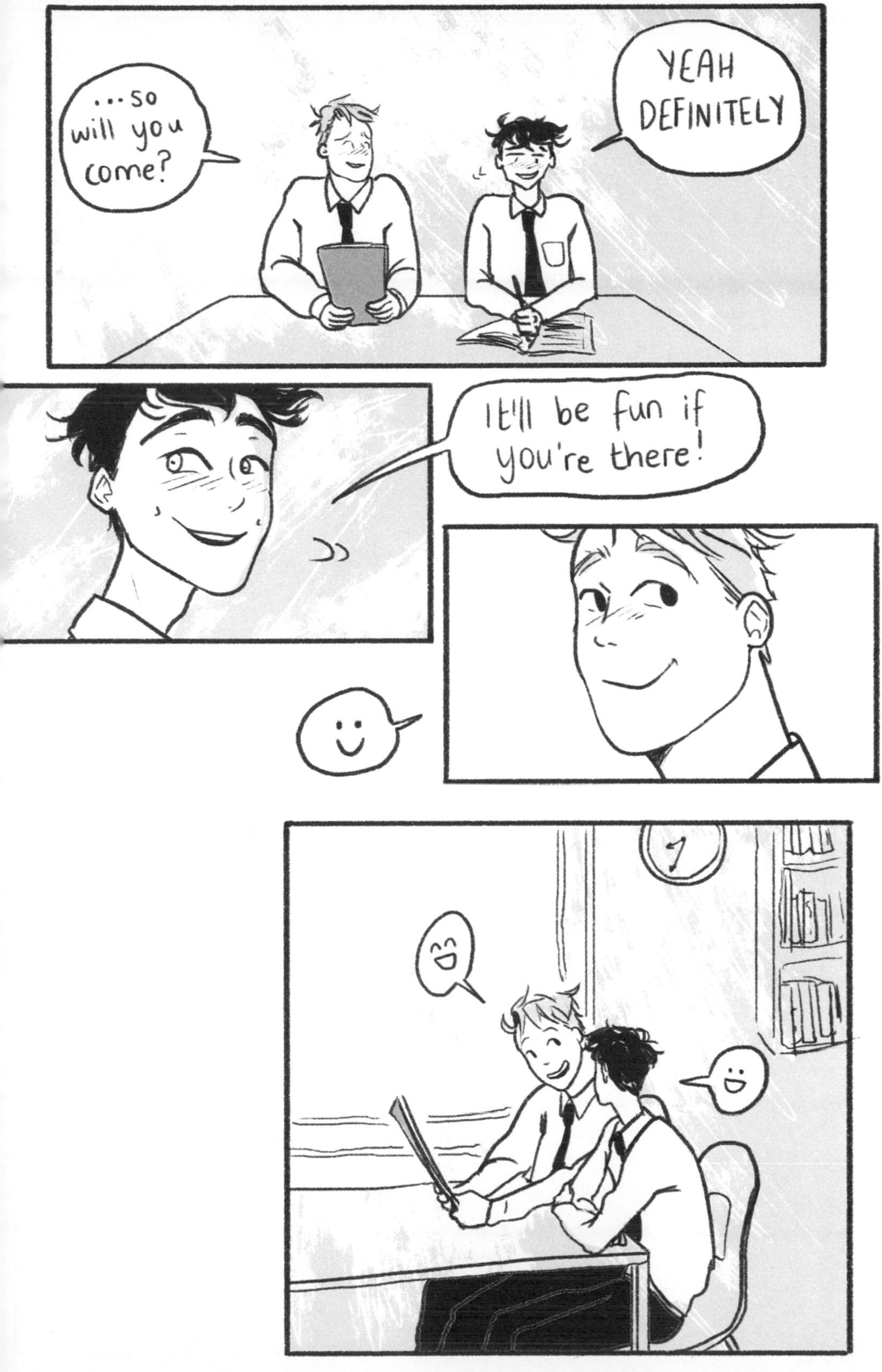
...so will you come?
YEAH DEFINITELY
It'll be fun if you're there!

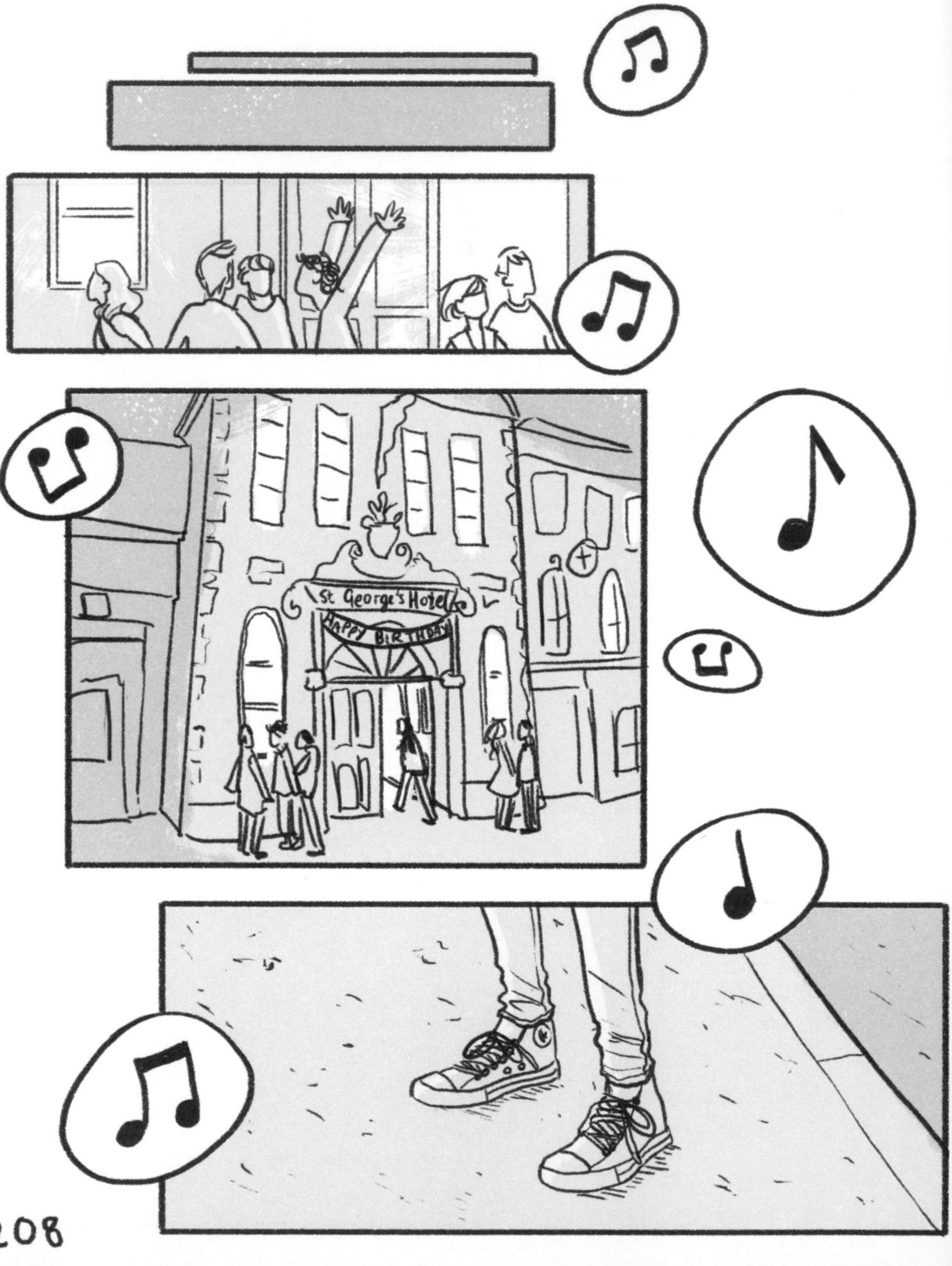
St George's Hotel
HAPPY BIRTHDAY

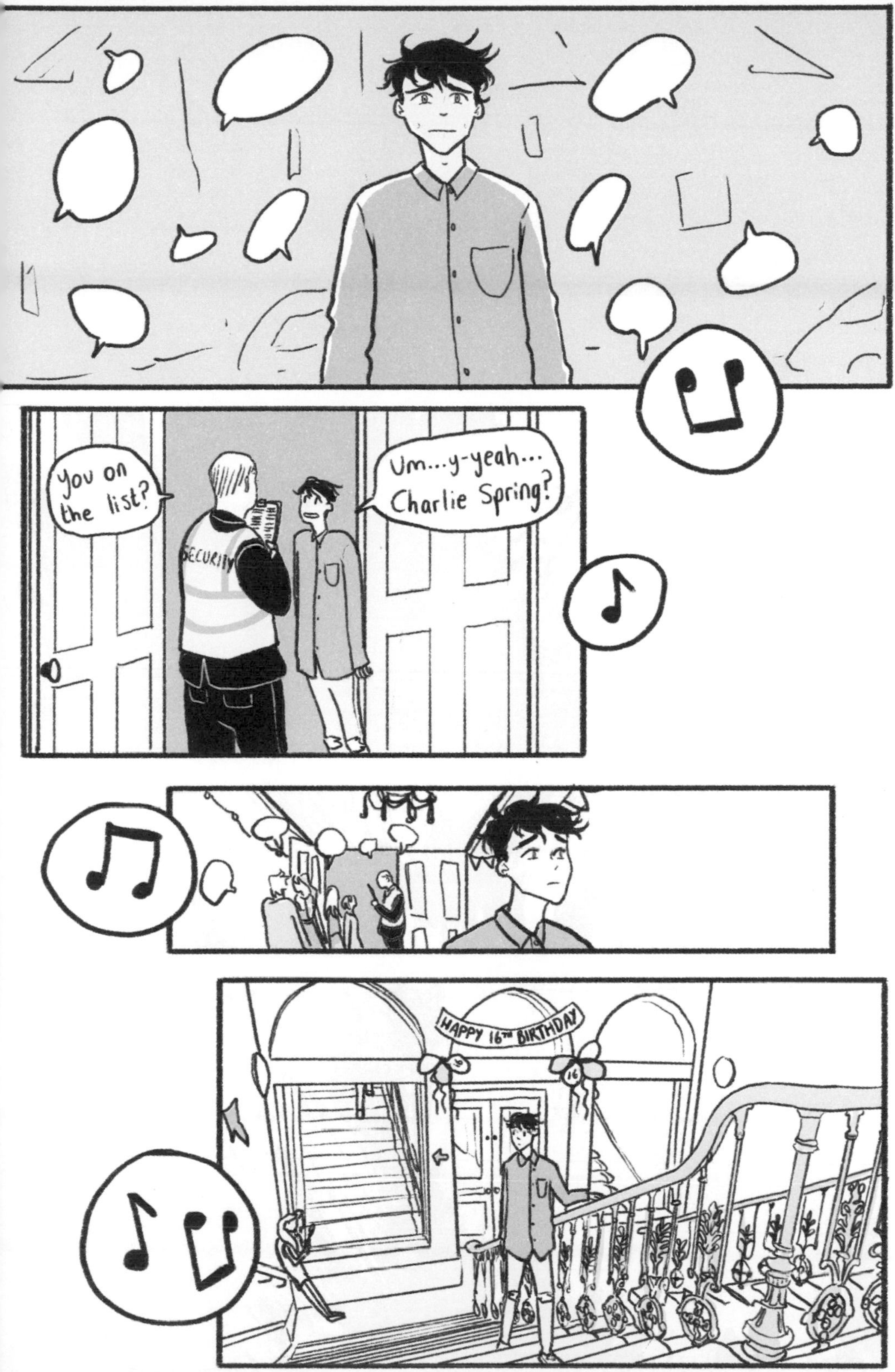
You on the list?
Um...y-yeah... Charlie Spring?
HAPPY 16TH BIRTHDAY

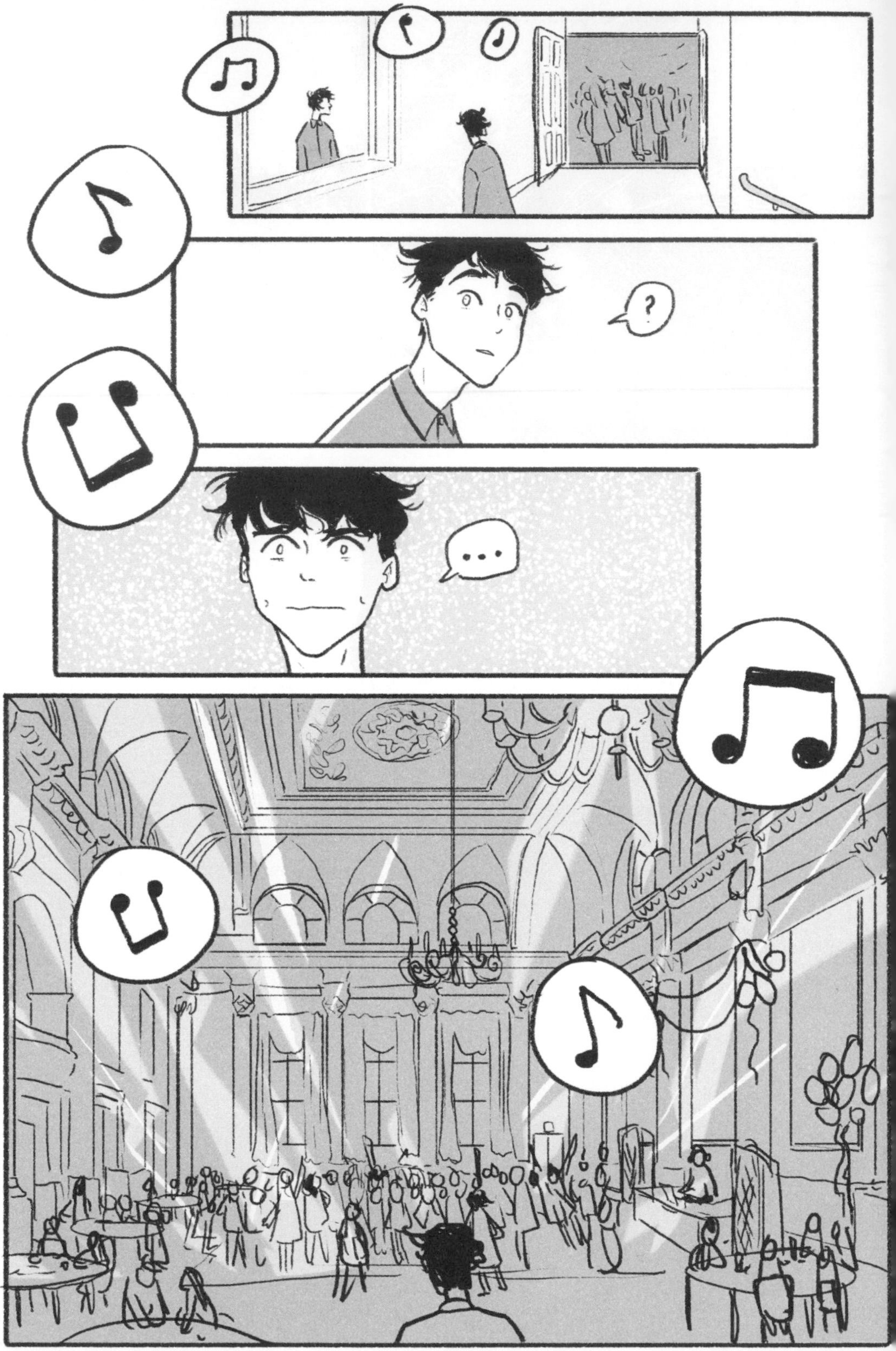
?
...

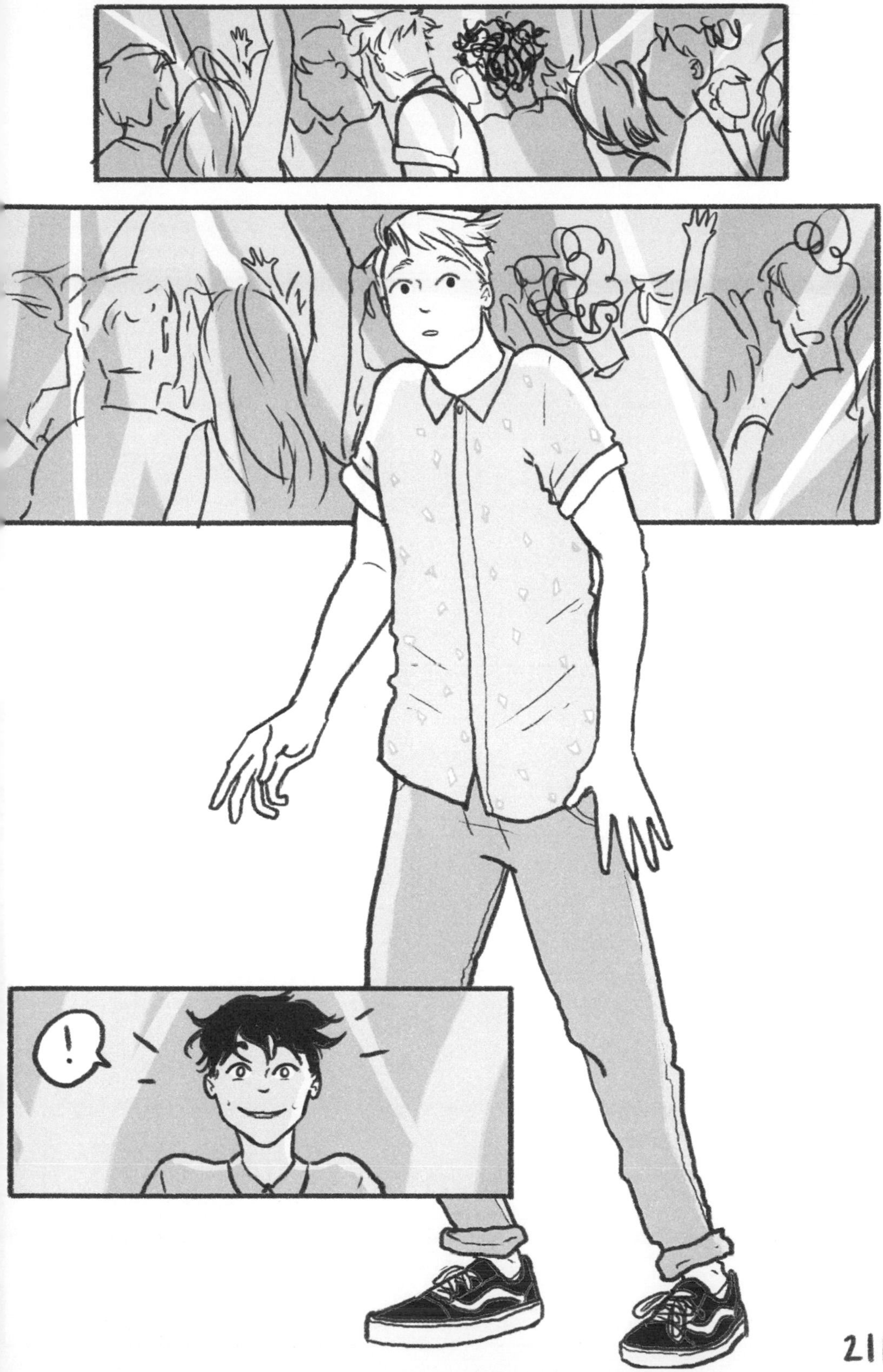
!

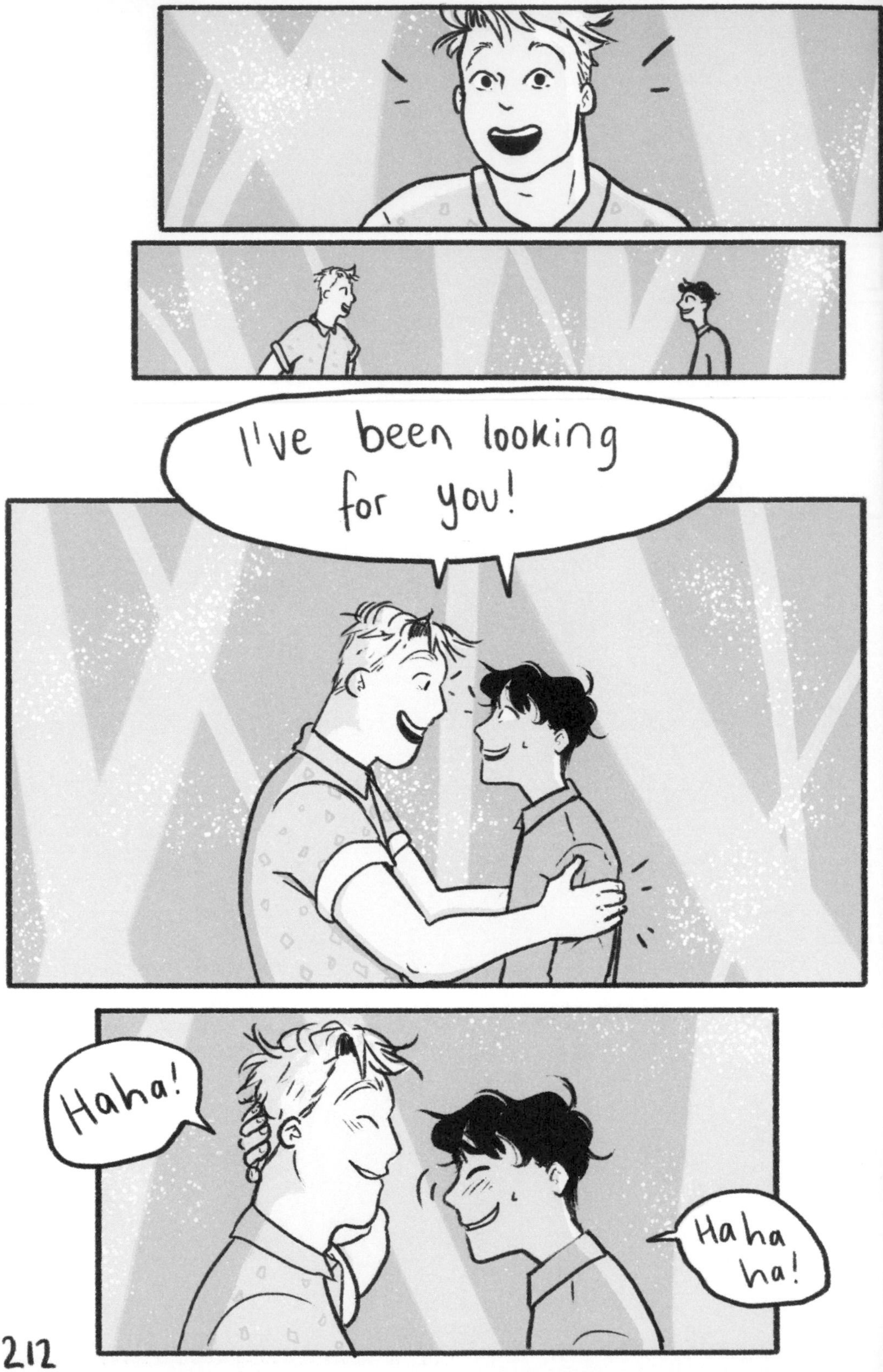
I've been looking for you!
Haha!
Haha ha!

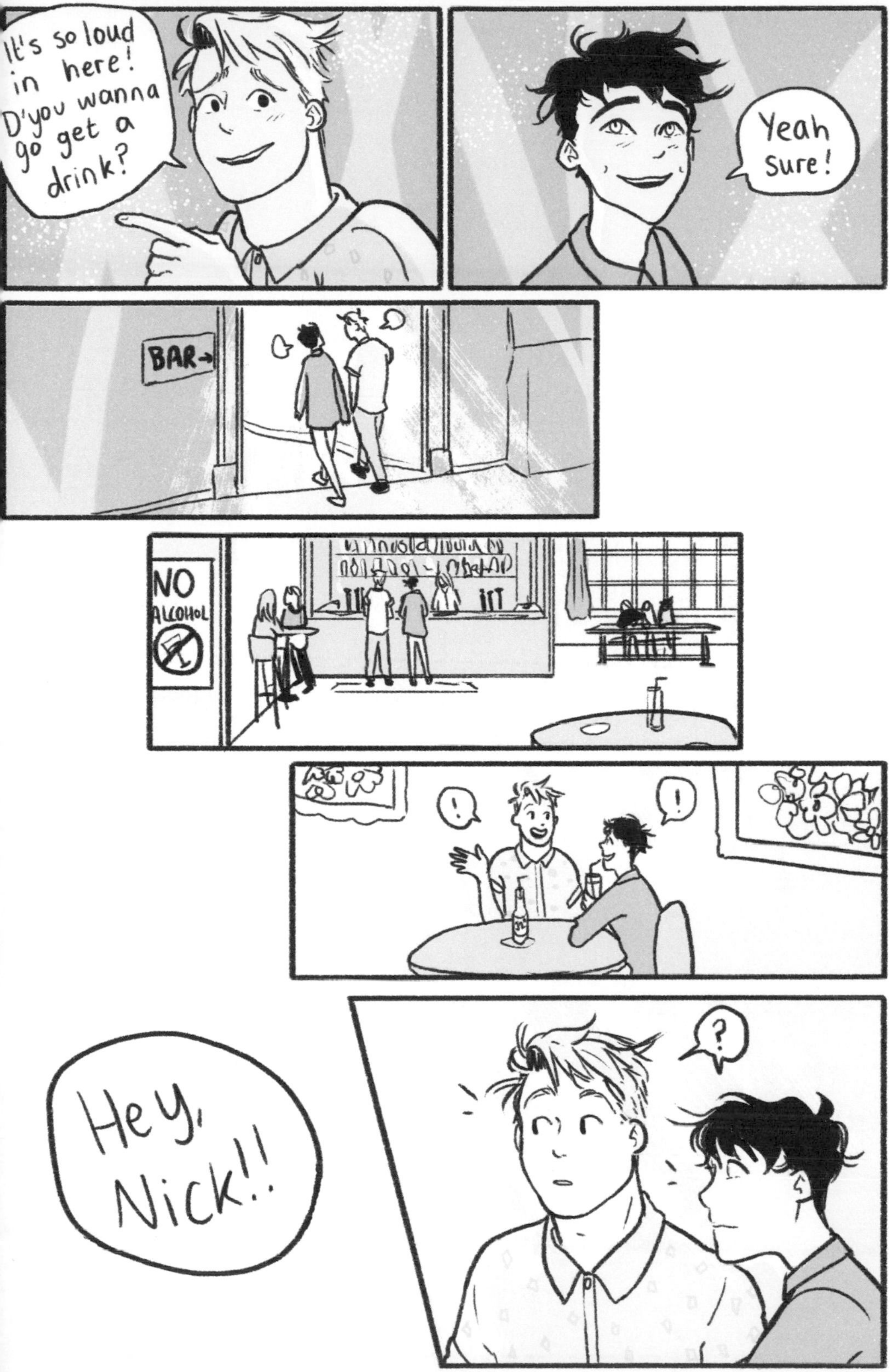
It's so loud in here! D'you wanna go get a drink?
Yeah sure!
BAR→
NO ALCOHOL
!
!
?
Hey, Nick!!

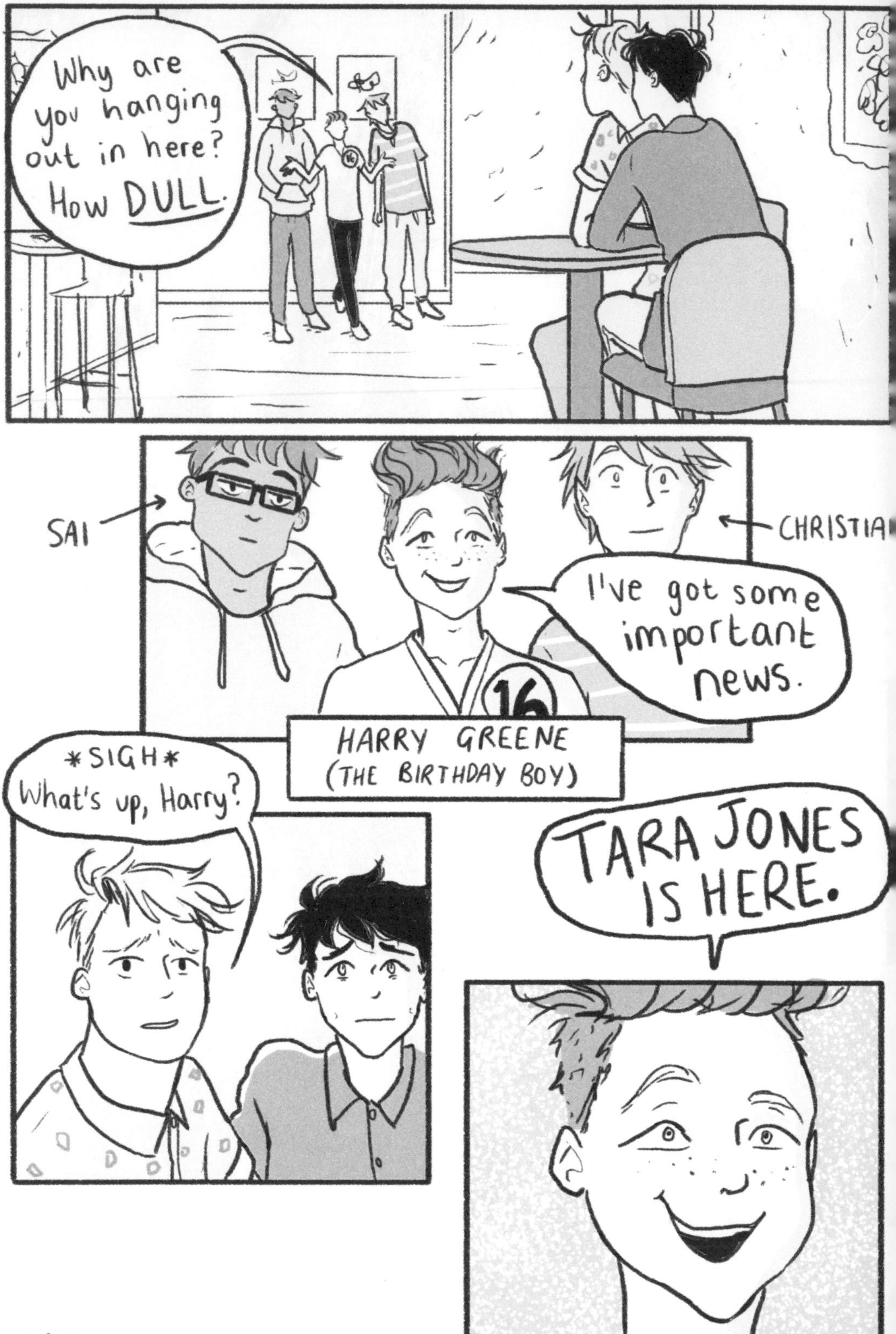
Why are you hanging out in here? How DULL.
SAI
CHRISTIA
I've got some important news.
HARRY GREENE (THE BIRTHDAY BOY)
SIGH What's up, Harry?
TARA JONES IS HERE.

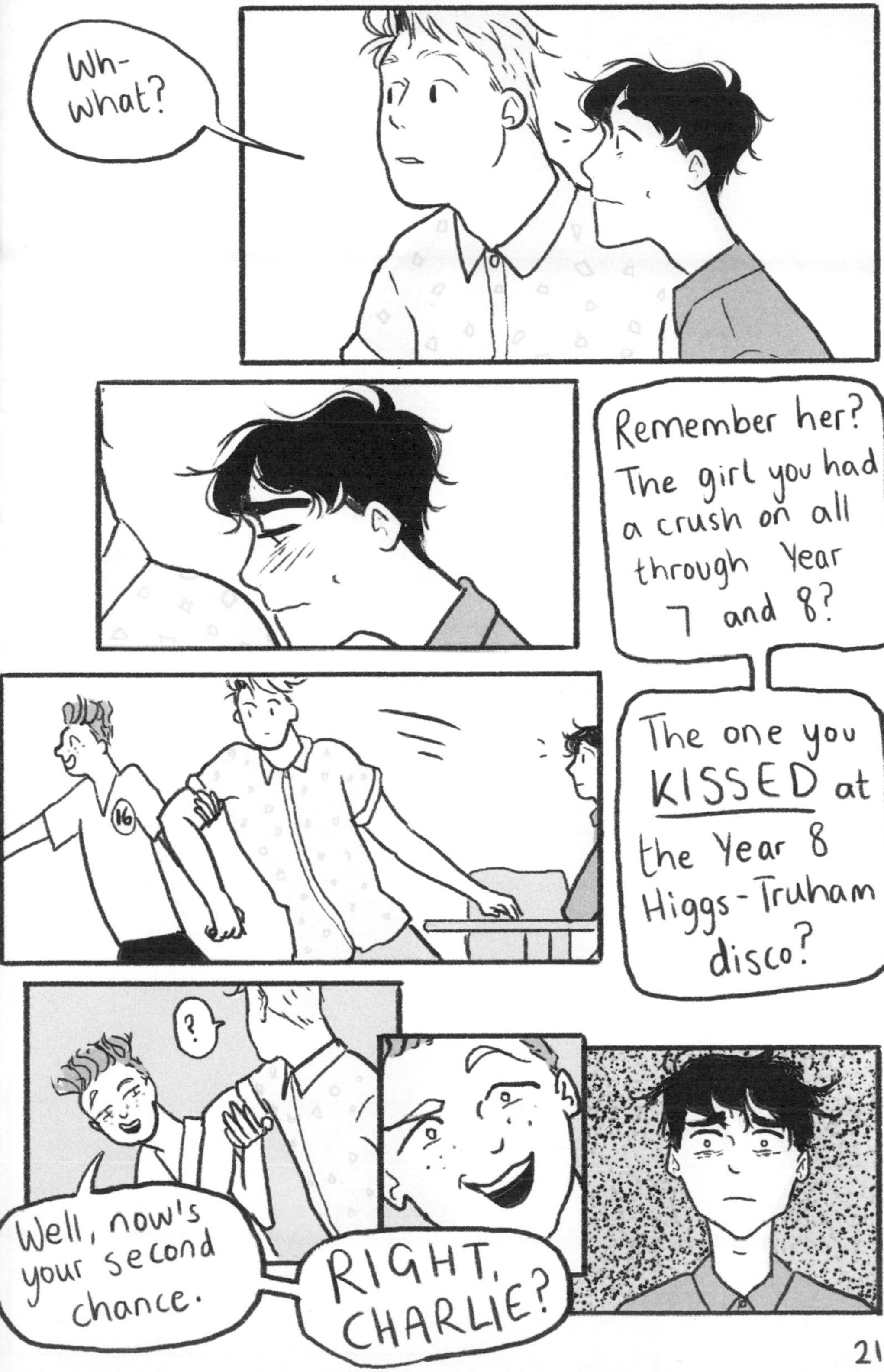
Wh- what?
Remember her? The girl you had a crush on all through Year 7 and 8?
The one you KISSED at the Year 8 Higgs-Truham disco?
?
Well, now's your second chance.
RIGHT, CHARLIE?

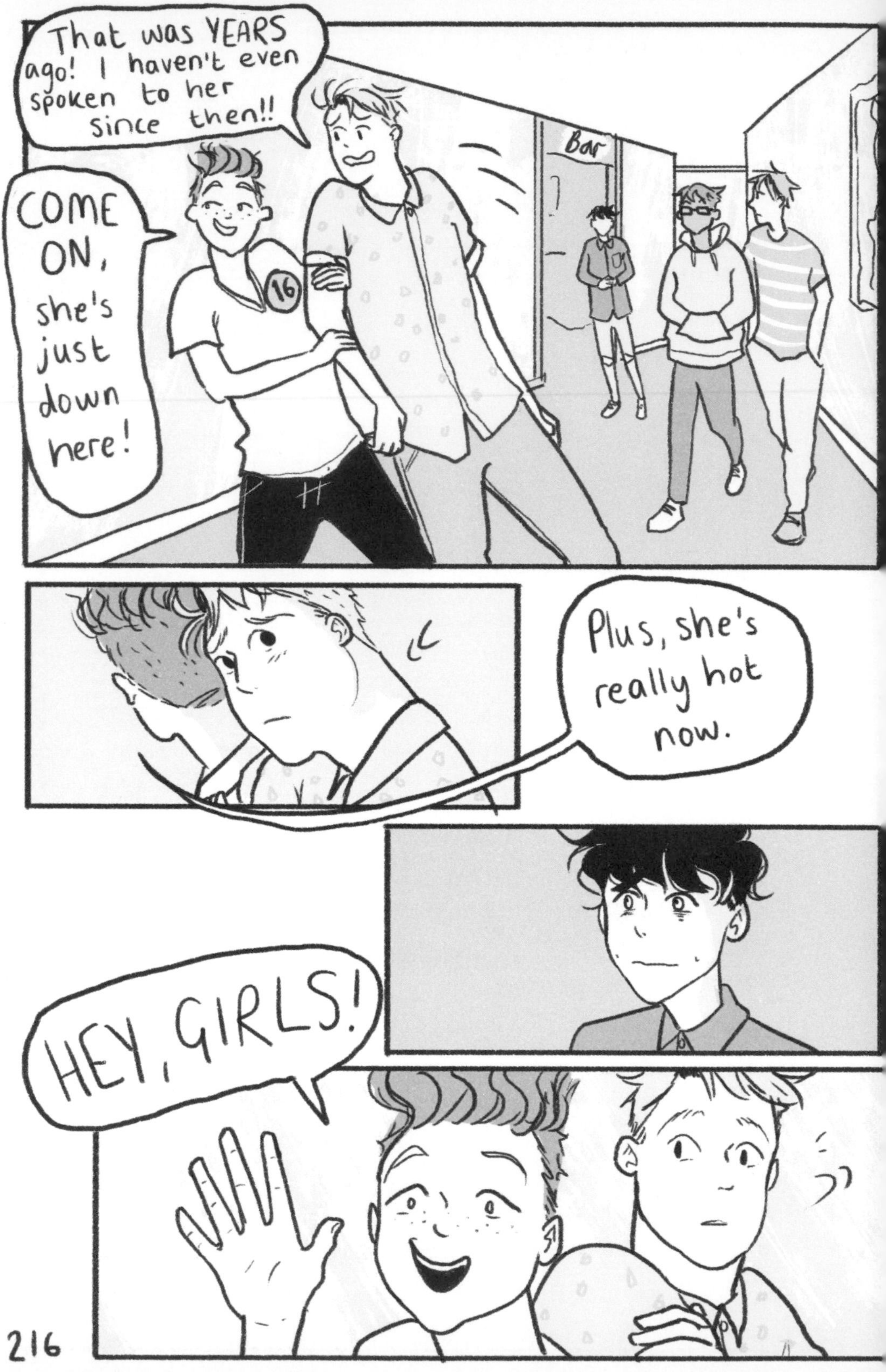

That was YEARS ago! I haven't even spoken to her since then!!
COME ON, she's just down here!
Bar
Plus, she's really hot now.
HEY, GIRLS!

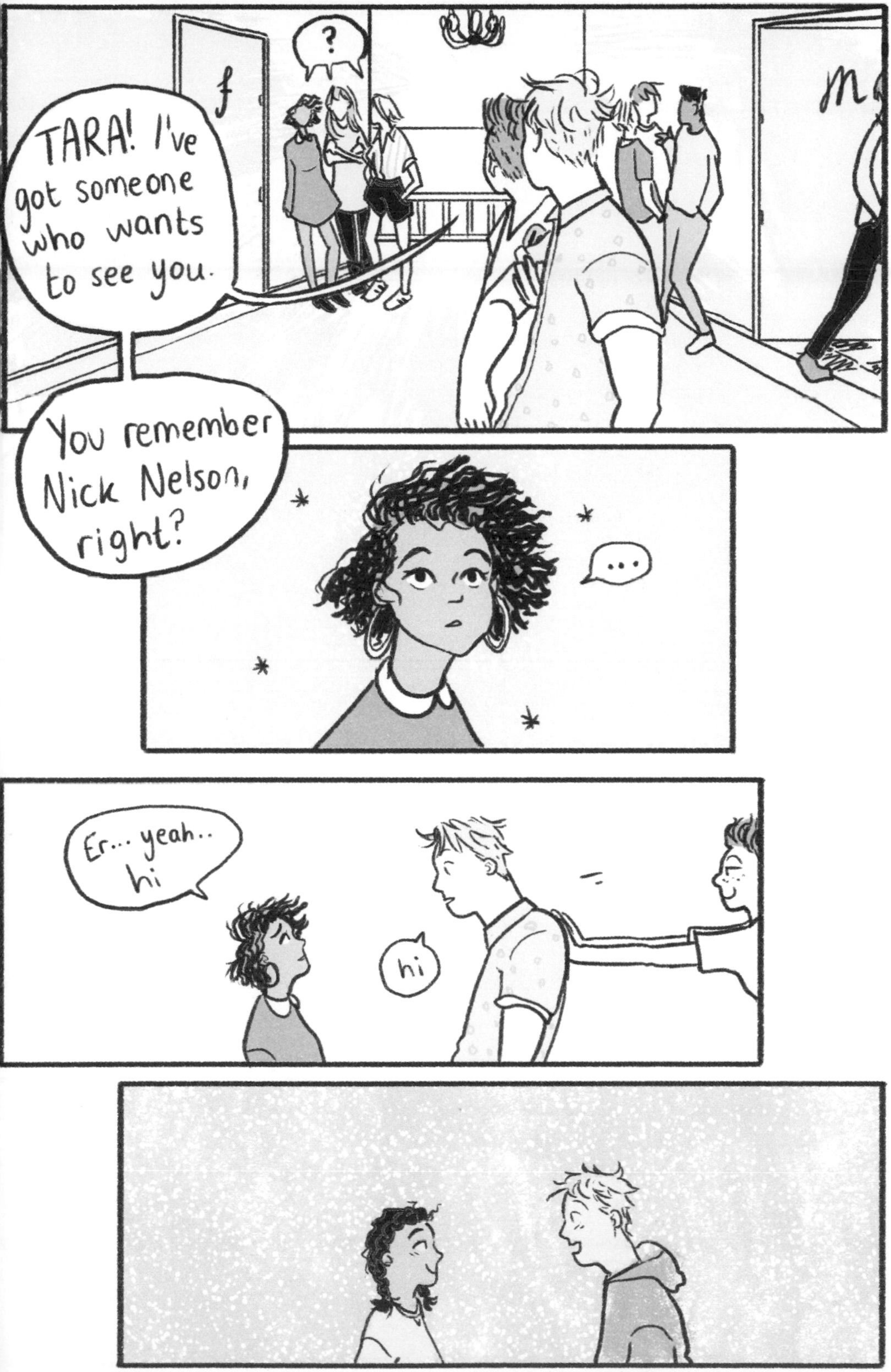
?
TARA! I've got someone who wants to see you.
You remember Nick Nelson, right?
...
Er... yeah.. hi
hi

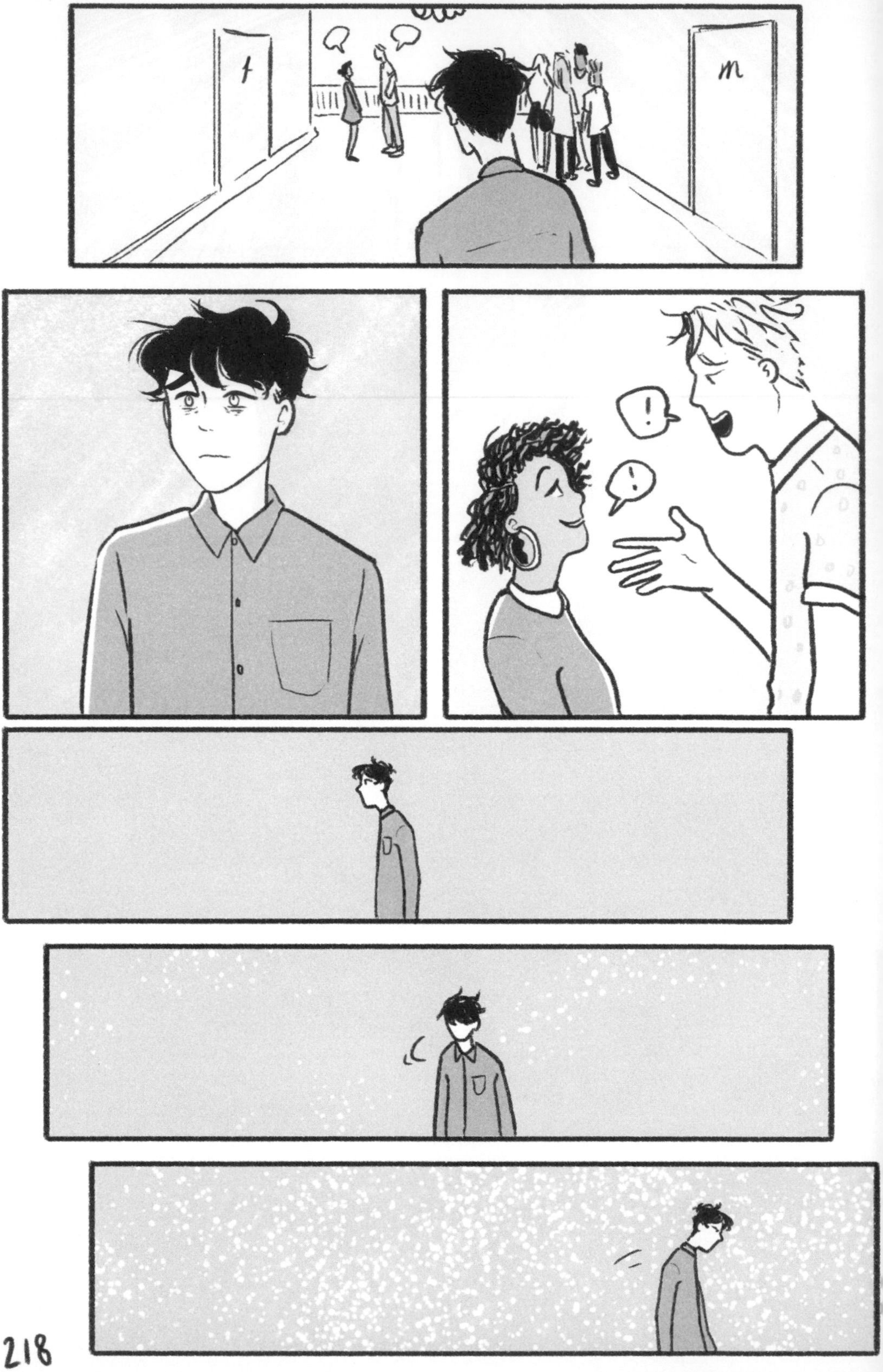
f
m
!
!

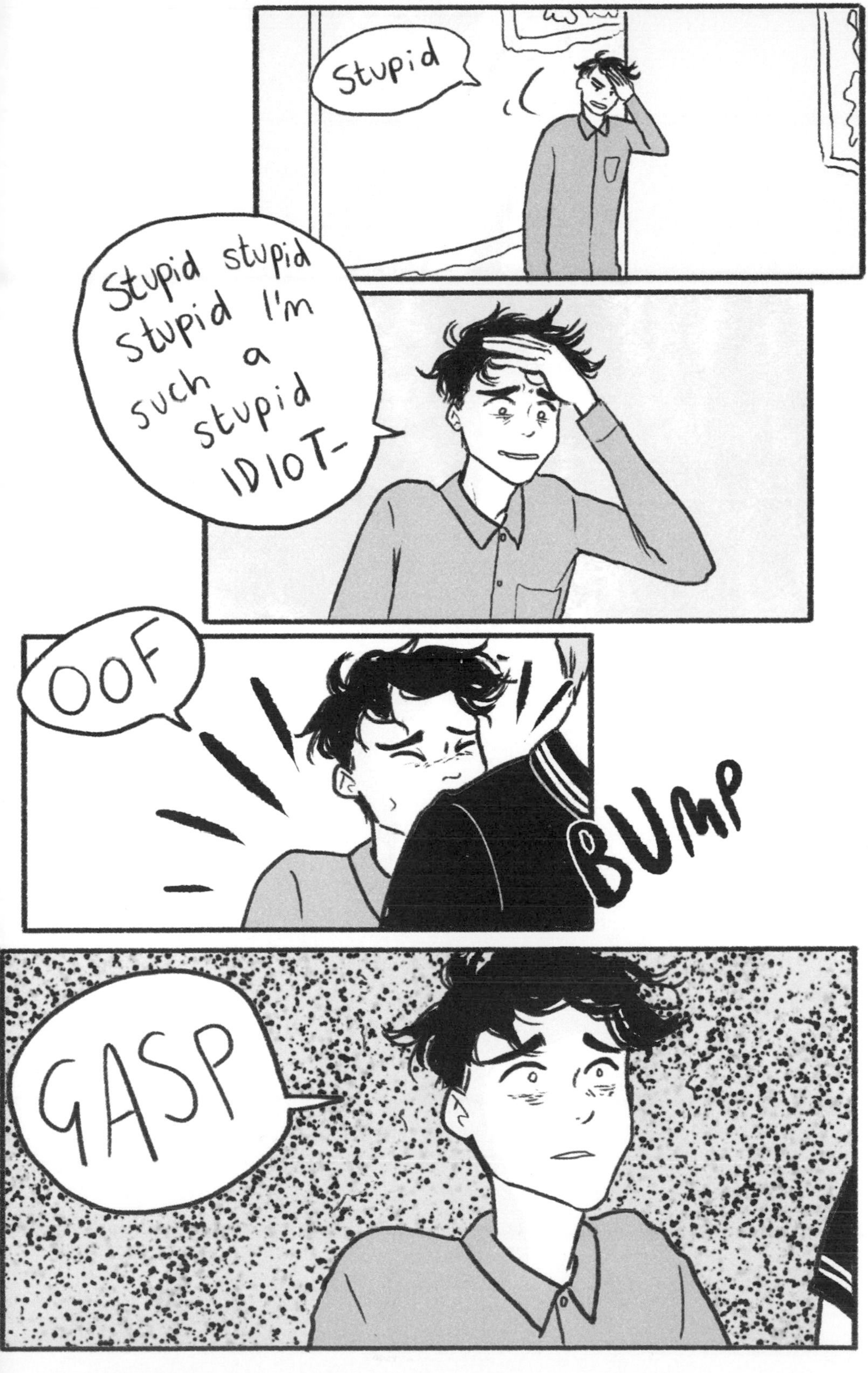
Stupid
Stupid stupid stupid I'm such a stupid IDIOT-
OOF
BUMP
GASP

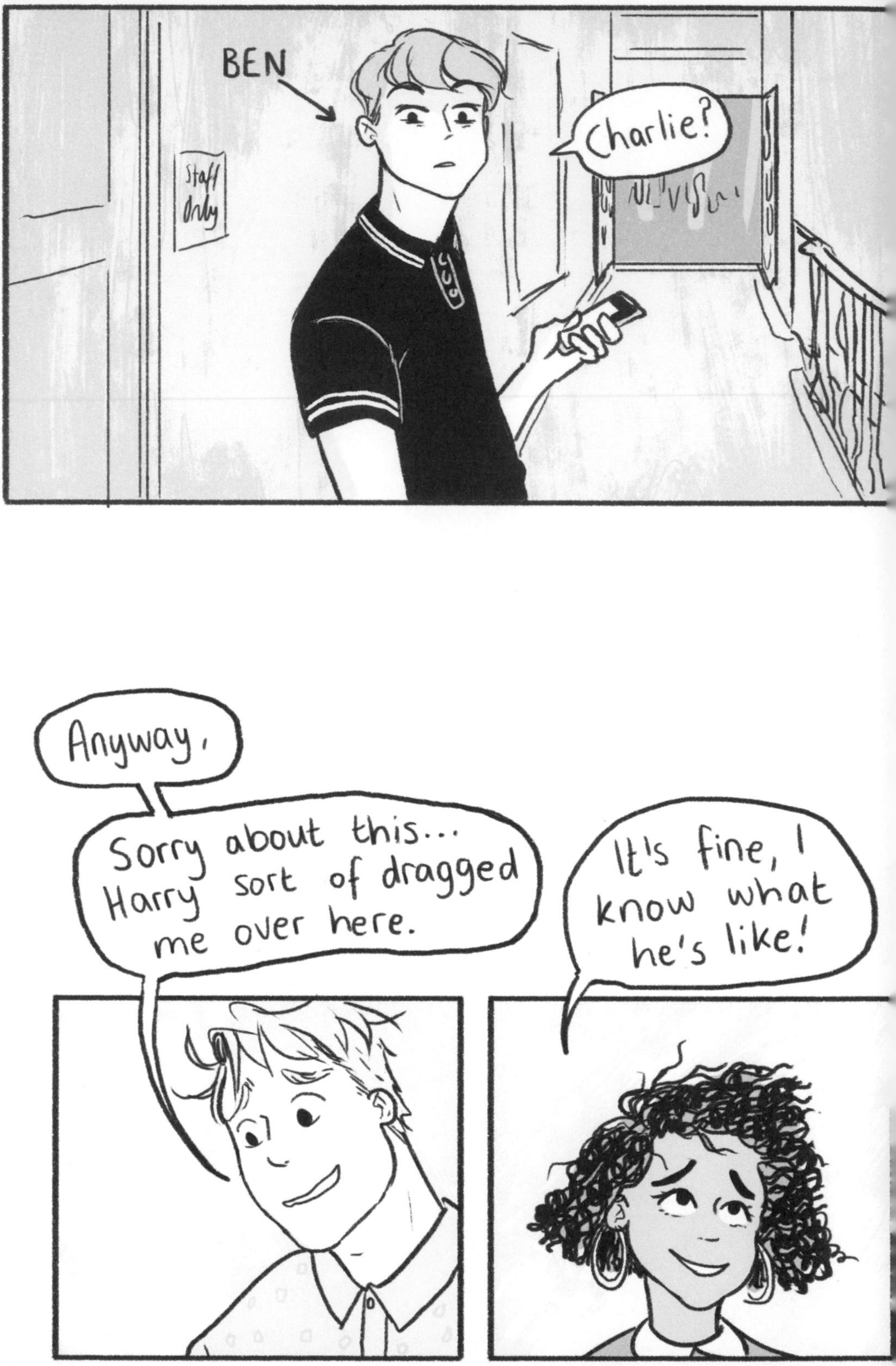
BEN
Staff Only
Charlie?
Anyway,
Sorry about this... Harry sort of dragged me over here.
It's fine, I know what he's like!

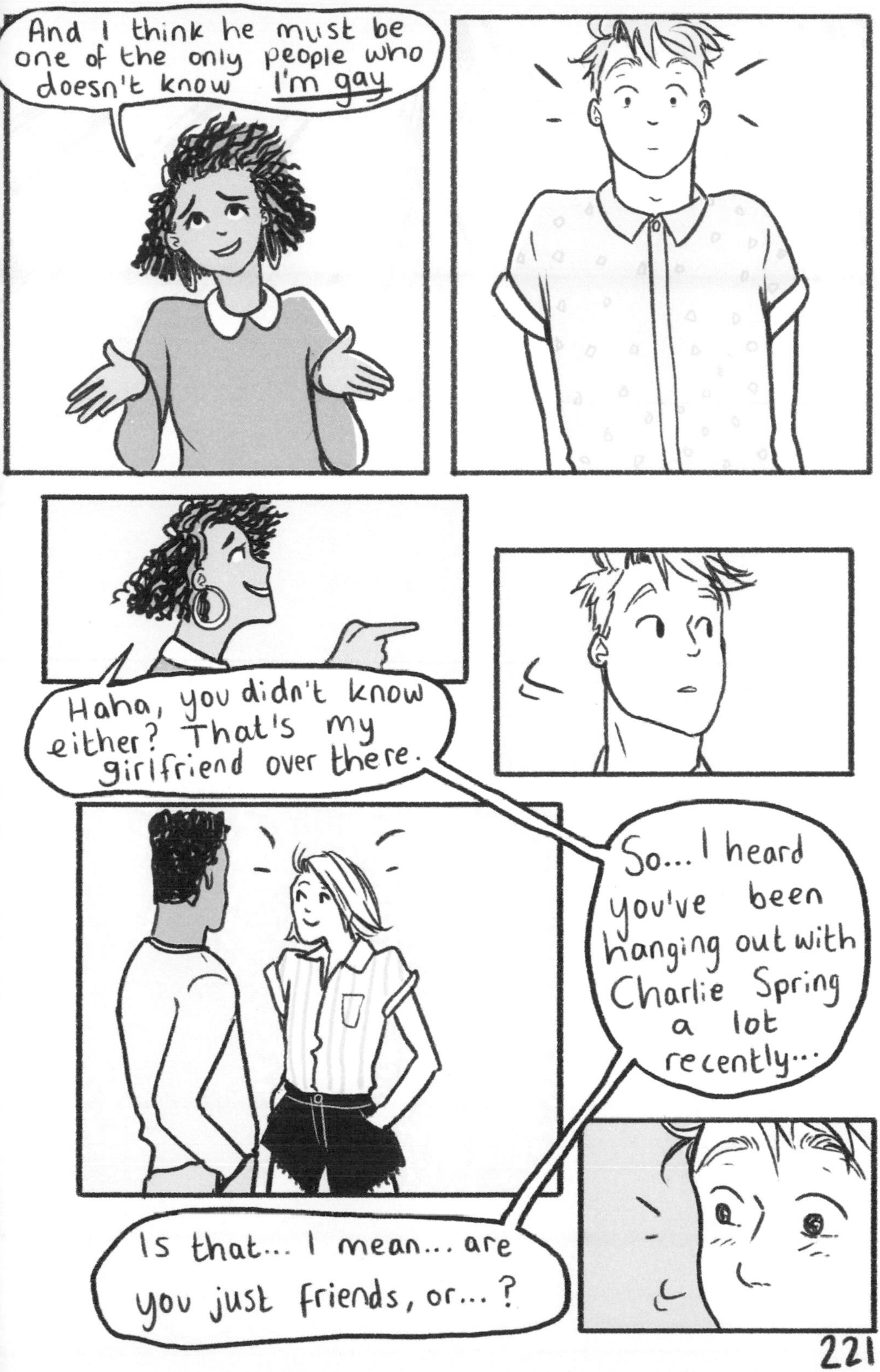
And I think he must be one of the only people who doesn't know I'm gay
Haha, you didn't know either? That's my girlfriend over there.
So... I heard you've been hanging out with Charlie Spring a lot recently...
Is that... I mean... are you just friends, or...?

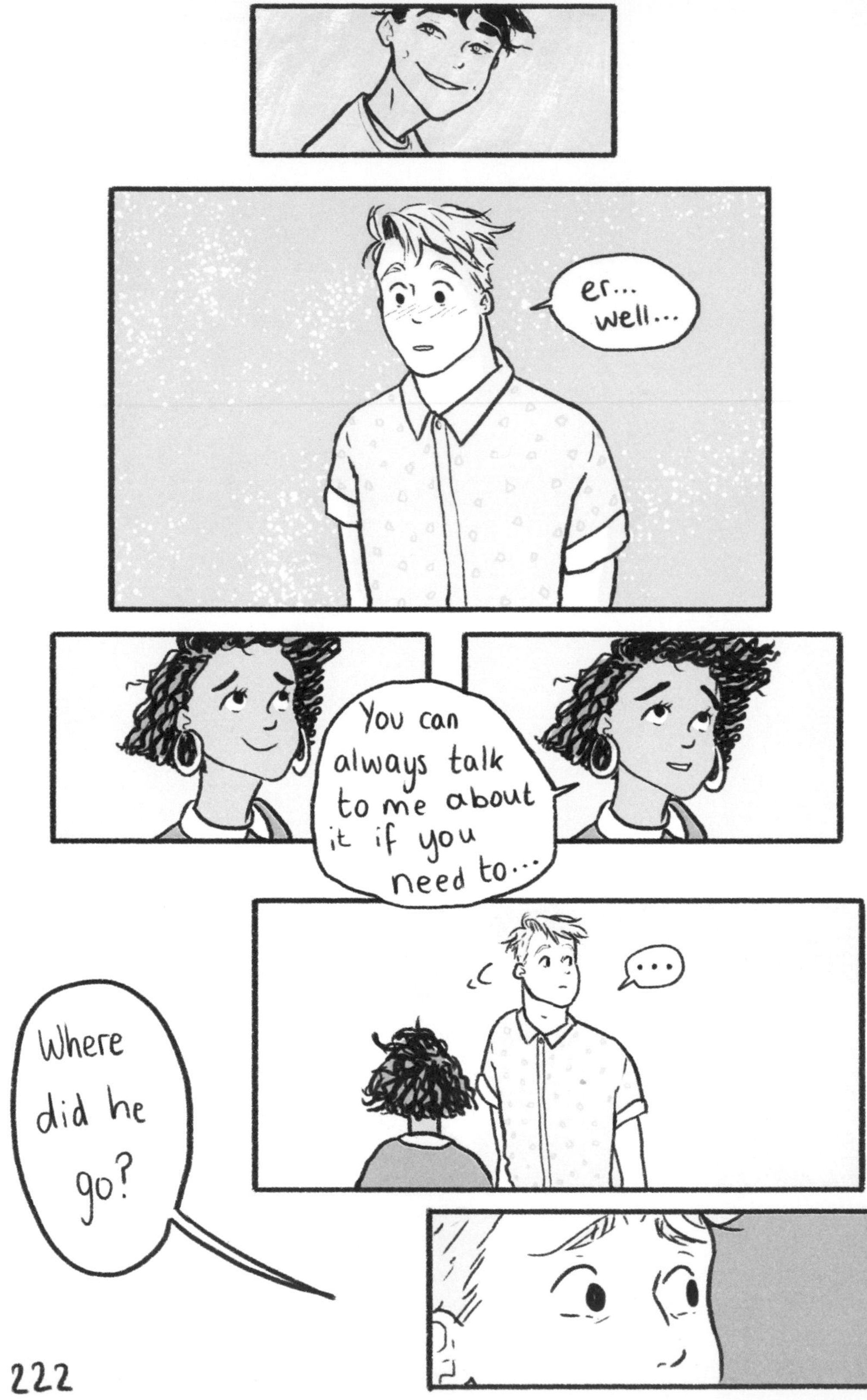
er... well...
You can always talk to me about it if you need to...
...
Where did he go?

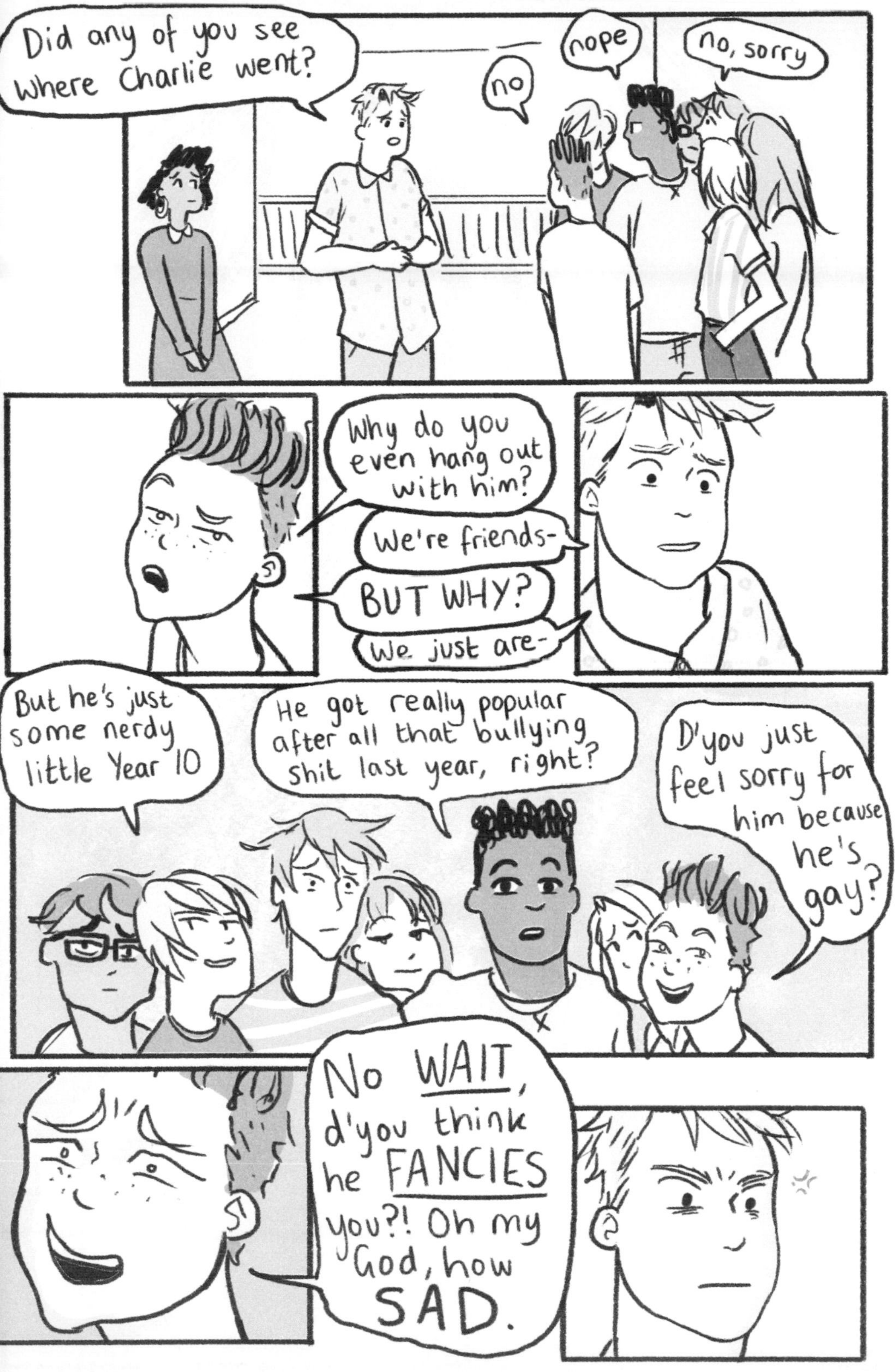
Did any of you see where Charlie went?
no
nope
no, sorry
Why do you even hang out with him?
We're friends-
BUT WHY?
We just are-
But he's just some nerdy little Year 10
He got really popular after all that bullying shit last year, right?
D'you just feel sorry for him because he's gay?
No WAIT, d'you think he FANCIES you?! Oh my God, how SAD.

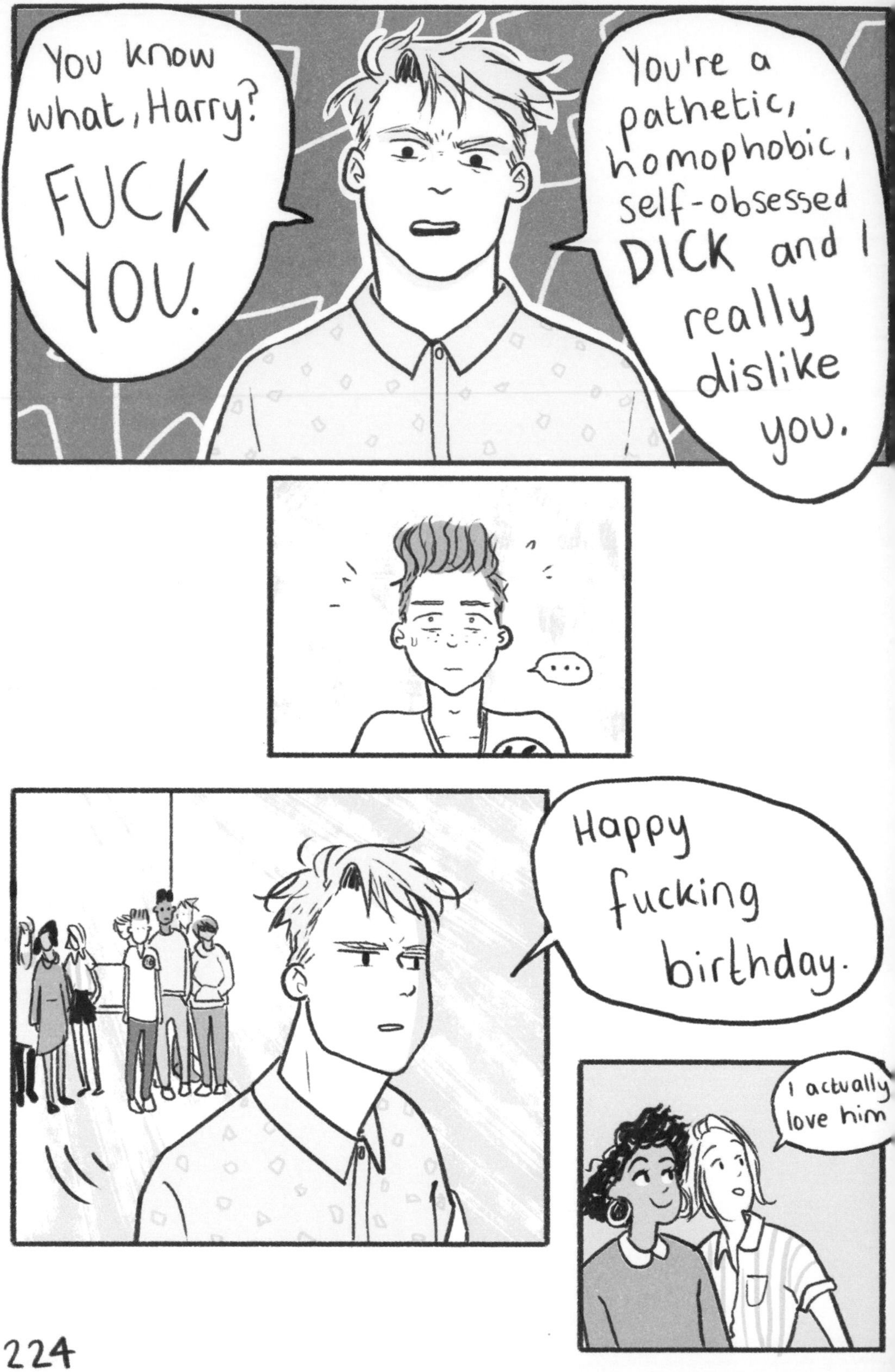

You know what, Harry? FUCK YOU.
You're a pathetic, homophobic, self-obsessed DICK and I really dislike you.
...
Happy fucking birthday.
I actually love him

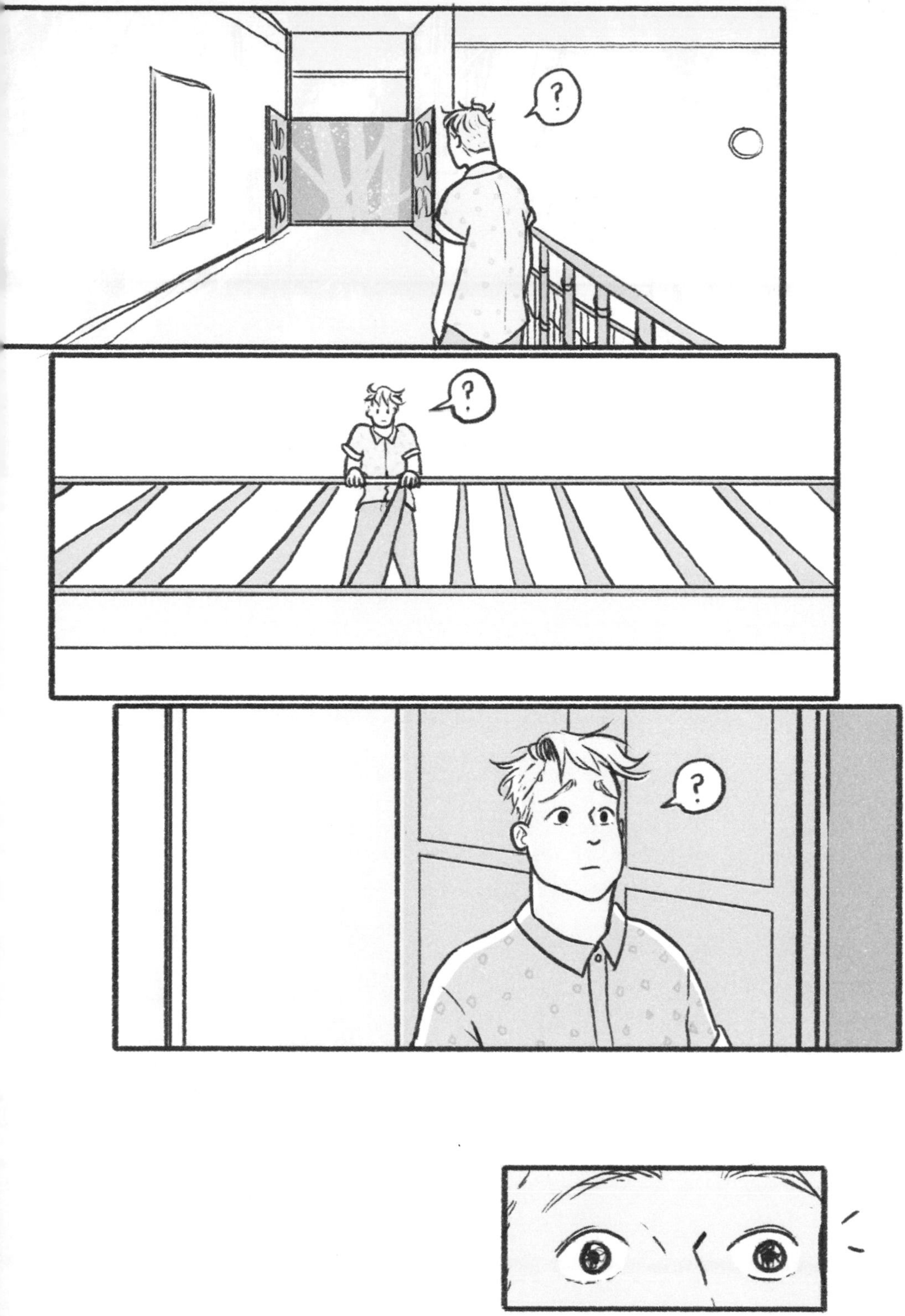
?
?
?

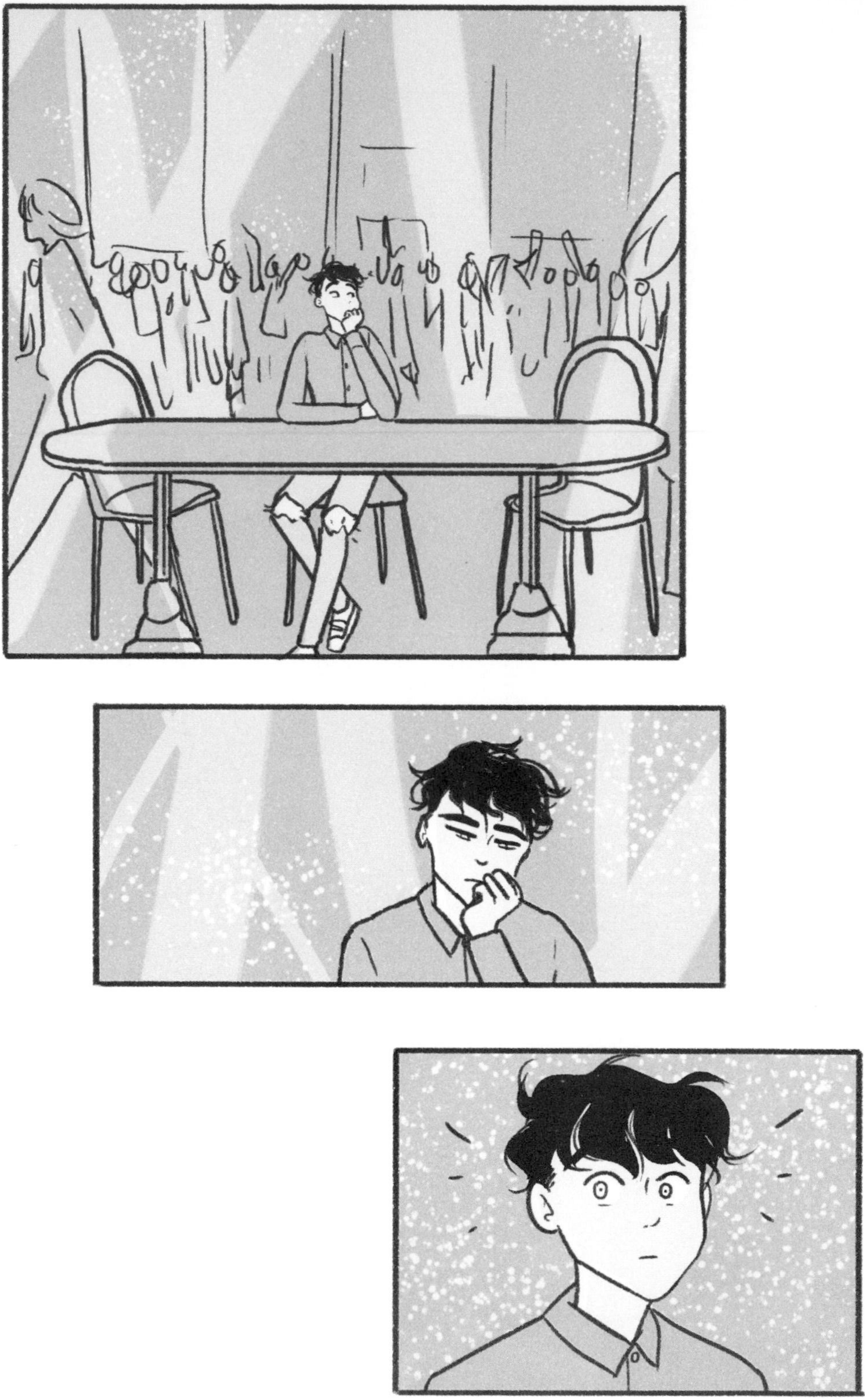

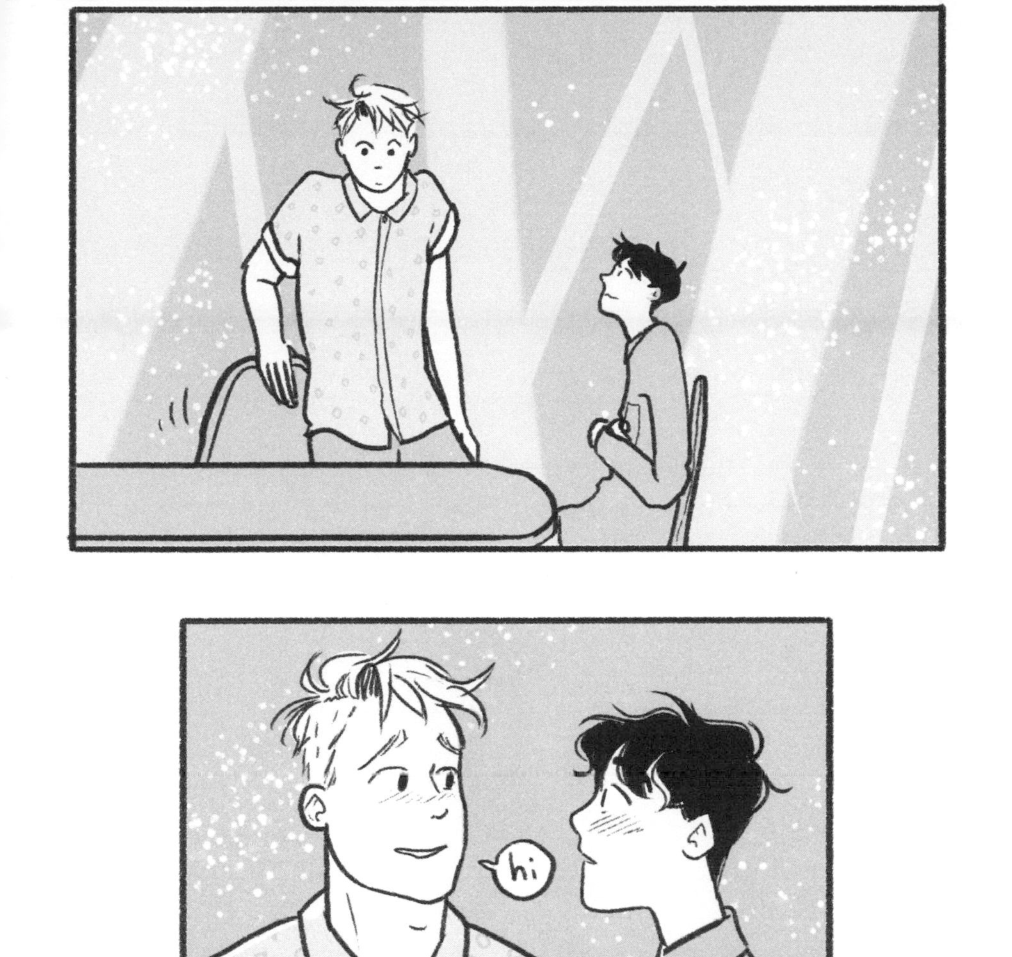
hi
um... sorry...

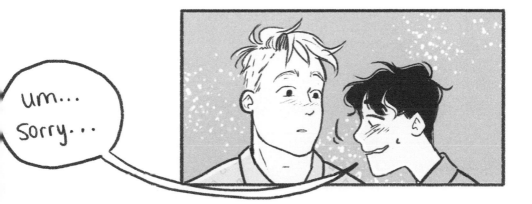

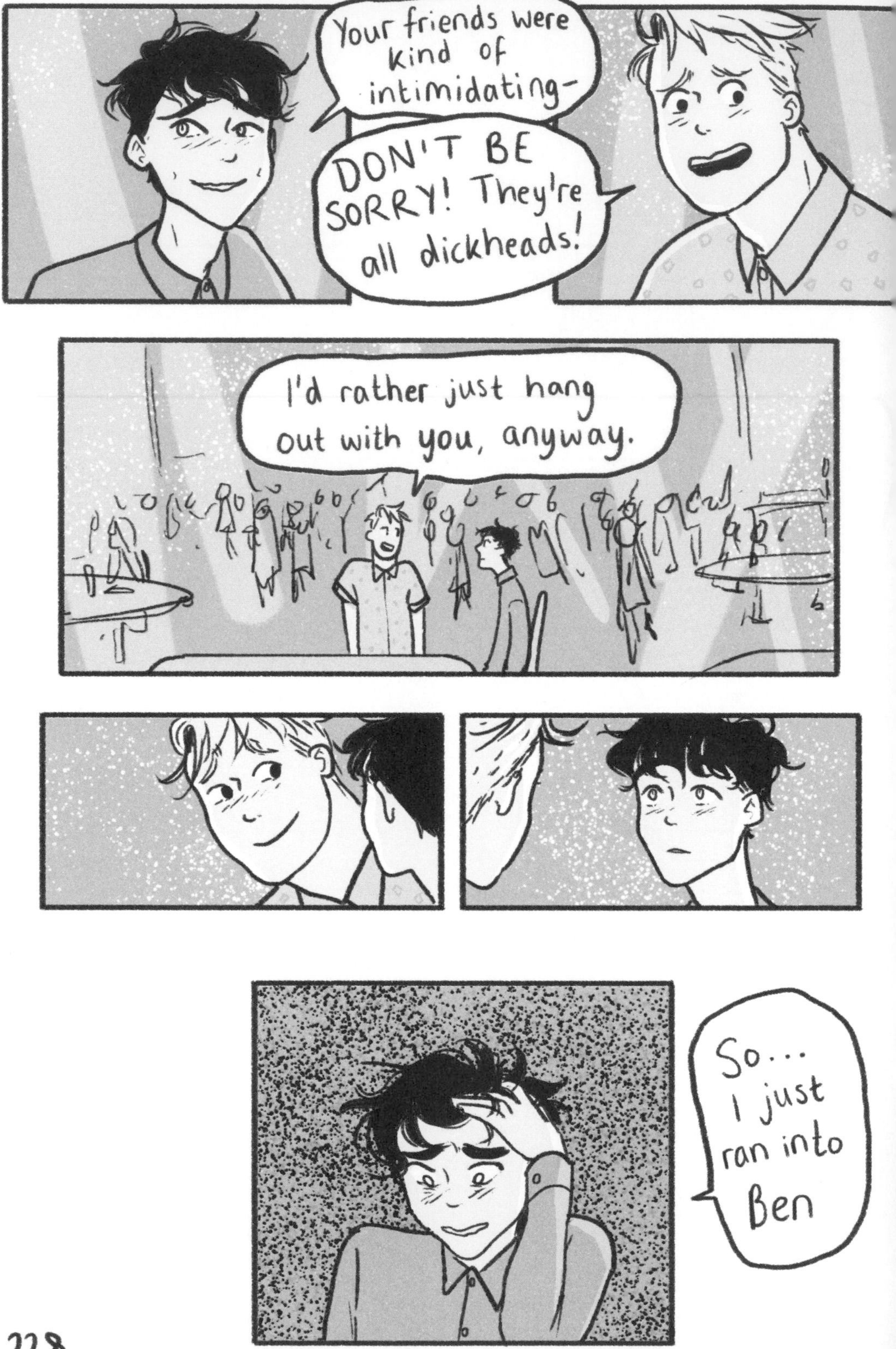
Your friends were kind of intimidating-
DON'T BE SORRY! They're all dickheads!
I'd rather just hang out with you, anyway.
So... I just ran into Ben

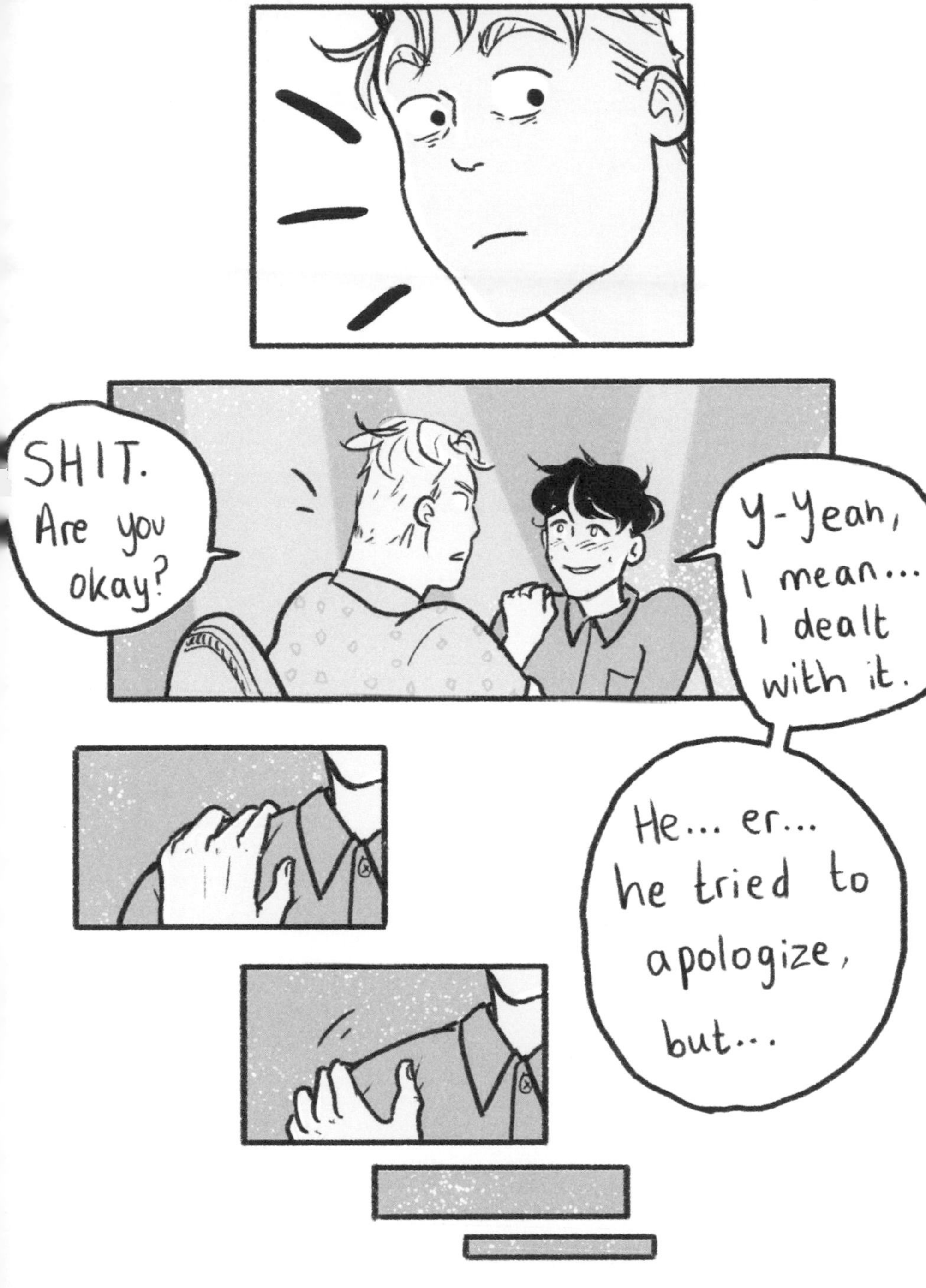
SHIT. Are you okay?
Y-Yeah, I mean... I dealt with it.
He... er... he tried to apologize, but...

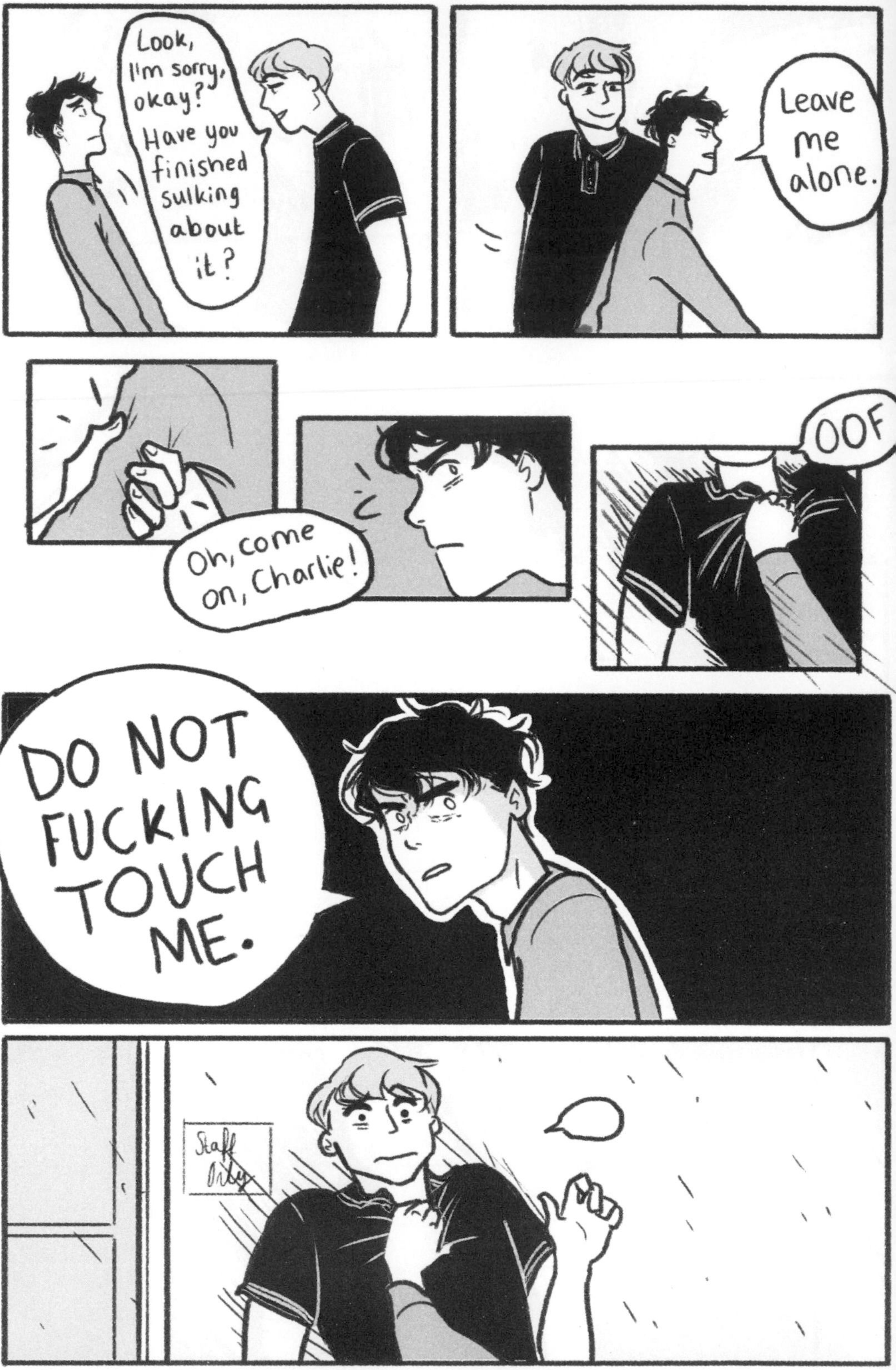
Look, I'm sorry, okay? Have you finished sulking about it?
Leave me alone.
Oh, come on, Charlie!
OOF
DO NOT FUCKING TOUCH ME.
Staff Only

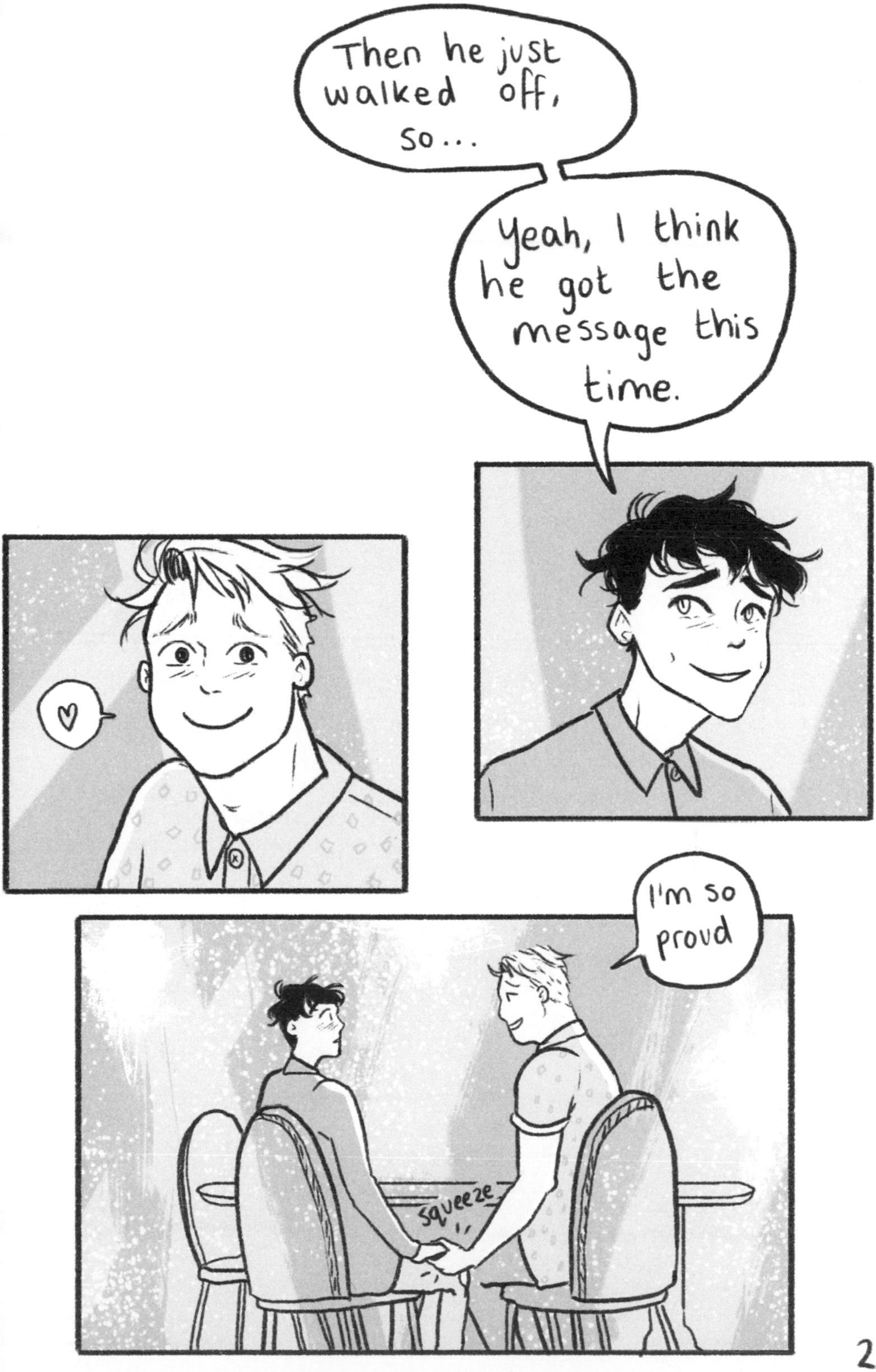
Then he just walked off, so...
Yeah, I think he got the message this time.
I'm so proud
squeeze

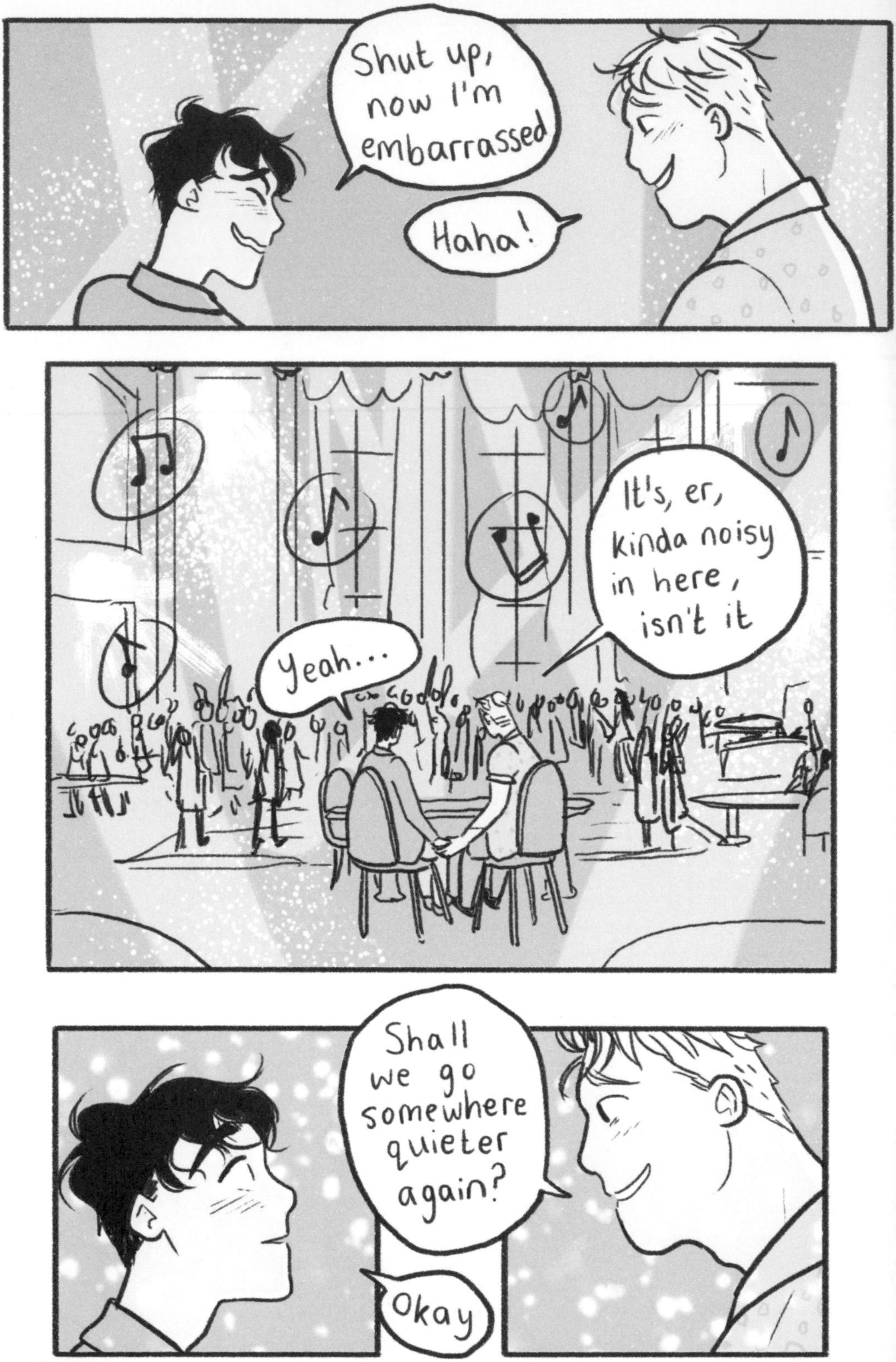
Shut up, now I'm embarrassed
Haha!
It's, er, kinda noisy in here, isn't it
Yeah...
Shall we go somewhere quieter again?
Okay

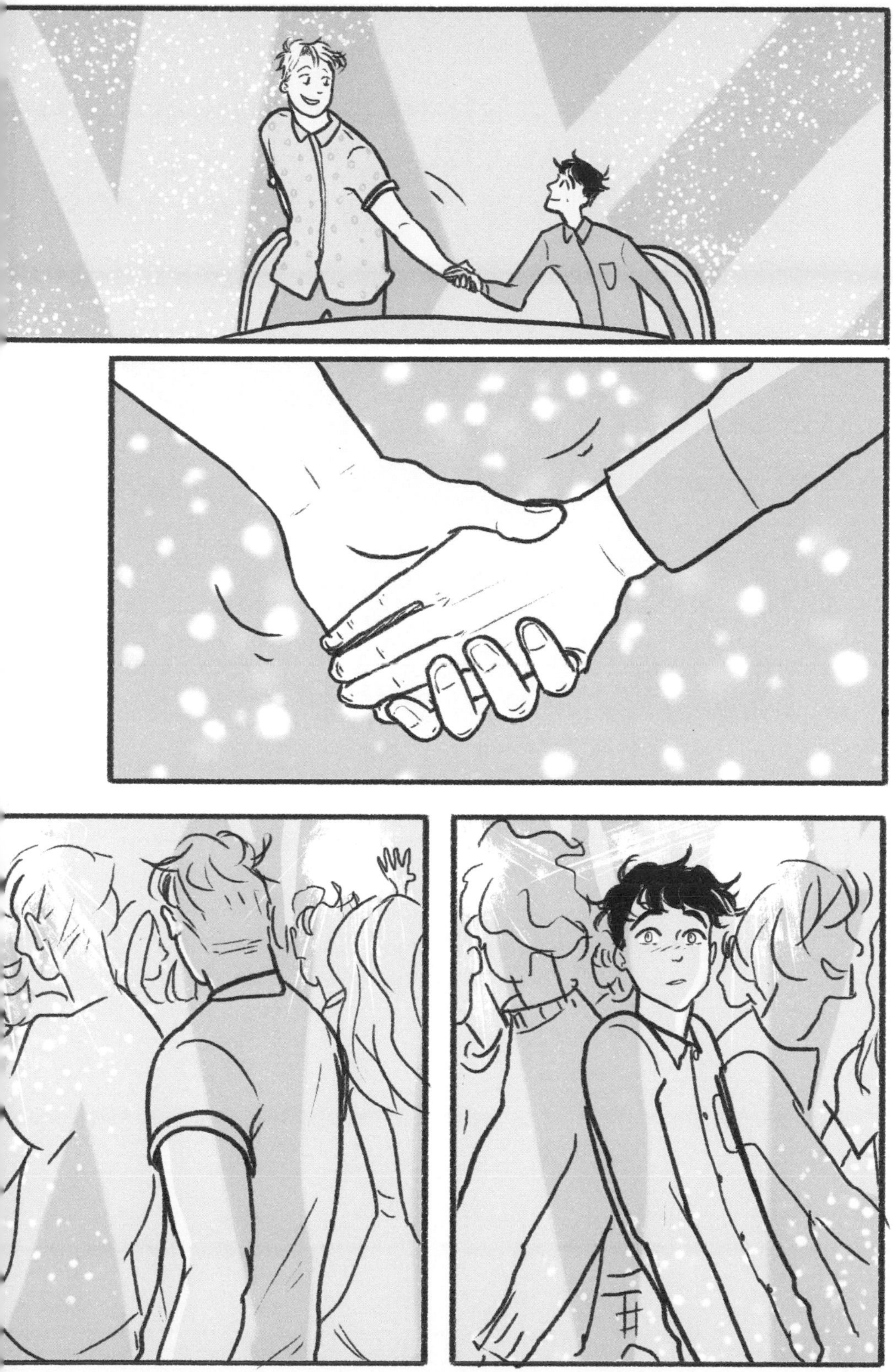

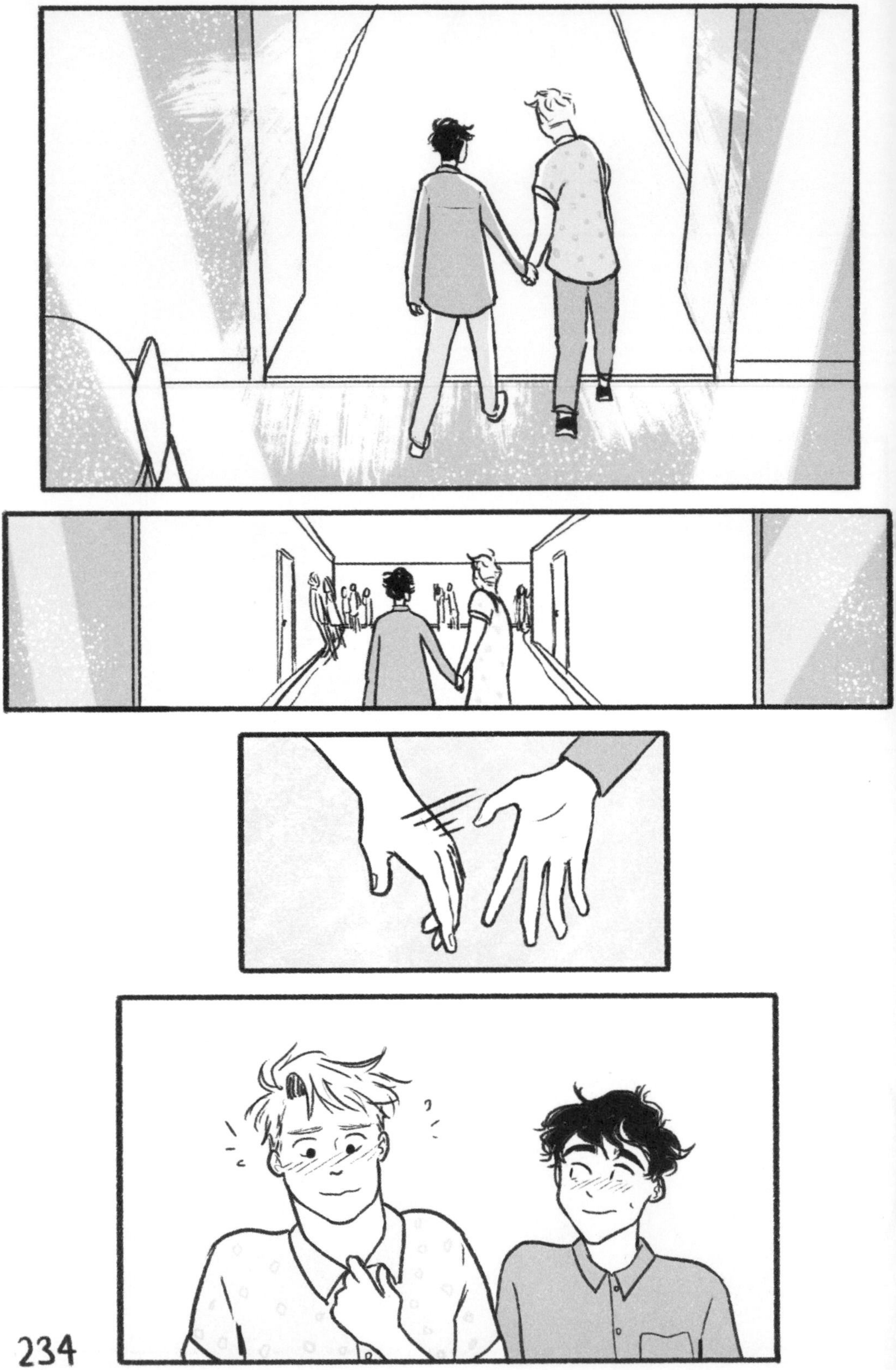

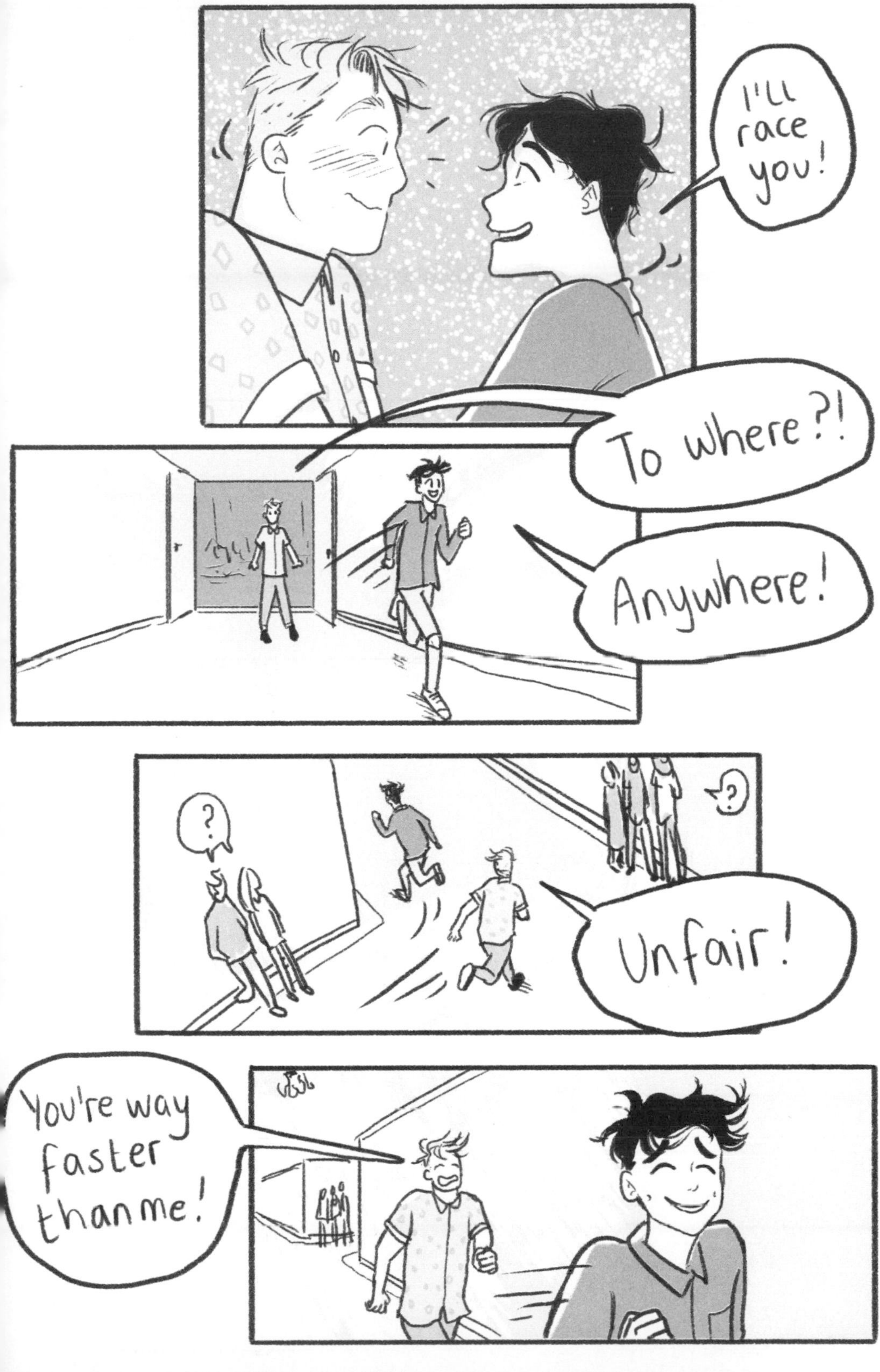
I'll race you!
To where?!
Anywhere!
?
?
Unfair!
You're way faster than me!

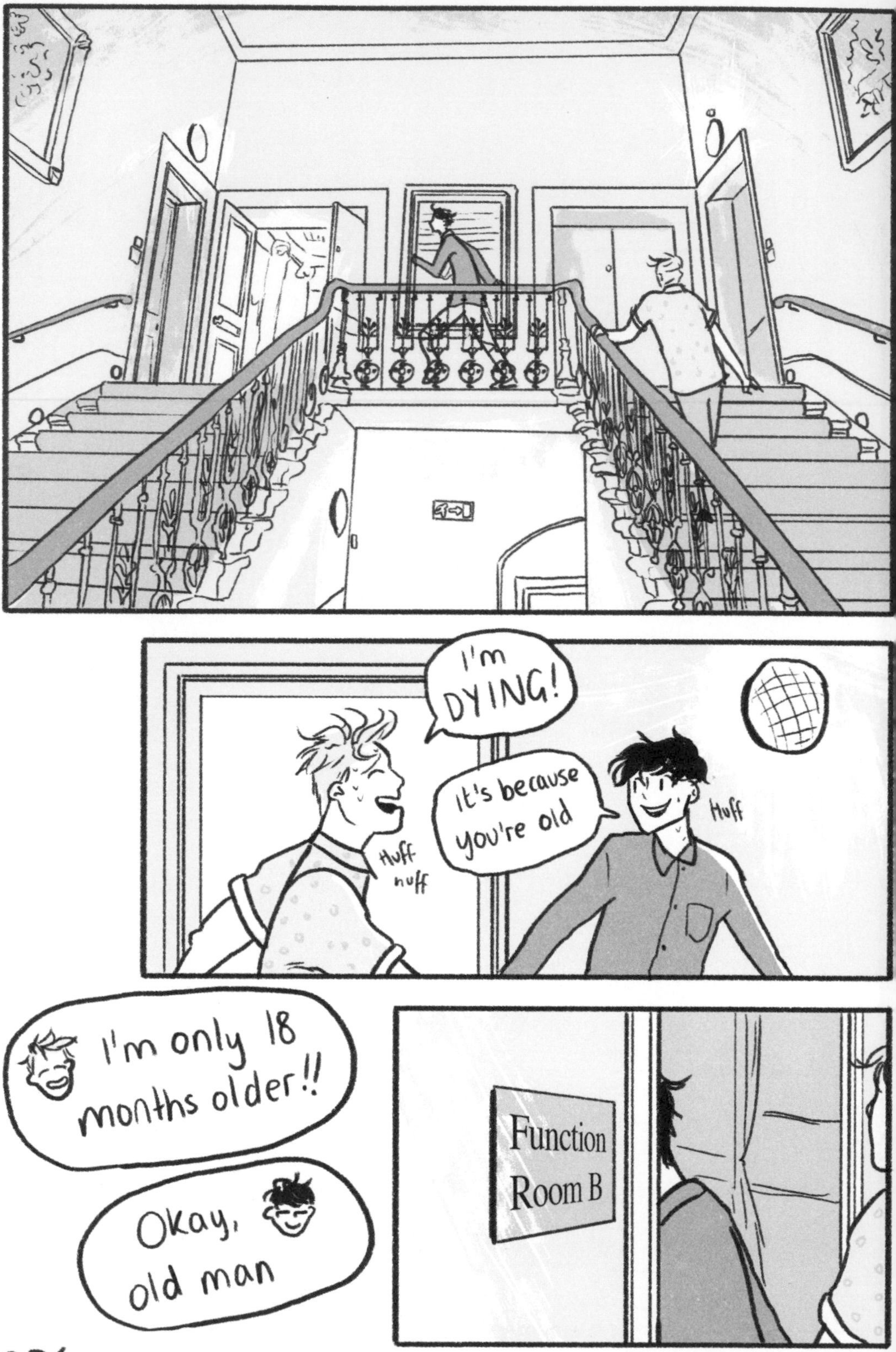

I'm DYING!
It's because you're old
Huff huff
Huff
I'm only 18 months older!!
Okay, old man
Function Room B

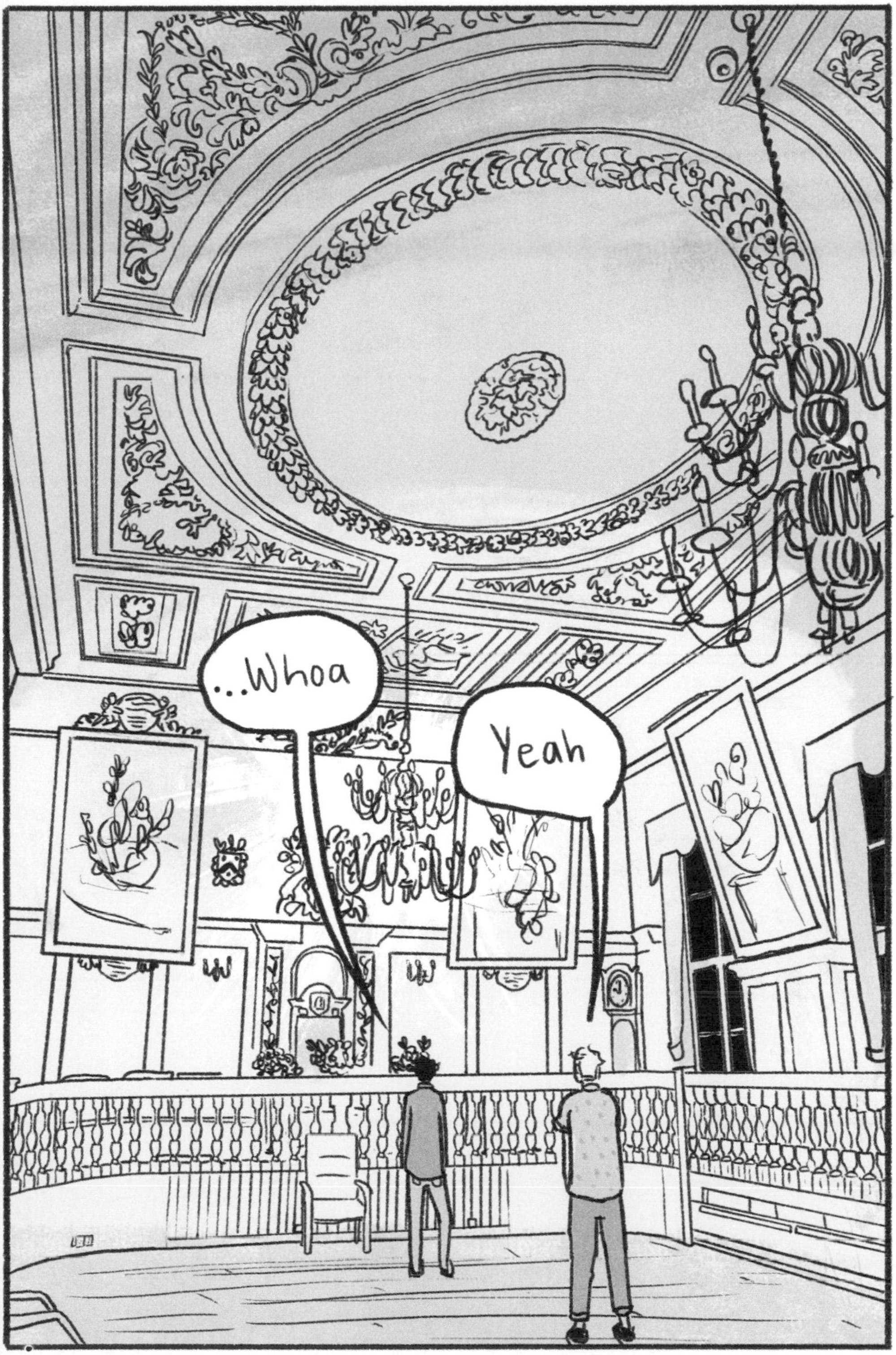
...Whoa
Yeah

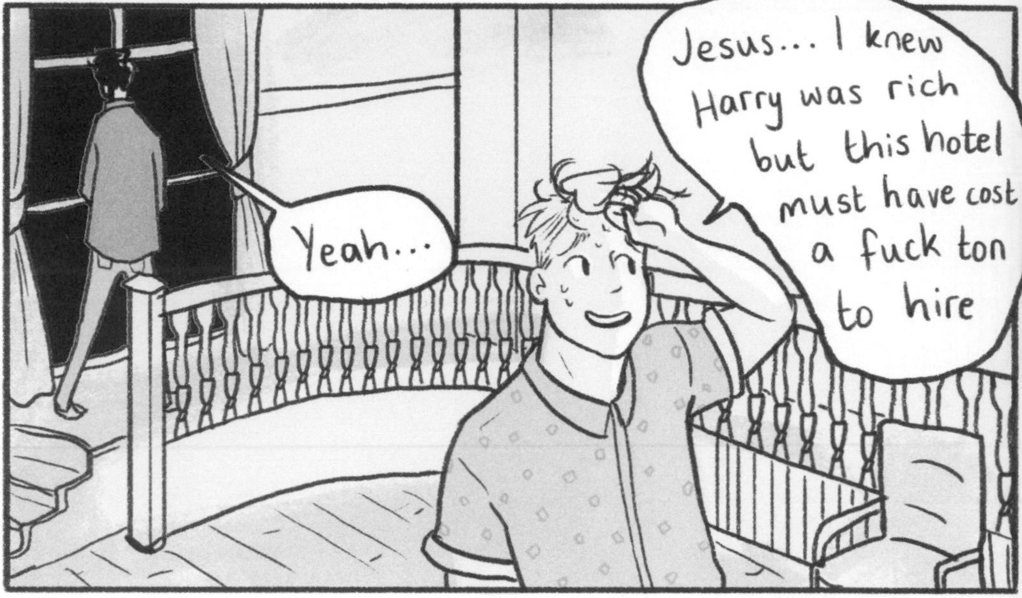
Yeah...
Jesus... I knew Harry was rich but this hotel must have cost a fuck ton to hire

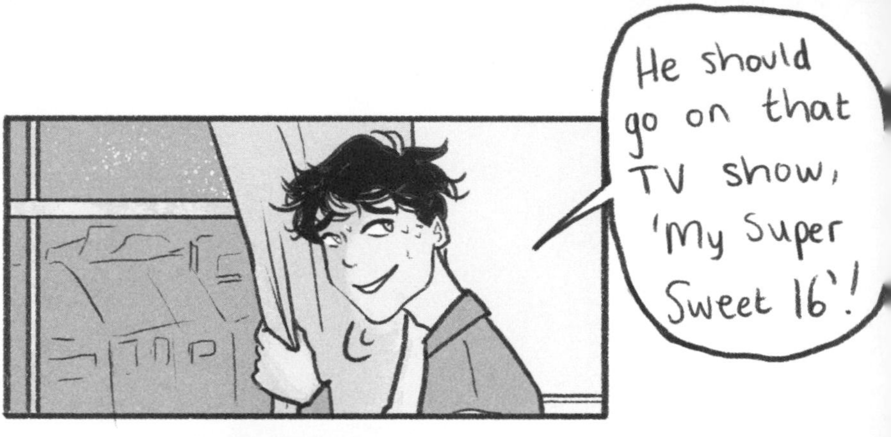
He should go on that TV show, 'My Super Sweet 16'!

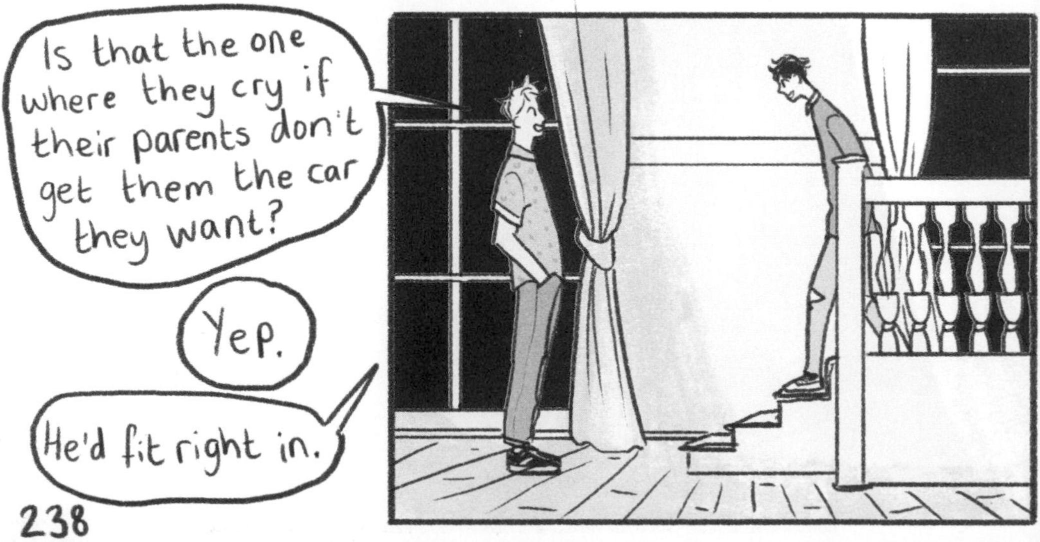
Is that the one where they cry if their parents don't get them the car they want?
Yep.
He'd fit right in.

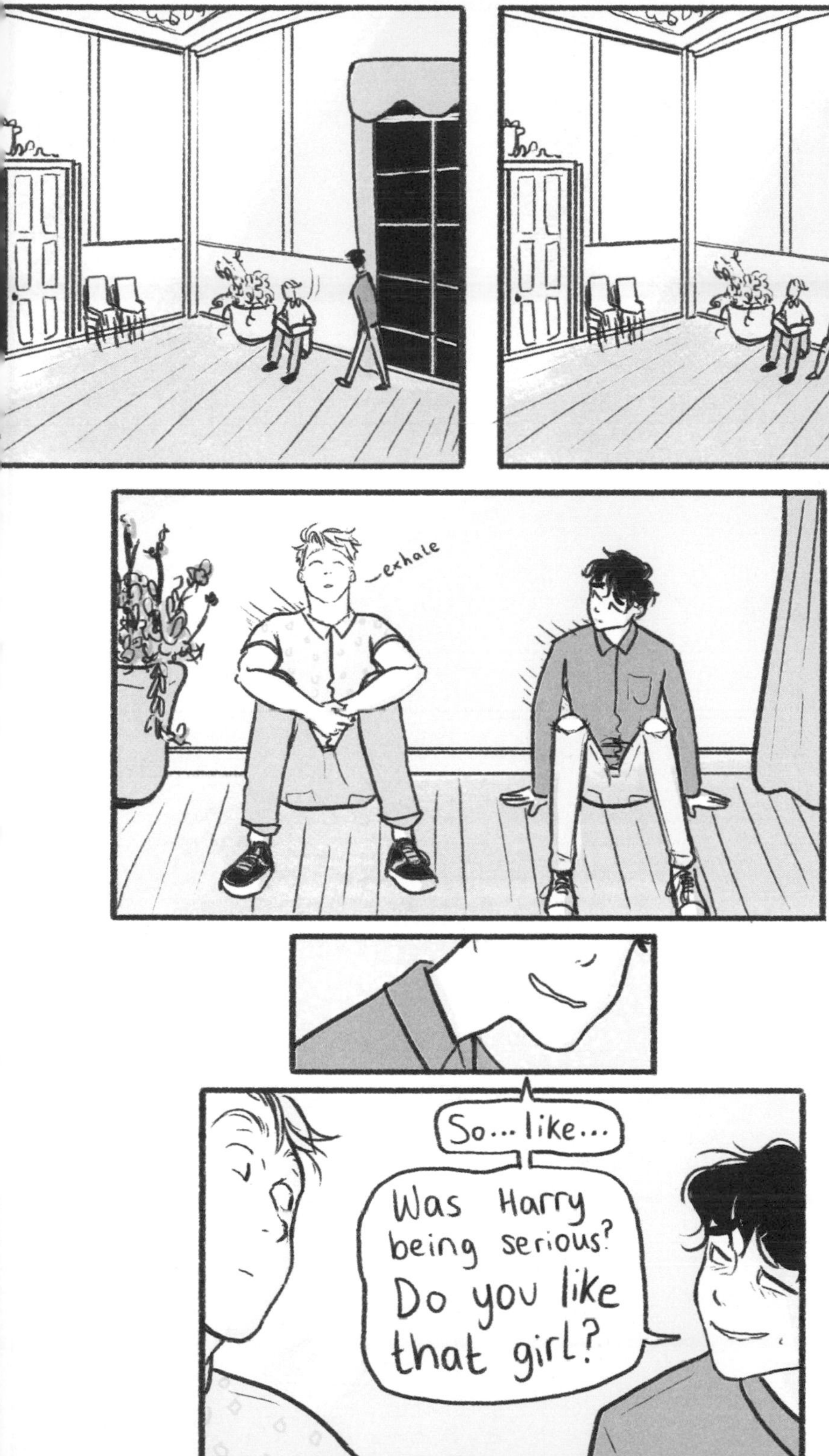
exhale
So... like...
Was Harry being serious? Do you like that girl?

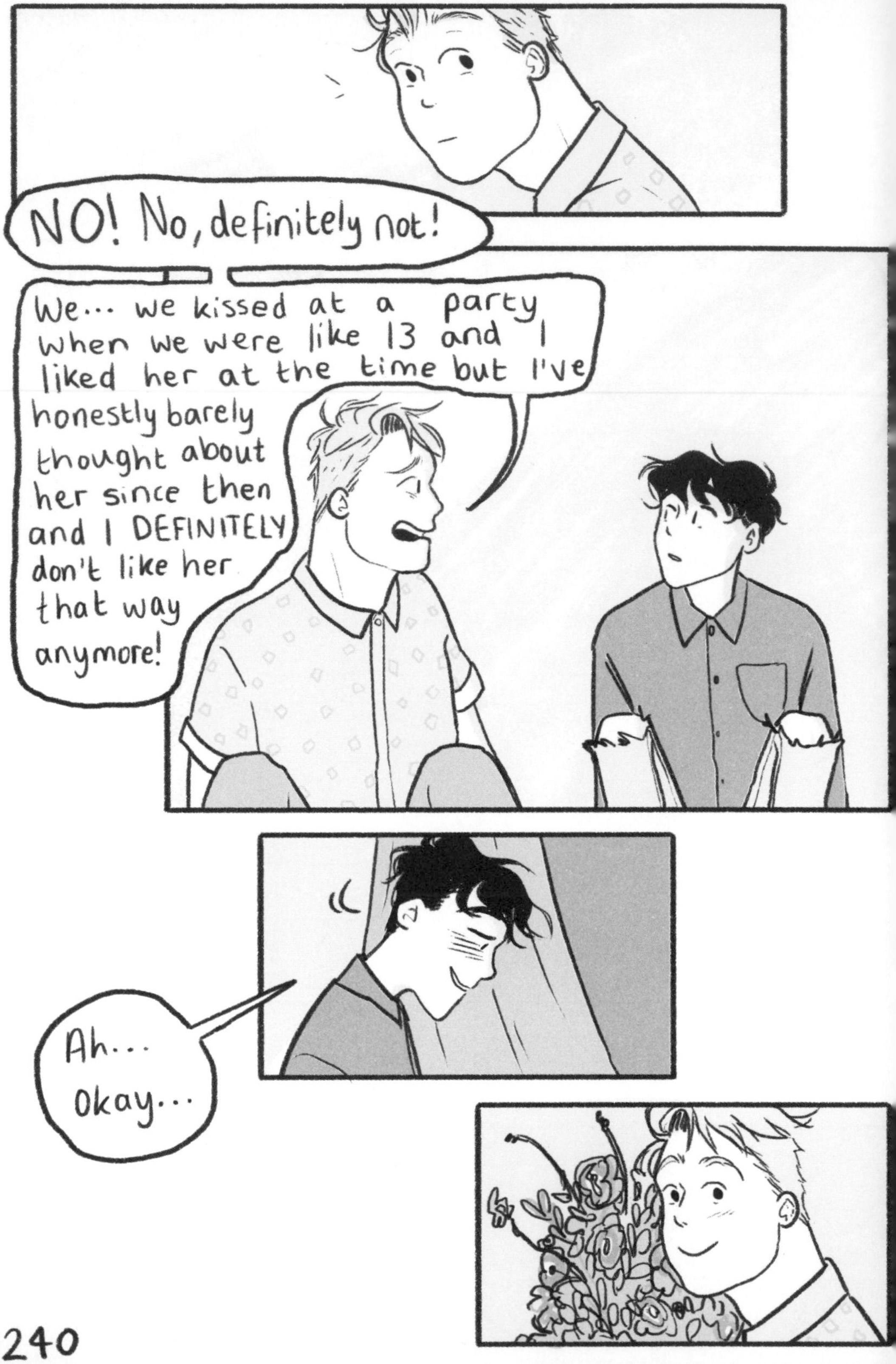
NO! No, definitely not!
We... we kissed at a party when we were like 13 and I liked her at the time but I've honestly barely thought about her since then and I DEFINITELY don't like her that way anymore!
Ah... Okay...

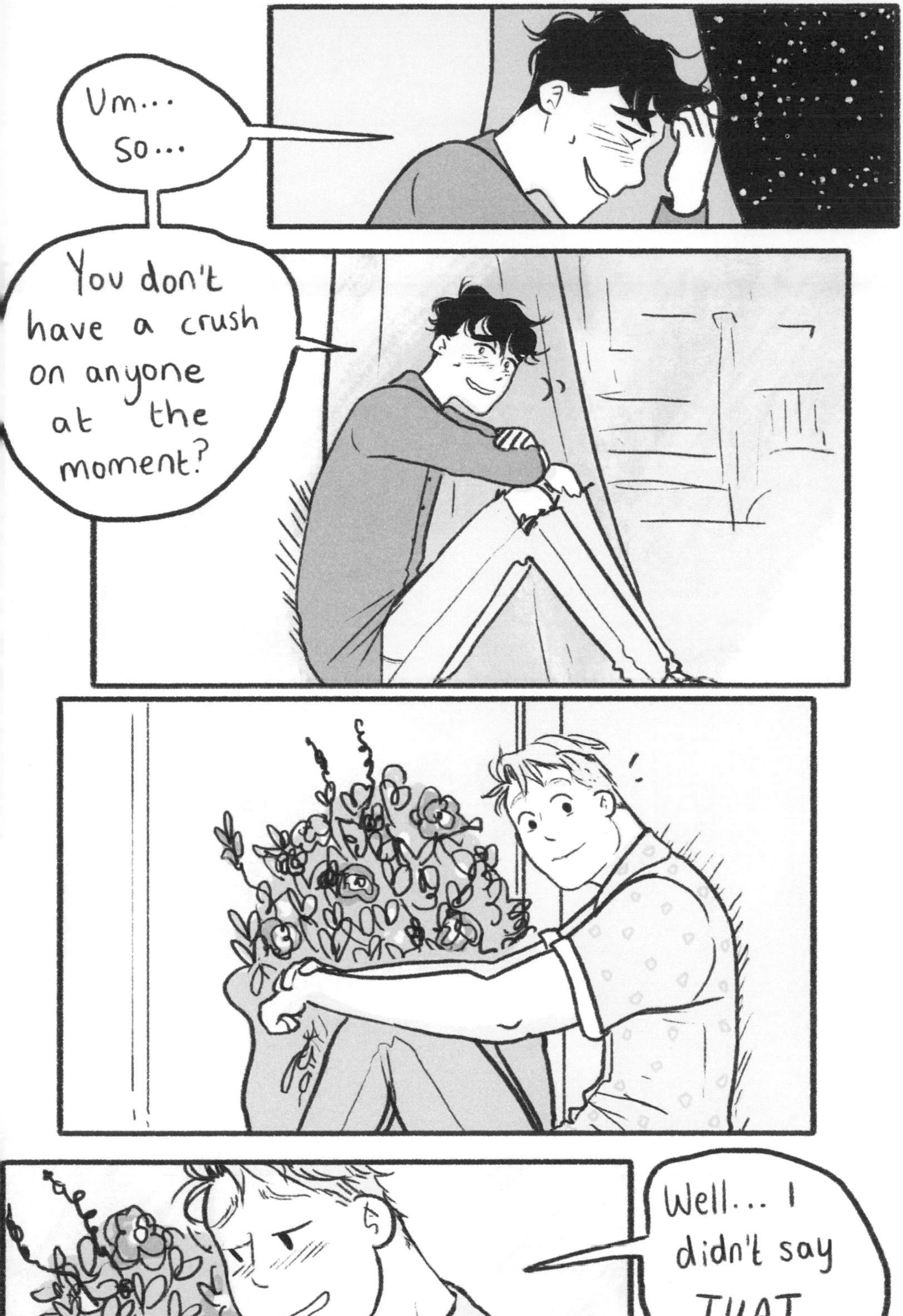
Um... so...
You don't have a crush on anyone at the moment?
Well... I didn't say THAT...

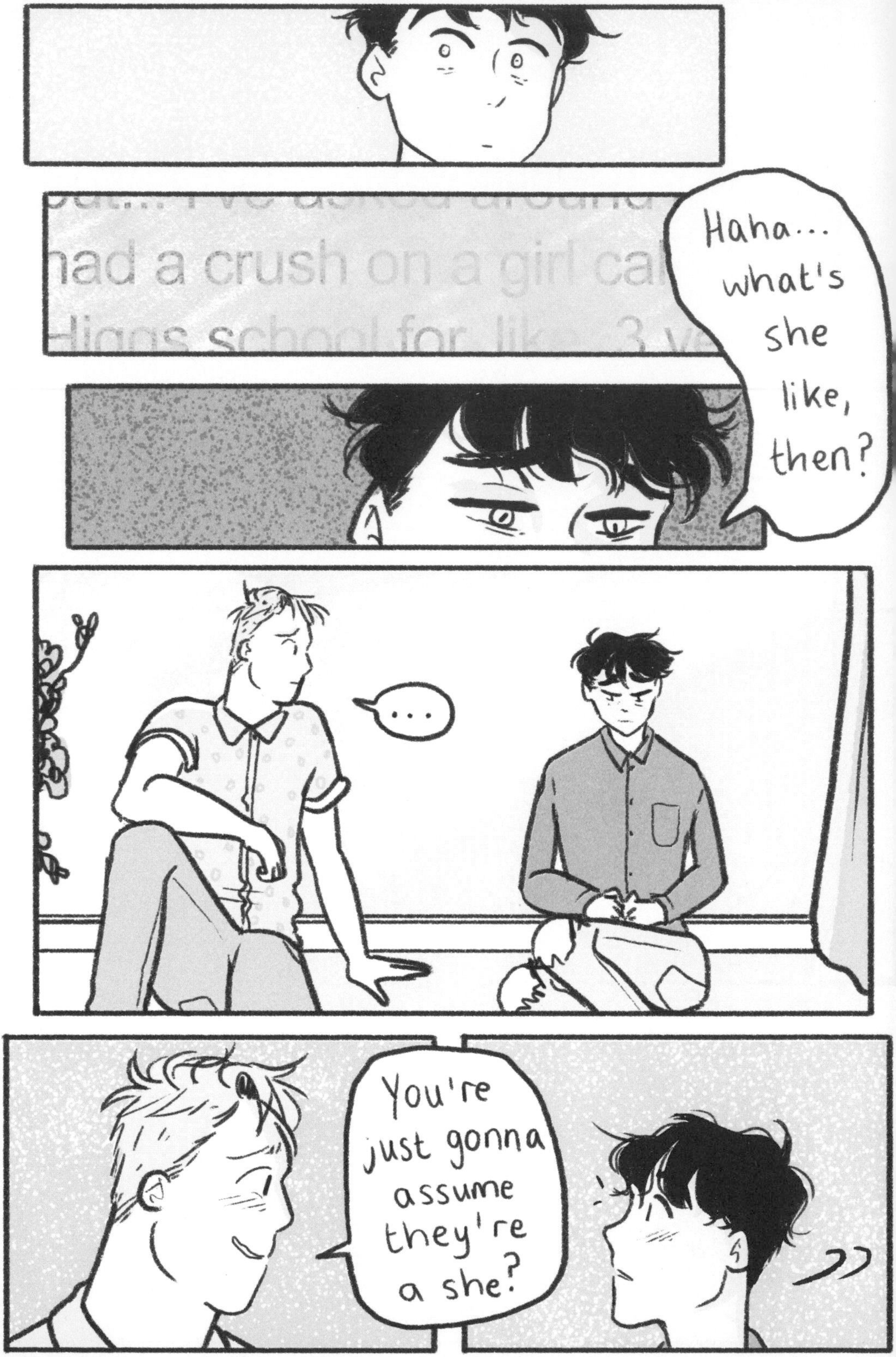

had a crush on a girl
Haha... what's she like, then?
...
You're just gonna assume they're a she?

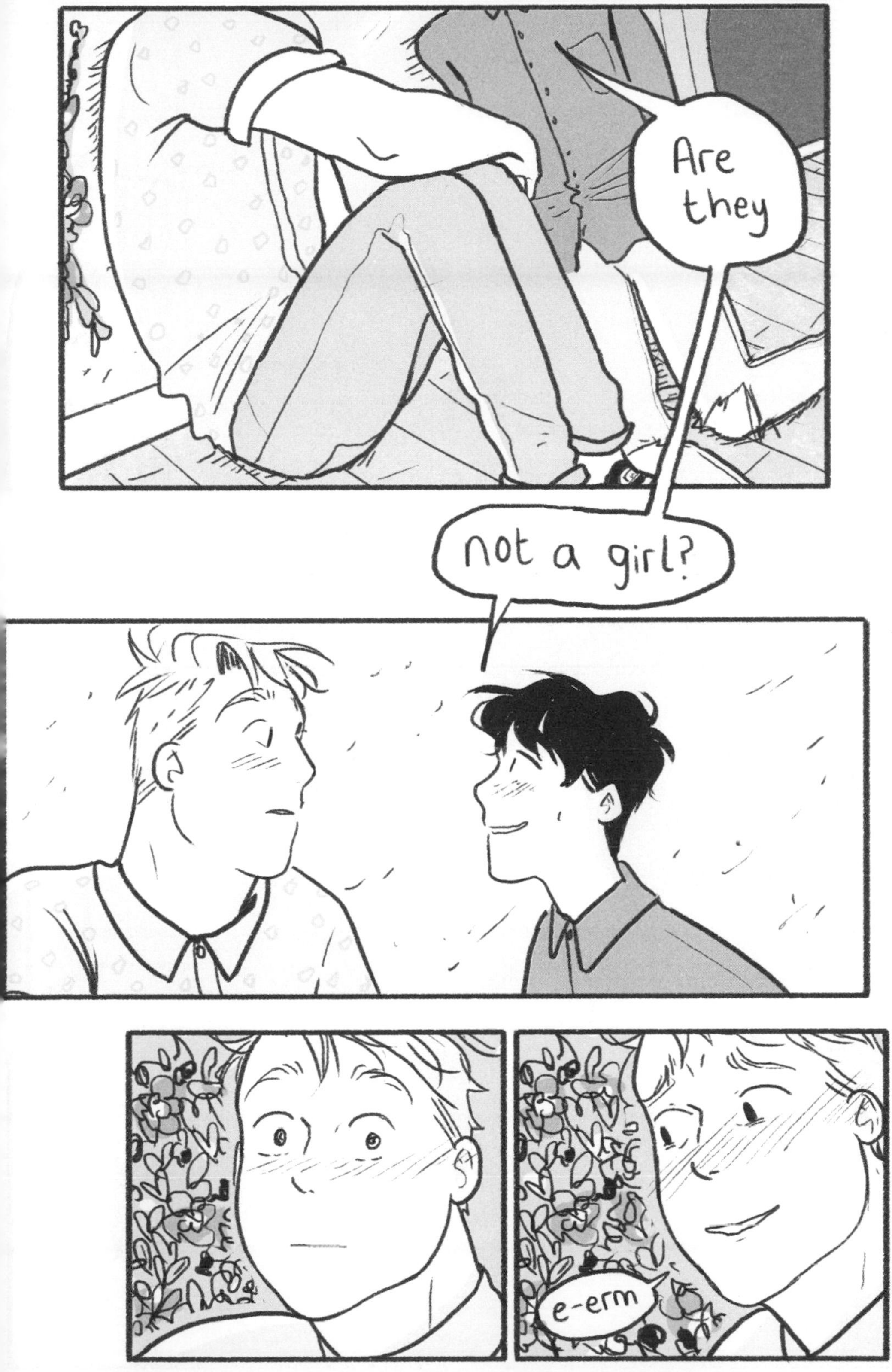
Are they
not a girl?
e-erm

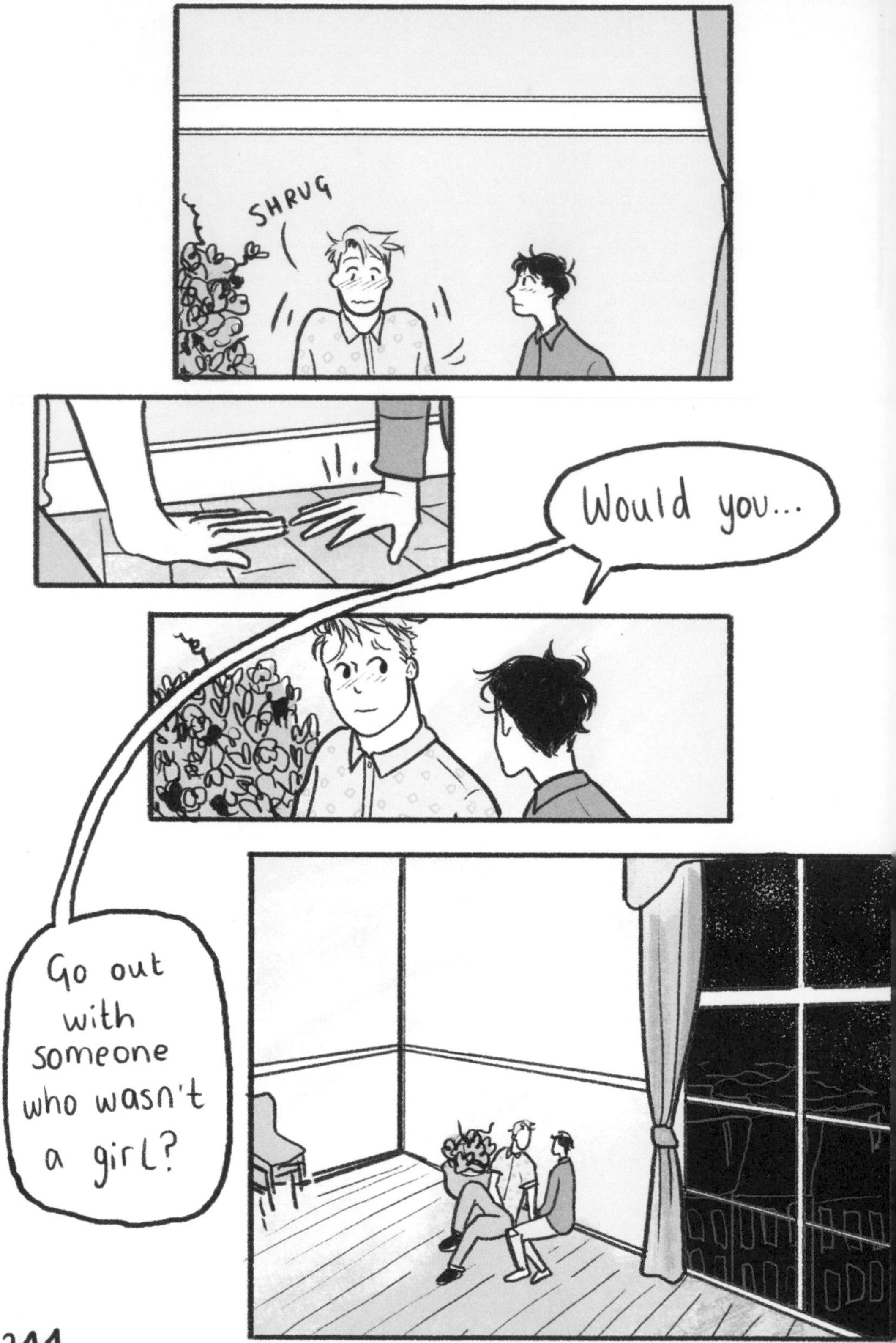
SHRUG
Would you...
Go out with someone who wasn't a girl?

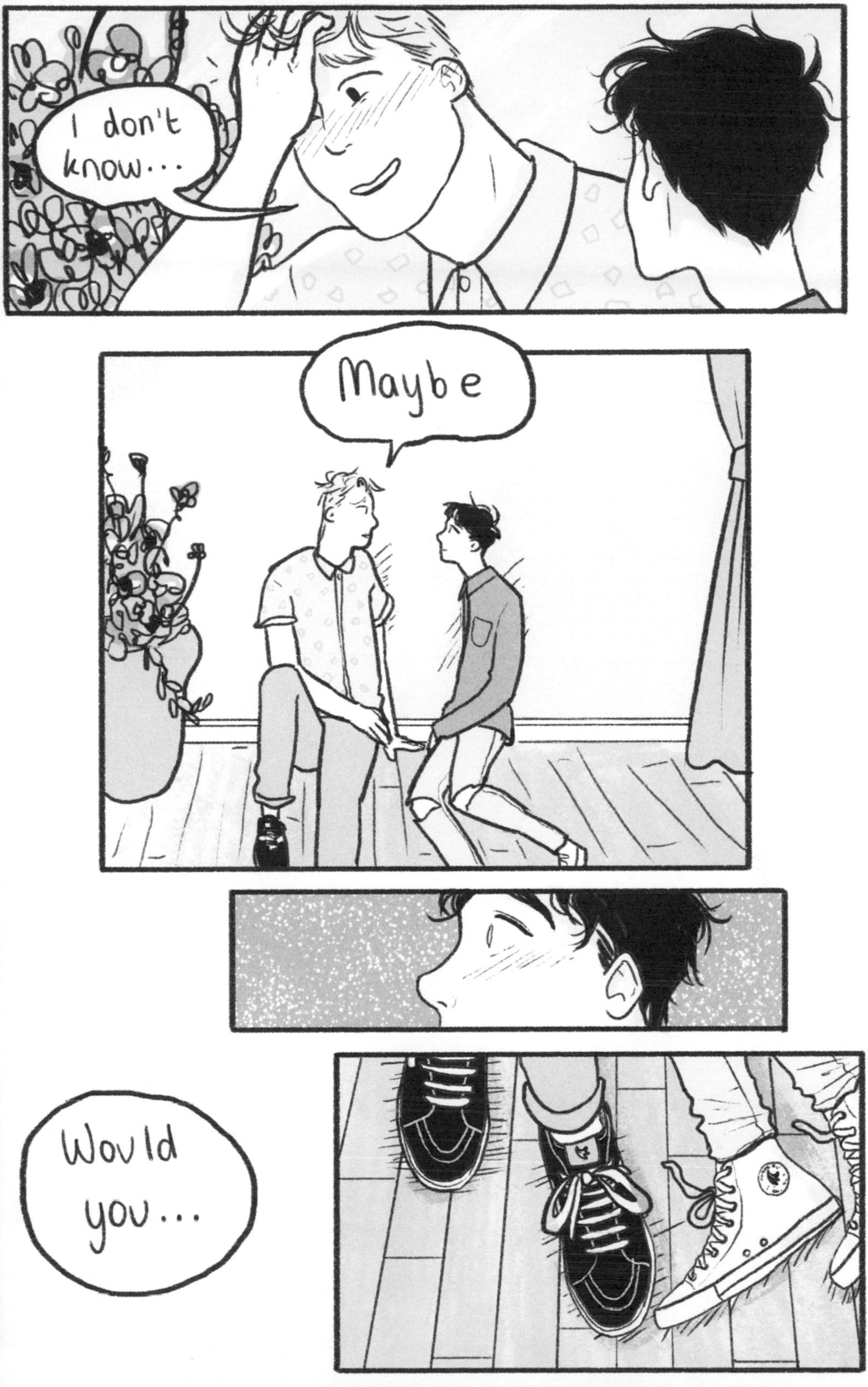
I don't know...
Maybe
Would you...

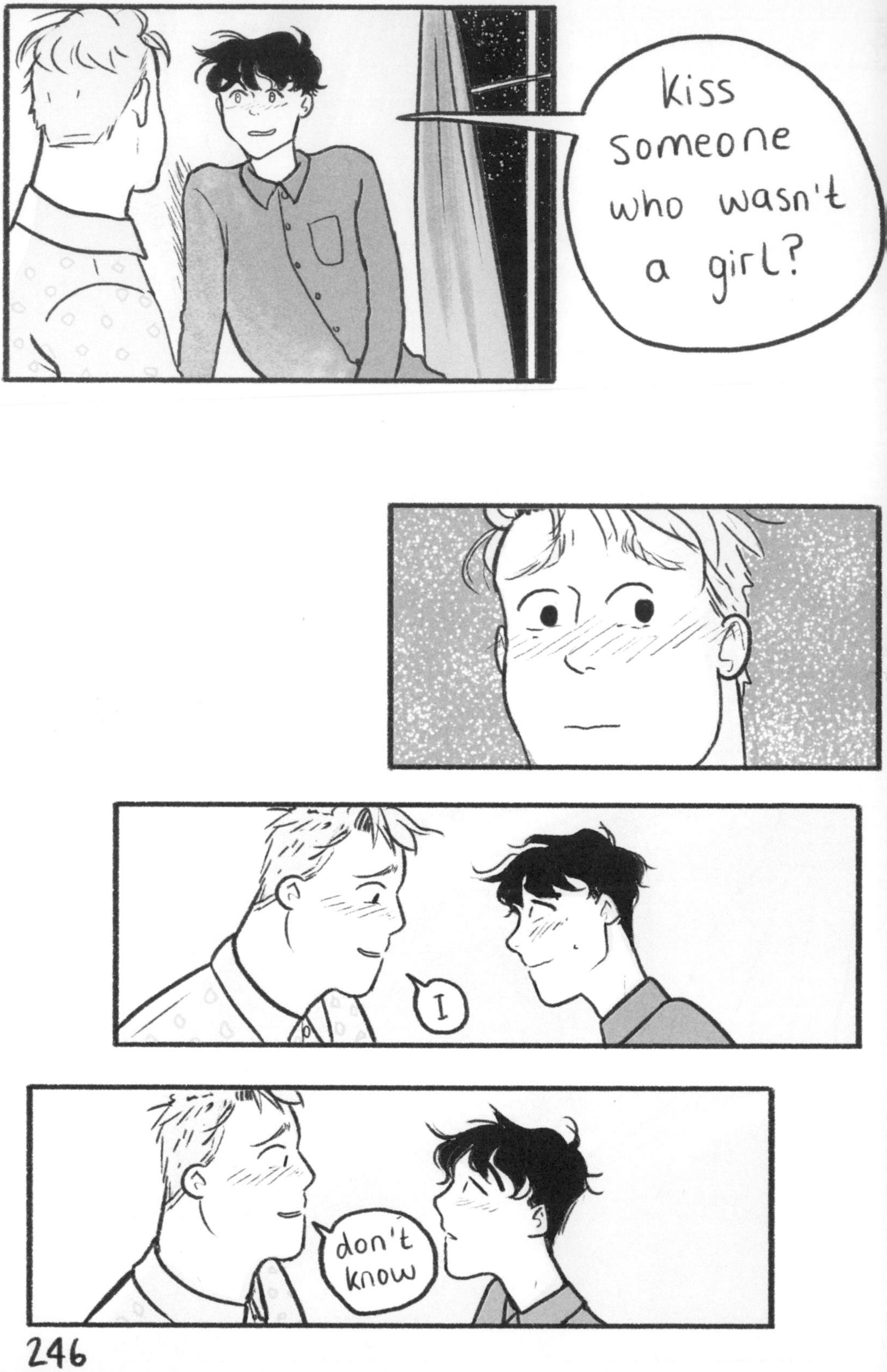
Kiss someone who wasn't a girl?
I
don't know

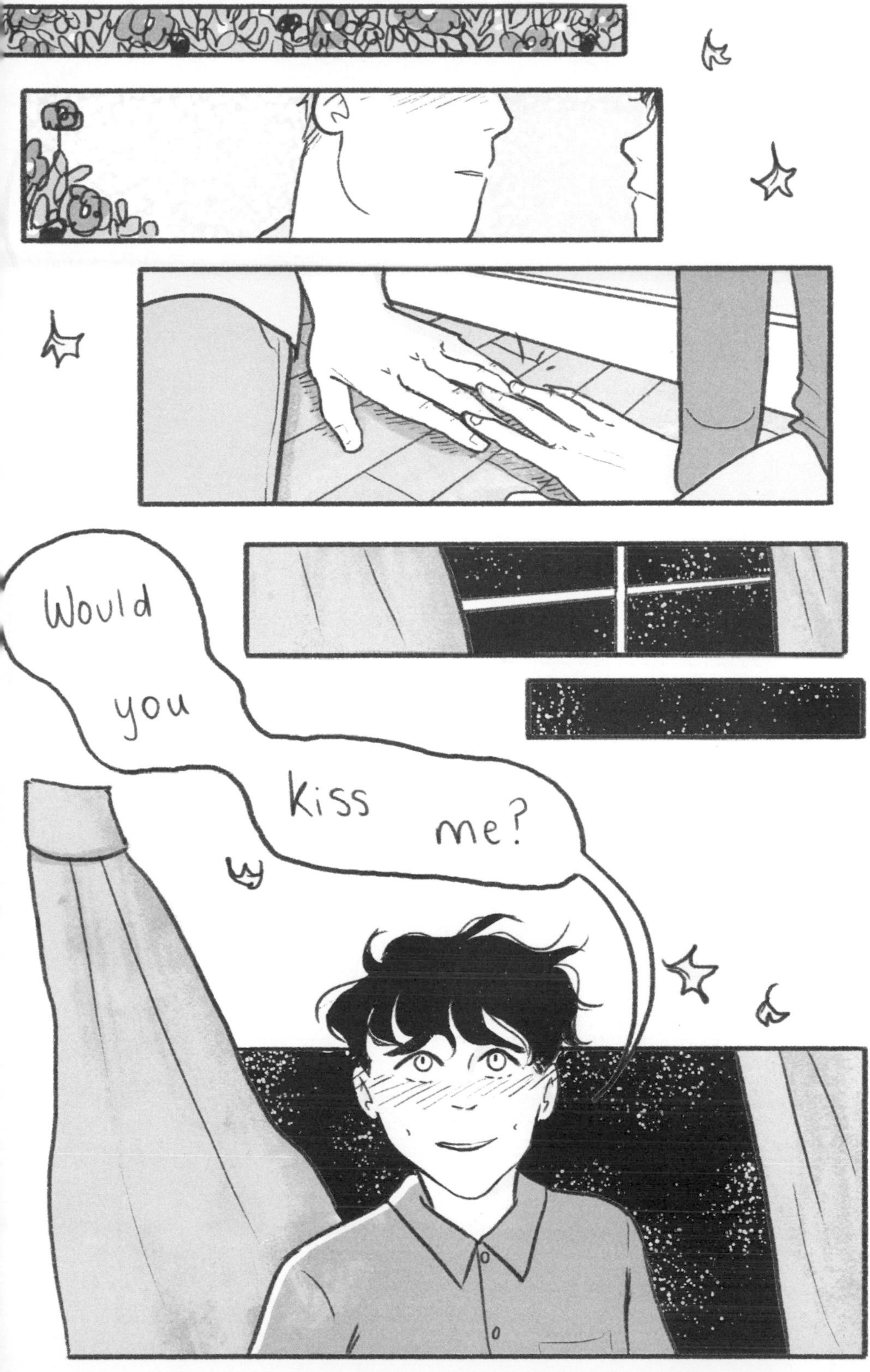
Would you kiss me?

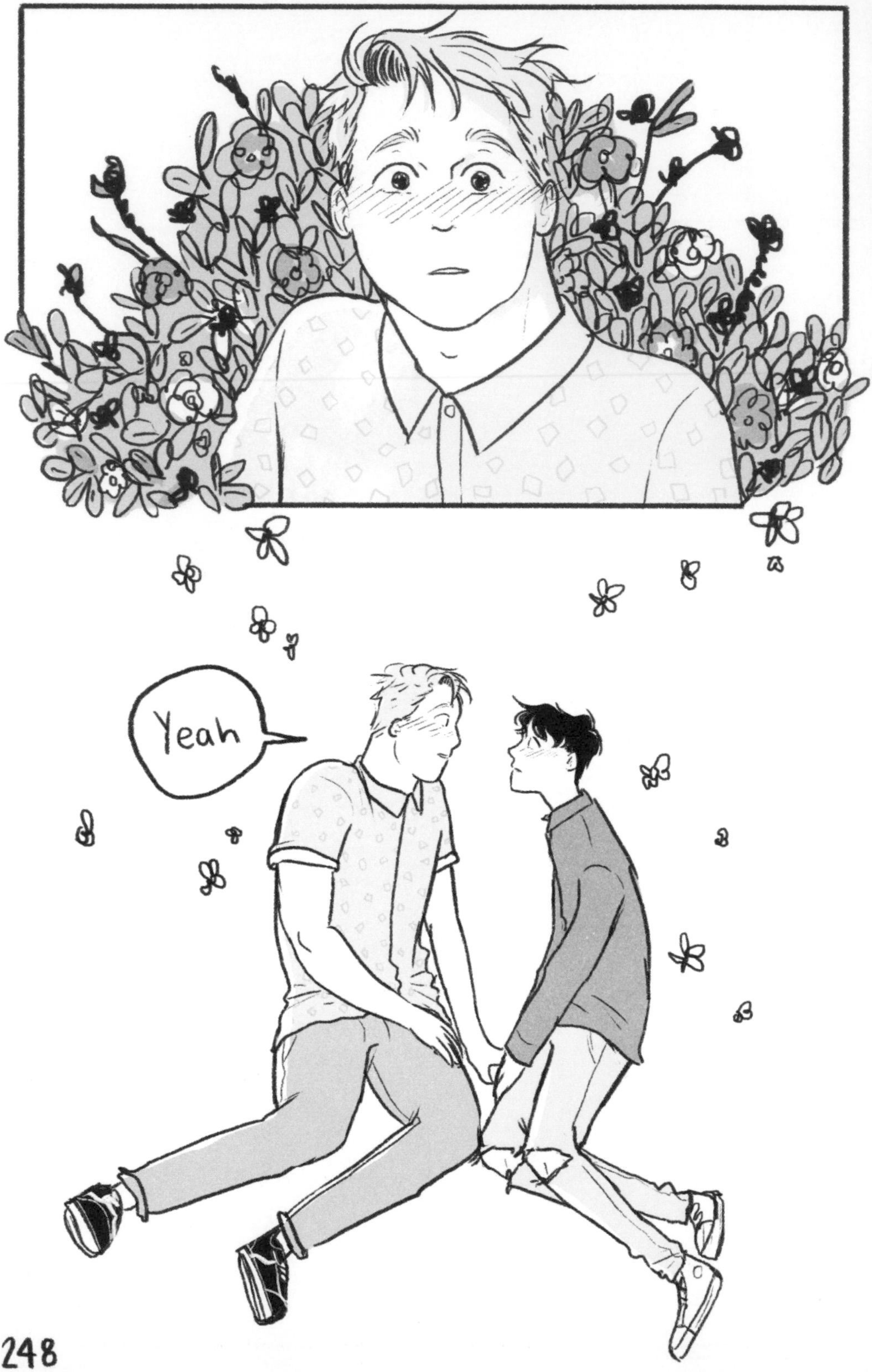
Yeah

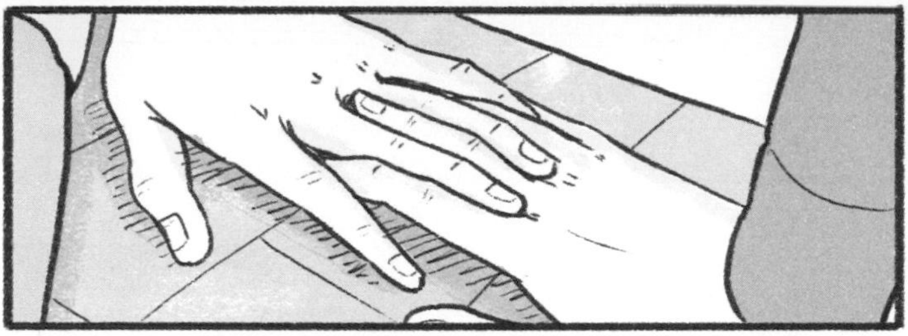

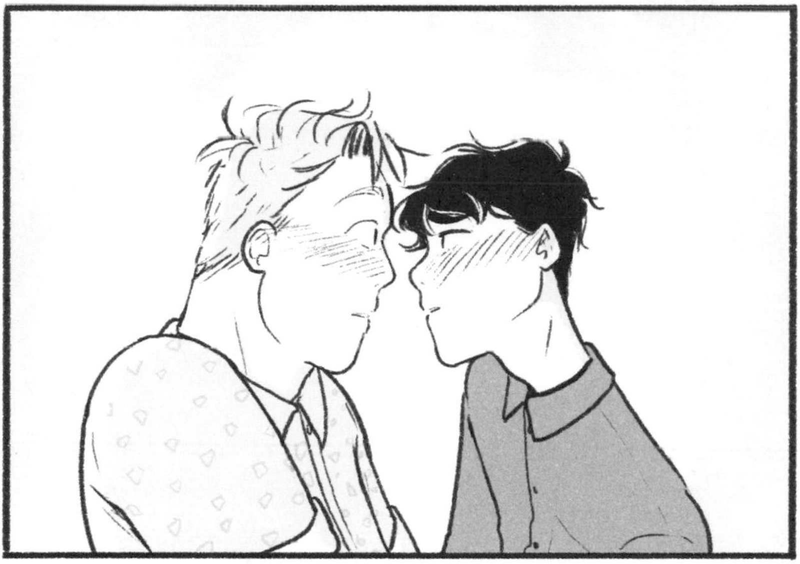

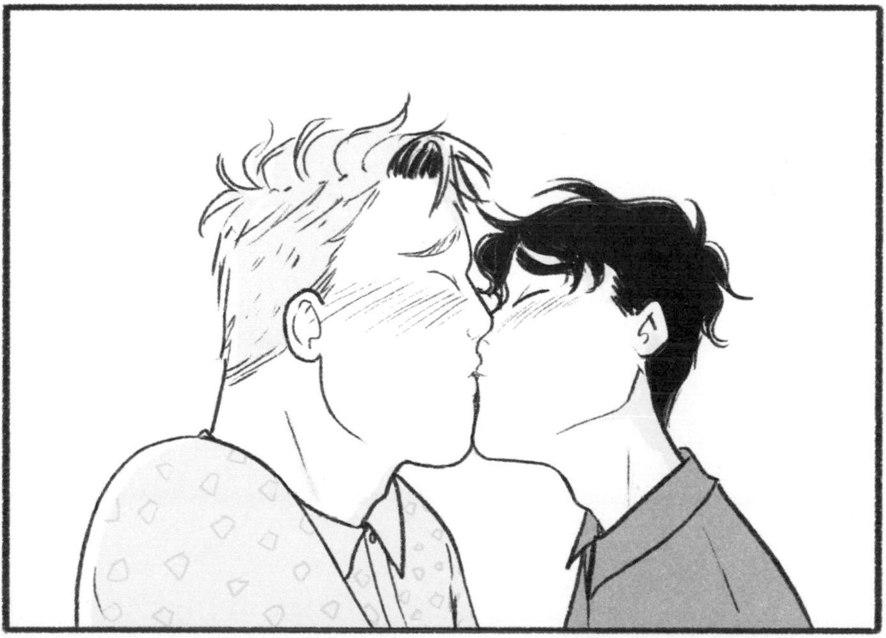

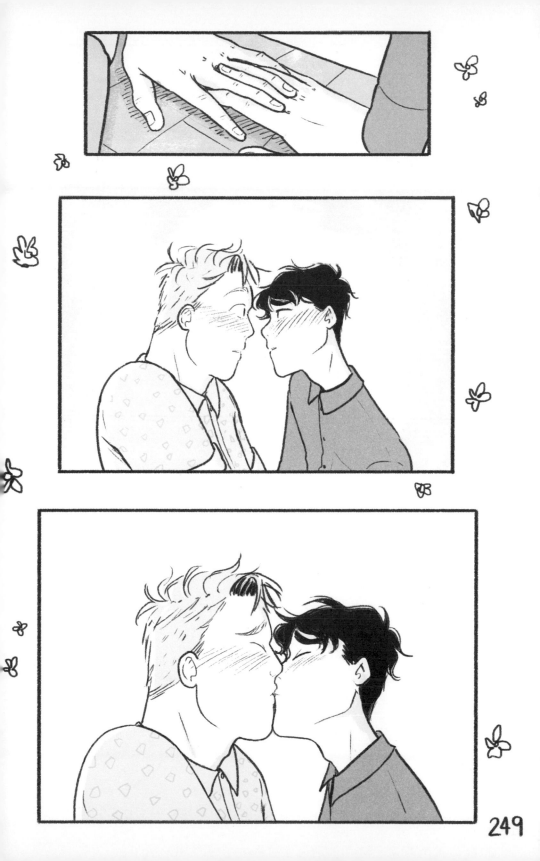

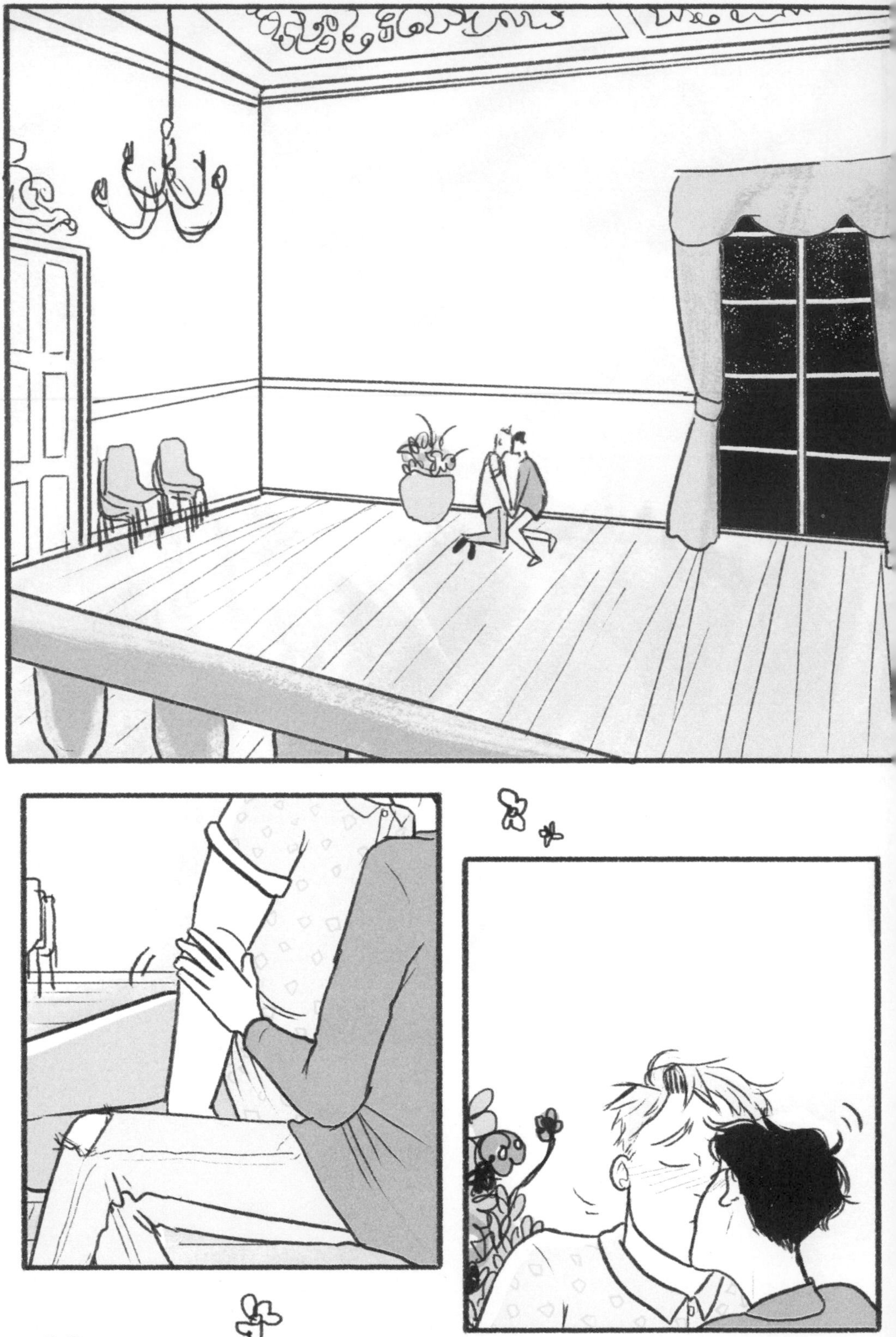

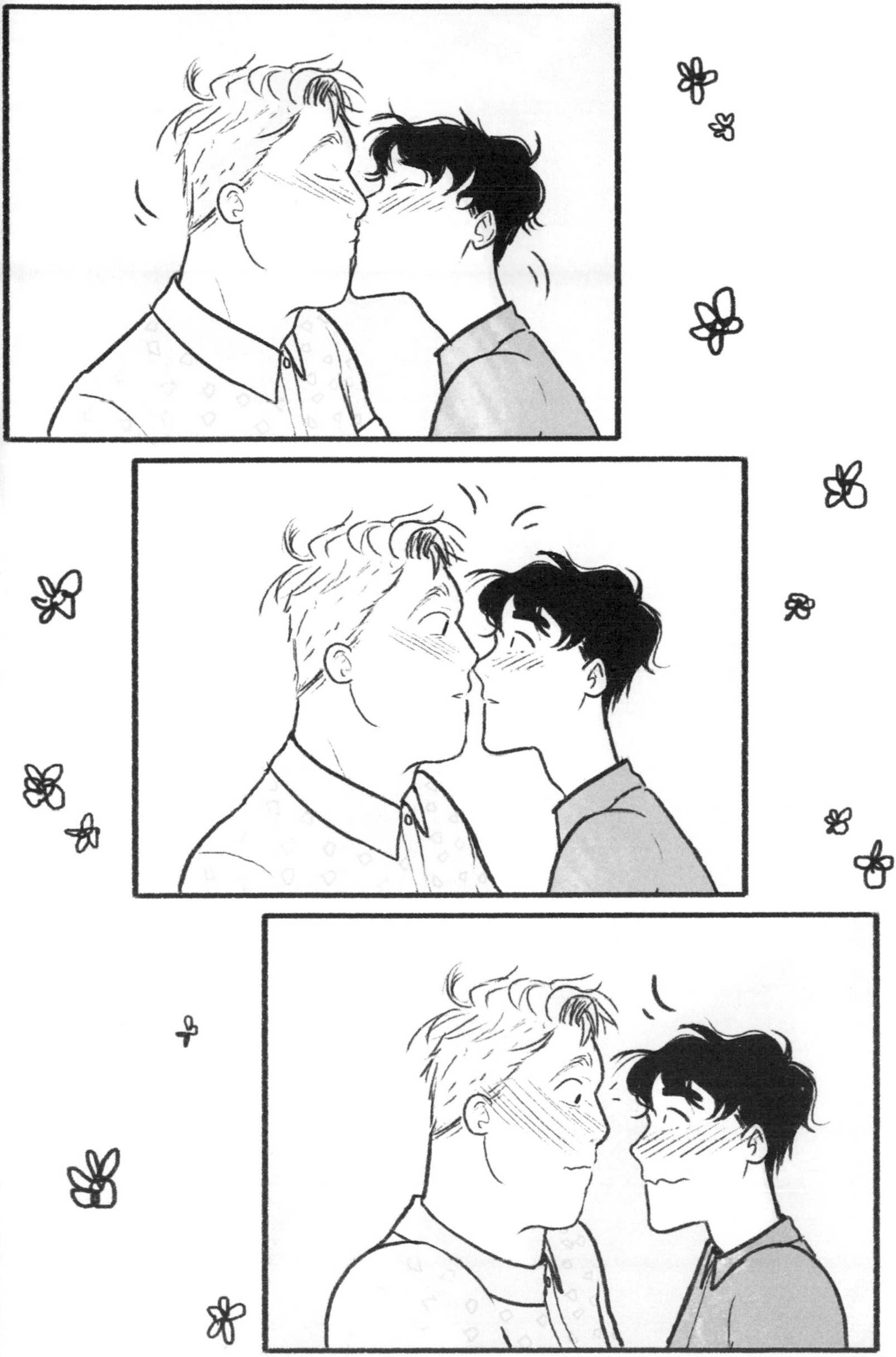

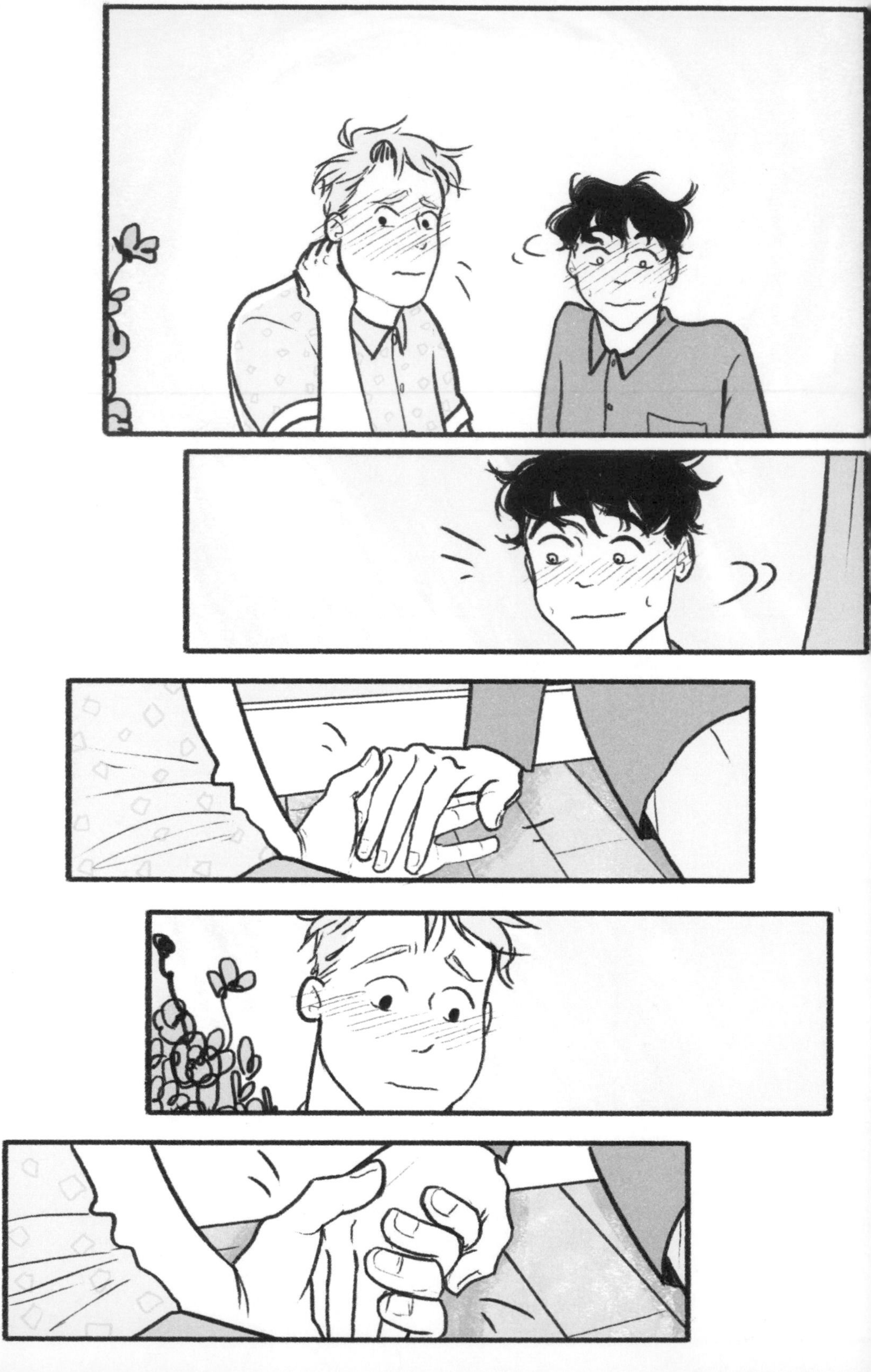

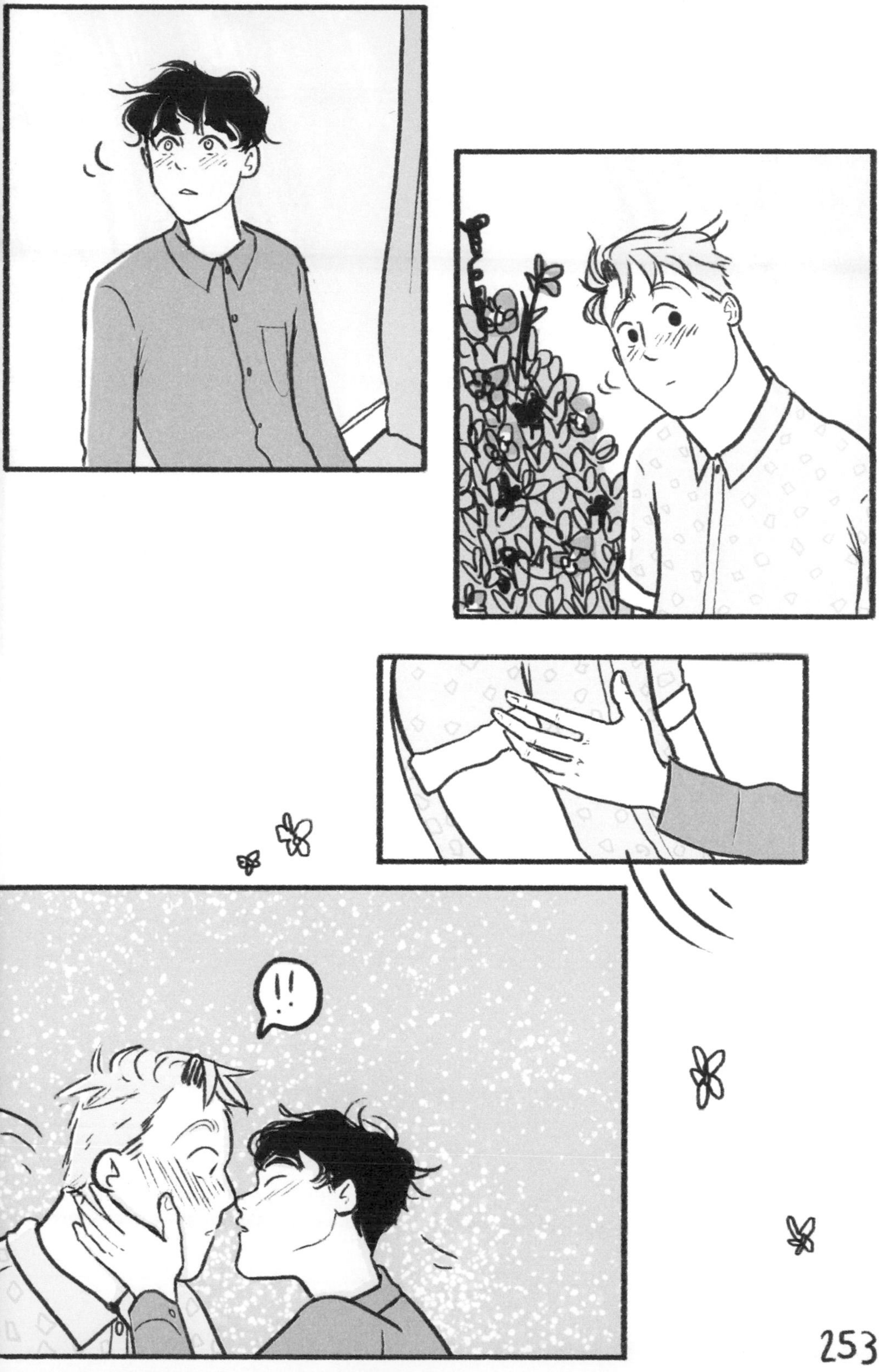
!!

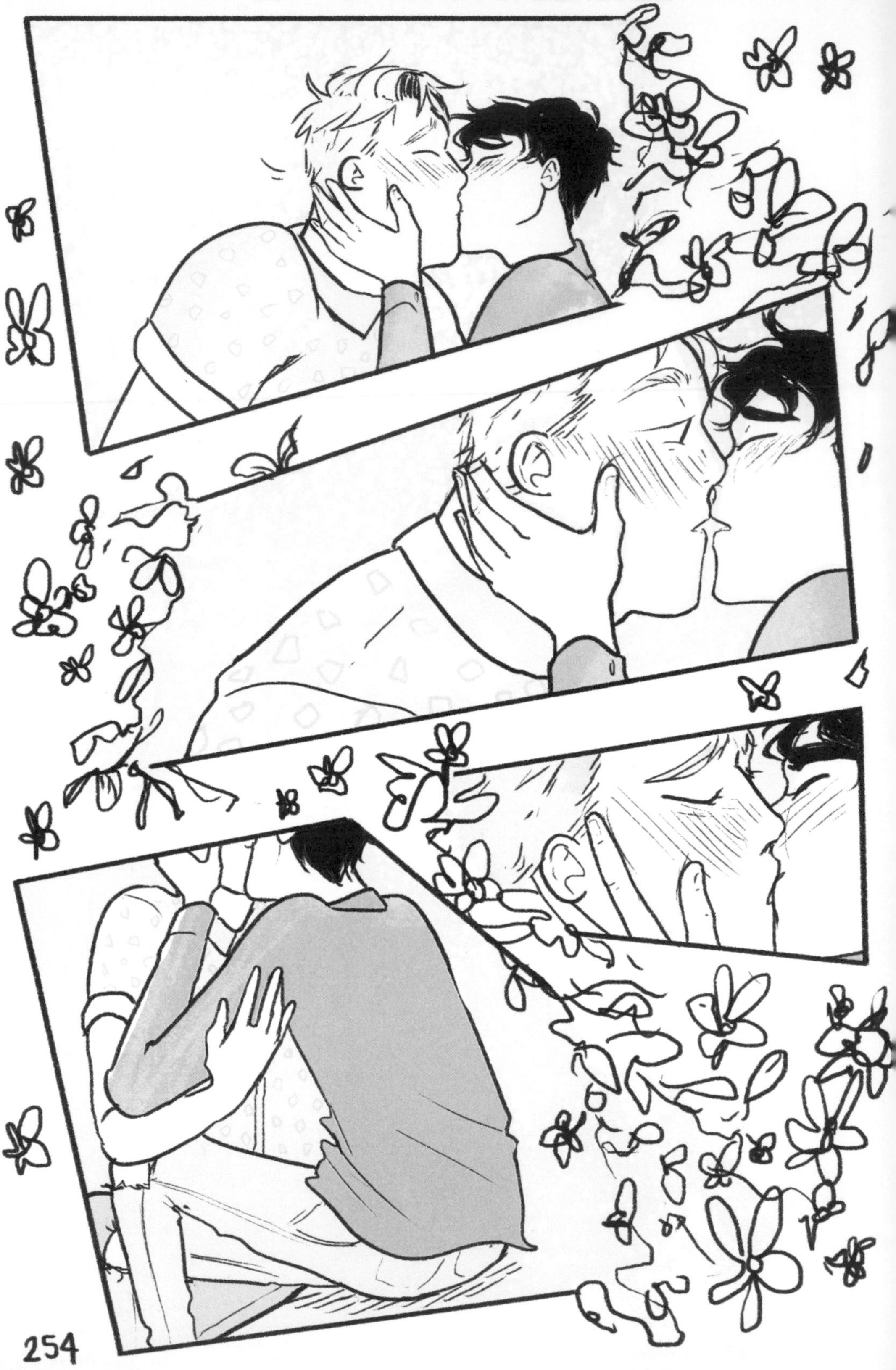

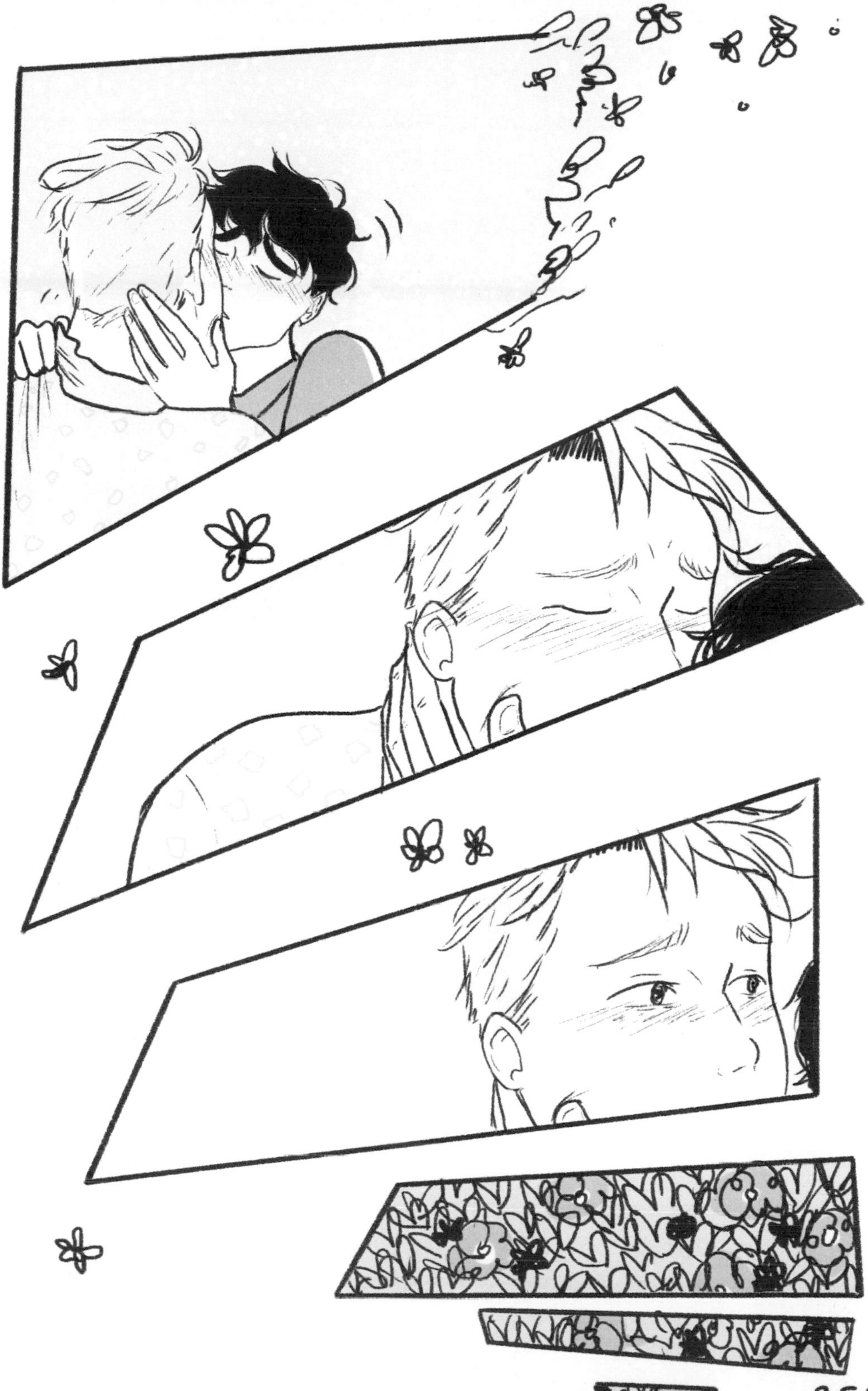

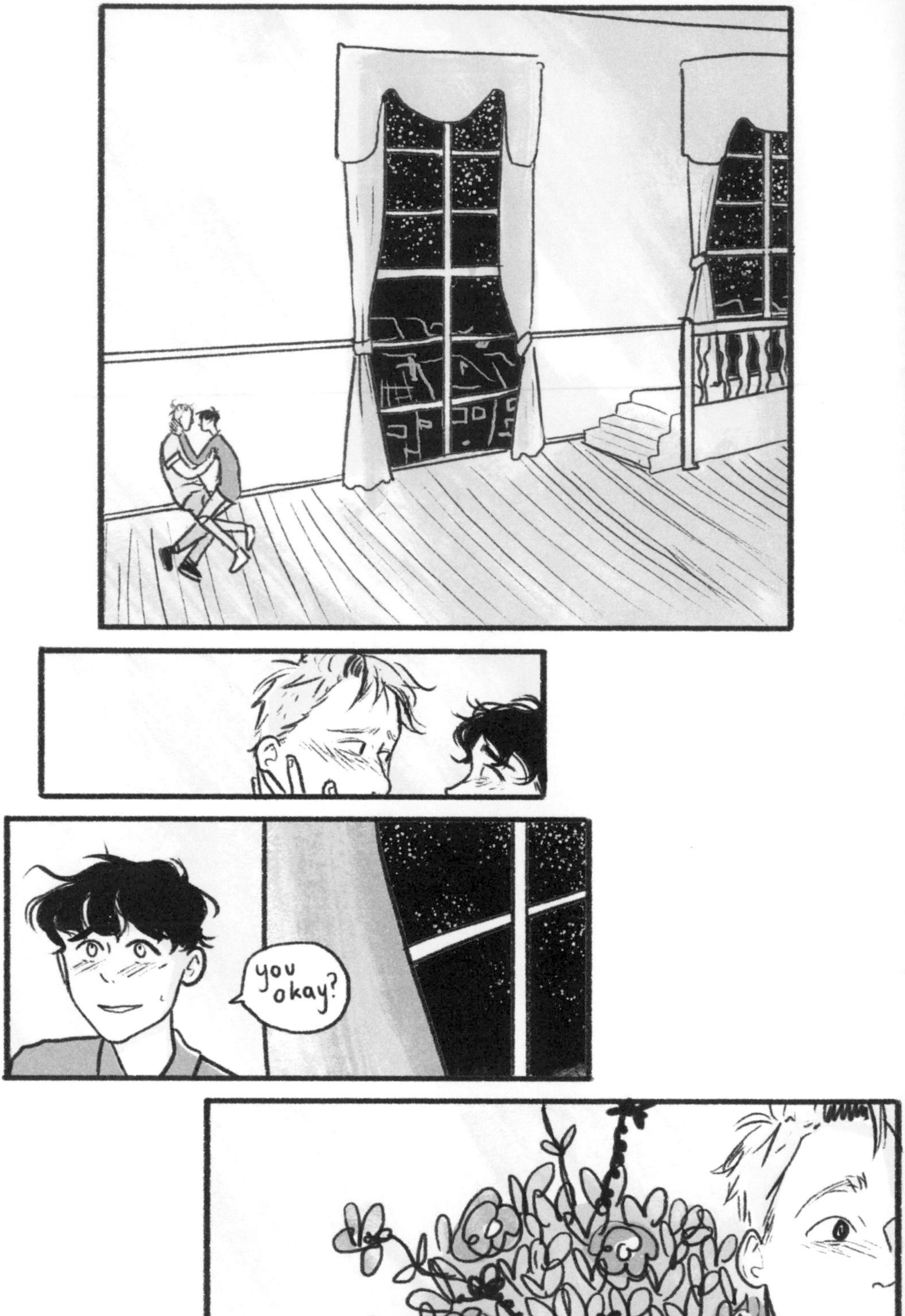
you okay?

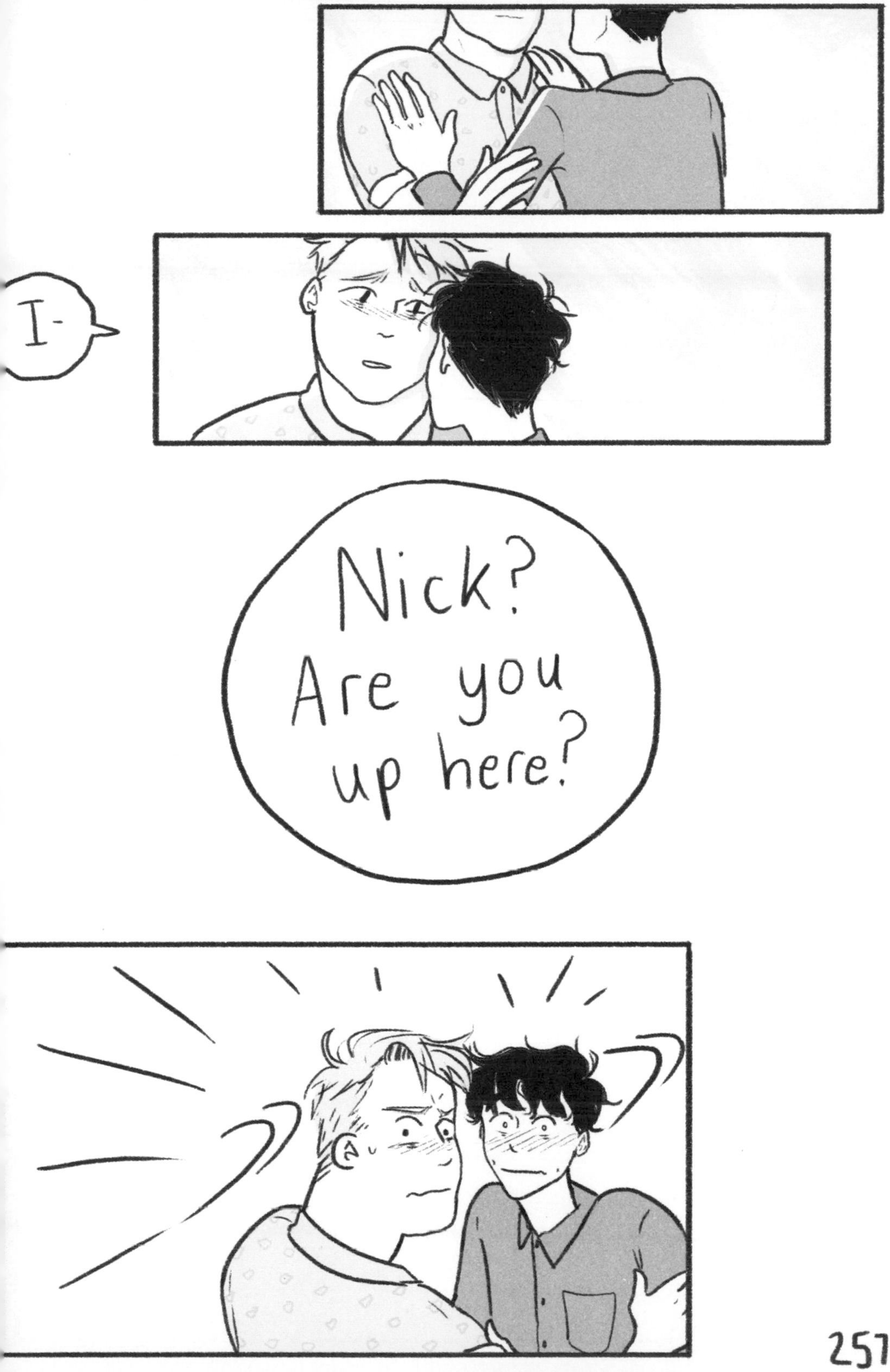
I-
Nick? Are you up here?

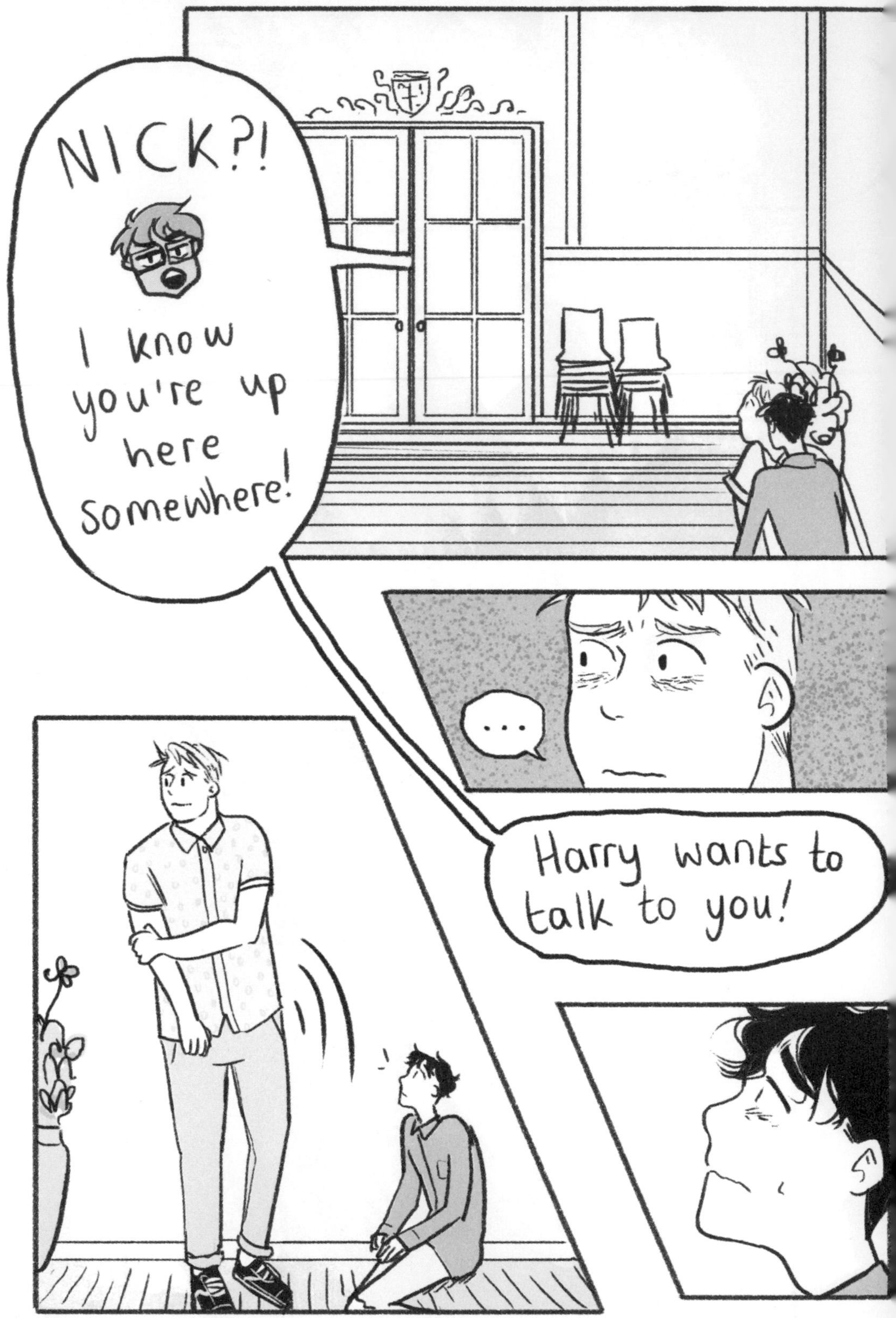
NICK?!
I know you're up here somewhere!
...
Harry wants to talk to you!

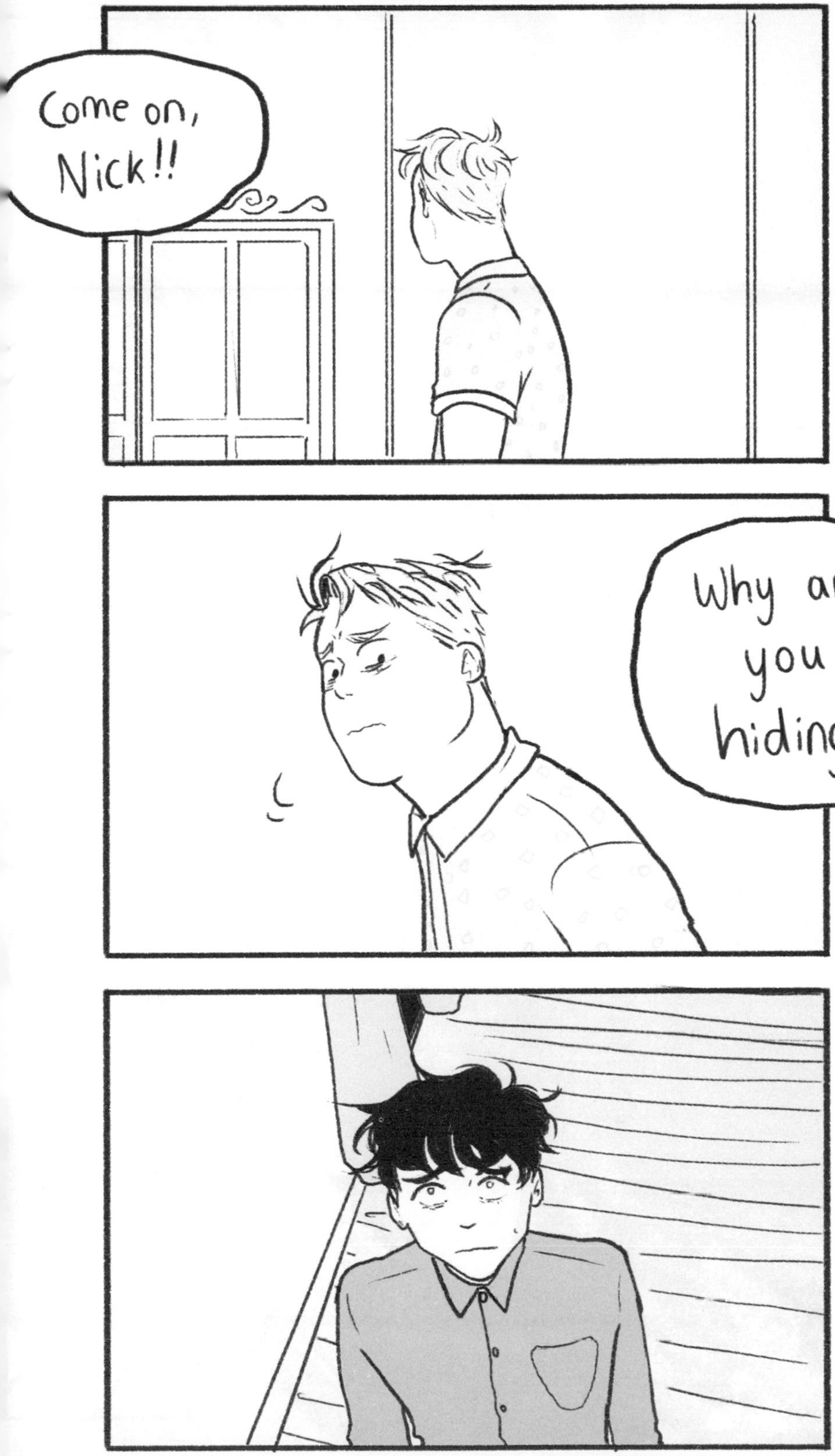
Come on, Nick!!
Why are you hiding?

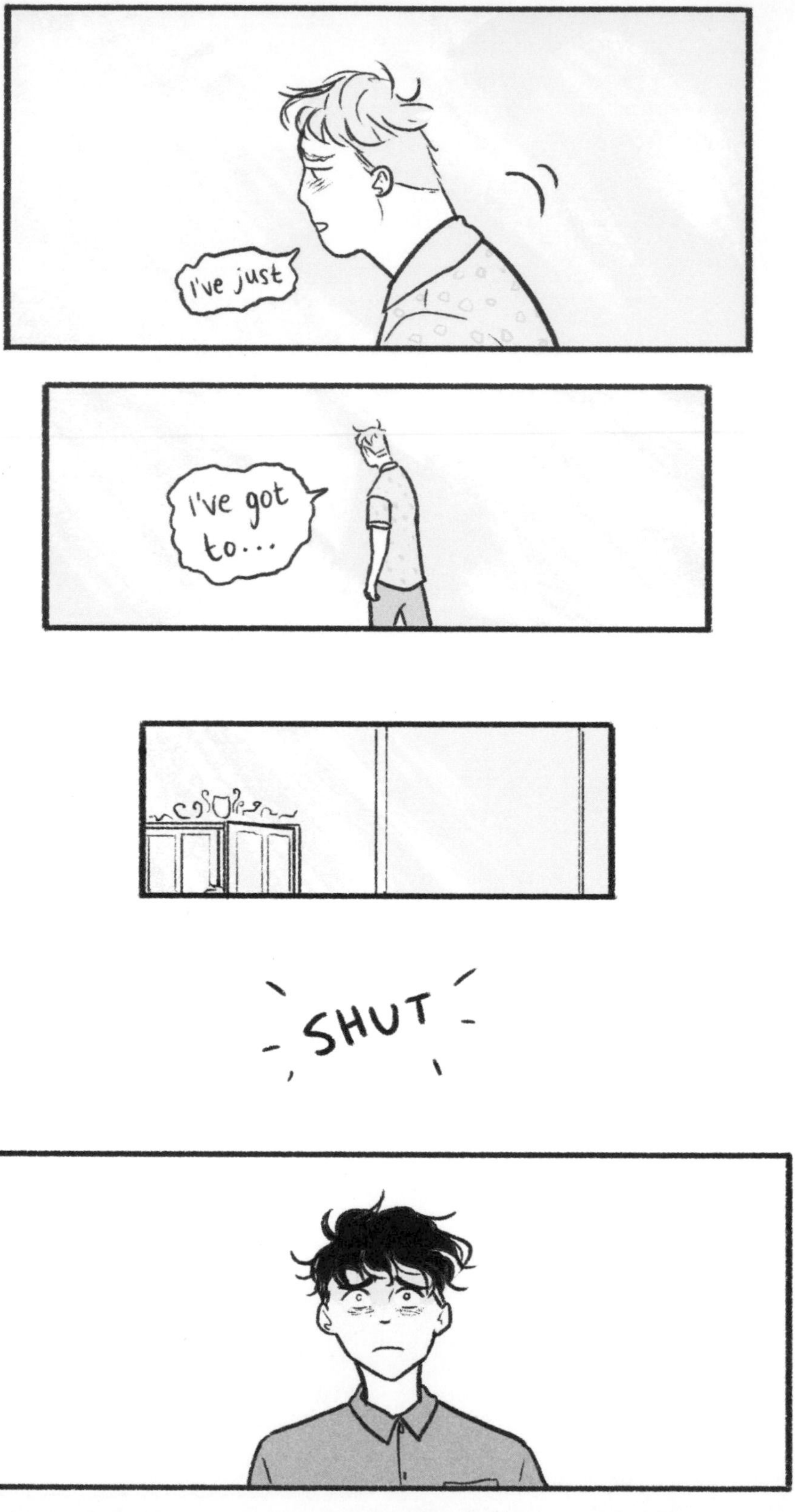
I've just
I've got to...
SHUT

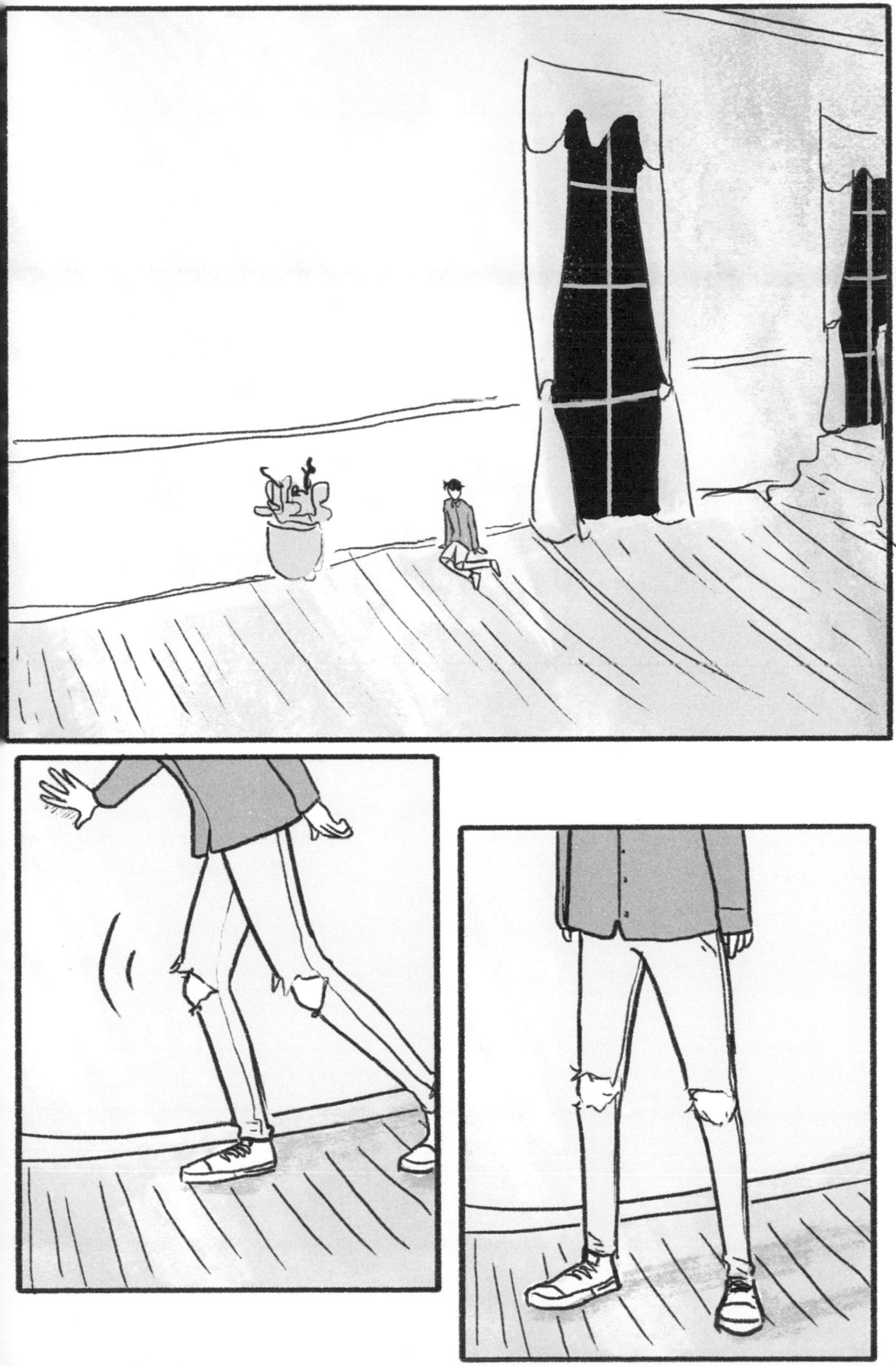

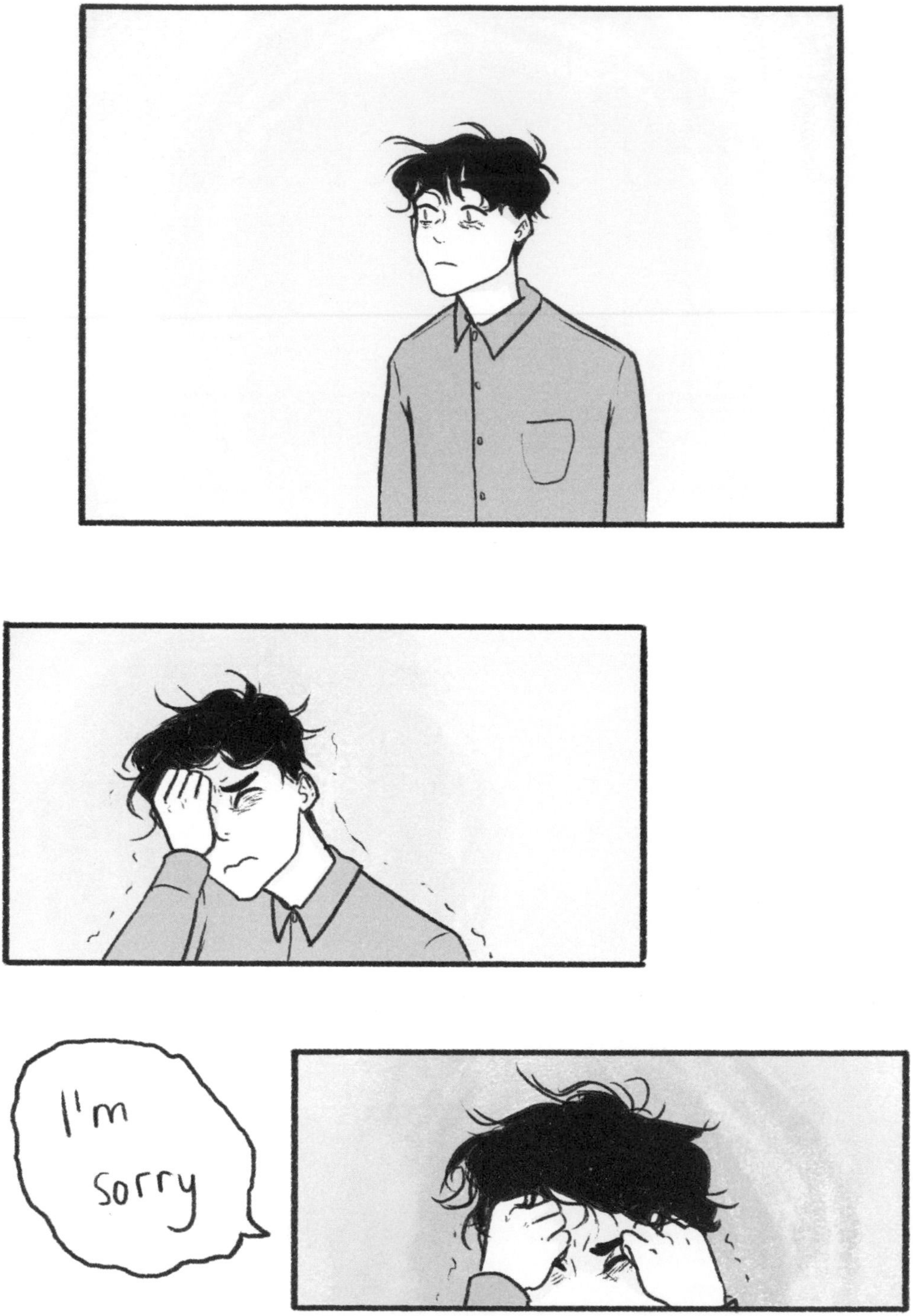
I'm sorry

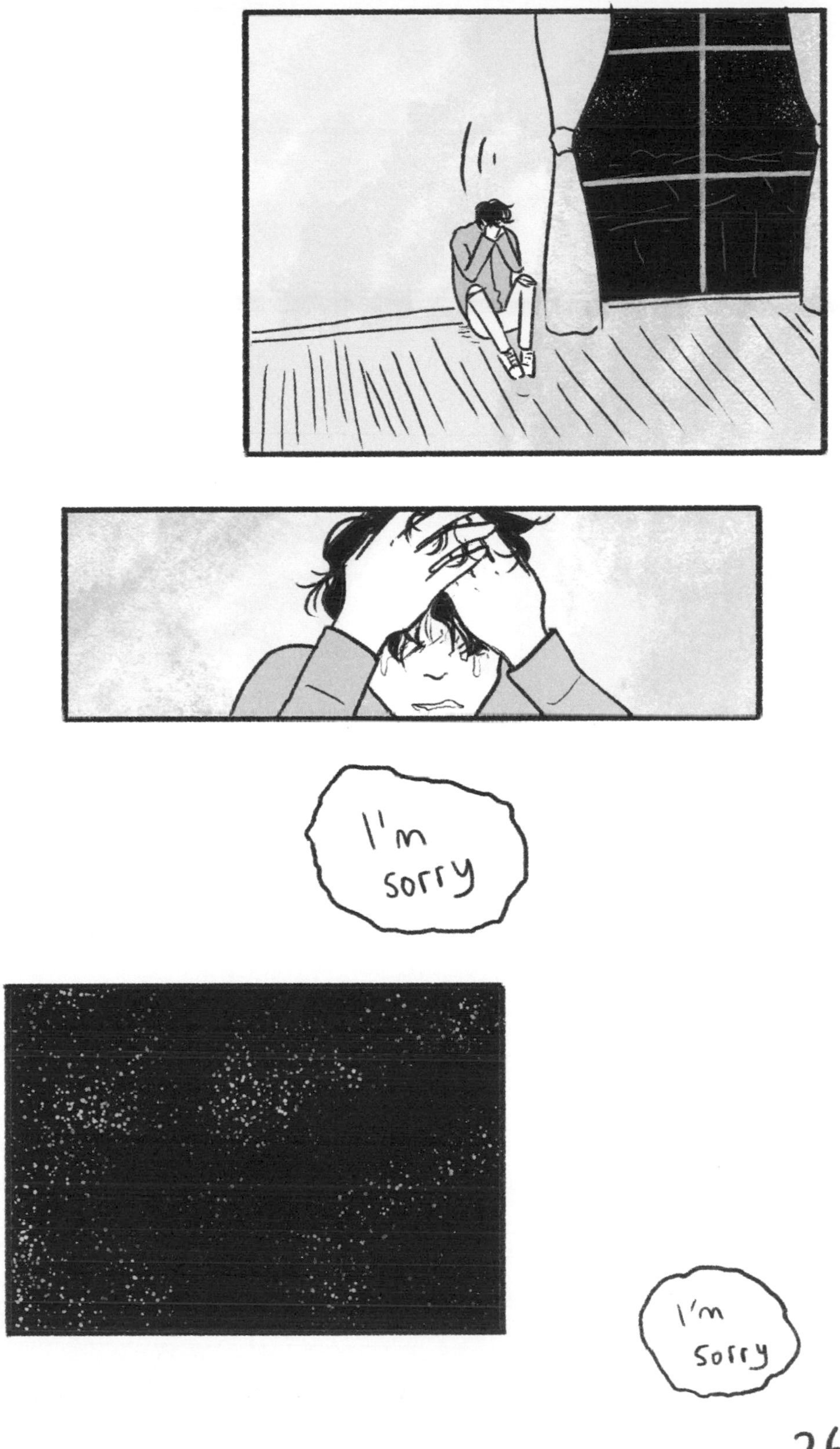
I'm sorry
I'm sorry

Heartstopper will continue...

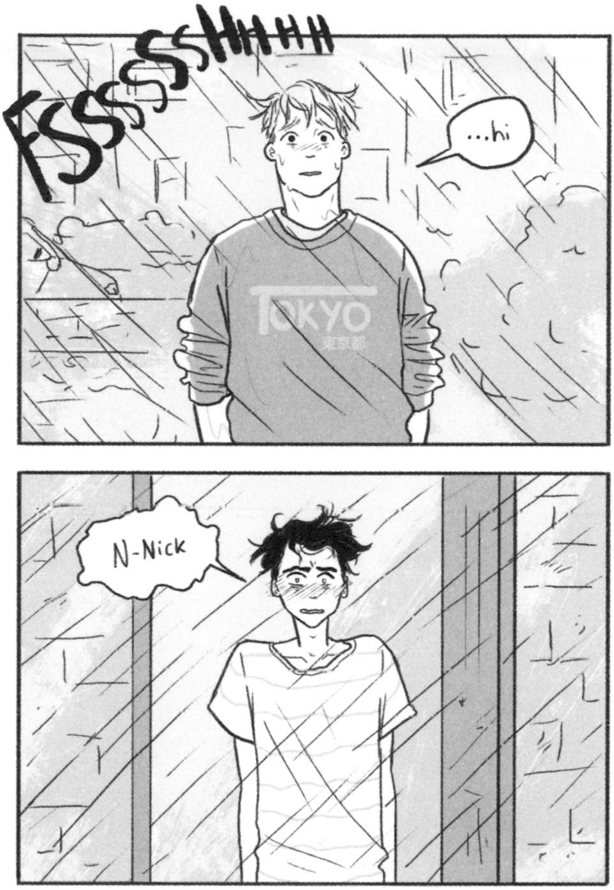
FSSSSSSHHHHH
...hi
TOKYO
N-Nick

Turn the page for a sneak peek!

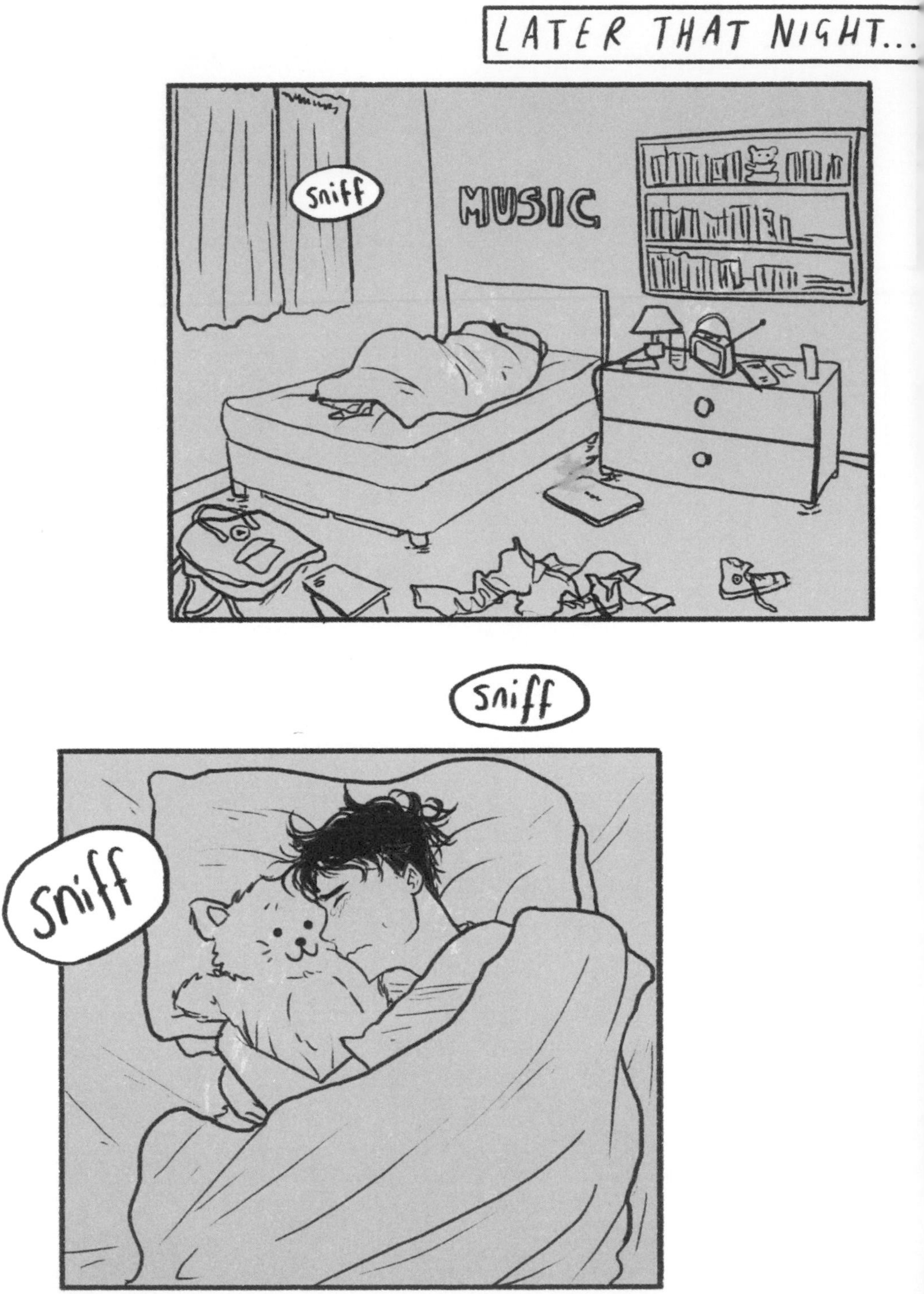
LATER THAT NIGHT...
sniff
MUSIC
sniff
sniff

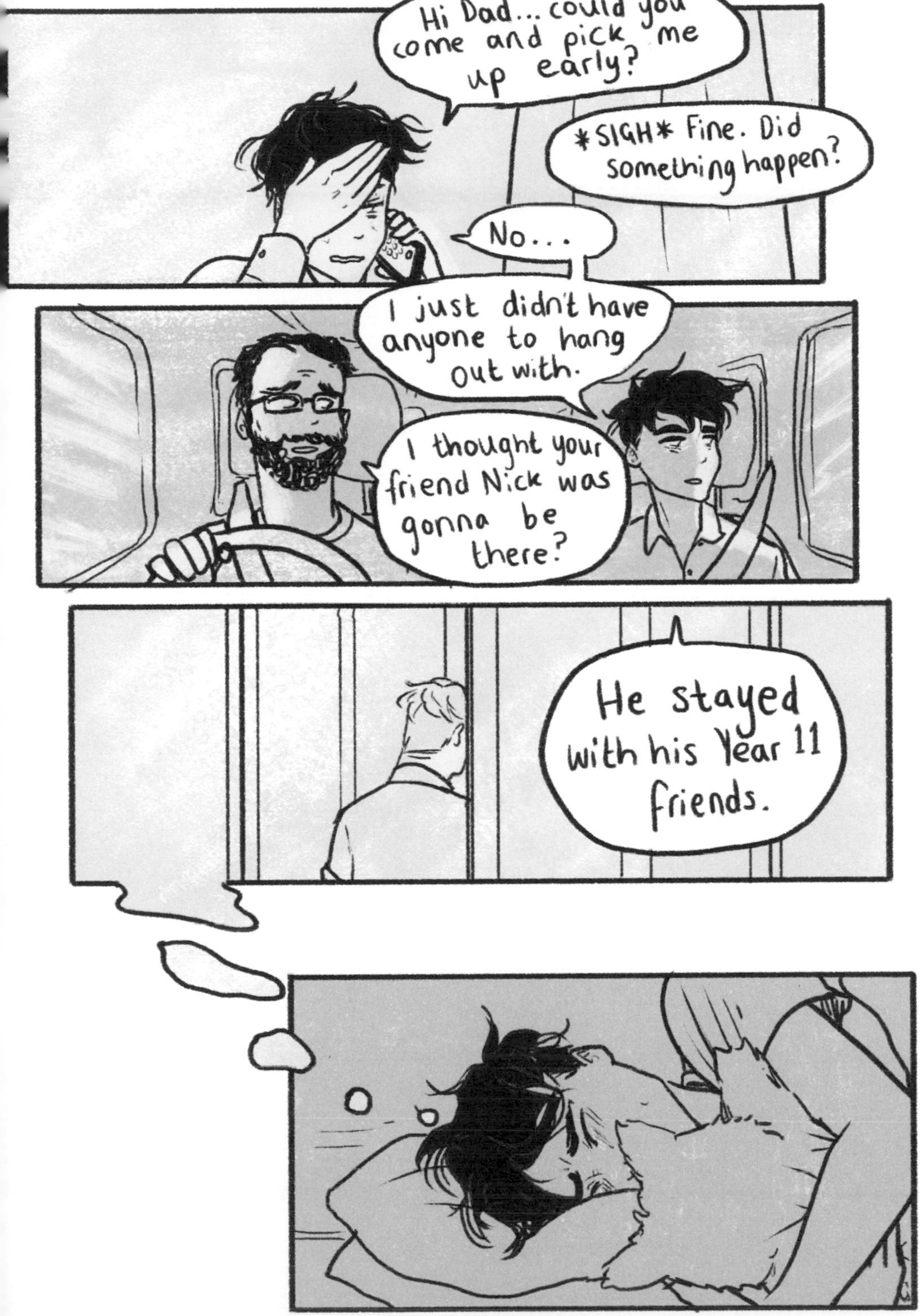
Hi Dad... could you come and pick me up early?
SIGH Fine. Did something happen?
No...
I just didn't have anyone to hang out with.
I thought your friend Nick was gonna be there?
He stayed with his Year 11 friends.

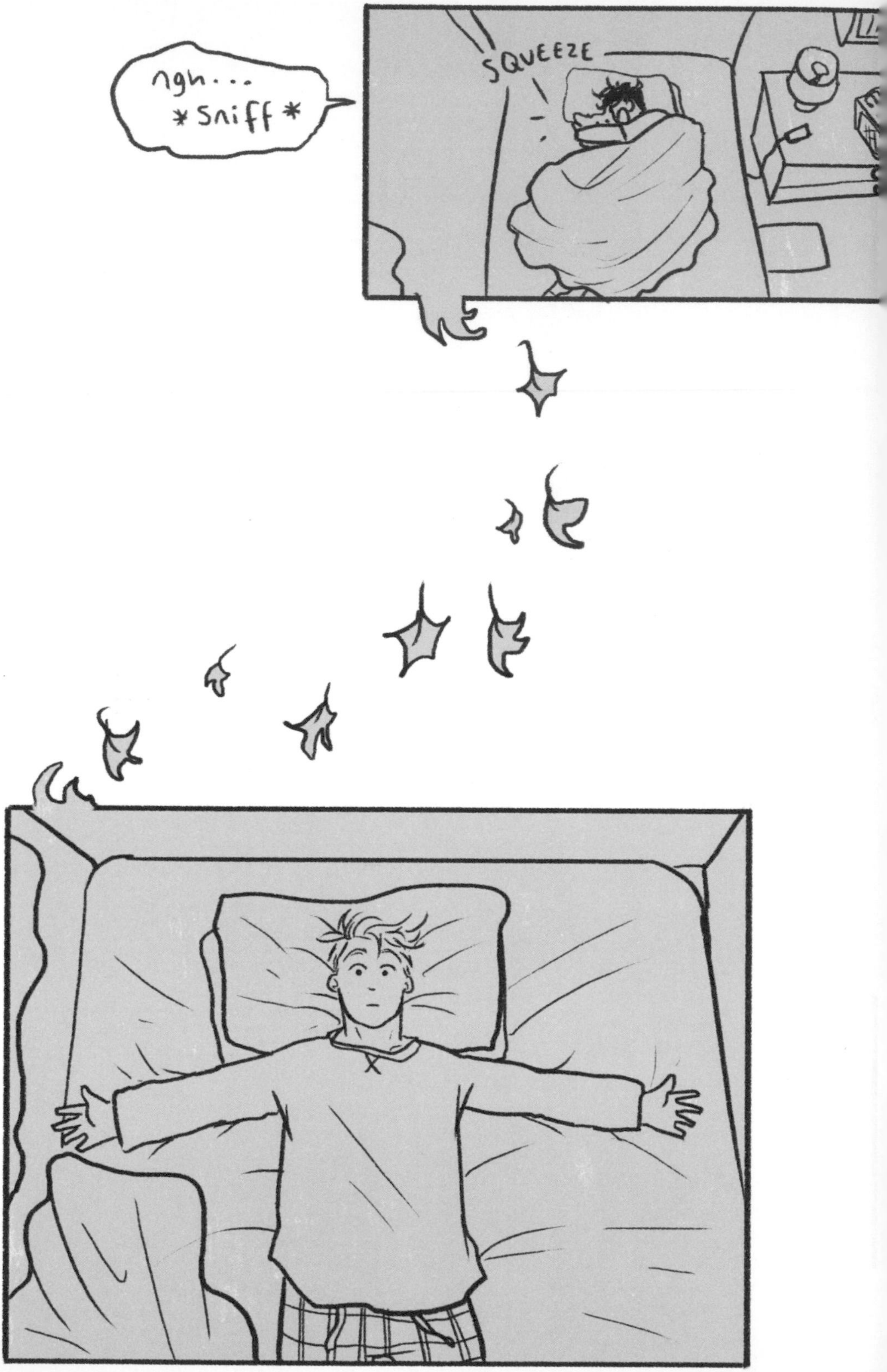
ngh...
sniff
SQUEEZE

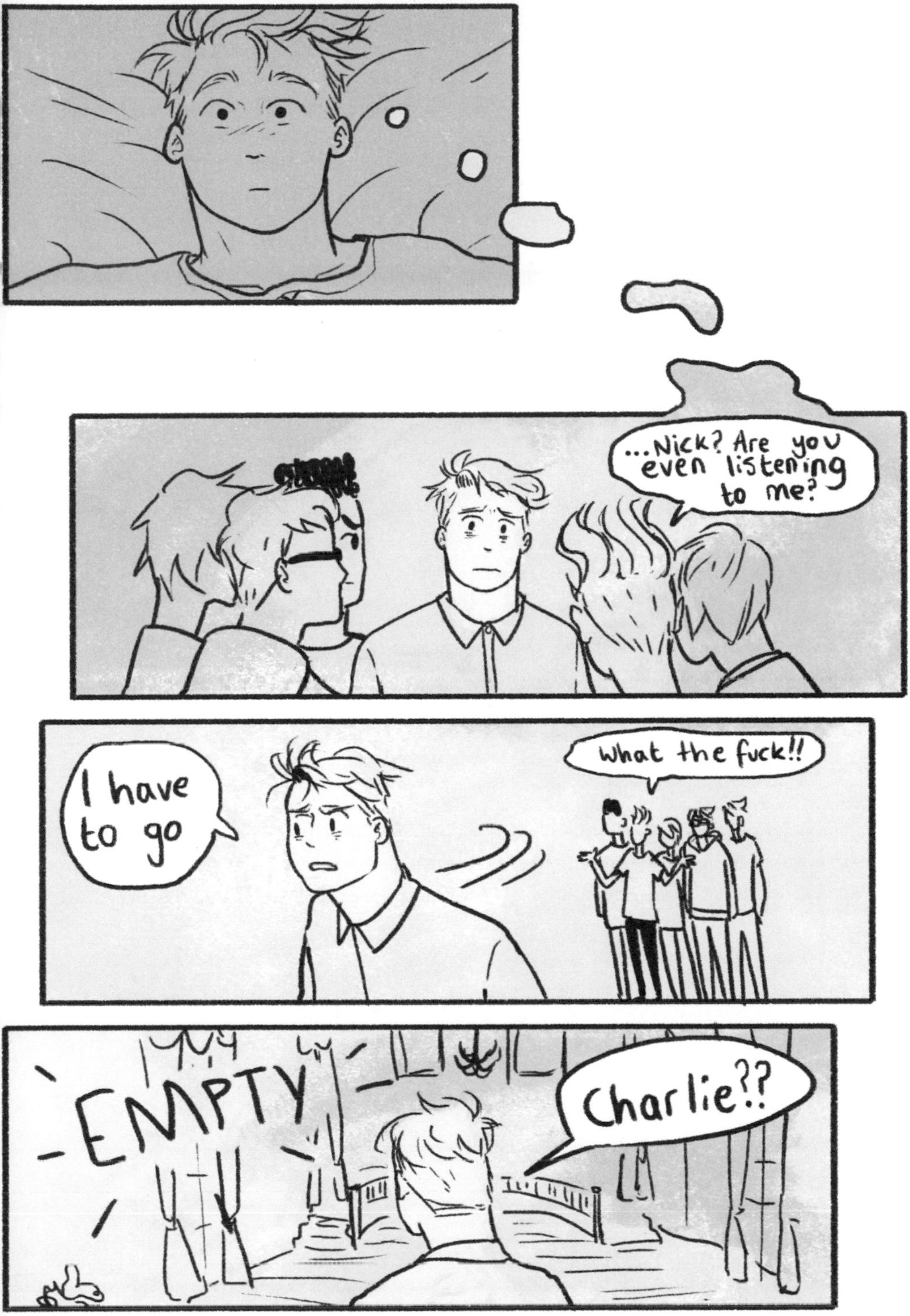
...Nick? Are you even listening to me?
I have to go
What the fuck!!
EMPTY
Charlie??

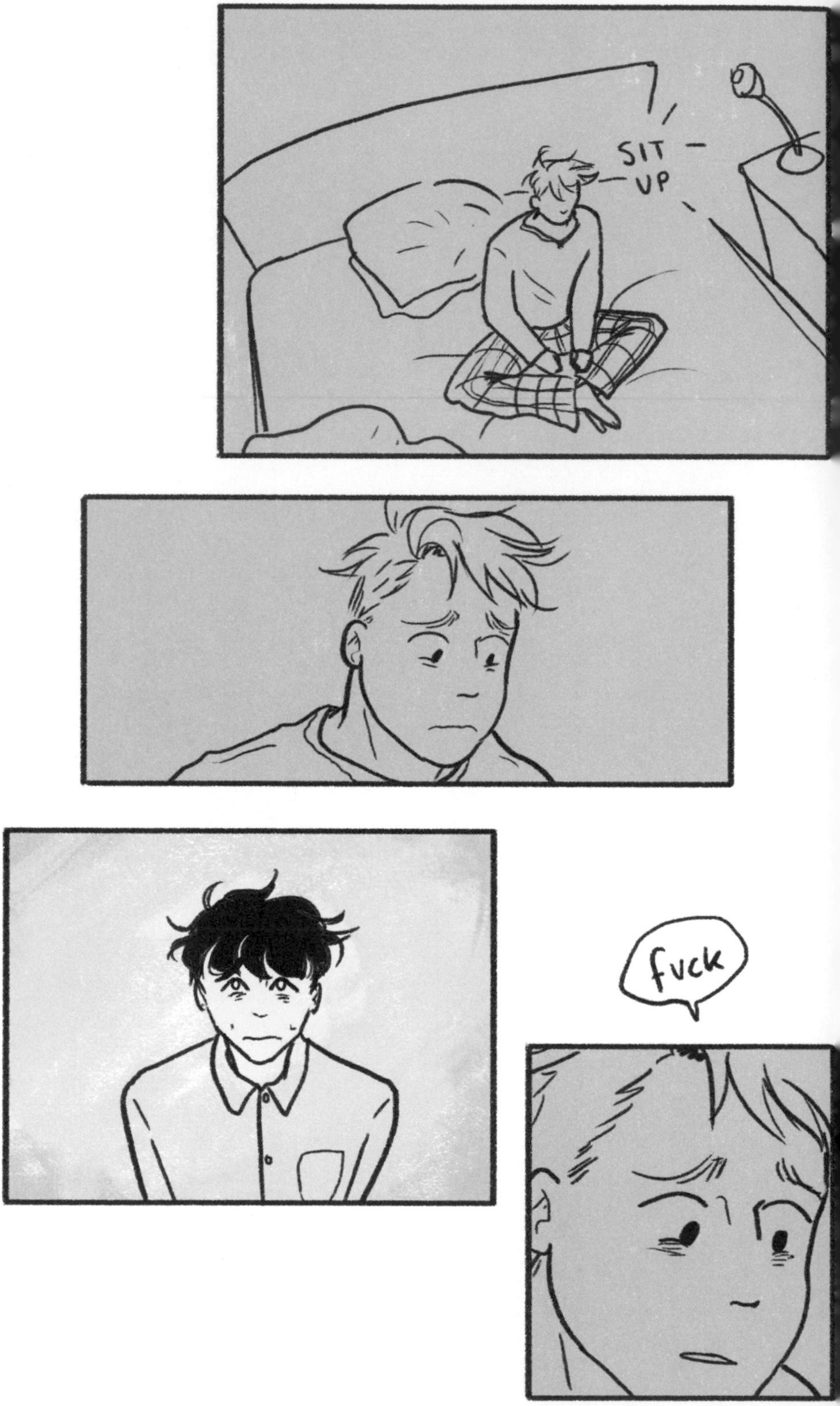
SIT UP
fuck

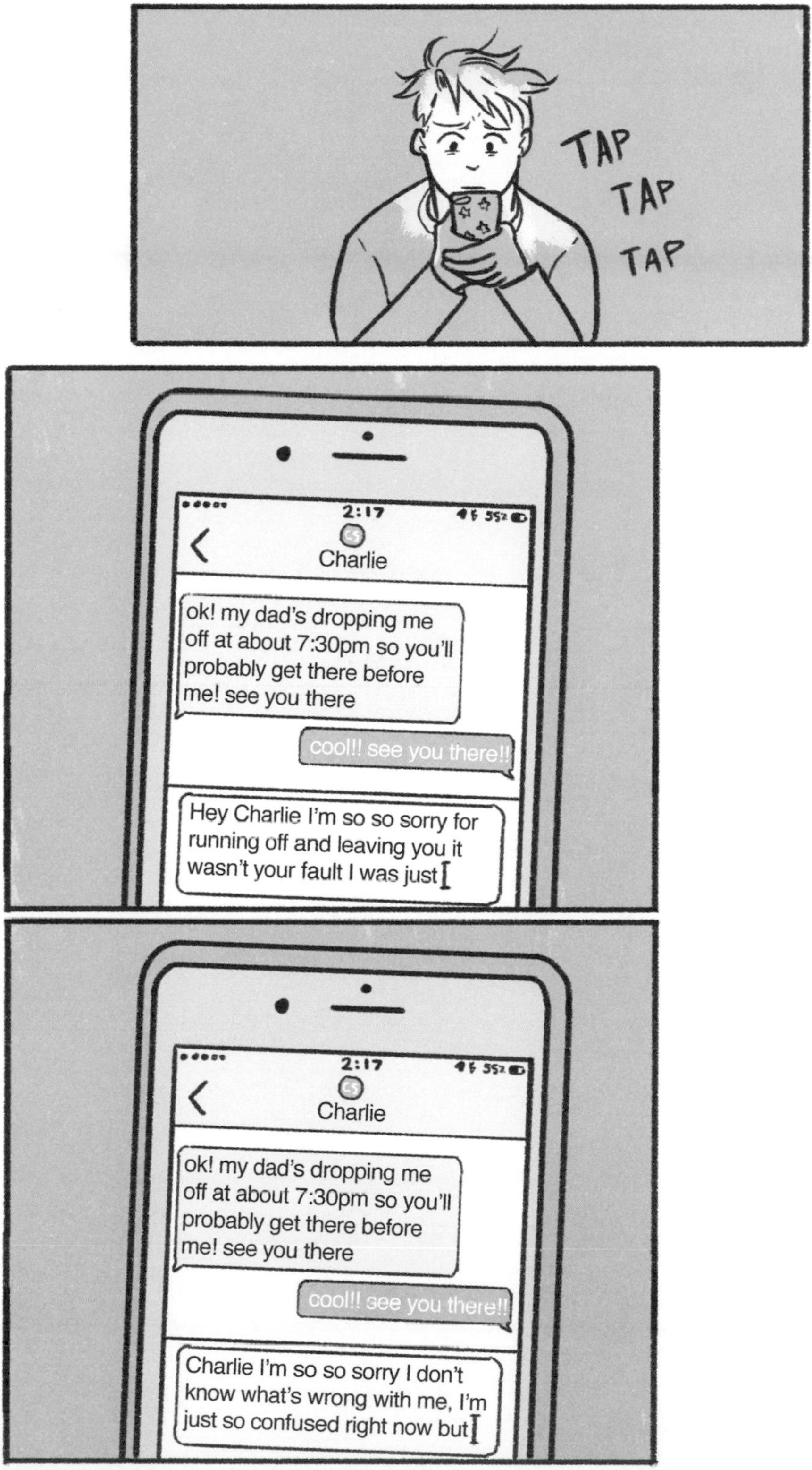
TAP
TAP
TAP
2:17
Charlie
ok! my dad's dropping me off at about 7:30pm so you'll probably get there before me! see you there
cool!! see you there!!
Hey Charlie I'm so so sorry for running off and leaving you it wasn't your fault I was just
2:17
Charlie
ok! my dad's dropping me off at about 7:30pm so you'll probably get there before me! see you there
cool!! see you there!!
Charlie I'm so so sorry I don't know what's wrong with me, I'm just so confused right now but

NAME: CHARLES "CHARLIE" SPRING

WHO ARE YOU: NICK'S FRIEND

SCHOOL YEAR: YEAR 10 **AGE:** 14

BIRTHDAY: APRIL 27TH

NAME: Nicholas "Nick" Nelson

WHO ARE YOU: Charlie's friend

SCHOOL YEAR: Year 11 **AGE:** 16

BIRTHDAY: September 4th

NAME: Tao Xu

WHO ARE YOU: Charlie's friend

SCHOOL YEAR: Year 10 **AGE:** 15

BIRTHDAY: September 23rd

NAME: Victoria "Tori" Spring

WHO ARE YOU: Charlie's sister

SCHOOL YEAR: Year 11 **AGE:** 15

BIRTHDAY: April 5th

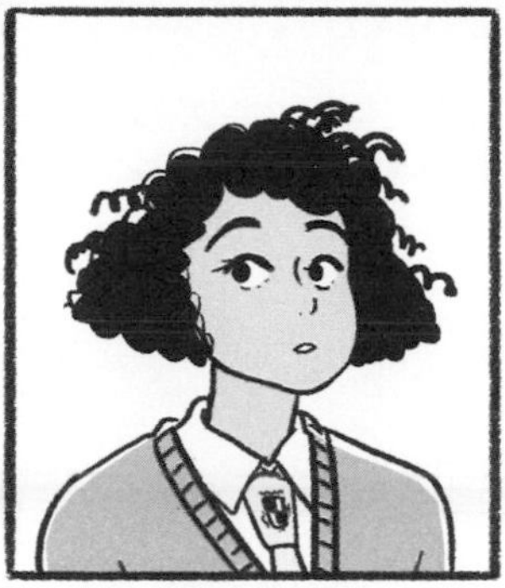

NAME: Tara Jones

WHO ARE YOU: Nick's friend

SCHOOL YEAR: Year 11 **AGE:** 15

BIRTHDAY: July 3rd

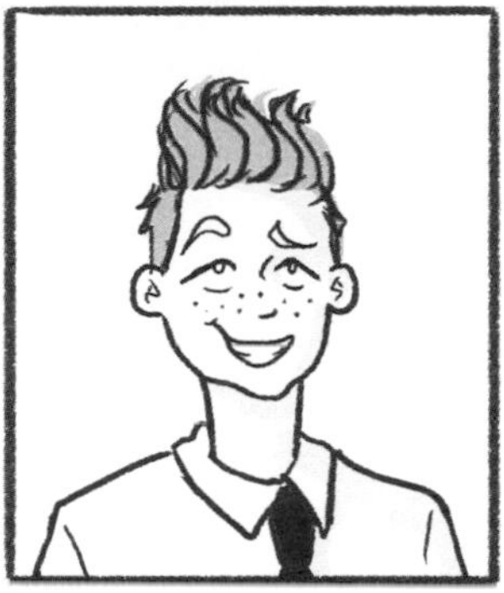

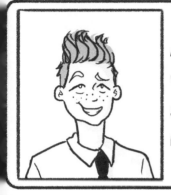

NAME: HARRY GREENE

WHO ARE YOU: NICK'S CLASSMATE

SCHOOL YEAR: YEAR 11 **AGE:** 16

BIRTHDAY: APRIL 17TH

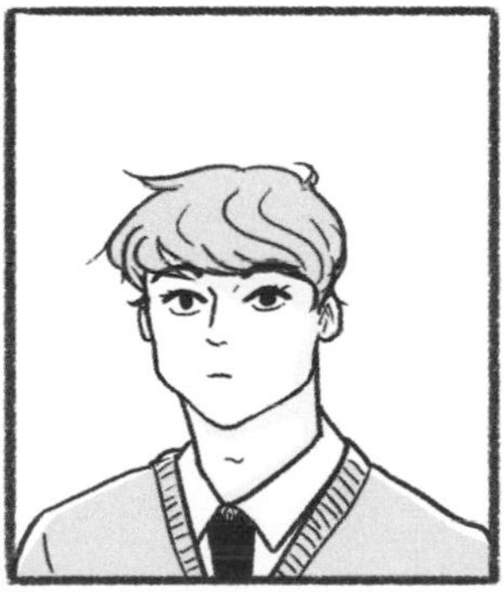

NAME: Benjamin Hope

WHO ARE YOU: Charlie's ex

SCHOOL YEAR: Year 11 **AGE:** 16

BIRTHDAY: December 1st

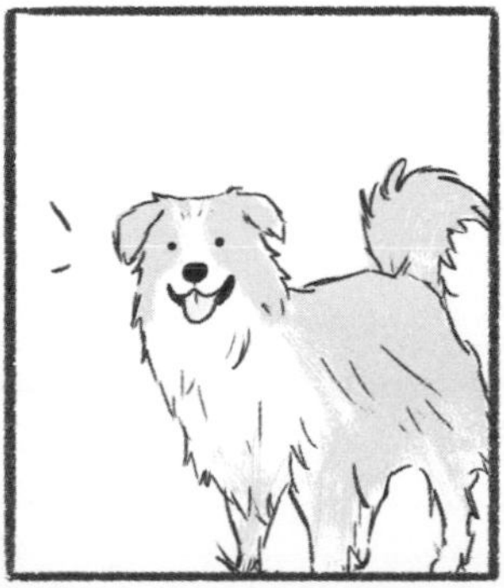

NAME: Nellie Nelson

WHO ARE YOU: Nick's dog

SCHOOL YEAR: N/A **AGE:** 65 (dog years)

BIRTHDAY: Unknown

Saturday March 20th

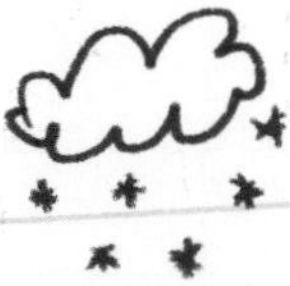

Hung out with Charlie all day!! He came over and we went out in the snow with Nellie which was so much fun!! I really like hanging out with Charlie, like WAY more than my other friends. I feel like I can actually just relax and be myself around him, and we still have such a good time and joke around, I swear I can't stop smiling when we're hanging out. I know it's weird but I honestly don't think I've ever liked a friend this much before... I sort of dread seeing my other friends, like they're kind of annoying and being around them is stressful.

But when I'm with Charlie I don't want the day to end??

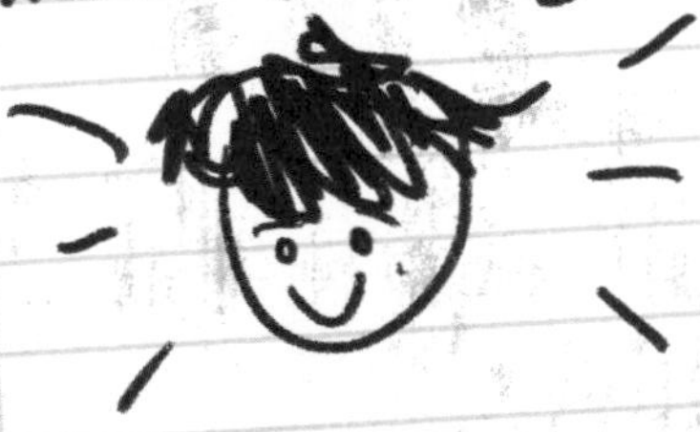

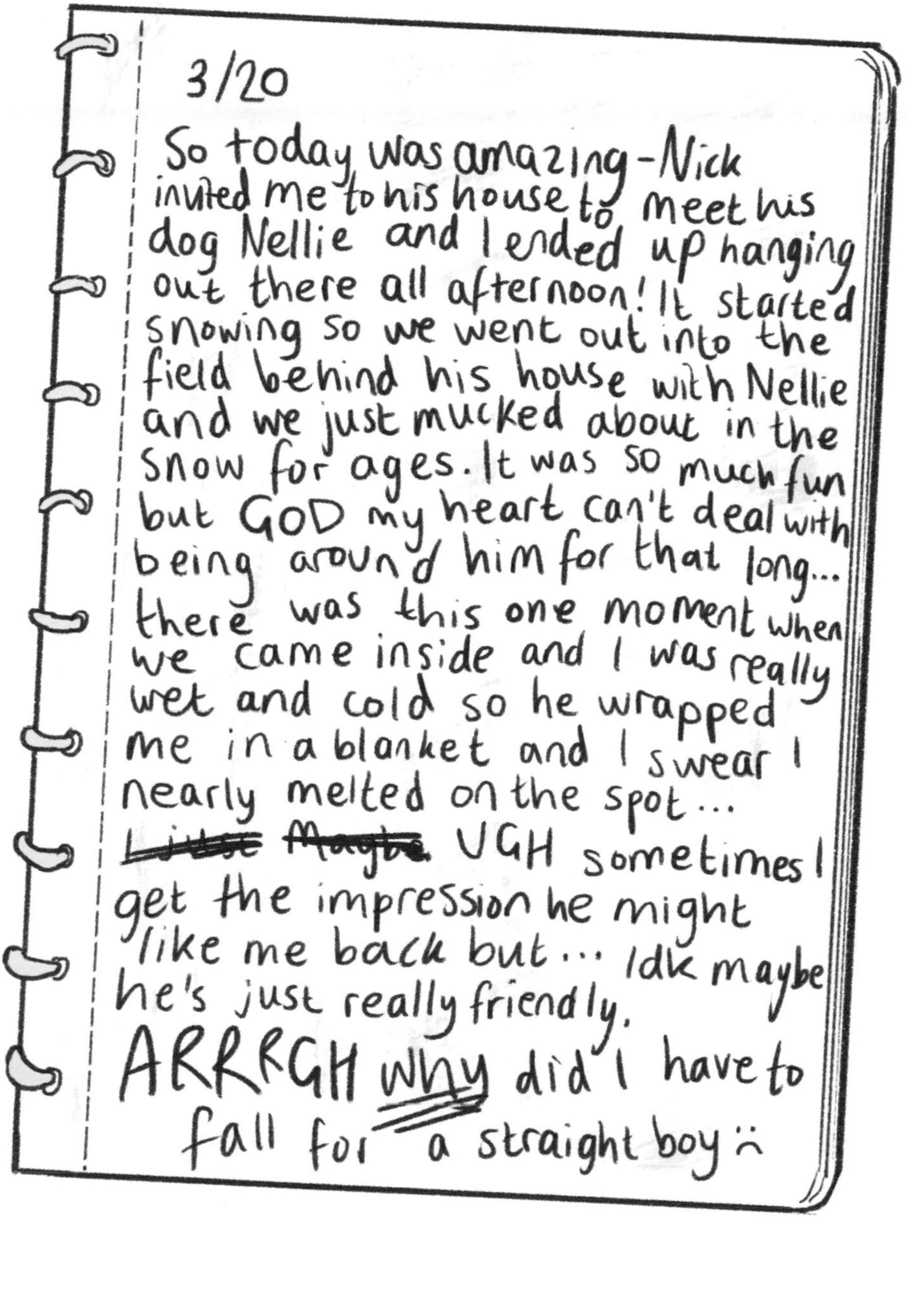
3/20
So today was amazing - Nick invited me to his house to meet his dog Nellie and I ended up hanging out there all afternoon! It started snowing so we went out into the field behind his house with Nellie and we just mucked about in the snow for ages. It was so much fun but GOD my heart can't deal with being around him for that long... there was this one moment when we came inside and I was really wet and cold so he wrapped me in a blanket and I swear I nearly melted on the spot...
~~Like~~ ~~Maybe~~ UGH sometimes I get the impression he might like me back but... Idk maybe he's just really friendly.
ARRRGH why did I have to fall for a straight boy :(

Author's Note

Nick and Charlie have been in my heart for a very long time.

As many of you know, they both first appeared in my debut YA novel, *Solitaire*. Charlie is the younger brother of the narrator, Tori, and Nick is his doting, protective boyfriend. Neither of them are particularly major characters, but in the novel, aged fifteen and seventeen respectively, they are in a firm, loving, supportive relationship. That's where my desire to tell their story began. How did they get to this point? And where will they go from here?

In my last year of school, I filled an entire sketchbook with my first attempt at telling the backstory of Nick and Charlie. Then I started again, my art slightly better, and filled another sketchbook with a second attempt at the comic. I remember spending hours at a time just sitting and drawing in bed, not even listening to music in the background, completely lost and in love with the story of Nick and Charlie. It brought me peace in a way not even writing my novels could.

In 2016, aged twenty-one and my art greatly improved, I launched Heartstopper. It started small, but slowly its audience grew and grew. At the time of editing this author's note, Heartstopper has almost 90,000 followers across Tumblr and Tapas. People come to the story for all sorts of reasons — for the realistic romance, for the LGBT+ representation, for the art, for the drama. But I think most of all, people have been drawn to Heartstopper because it brings them comfort.

It brings me that, too.

Alice
x

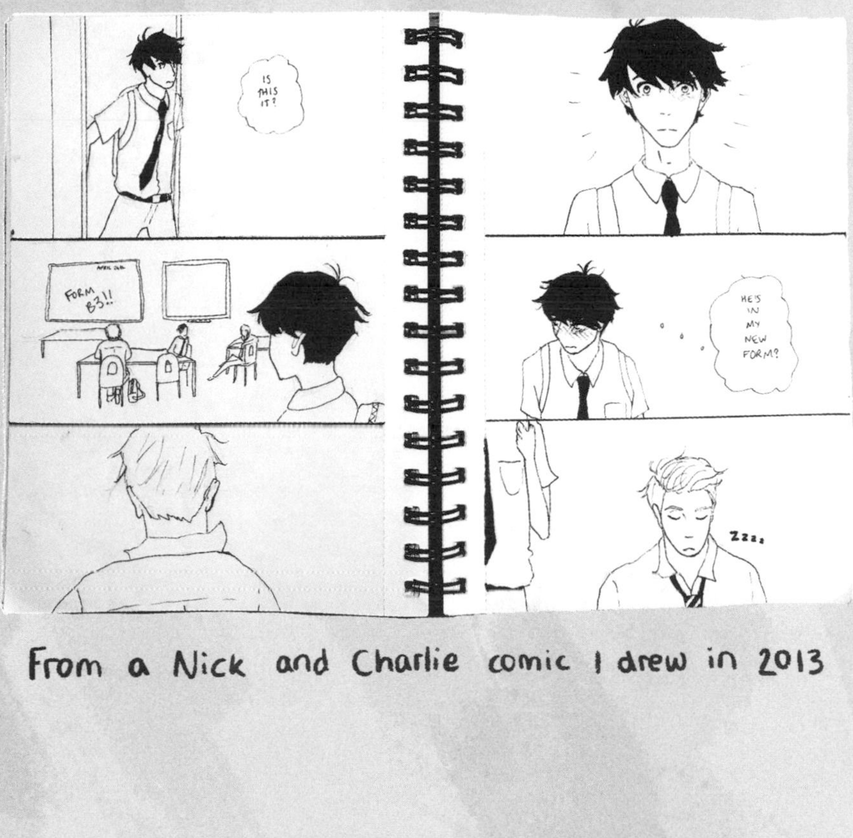
IS THIS IT?
FORM B3!!
HE'S IN MY NEW FORM?
Zzzz

From a Nick and Charlie comic I drew in 2013

Acknowledgments

Love and thanks to my Patreon patrons, Kickstarter supporters,
and all readers of Heartstopper over the past couple of years.
This book wouldn't have been possible without you.

A huge thanks, also, to my agent, Claire Wilson, and to the
teams at Hachette in the UK and Scholastic in the US.
Thank you for showing Heartstopper so much love.

Finally, a special shout-out to those amazing
people who gave a little more to the Kickstarter:

JT Taylor, Lorna Burch, Kyle Sanders, Ade Mayr,
Ruben Molina Fernandez, Lucy Powrie, Shannon Baillie,
Annie Furlong-Muir, David Browne, Isobel, Lucy McGlasson,
Jake Fraser, Charlotte Dreyfus, Manon Pothin, Lowen Crombie, Chloe
Zargarpour, Liang Hai, Katie Gibson, Whitney Gravelle, Daphne Tonge
(Illumicrate), Tory Schorsch, Jamie Destouet, Janintserani Herrera,
Peter Stromberg, Elise Buchanan, Bella Beecham,
Orlee Pnini, and John H. Bookwalter Jr.

See you
next time!
x

Alice Oseman was born in 1994 in Kent, England, and is a full-time writer and illustrator. She can usually be found staring aimlessly at computer screens, questioning the meaninglessness of existence, or doing anything and everything to avoid getting an office job.

As well as writing and illustrating Heartstopper, Alice is the author of three YA novels: *Solitaire*, *Radio Silence*, and *I Was Born for This*.

To find out more about Alices work, visit her online:

aliceoseman.com
twitter.com/AliceOseman
instagram.com/aliceoseman

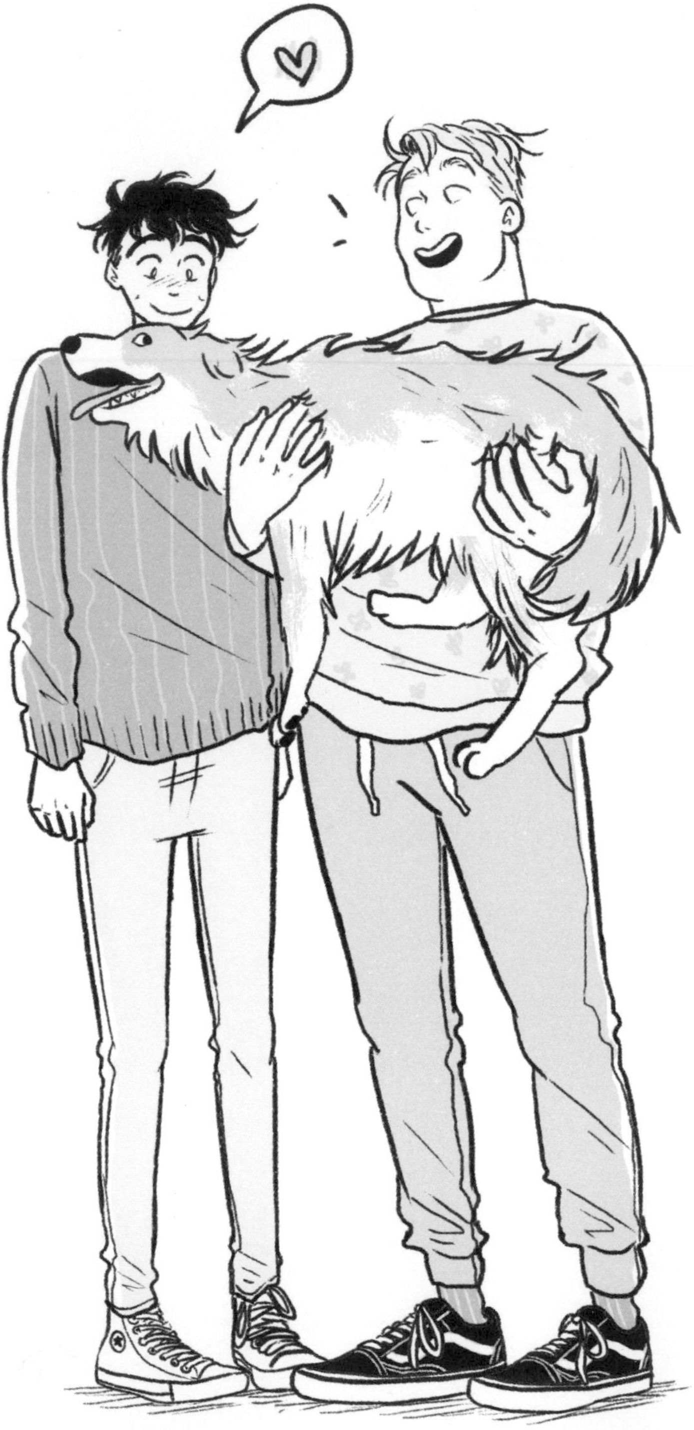